"A long loud cheer for the men and ships of the Navy's amphibious forces—the first good, honest novel about the Navy in World War II."

BOSTON POST

"Alive with the tense excitement and despair of the battle for the islands of the South Pacific . . . the story of the attack transport 'Belinda' and the men who grow to love her, to despise her and to be afraid of her, of Captain Hawks, who turns the fleet upside down in search of red ink, of Lieutenant Dave MacDougall, who rises to become commanding officer during a kamikaze attack off Okinawa, of the thousands of men who died on and off the forgotten beaches. A realistic chronicle of action . . ."

DAILY OKLAHOMAN

"Epic action . . . a great affirmative American novel . . ."

CHICAGO TRIBUNE

Big!

One of the biggest peace-time naval manoeuvres in recent years took place when AWAY ALL BOATS was filmed by Universal-International with the cooperation of the Navy Department. Stars Jeff Chandler, George Nader, Julie Adams and Lex Barker were involved with the war games held by the Navy in the Virgin Islands. Dozens of ships, hundreds of boats of all sorts from launches to landing craft, 20,000 sailors and marines took place in practice beach-head landing tactics. Some of the most impressive and authentic landing sequences ever filmed were recorded on thousands of feet of Vista-Vision film to make the movie based on

AWAY ALL BOATS

Away All Boats

A Novel by

KENNETH DODSON

BANTAM BOOKS · NEW YORK

AWAY ALL BOATS

A Bantam Book published by arrangement with
Little, Brown & Company, Inc.

Printing History

Little, Brown edition published December 1953
2nd printing February 1954
3rd printing March 1954
4th printing March 1954
5th printing April 1954
6th printing June 1954
7th printing June 1954
8th printing July 1954
9th printing August 1954
10th printing October 1954
11th printing October 1954
12th printing December 1954

Dollar Book Club edition published April 1954
2nd printing July 1954
3rd printing January 1955
4th printing April 1955

Excerpts appeared in *This Week* May 1954

Grosset & Dunlap edition published March 1956

Bantam edition published July 1956
2nd printing

The task-force movements, beachhead assaults and principal enemy air attacks described in this novel are intended to be historically accurate, and in other respects the author has attempted to tell a story which will ring true to veterans of amphibious landings.

All characters in this story are fictional and any resemblance to actual persons is coincidental. The U.S.S. *Belinda* is imaginary; there was no attack transport by that name. Many other ships in the story never actually existed, yet it is the author's desire that in these pages the reader will recapture the spirit of those ships of the United States Navy which sailed to victory through the Pacific islands.

Bantam Books are published by Bantam Books, Inc. Its trade mark, consisting of the words "BANTAM BOOKS" and the portrayal of a bantam is registered in the U. S. Patent Office and in other countries. *Marca Registrada*

PRINTED IN THE UNITED STATES OF AMERICA

BANTAM BOOKS, 25 West 45th Street, New York 36, N. Y.

For
Carl Sandburg
and for
my dear wife, Letha

THE UNITED STATES NAVY

GUARDIAN OF OUR COUNTRY

The United States Navy is responsible for maintaining control of the sea and is a ready force on watch at home and overseas, capable of strong action to preserve the peace or of instant offensive action to win in war.

It is upon the maintenance of this control that our country's glorious future depends; the United States Navy exists to make it so.

WE SERVE WITH HONOR

Tradition, valor, and victory are the Navy's heritage from the past. To these may be added dedication, discipline, and vigilance as the watchwords of the present and the future.

At home or on distant stations we serve with pride, confident in the respect of our country, our shipmates, and our families.

Our responsibilities sober us; our adversities strengthen us.

Service to God and Country is our special privilege. We serve with honor.

THE FUTURE OF THE NAVY

The Navy will always employ new weapons, new techniques, and greater power to protect and defend the United States on the sea, under the sea, and in the air.

Now and in the future, control of the sea gives the United States her greatest advantage for the maintenance of peace and for victory in war.

Mobility, surprise, dispersal, and offensive power are the keynotes of the new Navy. The roots of the Navy lie in a strong belief in the future, in continued dedication to our tasks, and in reflection on our heritage from the past.

Never have our opportunities and our responsibilities been greater.

CHAPTER 1

The first time MacDougall saw the *Belinda* was the night before her launching. He was master in the *Roamer* then, his ship in Moore's dry dock at Alameda after a voyage to the Coral Sea. It was late at night; restlessly waiting for word from Nadine, who was coming by train from Seattle, he was alone in his cabin. Near midnight, he went down into the floating dry dock and walked along the bilge chocks, looking up at sea grass and barnacles on the *Roamer's* bottom, and checking her propeller for nicks. One of the workmen down there mentioned a new Navy ship to be launched next day.

"A cruiser?" he had asked.

"No, one of these new attack transports."

"What are they?"

"They carry lots of guns and their own landing barges—land soldiers and marines right up on them Jap beaches. . . . Why don't you go have a look? She's in the first ways, right next to this dock."

MacDougall walked over to see the new ship. Larger than his command; new: no barnacles or sea grass; smell of new paint and that look of raw steel about her unfinished topside. While he stood looking, a gnarled little man approached him and asked, "Are you to sail in her?" Such eagerness, as if nothing could be more wonderful than to go to the beaches in this ship, yet unlaunched.

"No," MacDougall said. "I'm skipper of that ship in dry dock; just came over here to have a look."

"I see." Disappointment sounded in his voice. "I'd like to go with her. She's a good ship, a fortunate ship. I've heard her talk."

"Talk?"

"Yes, Captain; don't be laughing. Ships talk." The little man blew his nose on a soiled bandanna. "Come with me, sir. The men are gone now; nobody here 'til the day shift."

"Then what are you doing here? I thought that all you shipyard men wanted was to make money. You aren't getting overtime now, are you?"

"No, sir. I'm—well, money—You don't understand."

"I'm sorry. About the ship now. You say she talks?"

"Aye, she talks." The little man started towards the ship with MacDougall beside him. Dark eyes darted full at Mac-

1

Dougall as he added, "And I'm *not* daft in my old age." He led the way up a ramp onto some staging not yet removed from the vessel's midship section, where painters had been at work. "Here you are. Mind the paint now, but put your ear to her side; you'll hear her talk."

MacDougall had put his ear to her hull, cautiously at first, then, forgetting half dried anti-fouling paint, had held his cheek snug to the bilge. Sound there all right: rustling of autumn leaves, distant surf, sounds he had never heard before, restless whisperings, voices in pain, voices thrilling with eagerness, mixed chattering in some unknown tongue, calling to far off places. MacDougall knew what it was; could explain these sounds in cold, scientific terms; why then was his spine tingling? He took his ear away and looked down at the old man, who was carefully refolding a yellow telegram. "Those are locked-in stresses working out. They come out slowly in a part-welded hull."

"I know, son. Each part is trying to be free again, but they'll soon settle together; she's going to be a good ship, I tell you."

Arc lamps shone down, casting light among shadows. As the old man looked up there were tears sparkling.

"This ship really means a lot to you," MacDougall said.

"Aye, she does—especially now." The old man took out the telegram again, unfolded it, looked at it once more as if in unbelief, then folding it carefully, he stowed it once more in his shirt pocket. "You see, I have no one left now. My son and his wife—killed in an accident long ago. I raised my grandson. He went into the Marines, one of the first to volunteer. Today I got this: died of wounds, Guadalcanal. . . . I put everything I could into this ship, things learned slow in a long life of shipbuilding. Somehow I could see my grandson sailing in her, coming home safe from those beaches too, for she is a fortunate ship—I have always had that feeling since we laid her keel." The old man pulled out the blue bandanna once more and blew his bulbous nose.

At noon next day MacDougall had seen her launched: watched from high on the dry-docked *Roamer's* bridge while this new ship—flag bedecked, after appropriate speeches by dignitaries and traditional champagne treatment—slid down greased ways to meet salt water; proud name on her cruiser stern: U.S.S. *Belinda.* He had made another voyage in the *Roamer* while the *Belinda* went to outfitting dock. In the press of following events he had nearly forgotten this new attack transport, until, volunteering for active duty, he had by strange coincidence been assigned to her as boat group commander.

2

As the *Belinda* steamed out beyond the Farallon Islands on her shakedown cruise from San Francisco to Pearl Harbor, MacDougall and the ship's boatswain completed a careful inspection of the ship's weather decks. Under their watchful supervision, experienced boatswain's mates led green seamen in the unfamiliar work of securing the *Belinda's* topsides for sea. Lashings and turnbuckles were used liberally to snub down anything which might go adrift. Both men then climbed down the vertical rungs of fixed steel ladders, three decks down to the bottom of the after hold, where a working party had just finished re-stowing hastily loaded cases of beach party equipment so that they now reached snugly from side to side of the barn-like compartment. Above the throb of the propeller and intermittent rumblings of the steering engine, they could hear sea wash alongside the thin shell plating. Beneath their widespread feet the lightly burdened ship pitched and rolled in a lively manner, as if experimenting with the strange new element of salt wave through which she plowed at an easy clip of fifteen knots.

"Now let her roll," said the boatswain. "We've got our part of the ship secure for sea."

"I'm satisfied here," said MacDougall. "Every one of those thirty-two landing craft is snubbed down to the last inch of slack. Cargo booms are cradled . . . we're stowed wing and wing down here. Let's go up and give Jackson a hand in the storerooms. They're going to be a shambles if the ship starts rolling."

"Yes, sir—but the supply department . . ."

"I know. Remember, this is Jackson's first day at sea. Something tells me that he could use a little help." As MacDougall grasped the first rung of the vertical ladder and began to climb out of the after hold, a peculiar shaking of the hull and an otherwise unnatural lift of the port side indicated to him that a decided change in course to the left was being made. "The skipper's zigzagging," he said. "Hope he keeps her out of the trough until we get things buttoned up." The *Belinda* took a few preliminary swings and then lurched over on her port bilge and stayed there, trembling and shaking for several seconds while loose gear thundered and crashed. Troop bunks in the berthing compartment directly above clattered to the port side of the 'tween decks from their high stacks, paused there, then rushed from side to side with each succeeding roll. Three of these canvas covered pipe frames fell through the hatch

3

opening into the lower hold, barely missing MacDougall. He let go the ladder and jumped back out of the way, then cautiously led the way up to the berthing compartment. The place was a mess. Officers and men floundered and heaved together, trying to restore order while the ship rolled violently from side to side. During the third big roll to port a dozen large pasteboard cartons fell down upon them from other high stacks of lashed bunks. The cartons burst and their contents spilled upon and about them: hundreds of coat hangers. One of them hit MacDougall on the head. He picked it up and flung it against the opposite bulkhead.

"Five thousand coat hangers!" he exploded. "I wonder who ordered them."

"I don't know," said the boatswain. "You see a lot of funny things in the Navy these days." He listened to the sounds of smashing and banging carried to his ear from all over the ship by the steel hull, growling softly, "Why don't the Old Man bring her up into the sea? It'll take three times as long to secure everything that's adrift while we wallow in the trough like this. Surely the captain's no fool. Say! I wonder . . . ?"

"I've been wondering too," said MacDougall. "Perhaps the skipper is giving all hands his Object Lesson Number One."

"That could be," agreed the boatswain.

"Well, let's follow the noise and bear a hand," said MacDougall. "Jackson is in trouble."

When the *Belinda* took her first violent roll, Lieutenant Jackson, the supply officer, was in the crew's mess hall supervising details of preparation for the first supper to be served at sea. Together with some of his storekeepers and with Maxwell, chief master-at-arms, and his mess cooks, Jackson was taking hundreds of water glasses from large cartons and stacking them on trays in tiers eight high. Maxwell no longer argued with the supply officer, but carried out all his instructions and suggestions promptly and cheerfully. The decks had been swabbed clean with soap and water and now shone with a heavy coat of wax.

"I made quite a study of feeding crowds of men at Treasure Island," Jackson was saying. "I want everything clean and scientifically placed." He was concentrating hard on arranging mess gear and prescribing how the lines of men would pass, down ladder to steam table, then to mess table and finally to the row of large G.I. cans where scraps were scraped off and mass trays stacked beside the dish washing machine before sailors and troops climbed out of the mess compartment on the opposite side from where they had come down. From time to time he noticed that the ship moved strangely under his feet.

He had expected this, and found it not as uncomfortable as he had been led to believe.

Suddenly the ship careened to port. Jackson's feet shot out from under him. Glasses tumbled from stacked trays and fell in crashing fragments all about him. With frightening acceleration he coasted on the seat of his khakis the full seventy-foot beam of the ship and brought up with a thump against the port bulkhead, together with a conglomeration of knives, forks, spoons, stainless steel mess trays and broken coffee mugs. Before Jackson could pick himself up, the ship rolled violently in the opposite direction and lay shaking and quivering with a twenty-five degree list to starboard. This time he traveled on his stomach, returning in eighteen seconds to the spot where he had originally fallen. Broken crockery and two G.I. cans followed him. Again he lay in a pile of rubble, only this time there was more of it, additional gear having hit the deck with the second roll. Braced against a frame in the starboard bulwarks, Maxwell kept his footing while with a wide grin he watched the prostrate supply officer make the round trip across his waxed deck. When Jackson returned, face down, he helped him to his feet. Jackson mumbled thanks and sank to a nearby bench, fortunately secured to the mess table and bolted to the deck. Here he clung, examining minor cuts and bruises and reflecting bitterly upon his superior instructions, including the waxing of ship's decks. Exasperated and angry, he had bitter things to say, but realizing that he was the victim of his own inexperience, he swallowed them down. Then, as the ship continued to roll and crockery to smash, certain physical symptoms began to complicate his misery.

"Oh, no," he groaned aloud, "not now!" Yet it was true, he was getting seasick. Jackson gritted his teeth and staggered to his feet. Hanging on to the mess table, he grinned weakly at the master-at-arms. "You win, Maxwell. No more wax."

"Oh, that's all right, sir," said Maxwell, balancing his lanky frame easily against the roll. "We all learn the hard way."

But things were not all right, Jackson thought. No words could fix up this mess. At last he said, "Take your mess cooks, Chief—if they can still navigate. Get this mess cleaned up and when you break out new gear, be sure it's nailed down." Jackson started aft, clinging to tables as he went. At the bulkhead door he paused and blurted out, "I won't tell you how. You seem to know more about this stuff than I do."

As Jackson staggered off towards the galley, Maxwell gave a large chunk of shattered coffee mug a vicious kick which sent it spinning clear across the mess hall's waxed deck to crash into fragments against the far bulwarks. One of the storekeepers laughed. "Set her up in the other alley, Chief."

"These ninety-day blunders!" exploded Maxwell. "The wardroom's full of 'em—so all-fired efficient until they get to sea."

"That Jackson's a nice guy, though. This is my second hitch and I never worked for better."

"That's the trouble," said Maxwell. "Now if he was a termite like that Ensign Twitchell, I'd really make things miserable for him."

Jackson was miserable enough without help from Maxwell. When he opened the galley door, savory odors of cooking meats and vegetables, which just an hour before he had sniffed with critical appreciation, nauseated him unbearably. The very orderliness of the place exasperated him. How could the mess hall be a shambles and this place, just next door, as tidy as the kitchen at the Palace Hotel? Great kettles of soup and vegetables were firmly clamped into position. Pots on the great galley range were stopped short after an inch or two of horizontal travel by stout iron baffles clamped at intervals across the smooth-surfaced range top. Three white-dressed cooks, old-timers in the Navy, whooped with merriment as they slid from place to place, tending range and cooking kettles. A few quarts of soup, slopped over by deep rolling, ran back and forth on the deck; everything else was spotless. Jackson clung to the door frame, taking in the scene, while before him in the center of the work space, standing with feet wide apart as if glued to the deck was the short but massive figure of Rockwell, his commissary officer.

Rockwell looked calmly at Jackson. "Sounds pretty bad up there in the mess hall," he said with a twinkle in his brown eyes.

"Yes, it does," Jackson admitted, thinking, I suppose he knows all about the wax. I'll have to live it down, and other blunders to come, I suppose; but I'll learn, if I can just get over this nausea. . . . There's work to do. "We'd better go have a look at the storerooms," he said, gulping.

"Yes, sir," said Rockwell cheerfully. "Everything is under control here in the galley. I'll be glad to give you a hand."

Rockwell opened the after galley door, which led into the starboard passageway. Whistling a tune, he rolled along the narrow alleyway, balancing easily against each violent roll. Following behind, Jackson was flung from side to side and kept his balance only by frequent stops to steady himself with outstretched hands braced against bulkheads or clinging to the exposed fire main. Small workrooms were placed along the passage. Peering through their hooked-back doors, Jackson could see that they were all in a confused state, and in many of them pale-faced bakers, mess cooks and yeomen struggled to restow vegetables, bread, pies and mimeographed forms. Evidently the galley was an exception. As Jackson floundered past the butcher's shop he came face to face with a butcher's striker, gathering up pork chops. He was a tall, thin fellow and bore no physical resemblance to his average-sized department head, yet looking at the pale, unhappy face, Jackson seemed to see in it the mirrored image of his own misery.

Rockwell led the way down another ladder to the starboard dry stores compartment and unlocked the door. Entrance was barred by a tangle of flour sacks and cases of spam. He turned to Jackson. "I'll go round up a working party," he said.

Jackson watched the bulky Rockwell heave himself up the ladder and out of sight, then hung to the ladder's pipe railing. Combined smell of stores, fresh paint and fuel oil overcame him. At last the sound of feet coming rapidly down ladder caused him to jerk his head up and wipe his mouth. MacDougall was smiling at him, part sympathy and part amusement showing on his face.

"What's the matter, Jackson?"

"That's a silly question," said Jackson. "My stores and gear are scattered over ten acres."

MacDougall shook his head. "Trouble with you fellows, you never read about 'The Gun.'"

"'The Gun.' What's that got to do with this mess?" groaned Jackson.

"It's an old French sea classic—Victor Hugo, I think—tells about a massive ship's cannon in a corvette at sea—wasn't properly lashed; got adrift in a gale and crushed nearly everyone in the gun deck to a bloody pulp. They shot the gunner who failed to secure it. You've got one consolation: you'll survive this."

"I suppose so," said Jackson. "I'm . . . I'm responsible for this mess. I'll see it through . . . somehow."

"That's the spirit. Well, I've got to go have a look at the crew berthing compartments. Tough it out, boy!"

The *Belinda* had three crew berthing compartments, 306 forward, 309 and 310 aft. All three were on the first platform, two decks below the main deck. At port and starboard entrances to each berthing compartment were the "heads." Here at the starboard side of 310, MacDougall found the seagoing lavatory was well attended. The boat commander squeezed in to have a look at his boys. All present were very sick, and there was evidence on the deck that all had not made it in time. The ventilation was poor, and for all his experience with stormy weather, MacDougall was nearly overcome. He could visualize the same situation in all other berthing compartments. Unless heads were scoured out at once, the majority of greenhorns would soon be too sick to move.

7

Passing through a watertight door, MacDougall came into the brightly lighted berthing compartment: fresh-painted white bulkheads, rows of green-painted steel lockers and more than two hundred bunks, rigged three high. Unlike the pipe-framed canvas provided for sleeping troops, these bunks had flat springs and mattresses, rigged three high instead of four. Many seasick youngsters lay in their bunks. The place must be cleaned up in a hurry and these boys stirred to activity before it was too late. MacDougall looked about for able-bodied men. The first section, sick or well, was away on watch. Most older hands in the other two sections were busy with working parties, struggling to secure loose gear still crashing back and forth in the wallowing ship. At last he found two men who looked like old hands—big fellows, one sandy, one swarthy-complected. They sat across from each other on two upper bunks, enjoying the misery of a small, pale-faced teen-ager, sprawled on his stomach with his head over the edge of the bunk.

Approaching unseen, MacDougall swung around the tier of bunks and confronted them. Tingling at the nape of his neck, he reverted to the vocabulary of his own days before the mast. "You two donkeys get your tail bones down from those bunks and start cleaning up this place."

The dark fellow looked astonished, but said nothing. You could expect almost anything from officers, but this guy didn't even talk like one; sounded more like a bosun's mate. Wise guy: it would be fun to punch him in the nose—if only he was a bosun's mate. . . .

His companion was more articulate. "We ain't on watch, sir, and besides—"

"And besides, you aren't out helping your shipmates to secure this Noah's Ark for sea," MacDougall interrupted. "You two look like just the fellows to take charge of dunning out this compartment. You can start with the head."

"But—"

"Come on, both of you. Get moving. You round up the pollywogs that are still on their feet. There's plenty of buckets and swabs in the gear locker by the head. I'll see if I can get life into some of these boys and send them along to help you."

The two big fellows slid down from their bunks and started towards the door. The dark-complected one, a carpenter's mate, spoke now for the first time since being disturbed by MacDougall. "Funny thing," he said to his mate, "he never asked our names, just said, 'Get your tail bones off the bunk.' They generally take your name and put you on report for shirking duty. Guess he thinks he's tough; thinks he can handle us by himself."

"He thinks! We're heading for the swabs, aren't we?"

MacDougall worked his way along row after row of tiered bunks, shaking, coaxing, kidding the most likely cases back to their feet. "Come on boys, rise and shine! Show the Navy a leg; let's clean up this compartment so it's fit to live in."

Some remained in a stupor, but most made efforts to get up and comply. Still scared of those boot camp chiefs, MacDougall thought. In the last row of bunks he came upon a clean-cut fellow of about twenty-three who sat holding his head dejectedly.

"Come on, fellow," urged MacDougall. "Snap out of it. It can't be that bad."

"Aye, aye, sir," said the boy automatically, but did not move, his co-operative nature submerged by depression and utter loneliness.

"Come on, son. I need your help."

The boy looked up at MacDougall with dull misery in his dark eyes. MacDougall seemed to place him.

"Aren't you Jones, from the second division?"

"Yes, sir."

"Married, aren't you?"

"Yes. My wife was waiting on the bridge. She waved. . . ." The head went down again as Jones stared at the deck between his feet.

"Then you've got a lot to live for. I left a wife and kid back there. I know how you feel, but I've been through this before. The sooner you get up and try to lick this seasickness, the easier it'll be. A lot of the boys are worse off than you—down for the count like you'll be if you mope much longer in this stuffy corner. Let's clean this place up. Everybody will feel better."

On the next deck up, MacDougall paused to look in at the chief's quarters. The mess room, with long, white-covered table, was empty, as was the berthing compartment beyond. Everything was neat, rows of double bunks made up with clean linen, gear stowed away securely. In the large, clean head, a single toothbrush slid back and forth with the ship's roll, otherwise the place might be somewhere ashore.

Leaving chiefs' quarters, MacDougall heard something crashing about far up the passageway. Going forward he found an empty G.I. can rattling around. At the end of the passageway the door to the garbage-grinding room opened and an untidy seaman emerged, shouting down ladder to the mess hall, "Hey, you mess cooks, come get your cans. It ain't for me to tote 'em down to you." Evidently this was the garbage grinder; he had heard about him: mountain man from Tennessee. His work space must be a mess. MacDougall stuck his head through the doorway. The appearance of the place came as a shock. It was as neat as the pilothouse. Bulkheads and deck were freshly scrubbed; the grinding machinery shone. Loose equipment was lashed in an amateurish but effective manner. The only dirt visible was upon the person of the garbage grinder, whose hair, face and clothing were not merely spattered with garbage fragments but were filthy with accumulated grime. "You want something?" asked the man in a tone which implied that visitors were not welcome.

"No," said MacDougall. "I just want to see if everything is under control."

"This place is always under control—'cept when they leave bones and chicken guts in the garbage or don't come collect them G.I. cans like they's supposed to."

"Looks like you're doing a good job."

"Of course I am. This is one of the importantest places in the whole ship. I grind up all the garbage and mix it with water. Then it runs into the ocean and mixes all up with it so no Jap submarine can find us like they can if them mess cooks dump it overboard like they want to."

"Why don't they want to bring garbage here? It's closer than to pack it out on deck and dump it over the side."

"They don't like to sort it. I make 'em take out bones and chicken guts and haul 'em to the incinerator and they don't like it. So I watch 'em. I want all the garbage brought here."

"What do chicken guts do?"

"They plug the gears, that's what they do. Plug the gears like rubber and I have to take the machine apart to clear 'em out."

"Ever get seasick?"

"No, never been sick in my life—except my feet hurt sometimes."

"You're Hubert, aren't you?"

"That's right, Gilbert Hubert from Tennessee. Who are you?"

The boat commander grinned. "MacDougall, sir," he said, and headed around to the port side to have a look at the sick bay.

A long drawn out pipe from a boatswain's call blasted from a loud-speaker on the bulkhead above his head. There was a pause, a slight cough and then a cool, satisfied-sounding voice asked, "Do you hear there? This is the captain speaking." There was another pause; MacDougall could visualize Captain Gedney looking to windward over tossing sea crests before facing his PA microphone on the bridge to say: "Before the *Belinda* was cast off from the pier this morning, it was reported to me that the ship was ready in all respects for sea. If there now remains any doubt whatsoever that this report was over-optimistic, I will be pleased to remain on this course a little longer." Gedney paused, then, with all the emphasis he could put into

10

his voice, the order came ringing from this loudspeaker as from all the hundred odd throughout the ship, "All hands, secure the *Belinda* for sea!"

MacDougall felt the ship lift to starboard with that little tell-tale tremor—Gedney was bringing her up to the wind again. The character of the ship's motion changed radically. As she came out of the sea's trough and headed into wind and sea, extreme rolling gradually eased to an easy four or five degrees. Pitching increased, and occasionally the *Belinda* trembled after her light bow fell hard upon a wave top, but sounds of sliding and crashing gear were almost completely absent.

Meeting the boatswain and Jackson, MacDougall suggested, "How about a cup of coffee?"

"Good idea," said the boatswain. "I could use one."

Jackson merely nodded. The idea of sitting down appealed to him, but the very thought of coffee . . .

They crossed to the port side and headed forward for the ladder which led up to the passage just outside the wardroom. The entire outboard side of this main deck passageway comprised the ship's hospital unit: sick bay, main dressing station, surgery, medical lab, isolation ward and dentist's office. As they passed, the surgery door opened and an athletic-looking lieutenant of the medical corps stepped out.

"Hello, Dr. Bell," said MacDougall. "Sick bay in good health, or is major surgery indicated?"

"Oh, a few smashed bottles," laughed Bell. "Smells pretty strong in there."

"You should smell the berthing compartments. . . . Not so antiseptic!"

"I really should go down there," said Bell. "Are many of the boys sick? Most of my hospital apprentices are in no shape to help others. The pharmacist's mates are O.K., except those who have had nothing but shore duty."

"How's the senior surgeon?"

"Flynn? Oh, he looked a little pale for a bit, but fortunately none of us doctors got really sick. You'd think Ezra Gates had been to sea all his life." Bell walked along beside MacDougall. "I'm glad that violent rolling is over for a while. We heard the captain. Is the ship in a mess?"

"Fine mess for an hour or so. Learning the hard way." They climbed the ladder and entered the wardroom, a large place some fifty feet square, with portholes looking out over the foredeck, a pantry to starboard and a small officers' lounge to port. Only the four, long mess tables, which ran from side to side, were upright. The place was a shambles of overturned furniture, smashed chinaware and tumblers, silverware, magazines

11

and cribbage boards. In a brown puddle near the sideboard were fragments of all four glass coffee makers.

"Just look at that would you!" exclaimed the boatswain. "All this hullabaloo and now no coffee! Where's that mess attendant?"

MacDougall stepped into the pantry. "Here's two of 'em," he called.

The others followed. Two Negroes were sprawled upon the deck, cradling their heads in their arms.

MacDougall poked one. "Come now, lad. The storm's over." There was no response.

"He may really be ill," said Bell, kneeling down and reaching for the pulse.

The young Negro opened his eyes. When he saw the doctor he jerked his hand away and sat up. "No, sir, Doctor," he protested. "Don't stick that needle in me no more. I ain't really sick, Doctor, just resting, that's all."

"Go have a look at the wardroom," said the boatswain. "See what happened while you were resting. It's going to cost the officers about two bucks apiece for that nap of yours."

They boiled coffee in a pot and found some unbroken mugs. As they sat down, Quigley, the executive officer, a handsome six-footer in spotless khakis, came in and joined them.

"Ah, coffee!" he said, rubbing his hands together. Then, looking around, "What a horrible mess! Weather was quite rough for a while."

"Oh, was it?" cracked MacDougall.

"Certainly was. Lovely photo of my wife in a silver frame she just gave me—hit the deck and smashed the glass. I must get the carpenter to replace it. Then the coffee I had on the desk spilled all over my best shore blues, which the boy hadn't put away."

"That's too bad," said Bell.

"Yes," Quigley continued, "but the worst of it was that it woke me up from my afternoon nap."

MacDougall stared at Quigley. "Nap?"

"Certainly. I always try to get in forty winks on afternoons when there is nothing to do."

CHAPTER 3

The *Belinda's* first supper at sea was a poorly attended meal. Old hands, their appetites improved by exercise of securing for sea, hungrily received the offerings of Shadow Rockwell and his cooks, but the chow line was short. During the hour's respite before sunset battle stations, that majority of the crew who were as new to the sea as their ship, were in their bunks recovering from Captain Gedney's shakedown. Even lying prone, they were reminded of the day's experience, for Gedney addressed all hands in a personal announcement that the ship was on a ten-day shakedown cruise, and that the next port of call would be Pearl Harbor.

Ten minutes before sunset, the "all hands" pipe sounded again over the PA, then the voice of the watch boatswain's mate reaching every section of the ship with the order, "Now darken ship. Now darken ship." It had been previously explained that this order required every scuttle door and steel porthole backer to be closed and dogged down so that no gleam of artificial light could show outward from the ship. Lights in passageways leading to weather decks were to be dimmed, and rubberized blackout curtains rigged inside doorways.

Five minutes later the long pipe came again, this time followed by intermittent honking of general quarters alarm and the boatswain's mate's "All hands man your sunset battle stations." Since leaving port, division officers had worked with pencil on division watch, quarter and station bills and posted them so that every man aboard should know the location of his battle station.

After a clatter of men running and of helmets coming off gun tub hooks at each gun station, guns were reported ready within eleven minutes. "Manning the guns in eleven minutes," Gedney informed his crew over the PA, "is an improvement on the fourteen minutes which you took this morning; however, it has not the slightest military value."

The captain now turned his attention to the blacking out of the ship. The junior officer of the watch was sent on an inspection tour and returned to report over half the ship's portholes uncovered and lights still undimmed. Gedney, who detested overuse of the public address system, spoke to his crew once more. "It has been reported to me that the ship is less than 50 per cent blacked out. For your information and future guidance, it has been scientifically demonstrated that the light of a single match is visible to an enemy submarine for over two miles on a clear night. Now darken ship. Carry on."

Darkness settled about the ship. Decks were quiet; men standing in huddles behind their guns could hear the rush of water being divided by the stem and thrust astern by churning propeller. The moderating wind sang a gentle, tuneless song in the rigging. War seemed far away, and home far. One hour after sunset word to secure from general quarters was passed quietly over phone circuits. Condition Three was resumed and off-duty members of the crew were at leisure until called to stand night watches.

MacDougall rolled over in his upper bunk and looked down at the bridge messenger, who was shaking him violently. "All right, son," he said. "You don't have to shake my teeth out. Next time just call me."

"O.K.," answered the messenger, then realizing that officers rated a more formal reply and had nasty ways of getting you in trouble, he fled, leaving the stateroom door unlatched. The door swung back and forth, crashing alternately against the bunks and the twin steel lockers across the narrow room from the double-tiered bunks.

MacDougall swung to the deck, carefully avoiding overhanging portions of his roommate, sound asleep in the lower bunk. He washed some of the sleep from his face, dressed and headed down the dim-lit passageway to the deserted wardroom. After swallowing a cup of over-boiled coffee, he headed up steel ladders to the bridge. Among dim shapes on the bridge wing he identified the short, muscular figure of Jim Randall, an experienced junior lieutenant, who had the deck, put his hand on Randall's shoulder and asked, "How's she going, Jim?"

"Oh, there you are, Dave. Glad to see you. I'm ready for the kip after this screwball day."

"Yeah, the new Navy. . . . Little quieter than it was a few hours ago. Jackson must have his dishes corralled for the night."

Randall chuckled, then went on to the business of turning over the watch. "We're on course two-three-five true and gyro. No zigzag. Moon rises soon after two. Standard speed is fifteen knots; ship steaming at standard."

"How many revs, seventy-eight?"

"Engine room's been giving me seventy-seven. Proceeding singly and with ten days to get to Pearl, what's one little r.p.m.?"

"About two tenths of a knot," said MacDougall. "We'll let brother Harrison worry about that, poor guy."

"Yes, such a swell fellow—doesn't know one star from another."

"Good thing he's got two thousand miles of open water ahead. Couldn't be in a better place to learn."

"How in the world they made *him* navigator!"

"Rank, my good man. Haven't you ever heard of rank?"

"Somebody mentioned it to me once."

"Well, any night orders?"

"Not yet. Captain's in the pilothouse—sitting in that back-breaking high chair of his."

"What!" exclaimed MacDougall. "All good captains go to bed on nights like this."

"Oh, I'm sure he trusts us. Probably nervous, first night at sea, after what happened this afternoon."

"Perhaps he's waiting for her to break in two." It was now midnight. One by one, junior members of the watch reported that they had been properly relieved. After discussing compass checks, lookouts, gun watches, watertight doors and other small matters pertaining to the watch, Randall headed for his bunk. MacDougall checked bridge watch, lookouts and gun stations, then entered the pilothouse. In the far corner, level with pilot-house windows, the chunky form of Captain Gedney appeared to recline in space, ready to float away at any sudden roll. Moving closer, MacDougall could see the captain's high, swivel chair, fabricated by the *Belinda's* shipfitters to Gedney's own specifications. It looked like an uncomfortable barber's chair, set in a base which was welded to the deck. The back was adjustable so that Gedney could sit erect, watch the ship and reach handily into the dispatch case welded to the bulkhead. At present the chair was tilted back; Gedney was breathing steadily with eyes closed. Must have fallen asleep, though how anybody could sleep in that thing. . . .

"Good morning, MacDougall." Gedney's voice sounded calm and self-possessed. Must have been awake all the time, no doubt listening to what he and Randall had been saying.

"Good morning, Capt'n. I thought you were asleep."

Gedney's voice stiffened. "A captain never sleeps when his ship is underway. I was merely resting my eyes."

MacDougall cast about for a change of subject—surely he doesn't expect me to believe that. "Weather's moderated nicely, sir."

"Yes, fine weather. . . . The weather has been perfect ever since we dropped the pilot."

MacDougall wondered whether Jackson would go along with that. He smothered a chuckle. The Old Man might not appreciate jokes about his shakedown, at least not at this stage.

Wondering about the zigzag he said, "Moon will be up shortly after midnight, sir."

"Yes," said Gedney. "We will commence zigzag Plan Fox seven minutes before. I shall write up my night orders now." Gedney climbed down from his seat and disappeared into the chart room. Twenty minutes later he reappeared and stood silently beside MacDougall until he had regained night vision, then said, "My night orders are on the chart table. I will relieve you while you read and sign them."

"Aye, aye, sir." MacDougall stepped past the helmsman to the after bulkhead, opened the door and passed through folds of blackout screen. He found himself in a small and dim-lit passageway. To starboard was the radio room entrance; a babel of code signals came from the place—receivers busy, transmitters quiet, for the ship sailed under radio silence. At the end of

15

the short passage, a ladder led down to starboard—passage to captain's cabin and wardroom country. To port was the inside entrance to chart room and radar control. Entering here, Mac-Dougall was astonished to find Lieutenant Commander Harrison, the navigator, his tall frame bent in an angular fashion over the chart table, where he was puzzling over a star identification chart.

"Hello," MacDougall greeted him cheerfully, "you're a regular night hawk." Harrison nodded, a tight-lipped smile on his usually friendly face, then continued to concentrate on his chart. MacDougall read the long and involved instructions of Gedney's first night orders, signed them, checked ship's position plotted on the sea chart and returned to the pilothouse.

Gedney stood on his bridge, watching ahead and all around the horizon. While he waited for MacDougall's eyes to adjust to darkness, he said, "For some time to come, I will permit only you and the other three deck officers having years of experience to stand top sea watches. Each of you will have an assistant officer of the watch and two junior officers. This is done not because they are all needed on the bridge at once, but so that they may gradually qualify for top watches."

MacDougall said, "Yes, sir." These fellows in the wardroom —he had never sailed with a nicer bunch, but what did they know of the sea? How could a man teach them in a few weeks what he had painfully learned over a span of twenty years? Two Ph.D.'s, one in literature, the other in sociology; a master in romance languages, another in history. There were a couple of pricks in the bunch; that sadistic little Ensign Twitchell would bear watching. Most of them were thoroughly nice human beings, but they didn't ask, "What was your last ship?" They said, "What did you major in? What was *your* college?" All these campuses in mountains and valleys and out in the flat sweep of prairie grass—what had they to do with ships and the sea? Brains, he supposed; so many high-quality bins to shovel knowledge into in a hurry.

On the bridge with MacDougall tonight was Lieutenant, junior grade, Steve Sherwood, Rhodes Scholar and instructor in literature at Princeton, an easy-going but highly intelligent fellow who seemed, of all this lot in the wardroom, to come to the sea most naturally. The others were Ensign Karl Kruger, son of a Texas cotton rancher, and quiet Ensign Bud Foster, son of a Kansas farmer. Sherwood went into the chart room to prepare the zigzag plan. Kruger was sent out on a routine check of weather decks. Foster stood beside the bridge messenger on the port wing of the blacked-out bridge. In the shadows were enlisted men, boatswain's mate of the watch, quartermaster, two helmsmen, and there were fourteen lookouts: enough men on one bridge watch to run a small ship.

Nothing to do, just stars and sea—no enemy, no invasion fleet crowded all about. These things were to come, and when they did, he would be thankful for this period of quiet organization.

At last Gedney seemed satisfied and retired to his sea cabin, a room barely large enough for bunk, chair and wash basin, where the captain could be quickly reached in an emergency. "I will lie down with my clothes on, MacDougall. The light bulbs are unscrewed, the porthole is open; you may speak to me through the port at any time. I will be awake; I will just close my eyes."

When the sea-cabin door closed after Gedney, MacDougall sighed with relief. "After commanding a ship of my own," he said to Sherwood on the opposite bridge wing, "I can appreciate his sense of responsibility, but it's very annoying to have captains hanging around the bridge in the middle of the night when there is nothing for them to do."

"I'd think you'd feel better with the captain around."

"Not when you know ships. They can seem almost human. I like to be alone on a bridge at night; a skipper hanging around steals some of the feeling I like to share with my ship."

"You are a romantic lad," said Sherwood.

MacDougall laughed out loud. This Sherwood tickled him —such a fatherly attitude when he was at least seven years younger. "Was, perhaps," he said. "Things are changed now for all of us." Then Sherwood was gone back to the chart room and MacDougall stood alone now on the starboard wing, unmindful of men crowded into bridge shadows, his feet apart to get the sensation of his new ship's movements. New, she was, new but alive. He listened to wind in the top hamper and sea wash curling along the waterline, wondering what hostile shores they would visit and what action they would share.

MacDougall's thoughts went back to the first time he saw the *Belinda*: the night before her launching . . . that old man saying, "Ships talk." Tonight, as the salt wash pressed against the *Belinda's* bilge keels, she would be talking more, working out in this seaway all remaining locked-in stresses which would come free as long as her hull remained intact. While MacDougall gripped the bridge railing and felt the ship's vibrations he heard the words of the old shipbuilder whispering through the windswept rigging: "A good ship, a fortunate ship."

After one more voyage as master in the *Roamer* he had volunteered for active duty in the Navy, which involved removing two of the four gold stripes around the sleeves of his blues, and a cut in his income to less than one half of what it had been. Yet one thing had been added: the thrill running up and down his spine now that he was really on his country's team.

MacDougall remembered the next time he saw the *Belinda*,

17

on the morning of her sailing from the outfitting yard for this first passage and shakedown of ship and crew. Walking past a group of storage sheds, MacDougall had suddenly felt salt air whispering in from sea as he came upon a mooring slip. On the side nearest to him lay a neglected looking four-masted bark, stripped of her sails, white paint peeling from wooden hull, standing rigging hanging in slack bights, a martingale stay dangling from her bowsprit into tidewater which curled about her forefoot. Across from the bark loomed a much larger hull, freshly painted war-gray, her bridge deck higher than the squarerigger's topmasts, guns on her fantail frowning down upon the great wooden wheel on the bark's deserted poop. MacDougall rounded the sailing ship and glanced up at the Naval identification painted in white lettering six feet high on the *Belinda's* cruiser stern: PA 15. That stood for Attack Transport Number Fifteen, one of the first of a comparatively new type of combat ship, designed to land assault troops on enemy beachheads using her own landing craft. MacDougall looked up at these assault boats, nested on hatches or hanging overside from davits. They dominated the ship more than her guns or her radar antenna, which rotated one hundred and twenty-five feet above her waterline.

Speaking to his officers gathered in the shipyard briefing room the day before, the *Belinda's* commanding officer, silver-haired Captain Winthrop Gedney, Annapolis, Class of 1908, had said: "An attack transport's main battery is not her guns; an attack transport's main battery is her boats. The entire mission of the *Belinda* is to carry a combat-loaded battalion landing team of some fourteen hundred officers and men, and to land them, together with all necessary equipment, as it were in the laps of the enemy." Gedney had paused, smiling faintly as he dabbed at his tidy blues with a clean handkerchief. "An attack transport is the largest of all amphibious types. You might call her a beachhead lady. What she becomes will depend largely on you officers. You may make her a home, or if you so prefer, you may make her a madhouse and I will help you."

MacDougall's feelings as he looked up from dockside at the *Belinda* and her landing craft were less sweeping, more personal. He had been assigned duty as boat group commander, his responsibility to train boat crews and to guide these landing craft to shore in organized waves. There was much to be done before these boats, with their hinged ramps and sturdy diesel engines, were ready to carry the war to Japanese waiting on Micronesian islands.

MacDougall glanced at white draft marks painted next the rudder post: the *Belinda* was drawing only eighteen feet, four inches aft and less than that forward. He was familiar with the ship's characteristics, having commanded a similar type of hull

18

in the merchant service. With all the *Belinda's* additional top hamper of guns, three hundred and forty tons of landing craft together with six sets of heavy davits, innumerable gun mounts and additions to steel deckhouses on several levels, she was bound to be cranky. Requests for additional ballast had been denied, pending the shake down cruise to Hawaii. Most of the crew were green, and the ship was far from being properly secured for sea. That deserted old windjammer across the slip with her rigging hanging in bights was about as ready for sea as this newly commissioned ship of the United States Navy, due to sail within the hour. MacDougall looked up again at the wall of gray paint, thirty feet above him to main deck, eight feet more for each additional deck pyramided above—upper deck, boat deck, bridge deck and signal bridge. He noted rolled up debarkation nets, secured to bulwarks fore and aft and to upper deck railings amidships. Unfurled, these dropped to water's edge and shorebound infantrymen would clamber to boats waiting beneath. In his imagination he saw not khaki-clad men in helmets, but the white capped sailors now climbing shore brow to quarterdeck scrambling down these nets from a sinking ship.

Weather decks were crowded with sailors coming out scuttles from below-deck compartments for final muster before sailing. The last of the liberty section continued to climb the brow and step aboard, some dutifully, some proudly saluting colors and quarterdeck. MacDougall walked through the crowd and continued forward along the five-hundred-sixteen feet of the *Belinda's* length, and looked up at her bow, some twenty feet higher than the fantail aft. There was her starboard anchor, a three-ton affair which, being of different manufacture from the hawse, did not fit properly. Seen from the pier the anchor appeared incredibly high, yet soon it would be plunging up and down in the sea and if not secure, would soon work loose. MacDougall caught a glimpse of the warrant boatswain, intent as he moved about the electric-powered windlass with the carpenter and warrant electrician. I wouldn't be surprised if the anchor winch was haywire, MacDougall thought.

Nine-inch mooring lines surged alternately taut and slack; the ship was stirring at her moorings as if restless to get to sea. Engines must be warming up, propeller turning ahead and astern; it was time to get aboard. MacDougall swung on his heel and headed for the brow, dull ache inside for Nadine, his wife, and Robbie, his two-year-old son. As a sort of anesthesia to heart pain, his mind ground out lines of an old slaver's ditty, ending:

And then we put the hatches on.
It was time for us to go.

CHAPTER 4

Weather continued moderate, warming pleasantly as the *Belinda* approached the Hawaiian Islands. While the ship worked out her stresses, Gedney trained his crew intensively. Sunrise and sunset battle stations became familiar routine, daily drills exercised them in carrying out the ship's intended tactical duties and to cope with emergencies sure to occur in battles to come. Fire drill, collision drill, gas attack drill, abandon ship drill: day or night any one or more of these drills with attending problems in damage control were announced without previous warning. In one of many such alerts, PA speakers roused sleepers at one in the morning with: "Fire in combat gasoline stowage at frame one-four-six, second platform, number five hold. Watertight bulkhead at frame one-four-one ruptured. Damage control party number three, proceed to scene of the fire; all others proceed to fire quarters and stand fast." Bomb hits, engine failures, casualties to personnel, crashed bulkheads—hour after hour Gedney confronted his officers and men with simulated disasters, then watched them critically and held critiques on his bridge. After his chastened officers left, he sat in his high seat pondering over what had been done; thinking up new surprises to be suddenly announced by the authoritative voice of the ship's PA. Later, in surf-whipped Oahu and Maui bays, he would exercise his crew at the all important ship-to-shore movement. At present he concentrated on the ship herself.

Routine gradually wore into all hands until bewildering situations and commands became familiar, if not completely understood. One night, after a week at sea, a canvas target set up on a raft was dropped over the side. The *Belinda* turned and steamed back and forth on runs passing within three thousand yards of the raft. Star shells fired from Gun One illuminated the bobbing target with eerie, pale-green light. At Gedney's order, firing runs were made. The crew was stimulated by the sharp barking of five-inch guns, coughing rhythm of twin forties and rapid shock of automatic twenties as Gedney closed upon the target. When it was hoisted aboard, splintered and filled with holes, most of the crew felt confident that they could handle all comers. "Let us at them Japs," cried Ned Strange, a loader at Gun Two. "We'll do the same to them!"

On the tenth morning, off Makapuu Head, the *Belinda* was met by a low-flying B-26, painted bright yellow and towing, by means of a long wire cable, a canvas target sleeve about fifteen feet long, painted bright red. Weighted down with helmet, life jacket, sun glasses and binoculars, Gedney took station on the bridge wing and called all hands to battle stations. After giving specific instructions regarding angles of fire so as to hit the towed sleeve without endangering the tow plane, he said to alert little Art Hall, the gunnery officer, "Now get back to your control station and don't forget to lead the target."

"Aye, aye, sir," said Hall, holding his five-feet-six inches erect, "we'll punch that target full of holes, Captain."

The first run was horizontal, plane and target crossing ahead of the ship at about four thousand feet altitude. As the target crossed dead ahead, Gedney cried, "Gun One. Commence firing." His order went into the phone circuits. Almost instantly the long-barreled gun on the forecastle roared and recoiled. Again it fired, then eight more shots cracked in rapid succession. The sound was impressive, but each burst of exploding powder lagged further behind the target.

"Tell Lieutenant Hall to have his men lead the target," said Gedney to his talker.

Next came a similar run, only astern for Gun Two. In spite of warnings and careful instructions, the sleeve passed by unscathed. Tall Roy Alvick, gun captain at Gun Two, flushed red with anger and turned back from his position over the gun's breech to plead with MacDougall, his battery officer, "Let me point this gun, sir, with Doyle from Gun Three to train. We can knock that sock full of holes on the next run."

"No," said MacDougall sharply, "I know that you old-timers can shoot; the problem is to train these kids."

"But let us show 'em, sir. Just once."

"No. It isn't today that matters. What matters is teaching these men to hit Jap planes. They saw experts hitting targets at Point Montara gunnery school, didn't they? It's up to them now."

The target plane made glide runs for the anti-aircraft forties. After a few fitful explosions, these guns jammed at the breeches from improper loading and could no longer be fired. The tow plane came still closer to give twenty millimeter batteries a chance. As they burst into eager fire, the ship trembled, yet although the forward trajectory of tracer bullets seemed in line with the target, they swept backward from the speeding sleeve like water sprayed from so many hoses, and no hits were registered. As if encouraged by this miserable performance, the target plane flew some distance astern, then turned and came along the ship's port hand, passing close aboard and flying at masthead height. The bright red sleeve, rippling in the slipstream, seemed to be thumbing its derision at frustrated gun crews. Here was their chance! While the *Belinda* shuddered from truck to keel, every gun which could be brought to bear poured out a withering blast of fire, yet not one of these thousands of bullets reached the target. As the plane retrieved its undamaged sleeve

21

and returned to base, Gedney snapped on all groups of the PA system and said to his crew, "I thank God that we were attacked by fifteen feet of canvas!"

The litter of empty shell casings had been gathered up and stowed below. Decks had been washed down and the ship tidied for entrance into port. Waikiki Beach with its pink and white hotels lay abeam in a setting of coconut trees. Dead ahead, the flat, unimpressive entrance to Pearl Harbor was in sight. All hands had been called to quarters and division officers mustered on the bridge, waiting to receive orders for the day from the executive officer. Quigley stood beside Gedney's pilothouse chair. Despite the negative showing at gunnery practice, the captain seemed in excellent humor as he smiled and said in a pleasant tone, "The uniform for entering port will be service dress whites for officers and undress whites with neckerchief for the crew."

"Aye, aye, sir." Quigley saluted and returned to mustered department heads and division officers, passing on the captain's order in an equally pleasant voice.

The officers began at once to protest and to make excuses. "I left my whites in 'Frisco: thought we were going out to fight."

"Mine are crumpled in the bottom of a sea bag. That's where they belong for the duration."

"How about the line handlers? They'll be black before we get alongside."

Quigley waited calmly until silence was restored, then said pleasantly, "I repeat, gentlemen, uniform for entering port will be whites. I can't understand your objections; personally, I think it will look smart. Regardless what you may think about it, I am passing on an order from the captain. When the word is passed, all the crew not actually working the ship will be mustered on the main deck, by divisions, wearing whites. All officers will wear whites. All line handlers will wear whites. Is that clear?" Hearing no further comment, Quigley snapped out something which sounded like "Post." Thus dismissed, the officers returned to their divisions.

Curling breakers washed white reefs to port and starboard as the *Belinda* steamed carefully through green channel waters, entering Pearl Harbor. Her crew lined the rail two deep, facing outboard, their snowy whites sharply contrasting with battle-gray of decks and landing craft. At bow and stern, the boat-swain and MacDougall, in crumpled whites, supervised break-ing out of heavy mooring lines and wires by sailors reluctant to soil white trousers which they had carefully washed and pressed for liberty ashore. On the bridge, Gedney, dressed in perfectly fitting whites, beautifully laundered by his Chinese steward and decorated with three rows of multicolored service ribbons, looked down upon his crew with satisfaction. "Just what I wanted," he remarked to Quigley, who hovered at his elbow. "At least they look like sailors."

Randall, who had the deck, kept a close eye on the channel. The Naval harbor pilot who had come aboard was newly assigned to the Hawaiian area, therefore understandably nervous. A division of outbound LSTs wallowed down upon the *Belinda*. To squeeze past them it became necessary to steer to starboard, which was done just in time. Randall ran to the starboard wing and looked down. The *Belinda* was about to sideswipe a flotilla of mine sweepers moored alongside the channel. "Pilot," he called. "We'd better come left again."

"I can't," said the pilot. "These ribbon-clerk skippers are crowding me."

"You'll have to come left—push 'em over," said Randall striding towards the pilot. "We're going to crash into—"

Randall's sentence was never finished. Gedney's arm reached across his chest and stopped him abruptly. "Mr. Randall," said Gedney in a voice trembling with anger, "look at this!" He grasped Randall by the arm and pointed a finger towards the foredeck. Just forward of the bridge, two fifty-six-foot steel tank lighters were cradled upon number three hatch. A man dressed in a filthy undershirt and greasy dungarees, which were rolled halfway to his knees, sat comfortably in their shade on the edge of the hatch, enjoying the scenery. Black hair, badly in need of cutting, flopped over his eyes. He was apparently humming a tune, for he seemed to be keeping time with one of his dirty bare feet against the covered firemain which ran alongside the hatch. Indifferent to regimentation about him, he was whittling a stick with a murderous-looking jackknife.

Gedney was reduced to a hoarse whisper. "Randall, you are the officer of the deck. Go down and place that man under arrest. Bring him up here to me." Randall looked at Gedney in astonishment. Was it possible that the captain wished him to leave the bridge in a crowded, narrow channel to arrest a man for whittling a stick? The expression on Gedney's face convinced him that this was indeed the case. Randall turned and went down the ladder with Gedney's shocked voice following him: "What will Admiral Pettibone think!"

The barefoot whittler saw white shoes and creased trousers approaching: just let a body be comfortable and along comes an officer. He looked up at Randall, who was saying, "The captain wants to see you, up on the bridge."

"Oh, that's right nice of him. I never been up there."

Before the morning's over you'll wish you never had, thought Randall. Aloud he said, "Better leave your stick down here."

When they reached the bridge, Gedney was concentrating on the piloting and seemed to have forgotten all about the barefoot whittler. "I haven't time for him now. Can't you see I'm busy?" He gesticulated towards the after part of the bridge wing. "Have him stand there 'til I have time for him." Nevertheless, Gedney seemed to relax again. Leaving Randall to work with the pilot, he drew off a bit with Quigley and lapsed into reminiscence. "It's nice to enter port once more with the men at quarters in whites—reminds me of the admiral's pie."

"Pie, sir?"

"Yes, the admiral's pie. It was years ago—in the old Navy, of course. I was first lieutenant in the battleship *Colorado*. We were standing in to San Pedro after summer maneuvers. We were the flag: old Admiral Brash. You've heard of him, haven't you?"

"Oh yes, sir. Great on spit and polish."

"Indeed he was! The admiral had given strict orders that every man in the fleet should be mustered at quarters. The captain sent me about decks to see that the flagship complied. 'Every last man,' he said. Whom should I bump into on the quarterdeck but the admiral's steward, carrying a large lemon pie."

Quigley smiled. "I suppose you captured the pie, sir."

"No, indeed. The construction and repair people were mustered nearby and I put the steward in the front rank, next to the boilermaker striker. Of course he tried to wriggle out of it —you know how impertinent admiral's stewards can be. He said, 'Sir, the admiral ordered this pie.'

"I said, 'Was it a direct order?' He could not answer that. I had him there. I said, 'When all hands secure from quarters, you may tell the admiral that the ship's first lieutenant found you crossing the quarterdeck with a pie and placed you in ranks.' "

"Anything ever come of it, sir?"

"Nothing official; I knew my regulations. But for years after I was known throughout the fleet as the only officer who had ever mustered an admiral's pie at quarters."

When the *Belinda* had been securely moored, Gedney spun around on his heel and walked over to the barefoot nonconformist from the foredeck. Now he's going to get it, thought Randall. Dirty as a pig and no hat! The Old Man will fry him for sure!

"Well, son," said Gedney, still enjoying recollections of the admiral's pie, "what's your name and division?"

"I'm Gilbert Hubert, from Tennessee."

"From Tennessee, yes, but what division on the *Belinda*? What are your duties?"

"First division; I'm the garbage grinder," Hubert said proudly.

"I see, but you should keep cleaner," said Gedney.

"Oh, I keep that place clean, Cap'n. You should come down sometime and see for yourself. Only trouble is the chicken guts."

"Chicken guts!"

"They jam up them gears. I keep telling them cooks about the chicken guts. And them mess cooks, leavin' forks in the garbage. You wouldn't believe it—why, just this morning—"

"Yes indeed," Gedney raised a hand to put a stop to the garbage grinder's monologue. Then he turned to Randall. "See that this man gets cleaned up and into the prescribed uniform of the day." As Gedney headed down ladder for his cabin, Randall heard him muttering, "Chicken guts. Chicken guts, indeed!"

CHAPTER 5

Balancing on the decked-over bow of his command boat as it bounced in the chop alongside the *Belinda,* MacDougall anxiously watched the first attempt at hoisting out boats. Just before he had scrambled into the boat, Gedney had said, "I expect that this will take you a little over half an hour the first time or two." That had been an hour and seventeen minutes ago, and exactly nine of the *Belinda's* thirty-two landing craft were in the water. The rest still waited in chocks on deck, hung precariously from heavy framed arms of gravity-launching davits or dangled from cargo boom yardarms. Sunshine shimmered from the curving white beach line of Kaneohe Bay where MacDougall was scheduled to conduct the first practice landing of *Belinda's* boat group. Mountain peaks flanking Nuuanu Pali appeared to float in the summer haze while trade winds blew unchanging against Oahu's windward shore. The very air had the feeling of leisure, of languid resistance to change and sudden effort. Somehow, MacDougall knew, he must overcome this; the *Belinda's* first assault landing against Jap-held beaches drew daily nearer. It was up to him to train this boat group.

"Look at that VP, sir!" Al Hatcher, command boat coxswain, pointed aft. "Trouble!" MacDougall turned his head left. A thirty-six foot ramp boat swung and jerked at the ends of the heavy mechanical davit, which was slamming back and forth like two tremendous waving arms.

These davit crews: would they ever learn? "Goose her over there," MacDougall ordered. The two-hundred-fifty horse power engine roared; the command boat picked up way and swung in an incurving arc which brought them quickly within shouting distance of the davit. Hatcher was one of the few experienced landing-craft coxswains aboard. He was a smart and willing mountain boy from Virginia, with surf knowledge gained at Guadalcanal and Attu. As the command boat slowed again, MacDougall cupped his hands and yelled to the davit crew on deck above, "Pull the pin. Pull the strongback pin! Quit jockeying that davit winch and hold an even strain 'til you get the pin out! Let's launch that VP today!"

There were shouts on deck. Doyle, a boatswain's mate second, came on the run to take charge. A sailor bobbed up from within the hung-up craft, pulled the forgotten pin from the strongback center and the LCVP lowered in hesitant surges toward the water fifty feet below. MacDougall turned his attention elsewhere—six boats from the starboard side now safe in the water. He wondered how Sherwood was getting along on the other side. "Take her to port, Cox'n," he ordered. Again Hatcher gunned his boat, cutting around the bow of the drifting *Belinda*. Sherwood was with Randall in Boat Two, the salvage boat, an LCP with a shovel-nosed hard wooden bow, similar to the command boat except that it had no canopy. It was equipped with special emergency pumps and fire-fighting gear manned by a group of enlisted specialists under Randall, who were prepared to fight fire and to make emergency repairs to landing-craft engines and hulls. Things had gone better on the port side: seven LCVPs dutifully milling around in the prescribed boat circle ready for calling, while three more were halfway down the *Belinda's* side, all on an even keel. With a hasty wave to Sherwood, his assistant boat commander, Mac-Dougall hurried back to the starboard side.

Startled yells from the afterdeck brought his attention suddenly to number five hatch, where a ten-ton cargo boom crashed down through a tangle of parted rigging toward the ship's rail, while at the same time the landing craft which was being lowered overside dropped like a rock the last ten feet and landed in the water with a geyser-like splash. No need to signal Hatcher this time; the command boat was roaring to the scene. Mac-Dougall realized what had happened: some deckhand had mistaken clutch lever for brake. Now a boat and boom were ruined, no doubt—perhaps some of the crew badly hurt. All this in bright daylight! What would happen tonight when he was scheduled to launch these boats in pitch dark?

Passing under the end of the cargo boom, which hung overside in a tangle of guys and lifts, Hatcher brought the command boat smartly alongside the dropped craft. MacDougall jumped aboard and looked about. The coxswain was doubled over the horizontal steering wheel, gasping for breath. The bow hook was sprawled on the grating, near the ramp. The third member of the dropped boat's crew seemed unharmed and unconcerned. He sat on top of the large engine box, cushioned by a number of kapok life jackets.

The coxswain was getting his breath again. "Are you hurt, son?" MacDougall asked.

"I'm all right," the coxswain gasped. "Just that wheel . . . got me in the guts. . . . What happened?"

MacDougall was down inside the craft's deep well, where combat infantrymen would stand on the trip from ship to shore. He looked all about, not a leak. These boats were tough. The bow hook had a nasty gash over his left ear. MacDougall looked up towards deck. Boatswain Torgeson was looking down at the tangle. "Boom's bent about two degrees. I think we can fix it," he said laconically.

"I'll leave this boat," said MacDougall. "Looks O.K. but should be checked. Send the crew to sick bay for a check up, just in case."

From the hatch the command boat roared out to the rendezvous circle off the bow, where boats which had managed to reach water were idling in a ragged circle. En route, MacDougall asked Hatcher, "Who was that relaxed character doping off on the life jackets?"

Hatcher grinned. "That's Sacktime Riley."

"Sacktime?"

"That's what they call him. Sleeps night and day—supposed to be a boat engineer but he never moves a muscle if he can help it—always waits to see if the other guys will do it for him."

Somehow the rest of the boats were lowered into the water without accident. MacDougall rounded up the thirty craft, divided them into five practice waves, each in charge of a boat officer, and headed into Kaneohe Bay. The weather was pleasant; temperature, sun and breeze were just right. As the boat group drew away from the *Belinda* he could feel the tension running out of him. It was good to be away and on his own. Aside from his knowledge of boats and surf and his study of the new naval manuals on ship-to-shore movement, he was as green at this stuff as any of his crew. But there was no help to be had from the ship, from Gedney or any of them. This business was something new to the Navy; they would learn it in white water and on the beaches, not from books or from Gedney's lectures. He watched the boat waves following him, each a horizontal line of six boats. The first two waves looked good; that would be Sherwood and Kruger. The others were beginning to straggle astern. MacDougall took up his signal flags and ordered them to close up. Gradually third and fourth waves closed up somewhat, but the last one was not only falling back but individual boats in the wave were spreading further and further apart. There might come times when it would be necessary to spread boats apart to avoid enemy strafing, but first they must learn to act as a team. Soon they would be loaded with a thousand beach-bound soldiers or marines, and the landing would be a matter of minute scheduling. He could never maintain timed waves this way.

With a signal to Hatcher, MacDougall turned his boat around, cut throttle and waited for Sherwood's first wave to come up with him. Sherwood rode the nearest LCVP in the wave, long arms hooked over the ramp top as he watched the rocks about and shoreline ahead. "Lead the way in, Steve," MacDougall shouted. "I'm going back after those stragglers." As the command boat flashed by the third wave on her way seaward, the burly figure of Lieutenant Mike O'Bannion waved to him. Mike was taking his beach party in for orientation. They had the ship's jeep along to provide simple practice at landing a vehicle in soft sand. The jeep was loaded with high frequency voice radio equipment, with which Mike would establish communication with the ship from the beach.

The fifth boat wave was very slow to close up. No amount of signaling seemed to do any good. MacDougall cut his boat around and came close along side the last wave. "What's the matter, Bud?" he called to the boat officer. "Why don't you close up? That's what you're here for. Couldn't you see my signal?"

The ensign made no reply. A flow of angry words came to MacDougall's mind. Then he looked at Bud's face. It was not a face belonging to anyone who would be unco-operative or stubborn. It was just a kindly young face from somewhere in the middle of Kansas, completely lost in this stuff. MacDougall took a big gulp of fresh air, held it a moment, then exhaled and said, "Open your throttle four hundred revs more, Bud. That will bring you up to the rest of them. Bear right and bunch your boats together." MacDougall ran the command boat around to the other end of the loose line. "Squeeze 'em over, cox," he yelled. "They'll move over. It's just like herding cows." Hatcher, who had seen more cows than landing craft, grinned and rode herd on wave five.

Hatcher opened throttle on the speedy command boat and soon returned MacDougall alongside Sherwood's first wave, still in perfect alignment. They had rounded the point and were now deep into the curve of the bay, surf ahead and beyond, white sand washed by four-foot waves. Long ground-swell rollers lifted the line of boats abreast in unison, then slid on under, leaving them stern down in the trough. "Step her up," yelled MacDougall. "Ride her in on the back of that wave." Suddenly they were in white surf boil. MacDougall signaled Sherwood on, then cut his motor and watched the first wave go in for a landing while he waited for the second wave, checking three-minute time interval with the sweep second hand of his strap watch. Sherwood swept his boats in on a roller. Abruptly, bows grounded and ramps dropped down on wet, white sand in a

28

surprising stop to forward motion, denying the illusion given by wave motion that the boats would continue over dry sand until they landed in fragrant lantana shrubs beyond the beach line.

No boats broached to. Sherwood's wave retracted without difficulty and Kruger came in with the second wave for a similar landing. O'Bannion's beach party was landed without damage to their equipment. MacDougall began to feel better. Perhaps he had been over concerned during the bungled boat launching. His main responsibility was with the boats after they left the ship. He could visualize a thousand marines swarming up the beach, backed up by the ammunition, tanks and guns which his boat group would land. MacDougall's spine tingled. This job was just right for him; Harrison could have the navigator's berth.

O'Bannion's beach party set up canvas beach markers, each stretched between two stakes and painted with standard symbols for various stockpiles of material: gasoline, ammunition, water, provisions, medical supplies and tracked vehicles. Beach limits were vertical and horizontal panels of plain red bunting, which fluttered in the trade wind like great red sails. Assisted by Randall's salvage boat, the hydrographic party set obstruction buoys to mark rocks and coral shoaling which would endanger boat bottoms at low tide. A signalman stood at the beach line, directing landing craft to proper stockpiles. Ramps dropped, then raised again; boats backed off the beach to be replaced by others. It seemed to MacDougall that here at last were beginnings of system. "Beach her, Hatcher," he said. As soon as he felt jolt of sandy beach under solid bow, he jumped ashore and went to look for Mike O'Bannion.

O'Bannion had taken an active part in beach party exercises. He worked in the water with his men while they planted buoys and practiced holding the salvage boat from broaching to by means of steadying lines run from both quarters of the boat to shore. "Hold her, lads," he called. "When the surf rolls high, you'll need to hold her fast, or we'll be digging channels back to water."

O'Bannion waded ashore. He was soaked to the waist; better get his pants dry. Removing his trousers, he hung them up to dry on a driftwood snag. His voluminous shorts were plastered wetly against white skin of hairy legs; his shirttails rippled behind as he turned his attention seaward. There came MacDougall in the command boat. It would soon be time to round up beach party equipment and return aboard the *Belinda.*

Shadows moved across the sand from O'Bannion's right. Turning back to shore, he came face to face with two officers in khaki, gold lace on their cap visors. Scrambled eggs—must be some brass from Pearl come to check on the *Belinda's* first practice landing. Ignoring the absence of his trousers, he stiffened to attention and saluted smartly. They not only returned the salute but shook hands with him warmly. O'Bannion had not expected such cordiality; he looked at the devices on their shirt collars: the taller one was a captain in the supply corps; the stocky one was a medical officer with rank of commander.

"Have you had an accident, Lieutenant?" asked the doctor. O'Bannion looked down at his shorts. "Oh, no," the doctor hastened to add, "I mean your boat—it's aground, isn't it?"

"All those flags—" added the supply officer. "Are you signaling for help?"

O'Bannion cleared his throat. It was evident that these staff officers had no connection with the amphibious force. "Gentlemen," he began. "The ship you see out there on the horizon is an attack transport. In a matter of days she will be lying off an enemy beachhead—and I'll be standing on the sands with shot and shell flying all about."

"Indeed!" exclaimed the doctor. "And what are your duties?"

O'Bannion filled his chest with a deep breath, then exhaled. "I'm her beachmaster."

"Our staff duties at Pearl—medical planning—very dull —we haven't had opportunity . . . Just what does a beachmaster do?"

O'Bannion looked about the beach, picked up a stick and began to draw a diagram in the sand before the two officers, who had found seats upon a weathered log. In dramatic sentences, he outlined the ship-to-shore movement. "The attack force comes in from deep water," he said, pointing with his stick, first out to seaward, where the *Belinda* still lay, then to a spot in his diagram. "Battleships, cruisers, screening destroyers, here, here and here. They pour in a cross fire bombardment from both flanks. Now here in the center is the transport area. The attack transports lie here; each ship hoists out her own invasion craft; marines swarm down the nets into the boats." O'Bannion moved his stick a little closer to the diagrammed shore line. "Here's the rendezvous area, where landing craft from an entire transport division or squadron meet and form up in waves. The position of every boat has been planned, studied and practiced in what we call 'dry runs.' "

"I don't see how you do it!" said the supply officer.

"We can't see either," said O'Bannion. "It's all done in the dark—most landings. We get into position, hoist out boats, form up—all in pitch dark."

"What are these lines you've drawn?" asked the doctor.

"Those are the boat lanes from the line of departure to the beach."

"Line of departure?"

30

"Yes, that's what we call it. It is an exact distance off the beach, usually three or four thousand yards. A destroyer or picket boat is used to signal departure of timed waves. Then it is up to boat group commanders and their wave officers to get the boats to the beach at the exact instant."

"Why is the timing so important? It seems to me—"

"It has to be synchronized. Battleships, bombarding, planes, dive-bombing and strafing—it all has to be timed so that the assault troops land at the half minute interval between pause in bombardment and Japs getting their heads up again. If the first wave lands too soon, every man will be killed by the last run of our strafing fighter planes, or the last murderous thunder of rapid fire naval bombardment."

"And if they land late?"

"Mortars," said O'Bannion in a hushed tone. "Deadly accurate mortars. Snipers tied in the tops of coconut trees: some of them always survive until the landing. Then the Banzai charge, a fiendish horde, screaming and squealing like pigs—swords, bayonets. . . ."

O'Bannion was so engrossed in his narrative that he did not notice the return of MacDougall, who had walked up the beach from his boat and stopped just behind him. "The beach is the most dangerous spot in the whole operation," O'Bannion continued. "The naked, unprotected beach! It is there that the beachmaster stands, his duties so important that he is consistently protected by an armed sentry."

The doctor opened his mouth to speak. Sensing his question, O'Bannion hurried on, "The flow of vitally needed supplies—tanks, artillery pieces, shells, rifle ammunition, medical supplies, provisions, water, gasoline, even bulldozers to smash open Jap pillboxes—all this must flow like a vast river from the supporting transports, to the boats, to the shore and across the beaches. It is the beachmaster's job to see that the flow is efficient and uninterrupted, that the needed supply item gets to the right place at the right time. He is here for any logistic emergency. I tell you gentlemen," O'Bannion paused dramatically and gestured with his muscular right arm, "a beachmaster walks under a living canopy of fire. It is only by God's grace and the full fury of every gun in the fleet which can be brought to bear on the enemy at our backs that we have a chance of living to tell the tale of it."

The spell of his own eloquence was upon Mike O'Bannion. Shirttails flapping against hairy legs, he took a short turn up the beach, then swung about to seaward as if looking through bombardment smoke to see if the *Belinda* were still there. Then he saw MacDougall, and the dream faded from his eyes. Recovering himself quickly, O'Bannion introduced MacDougall to the two staff officers. He did it graciously, yet in the manner of an elder statesman presenting a worthy son. "This officer is our boat group commander. . . ."

"Yes, I bring the beachmaster his lunch," said MacDougall. "We just got the recall signal, Mike. Time to get everybody aboard."

When his command boat had been hoisted in, MacDougall climbed the ladder to the pilothouse to make his report. Gedney had just taken a shower and was already dressed in the bathrobe of snowy-white toweling which he often wore on the bridge during the night. He must have several of them, MacDougall thought; they're always spotless—even add to his dignity. He looks like an old Roman senator, sitting up there in his high chair. Gedney returned MacDougall's salute absent-mindedly. MacDougall coughed—he had better say something. "Well, sir, we finally got the boats away."

Gedney focused clear blue eyes upon MacDougall. "Yes," he said, "you got them away in exactly one hour and forty-three minutes."

The words soaked into MacDougall's brain like water penetrating a dry sponge. One hour and forty-three minutes: what a bust!

MacDougall waited for the last of it. He was one of the few officers aboard who had yet to receive one of Gedney's tongue lashings. Now it was his turn; the Old Man was selecting the bitterest, most cutting phrases he could think of. All that delay —what a sloppy rehearsal it had been. The *Belinda* was no more in shape for combat landings than a pink cloud. It was very quiet in the pilothouse. Enlisted men on watch there waited in pleased anticipation, thoroughly enjoying the prospect of watching another officer squirm. Even though they liked MacDougall, they were amused at his discomfiture as he stood beside Gedney's high chair, trying to hide his embarrassment from them. Color faded from the sky—still no movement from Gedney, no word. It became quite plain to MacDougall that his presence was no longer desired. While the enlisted men exchanged knowing glances, making the most of an entertaining situation which had turned out disappointingly, MacDougall walked slowly from the pilothouse and down the ladder.

CHAPTER 6

"Away all boats, away!" A hundred and more public address speakers shouted the order across night-black and wind-tossed waters of Maalaea Bay, Maui. A newly formed division of five attack transports, the *Belinda* among them, lay to in a line parallel with the shore, launching boats and embarking troops for the last of three scheduled practice landings. Three miles from shore loaded boats were formed into waves and led away from the transports by their boat group commanders. From the many loud-speakers on each of the five ships, from portable and built-in bull horns, came a bedlam of sound—amplified instructions hurled into the night. Then, at moments when all but one were silent, they heard clear, monotonous words of a mechanized voice calling out instructions and orders to boats and to debarking troops. The PA of each ship had its own peculiar tone, in which voice and personality of the speaker was submerged. Robots, thought MacDougall, visualizing five thousand soldiers crawling down fifty debarkation nets into a hundred and fifty landing craft; robot voices ordering human flesh to perform like robots.

A destroyer took station at the designated line of departure, two miles from the beach. Loaded landing craft wallowed in the chop at eight knots: thirty minutes from destroyer to beach. Boat groups from the other transports were converging. Wave tied to wave until there were five waves of thirty boats each, winged out and on their way to shore. MacDougall blinked a signal for the first wave, and swept past the destroyer. It was a chilly morning for August in the Islands. The command boat leaped and rolled, throwing off spray with each toss of her bow. Troop-laden LCVPs were less fortunate, moving sluggishly, seeming more reluctant to rise than to fall. As MacDougall moved to the right flank of the first wave and began to guide in to shore, he found himself abreast of Boat 22 with serious, dark-eyed Tommy Jones at the wheel. It was too early for color to show. Navy blue and Army drab looked alike. Men filled the rectangular cockpit, standing packed together. Wind-carried spray streamed over them so that helmets, faces, packs and backs dripped with salt water. Those faces seemed strangely alike; what a blank look men got while heading for the beach in a VP! Helmets seemed to tell more of a story than faces. A helmet did something to a man, pressing his brains down in uncomfortable protection, giving him stereotyped likeness to others about him, reminding him that he had become involved in some grim business whose exact meaning was not clear.

MacDougall spat out a mouthful of spray and wiped his face with a soggy handkerchief. For the next few minutes all these helmets were in his care; the helmets must arrive on schedule, here and at that enemy beachhead they would face together before many more days. He looked astern again—all waves coming along nicely, thirty boats in each, the last wave composed of thirty-six-ton LCMs with their heavy ramp gratings tracing the lightening sky. Bracing himself against lively movements of his command boat, MacDougall trained binoculars upon each wave flag. From one to six they were all there, all in order, all properly spaced; even Bud Foster from Kansas was formed up according to plan.

Shore line was much closer now—sand, trees and shrub taking on detail and beginnings of color in early morning. MacDougall checked his time and held up both hands in a slowing motion; with this following sea they were running a little ahead of schedule. He checked a visual range he had picked off the chart: seven tenths of a mile to the beach. Five degrees off his port bow the roof of a house showed through the trees. That would be Kihei village. Red Beach was two hundred yards south of Kihei. This rough position might do for a practice landing. On that unknown enemy beach he must pick out more accurate marks than this—from outdated charts, from photographs taken by speeding plane or hiding submarine—pick out the marks without ever landing first to look. Combat landings had to be right: you couldn't land men in front of defenses they were supposed to flank. If an old navigator had difficulty in getting oriented, how about these boys from the Middle West? Surely they were confused and concerned—or did they fail to realize yet the accuracies required of this sort of landing? No chance to ask them now. He felt premonition in the air; yet something was strange. Then he realized: no fireworks, no shooting—no sound except roar of engines. Dive bombers swooped down, but dropped no bombs over the landing area; fighter planes simulated strafing runs from one end of the beach strip to the other, yet fired no guns. Despite all efforts to bring realism to this last practice, the inhabitants of Kihei village could not be sacrificed. Battleships and cruisers, purged of their practice bombardment at nearby Kahoolawe Island, were returning to Pearl Harbor, leaving hard-working destroyers to guard rehearsing transports. The very silence of guns seemed like a sound, like the first rustling of leaves before a gale.

MacDougall looked at the radiolite sweep hand of his strap watch: ninety seconds until H Hour. Time to run the surf and hit the beach. He looked back at his boat group: all craft with the big white *B* painted full-size on bobbing ramps. Wigwagging *attention* with his signal flags, he then held out both arms horizontally in signal for each wave to move up from V formation to line abreast. He jerked a thumb to Hatcher, who opened his throttle more. "Try twenty-five hundred," MacDougall shouted above throaty engine roar. Then he pumped a vertically held flag up and down in the speed up signal to all boat waves. "Head right a little more, Hatcher. There; that's it. Steady as you go. Keep that tall tree dead ahead."

As the first wave cut into the surf line, Hatcher cut throttle. The command boat paused just outside the breakers, like a sheep dog watching a flock. Thirty VPs rose on the back of a

34

breaker and groaned towards shore with engines wide open. Running in a slightly ragged line curved to fit the bay contour, they hit the beach. Almost at once thirty ramps dropped upon wet sand; helmeted infantrymen with rifles ready jumped from ramps with seemingly mechanized unity. Splashing ankle or knee deep, depending on their luck, they ran up across the strip of loose sand with awkward, laboring steps, and disappeared into scrub vegetation beyond the line of algaroba trees which fringed the bay.

Wave after wave swept in through frothing surf and landed. Each time ramps dropped, men rushed forward to disappear into the brush. In twenty-eight minutes three thousand soldiers crossed the sand and disappeared. Landing combat supplies for them would be the slow and difficult job. In the *Belinda's* last wave came tall Ensign Marty with the four tank lighters: the biggest ensign with the biggest boats. In two he carried medium tanks and in two, heavy-bladed bulldozers.

By the time Marty arrived, O'Bannion had set up his communications post, beach markers and unloading signs. Randall's salvage boat planted obstruction buoys around a large coral head to warn landing craft. Most boats were able to retract without accident, but rough water swung some about and broached them to, beam on to sand and sea. There waves pounded them steadily, driving them higher up the beach and harder into the sucking sand. Randall came with towing lines, but unless he managed to start towing almost the moment a boat got into trouble, he was unable to get it off.

Leaving capable Dr. Bell to raise his own medical tent, O'Bannion stripped off his shirt and cap, then charged into the water. Waist deep, he bellowed orders to boat crews, beach-party men and shore-party soldiers alike. "Bear a hand here, men. Quick now! Take a strain on that towline, Randall. Now the rest of us here, rock her; rock her!"

Five LCVPs were gotten off in this manner and sent back with the rest to commence unloading the *Belinda*. One craft remained hard and fast, port side stuck in the sand, the other taking breaking waves aboard. MacDougall ran alongside Marty's tank lighter, pointing to the broached boat. Marty's coxswain, a man broader and nearly as tall as the six-foot-four ensign, jerked clutches and throttles, spun his wheel and beached the fifty-six-foot steel craft a few feet to one side of the broached boat. A husky soldier in olive drab coveralls started the bulldozer's engine roaring and lurched over the ramp grating and up the loose sand. The LCM's coxswain backed off his heavy craft, spun her around with her twin screws and backed her in with reckless accuracy to take a stout towline from the stranded VP.

O'Bannion shouted unheard against roaring twin diesels, "Set up on your towline and we'll rock her out of here." A jolt against the beached craft from landward flung O'Bannion away and down into the water. Rising, sputtering and wiping his eyes, he turned inland to see the giant bulldozer pressed against the plywood transom of the thirty-six-foot landing craft. Giant blade had bashed a large hole through which sea water was pouring into the cockpit. O'Bannion floundered ashore and ran up to the bulldozer, shouting, "No, no! You can't do that! This is a plywood boat. You'll smash her into kindling wood!"

High in his seat, the big soldier in coveralls looked down on O'Bannion and spat a stream of tobacco juice over the iron treads of his behemoth, then said, "Boats ain't no good on the shore, sailor."

"You back that bulldozer out of here right this minute."

The soldier stared back at O'Bannion, who was soaking wet, black hair plastered to his thick chest. "Who d'ya think you are, sailor? A chief, I suppose. Well, I don't take orders from no chiefs. I get my orders from Sergeant Kelly." The soldier opened and closed his throttle, allowing the machine to express his defiance and contempt of the Navy with thunderous roars, and exhaust popping. Then he eased in the clutch and began once more to push against the boat.

O'Bannion threw himself before the blade of the bulldozer, muscular arms outstretched and hairy chest heaving with anger. The bulldozer inched forward until the blade pressed against his chest, then stopped. The soldier on the machine and O'Bannion in the sand glared at each other. Rank and branch of service had less and less bearing on the situation; it was just one Irishman against another.

A major of engineers came running out of the brush and down the beach. "What's the trouble, O'Bannion?" he asked.

"This fool is trying to punch holes in one of my boats."

The major looked from the beached boat to the bulldozer driver. "You don't need to force Army co-operation on the Navy, Corporal."

"But, Major, I got my orders from Sergeant Kelly, sir. He ordered me to push this Navy boat back into the water."

"Malumphy," said O'Bannion angrily, "you've got to control your shore party. When I talked to you about us working together, I didn't mean this."

"The major can see I'm just obeying orders," said the driver sullenly.

Major Malumphy grinned. "This is the beachmaster you're arguing with, Corporal. He's in charge of everything here, up to high-water mark, where I take over. Looks like you're pressing beyond Army jurisdiction."

"I'm sorry, sir," spluttered the corporal, obviously not sorry. "I didn't know."

O'Bannion's anger had cooled enough to flash his thoughts back to the salvage job at hand. "Boski," he shouted to one of the beach-party men, "bring me an armful of spare life jackets." A hulking sailor dropped the signal flags with which he had been directing loaded landing craft to appropriate stockpiles on shore, jumped into the distressed boat and collected a big armload of kapok life jackets. O'Bannion stuffed three of them into the hole smashed by the bulldozer and used the rest to make a pad which he held against the boat's ramp. Then he signaled the bulldozer to come ahead. Chewing stolidly at his plug cut, the corporal brought the big blade carefully against the pad of life jackets and began to shove. O'Bannion gestured to Randall, who had clambered aboard the tank lighter and in a moment the big craft answered the bulldozer roar for roar as she took a strain on the tow rope. "Come on, boys," yelled O'Bannion. "Rock her. Let's break up this suction." Soldiers and sailors gathered around the boat and rocked in unison from side to side. The tank lighter pulled from seaward; the bulldozer shoved from shore. An unusually heavy wave broke against the boat, surging around and lifting it. Slowly at first, then faster, the boat moved. She pulled away from the bulldozer, dropping life jackets into the water. The tank lighter had her now; she was afloat.

Malumphy walked back to dry sand with water squishing in his boots. "That was real Army-Navy teamwork," he said to O'Bannion, who had retrieved his shirt from a nearby lantana shrub. "When my men get to know you, you'll have no trouble with them."

O'Bannion managed to smile again. "I've got enough to do without wrestling with bulldozers." He had his shirt on again. The bulldozer corporal stared at the twin silver bars on O'Bannion's collar. An officer! He should have known. He turned his bulldozer around with a clash of hastily shifted gears and roared off some distance towards the scrub lantana before pausing to spit another stream of tobacco juice in the general direction of the U.S. Navy.

MacDougall, who had come ashore to help with the boat, watched the corporal with amused interest, then turned to O'Bannion. "It's lack of clothes, Mike—just complicates life for you on the beach."

"What do you mean?"

"Remember the first dry run at Kaneohe? You meet the brass on the beach—no pants. Now along comes an Army bulldozer and gives you a bad time. You need a little rank, but your shirt with the collar bars is hanging on a bush."

The beachmaster looked out over his stretch of sand, where ammunition, drinking water, gasoline, provisions and artillery pieces were being moved shoreward across the ramps. Then he looked back at MacDougall and said, "Before this day is done, every soldier working on this bit of beach will know Mike O'Bannion on sight, with or without pants and shirt."

Mike sheltered his paper work and his rolled-up sleeping bag in a small pup tent. Although it was physically impossible for a man of his bulk to enter, he invariably referred to the place as his headquarters. While resting from frequent trips about the beach, he sat on a stout box in front of the diminutive tent, chest held high and knees pointing outward while his clear blue eyes surveyed the beach. Mike was at his best when seated informally. At such times his robust personality gave an aura of dignity to a packing case or a weather-beaten log which Gedney in his captain's chair aboard the *Belinda* might well have envied.

Dr. Frank Bell, the *Belinda's* assistant surgeon, established his beach-party medical aid station about thirty yards inland from O'Bannion's headquarters. He chose a site shaded by overhanging algaroba trees which gave protection from the sun and, theoretically, from enemy observation. Bell, an experienced surgeon who had left an excellent practice in Pennsylvania to serve in the Navy, was responsible for providing medical aid to casualties occurring on his section of the beach and those brought out from the line by Army medics. Selecting the most seriously wounded first, Bell and his Navy corpsmen would give emergency aid and load them carefully into empty landing craft for return to the *Belinda's* sick bay.

During the afternoon simulated casualties were brought to the beach by sweating stretcher-bearers who had little sympathy for the healthy bodies they were required to carry. One party of four bearers staggered over the last of the uneven ground and dumped a healthy-looking soldier unceremoniously at Bell's feet. "Look at that fat deadhead," one of them said, wiping rivulets of sweat from his face with a shirt sleeve. "I'll bet he gained five pounds on the trip."

Bell smiled briefly. He was a friendly man, but the handling of casualties, simulated or real, was a matter of absolute seriousness to him. He knelt down and read a tag on the man's shirt: "Compound fracture, left femur." Bell called for splints and bandages, then assisted by two corpsmen, he swiftly applied appropriate bandages and splints. The man was placed in a basketlike wire Stokes litter and his foot fastened to the bottom frame to extend the limb. "If this were an actual fracture, I would really set it tight," Bell explained as he worked. "We want to be realistic, but there's no sense in making this fellow more uncomfortable than necessary."

"It's all right with me, Doc," said one of the waiting litter-bearers. "You go right ahead; set him up good and tight."

Bell smiled again. "That's where I draw the line between
38

practice and actuality," he said, as he filled out the special diagnosis tag provided for the purpose. Then the man was carried to water's edge and placed in a VP for return to the ship, amid jeers and mock cheers from his fellows.

As Bell watched the boat retract from the beach, O'Bannion called his name urgently. "Come quick, Doctor. Someone's badly hurt." Bell ran up the beach and found O'Bannion looking into the brush. "Look up the trail there: man bleeding terribly!"

Bell tensed momentarily, ready for quick action, then relaxed. Something spurious about that blood. "Color and texture are wrong, Mike. Blood doesn't drip like that; doesn't coagulate that fast."

Some wag had brought red paint from the ship and poured a little upon a man marked "Flesh Wound, thoracic region." Bell applied suitable dressings without comment. He liked to joke about other things, yet, though he thought it quite natural for soldiers to joke about wounds to come, as a physician the prospect did not strike him as being at all funny.

Ammunition and provisions were now coming to the beach in quantity, most of it fastened by metal straps to sledlike skidboards called pallets. Except for small patches of coral protruding through otherwise smooth sand, the Maalaea beach was ideal for dragging palatized cargo ashore from opened ramps of landing craft. The bulldozer which had confronted O'Bannion earlier in the day was now making short work of the otherwise backbreaking task of moving tons of artillery ammunition from water's edge to ammunition dump. Still operated by the tobacco chewing corporal, it dragged twin cloverleaves of three shells each over ramps, out of shallow water and up the beach. Whenever a pallet caught on outcropping coral the corporal opened his throttle. "Something's got to give," he told Boski, the beach-party signalman, "and it ain't going to be the 'dozer." Splinters were shaved from runners of pallets, which sometimes overturned. After an unusually severe struggle, in which the stout wire towing strap nearly parted, the corporal looked down admiringly at the still unexploded ammunition. "That ammo is plenty tough," he said to Boski. "Why, it's almost as tough as the 'dozer."

Sandwiched between two loads of ammunition came a VP loaded with two pallets of actual human blood plasma. MacDougall shook his head. Gedney had officially protested against landing this precious stuff in its vulnerable glass bottles during practice landings. Evidently he had been overruled. MacDougall directed the coxswain to the section of the beach reserved for the medical stockpile. "Tell them to go easy with it. Carry it by hand," he shouted, seeing the bulldozer racing along the beach to meet the boat. Before O'Bannion or Bell

39

could reach the boat, the damage had been done. Warnings by the boat's crew were drowned out by the roaring bulldozer. With speed developed by practice on ammunition loads, shore-party soldiers hooked on the first pallet and the bulldozer yanked it out of the boat over the ramp and started up the beach, where it caught at once on a coral ledge. The corporal knew what to do about that; he opened wide his throttle. The wire towing cable tightened nearly to breaking point, then, with a jerk, the pallet came free and overturned, jerking the glass bottles across sharp coral. Every bottle in the pallet but one was smashed, and gallons of human blood plasma poured out on the sand.

O'Bannion went for the bulldozer driver. "You addle-brained idiot!" he roared. "Don't you know the difference between howitzer shells and plasma?" The corporal had nothing to say. He shut off his motor, then sat rubbing his chin and looking at the smashed bottles.

Bell paid no attention to the bulldozer. His eyes were focused upon one shattered bottle. The sand beneath it was wet with spilled plasma. Broken fragments of glass glistened wetly, reflecting the sun. Gradually the glass dried, dulling the reflection. Astonished at the silence of the corporal, O'Bannion cut his protest short. The corporal climbed down from his machine. Together with Boski and other soldiers and sailors gathered about, he lifted the second pallet bodily and carried it carefully up the beach to the medical station.

A neatly dressed Army officer came along the beach from the direction of other ship's shore parties and stopped beside Dr. Bell. "How do you do, sir," he said rather ceremoniously. "I'm from planning staff."

"I'm Bell, Navy surgeon."

"Fine practice landing." Then the colonel noticed the broken bottles. "What happened here?" he asked with mild interest.

"It's human blood plasma, smashed in a practice landing."

"Valuable stuff, but expendable," said the colonel crisply. "We allow for such mishaps when calculating logistics."

"People gave their blood for it," said Bell. "They might as well have taken so many pints of red paint to the blood bank."

"Oh, come now," said the colonel. "It was an unfortunate little accident, but these rehearsals have to be realistic." Bell had nothing further to say. The planning officer poked at the sand with the toe of a polished boot. Then he coughed. "Well, I must be getting on. Good afternoon, Doctor."

Bell's eyes followed the nattily dressed colonel as he walked along the beach. Then he picked up the bottle of plasma which had survived the accident and carried it to his medical aid station.

Landing on the practice beach for the last time, MacDougall

wiped salt water from his eyes with a sweat-soaked handkerchief. "We've got her licked now," he said to O'Bannion. "Eleven hundred tons of combat gear unloaded and hauled from ship to shore, dragged up your beach, dragged down to the boats again and hoisted aboard the *Belinda*."

O'Bannion tucked in his shirttails in readiness for his return to the *Belinda* and the critical scrutiny of Captain Gedney. "Two long days and nights of it," he said. "Even Mike O'Bannion is ready to wash the sand out of his hair. Let's load the troops and be done with it." Down to the beach came soldiers from the *Belinda's* battalion landing team, returning from practice deployment in the cane fields. They walked in small informal groups, drinking pop and eating candy bars. The Fighting Sixty-Ninth had "liberated" the Kihei village general store.

CHAPTER 7

During the short passage from Maui to Oahu, Gedney called O'Bannion and MacDougall to the pilothouse. It seemed almost like being home again, MacDougall thought: the Old Man in his high seat, freshly shaven and unperturbed by detailed bustlings of the watch. Sandwiched between the other four transports, the *Belinda* steamed over blue, sky-calm water which reflected cumulus floating above the bare and rocky shore of southwest Molokai.

"We have received unloading orders," said Gedney, his voice professional, yet pleasant. Yesterday's beach seemed far away. The two lieutenants were refreshed by a shower and sleep in good bunks. Watching Gedney reach into his dispatch case to withdraw the yellow commanding officer's copy of a message, both looked forward to simple discharge of troops and combat materiel at some cozy Pearl Harbor berth. Gedney glanced at the dispatch once more, though he knew its contents well, then asked, "Are you familiar with Pokai Bay, MacDougall?"

"Yes, sir. It's a small, unprotected cove about twenty miles along the coast from Pearl Harbor entrance. There's a sugar mill inland—no unloading facilities that I know of. Surely we aren't—"

"But we are," said Gedney with a pleased little smile. "We are a new transport. You two officers did very well during the landing exercise, considering the greenness of all hands. With a more experienced crew you should be able to do better. Therefore I requested permission to land both troops and combat load on a beach, using our own boats. The other four transports are going in to the supply docks at Pearl Harbor."

Beachmaster and boat commander exchanged unhappy glances. "These supplies, Captain," O'Bannion said in a protesting voice. "These same supplies are to be landed on enemy shores. There was a lot of damage, sir, in spite of all I could—"

"I am quite aware of that," said Gedney. "And you, Mac-Dougall; I suppose you are about to protest that your boats need overhaul."

MacDougall colored. "I was going to mention it, Capt'n. Bottoms are torn up, especially boats which broached on the beach. Engines are in bad shape and we only have one spare."

Gedney's smile broadened. "Excellent, excellent," he said. "Now we are getting somewhere. Do you gentlemen expect that we will go alongside a pier to unload for battle?" Gedney held up a hand for silence. "Of course I expect you to be anxious regarding boats and beachhead materiel. This is an opportunity to learn how to take care of both under sustained ship-to-shore operations."

"There was that plasma, sir," said MacDougall.

"Naturally, naturally," Gedney rose from his seat like a cantering rider, gazed ahead, instructed Randall, who had the deck, to slow down two turns, then faced MacDougall again. "Plasma and any delicate instruments will be held aboard until we enter harbor. It will not hurt the Army to replace a few cans of provisions and five-gallon tins of gasoline here. It will hurt the Army tremendously if we fail to put troops and equipment ashore expeditiously at our objective."

Well, that's that, thought MacDougall. I wonder what we'll smash up next.

By midafternoon the *Belinda* arrived off Pokai Bay, a small, sandy indentation in a rocky shore. Gedney left Quigley in titular command, with Fraser, the ship's salty first lieutenant, in actual charge of the bridge. Then, together with O'Bannion and MacDougall, he was hoisted out in the command boat, which also served as captain's gig. With Gedney seated in the stern sheets and Hatcher at the wheel, they set out for shore. Far to starboard the column of four transports, herded by destroyers, headed for Pearl Harbor docks and liberty for all hands. To port, and much closer, lay a former private yacht, now commissioned as a patrol craft, while offshore cruised a protecting destroyer-escort.

The bay was even smaller than MacDougall had remembered—a shallow, unprotected crescent, fortunately situated on the lee side of Oahu. Passing close aboard the patrol yacht, which was anchored some thousand yards from shore, they noticed some of her crew swimming over the side, others fishing from the fantail. Those on watch were dressed in gaily colored shorts or swimming trunks. Gedney noticed this informal discipline, yet made no comment. Drawing closer to shore, they found the central approach unobstructed, but waves breaking far to seaward indicated dangerous shoaling on either hand. Passing through the gentle surf, Hatcher grounded the boat. Gedney clambered out on the command boat's bow and jumped ashore. Failing to reach dry sand, he landed in knee-deep water. Ignoring wet shoes and trousers, Gedney walked ashore with what dignity the loose sand permitted him, and set out to explore the beach. Marks of tracked vehicles indicated that the beach had been used previously for a military practice landing. Puffing ahead some fifty yards, O'Bannion found a gravel road which led inland to a nearby railway loading platform.

The three officers retraced their steps to the beach. O'Bannion dug his toe deep into the sand. "We'll have to lay metal landing mats here, Capt'n," he said. "Otherwise we'll never get wheeled vehicles across this loose sand."

"Excellent," said Gedney. "A good exercise. I expect the beach at our objective to be much more difficult than the one at Maalaea Bay."

A skiff powered by an outboard motor landed not far from the command boat. Three men, one much taller than the other two, stepped ashore and approached Gedney. All three wore swimming trunks, and the big man also wore a floppy sun hat, plaited from native grasses. He tossed Gedney an informal salute which seemed more island greeting than military courtesy. "Good afternoon, Capt'n Gedney," he said in a deep, musical voice. "I'm Luke Stephens, skipper of that yippy out there. My regular assignment is patrol duty around the islands, but now and then I'm ordered to stand by a practice landing."

"Excellent," said Gedney, extending his hand. "My destroyer-escort is going in and I would not care to sit out there alone during a landing exercise. You have sound gear?"

"Yes, sir. We'll watch out for subs."

As Gedney introduced his beachmaster and boat commander, MacDougall had the feeling that time had rolled back a century. There was something incongruous about this meeting on the shore of the impeccable Gedney and this big man, casually dressed in swimming trunks and native hat. Stephens was undoubtedly islandborn—ruddy-bronze complexion and soft, yet limpid, brown eyes indicated that some of his forebears had belonged here for many generations. His commanding personality, not depending on clothing for dignity, was instantly felt. He seemed the host and Gedney the guest, as if he were a Polynesian king welcoming a twentieth-century Captain Cook.

"You'll have to be very careful with this beach, Capt'n," said Stephens. "No landing is possible during kona winds such as the one which blew out two days ago. Even in fine weather the surf is treacherous."

"But surely now . . ." Gedney paused. Authority stronger than naval regulation rang in this man's words.

Stephens looked out to sea and along the flanks of the small beach, saying again, "Even in nice weather the surf is treacherous here. Everything looks at peace, just as it is now. Then, without any warning at all, two or three big swells will run in and take charge of the place. They are dangerous here in the center of the bay, but the greatest danger lies on either hand."

Gedney nodded in polite but casual appreciation. "Thank you for the local knowledge," he said, twinkling blue eyes glancing at sand and surf but lingering on his little flotilla of three vessels. O'Bannion's attention was on the loose sand. In his mind he supervised the pegging down of great rolls of steel landing mats. MacDougall watched the curling line of breakers, considering Stephens' warning. This cove had a comfortable intimacy. Used as he was to the sudden treachery of wind and wave, MacDougall's senses were lulled by a feeling of security. There was no pressure here, no time schedule to meet. Surely everything would go well.

Stephens discussed details of the landing with MacDougall, offering to station his patrol yacht at the line of departure as a marker. As they said good-by, he reminded: "Don't forget to watch that surf." He pointed out to sea. "The reef extends further than you can see when it's calm like this."

"Won't that tend to form a natural breakwater?" asked Gedney.

"No, sir, it's just a sneaky sort of thing out there to trip the deep swells and send them crashing."

"I'll watch it," said MacDougall as they got back into the command boat. He thought Stephens was being a little fussy. Strange, too. That big, self-possessed man was not the type to try to make an impression on Gedney. Furthermore, he seemed so at home in this place. MacDougall watched Stephens dive into a wave and swim through it and over the next with casual skill. This was a nice little place. Landing here would be almost a picnic.

Early the following morning the landing got off to a good start. The weather was clear and calm. Boats were hoisted out in thirty-five minutes and without accident. Troops climbed down debarkation nets into assigned landing craft without fuss, mix-up or a single bad spill. Moran and Alvick got the first heavy lifts overside and into Marty's tank lighters without delay. Sherwood formed boat waves and brought them to the line of departure plainly marked by the patrol yacht. Stephens dispatched waves to shore according to the schedule MacDougall had given him. Going on ahead to investigate surf conditions MacDougall found them to be excellent. Waves splashed on the sand with velvety softness. By sunrise the beach was crowded with soldiers who were detailed to assist Malumphy's shore party until the arrival of the special train which would take them back to the fort. O'Bannion had landing mats in place, lacking only the anchor pegs which had been inadvertently loaded in the bottom of a lower hold. With the exception of this minor detail, unloading proceeded without a hitch. Now that forty-eight-hour passes were nearly within reach, soldiers happily mimicked officious orders of the *Belinda's* PA system.

Cloud shadows crossed the bay, followed by a light rain squall, then the sun shone clear and warm. The gentle land breeze was fresh and sweet with mingled island scents. Fine weather cumulus drifted along the horizon between blue sky and even bluer sea. The feeling of impending conflict, sharpened at Maalaea Bay, was softened here in the intimacy of this little cove. By noon the breeze shifted offshore and freshened, and languid shore scents were replaced by salt tang. Combat cargo came ashore in a steady stream, carried by a continuous procession of *Belinda* landing craft. Heading shoreward with their burdens they wallowed sluggishly, rising slowly, sliding deeply on the backs of following swells. Returning empty, they tossed buoyantly against head-on waves.

Quick work was performed in the surf and on the beach. MacDougall and Sherwood kept boat traffic moving and directed it in, as and where needed on the beach. O'Bannion and Malumphy, aided by the extra manpower, got boats unloaded and turned about in a hurry. Randall stood by in his salvage boat while the beach-party hydrographic crew were always at hand with steadying lines. The moment a boat coxswain began to lose control, he was thrown steadying lines—given a tow if necessary. His boat was straightened out stern on to sea before it could flounder beam on and be washed against the shore.

By midafternoon occasional groups of heavier swells began to run into the bay, tossing approaching landing craft high and pooping over the transoms of unloading VPs. The boat group was gaining in experience, and with the co-operation of the beach party it began to appear that all would be kept under control. Nevertheless, by 1600 hours, heavy offshore swells began to roll in. LCVPs were broached to in alarming numbers, and even the fifty-foot LCMs needed all the leverage of twin screws to hold bow on to sand while unloading. MacDougall began to understand what the islandborn Luke Stephens had meant about wave action in this small cove. O'Bannion and Randall were busy full time with steadying and towing lines. Men struggled waist deep in the water, tugging at the ropes and passing equipment as rapidly as possible from wave-washed ramps to shore.

MacDougall took his command boat out to within hailing

distance of Sherwood's VP. "You handle the rest of the boat traffic, Steve," he shouted. "I'm going to use my boat on salvage work. Randall is swamped."

"Are you punning, friend?" Sherwood waved a lanky arm in acknowledgment. "I'll police the surf line, Mac. Go ahead and rescue the perishing."

MacDougall grinned and turned to Hatcher. "Stand in close to the beach. We'll take the left flank and share salvage with Mr. Randall. Have your men break out the towline." As Hatcher complied, MacDougall added, "We don't want to spend the night here digging wrecked boats out of the sand."

MacDougall had left the removable canopy of the command boat ashore this morning, preferring the better visibility of an open boat. When midday sun had scorched down, he had momentarily regretted this decision. Now he was glad; an open boat was much better for salvage work. He and Hatcher could see all around, and the deckhands could get about to handle their lines in a hurry. He stood on the decked overbow, just forward of Hatcher and the wheel. Here he was clear of the towline and could watch beach, boats and sea. From time to time he threw heaving lines to landing craft in need of help. The towline was fastened to the heaving line. Deckhands in troubled VPs hauled it aboard and dropped the eye over their sternposts. After each craft had been safely retracted, towline and heaving line were recovered and gotten ready for the next boat.

Most of the cargo was ashore now. In the face of a freshening wind, soldiers and sailors alike were working in an excited, yet pleasurable frenzy: laughing, splashing and heaving with all their strength. The end of a week's grind was in sight; there would be liberty tomorrow. The landing spot for various types of materiel stretched along the central portion of the cove. At the extreme left flank was the ammunition dump. MacDougall watched with concern while two LCVPs, loaded with artillery shells, headed through the surf together. They could not be handled at once. Carried away by the excitement of throwing goods ashore, they must have disregarded Sherwood's instructions to land one at a time. He had better get over there. "Hatcher," he called sharply, pointing to the two boats. "Let's get them out of there. See those big rollers coming in along the shallows!" Hatcher opened throttle; the command boat rose on a swell and ran across the little cove just outside the breakers, then headed in towards the two VPs.

The rolling swell was much heavier here at the edge of the cove. The two boats were already in trouble. In spite of anything their coxswains could do, they drifted closer to the shallow rim where surf crashed frighteningly against sloping sand. When within hailing distance, MacDougall climbed upon the bow of the command boat, his back to the sea. He steadied himself with the raised barrel of one of the two machine guns which were just forward of the cockpit and hailed the two coxswains. "Ahoy in the VPs! Back out of there. You're in too far to straighten out now. You'll get pooped with a sea and broach hard on that reef. . . . Back clear of the surf and get out of there! Back out!" Both coxswains heard his shouts but did not seem to understand. They looked around at MacDougall, faces bewildered, doing nothing. Unless they acted their boats were doomed.

Now the command boat rose high on a rolling swell, lurched about, weathered the crest and dropped into the trough behind it. The machine-gun barrel to which MacDougall clung swung around. He staggered for a moment, then reached for a new grip on the gun and raised his megaphone—those VPs would never make it unless they turned fast between swells and got out of there.

Hatcher shouted a warning to MacDougall: "Look—the sea!"

MacDougall turned around and looked seaward. A solid wall of water rose directly ahead of his boat and almost upon them —this was what Luke Stephens had been talking about. There was no chance of escape from it. MacDougall shouted back to Hatcher, "Open her up and head into it!" With mouth wide open, Hatcher gaped at the enormous wave, yet gunned his motor at once and spun his wheel, swinging the command boat nearly head on to it. "Take it on the shoulder," yelled MacDougall, gripping his gun barrel and looking up at the sea. "That's it. Hold her there. Get some way on her, quick!" No time to scramble back to the comparative safety of the cockpit. MacDougall wrapped both arms around the machine gun and hung on. The boat had beam and power; if she could only plane over the top. . . .

They were into the first wave now. It did not seem possible for them to rise over it, but the bow continued to lift, higher and yet higher. The churning propeller thrust the boat forward and kept it planing. While Hatcher, MacDougall and the boat's crew held their breath, the body of the wave swept under them, lifting the boat by the middle, bow and stern hanging in space, propeller racing in agony until Hatcher was able to move his hand to the throttle. Squatting with feet braced apart, MacDougall rode the bow, clinging desperately to the gun. Thrust high, he caught a momentary glimpse of craft, shore and waves in the distance, but his attention was drawn to the deep valley of water before him. Then with a sickening sensation, as if the bottom had dropped out from under the boat, it plummeted into the deep trough and brought up with a shuddering crash which nearly knocked the breath out of him.

MacDougall looked up at the second wave. It was bigger and higher than the first, towering above them in a sheer green wall, with sunlight gleaming through from the other side and foaming crest leering down upon them. He knew that the boat would never get over this one. Still shuddering from the first wave, the bow rose too slowly. These new-made Hawaiian seas were steep and close together; the boat was out of timing with them. Nothing but a raft would have flotation to surmount this next wave. Instinct told him to dive overboard right through the sea and get clear of the mess; he would be much better off without the boat. No, he thought, I can't leave Hatcher and the boys. His mind was motivated not so much by solicitude for his crew, though he felt that, as by the very impropriety of such an act. Instead, he dived headfirst over Hatcher's head into the open cockpit, grabbed the coaming and hung on.

The green wall of sea broke all over the boat, submerging men and gear in a tangle under water which filled the cockpit. MacDougall expected the shock of cold salt wave; it was not the first time an angry sea had knocked him down. What surprised him was sudden pain from head to foot—the crushing blow which stole his senses as it flung him in the bottom of the boat.

Weak from shock and pain, he struggled to his feet at last and looked about him. Things seemed strangely out of focus. Through a blur of dizziness he saw the others: Hatcher's face had a vacant stare, as if looking but seeing nothing, yet he still clung to the spokes of his wheel, the motor-mac sat in a drooping posture over the engine box; the deckhand huddled further aft in the bottom of the boat, chest deep in water, staring at his buddy on the engine box. Nobody said a word.

MacDougall's face stung. It must be salt water, he thought, and wiped a forearm across his face, then looked stupidly at his arm. It was covered with blood; something must have hit him. There was an awful pain in his throat; the rest of his body felt numb. He looked around the cockpit. There it was: a machine-gun mount, scarf ring and all—the gun he had been clinging to up on the bow. It had carried away, rooted-out bolts and all, and buried in that green sea, had struck him down. A mirthless jest passed through his mind: I never knew what hit me. At last he looked out beyond the limits of his boat. The salvage boat lay to, close aboard, the two craft joined by a short towline. They were out beyond the surf line, wallowing in the trough, but safe. Randall had come in and towed them out of it; that had taken guts. Now Larson cast off the towline, threw in his clutch and came alongside. MacDougall could see several inches of water sloshing around in the salvage boat: they had taken one too, probably coming in to tow them out. Looking at Jim Randall he saw a trickle of blood running from his chin. MacDougall began to speak for the first time: "You're hurt, Jim." His lips formed the words but no sound came out. That's queer, he thought, I can't talk. He wanted to ask about the two ammunition boats, and he couldn't ask. Perhaps they were still in trouble—or down under. As he looked towards the left flank of the little cove, where huge breakers crashed on the reef, Randall read his mind.

"Those two boats are all right, Mac. They heard you in time; gunned it out of there beam on. They just got to deep water about the time you took that sea—shipped a little water, that's all. I'll bet it's a long time before they get caught—" Randall looked at MacDougall's face. "Why, Mac! The whole side of your jaw is laid open! We'd better get you in to the beach to Doc Bell."

That's strange, MacDougall thought. My throat hurts awfully but I don't feel anything on my face. He ran his fingers down his cheek and over the jaw. Something wrong there; the flesh was very uneven and his fingers came away dripping blood. This time he managed a hoarse whisper, using all his effort, "That's funny. Don't feel anything there. Throat hurts." Then he pointed to Randall's chin.

Randall nodded. "Just a little cut," he said. "Let's see, now. Everybody else O.K.?"

Hatcher got his engine started without difficulty—what rugged things those engines were! The two boats ran in and beached. O'Bannion got everyone out of the boats at once and put in relief crews from his beach party. "I've stopped all unloading," he said. Waves were crashing on the shore, now, reaching out at the men scrambling from the two boats as if reluctant to let them go. The enlisted men were soaking wet and shaken up, but seemed otherwise unharmed.

MacDougall tried not to show that he was hurt; he felt embarrassed by the accident. His position now suddenly reminded him of the time he once fell down a cargo hatch at Shanghai and fractured his arm, then climbed painfully out of the hold as if nothing had happened, not wishing to let the coolies know that he was hurt by the fall. Here now was Mike O'Bannion trying to get him to lie down on a stretcher. MacDougall waved O'Bannion and the corpsmen away, took a few tottering steps and fell. After that he let them put him on the thing and carry him to Dr. Bell's medical aid station. MacDougall's body was a mass of cuts and abrasions. He was beginning to feel the pain now, an overall sensation of sting and bruise—except his throat. That was a special sort of hurt. He began to shiver violently.

Bell took over at once. "Cover him up with blankets, boys, lots of blankets." Corpsmen who seemed quite comfortable in undershirts tucked the blankets about him. "Just a little shock, Mac," said Bell. "Here, let's get at your arm with this syrette."

Bell stuck a needle in his arm, then got busy with gauze and tape. "I won't fool around with this at all," he said. "Flynn will have to clean you up properly when you get back aboard—you're as full of sand as an oyster."

Sailors carried the litter down to water's edge again. O'Bannion eased in a ramp boat and they put MacDougall in the bottom, with Randall sitting beside him. The boat retracted from the beach. Soon he could feel it surging ahead. MacDougall shut his eyes and listened to the regular thump as the craft ran to windward. The trip out to the *Belinda* seemed long; the wait alongside to be hoisted aboard seemed interminable. From time to time MacDougall opened his eyes. The ship's rail was lined with men, all looking down into the boat. Some of the faces he recognized, but nothing interested him much except to get aboard and into a bunk. He heard voices: "Why, that's Mr. MacDougall." More voices: considerable discussion as to how he might best be hoisted aboard. Should they use the casualty davit and haul the litter up on a hand whip? Should they hook the boat onto a davit, or heave it up with a cargo hook?

At last Randall spoke up. "Hook her on and let's get it over with." The decision had been made to do this, and as he spoke the cargo hook came down. While the boat was being hooked on and hoisted aboard, MacDougall thought: We've got to work out a system. Some day there'll be a lot of fellows in litters, waiting by the boatload. But pain and fatigue bore in; he put the problem off for another day and shut his eyes again.

Now the litter was being lifted from the boat; he was being carried down the deck. Voices buzzed about him like bees in springtime: "Easy there. . . . Gangway, boys. . . . Watch that door." At last the surgery door shut and the buzzing faded away. The litter was at rest. MacDougall opened his eyes to a small world of whiteness: bright operating lights shining in his face from overhead, more lights reflected from spotless white bulkheads and corpsmen dressed in white. Then came Dr. Flynn with his teasing smile. "Well, Mac, you don't look tight enough for a good Scot. Think I'd better sew you up here and there."

They pulled off his wet clothes and joked about the sand. They put hot towels over his face—some queer stuff—it was hard to breathe, yet he was still shivering. He had a hazy idea of what went on: pressure here and there, sting of medication, sudden stabs of Flynn's needle—the thing was sharp enough. What was he sewing on that leg for? It was the other one that hurt. After much time spent in cleaning and probing, Flynn was sewing on his chest and, at last, on his face. Now the needle really hurt. "I'm just trying to improve your face a little," Flynn's voice was cheerful, casual between stabs of that needle.

50

"Don't want your wife to throw rocks at you when you get home." While Flynn snipped and sewed, MacDougall thought of home: what a nice place to be. For a few moments he was able to push away painful reality, remembering Nadine and her gentle hands. Then Flynn's needle brought him back to the *Belinda*. Another foulup in the boats. It could have happened to anyone, yet things like that shouldn't happen to him. Breathing seemed hard—almost as if he had one of those boats on his chest, he thought. Boats, boats . . . guide in the boats to the shore. Look after them. Bring them back safe.

At last they were done. MacDougall was wheeled to the empty isolation ward and put into a lower bunk. Here at last was rest. Drug-softened pain whirled around him, and in a relaxing blur he was carried off into exhausted sleep. About midnight he awoke to fresh pain: drugs and shock were wearing off. He moved his tortured body about, trying to find a comfortable position, but found none. From time to time he heard running feet on the weather deck above—shouting, the whir of davit motors, steel blocks banging, cries of men tossing in boats alongside. Sherwood must be bringing the boat group back on board.

It was a wild night on the beach. Five of the broached-to VPs were driven high and dry by wind and sea before the last boatload of Army materiel was landed. From then on it was a concerted salvage job led by O'Bannion, on the beach and as far into the water as he could wade—assisted by Sherwood and his boats. Marty brought in all four twin-engine LCMs for towing. An hour after Major Malumphy had gone—to the fort for a shower and a good sleep, they supposed—he returned with a borrowed cherry picker and helped get the stranded craft into the water. By four in the morning the last VP had been dragged, lifted and pushed off the beach. By five, all had been hoisted aboard the *Belinda*, battered up, but safe and well-worth repairing by Rinaldo and his crew.

Gedney gave orders to get under way for Pearl Harbor. Off the harbor entrance he signaled dismissal and thanks to Stephens's patrol craft, then stood in to quiet water. This time he did not order his crew into white uniforms.

That afternoon Gedney came down to the sick bay to visit MacDougall. As usual the captain was freshly shaven, his clean khakis neatly pressed. With blue eyes twinkling, he shook hands. "Welcome back aboard, MacDougall," he said.

As he chatted on, MacDougall began to sense that there was a deeper meaning underlying this casual greeting. There was no criticism of his handling of the boats. "You are a sailor and I am a sailor. We understand each other," Gedney said. Mac-

Dougall was thinking, how different can sailors be? Yet he noticed that Gedney's conversation, all of it on a friendly, man-to-man level, seemed directed towards the ship and problems of the ship, rather than the boat group, which he had previously insisted to be the *Belinda's* primary battery. "You must understand—an executive officer with only three months experience at sea—a navigator with deportment in keeping with Naval tradition, but inexperienced. I'm alone on that bridge, Mac-Dougall. There are some things that rank cannot— Suppose something should happen to me as it has to you? What then?"

Gedney paused, and a chill began to sink into MacDougall's aching frame. But surely, no, not that. The boats were a part of him now. He had sweat for them and even bled a little. The bitterness of exchanging command for a minor role on the *Belinda* was compensated for by those boats. Gedney continued to talk of the many complications connected with running a ship like the *Belinda*, then suddenly he asked, "What is your opinion of Sherwood? Do you consider him capable?"

"I certainly do, Capt'n. Don't know what I'd do without him. You'd think he'd been in boats all his life. He's a natural leader and a natural with those boats." MacDougall felt a warm glow for these men and boys who worked with him in the *Belinda's* landing craft. Together they'd make a team Gedney could be proud of.

Gedney changed the subject back to MacDougall's injuries. "Dr. Flynn is of the opinion that you should be ordered to the naval hospital at Aiea, at least for observation."

That would take weeks! Those hospital people never hurried. Once they got their hands on you. . . . "Oh, no, Capt'n," MacDougall said with his hoarse whisper. "Don't let them do that, sir. They're taking good care of me here—after all, four doctors—I'll be all right. I'm sure I'll be able to talk soon. I've got to get back in the boats."

Gedney smiled benignly. "I'm glad to hear that you want to stay with the ship. You'll have to go to the hospital for a check on your throat by specialists, but I'll make sure, unless special treatment is needed, that you can stay with the ship."

"Thank you, Capt'n. There isn't much time, I know. We have to get busy right away with those boats. Sherwood can help me until I get back on my feet."

Gedney's jaw set ever so slightly. Then he said, "You must rest your voice, MacDougall. Rest as long as you need; get your strength back again, for I am going to need you." MacDougall visualized himself in the command boat, flying over wave caps, lining up his landing craft. What was Gedney saying? "You have confirmed my own observations, MacDougall. I am going to make Sherwood boat group commander."

MacDougall rose up as if he were ready to get right out of

the bunk and run up on deck to retain possession of his boats. "But Capt'n!" he protested in an angry and dismayed whisper. If he only had his voice; if only he could explain. . . .

Gedney reached out and pushed MacDougall gently back on the pillow. "You have to be practical, MacDougall. Flynn reports that you will not be able to climb up and down nets for months to come. You will not be able to walk much for weeks, and you must rest what voice you have left or you soon will have none."

MacDougall struggled weakly against the pressure of Gedney's hand, then sank back in the bunk and whispered hoarsely, "I'll be all right, Capt'n. I'm just bruised up. I can get into the boats at the rail." He thought, I just love those boats!

Gedney sat still, waiting for this emotional outburst to subside. MacDougall heard running footsteps on the deck above, then sounds of a boat being lowered. Light coming in through the porthole was shaded momentarily by the passing boat hull. Then it was water-borne; engine started, boat roared away—probably after mail. But it seemed to MacDougall that it was leaving him—all the boats were leaving him stranded in this regulation-bound ship. When engine sounds faded, Gedney continued: "I need a real sailorman on the bridge with me. Quigley and Harrison can take care of routine duties but they cannot take the conn, particularly in times of stress. That is where you will come in. While you are recuperating, you can train new officers of the deck and keep an eye out for me."

So that was it, MacDougall thought bitterly. He had been neatly trapped. First by the sea—a man could expect that, for the sea was a sailor's natural enemy. Now these people who had rank but couldn't do their work had hit him while he was down. He had given up his first command for active Navy service, anxious to do something useful in troubled times. Now he was a two-stripe stooge. MacDougall scarcely heard any further words of Gedney's. After the captain had gone, he lay in the bunk staring through the porthole at a glaring patch of blue sky. Then he sighed deeply and managed a drink of tepid water from the carafe beside the bunk. Man, it's stuffy in here, he thought. I wish I was out with the boats on a nice dry run.

Later in the day a delegation of enlisted men came to call. There was Doyle, the lanky boatswain's mate, Hatcher, Tommy Jones, the dark-eyed boat coxswain from San Diego, and Whitey McClintock, a friend of Hatcher's who worked for O'Bannion in the beach party. They stood looking at MacDougall, holding out a large can of chilled pineapple juice, shifting their feet about self-consciously and having little to say, yet after they had gone, something of their friendliness lingered behind. Then a corpsman came and helped MacDougall to a shower. Cool, fresh water felt wonderful; the last of sand and salt were washed away, and with them, so it seemed, a measure of his bitterness.

CHAPTER 8

Radar found Makin first. The radarman on watch pointed to the PPI scope while Harrison, the navigator, peered nervously over his shoulder. It was amazing, almost frightening to Harrison: that shovel-shaped surface antenna turning slowly at masthead height had picked up faint echoes from the tops of coconut trees growing on an island which was nowhere more than fifteen feet above the sea and twenty-three night-black miles away. The *Belinda's* long sea passage from Hawaii was nearly ended; the beaches lay not far ahead. Harrison made his reports to Gedney: distance and bearing to land. Other ships in the attack force also saw indications of land by this electronic mumbo jumbo and on the strength of pale green pictures seen in polar projection at the flattened end of a cathode-ray tube, the admiral sent out tactical orders in coded voice over the TBS. On "Execute the order," the assault force of four battleships, four heavy cruisers, six troop-laden attack transports with their nine screening destroyers, turned in wheeling columns and headed for coconut treetops. Three escort carriers with their four destroyers turned back into the trade wind and began to launch planes.

Captain Gedney, wearing helmet and kapok life jacket, stood on the wing of his bridge, watching dark shadows of ships ahead while he chewed absent-mindedly on a bit of cold toast. He was conscious of the mass of soldiers grouped quiet beside combat packs on the weather deck just forward of the bridge. He felt these men, his crew at battle stations, the other ships around him and the distant land. Only a dim shadow here and there for his eyes, the rest remembered reports and instinct of a seaman. It seemed long and slow to the transport area and hoisting-out of all boats. He had trained his crew for this day; much of what they did in the next few hours would be beyond his personal control. He had checked off details to be performed by each department of the ship to bring the *Belinda* to that precise spot marked with a penciled *X* on his chart, and from there to get boats away, troops debarked and landed at exactly 0930, on the precise strip of sand marked on his operation plan as Beach Red Two. Hearing rather than seeing his ship's company busy in the dark at specialized tasks, he felt a surge of pride that they had learned so fast, then choked it down, remembering all that they still must learn. They were green and inexperienced. If only they could do well during the *Belinda's* first

54

introduction to combat, they might one day develop the efficiency of which he dreamed and towards which he worked.

MacDougall broke into his thoughts now, whispering, "Radar has something out at thirty-thousand yards, one-one-five true—not positively identified yet, but it looks like the LST group, sir."

"Good. They'll be there for Yellow Beach inside the lagoon. There is nothing to hold up the landing now. The bombardment is scheduled to start in a few minutes." MacDougall rested his injured leg on a stool at the extreme bridge wing. Gedney glanced towards the pilot-house. All was in deep shadow, but he heard Randall's voice, keeping the *Belinda* on station in the column. For the moment there was nothing for Gedney to do. He had a little time for the relaxations of reflection. This atoll, main group of the Gilberts: he considered what little he knew of its history and culture. The operations plan called for delivery of seventeen hundred and seventeen tons of projectiles to the low and narrow shores of Butaritari. It was inconceivable that only Japs would be hit by them. Before the Japanese had come, it had been the quiet home of some seventeen hundred Gilbertese. White men had come before the yellow. Quiros, dreamy navigator of Portugal, had blundered upon this place early in the seventeenth century, but his visit had little or no permanent effect on the brown natives living there. They continued living their isolated lives according to their own freedoms and taboos, adjusting themselves successfully to life on a sandy strip of island which at no place rose more than fifteen feet above the sea. They subsisted on coconut, edible tips, pulp and seed of pandanus and upon an inferior taro which they learned to grow in shallow pits. Surviving, they grew hardy and fearless. Scorning delicious flatfish easily caught in the lagoon, they risked their lives in deep water beyond offshore reefs to capture tiger and gray nurse sharks, whose reeking flesh was savory to them. In eating these creatures, they believed that the man partook of the shark's courage.

Gedney peered about into the darkness: ship on station. He listened automatically to messages from the TBS and from his own radar. His active mind dwelt on sharks. He had no desire to catch one; he did not like fishing. Yet the thought of those brown men making such dangerous effort for something they believed worth while appealed to him. They were good people, he was sure; good in the sense of a good Navy man who abided not only by rules and regulations but by ancient customs. A man had to have instinct for these things. Yes, decent folk, these Gilbert Islanders. Their struggle was with the elements. Except for readiness to fight in defense of property—including wives —and to repel the more avaricious traders from their shores, they lived in peace: island with island and family with family, respecting even to the square foot that space assigned in the thatched public house of each island to the members of a certain family. They sailed their canoes in deep water, miles from any sight of land, navigating by stars without aid of chronometers or trigonometry. And they sang to their children in one of their chants . . . Gedney thought for a moment. He had the thing in a book down in the cabin. What were the words? Oh, yes, something like this:

> Mr. Star, thou, the little one,
> Wink once, wink twice.
> Thee I have chosen; thou art sleepy!
> Thou sleepest, Mr. Star, thou the little one
> O-o-o-a-a-a! Sleep!

Gedney paused, pleased at his excellent memory. Voice of the TBS broke in: directions to the minesweeping DD and to the bombardment group. Now a message for the *Belinda*. He supervised Randall in a course change, then, sensing the long hours of concentration soon to begin for him, he sank back into his contemplation. It was because these natives had so little that they had been left alone for centuries, unmolested by the more quarrelsome of the world's inhabitants. Living upon mere pinpricks of land, nearly lost in this greatest of all oceans, their security lay in remoteness and in undesirability to others. At last the English traders came, hunting copra and bringing tradecloth in exchange, introducing strange ideas of work—yet the pleasant routine of island life was little disturbed. Butaritari remained in peace until December 1941. While Manila and Hong Kong fell, Japanese came here to establish a seaplane base. They took what they wanted and dug in. Now the natives learned harsher meanings of work. A few months later, Americans came in a sudden raid: Carlson's Raiders, brought here by submarines. Landing quickly, they killed many Japanese and destroyed what they could of their works, then left. After that, Japanese reinforcements arrived here and at nearby Tarawa. More elaborate defenses were made. According to intelligence reports brought in to Espiritu Santo by a former Burns Philip South Sea trader, most of the natives had been moved from the village of Butaritari to more remote islets across the lagoon. Some appeared to have clung to their familiar home sites. Gedney wondered about them. Would they suffer with the Japanese on this day of reckoning?

Now the bombardment began, first scattered shots as battleships and cruisers got the range, then, with thunderous explosion, smoke and flame flashed from long rifle barrels while shells began to crash into the unseen shore ahead. The first visual indications of land were great fires flaming upwards from Japanese oil dumps. Soldiers waiting to climb down lowered debarkation nets watched in silence; there was nothing to reassure them in their first sight of the landing place. Sailors cheered—sailors waiting behind silent guns on the *Belinda's* weather deck, sailors on the signal bridge, sailors waiting to launch boats, boat crews sitting in their nested craft—they cheered and yelled like schoolboys at a game. Gedney went at once to the PA microphone and snapped on all groups. "Stop that shouting immediately," he cried. "It's disgraceful!"

The enthusiastic din died away, yet on the deck below Gedney's bridge, some undisciplined voice yelled, "There goes another one! Boy, oh boy! Look at the Japs burning!"

Human sounds were soon under control aboard the *Belinda*, but the tempo of electronic din increased. Voice struggled with voice and all struggled with tropical static as the TBS speaker on the pilothouse bulkhead repeated orders of division flagships: orders to launch more planes; orders to sweep mines, to close the beach with rapid fire of all caliber; orders of ship maneuvers. Then came the secret signal for the landing to proceed as planned. It was up to each transport now. Sweep second hands on big brass clocks in each dimmed-out pilothouse had authority greater than captains. The clock on Gedney's bridge was set to the exact second; it ruled precisely and unemotionally.

Now Gedney stopped before the clock. The sweep second hand was going around the right side of its large, illuminated face. "Stand by, Bosun's Mate," he ordered. The boatswain's mate snapped all groups of the PA and stood ready with his silver pipe. The sweep hand on the clock was rising. MacDougall, who had been backing the *Belinda's* engines to get way off the ship, now pulled the handle of the engine-room annunciator to "Stop." Gedney swung his right arm up vigorously, fingers pointing upward. "Away all boats, away!" he cried.

Standing before the PA microphone, the boatswain's mate put the silver pipe between his lips and blew the long, wailing call for *attention*. Then he repeated the captain's order, "Away all boats, away." The PA shouted the words from truck to keel, from bow to stern. No man could escape the sound of that order, "Away all boats."

Instant response came from the davits and winches: humming of drums released from brakes, whine of winch motors, hollow metallic clang of blocks against steel hull and cargo booms. Men shouted; boats splashed into the water; motors roared. The *Belinda's* boat group was getting away. Soldiers milled about, pushing their way towards assigned debarkation nets. In the same restricted areas, boats were being hoisted out, hatches uncovered and military vehicles having top battle priority were being lifted from the holds.

When the PA cried, "Away all boats," Sherwood was leaning against the canopy of the command boat, which hung in davits just abaft the bridge. He had checked every possible detail, had spent hours with MacDougall studying charts and photographs which had been taken recently from submarines and from the air. "There are going to be a lot of discrepancies between what we see here and what you'll see tossing around in that boat," MacDougall had told him. "When the time comes, you'll have to do it like the birds do when they migrate. Nobody can pound this stuff into you with a book or even with a chunk of coral. A fellow has the feeling for it, or he doesn't. My two bits are on you."

"Thanks lad," Sherwood had said. "I'll try and *return* like the swallows, too." Now he was being lowered swiftly down, hooks released, engine roaring and Hatcher tooling him out to the starboard boat circle off the bow. Kruger was in charge of a similar circle off the port bow. As boats were loaded with troops, medium tanks and light artillery needed with the first combat teams, Sherwood formed them into waves. From time to time he glanced at other ships also lowering boats and debarking troops, but his full attention was required now to make sure that all *Belinda* boats were formed up properly so that units would go into combat intact.

From the boats the whole panorama was changed; shore seemed further off while the *Belinda* loomed before him. How graceful her tapering bow looked from here at water's edge! The ship was his reference now. Sherwood tried to keep his boats together while MacDougall backed and filled carefully, keeping the *Belinda* on geographical station despite moderate trade wind and strong coastal current. It seemed to Sherwood that debarkation was lagging. He looked at his watch, carefully synchronized with the pilothouse clock. No, plenty of time. It must be him: impatient today—yes, nervous. He was chilled by frequent passing rain squalls, of short duration yet sufficient to soak all hands in the boats. Concussion of bombardment was in the air. He would be glad when it was time to go.

At last that time came. Sherwood wigwagged attention with his signal flags, then made the tight little circling motion with a single flag held over his head which meant, "Follow me in column." Marty and his big LCMs, carrying medium tanks, Kruger and the first VPs, wave after wave, each in a group with the lead boat flying the wave flag, bobbed along after him.

They made it to the line of departure with one minute to spare. Sherwood dropped back to the first line of his own boats while the amtracks clattered on in a ragged line abreast towards the destroyer, which was now on precise station at the departure line. A signal hoist fluttered from her yardarm. When the flags were snapped down it would be time for the amtracks to head for the beach.

The rain squall passed inland, leaving boats and men dripping and drying in bright sunshine. Nothing could be seen of the island now. Then the squall crossed the lagoon and the entire island shone fresh green and white, lying in a gentle curve from point to point and washed of smoke except for three burning oil dumps. Bombardment tempo increased now, so that while the island remained in view, it was not so clear and sharp. Entire coconut trees were tossed high in the air, turning slowly end over end. Distant battleships belched thunder and flame from fourteen-inch gun barrels. Yet more noticeable to men waiting in boats at the line of departure were sharp cracks from the nearby destroyer's five-inch guns, pouring rapid fire low along the beach. Sand and chunks of coral flew: Japanese defenses, perhaps. Sherwood wondered.

Now, while other firing continued and carrier planes darted down from aloft to take over beach pounding, the nearby destroyer ceased fire. Smoke sailed away from hot gun barrels. Down snapped flags from her yard. Execute the signal! Time for the amtracks to go. Away they clattered, beach-bound. No more orders or help; nothing but engine failure, coral or Japs would stop them now.

Sherwood moved his first wave of VPs and LCMs up into position. He looked back at the others: a little ragged but they would do. He looked at his watch. Two minutes more. Amtracks far ahead now—a half hour's run for them. He would nearly catch them with his faster boats before they crawled ashore. Those battleships were really going to it now. Flags again: Execute second wave. Sherwood signaled to Hatcher with his hand, then shouted down from the canopy top, "Remember, twenty-three hundred rpm." His boat wave surged past the stationary destroyer. Some sailors on her decks waved, but no one in the boats waved back. They were under the shore's spell now.

Strips of sand and groves of trees which looked like green and white ribbon from the line of departure gradually began to take on definition. Trees showed up as individual units, some taller than others, some with curved trunks leaning out over the sea. The beach looked very rough; much worse than Sherwood had hoped. A ragged staccato of explosions drew his attention back to the amtracks ahead: rockets fired from improvised racks. They landed far short; probably trigger happy. They were supposed to fire one now and then as they closed the beach until they got the range; then all were to be let go. They certainly weren't waiting. Rockets shot up at a forty-degree angle, squatting on their flaming tails as they lobbed shoreward in a high arc, landing in shallow water with all the explosive force of five-inch shells. Might be a good idea at that; any underwater mines off the beach would surely be detonated now.

Hatcher was pulling at his trouser leg. Sherwood looked down, saw him making expressive ducking motions with hands spread above his head, then pointing towards shore and making jerking motions toward himself with fingers opened to represent bullets. He shouted something, but Sherwood did not hear. The hand signs were sufficient; yes, better get down. Japs would surely return fire soon. Sherwood scrambled around the canopy. Before getting inside he took a good look at shore through his binoculars. Off to port he saw a clump of especially high coconut trees with a big lumpy shrub in front of them which seemed to reach out over the water. Lots of rocks and big chunks of coral cropping up in the sand. That must be the left flank. Sherwood looked ahead: more rocks showing up. Say! This wasn't going to be good. Something over to starboard —hard to make out much through his binoculars with the boat bouncing around in the chop. Yes, grass roof. A native hut; that's what it was. He rested his eyes. Now Hatcher was yelling at him to get inside. Sherwood raised the seven-fifties for a last good look, steadying elbows on the canopy top. Several native huts. The beach looked better there; of course, it would be. Natives would build on the good beach where they could launch canoes easily. He'd move over that way. It was not according to plan but the plan was no good if it hung him up in the coral. Perhaps he *was* supposed to land where the huts were. He doubted that; swift shore current was carrying him to starboard all the time. He could not be left of course. Aerial photos wouldn't show the huts; they'd be under the trees. Right or wrong, he would head that way—have to take a chance on snipers in the huts. Surely they couldn't survive this bombardment he had witnessed. The huts were all but demolished. Yet they might survive; strange things happened in combat.

Those amtracks were off to the left again. They'd have to scramble for themselves; his job was with the boats. About two hundred and forty men with all their gear in each of his waves. Well, get 'em in there, fellow. Now he could see patches of blue sky through the trees, glimmer of lagoon beyond, but most of this low ground ahead was thick with vegetation—no use wondering what might be hidden there; they'd soon find out. Sherwood's boat was running right wing to the first wave of VPs now. Those boats were working too far left. He wished that he were on the opposite flank so that he could push them over this way, the way MacDougall used to do it. Sherwood scrambled aft to the open cockpit and beckoned vigorously with his signal flags. Marty was staring at the beach ahead of him, running in with his four tank lighters—everybody was looking at the shore. No use yelling—thunder of guns and bombs bursting in the sand. Kruger was on the left wing. Look over here, Karl. Look, man! Ah, there he was, nodding and motioning his coxswain to come right. Sherwood pointed to the huts, now plainly seen with the naked eye. Kruger got the idea; he was pushing the VPs over now. For a time they bunched closely together; coxswains exchanged irritated glances, then, understanding, began to guide right, coming in obliquely on a course to bring the lot to the only decent section of beach. Landing craft from other ships were bearing left to other feasible landing spots. It was going to worry the Army, but better to land too far down or up beach than to be hung up in coral.

The VPs—something knocking on Sherwood's mind—now he got it: soldiers crouching down, just eyes watching the beach from under those helmets. He got the feeling that they were already personally committed to that beach, willingly or unwillingly. The boats were just filling in time: three and a half minutes to go. Now Hatcher was poking him again and pointing at the water. Something skittered along the surface of the water like minnows running from feeding tuna. Those were bullets; Japs firing back. Nothing to do but bore in. Machine-gun bullets ricocheted all about them now; red tracers coming from those thatched huts. Vinson, coxswain of the nearest VP, slumped over his wheel—must have been hit. They were pulling him away. A soldier had the wheel; he'd have to watch that boat! Now one of the deckhands had taken over; the boat was straightened out now, boring in for the beach with the rest.

Sherwood looked ahead again: amtracks rising out of the water like hippos after a bath. They rose higher and higher, lurching awkwardly from side to side as they crawled over uneven coral boulders. They were firing into the huts with their machine guns, but Jap fire had already slackened—perhaps the last strafing run of those hellcats . . . he'd never know. Off to the left one amtrack was stuck. He'd have to take care of himself until the VPs were in. Soldiers scrambled over the boxlike sides and dropped to the sand. Some ran for the bushes; some hesitated momentarily as if confused, then followed the rest. Straight ahead was a beaten-up breadfruit tree, something Sherwood saw at a quick glance but would remember the rest of his life. Every branch was stripped naked of leaves, yet a few disconsolate looking breadfruit hung from some of the broken tips like jack-o'-lanterns which had been left out in a storm.

Watch the rocks, Sherwood. Don't get sidetracked now. Over a little more—reef on each side; split the space. Water shallowing now, bottom showing—rough looking stuff—rocks and coral heads. That one bit of clear beach ahead was very narrow; he'd have to crowd the boats together. These were assault waves; they had to land together and on time. Here they were at the surf line. Ninety seconds of time left. Let 'em go. He motioned Hatcher to cut throttle and the command boat slowed while the wave of landing craft swept on. No turning back for them; they were bound for the sand. Sherwood looked over his shoulder; second wave coming along all right. Time for them later; he must watch for the first wave of ramp boats. It was high tide. If they didn't make it now they never would. One boat came to a jolting stop, hung up on something. The others slid in almost to the sand. Ramps dropped one after another. Soldiers splashed out with their rifles ready. Get those boats out of there, Karl! You've got three minutes to get 'em out of there for the second wave. Marty had the big tank lighters well in; big ramps clattered down, and almost at once medium tanks ground over ramps, splashed, jolted and climbed forward to join the fight. The second wave was almost in now and the first wave not yet retracted. One of them backing out . . . now two more. It was going to be close. Sherwood was tempted to rush in, shout orders and advice. No, that would mean just one more boat in the way. It was up to Karl.

Three VPs and two tank lighters backed clear before the second wave bore in past Sherwood's waiting craft. Suddenly he was looking at helmets again: boat after boat studded with helmets and set faces. He'd already forgotten the soldiers of the first wave. It was boats, boats—get the boats in and get 'em out again. Boats were his job. "Get the tow rope and heaving lines ready," he said to his deckhands. "We'll have to do salvage work until Randall gets here." He'd like to keep the tank lighters here; they were the best salvage boats, but needed to bring in bulldozers, more tanks and heavy mortars. All second-wave boats made beach, but three broached to before they could back out again. Excited, probably. "All right, Hatcher. We'll go in now and drag 'em out."

Sherwood managed to tow two VPs out. He was vaguely aware of thatched huts and of crippled coconut trees, one of which leaned a shattered trunk almost over his head. Boats, boats—get out the boats. "Take that line, boys. Throw it over your stern bitt. . . . Hook her on, Hatch."

The third wave swept past him, boats striking each other glancing blows as they forced in to remaining holes. Rocks, boats and coral: what a mess! Here came O'Bannion, and Randall with his salvage boat; he'd have some help now. Two minutes later Sherwood realized that he'd have to stop the fourth wave. Beach congestion was nearly complete. He'd have to stop them. Those soldiers were needed in the fight and somebody would sear his hide for this, but he'd have to stop them and send one in at a time, wherever he could find a hole to poke them. "Hurry up on that salvage, you fellows," he yelled, despair in his voice. Nobody heard him: explosions, confusions, intensity. Every man straining his guts. Nothing in the landing manual about this sort of mess, but he'd get the boats in somehow. They must get the boats to shore!

As Mike O'Bannion's third-wave boat neared shore he forgot din and smoke of naval bombardment, he even forgot ground fighting now beginning under coconut trees close ahead. Beach, coral, salt water, hull of landing craft grinding on coral, weight of materiel to be transferred from boats to beach—these were the things now. Gunfire seemed like distant thunder; his attention was given to the water under his boat. It was crystal clear, and peering down he could see lumps of coral, hundreds of small coral heads. If shallow water at beach line was like this, he was in for trouble. Coral heads would not overturn a boat, but they could stop her before she could reach shore. Here was a nasty lump! "Right, Cox'n! Quick!" They scraped by just as the boat next in line struck coral and brought up to a jolting stop. The rest of them swept on. He glanced back quickly and saw the coxswain trying to back off for a fresh start.

Now O'Bannion looked carefully at the beach: rocks and coral. Two boats of his wave managed to get in close, and dropped ramps. Soldiers splashed out, knee deep in water, holding their rifles well up as they had been taught in countless dry runs. Some fell down in deep holes, but managed to flounder out, rifles held over heads, faces set and tense. One after another they gained shore, ran forward to cover and dived flat. A bomb landed ahead—explosion followed by sounds of fragments returning to earth. Mike ducked instinctively, then realized that the stuff was inland. Something might hit them, but not that bomb. Good thing they only go off once. Something was missing—that glorious panorama he had expected. Nothing heroic about this confusion. It seemed to be the last of something and the beginning of something. Now his own boat struck coral with a fearful jolt. O'Bannion was thrown forward on top of Boski, the hulking signalman. Scrambling to his feet he shouted, "Back out, Cox'n; back full!" Oh that ramp—deep water all about them. "Stop it, you fool!" he yelled to the deckhand who was releasing the ramp catch. "Back out, Cox'n. We can't drop the ramp here."

Obedience: good thing. He could see that the boat's crew wanted to drop the ramp, get rid of them and get out of here. Instead the coxswain nodded, threw his clutch into reverse and backed clear. The VP swung beam on to shore, then as the propeller drove ahead again, she bumped around the coral head. "Fend off," O'Bannion called. Boski was already busy with a boat hook. Others, following his lead, picked up posts for setting up beach markers. Working together, they shoved the boat clear of one coral head after another. Coral scraped and ground under the wooden hull and along the steel-faced keel and skeg. The propeller sounded lopsided as if blades had been bent. The boat vibrated heavily; yes, bent prop. Well, get her in and get the beach party ashore. "How deep is the water under the ramp, Boski?"

The big signalman reached over the ramp and thrust down a boat hook. "Two or three feet."

"All right. Drop ramp!" Rattle and splash—whole boat seemed changed with the ramp flat, giving a sudden look direct into a coconut grove. A few trees down, tops shot from others, a few shell craters—otherwise surprisingly neat. Boski was in the water now, wading the ten yards to shore, testing the depth —then back. They had a lot of heavy equipment to carry ashore.

For the time O'Bannion ignored all other boats and running men. "Work fast, men. Get the stuff ashore. Pass it along. Lively, now—another man here on this radio." Time for him to go now. O'Bannion jumped off the flat extension of the opened ramp, sank to his waist, slipping, sliding, floundering. Easy now, O'Bannion. You're leader here. Go ashore right end up. Beach now: rough, unfriendly stuff. Sand under his feet, sand and rough coral. At last he reached dry ground. Now to orient himself. Whereabouts on the beach was he? He was the beachmaster—it was up to him to determine beach limits. Trees looked alike; rocks looked alike; the two tangents of land he had guided on were lost beyond overhanging vegetation. The beach curved; he couldn't get lined up by the ships, which might have drifted out of exact station.

A sharp *wham* spun him around. What was that? Close, anyway. Never mind, O'Bannion. Look at the beach, man; quick now! Over to the right a bit—in front of those huts—that was the only decent landing place. Never mind air maps and battle plans: so many yards measured off with calipers. That was on paper, most of it educated guesswork. This was wet sand and rough coral; the stuff had to come in here.

Here was Dr. Bell beside him, calm as usual. A man can look calmer than he feels; perhaps he looked calm too. "Right here, Frank," he said, "find a place to suit you near here and set up your aid station—you'll be out of the way of traffic." Palmer— where was he? Oh, over there setting up his transmitter. O'Bannion started towards his radio officer. He wanted to run, but his feet sank deeply into coarse sand. He was puffing as he said, "No, Chuck, not here. Tracked vehicles have to come through here. Get a place by the coral—that won't make any difference to your gear."

Now for the markers. He'd post limit signs as planned, but landing flags would have to be bunched in that one small place where boats could come all the way in. What a beach! Nothing but coral boulders. He wondered how they were managing on the other beach. Well, this beach, now. "Boski. McClintock. Bring the markers. There and there. Here and here. Yes, that's right."

Here came Malumphy. "Ready to go, Major? . . . Fine. We'll bring the stuff in through here. It's the only place just now. We can explore when things quiet down a little."

"Quiet down, Mike?" Malumphy kidded. "This is the pay run."

Looking seaward, O'Bannion saw Randall busy setting buoys along each side of the narrow passage into the beach. A mess of boats were stuck on coral. The last waves were coming in now between grounded and retracting boats. Sherwood was out there with Kruger trying to untangle the mess. They would have to hurry. Tide was ebbing now and low water would bring more trouble with the coral.

Suddenly O'Bannion became aware once more of things more distant. Combat teams had moved on in. Engineers of the Army shore party were running, heaving and pulling. The stuff was beginning to come in. Then he looked out at the ships, nearly hidden in smoke. Quick flashes of fire leaped out from their hazy outlines. Blue of the sea with sun glistening on wave slopes. Somewhere he had felt like this before—glory and the flag flying from the stump of that shattered coconut palm. . . . "Look out!" somebody yelled. O'Bannion spun around. A bulldozer swept at him, dragging a pallet of ammunition. He floundered out of the way, barely avoiding being knocked down. No, this was different, yet somehow strangely like some feeling he had known before. Queer, he thought as he went down to take active charge on the beach, I feel like I've been here before, yet it's all so strange.

CHAPTER 9

Locating a site for his medical aid station, Dr. Bell missed the shady algaroba trees lining Maalaea Bay. It was quite warm already and would soon be suffocatingly hot for wounded men under an unprotected canvas fly. Stray bullets and occasional Japanese sniper fire pinged in the nearby coconut grove. Finding a large shell crater, he called to his corpsmen. "We'll set up here, boys." Boski and McClintock came up from the beach to help. They drove stakes and set up a canvas fly. Corpsmen prepared instruments and dressings. Before the tent was up, somebody poked Bell. He turned around to see four men carrying two litters. "From the boats, Doc." They looked at him for instructions. Nobody seemed to be talking much. These lads had a bewildered look on their faces as if they didn't think a buddy could actually get shot—even here.

"Let's have a look," said Bell. The little fellow was a goner—shot right between the eyes. He looked familiar, but Bell couldn't place him except as from the *Belinda*. Inoculations or perhaps cat fever: one boy in a line of boys at sick call. Whatever it had been wouldn't matter now. Bell turned to the other one, a tall coxswain badly hurt. Looked like a deep flesh wound. Bleeding badly—shock, too. Get busy. "Compresses, Harmon. No, the large ones. Syrette, plasma—that case of sterile instruments."

While Bell worked, Boski put up the tent overhead, staking long canvas flies horizontally to allow light and ventilation while protecting the place from direct sunlight. Long before Bell finished with Vinson, the coxswain, and sent him on his journey back to the *Belinda,* the first soldiers to be wounded were brought in from the line. Army surgeons, waiting for their equipment to be landed, worked with Bell. Two were experienced surgeons; the young intern worked rapidly on superficial wounds, and wrote up tags. Bell had a little singing feeling within him as he worked; no specific words or music—something like breeze working through palm fronds outside the tent, and sunlight filtering down; nothing that he could hear above gunfire—just felt. He had expected to be depressed. Perhaps later on he would be, but now he was busy healing men's bodies, feeling needed and strangely happy.

At about 1100 Bell was finishing emergency work on a young private with a compound leg fracture. Bone fractures were his specialty; his prewar practice had been in a small Pennsylvania mining community where broken bones were almost a daily occurrence. Winding last turns of adhesive around the splints, Bell remembered his clean little surgery with the south windows; the smell of the place. It was something he liked to think of. Usually his memory slipped back to it easily; now something interfered with the trend of his thoughts, something near. He had the feeling that he was being watched. Not by the usual onlookers—he was used to that. This was more like a finger poking him.

Bell looked up. An elderly native was standing about ten feet away, regarding him intently. He was a dark brown man, wearing a single garment of beautiful soft matting which was wrapped about his waist and secured with a belt of woven hair. His head was grizzled and his face deeply wrinkled, yet the flat curves of his wiry frame had a look of hardness and supple strength. Wonderful muscle tone, thought Bell—amazing in such an old man. He must be over seventy, but I'd think twice before taking him on. Perhaps it was the eyes, clear dark brown and almost twinkling. The old man was self-possessed, apparently unafraid, although his little island had suddenly become a blazing battleground, white men fighting yellow. Bell smiled at the old man, who continued to stand there erect and to regard him seriously, intently. At last he squatted in the sand, being careful to move no closer. Perhaps he wanted help. Some of his people must have been wounded by the bombardment. Speech barrier—no way to talk to him.

"Will you gimme a drink, Doc?" It was the boy with the leg fracture. Bell reached for a paper cup, filled it from a five-gallon can and supported the young private's head while he drank the water. Then he looked at the native again. The old man seemed to be concentrating on something very hard. At last, reading inquiry in Bell's face, he pointed to the water can.

Bell stepped across the shell crater, picked up a mess kit, filled it with water, turned the handle around and offered it to the islander. The old man took it with a steady hand. His movements were unhurried, almost casual. He tipped it until a few drops ran over the brim and fell to the sand; then watched sand soak them up. "That's good water," blurted Bell. "Distilled on the *Belinda*. Tests less than two grains of salt." Then he wondered why he had said the words; they would mean nothing to this old man.

The islander raised the mess kit to his lips and took a careful sip, savoring the water in his mouth. "Good." He said the single word in English, then turned and walked towards the village with rapid steps, carrying the mess kit steady in his hand.

"Well, what do you know!" Bell exclaimed. "Speaks English!" After all, how was he to know what language we speak, barging in here with our fourteen-inch guns. A few minutes later the old man returned with the empty kit. This time he was accompanied by three women and several children. The women were much younger than he. One of them, obviously pregnant, wore what looked like the top of a loose cotton dress cut short at the navel. Her distended midriff was bare and a short grass skirt hung from her hips. She wore a necklace made from teeth of some sort—probably an amulet, for she fondled the thing as if seeking from it some measure of protection. The other two women were similarly attired, but wore no ornaments. All three had a certain degree of the old man's assurance, but they stood back, waiting for him to make the next move. The way they looked at him he must be a chief. The children showed less restraint, smiling and squirming bare toes in the sand after the manner of all children when in the presence of strangers. The bodies of all these people were clean and their simple garments remarkably neat, Bell

67

thought, considering the bombardment which they had somehow survived.

"Water, sir," the old man said, holding out the empty mess kit. A jeep bobbed over rough ground towards the tent, stretcher lashed across the engine hood: another casualty. Bell returned the mess kit to the elderly native and pointed to the water can. They would have to help themselves. Soon Bell was busy with another wounded soldier and all thought of the natives was pushed out of his consciousness. When he turned back to the tent door again, he was astonished to see a muscular Gilbertese, dressed in blood-stained shorts, lying on a mat just outside the tent. The old native was there again with the three women behind him, none of them showing any signs of exertion.

Bell knelt down to have a look at the native on the mat. He was young and husky—a handsome fellow—yet his dark brown face had something of the bloodless look of ashes. Even now, when obviously in deep shock, there was a trace of twinkle in his clear brown eyes—as if to say, "I made it, didn't I?" He had a nasty abdominal wound, probably shrapnel or a bit of shell casing. Bell got busy in a hurry—couldn't let a fellow like that slip away. He hoped they hadn't given him too much of that water. "I'll patch him up and send him out to Flynn," he said to Palmer, who came in with a message from the *Belinda*. "Pat is a good bellyman; he'll do a good permanent repair job on my friend here."

It was hot deep in cargo holds, where soldiers and sailors struggled together in the interminable job of getting out tanks, artillery pieces, gasoline, provisions, small-arms ammunition and heavy clover leaves of artillery shells. It was hot in the *Belinda's* gun tubs, where tropic sun beat down almost vertically, reflecting waves of heat from steel splinter shields, yet it was more pleasant than engine room or cargo holds. During Condition One Able, the official watch status during ship-to-shore movements, nobody was ever off watch. Boat crews, beach party and bridge specialists worked the clock around without letup. The rest of the crew were rotated. Communications people manned lookout stations and helped out on deck. The black gang alternated four hours in the engine room with four hours at the guns. The deck force alternated eight hours at cargo and boat handling work with four hours at the guns. Thus gun crews, while required to be alert against surprise Japanese attack by submarines, planes or surface craft, were also resting from more strenuous work.

Up on the bridge there was a little shade and breeze, but no relaxation. Messages came in continually from voice radio, flag hoist and blinker searchlight, which was used during daylight—orders from admiral and commodore; reports and requests from beach and boats.

MacDougall was at the starboard bridge wing, watching bearings of shore through pelorus sight vanes. The ship was drifting again: there must be a two-knot set along shore towards Ukiangong Point. He looked down over the side. Several landing craft, recently returned from the beach, were drifting in the water within hail, waiting to be called alongside for loading. Tired sailors sprawled in boat bottoms and across engine boxes; even coxswains were as nearly prone as possible, making languid movements from time to time to prevent their craft from drifting away. Here, alongside the *Belinda* once more after the landing under fire, they felt secure enough to remove helmets and life jackets during this short respite before they returned to Red Beach. Three VPs and a tank lighter were tied alongside, being loaded; a fourth VP was being refueled through a hose at number four hatch. MacDougall took another look at bearings: still drifting. Time to get ship on station off Red Two—submarines had been contacted off the point by a patrolling destroyer. Yet if he came ahead on the engines now, all unloading would have to stop until the ship settled down again. He decided to wait a little longer.

The Old Man was yelling again. MacDougall swung inboard as Gedney came down from his seat and out the bridge wing on the run. "Megaphone," cried Gedney angrily as he brushed past MacDougall and jumped upon the bridge-wing platform. "Someone get me the megaphone . . . please!" Gedney hissed out the last word. A messenger came running with the megaphone. Gedney grasped it, dropped it across the bridge rail with a hollow bang and shouted through it to the men drifting in landing craft within hail. "Ahoy in the boats. Put on your life jackets. Put on your helmets. Keep them on; keep them on!"

Faces turned up to the bridge. Men called to their mates, sprawled in sleep. There was a general yet a very slow movement towards compliance with the captain's order. Had these men been on the bridge they would have answered, "Yes, sir." Regardless of resentment or physical discomfort they would have quickly scrambled into battle dress. In the boats there was a feeling of remoteness from the bridge. Boat engines hummed their idling song and exhausts sputtered with impersonal indifference. Boat crews were weary from vibration and rolling about—from exacting demands of timed wave landings—from roar of gunfire and lack of sleep. They obeyed their captain, but it took a little time.

Gedney realized the futility of arguing with his enervated boat crews. Having given the order, he ignored the subdued murmur of grumbling which carried up to the bridge, yet felt the necessity of explaining his attitude to somebody. Turning to MacDougall he said, "A ship sometimes sinks in two minutes; a ship's boat may be wiped out in the wink of an eye. We never know when a bomber or a torpedo may get through." After a pause, Gedney added, "And were it not for that, the wearing of battle dress is an order from higher authority."

Now Gedney's thoughts turned to boat repair. Two landing craft which had come to grief on the coral were in the skids, where shipfitters and carpenter's mates hurried repairs. "When you get the ship back on station, go down and see what progress is being made with boat repairs," he told MacDougall. "I'll watch ship for you until you get back."

MacDougall limped aft to the fantail, where he learned that both boats would be ready within the hour. Returning, he squeezed between slingloads of gasoline and ammunition, managed the vertical ladder to the boat deck and limped forward towards the bridge. Here he met Boatswain Torgeson and, turning to speak to him, neglected to raise his game leg over one of the steel cables which crossed the passageway abreast each davit arm some ten inches above the deck. Too late, he tried to lift his leg clear, tripped and fell flat on the deck. More surprising than the fall and the pain was the blast of heat radiating from the steel deck.

"It's that trick leg of mine," MacDougall said, as Torgeson helped him to his feet. "If that knee puffs on me again, Flynn will probably try to throw me back in the sick bay. . . . Well, I'm not going to the sick bay; I'm going back to that bridge if I have to crawl." MacDougall took an experimental step. It was painful, but he'd make it.

Torgeson was laughing. "Anyway, I see you stenciled on your amphibious insignia."

MacDougall looked down at black tar marks running across his trouser legs at the height of the wire. He grinned, "This was the last pair I had that wasn't marked." Limping towards the bridge he reflected on the boatswain's remark. It was true: of twenty-two hundred men who had arrived in the *Belinda* off Makin that morning, nearly all bore horizontal tar marks on their pants. Davit cables were no respecters of rank or service —they just threw you and branded you with the insignia of the amphibious rabble.

Climbing the bridge ladder, MacDougall's eyes came level with Gedney's neatly shined shoes, then he noticed the captain's trousers. Carefully washed, starched and pressed by his Chinese steward, they bore faded but unmistakable evidence of contact with a davit cable. "What are you grinning at, MacDougall?" asked Gedney. His good humor had returned, but the lieutenant knew better than to strain it.

"I just hit the deck and Torgeson was kidding me about it,"

he said, but he was thinking: Don't tell me the Old Man has joined the amphibious rabble, too!

Standing on a slight rise above the beach, O'Bannion paused to wipe his sun-raw face and neck with a sweat-soaked handkerchief. The tide was nearly out, and he was having trouble with coral. For as long as possible he had managed to get landing craft in to shore, one at a time. In spite of coral and rocks he had been able to land field artillery guns. Major Malumphy set up supply dumps behind the line which were soon receiving gasoline and water in cans, ammunition, provisions and repair parts for the machinery of battle. Boats from Red Beach One, which was even worse, added to the congestion. Salvage boats worked full time.

"We need a channel blasted through this coral," O'Bannion said to Malumphy, who joined him on the rise. "You see what I'm up against. No amtracks and no bulldozer. It'll take forever to wade in with the stuff."

"I'm doing what I can, Mike. We've got dynamite now and I'll get right after that blasting. They've given us priorities on amtracks and a bulldozer."

"I can't drag ammunition ashore with priorities. I need a bulldozer. Look at those men of yours floundering over that slimy coral trying to carry 105-mm clover leaves; they weigh about two hundred and eighty pounds."

"Battle has priority, Mike. It's about time for the secondary landing inside the lagoon. Listen to the bombardment over there."

"There won't be much battle anywhere if they run out of ammunition." O'Bannion pointed disgustedly towards the two broken-down amtracks parked above the beach line. "I suppose they'll let us have that one with the broken shaft!"

A group of native children, dressed in short grass skirts, approached one of the broken-down amtracks curiously. One boy of about ten years, bolder than his fellows, reached out and touched the amphibian's steel side. Startled at the heat, he withdrew his fingers quickly. Nevertheless, the amtrack challenged him; a few moments later he climbed up the treads and scrambled aboard, looked down triumphantly at his playmates, then with a yell of delight jumped down into the deep cockpit. Other children followed, and soon both amtracks were swarming with squealing, bright-eyed children. Reassured by the children's advance, increasing numbers of islanders appeared. These older ones seemed stunned by the strange and awesome happenings to their island. Some asked for water in fairly good English, saying it had been denied them by the Japanese during the last three days. They made motions indicating that rain was the only source of supply. "Japs probably saving it for combat," O'Bannion said to Malumphy. Then he called Mc-Clintock and instructed him to dole out water from a five-gallon tin. After polite thanks by their spokesman, the natives withdrew from the beach and squatted together under the shade of battered coconut trees, watching ships, boats and these strange white men, comparing differences in their appearance and actions with the Japanese who had preceded them to this beach.

═══ CHAPTER 10 ═══

The LST vibrated and heeled over as she followed two destroyers into the lagoon on the opposite side of Butaritari Island from the *Belinda* and Red Beach. Ensign Bud Foster, who, with his pal Ted Fauré, had been assigned from the *Belinda* at Pearl Harbor, swallowed at the lump in his throat and climbed into the small control cab of the lead amtrack, soon to be launched into the lagoon to lead the first wave of the second landing into Yellow Beach. In a way the trip from Hawaii had been a vacation: no watches to stand, no senior officers acting superior, and little to worry about until that big four-engined Jap "Mavis" and the three "Bettys" made a run on them the day before. Now was different. With Fauré to assist, it was up to him, Ensign Bud Foster, to guide in the important first wave of sixteen amtracks to the landing at Butaritari village. It was here that the strongest Jap defense was expected. That's about all he knew, except for a half-hour lecture before maps and photos of the island before they left Pearl.

"There are four wharves inside the lagoon; all off the village and spaced well apart," the briefing officer had said. "Yellow Beach is between On Chong's and King's Wharves—these two to the west. There's a sandspit with machine gun emplacements here between the two. Don't land there; guide right, next to On Chong's Wharf. That will be your best mark to look for when you come in." Even looking down the commander's pencil to the flimsy paper with its legend of pillboxes, rifle trenches, tank revetments, barbed wire, coast defense guns and so on was frightening enough.

Bud was no fool; he understood clearly why Gedney had selected the two of them for this job. As they left the briefing room and headed for the LST which was to take them two thousand miles to Yellow Beach, he said, "You know why Gedney picked us, don't you?"

"Sure. We won the competition on the shakedown cruise: two ensigns most likely to foul up."

"Remember that story he told in the wardroom: every ship always sends its best men. That's what we are, Ted, best men, the most expendable."

"I don't *feel* expendable."

"I don't either, of course. What I mean is—this Yellow Beach and all—lot of responsibility we've got. 'Got to be timed just right,' he said. 'Everything's synchronized.' I don't think we've got very much to go on. Imagine a civilian contractor giving a job like this to us!"

"Imagine any civilian getting near Yellow Beach if he could help it!"

As the LST shuddered astern inside the lagoon, Bud still felt that he had very little to go on. He wanted to run up on deck and have another look at smoke-obscured shore lines. Everything was buttoned tight inside this floating warehouse. He had to stay with the amtracks now. LST sailors ran about the tank deck while her first lieutenant yelled orders. Doors swung wide and the big ramp clattered open, revealing lagoon in bright sunshine—deep blue water, shallower emerald paling to white on the reefs. Butaritari village was obscured by a dense pall of smoke, gray here, black there, rising high, then coming towards them with the light breeze. At last he made out a wharf, but which wharf of the four he could not tell. Where was On Chong's Wharf? Suppose he landed in the wrong slot!

"Well, Navy. You ready?" It was Captain Lang, the company commander. He climbed up and squeezed in between Bud and the driver in the amtrack's diminutive control cab. The deep well behind them was filled with combat infantrymen. Lang's usually pleasant face was set, almost expressionless. His mind was fixed on the beach, on what he would do when this amtrack got there. It was just like a record: the turntable is revolving; you set the needle at the edge of the groove and it grinds on in. The tune is there; the notes are set. What he would do when they landed—that was his record. Nothing on that record about today's chances or how he felt about home, his wife and kid. Those thoughts had been with him during wakeful night hours. They were put away now; his thoughts were grooved to the inside of this lagoon off Yellow Beach.

Bud had been watching the shore. Between drifting smoke clouds he had finally located all four wharves. They were all low: small-boat stuff, with the two biggest ones to the right. Yellow Beach lay between these two. His stomach seemed to whirl in space—this uncertainty. Bud turned his slow, boyish grin to Lang. "I'm ready," he said. "Ready as I'm going to be."

Then the PA whistled—even LSTs had PAs. "Away the amtracks." Engines roared and echoed in the tank deck; treads clattered as Bud's amtrack lurched down the ramp, then splashed in the water nearly up to her coamings. Sudden change from riding high to deep immersion in lagoon waters was confusing to Bud. With his eyes so close to water, landmarks were much harder to identify than from the higher tank deck.

73

Strongest impressions now were sun glare and dark smoke drifting from shore. Bud looked at lagoon water lapping near his face—like drifting downriver in a bathtub, he thought. Now where is On Chong's Wharf? Somehow he found the wharf again, and somehow got all sixteen amtracks in line abreast and reasonably lined up with shore. Ted Fauré was at the other end, his job to squeeze the amtracks over to the guide. It's up to me now, Bud thought. Just three weeks ago MacDougall was jumping me for straggling, and now I'm guiding in a pay-run first wave! Bud felt no elation whatsoever; he would willingly exchange jobs with almost anybody, even with one of those fellows clutching rifles in the deep cockpit behind him. Two destroyers were pumping shells into Yellow Beach now. They also acted as control craft at the line of departure. Bud headed his wave to pass between them. Roar of battleship gunfire, which had slackened after the Red Beach landing, thundered all out again. Smoke obscured beach and wharves more than half of the time. Shells exploded against the corner of On Chong's Wharf and, while Bud watched, one entire corner of it collapsed. Golly! he thought. If they shoot my wharf away, what will I use for a mark?

The DD gave the signal, and Bud started the ragged line of amtracks churning shorewards. Things were hazy in his mind from then on. He listened to the amtrack's clattering treads, thinking how odd that he could hear them above the bombardment, then wondering whether he really heard the treads or just felt them: push, push, push, push—little handfuls of water thrust astern on either side of the amtrack as it crawled across the lagoon towards the reef. Bud looked back at the second wave: tank lighters with big ramps, rising and falling deliberately over the smooth-surfaced ground swell rolling into the lagoon from sea. Turrets of medium tanks they carried protruded above their sides as if already searching for targets. He spared one glance for soldiers in the deep well at his back. Two seemed to be sleeping, perhaps they were seasick. Others just looked at each other with expressionless stares, or stretched eyes to the level of the coaming and stared at the shore they approached. The Army driver was having trouble steering the amtrack; they were supposed to be guide, yet their clumsy vehicle wallowed from side to side like a rooting hog.

Complying with bombardment schedules to a split second, all naval gunfire suddenly stopped. After a few moments of quiet came the roar of carrier planes diving down, followed by the multiple shock of exploding bombs. Then more planes, one at a time out of group after group, diving down, pulling out, some treetop low; falling sticks of bombs; more explosions and more smoke, fewer trees along the beach ahead. Before Bud could accustom his nerves to this, a signal rocket went off down the line, curved up and landed nicely at the beach line. Then all the amtracks let go with their rockets: flames thrust back, an inhuman whooshing sound, up, up, seeming to hang in air, then quickly down, and more reverberating thunder along the beach.

Bud looked at his watch: seven minutes to go. Bombs still falling and newly arrived Hellcats strafing the beach with chattering machine guns: beach sand packed with sand spurts, shallow water, where they were due to land, now riffled with thousands of driving bullets, tracers hissing as they quenched. All this lethal rain was to stop just before the amtracks arrived—the briefing officer had explained it casually with a pointing pencil. Bud's line of amtracks were less than a thousand yards from that beach; they would soon come under the bombs, the spatter of machine guns on diving planes. Bud wondered if his watch was right, if the planes could be late—delayed en route somehow and now going through their part. Perhaps the amtracks traveled faster in this smooth water than planners expected. On the LST coming down from Pearl he had asked these questions and many more. Nobody seemed to know; they just rode the thing. He hadn't realized about this strafing. How close were they supposed to come anyway? Did the pilots know? Perhaps some of those pilots knew less than he did about the timing of this landing; perhaps while traveling at high speed over a strange area it was impossible for them to judge distances. Bud became more concerned with these carrier planes than with the unseen Japanese enemy. He wished that he could ask somebody now; he was just a green ensign. Always before there had been some big shot around to make important decisions. Here was an invasion coming in to land with Bud Foster to guide it. He felt like a man sitting astride a rocket, steering it somewhat this way and that, yet having no control over its speed or ultimate destination. Find On Chong's Wharf, that was his job. He had studied plans and photos, recognized the wharf and hung on to it with his eyes. The landing just ground on; somebody had started it and he was in it, steering a ragged line of floating bathtubs, just a part of the whole. Maybe something had got out of gear somehow. Bud looked up at the sky again: little black specks of dive bombers sitting up there, still waiting to come down. He reached over and grasped Lang's shoulder, shouted, "I think we're ahead of schedule. Those planes will blow your men to bits."

No change on Lang's face, still set with that fixed expression. "Think we'd better slow down?" Lang, too, was shouting to be heard, but did not seem to be excited. Bud nodded and the driver cut his throttle. Other amtracks surged ahead, bulging the line. Bud stood up with his signal flags and waved them down. Ted Fauré at the other end of the line had been watching him; he too slowed his end of the line. Tank lighters in the following wave surged up close, looming as if their great ramps would crush low amtracks under water; then they too slowed, keeping a reasonable distance astern. That would save a foulup in the water, Bud thought; but while he waited he worried about the shore, wondering whether he was doing something necessary, perhaps brilliant, or something that would further foul up this biggest job the Navy had given him—had given him because he was considered more expendable than other of the *Belinda's* boat officers. He felt no elation or power over men and machines—only pressure, pressure.

Ten minutes later the air strike slackened and Bud started the first wave forward again, hurrying them now, for if his watch was anywhere near accurate, he was late where no tardiness was considered excusable. Standing up on the small foredeck of his wallowing craft, he watched to make certain that all the others were moving. Lang yanked him down, pointing to quick, small splashes in the water just ahead: machine gun fire coming at them—he wondered where from. Wreckage on the wharf ahead as well as to the left of what looked like a seaplane ramp at the end of King's Wharf. To the right of On Chong's Wharf were two sunken hulls, beached in the shallows. Splashes reached out across water towards him from that direction. Bullets spattered against the amtrack. Bud ducked automatically. Once more he looked out. Shore breeze roughed swell tops now; it was hard to trace bullets. He kept his head down for nearly a minute, then felt the jolt as the amtrack struck coral and ground slowly up and over the reef's ledge. One amtrack far down the line scrambled up the seaplane ramp off King's Wharf. Transition of Bud's vehicle from unskilled swimming to lumbering travel on land took place in shallow pools and reef flats. Thrown around by one especially heavy jolt, Bud looked back and saw tank lighters make sudden stops at the reef ledge; those heavy ramps dropped and medium tanks rolled out. One he watched wallowed ahead a few yards, then dropped nearly from view into a deep coral-bound pool, and stopped. Heavy explosion ahead brought Bud's eyes front. No telling where that came from. As he raised his head to look, another spatter of automatic fire crashed against the unarmored amtrack. Bud ducked again, keeping eyes barely high enough to see ahead through slits in the steel plate now closed across the windshield.

The amtrack lumbered up to dry land; now the Army was on its own, Bud just a passenger. He hung on as the vehicle careened around or over wreckage of demolished native buildings. The driver seemed to have forgotten his throttle, which remained wide open. He steered this way and that as if anxious to get through the strip of village. Ignoring gunfire, Lang raised up and looked all about, trying to orient himself. Now he tapped the driver's shoulder. The amtrack stopped suddenly, throwing Bud violently forward. Shattered coconut logs lay in a crisscrossed jumble ahead, some resting on remains of buildings they had once shaded. Progress ahead or to either hand was impossible. An umbrella of explosions in the air about them tore at Bud's ears. Lang yelled to the driver, "Back out of here and try again." The driver clashed gears, got the amtrack in reverse and lurched backwards. Bullets spattered the side again. "Duck!" yelled Lang unnecessarily. Then, "Back up some more. There's a hole to the left. We can round it and go ahead again." At this moment Bud scrambled out of the cab without a word to Lang and dived for shelter amid rubble of a wrecked dwelling. The amtrack moved on out of his sight.

Bud lay still under cover of coconut logs and a section of weathered frame siding until gunfire in his vicinity slackened. How long he waited he had no idea. He had lost all sense of time and had forgotten about his watch. Once the wave had landed, time had returned to casual importance again. Bud stood up and looked about. Fighting seemed to have moved eastward and somewhat inland on this narrow strip of the island's middle. Looking up at trees still standing, he thought about snipers, then shrugged. Nothing had hit him yet—amazing at that. He started back towards the beach; to do so seemed a natural step towards return to the *Belinda*. He had been given no specific instructions regarding this. A rifle cracked sharply; Bud dived for cover—perhaps this wasn't going to be so easy. After a few minutes of silence in the vicinity, he crawled cautiously forward. Coming to a small clearing, he saw one of the amtracks—hit by a shell, one entire side blown open and the endless track torn off. Three bodies lay on the ground beside it: Americans. Bud inched his way around the clearing, eyes examining trees—anything which might provide hiding to snipers. Looking up, he stumbled over something soft and warm. A shudder swept through him, shook him—body of a little Oriental lay there. The chest was nearly blown away, ribs and lungs a bloody mess, yet the ashen face looked unharmed. Upper lip curled back, exposing buck teeth. The eyes were already glazed; otherwise the facial expression was natural: remote, almost contemplative, showing neither anger nor fear.

Bud managed his way through rubble of village and grove. Regaining the beach area, it was a relief to see Americans on the move again. Nobody paid attention to him other than a quick glance at his blue-gray helmet. Men and materiel were moving in across the lagoon reef. Outward bound, he seemed to be breasting the human tide alone. At water's edge he found Lieutenant Finnigan, force beachmaster, remembered from dry runs in Hawaii. Busy establishing the beachhead, adjusting theories of plan to D Day realities, Finnigan had no time for casual talk. Depth of water was two feet less than expected; only a few spots allowed landing craft to cross the reef. Low tide would be better here; boats could come to reef edge, then cargo pallets could be dragged to dry ground by amtracks. Until then men must wade to shore, carrying heavy armloads from broken-up pallets. Bud knew nothing of the over-all situation. He waded out to a boat and struggled back over rough coral with all the 37mm ammunition he could carry. He felt better doing something. As Bud passed Finnigan on his return for a second load, the tall beachmaster reached out an arm and stopped him.

"I've got a job for you, Ensign. You're from the *Belinda*, aren't you?"

"Yes, sir."

"The flame throwers are fouled up: no oxygen tanks—don't know where they are. Take one of those empty boats, go outside the lagoon to the *Belinda,* and bring me back a load of oxygen tanks as fast as you can. I'll radio ahead; they should be ready when you get there."

"Yes, sir," said Bud, eagerness and relief in his voice. Work to do and a big two striper taking the responsibility. And the *Belinda* . . . After these two strange weeks away it would be swell to see the familiar ship, to see the gang for a few minutes while the boat was loading. He ran down to the beach and splashed out towards reef edge. His feet hurt: sweat and now sand in his heavy beach shoes ground salt water into blisters. Say—he could get dry socks from his locker! His mind jumped ahead to the crowded little room he shared with Fauré, Kruger and another ensign. It would be almost like coming home.

The first empty boat he reached was from an LST. Bud scrambled aboard, explained his mission to the coxswain and was soon on his way out of the lagoon. Sky which earlier in the day had been blue and clear was now obscured with dust and smoke; air smelled of gunpowder and burning oil. Waters outside the lagoon looked sparkling clear. It would be good to get away from here and out into clean, unobstructed water once more.

Once aboard the *Belinda,* Bud was greeted warmly by his friends. Heading for his stateroom and dry socks, he was confronted by Biggs, captain's orderly. "Captain wants to see you, Mr. Foster. . . . Starboard wing of the bridge." Bud nodded. He wanted those socks, but ensigns don't change socks while commanding officers wait. Climbing ladders to the bridge, he wondered what the Old Man wanted—never a good word from him yet. Perhaps this was the day of change. Those two weeks away from the *Belinda* had been rugged, except for lazy sunbaths the first week out—air attacks of four big Japs on one poor little LST, then this morning to top things off.

Bud found Captain Gedney shouting admonitions through his megaphone to the LST-boat's crew. "Put your bowfast on the outboard cleat. You'll never get alongside under the load the way you're doing it." Gedney turned to MacDougall, who was at his elbow. "We shouldn't blame these lads. They don't get proper training on LSTs, with Bachelors of Art for commanding officers."

MacDougall grinned, then seeing Foster, slapped him on the back and shook his hand. "Welcome home, Bud."

Gedney gave attention to the landing craft until the first slingload of oxygen tanks had been successfully lowered into it, then he turned and saw Bud. Gedney seemed to be waiting for something. With a start, Bud remembered and managed a salute. Returning the salute casually, Gedney allowed him a benign half smile. "Congratulations on a safe return," he said.

Bud beamed; a warm, wonderful feeling flowed through his being. "Thank you, sir." The words breathed out like a relieved sigh.

Now the little smile was gone from Gedney's face. Blue eyes probed into Bud's. "Ensign Foster, can you explain to me your reasons for holding up the landing on Yellow Beach for eleven minutes?"

Bud's golden glow was replaced by the old familiar chill. How could a green ensign explain anything to a four striper? "Well, sir. It was the planes. They kept on coming and I thought that if those soldiers got strafed . . . I thought . . . Well, you see, Captain . . ."

Gedney held up his right hand for silence. During the following pause, Bud took a quick gulp of air which hurt his throat as he tried to swallow. Well, let's have it, he thought. I'm really on the Old Man's list now. "Young man," Gedney said at last, his tone fatherly, almost kind, "when Admiral Nimitz requires your advice he will send for you. Meanwhile I direct your attention to his operation plan, which required planes to bomb and strafe the beach area until the first wave approached within one hundred yards of the beach, a distance safety factor calculated to protect our own assault waves from friendly fire. Those planes were waiting for you to close the beach within one hundred yards. Your delay in landing on schedule held up the entire Yellow Beach landing eleven minutes, thus allowing the enemy to recover somewhat from effects of our naval bombardment. Evidently Providence saved you from the effects of your own poor judgment."

The bridge was very quiet. Thus endeth the lesson, thought Bud. It could have been much worse. MacDougall pretended to be busy with his binoculars. Gedney looked over the side, frowning at the LST's boat once more. Without turning around, Gedney said, "Get down to your boat now, Foster. It is nearly

79

loaded. When you have delivered the oxygen to Yellow Beach I expect you to board *Belinda* by first available ship's boat."

"Aye, aye, sir." Foster saluted Gedney's back and ran down the ladder. No time for coffee in the wardroom now, but he was determined to get those socks. He rushed down dark passageways to wardroom country, nearly knocking down a Negro mess attendant, then swung open the door to his room.

Kruger was there in salt-stained khakis, strapping on helmet and forty-five. "Hi, Bud." His voice was friendly but casual. Then Bud remembered that Kruger had made a landing too and was probably just as tired as he.

"Just in for chow, Karl?"

"Yep. Got to get back in that boat now. We got a rock pile on Red Beach." Kruger started through the door, then hesitated. "Say, what did the Old Man want—give you a medal?"

The grin returned to Bud's friendly face. "Not exactly, but it was the most attention he's given me since I reported aboard. Up to now I've never rated more than a dozen words out of him at once. . . . 'The bearing is moving to the left, not to the right.' You know the routine—used to scare me."

"What did you get this time?"

"Oh, he made me kind of proud. After all, it isn't every miserable little ensign that gets to hold up an invasion for eleven minutes."

CHAPTER 11

Light of D Day was fading and there was no moon, yet over Butaritari Island bright planets burst into temporary being, hung suspended, then drifted gently downward, carried towards the lagoon by a quiet sea breeze. When the last of their parachute-borne magnesium was consumed, these earthly luminaries —shot from guns—completed brief life cycles and gave way to darkness; yet eerie lights continued, for as each star shell faded, its place was taken by another and yet another.

While battleships, cruisers, transports and destroyers formed up for night retirement and steamed away from island battleground, MacDougall watched intently from the *Belinda's* bridge. Tropic night came quickly; outline of Makin Atoll faded into darkness and distance, yet star shells showed the island's location plainer and further than light of day. The ships zigzagged southward, scheduled to turn at midnight and zigzag back, arriving at dawn off the beaches. Red Beach was cluttered with unloaded boats, waiting while engineers blasted passage for them through the coral. Retirement for the invasion fleet was a prudent tactical move. No more supplies could be landed until the bottleneck at the reef was cleared; warships could not bombard such a small strip of land without endangering Americans. Several Japanese submarines had been detected by destroyer sound gear. Therefore, with the exception of two destroyers remaining in the lagoon, the attack force steamed away overnight, while sputtering star shells hovered over men nervous in sandy foxholes.

O'Bannion lay in his foxhole, next to that of Major Malumphy, on Red Beach. Star shells floating down from sky like ghostly lanterns illuminated silhouettes of tattered palms. Groups of Japanese marines had been by-passed during the advance from Red and Yellow beaches towards the western tank barrier, an enemy-built defensive line. Others of the enemy had infiltrated the lines—having the advantage of knowing the terrain intimately, they wriggled and glided through Butaritari's swampy marshes, moved stealthily from shrub to shrub, from tree to tree, even getting into foxholes occupied by invading Americans. Near Red Beach, some Japanese hid under fallen palm fronds, waiting chances for some last desperate effort. One of them was hidden in an undiscovered machine gun emplacement, watching comings and goings on the beach for hours. At last, hearing movements and hushed voices near at hand, he cut loose with his machine gun. Chattering shots ripped through the shrubbery behind O'Bannion. Malumphy swore under his breath. A sergeant crawled around and flanked the gunner. Well-thrown hand grenades silenced him forever. Now there were voices in the night: fantastic, mocking voices. "Haro, Yank. Haro, haro. . . . Psst! . . . Hey, Sarge! . . . Medics! Send medics; I die, I die!" Voices in English—English with a Harvard accent; English with an unmistakable Kobe hiss; English with *r* substituted for *l*—English of snipers, of desperate and disorganized Japanese.

Obeying strict orders, Americans gave no reply. They lay in foxholes, dry or swampy according to their luck. Some holes were shallow, carelessly dug during comparative safety of evening twilight. Too late now to dig: any sudden movement, sound or cry brought the crack of a Japanese rifle, even of an American rifle. It was a nervous beach; sleepless men longed for dawn, for action, for anything except lying still in a sandy ditch where at any moment they might be shot or have their throats cut.

Mike O'Bannion was a big man. He had prudently dug for himself a big foxhole, and had made sure that every man in his beach party followed his example. O'Bannion and Malumphy had dug a small ditch between their two foxholes so that they could lie facing each other and whisper back and forth. They said little, and most of that concerned the situation and their men. Sherwood had taken all remaining landing craft, most of them still loaded, into the lagoon overnight. Soldiers and sailors assigned to the beach could do little until daylight. Their duty now was to survive the night and rest for the rigors of the second day. After one of the intermittent combinations of cries, movements and rifle shots had subsided, O'Bannion reached across the ditch and poked Malumphy. The major stirred; O'Bannion could see the outline of his helmet, placed like a sheltering roof over his face. Malumphy lifted the helmet enough to turn his face. "What is it, Mike?" he whispered.

O'Bannion felt intense desire to communicate his inner thoughts with someone. "I had the queerest feeling after we landed this morning. I was looking out at the ships, half hidden in smoke. It seemed as if I had been here before."

"You couldn't have been here, that's a cinch."

"That's what I couldn't figure out at the time—of course I've seen plenty of islands with coconut trees on them. . . ."

"Well, where was it, then?"

"It was the first dry run we made from the *Belinda*—back in Hawaii. I got wet working with the boats . . . drying my pants on some driftwood when two staff officers from Pearl came along. I told them what a landing would be like: the ships, the smoke, the men and guns coming ashore. I could see all that—just see it!"

"Was it like this?" Malumphy's voice had a slightly teasing intonation. No foxholes there, he was thinking.

O'Bannion remained quiet for several minutes, then said slowly, "It's so different at night. Those star shells, that greenish devil's candlelight! Doesn't it give a man the creeps?"

Clouds hung over battle smoke as the attack on Butaritari went into its second day. Gunfire, moving slowly northward, sounded more distant to Captain Gedney. At dawn he brought the *Belinda* back to Red Beach. Bathed in bright sunshine, the ship drifted alone in the clearest of blue water. Other transports lay off the lagoon entrance, several miles away, to finish their unloading by way of Yellow Beach inside the lagoon. The *Belinda's* winches were busy again, swinging combat cargo overside into the boats. Landing craft shuttled between ship and beach. Malumphy's engineers blasted a small passage through the reef so that boats could get in to Red Beach one at a time, even at low water. Unloading was not going fast enough to suit Gedney, yet as long as some progress was being made he could maintain reasonable calm. It was these full stoppages at the coral-studded beach that were so maddening.

Conning ship, MacDougall took a quick bearing of Ukian-gong Point, right tangent of visible shore. The *Belinda* was close: thirteen hundred yards by last radar check and drifting fast towards the point. Strong current here, but parallel with shore. No danger of going aground, rather that of drifting away from Red Beach so that landing craft had further to run —and there were Japanese submarines reported off the point this morning. He would have to be careful. Bearings indicated the *Belinda* to be a thousand yards from assigned unloading spot. MacDougall looked over side again: the last of the bull-dozers still hung overside while LCM Number Two maneuvered alongside. He decided to hold on a few minutes longer; if he started up engines and swung the ship back towards assigned position now he would throw off the tank lighter and delay that bulldozer, badly needed ashore.

The signal bridge bell clanged. The first-class quartermaster answered, "Pilothouse, aye," listened to the message, then came out to MacDougall. "It's the flagship, sir. Orders to take station at once."

"Very well. I'll get moving as soon as Moran lands that bull-dozer in the LCM. . . . Jerk up the helmsman and stand by the annunciator. We'll move in a minute."

MacDougall's injured leg ached from the standing required by night-long maneuvers. He looked overside. They would soon have that heavy bulldozer in the tank lighter. Turning inboard again he was confronted with the surly face of Ensign Twitchell, the signal and recognition officer in the ship, his protruding eyes seemed to be constantly searching for a situation of which he could take some advantage. His usual expression to enlisted men was a leer. Even when nearly blank in the presence of his seniors, a trace of sneer remained. Nasty little punk on the make, MacDougall thought now. Wonder what he wants.

"Did you get that signal from the flagship, Lieutenant Mac-Dougall?" asked Twitchell.

"Yes, I did."

"You didn't obey it. I gave you the message four minutes ago."

"Listen, son. You report messages to the bridge. We acknowledge when the message is understood. That's the end of your responsibility and the beginning of ours. Savvy?"

Twitchell flushed. "You didn't obey that order yet," he insisted. "I'm not going to let you or anybody else get me into trouble."

MacDougall pointed into the pilothouse. He shoved his face down toward the signal officer and lowered his hoarse whispering voice until it was nearly inaudible. "There's a man sitting in that chair in the pilothouse, Ensign. Suppose you go tell him your troubles."

The captain! Twitchell had thought him down below. The frustrated ensign shoved his lower jaw out sideways and worked it back and forth, then turned his back on MacDougall and

83

climbed the ladder to the signal bridge. MacDougall looked overside; the tank lighter was gone. He looked at the bearing of the point, then at his watch. "I'll wait for three minutes more, just to show little Nero who's running things here," he muttered to himself. At last he ordered engines ahead and rudder full left. The *Belinda's* stern came round and she gathered headway toward her assigned station.

Gedney came out to the bridge wing and looked at Ukiangong Point. "We've never been so close to it before," he remarked. MacDougall did not reply. Now Gedney turned binoculars upon the flagship *Pennsylvania*, brooding guns temporarily silent, her wide signal yardarm naked of signal bunting. "Two enemy submarines were sighted off the point at dawn this morning," Gedney remarked casually. MacDougall thought, he knows that I knew that. He's going to chew me up and down for delaying compliance with orders from the flagship. With a measure of guilt, MacDougall considered those lurking Japanese submarines; it seemed difficult to picture such menace under this sparkling water, yet of course they might still be there. He had eight surface lookouts constantly alerted for periscopes, but if they did see one it would probably be too late. Then he thought of Twitchell. Well, let the Old Man chew me. It was worth it—the ship's still afloat. Gedney took a sheet of rice paper from his pocket and wiped the lenses of his binoculars carefully. "Many flag officers have a most annoying habit," he said reflectively. "They put some inexperienced junior on the signal bridge and tell him to keep the disposition on station. Such subordinates have neither navigational experience nor judgment as to relative importance of station-keeping according to plan as against this unloading of combat equipment for which reason only we are here." Gedney cleared his throat, looked at the battleship once more before adding, "I presume it was some such junior-grade lieutenant who ordered us to take station. Except for straining safety factors, I would be inclined to remain here a little longer."

MacDougall felt relieved. Gedney must have heard what he said to Twitchell, and this was his way of expressing his approval. He ventured a smile which Gedney returned. "You are a seaman, MacDougall," he said. "I am a seaman." His words seemed to imply, we see eye to eye on this.

Twitchell watched the ship creep up to her assigned position off Red Beach. Landing craft, which had followed the ship like pups running beside a mother dog, were now alongside. Twitchell was angry with MacDougall and looking for a victim among the enlisted men. Perhaps he could put somebody on report, get him some extra duty or loss of liberty. He had been all around his division, but everything was in order. The men were smart enough to see that he meant business this morning. They didn't dare get out of line. There was a little satisfaction in that. Just a little.

Twitchell looked over the side. A big sailor was climbing up number three debarkation net from a VP. It was Boski, one of his signalmen, on temporary duty with the beachmaster. At the thought of O'Bannion, Twitchell's anger flared. That big Irish pig. The way he acted, the signal officer didn't have anything to say at all. Well, some day he'd show him.

A few minutes later Twitchell saw Boski on the deck below. He was with one of the radio men, pulling something out of the radio storage locker. Twitchell called out sharply, "Boski. Come up here."

The big signalman straightened up, wiped sweat from his eyes and nodded. Then he lumbered forward, climbed the ladder to the signal bridge and stood before Twitchell. "Yes, sir," he said. The *sir* was slurred off almost into nothingness.

"What were you doing down there, Boski? Why didn't you report to me when you came aboard?"

"I was getting out a battery for the beach-party transmitter. The one ashore has gone dead."

"That's a job for the radioman. You're supposed to be on shore to take my signals. You had no business to come aboard here. You deserted your post."

Boski looked down at Ensign Twitchell. "Is that all, sir?" He asked the question in the same dull voice.

Twitchell sneered up at the signalman; his lower lip took on a nasty curl. "No, that is not all. Why did you come aboard?"

"Sir, Mr. O'Bannion ordered me to get them batteries. Mr. O'Bannion is a full lieutenant and he is in command of the beach party. I am in the beach party and I do what Mr. O'Bannion tells me to do."

"I'm the signal officer," said Twitchell. "I'm the signal officer." There was defiance in his tone. That was wrong. Why did he have defiance in his tone to an enlisted man? It wasn't going the way it should at all. Boski stood still without further reply, then turned and started down the ladder to the navigation bridge.

"Come back here, Boski," ordered Twitchell in a dull, flat voice. The hulking signalman stopped, turned slowly and retraced his steps. He was nine inches taller than the ensign and some seventy pounds heavier. Yet his weight and power did not seem to menace the officer. It was as though Twitchell were standing alongside a seagoing tug of over a thousand horsepower. "Why did you walk away from me like that? Why did you walk away?" Twitchell's voice rose at the end of the repeated question. He was very unsure of his ground. He wished that Boski were back on the beach—anywhere. But he could not run from this man now, this man who just looked down at him, waiting.

"Why did you walk away?" repeated Twitchell once more. His voice sounded like a damaged record—repeat, repeat—why, why?

Boski seldom spoke; words came hard to him. His mind was deliberate, his speech still slower. It was his body with the big flashing muscles that was fast. He spoke slowly now. "I walked away so I wouldn't hit you, Mr. Twitchell."

A surge of fear swept through Twitchell; then it passed. Boski would not hit him now. The moment for that had come and gone; yet the very thought of it weakened him. The power of this man—the strongest man on the ship—this quiet man who hated him. The others hated him. They all hated him. Most of them he could handle. But he was afraid of this Boski. If he could just get something on him. . . . But Boski had the cunning of a wild animal. He knew what he could do and say in this Navy.

"If I stood there, Mr. Twitchell, when you talked to me like that, I would just flatten you—I couldn't help it. So I walked away."

"But I'm the signal officer. You disregarded me."

Boski took a deep breath, then placed hamlike palms against his flat hips and looked down again at Twitchell. There were little speckles in his otherwise clear brown eyes; they seemed like tiny arrows—like lethal rays of some sort which could pierce Twitchell, transfix him, make him completely helpless. "You never ordered me to stay, Mr. Twitchell. You order me to stay here now and I'll stay here as long as you tell me to stay here." Boski turned around very slowly and walked across the hot steel deck of the signal bridge, his broad back turned to Twitchell. He heard no order to stop, so he continued deliberately down the ladder and out of sight.

CHAPTER 12

Later that same morning Dr. Flynn was in the surgery, checking the condition of his surgical instruments. The place was spotless and quiet—much too quiet. Most of the wounded had been taken to the division flagship. Flynn knew that many of them still waited for attention there while he waited here in his empty surgery, like a barber on a Monday morning. Why didn't they send some of them here? Was the fleet surgeon trying for a record? The only casualties brought to Flynn so far had been sent out directly from Red Beach by Dr. Bell. Vinson, the boat coxswain wounded during the landing, was in the sick bay now, well taken care of. Vinson's little deckhand had been done for. Eight soldiers from Red Beach were resting in clean bunks, wounds dressed, fractures attended to. Then the native from Butaritari—he was the most interesting of all. Surely never before aboard a ship like the *Belinda,* he had seemed composed and unafraid, even when the ether mask had been placed over his face. He would recover—a long pull, but he had both the constitution and the will to survive.

Now the surgery was empty again. Restless after a good night's sleep in his cot on the open boat deck, Flynn picked up an old copy of the *Journal of the American Medical Association,* scanned familiar pages and tossed it back on the cabinet. He knew that this very moment wounded men waited in litters. while he, trained to help them, had nothing to do. I might as well be back in San Diego, delivering babies for dependents, he thought.

The wide surgery door opened on silent hinges. In rushed heat and sound from the nearby engine-room hatch, together with sticky, oozing heat from inner passageways of a ship becalmed in the tropics. Some voice shouted instructions deep in that devil's kettle of an engine room. Shut off something. Even while the ship lay dead in the water, pumps thrust and motors hummed, fires burned and steam pressure was kept up: organs functioning in sleep, Flynn thought. His mind twisted thoughts lightly. They were making fresh water from the sea so they could report to Captain Gedney so many thousand gallons on a slip of paper, then turn off the water so that there was none for washing. Of course the crew would get more prickly heat. Send them to Flynn; he will prescribe for them—nothing else to do.

The door was swinging back and forth with the ship's lazy rolling. Would these corpsmen never learn to hook a door back?

"Dr. Flynn." It was Wilkinson, surgery pharmacist's mate—blond head popping in the door, then withdrawing.

"Yes," Flynn answered cheerfully. Another casualty, perhaps—not that Flynn wanted bodies to operate upon, but if men were wounded, needed attention from trained hands, they might as well bring them to Flynn—anything but more prickly heat, cat fever, inoculations.

"Dr. Flynn!" Wilkinson again—excitement in his voice.

"What is it, Wilkinson?" Flynn was getting impatient—this bobbing in and out . . .

"It's a Jap, Doctor—a wounded Jap prisoner! Alvick's men are picking him out of the boat now."

Work to do—something interesting: a prisoner. How did they capture him? The stories they told about these Japs: fanatics, dangerous to their last breath. Flynn followed Wilkinson. Sunny out on deck—morning air fresh. Blinking at sudden light, Flynn found himself at the edge of a milling crowd of men: workers and watchers in khaki and dungarees. The nucleus of the crowd was at the rail abreast number five hatch. Flynn moved forward into the crowd; men looked up quickly, enough of them recognizing the doctor and making room for him so that he soon stood at the *Belinda's* railing looking down into an LCVP which was alongside. The casualty was in a wire Stokes litter, strapped in so that he could not fall out—strapped in so that he could not escape, Flynn realized. This man was an enemy.

The prisoner's body filled the length of the basketlike stretcher. He was tall for a Japanese, dressed in the faded blue uniform of an Imperial marine—one leg in bloody splints and a large dressing on his head. He seemed groggy; perhaps he had been struck on the head. Flynn hoped that there was no concussion—nasty stuff.

The wounded Japanese muttered something, moved his right arm slowly back and forth. Excited murmur through the crowd like a puff of wind rippling a still pond. There was feeling here at the rail. What was it? Surely not fear. It had the feeling of fear—ridiculous—yet Flynn began to sense it within himself. This was the enemy so long talked of, thought of. Most of these men had never seen a Jap before: back in the States they had them all corralled out in the desert somewhere. This was the enemy feared and hated in an impersonal but in a terrible way. When you came right down to it, here was one of the people who were responsible for this shipload of sweat and bitching—unfamiliar military life and discipline. Anything a fellow didn't like about the Army or the Navy from here to Kansas you could blame on the Japs. Here was one of them, the first one they had seen. Lashed in a stretcher like that, he just moved his arm and it scared them—a tiny little fear—just nothing measurable in the strength of all these American boys standing under the shadow of their own gun barrels, but it was there. Flynn could feel it, share it: would this enemy rise now, suddenly brandishing a banzai sword, and leap out at them with some fanatical cry, to kill and die for his emperor?

Alvick was hoisting the prisoner aboard now, his hatch crew well trained at this maneuver. Together with the corpsmen they would get the Japanese to the surgery. Until then Flynn was free to be a spectator. He looked now at the face of this Japanese: thinner than most, nose long for an Oriental, but nostrils typically flat. The thyroid type—not at all like pictures on the posters at San Francisco, ferocious buck teeth dripping with the blood of a Chinese child. For that matter he didn't look at all like the short, amiable little Japs Flynn had known casually before the war. Something inscrutable about this fellow—something beyond the shock he was suffering. He seemed to be in another world, remote from this ship and watching crowd as if the soul had already departed the body. Flynn shivered, then shook himself from the obscure trend of his thoughts. He looked at the ring of American faces about the stretcher. Curiosity—that was the key note. It was on all the faces: on the ones which showed derision, on the face of the dark-skinned soldier who spat in hate upon the deck. It was written there in all the faces—no sympathy that he could see, hate in a few, satisfaction in many, but curiosity in all. Perhaps this was why not a word was spoken, except only the crisp orders of Alvick to winchmen and line tenders. Now the litter was on deck, crowd opening wide, corpsmen watching the Jap's face at every other step. Into the darkened passageway, stale sticky heat, then the wide surgery door again—opening, held open for the litter, for Flynn, then closing to exclude some of the heat and some of the excited chatter now crackling through the group of men left outside.

Flynn was not alone with the prisoner. Wilkinson and his mates scurried about, getting ready. A big man, dressed in the universal white of a surgery, was scrubbing up at the sink. Flynn's colleague, Dr. Ezra Gates, getting ready.

The only person not in white was the prisoner. His blue uniform was faded and torn, stained from struggle on the island, from sweat and blood. Flynn looked curiously at the man. He seemed to be some sort of officer, probably not very important. The fellow's ribs protruded and he looked undernourished, though of course he might just be that type; some of them never fatten up. Cheek bones showed clearly under tightly drawn skin, which was tanned and parched, yet had a slight blush of color under it. Sparse black whiskers stubbled the small chin. Now the eyes opened, just a crack at first, then as wide as they were accustomed to open in their almond frames. Deep brown eyes looking at him. What was it they showed? . . . Fear? . . . No. Doubtless enough he was scared stiff, but no trace of it showed in those eyes. They were like the expressionless eyes of a treed squirrel looking out from a branch hollow. The wounded prisoner was deep in his shell. It was as if he were looking out at death, had already written himself off. Flynn started. Why, it's me, he thought. He thinks I'm going to kill him. But why should he? I wonder if they showed him some posters of *us* before they sent him out here to Butaritari.

The only place where the wounded prisoner could be safely confined, yet properly cared for, was the ship's insane room, across the passageway from the *Belinda's* medical laboratory. Here, behind a locked and barred door, the Japanese had been placed in a comfortable hospital bed. Larry Jordan, on guard outside this door, was getting nervous. It seemed to him that half the *Belinda's* crew was crowded into this portside alleyway, hoping to get a look at the captured Jap. It was all right for them to look—a couple at a time—but he didn't like them to crowd him so closely. He wasn't used to having a loaded gun in his hands and wanted a little space about him. Larry grounded the carbine on the deck and held the barrel in front of him with both hands. "Take it easy, fellows. No use trying to batter down the door. Dr. Flynn has the key. Why don't you go ask him for it?"

Quieter now, moved forward by ones and twos, curious sailors looked through the glass port. The small room had no other windows. A single electric light in its watertight glass protector shone down from overhead upon the Japanese, who lay on his back in the hospital bed. Enveloped in a heavy plaster cast, his fractured leg was elevated by ribbons of bandage suspended from pipe brackets in the overhead. The prisoner's head was nearly covered with bandages. He faced toward the door with eyes closed. It wasn't much to see.

On his way from the stuffy medical office to the wardroom for lunch, Flynn paused at the surgery door, then stepped inside. Once more the place was quiet and spotless, even the dog-eared back number of the medical journal had been placed neatly on top of the white enameled cabinet, exactly perpendicular. Flynn reached up absentmindedly and thumbed familiar pages—new antiseptic procedures . . . He tossed the pamphlet back on the cabinet, noting with satisfaction that it now rested at an untidy angle upon the gleaming enamel. Then he heard his name called—sharply, urgently: "Dr. Flynn. Dr. Flynn! The keys . . . Come quickly!" Flynn stepped outside the door just in time to collide with a clean-cut young sailor carrying a carbine. "Quick, Doctor. It's the Jap. He's hung himself!"

Flynn reached into his pocket for the key, felt its small hardness between his fingers, then ran forward along the passageway after Jordan. Without waiting to look through the inspection port, Flynn unlocked the insane-room door and flung it open. A strip of bed sheet was tied tightly around the wounded prisoner's neck, its other end secured to a pipe bracket in the overhead, near the one from which they had suspended the leg. The Japanese marine sagged in the bight of a grotesque arc: bed sheet, then dark head, curved trunk, the buttocks at the curve of the arc, then plaster cast—uninjured leg hanging free like the tail on a printed letter *Q*. The

Japanese was choking convulsively, gasping for air. "Here, help me!" cried Flynn. "Lift him here . . . now hold him." Flynn reached a hand to his belt and pulled from its sheath the knife which every man aboard the *Belinda* wore constantly, in case of shipwreck or other emergency. With a single slash he severed the sheet. "Now hold him up here." With a second motion he severed the bandage sling suspending the plaster cast. Now the man was free and they lowered him to the cot. His face was sallow and he gasped for breath in a feeble, ragged manner. He was nearly done for. "Go yell for the corpsman," Flynn said, "then run to the wardroom for Dr. Gates."

Jordan left the small room with a single bound, glad for relief in action from the despair of an accident allowed by his own momentary carelessness. Flynn could hear his shouts, "Hey, corpsmen, Wilkinson, anybody—quick!"

Flynn struggled to turn the Japanese over on his stomach. Artificial respiration—that's what he needed. But the heavy cast made things awkward, and bedsprings gave under thrusting hands. The man seemed to be losing out. Now footsteps. Several corpsmen, then big Ez Gates pushing through. "He hung himself with the bed sheet, Ez. He's near done in—needs oxygen. Let's get him to the surgery."

"Yes," said Gates. "I'll take him." The big doctor gathered the tall Japanese in his arms, plaster cast sticking awkwardly out to his right, and stepped into the passageway, once more crowded full with suddenly arrived spectators.

"Clear the way," cried Flynn.

"Gangway. . . . Clear the way. . . . Stand back, sailors." Other voices took up the cry. Almost mechanical co-operation, now part of daily routine, took over. Men rushing up out of curiosity turned suddenly and shouted to their mates to stand aside. All who could, retreated, while the rest flattened themselves against the passageway bulkheads. Standing thus, their eyes followed Gates as he edged sideways toward the surgery with a quick, crablike shuffle.

Oxygen! Sudden fact slammed home at Flynn: they had no oxygen! All the stuff they had, but not that. "We need oxygen," he said simply.

"I'll get oxygen," said a quiet voice behind him. Flynn turned. It was Lieutenant Ingalls, the engineering officer, standing in the doorway to his stuffy log room across from sick bay.

Flynn began to thank him, but Ingalls was already calling over the heads of the crowd to tall Jerry Rinaldo, the chief shipfitter. "Bring the oxygen tank with a gauge and hose from boat repair, Jerry."

Satisfied, Flynn stepped quickly into the surgery. Gates had the Japanese face down on the warm steel deck and was astride him, pumping the lungs with his hands. No sign of returning consciousness yet.

Rattling and shouts outside the door now opening. Roar of sounds and rush of heat again. A new clatter—wheels of a hand truck on the steel deck: the oxygen tank. Flynn gave quick instructions. An emergency tent was rigged over the prisoner's head and shoulders. Gates turned the man over as oxygen hissed from the rubber hose.

Careful watching, then Flynn said, "Pulse is stronger. I think he's going to make it."

Gates ducked out of the oxygen tent, where he had been making final adjustments and stood up slowly. The breathing was more nearly regular now. Flynn dropped the man's thin wrist and looked up from his strap watch. "Pulse seventy-eight and much stronger." Immediate danger to this life was past. Gates's mind felt free to roam again in the green valley of his thoughts. Saint or rogue, friend or enemy—it made no difference to a doctor. Life was the spark they shielded here from the winds of circumstance. Until the last inevitable moment when it must die out, they cupped their hands about it.

Larry Jordan had been relieved of the guard; in fact twice relieved, for Chief Maxwell had been instructed to double the guard. When the prisoner had recovered sufficiently to be returned to the insane ward, a constant eye was to be kept at the inspection port, so that any further attempt upon his life could be prevented immediately.

Jordan still waited outside the surgery door, his dinner completely forgotten. He knew that word of the attempted suicide had reached the captain. There would be a stink about this and he would be held responsible. He expected to be severely punished for those few minutes in fresh air away from the inspection port. He felt an unhappy chill—Captain's Mast: at the very easiest loss of five liberties. With liberty one day out of four while at Pearl—if the ship ever got back that far—that would mean twenty days confinement while in port. The ship wouldn't stay in nearly that long; it might take him six months or even more to work off loss of five liberties. Six months of never leaving the ship in exchange for three minutes in the fresh air. Well, that was just part of life in the Navy. Hawaii and possible liberties seemed remote; the whole business of punishment was shoved into the back of his mind together with all other unhappiness and frustrations this war had brought him. He waited here to see how the Jap came out—not that he felt any great sympathy for him, nor any particular resentment for the trouble which the attempted suicide had incidentally brought to him. It was something like sitting in the dugout at a ball game, wondering how your side was going to come out in the last half of the ninth. Jordan did not consciously think of the *Belinda's* crew as a team, yet that was really the way he was beginning to feel about it.

While Jordan hesitated outside the surgery door, Flynn went to check on the Japanese prisoner. The Jap seemed conscious, but his eyes remained closed. Perhaps he had sunk into an exhausted sleep: sedatives taking hold. Flynn wondered what his thoughts would be when he awoke. Would there be resentment now that death, like freedom, had been snatched from him?

The Jap's eyes were opening: first those thin slits, then, with cautious acceptance of time and place, dark eyes looked at him without a flicker. Fear, hate, reassurance, gratitude—Flynn saw none of these things in the eyes of this enemy whose rejected life had been returned to him. If Flynn saw any emotion at all, it was the complete alertness of the squirrel cornered in his hole.

In the stagnant tropics odds are all against any air movement penetrating inside a drifting ship, yet the whim of a fitful breeze had made the inside of the *Belinda's* pilothouse a pleasant place. Unrefreshed, nevertheless, Quigley shifted his weight uncomfortably from one well-polished shoe to the other; he was toasting on the Old Man's grill and he didn't like it. Gedney glanced briefly at the executive officer, for whom he had sent, took a quick, appraising look at the position of his ship relative to other ships of the task force and to nearby Butaritari, then leaned back in his high seat and closed his eyes. Finger tips pressed together in contemplation, he relaxed momentarily into his innermost thoughts. Quigley stood straight on the balls of both feet and coughed delicately. Gedney remained completely indifferent. I might as well be up in the mountains of Tibet, Quigley thought. His geography was hazy, but that was the most remote place he could bring to mind and he was beginning to think that Gedney would have made an excellent lama.

At last the captain sat up, glanced quickly at the horizon, then brought his eyes to bear exactly upon those of his second in command. "Quigley," he said, "have you ever considered the purpose of your being here in the *Belinda?*" Blue eyes were boring into Quigley now. Hunting for a suitable reply, Quigley thought how different this was from sociable conversations in some officers' club, where he could spread it on a little thick to fellow officers casually met and seldom seen again. This was sharply different; he stood before Gedney as if naked. Through his mind flashed a series of his insignificant contributions to this ship. He knew that he was not a working officer, and that

Gedney was well aware of that fact. Yet there were modesty and personal honesty underlying Quigley's love of rank and show. He hoped that he did contribute something to dignity and discipline on this ship, if not to the know-how and the sweat. These he could hardly mention here. He knew that Gedney meant something else—something which he would pronounce when he got around to it—which would surely have a refined but unpleasant connotation for him.

A twinkle appeared suddenly in Gedney's eyes; he was ready now with his boiling oil. "You know, Quigley, there has to be a goat for everything. I am the over-all goat for things which go wrong in the *Belinda,* but you are my executive officer, the specific goat for things which go wrong within the working administration of the ship." Gedney suddenly pointed to shore. "A battle is going on there against our enemy, the Japanese. In battle we bring everything possible to bear against the enemy: careful planning and rehearsal, ships, men, arms, materiel and military intelligence. All these things are important. Failure of any one brings added weight to the others, possibly failure to the entire effort, at the very least, increased casualties and delay in completing the action. Delay here at Makin may bring increased casualties from the enemy entrenched ashore out there under those coconut trees, from Japanese planes or submarines. Delay here will also hold back release of the combat team now being held in floating reserve, which is badly needed at Tarawa. We are nailed down this morning at Tarawa, less than an hour's flight from here. Our losses there are heavy and mounting."

Quigley shivered. He felt the breeze now, cool against his shirt. Could he be perspiring? No shower—water hours. Gedney was putting a weight on him, a big, remote weight. His connection with it was as yet uncertain, but he knew that Gedney would clarify that. The commanding officer is not to be interrupted. Given time, Gedney never failed to make his point.

Gedney stirred in his chair—some distracting activity in the pilothouse—his Chinese steward with coffee. Gedney wanted the coffee, but he did not wish to lose the organization of his thoughts, or to break the spell he had thrown like a net about his executive officer. He waved the coffee aside and continued: "In this action we have captured one prisoner. He is obviously an officer and undoubtedly knows much of Japanese strength and defenses here. Such a prisoner is worth more than gold to us now. By the international agreement of the Geneva Convention, and by unwritten laws of humanity, we are required to attend to his wounds and if at all possible to preserve his life. Beyond all this we must save his life, for by doing so we may save many lives of our own men."

Quigley began to shift from one foot to the other and then back again. Pressure was becoming specific; Gedney's finger was pointing. Quigley wished that he could say something, anything, to break this up, but he knew that it would be worse than useless to open his mouth now. He stood quietly, contracting the muscles of his buttocks, feeling the strain, wishing that he were down in the wardroom away from these blue eyes and the inevitable pronouncement of his guilt.

"The only prisoner captured was entrusted to the *Belinda*," said Gedney. "Here he was allowed to hang himself." Tempo sharpening, Gedney's voice went on: "The Japanese give no instructions to their people in case of surrender, in fact they have no word for surrender in their language. Therefore, two things are likely to happen: the prisoner may attempt to take his own life, or he may talk very freely. In the Japanese military organization it is impossible to instruct men not to talk in case of surrender, the possibility of which they refuse to admit. They are victims of their own psychology. Therefore, if we capture a Japanese we must do two things: preserve his life and persuade him to talk."

Jim Randall, who had the deck, stuck his head in the pilothouse door. "Amtrack coming alongside, Capt'n—some Army officer and a Japanese-American noncom. Might be an interpreter, sir."

"Thank you, Randall," said Gedney, and turned again to Quigley. "Because an adequate and properly instructed guard was not set by the executive officer of this ship, the prisoner is in no condition to talk, even were he inclined to do so." Gedney grasped the armrests of his seat and prepared to swing down to the pilothouse deck. Pausing, he transfixed Quigley with all the power of his rank and personality. "Quigley," he said, "don't you dare to bring the seaman who had the guard duty up to me at mast. You are the one who should be punished." Gedney sprang lightly to the deck, absorbed the shock of the fall with a slight give of his knees and then trotted quickly out to the bridge wing to watch the amtrack's arrival. Ignoring obvious snickering from delighted seamen on watch about the pilothouse, Quigley shrugged his shoulders, took a deep breath and headed down toward the wardroom. Well, that's over, he thought.

On his way below, Quigley paused on the boat deck just below the bridge wing where Gedney stood and looked at the scene below. The amtrack muddled alongside and *Belinda* sailors tossed down bow and stern fasts. A soldier on the amtrack floundered about, trying to secure the clumsy craft. There was an eye spliced in the end of each line. Grasping one, he looked about for some cleat or projection to slip it over, but found none. At last he spotted a pad eye near the craft's blunt nose. He managed to pass the line through the pad eye, attempted a hitch, fumbled it and gave up. The amtrack was swept away by the current and, after delays, managed a return approach. By this time the soldier had spotted a paintbrush lying on deck near the cockpit, dropped there by some careless seaman on the LST which brought the amtrack from Hawaii. A paintbrush landing on Yellow Beach with the first wave—there it was! The soldier grabbed it, took up the bow fast and pulled it through the pad eye again. Using the paintbrush handle for a toggle, he secured the amtrack to the *Belinda*.

In spite of his vague knowledge of seamanship, Quigley knew that this maneuver of berthing an amtrack had not come up to Navy standards of smartness. How pleasant now to wait, knowing that Gedney would soon let fly the darts of his wit upon somebody else.

Gedney was merely amused. "Look, Quigley," he called down pleasantly. "The Fuller Brush man has arrived at Makin Atoll." Then he turned to greet the intelligence officer who had come out from shore to interrogate the wounded prisoner.

CHAPTER 13

About midnight of the fourth night off Makin a loud underwater explosion shook the *Belinda*. Submarine contact. They would get emergency turns from the flagship. MacDougall swung around to call Gedney, and found the captain already beside him. How that man could move! "Submarines," said Gedney. "I've been expecting them before this.· . . . Call battle stations."

TBS orders now: crisp, yet without a trace of excitement. Emergency turn to the left. All ships turned at once, cutting off at an angle from the danger without changing column axis. Two destroyers fell back from the fanlike screen ahead and steamed in figure-eight patterns at high speed, dropping one depth charge after another. Each explosion struck the *Belinda's* hull like a giant hammer. Battle-alarm honker called an insistent order to man guns; boatswain's mate's shrill pipe was followed by, "All ha-a-ands, man your battle stations!" Ship alive with helmet clatter, quick tramp of feet on steel ladders and decks, ready-box covers slammed open, guns loaded quickly in the dark.

Another emergency turn to the left—task force now steaming at right angles to its original course—ships ahead and astern of the *Belinda* now on either hand. Then back right once more: quick, unpredictable changes both left and right to throw off torpedo aim. Exploding depth charges sounded far astern now. "They've got him in a deep dive now," said Gedney. "No danger from that one for a while. There must be others about, however. Alert lookouts again, MacDougall."

"Aye aye, sir. . . . Talker. Order to all surface lookouts . . ."

At last all ships returned to fleet course, heading for Makin once more. Gedney waited half an hour more, then secured from general quarters. Even then he left half the crew at the guns while the other half stood watches or rested. "A gunner in his bunk is absolutely useless in emergency," he said to Quigley.

"That's right, sir," answered Quigley, sleepy enough to agree with anything.

By four in the morning the *Belinda* had settled into an uneasy routine. Gedney was back in his chair. While a sliver of moon rose in the east, the disposition zigzagged nervously. Jim Randall had taken over the deck from MacDougall, who sat on the camp cot and looked toward Makin, located on the horizon by three pale star shells. Radar had reported another disposition. Randall came over to the cot to discuss it with Mac-Dougall. "Must be the carrier group, Dave."

"I suppose so. . . . Couldn't be anything else. Those emergency turns . . . We ran off to port. Perhaps they ran over this way from another contact. That would bring the two groups of ships closer together than planned."

"Well, there they are; we'll soon be within a mile of them. I hate to call the Old Man. He hasn't had much sleep these last four days."

"Why don't you wait? The admiral will shove us over if we get too close." MacDougall had seen carriers underway a hundred times before, yet his curiosity was again aroused. He wondered how they looked now against black of night; planes on deck ready to warm up and take off to relieve the combat air patrol now aloft. It was about time for the carriers to swing back into the wind. He felt the urge to get up and hunt for them with his binoculars, but aching body and fatigue pulled him down. Still he sat on the edge of the cot; it seemed too much effort to lie down. He gazed vaguely into blackness of sea and horizon, broken occasionally by another star shell over Butari-tari. Then he saw a quick little flash, a lightning thing, come and gone. He wondered what it was, then heard an explosion, softened somewhat by distance, yet having a different quality of sound from underwater depth charges. There was something odd about it—something ominous. "Jim," he called. "Jim, I saw—I think—"

A soul-searing flash of sudden flame shot high into the sky. Death! . . . There had to be death in such flame! Then, as MacDougall watched in awed fascination, sound of a tremendous explosion reached him across water. This was no sharp crack of gunfire; it was a deep, upthrusting *whoom*. There was power in it—power to toss a ship as an angry bull could toss a man.

"They've got to one of the carriers!" shouted Randall. "That's her gas tanks going up!"

Gedney appeared, called crew to battle stations once more. Helmets clattered, TBS shouted sharp orders for emergency turns, calls for help, instructions to destroyers, to battleships, to transports. Pattern of rigging, ships and flames changed as the *Belinda* wheeled to each new order for emergency turns. Explosions came fast now. Submarine contacts were reported all about—destroyers running like mad dogs on the loose, tracking them down, dropping depth charges, eight to a pattern. Randall laughed a nervous laugh stripped of any happiness. "Every whale within fifty miles will be getting it now," he said.

Excitement plain in voices from the flagship stabbing from TBS speaker to anxious listeners on the *Belinda's* bridge. Excitement in Gedney's voice as he conned ship and saw to detailed manning of guns and damage control stations. Ships of the fleet maintained order and discipline; each group kept careful station, turning together precisely on order. Large ships —carriers, battleships, cruisers, and transports—wheeled in response to orders for mutual self-preservation. Destroyers divided among themselves without a moment's hesitation three tasks necessary to protect the fleet and to rescue the shipwrecked. Some maintained a tight and orderly screen about the larger ships; some ran depth-charge patterns over submarine contacts; others ran close aboard the doomed carrier, searching flaming waters for survivors.

"There is no chance in the world to save that ship," said Gedney. A second terrific explosion rose half a mile skyward: flames bright orange, with flecks and streaks as if ammunition were hurled up to explode while sailing upward in this geyser of fire. Secondary explosions were coming faster now; there were so many things to explode: planes on the flight deck with full gas tanks and loaded bomb racks, ammunition and bombs in the hanger deck, great storage tanks filled with high-test aviation gasoline, highpressure steam boilers run out of water, ready boxes filled with high-explosive shells placed at guns all about the ship, powder magazines deep under the waterline filled with tons of explosives—when those went up it would soon be over.

Explosions were getting heavier, more fiercely staccato. New bursts of flame shot higher and still higher. Debris showered from the sky, landing on the decks of the battleship *New Mexico* nearby. MacDougall strained his eyes against the lenses of his binoculars. He knew that nearly a thousand men were aboard the *Liscome Bay*. Many faced the choice of burning or drowning; others would meet one fate or both without choice. Nothing but flames! Could it be possible that men still struggled to put out fire like that—fog nozzles spraying red-hot bulkheads, foam pumping to smother burning oil? Surely not. Pumps and firemains would be gone by now. The captain must have given word to abandon ship. What man, pursued by such flames, could humanly wait for an order? They must be jumping into the sea—God help them then! Flames leaped up from the water where oil floated. The fear of sharks with which the *Belinda's* crew were so preoccupied in idle moments—where was fear of sharks in the face of fire like this! Straining through his glasses, MacDougall saw only flames and low black silhouettes of rescuing destroyers hunting for survivors in the flaming sea.

Then fore and aft on the dying *Liscome Bay* flames shot higher than any others, higher it seemed than flame could possibly reach. Across water came reverberating thunder. No mistaking that sound; it was the death agony of a ship. "The magazines," Gedney said quietly. "She can't last much longer now." As he spoke there was a lessening in the height of flames. Then the burning hulk rolled over and the flames were quenched forever in the sea.

How chilly it was, MacDougall thought. How dark the night! Not far away hundreds of men struggled for their lives in oily water, drowning, choking on fuel oil which doomed a man once it got into his lungs—exhausted sailors letting go some bit of wreckage, slipping down. Here was the *Belinda,* floating high with her life rafts and landing craft, yet he could not pull an oar or throw a line to help them. That was up to assigned destroyers; *Belinda's* duty to keep formation. MacDougall looked to the east for signs of coming sunrise, but all he saw were the disconsolate looking sliver of moon and a group of three pale star shells hovering over Butaritari Island.

At daybreak the *Belinda* drifted slowly in to Red Beach, hoisting out boats which had been repaired under tarps during the night. Gedney's voice carried over the PA: "This is our last day here. We must finish unloading with all possible speed, then be prepared to reembark troops." From his bridge, Gedney scanned the horizon for sight of the troop convoy due to arrive: garrison forces to relieve combat teams. There was a single plume of smoke out on the horizon: some ship steaming independently. It was unusual for a ship to steam alone in these contested waters, still more remarkable that she should allow her boilers to send up a smoke signal visible to every enemy periscope within thirty miles. Gedney shook his head, muttering, "Such negligence!" Then he sighted two destroyers coming in from seaward: undoubtedly the two which had remained behind to pick up survivors from the *Liscome Bay*. "Biggs," he called. "Ask Dr. Flynn to step to the bridge."

Standing beside Randall on the bridge, Flynn waited impatiently for the destroyers. He had been up since five o'clock, getting his surgery and sick bay ready for a flood of casualties. He had abundant stocks of plasma and surgical dressings, and two excellent surgeons to assist him, for Dr. Bell had just returned from the beach. Flynn accepted a pair of binoculars from Randall and, after a little fumbling, got them focused on the nearest destroyer. It moved slowly, low in the water, weighted down with its burden of wounded sailors. The rescued were crowded in every feasible space: gun tubs, turret tops, scuttles and depth-charge racks. Standing with bandaged heads and arms, sitting, lying in litters—bandages, bandages, fuel oil-streaked bodies.

"Look at them, Jim," said Flynn. "Burns, lots of burns. Shock, too. Look at those fellows wrapped in blankets, jackets, anything. This climate: sun shining warm again. Bad sign to a doctor."

"They're sure messed up with fuel oil."

"Yes, fuel oil kills more than drowning, once they hit the water. If it isn't burning they inhale it while they struggle in the water, or at least swallow a lot. Effects last for months— sometimes slow death. I was reading just yesterday in the medical journal—battle experience at . . . Well, never mind now, Jim. I've got to go down and get all set for these fellows."

After the destroyers entered the lagoon, Gedney raised his binoculars again to take a long look at the single approaching vessel which had been smoking so heavily. Masts and funnel showed well above the horizon now. The angle of her approach as she also headed for the lagoon disclosed large red crosses painted on snow-white sides. "A hospital ship," he said. "Of course. . . . What other type would blow tubes in broad daylight out here in the forward area?" Robinson, the communications officer, ran out of the coding room with a message, which Gedney read, initialed hurriedly and said, "Route this to the medical officer at once."

Flynn signed the message board, took his copy and closed the surgery door. Leaning against the sterilizer, he read the pink action slip, then without comment passed it to Bell, who was checking surgical instruments. Big Ezra Gates turned from the porthole, where he had been watching destroyer masts moving on the opposite side of a thin coconut grove. "What is it?" he asked.

"We've been robbed," said Flynn. "A hospital ship is coming to take all the casualties."

"All of them?—I mean, at once? Just think of it!" Gates exploded. "All those men: wounded, burned, gasping for breath, suffering from shock—lying on litters for hours, waiting turns. . . . Here we are with nothing to do!"

Bell spoke now, softly, although his surgeon's hands had unthinkingly folded the message into a hundred careful, tiny squares: "Take it easy, Ez. You never can tell. Perhaps they'll send us another prisoner to work on."

Ensign Karl Kruger looked over his shoulder at the six VPs bobbing in the wake of his lead boat, as he came alongside the nearest destroyer.

An officer in oil-stained khakis, wearing web belt and forty-five, hailed him in a tired and casual voice.

"You for the casualties?"

"Yes, sir. Want me to bring my boats alongside now?"

"Not yet. I'll hail you. Paper work for the transfer isn't ready yet."

Kruger raised his hand but made no other reply. "Ease over with the other boats, Tommy."

Jones gunned his motor briefly and surged close to the other six boats. "What's the papers for, Mr. Kruger?"

"They have to keep track of everybody. Every ship in the Navy logs you over the side, coming and going—you know that."

"But these guys are wounded."

"That's right, Tommy. They got to find out who the survivors are. That hospital ship isn't anchored yet. We'll get 'em over there." Kruger looked at the hospital ship's gleaming sides, then back to the dark gray destroyer, waterline stained with fuel oil from the lost carrier, decks crowded with men in oil-soaked dungarees, many bandaged extensively with white surgical dressings which contrasted strangely with their filthy bodies and clothing. "I'll bet that DD's doctor is busy," he said at last. "One doctor and about three corpsmen to handle all those casualties."

"Yes, but you'd think they'd give them a little water to clean up with."

"Where are you going to get the water on a little old can? They haven't got it, Tommy." Rattle of chain sounded across the lagoon: hospital ship anchoring. Kruger looked impatiently at the destroyer—they should have those orders now. Surely nothing fancy was needed for this. Paper work, paper work— "I wonder how many filing cabinets went down with that carrier," he mused aloud.

"What's that, sir?"

"Oh, nothing. I was just thinking about the forests."

"Sir?"

Kruger grinned. "They say those guys in the north woods are cutting down the forests to make paper so we can fight a war. When all the trees are gone we'll run out of paper, and then the war'll be over. Can't fight a modern war without carbon copies of everything."

"Oh," said Jones, uninterested now. Mention of paper had taken his mind to San Diego and his wife. "I'd sure like to get a letter from Lorraine."

"Ahoy, *Belinda* Seventeen," hailed the destroyer's O.O.D. "Bring your boats alongside now."

Kruger took his boat in first. Sailors at the destroyer's rail tossed lines. Quickly, gently, the wounded were lowered into the boat, one at a time. "Steady the boat, fellows," Kruger cried urgently. "Don't let her bump the side now." Many hands were thrust out from the low-lying destroyer and from the boat—more hands than were really needed. Sympathy and curiosity showed in young faces—voices of advice and encouragement.

"Watch out, you donkey. You'll knock his brains out against the side."

"Gimme that steadying line, Mac. Give it here."

"Easy up there, take it easy."

Kruger looked at the first casualty. Swathed in white bandages, he looked more like mummy than living man: head wrapped round and round with gauze, eyes and cheeks covered, only broad, short nose and swollen, cracked lips exposed and shining in the sun under a thick coat of petrolatum. Jones had forgotten about San Diego and mail. Staring in horrified fascination, he thought: he looks like a boiled lobster—what you can see of him. Then Jones trembled: from now on he would never sleep so easy in his third-tier bunk in compartment three-ten. Those dirty Japs! This could happen to the *Belinda*—to him personally. He might never get back to Lorraine again—might be drowned under a huge puddle of oil, going down to the sharks.

"Come on there, Tommy! Watch your boat!" Jones nodded to Kruger and jumped to his controls, spun his rudder over and kicked ahead to ward off the thrust of a passing LST's bow wave. Seven other litters were quickly lowered into his boat—arms and legs strapped in gauze-covered splints, but fuel oil still staining injured limbs. They hadn't had much time. One young kid, who also had heavy dressings around his belly and groin, groaned continuously, screaming in pain when his litter was jerked or bumped. Tommy yearned either to be able to help him in his agony or to slap him quiet like the others. Most of them just lay in the litters, staring at blue sky, tanned faces drained of color except for smudges of oil, washed-out looking under their dirt. Something strange and distant about these

102

wounded fellows, Tommy thought. They seemed so far away from everything, but when they yelled in pain it made you want to just kill somebody—Japs or somebody. Somebody started all this—he never could figure just how, but they couldn't tell him this was right.

When the boat was loaded, Kruger nodded to Jones and they shoved off for the hospital ship, giving place to another VP at the destroyer's side. The DD's officer-of-the-deck had not given the customary naval order—perhaps it seemed superfluous to him. They just shoved off with their wounded. White sides of the hospital ship soon blanked out lagoon and other ships. Jones brought the boat alongside a wide ramp, lowered exactly to water's edge. Navy corpsmen in spotless white ran down the ramp, grasped handles of the first litter and, moving in perfect unison, swung it out of sight into the hospital ship's spotless interior. Contrasted with the babel of conflicting instructions from survivors and friends on the destroyer, wounded were received here in silence, so that they seemed to lose any trace of remaining personality. "These pharmacist's mates must have had plenty of practice," Kruger said to Jones as the last litter was swept up the ramp with a muscular co-ordination which seemed nearly mechanical in its perfection. Faces of the hospital ship's crew were expressionless, as if they were taking aboard so many bundles of ship's laundry. "Shove off, Tommy," said Kruger.

Now a chief pharmacist's mate hurried down the ramp. "Where are the orders to cover these men?" he asked.

"I just brought them over from that can," Kruger said.

"But we must have orders."

"That can didn't wait for orders when she picked them out of the water. . . . They mentioned paper work over there. I guess you'll get your orders all right."

The chief regarded Kruger with a pained expression, as if he had failed in a most important matter, but withheld further comment. Kruger looked across the water: widely spaced landing craft coming from each anchored destroyer towards the wide ramp and efficient litter bearers. This chief—probably from some big base hospital—he'd learn. "All right, Tommy," Kruger said, "let's go back for another load."

CHAPTER 14

Five days after the first landing, soldiers from the battle line returned suddenly to the *Belinda*. In a matter of minutes boats loaded with them swarmed about the lowered nets. They climbed aboard slowly, like men who were very tired, who no longer felt a life and death necessity for sudden action. One

103

young private paused at the top of the debarkation net, hands resting on the *Belinda's* rail. He was not wounded, but seemed near the point of exhaustion, feeling that the last steps over the railing were too much, that he would lose his grasp and fall back into the boat below. Men in dungarees reached out and helped him. "That rifle and pack getting heavy, soldier?" one of them asked. If the young soldier heard, no reaction showed in his mud and sweat-stained, unshaven face, in glazed, staring eyes focused far beyond the *Belinda's* beam as if still searching for another hidden foxhole. Once over the rail, he paused with feet planted wide while other soldiers in helmets and stained fatigues worked around him in the patient, yet insistent manner of closely packed troops. The private waited for nearly a minute, shoulders hunched, weighted by some unseen burden much heavier than pack, rifle or the helmet which seemed to thrust his neck down between his shoulder blades. At last he shuffled aimlessly onward, moving which-ever way he was pushed until lost in the crowd's anonymity.

A squat LCT chugged alongside number three hatch, bring-ing several hundred troops from inside the lagoon, together with an enormous pile of khaki duffel bags. Pappy Moran jumped up from the hatch and called to his men. "Stand by your winches, Prosser. Slack away on that midships guy, Red. Stand clear, soldiers; give us room to work. . . . Get hot, sailors. Drag that cargo net aft. . . . No, not there. Get it under the hook. Let's get loaded and out of here!"

Roy Alvick, leading petty officer in the second division, wiped perspiration from his face with a soggy handkerchief. It was uncomfortably hot in compartment 212, where humid air now carried the earthy smell of island soil and vegetation, mixed with strong odors of stale sweat. Alvick was anxious to get bunk stanchions set up over the covered square of number five hatch, so that he could send his tired men to chow. A large pile of duffel bays lay in the hatchway where bunks must go. The tall boatswain's mate looked about the compartment until he spotted a gray-haired man wearing the chevrons of a first sergeant informally painted in black on the sleeves of his fa-tigues. Alvick walked over to the top sergeant.

"Know who this gear belongs to, Sarge?"

"Yes." The sergeant's voice sounded flat, disinterested.

"Will you get 'em to move their gear out of here? We've got to get these bunks set up."

The sergeant spoke with an air of finality. "No, I can't do that."

"Listen, Sarge . . ." rising irritation in Alvick's voice. "My men are late for chow already—we've got to get these bunks set up. Where are the men these bags belong to? What are they doing?"

"They're dead."

"Oh. . . . I'm sorry." Alvick crossed the hatch to a group of his men. "Come on, sailors. We've got to move these bags."

The ship's galley was uncomfortably hot, but steam-laden air was fragrant with cooking juices: chicken and the last fresh vegetables, so-called, which Shadow Rockwell, ship's commissary officer, had saved especially for this occasion. Passing through the galley, the rotund Rockwell paused to inspect roast fowl coming from great ovens, looked at rich soup and at somewhat shriveled but carefully cooked vegetables being ladled from a long row of shiny steam kettles. "Them soldiers had better like this," he said to Rostelli, the watch supervisor. "We're really putting on a feed. I know they ain't had anything like this to eat up in the line."

Rockwell continued forward into the crew's mess hall. Tired soldiers in filthy jungle-green jumpers and trousers, stubbled with four days' beard, hands and faces still dirt and sweat smeared, moved slowly along in a twisting serpentine, down ladder from the weather deck and around dish-washing machinery to the line of steam tables. Here Navy mess cooks, dressed in clean white undershirts above working dungarees, served dinner cafeteria style, each soldier moving along with his Monel-metal mess tray while suitable indentations were filled with large portions of Rockwell's offering, topped off with homemade ice cream and a steaming mug of coffee.

Hundreds of battle-worn soldiers ate at mess tables reaching athwartships to ship's sides from a broad central passageway amidships. Rockwell walked between tables, one after the other, making certain that there was plenty of food, and noting how it was being received. Quite at home with fellow officers in the *Belinda's* wardroom, Rockwell nevertheless spent very little time there. He ate a tremendous amount of food in the course of a day, accumulation of numberless samples of nearly everything prepared by his cooks. Sometimes he sat down to eat, but this was usually to rest his feet, the food he took on such occasions was merely a snack to top off prodigious amounts consumed while on his rounds.

Rockwell stopped at one of the mess tables. A dark-complexioned soldier sat at the end. He might have been thirty or forty—nothing whatever of youth in his face. He gulped down chicken and potatoes with cream gravy in large mouthfuls, yet not paying the slightest attention to what he was eating; his dark eyes were focused upon the mess table about a foot beyond the edge of his plate. A much younger soldier sat at

105

his right: boyish snub nose and large ears, little tufts of brown fuzz stubbling a dirt-smudged face. His fatigue jacket, like his hands and fingernails, was black with ashes from crawling in some burned ruin ashore. Cupped between filthy hands he held a thick porcelain soup bowl a few inches from pursed lips in a sort of frozen motion, while blue eyes stared fixedly at the broth. A third soldier sat opposite the boy. Naked to the waist after an unsuccessful attempt at washing, he had long, flat muscles—a St. Christopher seal hung, together with dog tags, about his neck. He was tough, aggressive looking—reckless face, large, straight nose and lips which looked as if they could be cruel. No passion showed in his face now—no humor, no interest in the busy mess hall, no interest in food. He was looking very intently across the table at the young soldier's face, remembering the battle—that time the kid covered him when he stuck his neck out at the wrong time. He wouldn't be here if it wasn't for the instant way the kid threw that grenade —blasted that Jap sniper out of his concrete cistern. Relive the hour, the minute. Breathe slow, glad to live.

Preoccupied with food, Rockwell nevertheless detected communion and comradeship between these three. Wishing only to be friendly, he raised his voice above the clatter of mess gear, shouts of mess cooks—just enough to be heard. "How's the chow, fellows?" No reply; the three soldiers did not seem aware of his presence. Rockwell was a warmhearted man, usually patient. He repeated his question in a somewhat louder voice without losing a trace of good nature. "How's the chow, fellows? . . . Chicken all right?" Still no answer; none of the three moved his gaze so much as one inch. Rockwell began to feel ignored; with anger in his voice he fairly shouted at them, "What's the matter with the chow?"

The tough-looking soldier turned his face very slowly and looked Rockwell directly in the eyes. "The chow?" he asked. "Oh, the chow's all right. . . . I guess." Then he turned slowly back and resumed staring at the kid across the mess table.

Combat troops nearly all aboard—it would soon be time to go. The attack force would leave four graveyards behind, three of them named by men who had fought for possession of Butaritari, then helped bury the dead. Massed artillery had been dragged from Ukiangong Point. The cannon were now replaced with neat rows of graves. One of the burying detail had named it Gates of Heaven Cemetery. Just under the trees behind Yellow Beach, twenty-one soldiers were buried in Sleepy Lagoon Cemetery, this name also suggested by one of the men who had stacked rifles and taken up shovels.

The boatswain of the *Alcyon* and one of his sailors had died of wounds after making a run in a tank lighter on the hulks within the lagoon, answering Japanese sniper fire with two machine guns mounted on their craft. They now lay in shallow graves on little Kotabu Island, at the opposite side of the lagoon entrance from Flink Point. There are no valleys on Makin and no point of Kotabu rises higher above the sea than the shoulders of a tall man, yet a beach-party sailor from Ohio straightened up from smoothing a mound over the boatswain and said, "Let's call this place, Happy Valley."

The fourth burying place received no name other than the one which marked it on battle maps, and no shovels were used for the interment. Fifty natives labored willingly under an Army major and a Marine captain, succeeding after two days' work in burying less than one third of hundreds of Japanese dead. Unattended bodies decomposed rapidly in warm, moist air, endangering lives of natives and of garrison forces who would remain on the island. It was therefore decided to collect these bodies and to bury them in a common grave. The West Tank Barrier, a major link in defensive intrenchments dug by Japanese months earlier, was considered best suited to this purpose, and bulldozers were used to cover the grave. Garrison forces carried out the post-combat treatment plan, which entailed disposing of fecal matter and collapsing and sealing with bulldozers all enemy shelters, which might contain undiscovered dead and cause an epidemic. Thus, many Japanese were buried without been seen or counted.

"Look at 'em. . . . Look at 'em. . . . Japs!" Word passed from mouth to mouth along the *Belinda's* afterdeck. In less than a minute the rail at number five hatch was crowded with sailors and re-embarked troops, each man shoving and worming his way outboard to get a better view of the tank lighter tossing in choppy water alongside. "Stand clear, men. . . . Gangway. . . . Give us room to work. . . ." Great hook lowered overside . . . thirty-six ton craft plus load hoisted to the rail.

Suddenly watchers aboard the *Belinda* were confronted with fifty-one stocky little men, dressed in new dungarees and blue chambray shirts. Few watching Americans realized that these were not Japanese combat troops or Imperial marines, most of whom were now dead—the last in a Banzai charge on what was ever after called Saki Night—but Korean laborers, brought here to help build fortifications. With excited comments, watchers on board tried to reconcile these docile, moonlike faces with their previous conceptions of a leering, buck-toothed enemy.

"Kin them critters fight?" one soldier exclaimed in amazement.

"Well, you been ducking bullets, ain't you?"

"Yes, but—well, just look at 'em!"

The prisoners were guarded by a single squad of infantrymen who watched their charges carefully while at the same time feigning casual indifference for the benefit of spectators. Guards nodded to the prisoners, indicating the rail. The Koreans clambered meekly over and were herded through the curious crowd on the *Belinda's* afterdeck. A lanky corporal poked at one of them experimentally. "Show me your buck teeth, Joe," he said. It is unlikely that the prisoner understood English words; perhaps with a feeling of relief at unexpected lack of hostility he complied with a silly, vacuous grin.

Still grinning, the prisoner started forward after his fellows, passing an American with a hard, unsmiling face. "Smile, you yellow belly," said this soldier, spitting out the words bitterly. "You're lucky you aren't stinking like the rest."

All Japanese remaining on Makin were not dead. Small unorganized groups still survived—some hiding in undiscovered holes, others having fled by night to smaller, uninhabited islands of the atoll. Garrison forces would be occupied for weeks in discovering and subduing them. Due to communication difficulties and to Japanese combat psychology, it was almost impossible to persuade them to surrender. On the day before his death, the executive officer of Japanese forces wrote in his diary, "Today looks like another clear day. I feel like singing a song. There is a breeze coming from the northwest. I hope the tanks won't come today so that I can rest my bones in peace."

Bright-colored bunting snapped up and down from signal yardarms as transports formed up for final departure. Most of the support group of carriers, battleships, cruisers and destroyers remained behind to protect the new American garrison from counterattack, or to strengthen the difficult offensive at Tarawa. Only one battleship accompanied the transports now. The *Mississippi,* damaged by a turret explosion during the bombardment which killed forty sailors, steamed quietly abeam of the *Belinda,* all her fourteen-inch guns leveled at the horizon save the crippled one, which pointed up at lowering clouds like a sore finger.

Captain Gedney sat in his high seat watching the station keeping of Mike O'Bannion, who now had the deck. Gedney began to feel drowsy. The watch had been set and the ship was settling down again into the pleasant monotony of sea routine. There was finality in the steady pulsing of her engines, as if they knew that two thousand miles of open sea lay between Butaritari and Pearl Harbor. Gedney settled himself more comfortably in his high seat and soon began to snore.

CHAPTER 15

"It's right thinking will turn the bullets aside, Flynn. You'll have no work to do on me." Mike O'Bannion mopped at sweat trickling down his hairy chest with the limp ends of a damp bath towel which hung about his neck.

Air in the *Belinda's* officers' quarters was clammy and stifling. Steel backers dogged tight over portholes not only contained light within the ship from enemy prowlers without but also prevented the slightest trace of fresh air from entering. A feeble breath of hot, machine-processed air struggled from an opening in the overhead pipe which theoretically provided ventilation to the place. Dressed in his capacious undershorts, O'Bannion was seated without the slightest loss of dignity upon the closed toilet seat in the small head common to the room which he shared with MacDougall and also to the one adjoining, which was shared by Dr. Flynn and the ship's languid dentist, Dr. Newth. Chairs were available in both narrow rooms, but O'Bannion preferred the toilet seat; with doors hooked open on either side, it gave him a commanding position and the desirable feeling that he was presiding over this informal gathering. Furthermore, the light was better for the exact work required by the needle point chair cover he was making. Dr. Flynn, also stripped down to his shorts, sat at his desk in front of a photo of his wife and two children, writing a letter which could not possibly be mailed for several weeks. The skinny frame of Dr. Newth, or *The Body,* as he was known in the wardroom, was stretched out limply in the lower bunk, naked and breathing with utmost economy of effort. MacDougall, recently down from the bridge, sat at the small foldup desk in the other room, legs extended and feet resting on top of the wastebasket. With occasional pauses to rub aching muscles of his game leg, sore from the constant standing required on the bridge, he was thumbing through pages of a bulky operation plan, getting a final check on details he would need during assault landings to be made on Kwajalein Atoll, now some two hundred miles away.

After a final look at diagrams of the transport area off Red Beach One, MacDougall closed the book and took his feet off the wastebasket. "What's that, Mike?" he said, joining in the conversation. "What are you going to bend the bullets with— that fancy bit of needle work you've got there?"

O'Bannion shoved his needle carefully through the center of a pink rosebud he was just completing, then held up the needle point, regarding it admiringly. "One more to go and I'll have enough for every chair in our living room . . . back in Boston." Placing the needle point carefully across his hairy knees, O'Bannion wiped his face on the towel ends. Without the slightest trace of a smile on his face he looked MacDougall in the eye. "Kwajalein is going to be hell on the beach, Mac, but I'll stand there with shot and shell flying about me, just as safe as I am in this head. I'll keep my thoughts right and the bullets can't hit me; they'll be swerving to left and right but not one of them will hit Mike O'Bannion." The beachmaster thrust extended fingers directly at MacDougall, in a dramatic curving motion which barely missed his nose. "See," he said. . . . "Just like that! The bullets will never hit you if you keep thinking right."

"That's downright decent of you, Mike," said Flynn. "If this heat keeps up I won't feel like performing any avoidable surgery."

MacDougall got up from the desk, passed through the two doors of the head and sat down beside Flynn. It had been much cooler on the bridge, but things were tense up there and the strain wore on a man. The attack force in which the *Belinda* now sailed was many times larger than the one in which they had gone to Makin. They were now steaming between Japanese-occupied Marshall Islands for the attack on strongly defended Kwajalein in the largest amphibious operation in the Pacific to date. Menace electrified the air; some Jap disposition would surely jump them. The ship was steaming in Condition Two: four hours at the guns and four off. Peacefulness of stars peeking between cotton-cumulus clouds seemed false, out of place. Surely if a man looked hard and long enough there must be something lurking in this darkness. . . . If you could only see it; that was the trouble. Nothing to be seen all around the horizon save two hundred ships, large and small, moving along together in precise formation. Hot down here in the room, yet good to be able to rest and to kid along with fellows like Flynn and O'Bannion.

A double knock sounded on the door leading into the passageway. The door opened sufficiently to admit shoulders and one arm of Steve Sherwood. "The exec wants to see all officers in the wardroom at once," he said quietly.

"What's up?" asked MacDougall.

"I don't know—something about the operation, I think." Sherwood indicated the prostrate dentist with a long index finger. "Is it alive?" he asked.

"I'd have to make an examination to be entirely sure," said Flynn. He got up and poked the dentist experimentally. "Yes, it breathes; nevertheless, I think we'd better leave the body here on detached duty." O'Bannion and Flynn pulled on khaki trousers and shirts, for Quigley would not allow officers in

110

the wardroom unless fully dressed, then followed Sherwood and MacDougall into the passageway, leaving the sleeping dentist in his bunk.

Fans in the wardroom merely stirred the humidity. Supper and sunset battle stations were long over and, except for one large pile of uncensored letters, mess tables were bare. In the alcove lounge, comfortable chairs, upholstered in imitation leather, overflowed with perspiring officers in limp khaki. Many who could find no seat, no armrest to do for a seat, squatted on the deck, resting their backs against bulkheads or knees of fellow officers. A small record player lashed in a corner of the alcove was trying to maintain even rotation against the ship's slow rolling. The tune came out faster and higher, then slower and lower, but it was unmistakably from the *Oklahoma* album which Ensign Gene Cooper had picked up in Honolulu during dry runs for this operation—a clear, leisurely voice singing, "Oh, What a Beautiful Morning."

MacDougall looked about quickly—the exec had not yet arrived—then walked over near the record player and leaned against the bulkhead, beside Dr. Bell. Cooper sat across from them, listening carefully, eyes distant and soft. Bell winked at MacDougall. "Pretty stuff," he said.

The record player was struggling with "The Surrey with the Fringe on Top" when a feeling of alert expectancy came over the wardroom. Someone shut off the music and officers came slowly to their feet. Lieutenant Commander Quigley stood inside the doorway, smiling in a light and friendly way. He seemed pleased about something—had not even noticed that Robinson, the communications officer, was wearing carpet slippers and enlisted men's white socks.

"Gentlemen," said the executive officer, "the captain has sent me to ask for volunteers for a special mission." It was very quiet in the place, ventilation blowers plainly heard. No immediate response. . . . Quigley smiled in a tight-lipped way. "Why, gentlemen, remember the Alamo—aren't you all going to volunteer?"

"What's the job?" asked Sherwood. "Some bright lad to capture the island singlehanded so the rest of you can go home for thirty days leave?"

Quigley coughed. "Not exactly. It's a little reconnaissance mission. As you know, available charts of this area are very poor. Little is known about actual beach conditions. The public is indignant over heavy losses at Tarawa. Kwajalein must be captured and the landing operation must not be fouled up."

"Somebody go get a flag and wave it a little," growled a dour voice at the back of the group. Quigley looked towards the speaker: Fraser, ship's first lieutenant. These Merchant Marine reserves were always needling him, forever ramming their confounded seamanship down his throat and annoying him with caustic remarks. Well, there wasn't much that he could do about it; they growled, but they produced. Yet sometimes he thought that it would be nice to have a wardroom completely filled with respectful young ensigns.

Quigley tried again, his words so well rehearsed that they sounded almost memorized, like the chatter of a green salesman —giving the impression that he did not have the slightest knowledge of what he was talking about. "Four attack transports, the *Belinda* among them, have been instructed to each equip an LCVP and to recruit a volunteer crew to take it through the surf off Red Beach, examine the reef and plot optimum boat channels into the beach. As you all know, the main landing will be made on D Day plus One. The reconnaissance on the main beach will be made tomorrow, D Day, at fourteen hundred. The captain has instructed me to ask for officer volunteers. He will then select one from the list. This officer will take charge of the *Belinda's* reconnaissance boat and will select his own boat crew from enlisted volunteers." Quigley paused a moment, enjoying the element of drama. Then he said, "All volunteers please step forward."

MacDougall stepped forward at once. "I'll go," he said. Here at last was a chance to get away from the ship again, to go on his own and have a little adventure. He was thoroughly trained for this sort of thing; of course they would pick him from the group of volunteers. Then he noticed that it was very quiet in the wardroom; no one else had stepped forward. This amazed MacDougall at first. What was the matter with them—didn't they want a little fun? How many times had he read about things like this? The Alamo—a hundred other places . . . Everybody was supposed to volunteer; but these guys didn't want to go. Were they scared? Then he began to realize that there was another reason. They weren't trained navigators. It wasn't fear of Japs but prospects of having to chart a reef that frightened them. Still, it was embarrassing to stand alone in front of them all. If only one more would step out, he would feel much better.

Quigley coughed again. "Anyone else, gentlemen?" The silence became uncomfortable. He tried to assure them, "Actually there will be very little danger."

One of the officers snorted derisively, "Broad daylight—no danger!" Quigley was not quite sure who it was, but he suspected Hall, the gunnery officer.

Speaking more quickly now, as if anxious to assure all present that there were no grounds for apprehension, Quigley added, "Oh, I know that the beach is strongly fortified with artillery and machine gun emplacements, but our battleships

112

will be off at one side, pouring a withering fire along the beach. The Japs will be nailed down completely."

"Why don't you go, if it's all so simple?" asked Fraser.

Quigley was beginning to get angry. He wanted to shout at Fraser that the executive officer could not be spared. But he knew that this would only make him appear more ridiculous than ever. He knew that he was the kind of officer who could always be spared. They wouldn't even miss him. Well, he had to say something. He said, "I wasn't asked. I was sent by the captain to ask you gentlemen."

"I don't want to go, but I'll go if I'm sent." It was Ensign Tony Brooks, Sherwood's assistant boat commander. Popular with nearly everybody on board, he was capable to the full limit of his knowledge and experience.

"A brave and honest young man," said Sherwood. Mac-Dougall and Brooks grinned sheepishly at each other. Quigley waited a moment longer. Then, without another word and as if triggered off by some invisible force, he leaped through the blackout screen and ran up the ladder to the cabin.

The atmosphere in the wardroom remained awkward. Some of the officers stepped over to the coffee maker and began to pour out coffee. MacDougall joined these. Someone thrust a full cup towards him. His head was buzzing with the excitement of the prospect ahead—gear he would need, men he would want with him. Cooper walked over to the record player, reached for the "Scheherazade" album, weighed it in his hands and put it back on the shelf unplayed. Then Quigley returned as suddenly as he had left.

"Brooks, you are to go," he said.

MacDougall banged his cup on the mess table, spilling the coffee. He rushed up to Quigley. "What's the matter with me?" he asked, anger rising together with disappointment in his voice. "Why won't he let me go?"

"He said he can't spare you," Quigley said casually. "He said he needs you on the bridge. And then, there's your leg. You're still crippled up, you know."

"Baloney!" MacDougall spat the word out at Quigley. "What's he need me up on the bridge for? He's got a navigator up there, and there's Randall. As for the leg . . . if I can climb the ladder to the bridge, I can swing a leg over the rail into a boat, can't I?"

"The captain says he needs you." Quigley was glad that somebody else was uncomfortable and angry; it helped him to regain his composure. He had said his piece. It was as if he had washed his hands of the whole business—as if, so far as he was concerned, the thing was as good as done. He had passed the captain's word along. Now it was up to subordinates.

"I'd like to speak to the captain," said MacDougall.

113

"Go right ahead. You have my permission."

MacDougall limped out of the wardroom and hurried up the ladder to the cabin. The door was hooked open as usual; a gray curtain hung across the entrance, swaying sedately with the ship's movements. MacDougall knocked. "Come in." The captain's voice, calm, unruffled, reached out to him from within. MacDougall stepped inside. Gedney sat at the conference table which dominated the cabin. A precise arrangement of Navy manuals, bound operation plans, maps and charts covered the table, radiating efficiently from a large sheet of clean, white paper placed in front of the captain, upon which he had been making notations in his clear, extremely neat handwriting. MacDougall mentally compared this with the crumpled, sweat-stained notes which he had taken from a similar set of plans. Faint hopes of going in the boat, engendered by rushing up to the cabin to appeal the decision, began to fade. Gedney looked up from his notes and regarded him with his most benign smile.

"Yes, MacDougall. What is it?"

"The boat, Capt'n. I want very much to take that boat."

"I'm sorry, MacDougall. I can't let you go. Almost any of the others, but not you."

"But, Capt'n, those fellows can't even navigate a ship! They can't be expected to go out in a heaving VP, where everything is confusing, and still plot an accurate chart of the beach. You know I've navigated ships for years, Capt'n—taught navigation too—but this will be tough, even for me."

Gedney smiled. "I'll tell you a secret." Pointing his fountain pen, he said in a low voice as if imparting information of an extremely confidential nature, "Do you know, MacDougall, I would very much like to go myself. I think it would be fun. But I can't go, and I need you, so you can't go. Brooks will have to do the best he can. But I'll tell you what I'll let you do," he said, smiling like a mother promising candy at another time. "You may go down and take charge of preparations. Get a good crew for Brooks, procure or have made any equipment you think they will need and show them what to do."

MacDougall's heart sank. There was no higher appeal for him; he could not go. He could not go but he could do all the dirty work. He began to get angry all over again, reaching here and there in his mind for some new argument which might change the captain's decision. He looked at Gedney, busy once more with his operation plans, putting down neat lines of notes in that bold but tidy handwriting. MacDougall felt the chill and disappointment of failure. He was dismissed; orders were orders. Without another word he left the cabin and went down to get a volunteer crew for Brooks. At least, he thought, the Old

114

Man was honest about it. He didn't throw that bum leg at me.

It seemed as if all the enlisted men wanted to go. They shoved and pushed each other, trying to work forward through the crowd in the mess hall where MacDougall stood. Among them he saw faces of men he liked and trusted, but for the moment he nearly hated them, for some of them would go but he could not. This was so different from the wardroom. These fellows in dungarees wanted to go, while officers, who were supposed to be leaders, hung back.

"Hot dog! Let me through, boys. I want to see my little slant-eyed friends on the beach!" Lew Doyle, rangy cowboy from Texas, now Alvick's righthand man in the second division, pushed to the front of the crowd. "Don't forget me, Mr. MacDougall. I don't want to miss out on this." It was just a ride to these boys. They were eager to help all they could, but it would not be their responsibility to find channels and spot potholes in the reef off Red Beach One, or to plot them accurately so that infantrymen would not drown. . . . Well, he had to pick a boat crew now, and here were enough volunteers to fill fifty boats, all yelling to go. Pulling a crumpled bit of paper and a stub of pencil from his shirt pocket, MacDougall smiled for the first time since Quigley had come down from the cabin. They could not all go; some of these boys were going to be very unhappy. Flattening his paper against the mess hall bulkhead, MacDougall began to put down the names of Brooks's boat crew.

A somber, dripping curtain hung over and all about the *Belinda*. Except for misty shapes of sister transports, dimly seen in squally night, she was isolated from all else about her—intense feeling on her bridge of busyness and suspense reaching far beyond limits of visibility. Somewhere beyond that dank veil was Kwajalein, principal and most strongly defended island of the atoll from which it took its name. It was a cucumber-shaped citadel, seven miles around the rim, forming the atoll's southeastern corner. Japanese headquarters for the Marshall Islands, bristling with guns, many of the strongest defenses underground and out of sight to curious cameras of American reconnaissance planes and submarines, Kwajalein Island presented fearful questions to the attack force now closing in. All that was known or anticipated had been carefully evaluated, yet only intimate, perhaps costly battle experience would reveal what these Japanese had actually done against attack. This assault operation would be the first American attempt to dislodge Japanese from territory they had occupied previous to their sneak attack upon Pearl Harbor. Not lacking time to fortify

Kwajalein, the Japanese were surely well dug in, yet it was doubtful that they had anticipated the extent or the fury of the mechanized hurricane soon to sweep over the reef.

Notwithstanding its coral and coco palm flatness, Kwajalein Atoll is a tremendous area: great lagoon like a vast inland sea reaching far out of sight, a sea with choppy waves built up by the wind within its borders; circling this sea a necklace of reef-connected islands, varying in size from seven miles down to tent-sized high spots on the encircling reef. Except for two deep-water entrances, the reef binds islands and sand bars together, forming an irregular-shaped enclosure, twenty-five miles wide and eighty miles long. Twelve of the twenty-six islands composing the southern portion of the atoll were to be captured by the Army, carried in the attack force of which the *Belinda* was a unit. Another attack force would land Marine combat teams on Roi and Namur Islands at the northern tip of the atoll. So extensive was the vast lagoon that the two attack forces would not only be out of sight to each other, but beyond the range of tactical voice radio. What happened on Roi might as well be a thousand miles away as far as the *Belinda* was concerned.

Minor landings were scheduled for the Southern Attack Force on D Day, 31 January 1944. These included capture of small islands bordering Gea Pass, a narrow channel west of the main island and Enubuj, site of Kwajalein's main radio station. Enubuj was situated five thousand yards westward around the reef from the southern tip of Kwajalein Island, where the main landings were to be made the following day. Planners had studied long over such inaccurate charts as were available, over photographs snapped from air and from periscope. These men knew that main Japanese coast artillery was placed at the main island's southwestern tip. They had to balance long stretch of reef and chances of being flanked against struggle for a landing at one end of the cucumber: most obvious landing place and therefore most strongly defended by the Japanese. They decided to make the main landing at Kwajalein Island's southwestern tip. To assist this, two days of bombardment were to be implemented by the landing of sixty field artillery cannon on Enubuj, set up where they could be brought to bear upon the landing beaches of Kwajalein and upon enemy positions further inland. While of lighter caliber than naval rifles, these guns, once landed, could deliver more accurate fire than the moving gun platforms of ships or planes. As landing infantrymen advanced, field artillery on Enubuj would handle barrage and call fire in congested areas, lessening the danger of killing Americans with so-called friendly fire. After the landing bombardment, thunder of Naval barrage would move ahead at a safe distance, or remain on Army call. Detail on detail, beyond remembering of any one man, written, approved, printed; kept in locked safes, promulgated with careful secrecy down chains of command. Minute-to-minute operation of planes, ships of every kind, landing craft, beach parties, approved weeks in advance by admirals. So also with the Army, proposed advance day by day, hour by hour, reaching down the chain to each combat platoon of forty men. Study operation plans; search out details to be demanded of your brain and your flesh. Gather about relief maps of painted plaster, before blown-up battle plans displayed on hatches of transports for study by sergeants, corporals, privates. Suck in your guts and breathe slowly. You're on the best side of this thing, boys. Better to wait here, uneasy, nervous, than to be waiting on Kwajalein behind reinforced concrete, behind walls of felled coconut logs, in foxholes, spiderholes, in cellars, in cisterns. Better not to be on the taking end of this thing.

Transport groups arrived off Kwajalein long before dawn on D Day. Gropings of ship following ship were aided by radar, whose polar projections showed both islands and ships, by day and by night alike in the same monotone of pale green. But now, watchers on weather decks saw great red fires leaping upward into the night and strange red tracks against black of night traced by fourteen-inch shells speeding from battleship gun barrels towards Japanese defenses, fuel tanks, ammunition dumps. Drone of carrier dive bombers circling and diving down in turn were blanked out intermittently by explosions of dropped bombs; sounds preceded by quick flashes and occasionally by pyramids of new flame from ignited oil and gasoline, now and then from great pyrotechnic displays produced by lucky hits on Japanese ammunition dumps.

A continuous succession of rain squalls swept over the fleet, soaking all hands exposed on weather decks and lending an atmosphere of mystery and unreality to the night action. Nothing was seen except shell tracers, explosions and fires on shore. Every ship was completely blacked out so that not even the slightest glow of compass light was exposed. Yet each group of ships deployed according to plan, performing complicated maneuvers in congested waters, guided by electronic eyes. From his bridge, Gedney wiped squall water from his eyes and gazed into murk ahead in which he could dimly see partial outlines of his transport group flagship, five hundred yards ahead. Here and there in obscurity he could find a spot even blacker than the night, indicating another ship. He could only sense the vast bulk of fleet units all about, as if his eyes, peering into dripping night, could visualize what his radarmen reported. This substitution of feeling for sight was the product of careful orientation and years upon the bridges of many ships. Gedney's active thinking was directed to debarkation of troops aboard. Sherwood and his boat group were standing by to transfer a portion of the *Belinda's* Army landing team to an assigned LST, one of a group which lay close in to unseen Enubuj Island. Gedney visualized the organized scramble down nets, the transfer across tossing black waters and final emergence from the LST's ramp in armored alligators, clattering towards the radio masts of Enubuj, clearing way for Army cannon, for landings next morning on Kwajalein Island itself.

With daylight, first glimpses of Kwajalein Atoll gave the same general impression as had Makin, only on a much larger scale: flat islands crowned with coco palms; wind-driven white water breaking along the reef line. There was a lack of freshness here: carrier planes dived out of an overcast, squally sky upon coco palms, tattered, uprooted here, cut off at the stump there by two days of constant bombardment carried on by groups of old battleships, heavy cruisers and efficient new destroyers before this arrival of the attack force. Smoke from blazing oil dumps drifted for miles. Against this dismal backdrop, battleships and their lesser kin paraded slowly off assigned target islands, belching smoke and flame. Dive bombers streaked out of the sky to the very fringes of tattered palms, dropped lethal burdens, made zooming, twisting escapes from fingered spurts of Japanese anti-aircraft fire which rose to meet them. All sounds and sights seemed blended together by the steady, never-ceasing drone of more carrier groups coming in from sea, circling in precise formation high aloft, like eagles waiting for the strike.

Transports and LSTs carrying troops bound for the capture of Enubuj, Ninni and Gea islands were launching boats from davits, amtracks from ramps. Transport divisions committed to tomorrow's main landing stood in and out, maintaining fleet speed and zigzagging to lessen danger from Japanese torpedoes. Minesweepers in staggered line abreast cruised carefully along the reef preparing the shallows for invasion. Mistress of every ship in sight was the old battleship *Pennsylvania,* here as at Makin the admiral's flagship. Her broad signal yards blossomed with streams of bunting which were promptly copied by other ships. As if in example, her guns thundered loud; quick flashes of fire and billowing smoke from her great rifles leaving no doubt as to her authority.

Captain Gedney conned the *Belinda,* next in column to the squadron flagship *Woodbridge.* Instead of five transports in the squadron there were three columns of five, and their squadron was now but one of many. More dots showed on the *Belinda's* radar screen than had been seen on the approach to Makin three months earlier: dots representing more islands and more ships. There was a businesslike attitude on Gedney's bridge this morning—no undisciplined shouting heard about decks. Yet a troubled undercurrent flowed beneath this apparent calm. Scuttlebutt, that true or fancied rumor which is as much a part of every ship as her frames and bulkheads, spread like a grass fire from deck to deck, from compartment to compartment. Among twenty-six hundred souls aboard the *Belinda* was a generous sprinkling of calamity callers, consciously or unconsciously serving as ship's jesters. Death and disaster to all aboard was predicted, each myth gathering more barnacles of lurid detail as it penetrated into remote compartments of the ship.

Down in the boiler room, Blackwell, fireman first class, could see nothing going on beyond the limits of his ovenlike working space; he could only feel and hear great explosions rapping sharply against the bulwarks where he stood, twenty feet below water level. There was tension, expectancy down below quite different in character from that experienced by watchers on deck. Danger felt all around, pressing in like sea water outside that quarter inch of shell plating. A fellow could believe anything down here; at best he would wonder and worry as Blackwell did now, listening to Zereko, the watertender, who had just come in from the engine room with the latest dope:

"Five transports torpedoed—just like that, before dawn. Grandy saw the explosions. . . . Big Jap fleet waiting in the lagoon."

Blackwell bit his lip. "We got battleships," he said uncertainly.

"Yeah, but that ain't all. Seven hundred of them Nip bombers coming this way from Truk. We'll all be swimming by afternoon —if we don't cook in steam and burning oil first."

In the two-squad boat team waiting outside the head at compartment 206 a corporal from New Jersey told a private from Montana:

"They'll sink this ship, that's what Dalton heard the major say. That suction carries you down, fella, down to where it's dark and slimy and the sharks are waiting."

"Naw, that ain't it. We'll float, maybe . . ." voice of Private Albright, face twisted so you couldn't tell whether he was kidding, whether he had really heard the dope—whether he was scared himself as he said, "The beaches are all mined, Toby. Them Japs will wait 'til we hit the beach and then—pouff— arms and legs and heads flying through the air. We ain't got a prayer, Toby. We ain't got a prayer."

The very exaggeration of these innermost anxieties relieved rather than added to unspoken fears. Idle waiting for the signal to go was the worst of it. Seamen busy on the weather deck and soldiers making last minute preparations before climbing down net watched the bombardment with outward casualness of sidewalk superintendents viewing an excavation. What gnawing fears each man suppressed were a secret of his own heart, hidden from others, possibly from his own mind.

The *Belinda's* afterdeck buzzed with activity as the second division, the boat repair crew and volunteer helpers fitted out an LCVP which was slung outboard alongside the starboard rail at number five hatch. This was the craft selected for the reconnaissance trip to the reef. There were no blueprints, specifications or mimeographed operation plans for this job. MacDougall sat on the ship's rail alongside the boat with his game leg resting on the gunwale while he coordinated the activity. There was no reminder that this was a pressing military matter, no forecastings of doom; rather a pleasant air of informality. "Good thing the Old Man's too busy on the bridge to come down here," MacDougall said to Tony Brooks, who stood beside him. "Gedney considers leaning on the rail very unseamanlike; I'm sure he's positive that only a soldier, and a dumb soldier at that, would sit on the rail like this."

Brooks laughed, but the worry lines never left his face. "How do you think *I* feel about this little expedition? Why didn't I keep my big mouth shut? Then some other guy would be trying to figure out where to take this boat and what to do when he got there."

"You'll be all right, Tony. Just take one thing at a time as you go along."

"That's all right for you to say, Mr. MacDougall. I'm going to foul this whole deal up, that's for sure."

MacDougall looked at Brooks's clear blue eyes and grinned. "You've got what it takes, Tony. Don't sell yourself short."

MacDougall swung around to have another look at the boat. Men swarmed over it from ramp to stern. Protective bulwarks of light armor plate surrounded the cockpit, which was lined with sandbags. More sandbags were carefully stacked about the engine box. The anchor line was new and an inflated rubber raft with a long, light painter attached was stowed beside it. Gunner's mates fussed with the two thirty-caliber machine guns mounted aft.

"It's plain enough we aren't going on a picnic," said Brooks with a nervous laugh.

"Can't be too sure about that," said MacDougall. "Shadow Rockwell is likely to show up any minute now with turkey sandwiches and a thermos jug of coffee."

"That's good. No use dying on an empty stomach."

Tony Brooks flinched as another great broadside exploded in his ear. He had just landed O'Bannion aboard the flagship and was now on his way to the reef. Chesney, the flag boat commander, had been no help at all. Brooks expected definite

120

instructions, desired them as earnestly as MacDougall would have avoided them, but Chesney seemed bewildered, and for once had little to say. None of the three other boats had any navigational equipment or plotting sheets. Chesney had a small scale chart of the island, nothing more. MacDougall had told Brooks, "These charts we have of Kwajalein aren't worth a nickel for close work like this. There never was enough trade here to warrant careful surveys—until the Japs came. They're very diligent boys about this chart business; you can bet they have good ones! . . ." It's a cinch we don't have either the charts or the island, Brooks thought as he hunted earnestly for a recognizable landmark—otherwise there'd be no reason for this questionable expedition. Well, here they were and it was going to be every boat for itself, by gosh or by guess. Brooks was beginning to feel that it wouldn't matter much now whether or not the *Pennsy* and her friends shot away the trees.

Two battleships and five destroyers concentrated their fire on the southwestern tip of Kwajalein, where the main landing would be attempted the following morning. The reef was broad and solid here, shallowing gradually as it neared shore. A long, rolling ground swell lifted Brooks's reconnaissance boat and shoved it along, half willing, half reluctant, towards Japanese coastal guns: bow suspended in space while the stern transom buried deep in the swirling trough, then the stern lifted sluggishly—for weight of armor plate and sandbags pressed it down heavily—yet up it went while the bow dropped from under until the boat's occupants found themselves looking uncomfortably over the ramp at Japanese defenses with the feeling that they were being catapulted onto the enemy beach.

Brooks veered the boat sharply to port, heading for the reef where it linked Kwajalein and Enubuj Islands. Rain still pelted down from a gloomy and ominous-looking sky, product of squall cloud and bombardment smoke. Reflecting this grim mood, deep water off the reef had exchanged its usual brilliant blue for a dull gray both sullen and disturbed. The boat ran over the reef line. Restlessness of the sea was now compressed in shallowness, water hissing in a heaving mass of pale browns and dirty whites. No heavenly emerald of tropic reef here, but wild sobbing of waters as if shuddering at thunder and concussion of bombardment. Battleship projectiles, ejected from gun barrels with tremendous explosive shock, screamed close overhead as if trying to suck Brooks and his crew from their craft to fling them in pulp upon the battered stonework of enemy fortifications at the southwestern tip of Kwajalein. It's a strange feeling, Brooks thought. I've never felt so temporary in a boat in all my life.

Reef must be shoaling. "Watch out for the bottom, fellows," Brooks shouted. "We don't want to get hung up here." His ears rang with the violent detonations and there was a constant buzzing in his ears, so that he was not sure whether he had been heard. Then to his relief he saw Moran and Rinaldo lean out quickly to port and starboard where they could keep a better watch for coral. The tide was high. Had the day been sunny they might nevertheless have seen bottom; but here in this dripping, clouded little world, sea was opaque and bottom lost to view as completely as the ship they had so recently left.

Brooks forced his mind away from the comparative comforts and security of the *Belinda* and fixed his eyes upon the shore. The boat was nearly across the reef. Deep water inside the lagoon was clearly marked by the sudden regularity of brown swells which rolled across the great atoll towards islands out of sight beyond the northern horizon. He watched the left tangent of Kwajalein, the battered trees. Yes, some trees were still left standing, though most of their tops were tattered like torn sheets left out in a gale. Then, as the boat moved along, other trees emerged from the background: fresher, undisturbed. The craft came in line with Kwajalein inner shore and it was time to turn. Brooks placed his hand on Alvick's shoulder, leaned down and shouted in his ear, "Head her for the beach." Alvick nodded and spun the wheel. The boat came around, rolling sluggishly now: wind on her starboard beam. Red Beach lay dead ahead some fifteen hundred yards away— seeming even closer across open water. Brooks looked over the ramp at the muzzle of an ugly coastal gun barrel pointing directly at him from a heavy masonry revetment. He need do nothing now save keep the boat on present course, and within four minutes the engine would take them to that cannon's mouth. Brooks shivered, looked at his strap watch. He could not hear its ticking above the bombardment but the sweep second hand moved steadily around with each accumulating second, utterly indifferent to what fate succeeding minutes might bring to Boat Twenty-Three, U.S.S. *Belinda.* Brooks looked at the beach again. The top of a tall coconut tree, cut from its trunk, rose, then fell against backdrop of smoke-laden cloud and dropped upon the shell-pocked sand.

Pappy Moran raised his head suddenly and shouted something. His gravel-voiced bellow was lost in a broadside, but his lips and expression seemed to indicate bottom. Brooks leaned over the side, looking intently downward. At first he saw nothing but surging water, then a coral head and movement under the water—something obscure, possibly fish or seaweed. The boat plowed onward. Two minutes had passed and they were within eight hundred yards of shore. What was that? . . . Bottom? Yes, bottom—round little nubbins of coral, deeper places, definite seaweed streaming with the tide between pinnacles of sharp-toothed coral. Brooks raised his head to order out sounding gear, then saw that they were already at it. Moran, Rinaldo and McClintock had the gear ready. Hatcher, experienced in surf work, took over the controls from Chief Alvick and nudged the boat gently shoreward. The heaviest part of the extensive rain squall was now passing over. Wind-driven pellets, surprisingly cold, beat down upon them, soaking their clothes and everything in the boat. While Brooks and Scott struggled with sextant and stadimeter, the others began to take soundings: ten feet shoaling irregularly to seven feet, then to six. They tossed the sounding lines back into the boat and took up the marked bamboo poles, sounding solemnly and mechanically, holding up dripping poles and indicating depths with their hands so that Brooks might see. Brooks nodded, marking down soundings as best he could, until the plotting sheet became one soggy mass of indecipherable pulp. He looked at Scott for some indication as to what they should do now—naturally the chief quartermaster would know more about instruments and plotting. Scott had taken off his helmet, which interfered with the eyepiece of his sextant. Water streamed from his close-cropped hair and ran down both cheeks to the corners of his mouth. He dabbed at fogged sextant lenses with a soggy handkerchief, aimed the instrument horizontally at the coconut trees, twirled the burled thumb-screw back and forth as he tried to bring the reflected image of one tangent of the beach into superimposition upon the other at which he looked directly. Scott took the instrument from his eye, noted water flooding the mirrors again, glanced at micrometer readings on the tangent screw and shook his head. More water cascaded down his face. He wiped it with one motion of a sopping shirt sleeve, then, resting the instrument on his knee, he looked up at Brooks, shaking his head again. All pretense of scientific accuracy ended here, Brooks realized. From now on it was just a matter of muscle and nerve outlasting the difficulties. He put the waterlogged chart back into its canvas cover—just why he did not know, for it could not possibly get any wetter—then tried to concentrate on remembering the soundings.

Hatcher poked Brooks and pointed off to starboard. Men in the next boat, now some three hundred yards distant, had launched their rubber raft and were towing it alongside. Brooks shook his head. "Not yet," he cried. "Too deep yet. Wait a bit." His eyes darted from one pole to the other. It was not the depth that mattered the most but whether or not the reef floor shallowed gradually, free from potholes or coral heads which might spell the difference between success or disaster during tomorrow's landing. Suddenly Rinaldo's pole sank, so that the shipfitter lost his balance and nearly fell overboard. Deep pothole. Brooks looked quickly at tangents of coral

123

shore and at the angular height of trees, endeavoring to mark the spot. Remembering MacDougall's instructions, he reached for the stadimeter, wiped its lenses with a corner of his shirttail and put the rectangular-shaped instrument to his eye. He turned the thumbscrew until the top of a tall palm tree sat at the water's edge. The instrument was set for a height of sixty-five feet, the estimated distance from water to treetop. The distance scale showed six hundred and ten yards. Brooks reached into his breast pocket for his notebook, but the pages were saturated with rain water and spray so that the pencil made no legible mark. He shoved the notebook back into his pocket and concentrated once more upon the soundings. The mean floor was now only four feet below the surface and seemed to be consistent. Brooks measured the tall tree again; the stadimeter now read three hundred and seventy yards. He looked carefully at shore. Just above the battered sea wall was a row of pillboxes, most of them still intact. Brooks imagined eyes, thousands of eyes peering out upon his boat from behind those defenses. He looked for the muzzles of rifles and machine guns, but saw none—only cannon, pointing somewhat over their heads. Brooks wondered what the Japs were waiting for. Why didn't they shoot? Mind whirling with conjectures, he looked for stubby mortar barrels; of all hellish things on a beach they were the worst. The Japs marked off water areas into small squares, knowing from long practice exactly what trajectory was needed. When you reached the little square— poof—boom! Up you went like a bloody rosebud! Brooks looked over the surface of the water about him, searching for markers of any kind, then shook his head and laughed mirthlessly, telling himself: *Don't let it get you, boy.*

Hatcher looked at Brooks, expression on his face clearly asking for the meaning of the joke. Brooks groped for a wisecrack but could think of none. He raised his stadimeter again towards tattered palm tops: three hundred yards and the water still between three and five feet deep. This was close enough to take a boat. Landing tomorrow, not today; landing by thousands of infantrymen, not a single boatload of half-drowned sailors grasping sounding poles! During a momentary lull in the bombardment, Brooks heard small waves breaking on shore. "Come left and run parallel with the beach," he said to Hatcher. "This is far enough. None of us can speak Japanese." Then he noticed that all the men in the boat were looking at him and grinning. Some of the nearly unbearable tension ran out of him and he grinned back at them, momentarily happy. At last he had gotten off his wisecrack.

There had been a reason for the short lull in the bombardment. All ships fired broadsides now in rapid succession. Entire trees together with huge chunks of mortar and clouds of rubble sailed high into the air from the sector of beach abreast the *Belinda's* boat. Brooks felt buzzing in his ears again: concussion, shock. He gulped, trying without any success to swallow the lump in his throat. Rubble and trees settled to earth. Then he noticed that the cannon which he had been watching most particularly had been knocked from its mount and now pointed up the island instead of towards his boat. He wondered what spotters on the battleships had seen . . . perhaps some movement threatening his craft. Brooks shivered again, wondering whether his chill was caused by cold rain, then knowing full well that it was due to fear of those silent, pointing guns.

Movement close at hand brought Brooks's attention back to his boat: big Foots Boski lifting the rubber life raft experimentally and looking to him for the word. Brooks nodded; yes, this was the time to get it out. When Boski lifted the raft —as if it had no weight whatever—Brooks pointed towards the offshore side. Boski flipped the raft over and Moran secured it alongside by the painter. Two canoe paddles were lashed inside the doughnut-shaped raft, which had been painted battle-gray over its former bright orange color. "O.K.," shouted Brooks. "Two men in the raft."

Nearest to the raft, Boski leaned over the side of the landing craft and rolled his hulking body onto the rubber raft. Moran began to follow in his usual deliberate manner when, with a sudden movement from behind him, tall and wiry Rinaldo placed one hand on his shoulder, the other on the craft's gunwale, raised his feet and scooted overside. The raft lurched and sank low at one edge with Rinaldo's sudden weight, so that sea water began to pour over the doughnut side and rise above the canvas bottom. Moran muttered angrily at Rinaldo, and the two chiefs glared at each other for a moment, then both laughed. Moran whipped off his helmet and gave it to Rinaldo to bail out the raft. After a few scoops of the bailer, Moran reached out and grabbed up his helmet again. "That's good enough, you claim jumper," he growled. "Do you good to get your ass wet."

Brooks considered the situation. If the men sat upright in the rubber raft and paddled closer to the shore they would almost certainly be shot. "Wait a minute," he shouted. "This won't work. You guys can swim, can't you?" The two men nodded. "Well," said Brooks, "just slip over the side and wade. Hang on to the raft and keep it between you and shore so the Japs can't see where you are." Brooks turned forward to McClintock. "Get that coil of light line and bend it on to the raft. Pay it out as they need the slack." Rinaldo and Boski were standing up to their armpits in the water. "Hang on to that raft," said Brooks. "Don't let it get away from you. If you get into trouble, just hang on and we'll tow you out in a hurry. Understand?"

The two men in the water nodded and began to push the raft towards shore, using their bodies for sounding poles. With a splash, Moran jumped overboard and floundered towards the raft. Boski and Rinaldo made room for him in between them, Boski with his usual dead pan, Rinaldo grinning: "Why, Pappy, I think your ass is wet!"

Between sudden, shocking broadsides, the roar of approaching planes. Something compelling in the sound so that Brooks interrupted his anxious concentration on soundings with occasional glances upward. Dive bombers coming in high, winging over one at a time, plummeting towards targets close behind the beach: probably fringes of the airstrip. Exploding bombs added to bombardment din, filling in any sound gaps neglected by battleships so that Brooks's men could no longer hear his shouts and he was reduced to giving hand signals. Then, from within jagged fringes of coco palms, up into the murk of rain and smoke came spurts of flaming orange tracers —Japs firing at last. For the space of a few gulping breaths, Brooks felt a measure of relief. These swift, flickering bullets were real, not ghostly anxieties in the back of a man's mind. He was still here—his heart pounding a little perhaps—and his men still waded slowly along the reef. But what next? Surely every undamaged gun along the reef would cut loose now— just waiting for the word. He visualized a mass of bloody wreckage floating over the reef. Then he closed his mind to it, shoved it back out of his conscious thinking.

Tracers continued upward, planes downward. Brooks could not tell whether they met, whether any planes were hit. Out of the corner of his vision as he stared towards shore, taking in raft, guns and tracers, he saw numbers of carrier dive bombers making their getaway in a series of steep, climbing turns. The whole thing was too much for one man to watch. With a general impression of wild activity aloft and deafening sound all about—except for the frightening sector of silence along the nearby shore line—Brooks turned back to concentrate fully on his own job. Boski, Moran and Rinaldo waded deliberately along the reef. Now and again one of them would sink up to his neck in a small pothole, grasp the rubber raft and work carefully out of it. Brooks looked beyond the raft to where brownish-white water lapped against the tumble of masonry sea wall, waiting for little spurts of orange flame until it became more impossible than ever to swallow the lump in his throat.

Aboard the flagship the staff navigator, a gray-haired commander in neat khaki, received from the dripping and disheveled Brooks his report of the beach approaches. The commander sat at a large table in the admiral's plotting room, receiving the boat officers one at a time. Before him was a large and spotlessly neat chart of Kwajalein Island upon which lay the precisely oriented metal arm of a universal plotting machine, a pair of dividers for stepping off distances and a perfectly sharpened pencil. Brooks looked at an unoccupied chair on his side of the table, but as he was not invited to have a seat he remained standing, feeling uncomfortable and out of place, anxious to get back to the *Belinda* and some dry clothes. "May I see your plot?" the commander asked. His tone was mild, almost casual, as if he fully expected Brooks to produce a chart as neat and as dry as the one which lay before him on the table.

Brooks cleared his throat; that confounded lump was there again. He wished that he could have a drink of water. Funny, wanting a drink of water when he was sopping wet and shivering from exposure. "Well, sir," he said after a pause. "I started out with a plotting sheet our navigator made up for me, but it got so soaking wet the pencil made holes in it . . . and finally I couldn't—Well, sir, it was hard to work out there, tossing around without a compass."

"With ranges and triangulations it is possible to make a perfect plot without a compass," said the commander, dismissing Brooks's excuses with a negligent wave of a hand. He began to ask penetrating and specific questions regarding the beach approaches, which were difficult to answer. His manner was polite but impersonal, so that Brooks had the feeling that he might be reporting a routine inspection of the flagship's paintwork. When Brooks had given as best he could the information the commander desired—no questions being asked regarding severed tops of coconut trees—he was dismissed with cool thanks, and stumbled across snowy planks of the quarterdeck feeling untidy, and out of place. He managed a salute to the colors and another to the snappy-looking junior O.O.D. at the accommodation ladder, then got down into his boat and shoved off for the *Belinda*.

The men in his crew were laughing and slapping each other on the back. They were still soaking wet but had been warmed internally by mugs of hot coffee in the chief's quarters while Brooks had been facing the commander. Lieutenant O'Bannion was in the boat once more, seated comfortably on the transom, legs braced inside the cockpit. "You're wet, my lad," said O'Bannion. Brooks laughed absently, his mind back at the reef. I wonder why they didn't fire, he thought. O'Bannion looked astern at the flagship. "It was fine on the bridge of that battleship," he said. "Wide sweep of decks, everything tidy and shipshape, those great guns belching fire and thunder at the shore. What a grand sight! It put me in mind of the Fourth when I was a lad in Boston." O'Bannion shook his head as if overcome by the wonder of it all. "It would have done my father proud to see his son, Mike, aboard a battleship in action."

Brooks wiped the water from his face with the back of his hand. "I think I'd rather go back to the beach," he said.

CHAPTER 16

Manmade thunder, greater in din and scope than anything previously experienced, announced the dawning of D Day plus One, day of the main assault landing on Kwajalein. Since Brooks and his men had explored the reef the previous afternoon, small but important landings had been made on five lesser islands which dotted the reef clockwise to westward. Official plans called for capture of only four of these, but in the darkness, during a blinding squall of wind-beaten rain, strong current setting northward along the seaward face of the reef carried rubber rafts filled with men from the 7th Division Reconnaissance Troop to an unscheduled destination. Intending to land on Ninni Island, which flanked the deep-water pass through which the fleet must steam in order to enter the lagoon, they landed unknowingly on Gehh Island, where a sharp little skirmish took place which had been planned neither by Americans nor Japanese. Japanese military personnel, fishing in the nearby lagoon, had been caught in the hail of the early bombardment. Survivors fled for safety, hiding under the coconut palms of Gehh Island, where they were tracked down and with few exceptions were exterminated by Americans who accidentally stumbled ashore in the darkness.

After small but intense skirmishes, all five islands were captured, providing invasion forces with a preliminary toehold on the tremendous atoll. Flanks of the narrow deep-water entrance into the great lagoon were now protected. As soon as minesweepers cleared a passage, transports, carriers and men-of-war could enter. Enubuj, next to Kwajalein main island, had been captured, but not without the loss of two great radio towers which, in a ringlike waste of flat islets, nearly awash, had been a great help in identification. A battery of some sixty 105-mm howitzers, boated from transports, carried across the reef and landed on Enubuj, was now set up wheel to wheel, facing Kwajalein landing beach. Sharp barking of these cannon now joined the swelling chorus of Naval explosions and their bite was felt on the strongly built but now crumbling defenses at the main island's southwestern tip, scene of Brooks's wading exploration the previous afternoon, and where the principal assault landing was to be attempted this day.

Yesterday's threatening weather had cleared, replaced now with a manmade hurricane stirred up by naval gun barrels and the artillery landed on Enubuj. Sulfurous fumes and smoke billowing from burning Japanese oil dumps almost completely clouded the fresh blue sky. Aboard the *Belinda*, in turn drifting and jockeying for position in the transport area, debarkation nets hung overside, sagging from recent clambering of soldiers debarking for island battle. Boat davits were empty, long arms of gray steel reaching overside like gigantic claws, wire boat falls with their heavy steel blocks swinging out then back, with doleful clatter against the hull at every roll. Watching from his bridge, Gedney divided his attention between the bustle of unloading preparations on his weather decks and on Sherwood's boat waves, now moving along the seaward side of the reef towards Kwajalein Island, some five thousand yards distant. MacDougall stood beside Gedney, his binoculars also trained on the distant landing craft. "Can you make out Sherwood?" Gedney asked. "Are you sure those are our boats?"

MacDougall lowered his glasses and wiped the lenses with a dry corner of shirttail. After all night on the bridge his sight was blurred from constantly watching the bobbing command boat. "Yes, sir. There he goes, just ahead of the amtrack waves—right in line with Enubuj Island."

With pleased sounding, metronomic tones, Gedney began to review the operation out loud: "Bombardment groups deployed on both flanks. DDs 673 and 478 marking the line of departure off Red Beach. First assault waves transferred from *Belinda* to LSTs 1020 and 1026, thence to Army alligators guided in by *Belinda* boat group. Brooks and Kruger to guide first wave. Boat officers from *Mears* and *Woodbridge* to guide second and third waves to Red Beach One. Sherwood then to bring troops for fourth, fifth and sixth waves to line of departure for transfer to LVTs. Tanks and bulldozers in LCM wave: Ensign Marty. Sherwood to co-ordinate. . . ."

MacDougall paid no particular attention to Gedney's measured tones. It seemed to him that they were part of this gigantic machinery for invasion, as if all of them were puppets moved about on endless treads, fear compressed within, actions automatic, in accordance with operations plans. Yet in spite of this he knew that Sherwood was out there on his own. Nothing said here except into the mike of the landing craft voice circuit could have the slightest effect on Sherwood's actions. *I wonder if he's still trying to sing against all this racket,* MacDougall thought, remembering Sherwood's predawn departure from the *Belinda*. Sherwood had climbed into his command boat singing, "Oh, What a Beautiful Morning"—singing at four in the morning before shoving off into the rainy, black unknown.

Daylight now, sun and blue sky after murk and rain, ephemeral beauty of clean white cloud scurrying from the windward horizon to join smoke of exploding bomb and shell and great smudge pots of burning Japanese fuel storage. Battle would change this beauty soon enough, yet while it remained, words of Sherwood's song returned to filter through MacDougall's thoughts. Sherwood was out there now—out where Mac-Dougall would like to be—taking the greater chances, herding boats and men in helmets along that offshore reef towards the inevitable moment of H Hour—floundering and splashing over coral and out to the sea to attack an enemy dug in behind battered concrete and twisted steel. The carefree tune from Sherwood's lips returned to MacDougall now, intensified, beat out with the tremendous authority of one-ton projectiles, carried by the wind blowing from clean, open sea, passing over gray ships now belching not only projectiles and burned gunpowder but men, materiel . . . passing over boats and crawling amtracks, flung with the awesome speed of bullets upon frightened little men on the island shore who waited for invasion and death. . . . Ridiculous thought, yet so real to Mac-Dougall now that it seemed to him all must hear it, friend and enemy: the little Jap, ducking shot and shell, he must hear it too, and joining in the tremendous, mechanized chorus with his squeaking little voice must even now be singing a repetition into the winds of circumstance, committed beyond recall to his death:

> *Oh, what a beautiful morning,
> Oh, what a beautiful day
> I've got a beautiful feeling
> EVERYTHING'S COMING MY WAY!

MacDougall looked at Captain Gedney. Surely he heard the song screaming out in the whine of passing shells. It was louder than earth-shaking explosions they watched; it was the loudest thing in the world.

Gedney's face was impenetrable; whether he was making complicated mental computations of time, speed and distance or merely following progress of Sherwood's boats along the reef, MacDougall could only guess. At last Gedney said in a casual tone of voice, "It's a nice morning." Then he noticed the startled look on MacDougall's face. What's got into him, Gedney wondered; he's usually calm enough.

Seconds of the final hour ticked by while widely dispersed units of the Army and Navy approached the culmination of months of planning and practice. The scene was like the reconnaissance photos and battle maps expanded to full size and seen in three dimensions with sound and smell added. Regardless of the hesitancy of any given unit, or of fear in individual human hearts, the over-all impression was one of relentless mechanical precision and overwhelming power. So it appeared from the bridge of the *Belinda*, even as bells jangled and excited orders were given to keep her on station and to prevent collision with sister ships often drifting closer than a single ship length away. . . . And so it must have appeared to the enemy crouching behind crumbling revetments at Red Beach —to those who were still physically able to see the tidal wave of invasion before it swept over them.

While artillery set up on Enubuj, lobbed shells across the reef to drop on the focal point of attack, naval gunfire reached a crescendo of rapid fire. Hellcats dived, bombing and strafing the landing beaches. Ships numbered in the hundreds moved deliberately on exact missions prescribed by the operations plan, or else lay to in ordered groups, waiting like substitutes at a football game for word to rush into action. Hundreds of alligators clattered along the reef, herded by the Sherwoods, the Brookses and the Krugers from many ships, looking like columns of industrious ants. From close up this ant-like behavior was emphasized by the meandering approach to the beach of the almost unmanageable amphibious tractors in ragged lines abreast. Yet these clumsy armored craft were the heart of the expedition; it was for them that large ships deployed, and in preparation for their landing at Red Beach that the pre-landing bombardment thundered.

Finally, for the last time before landing hour, the sweep second hand in the large brass clock, eagerly watched now in the *Belinda's* pilothouse, made its round. Gunfire lulled to an unaccustomed silence, awesome as the quiet blue eye of a hurricane. Their last bullets expended, strafing planes zoomed upward from the beach and returned to their carriers while the first wave came in. Amtracks lurched and floundered, boxlike bodies rising unevenly from the water, slithering across wet coral, pressing onward as close as they could get to the battered sea wall. Out came the infantrymen, moving quickly, without apparent hesitation—some swarming ashore from knee-deep water, others less fortunate dropping into potholes, staggering out dripping salt water, stripping protective pliofilm from their rifles before crossing wavelike heaps of rubble and moving on into the graveyard of shattered coconut trees and men which was the southwestern tip of Kwajalein.

After the two minutes of silence required by plan, the guns opened fire again. Gone the tumultuous crescendo; fire deliberate now, sometimes in salvo, more often the startling crack of a single great fourteen-inch rifle, carefully aimed beyond friends and upon the enemy. The radio air was filled with messages from gun spotters, some on foot with the infantry,

131

some aloft in toylike Piper Cubs: *Up five hundred yards.* . . . *Left two* . . . Shoot the enemy, not the friend. Over the island of Kwajalein spread a stinking pall of smoke which the trade wind would not blow away for five bloody days.

At two in the afternoon, order came for transport groups to enter the lagoon through the narrow deep-water entrance between Ninni and Gea Islands, each ship to proceed independently. Shrill boatswain's mate's pipe sounded over the *Belinda's* PA, "Now trice up all debarkation nets. . . . Now go to your stations all the special sea detail. All hands man your battle stations." Tanks, field guns, ammunition and cans of water for troops in the battle line were left hanging in cargo slings while the *Belinda's* crew ran to battle and anchoring stations.

Gedney was pleased. "We've had enough of drifting outside the reef," he said to MacDougall. "We'll soon be anchored inside the reef, comparatively safe from submarines. . . . All engines ahead full."

Harrison, the navigator, raised an anxious face from his charts. "How about shore batteries, Captain?"

Gedney waved a negative in the air with his hand. "Shore batteries are the lesser evil. We can always move out of range. Besides, a shore battery is much easier to locate and engage than a submarine. . . . Flank speed, MacDougall. Come around on full right rudder."

"Right, full rudder, sir." Engine room annunciator clanged, ship surged ahead, swinging about her pivot point, then ranging along the reef towards the narrow entrance into the lagoon. Gedney began to hum a tune, startling the bridge messenger, who leaped out of the captain's pathway, then turned to stare.

"Proceed independently," said Gedney reflectively. He flavored the words, running the tip of his tongue about his lips as if they were sweet to taste. "Proceed independently. That's the order I like to hear. While we proceed independently, International Rules of the Road apply, and not even a battleship has precedence over the *Belinda* unless it is given to her by those impartial rules."

Bow began to cut the waves and fresh breeze whipped spray over the foredeck, soaking the anchor detail.

Harrison's lanky frame bent over his chart, his brows furrowed with concern while he plotted and replotted sets of hearings which refused to intersect on his inaccurate chart. "Watch your plot closely, Harrison," ordered Gedney. "What is the course and distance to the entrance?"

Harrison raised an unhappy face from the maze of bearings which gave him no definite answers. "I'm not positive, Captain . . . matter of island identification, perhaps. The operation plan clearly showed two large radio towers on Enubuj Island. I do not—"

"Get busy, Harrison, get busy. We will be at the entrance within three minutes." Gedney trotted out of the pilothouse to where MacDougall stood on the bridge wing, watching his bearings over the pelorus and estimating safe distance from the reef by eye. Gedney's eyes were shining with excitement. "I'm not worried about Harrison's plot," he said under his breath. "I just want *him* to worry a little. . . . His navigation at Maalaea Bay: *'The large island is Maui.'* I'll not let him forget that in a hurry."

MacDougall grinned, "With the sun shining we can see the reef line clearly, sir."

"Exactly. Much better than the charts. Hold her as close as you think safe. I want to beat the commodore inside." Gedney looked off to port. The squadron flagship *Woodbridge* was racing for the lagoon entrance on a more direct line than the *Belinda,* now streaking along the reef. "Watch the *Woodbridge,* MacDougall!" Gedney cried, ducking back to take his place at the pilothouse windows. "She's a little closer to the entrance, but the *Belinda* has the right of way and I am going to take it."

MacDougall watched the *Woodbridge* through his pelorus's sight vanes. He kept the hair wire on the flagship's white-frothed bow, watching the reflection of the compass bearing in the tiny mirror beneath the sight vane. "We're on collision bearing with the *Woodbridge,* Capt'n. Two-six-eight; no change."

"What are the engines doing by tachometer, Randall?"

"Eighty-three rpm and a bit, sir."

"Call the engine room; tell them we must have two full turns more."

"Aye, aye, sir."

Excited looks were exchanged between junior officers and enlisted men in the pilothouse. Only Harrison remained serious, frowning over his bearing plots, certain that the *Belinda* would crash either into the reef or into the flagship. The *Belinda* shuddered from the extra thrust of her screw. Shouts and clanging could be heard coming up through engine room ventilators. The bow rose higher, then fell deeper, slicing the clear sea water and sending sheets of wind-blown spray over the foredeck. The two ships were racing nearly at right angles to each other: *Woodbridge* heading straight towards the lagoon entrance, *Belinda* running parallel and just outside the reef. Randall stood on the port wing, taking distances with a stadimeter. "What is the range to the *Woodbridge?*" Gedney asked.

"Fifteen hundred yards, closing rapidly, Capt'n."

"Bearing, MacDougall?"

"Still steady, Capt'n. . . . Collision bearing. . . . Now it's moving a bit." MacDougall's voice rose with excitement. "We're beginning to draw ahead now, sir."

Gedney took a quick look at the gap in the reef through which he must thrust his ship, then swung about on his heel to watch the racing flagship. A dozen binoculars were focused upon him from her bridge. "Look at them!" Gedney cried. "Staring at *me;* examining *me!* Why don't they put their noses into the International Rules of the Road, Article Nineteen: *When two steam vessels are crossing so as to involve risk of collision, the vessel which has the other on her own starboard side shall keep out of the way of the other.*"

The two ships rushed towards a point of intersection. "Range, nine hundred yards," called Randall.

"Bearing moving more rapidly now, Capt'n," called MacDougall, adding anxiously, "It doesn't look good to me. They should slow down and sheer astern of us."

Gedney seemed to ignore his officers. Except for quick glances at the narrow lagoon entrance to starboard, he kept his eyes on the flagship. At last, no longer able to contain himself, Gedney jumped up and down, pounding his right fist into his left palm, binoculars swinging violently from side to side like the pendulum of an old clock while he shouted across the water in the general direction of the *Woodbridge*, "Article Twenty-Two: *Every vessel which is directed by these rules to keep out of the way of another vessel shall, if the circumstances of the case admit, avoid crossing ahead of the other.*" The bridge watch, who with the exception of Willicut, the quartermaster, had never heard of the Rules of the Road, gaped at their captain with open mouths. Gedney paid no attention to them. His eyes were shining: his ship drawing ahead now; war, invasion, death on the beach—even the safe full of operation plans—all forgotten in the excitement of this moment. Once more the fist pounded into the palm as Gedney continued his chant. "Read Article Twenty-Three: *Every steam vessel which is directed by these rules to keep out of the way of another vessel shall, on approaching her, if necessary*"—Gedney's voice rose now to a triumphant shout—*"SLACKEN HER SPEED OR STOP OR REVERSE!*"

MacDougall and Randall exchanged glances, both entertained and concerned by Gedney's suddenly precipitous behavior. Such a stickler for rules! MacDougall was thinking. Yet he must hate them, he must. Look what he's doing with his precious ship when he gets a chance to throw rules back into the teeth of a commodore!

If Gedney felt any concern he failed to show the slightest inkling of it, even while the speeding ships closed to within eight hundred yards. "The commodore knows he's wrong," Gedney announced to his officers. "Look at that signal yard.

Nothing there. If he had any rule back of him—any favorable interpretation of an unfavorable rule—he'd be throwing bunting at me by the mile. He's just bluffing, throwing his rank, which is not a rule of the road. He gave the order to proceed independently and I have the right of way. His officer of the deck may not know it, even his navigator possibly may not know it, but the commodore knows it. He knows the rules and he knows that he has allowed himself to get into an untenable position."

The ships still raced towards intersection. MacDougall sucked in his breath. The situation would be serious in a matter of seconds. Gedney, model of correct behavior that he was, was dangerously out of character. Could it be possible that the bombardment . . .

"Distance, seven hundred yards," called Randall.

"Time to head for the entrance, Capt'n," cried MacDougall.

"Not yet. . . . Not yet," shouted Gedney. "Steady as you go, quartermaster. . . . He must slow down first."

"Ha!" exclaimed Randall. "He must have heard you, Capt'n!" The flagship was coasting now, her propeller dragging, rudder swinging her conservatively and in accordance with Article Twenty-Two, towards the Belinda's speeding stern. Then a cloud of escaping steam shot from her funnel with a loud pop.

Gedney put his hand on the stooped shoulder of the navigator, who still struggled with his bearings. "Look, Harrison," he said. "The commodore has popped his safety valve! Right full rudder, quartermaster." Gedney rubbed the palms of his hands together as he watched MacDougall bring the ship's head up for the narrow lagoon entrance. "Relax, Harrison. Just look at the flagship, sitting on her tail while we lead the way in to the lagoon. I remember back in Nineteen-Twelve . . . old Captain Gow got Admiral Brashler in a box off Hampton Roads, made him pop his safety valve. Of course that was in the days of coal burners—" Gedney broke off to point with happy satisfaction at the mixture of white steam and black smoke pouring from the Woodbridge's funnel—"even more spectacular than this."

Still at flank speed, the Belinda shot into the narrow breach between Gea and Ninni islands. Gedney's eyes still danced with excitement and pleasure, risk to his ship in a narrow and poorly charted channel did not seem to concern him in the slightest. "It's a clear day with the sun at our backs. We can see the reefs, MacDougall. You watch this side, I'll go watch to port." Gedney skipped lightly back through the crowded pilothouse, went to the bridge wing where he could look for coral close ahead. Still unconcerned he pointed along the reef. "There's Gehh Island," he said to Randall. "The second one to port. They captured it by mistake this morning—rubber rafts drifted past

135

Ninni in the dark. Easy mistake to make on a black and windy night, drifting along in a rubber raft. Just as well, too; the place was thick with Japanese."

MacDougall stood behind the pelorus, watching the reef, making sure that the *Belinda* kept in blue water and skirted the green and white shallows which would rip her bottom open. Gea Island was close to starboard now: pretty little place with a lookout dwelling high on stilts, poking above tops of un-harmed coconut trees. He noticed a beached tug off Gehh—several Japanese dancing in and out of the pilothouse in wild excitement. "Captain," MacDougall called across the bridge, "there's—" His voice was drowned out by sudden clamor from the gun crews on the signal bridge above him.

"Look at them Japs! Can I shoot, Mr. Kelly? Can I shoot? Hey! Look at 'em, look at 'em, look at 'em!"

"No, no! Wait for orders."

A new voice above the others: "Shoot the yellow bellies!"

"Aw, Mr. Kelly, I got 'em in my sights. Lemme shoot."

Gedney jumped from bridge wing to pilothouse, sending his orderly spinning into a bulkhead, knocking a messenger flat. Gedney snapped on the PA and stuck his lips angrily into the microphone. "All guns hold fire. All guns hold fire. I will give the order to fire. No gun will be fired without orders. Our ob-jective is Kwajalein, not a beached Japanese tug." Gedney step-ped back to the open wing of the bridge, blue eyes mild again; all the anger had poured out of the man. He looked around at nearby land, coconut trees, native huts, canoes, bits of clearing all flowing back from his fast-moving ship. "Fine place for bearings, Harrison," he remarked mildly. "If you don't know where you are now, you'd better toss your binoculars into those coconut trees."

Fresh wind blew in from seaward, pressing battle smoke back upon Kwajalein. Clear, deep water reflected blue sky; shallows revealed themselves in lustrous emerald greens; white sand bars dazzled the eyes. MacDougall was happy, unworried in the sure knowledge of his work, the battle momentarily remote. Keep in blue water and be safe; use the eyes seamen had before charts. Harrison stood beside him, looking unhappily at the coconut trees. MacDougall liked the kindly Harrison, yet he was amused that science had failed this former schoolmaster to midshipmen. If Harrison could only realize that sometimes you drive a ship just like a car down a country road—only Gedney would never let Harrison guess. Harrison was the assigned navigator, officially responsible for operational exacti-tudes. Here on the bridge were three other men who could have done the job for him, but one was his commanding officer, the other two his juniors in rank. It was a crazy system.

The last yard of white reef came abeam. Right ahead lay a sand bar. "Time to turn now, Capt'n," called MacDougall.

"Right full rudder," shouted Gedney. The *Belinda* came around, steaming close along the reef once more, but this time doubled back on her track and within the lagoon. Ahead was Kwajalein Island, torn and shaken with explosions, nearly covered with a murky blanket which was half burning oil, half burned powder.

The fresh beauty of Gea Island faded astern. The *Belinda* steamed alongside Enubuj Island, where a landing had been made the previous afternoon, now a shambles of broken palms and wrecked buildings. Over the whole drooped ruins of the two giant radio towers for which they had looked. "Oh!" exclaimed Harrison. "There's my landmark. No wonder I couldn't find the towers." MacDougall barely heard Harrison's words. More than sixty cannon, placed wheel to wheel near the eastern tip of Enubuj, cracked in a ragged staccato of rapid fire as they poured a barrage just ahead of the slowly advancing battle line of Kwajalein. The *Belinda* moved on, paralleling the bare reef where Brooks had made his reconnaissance the previous afternoon. Fresh wind blew over this bare reef between Enubuj and Kwajalein, yet it could do nothing with the death pall which hung over the battlefield. Carried by some fickleness of the upper air, pressed downward by the weight of its noxious gasses, littered with scorched paper and tiny fragments of tree and dwelling, it fell now upon the decks of the *Belinda*. It brought the smell of many burning things, a sweetish, kerosenelike smell. . . . And mixed with it was the stink of death.

Gedney anchored the *Belinda* close to Kwajalein in fifteen fathoms of water, using barely enough chain to hold her there, keeping an anchor watch at the windlass to heave up should the *Belinda* be required to run from air or submarine attack—it was conceivable that Japanese submarines lurked within this great lagoon—or to veer more chain should the ship drift towards the reef. After them followed other transports, and squadrons of LSTs. Anchors splashed and chain rattled from hawse pipes all about. Carriers steamed nearly to the north horizon within the lagoon, then turned and headed full speed into the wind, launching and taking on planes. Battleships, cruisers and destroyers paraded along the beach, half hidden in smoke from their own guns and from the dying island.

"No word yet from Sherwood or O'Bannion?" asked Gedney petulantly.

"No, sir. Not yet."

Gedney stamped his foot angrily on the deck, jumped back into his high seat and began to thumb rapidly through a stack of radio dispatches. At this moment an inexpertly handled landing craft, returning from the beach, crashed into the ship's side, just below the bridge. Hearing the sound and feeling the light shudder echoing through his ship, Gedney came down from his chair again, rushed to the wing and looked down angrily. "Get me a megaphone—a megaphone," he demanded in a furious whisper. When a messenger brought one on the run, Gedney grasped it, aimed it at the dungaree-clad coxswain. "Put on your helmet and life jacket don't you know how to handle a boat where is Mr. Sherwood?" Gedney shouted in one angry exhalation. The coxswain stared up at the bridge, mouth half open, tanned young face smeared with grime and dried sweat. The boy looked completely baffled. It was obvious that he had no information for his captain. Gedney threw down the megaphone, allowing it to bounce towards the corner of the bridge while he returned to the stack of dispatches.

Randall came over from the port wing. "Look at the *Woodbridge*," he said to MacDougall. "She's calling us; looks mighty important, bridge almost covered with flag hoists."

"Trying to make up for losing that race with us."

"No doubt." A bell clanged sharply in the pilothouse. "Signal bridge," said Randall, heading for the pilothouse. "Bridge, aye."

"Signal from the *Woodbridge*, sir. LST 627 ordered alongside *Belinda* to take on thirty-thousand gallons fresh water."

"Understood," said Randall, making a face. "That takes care of the shower I was going to have tonight." Gedney glared at Randall and jumped down from his high chair again. He's stewing over the boats and this uncertain anchorage, thought Randall, quite undisturbed. "There's the 627, Capt'n, board on the starboard beam."

Randall gave instructions to a boatswain's mate and the PA called out: "Now the first division, stand by to receive LST 627 alongside, starboard side number three hatch. . . . Now the water-king report to the log room." The bald-headed watertender who was charged with the pumping of all water tanks turned from the rail where he had been watching the burning shore line and headed on the run for the chief engineer's office. Seamen climbed down from gun platforms and left cargo winches to get mooring lines ready.

Pappy Moran rolled down the foredeck, shouting, "Stand clear, soldiers. Stand clear of the side."

Infantrymen from platoons being held in reserve moved grudgingly back from the rail. Up on the bridge, Gedney and MacDougall watched the approach of LST 627. "She's coming in too fast," said MacDougall.

"Yes," said Gedney, "much too fast. When he backs down, his bow will fall off the wind." True to prediction, the LST swept up splendidly, while her engines churned madly astern in an unsuccessful attempt to overcome headway. Then the wind caught her high bow. LST 627 shuddered, wavered, then swung rapidly towards the *Belinda* in a wild yaw which could never be controlled by engines or rudder.

"It's one of those ribbon-clerk skippers," said MacDougall in angry concern. "Shall I yell at him to drop his port anchor, Capt'n?"

"Certainly not," snapped Gedney. "That young fool may indeed be a ribbon clerk, but remember, he is the commanding officer of that . . . commissioned . . . thing. Rank does not permit us to give orders to a commanding officer, no matter how junior, no matter how ignorant, as long as he is at the conn of his own ship."

By this time the LST was too deep into trouble for either advice or anchors to do any good. The young junior lieutenant on her foredeck froze into immobility. Around him were line handlers, rushing up now with limp-looking fenders which they hung overside. "Lot of good that will do," growled MacDougall. "Look at the boy on the burning deck!" Randall called out a warning through the *Belinda's* PA and Pappy Moran's gravel voice urged his men to get hot with fenders: substantial lumps of old rope woven together. These were gotten overside just as the LST crashed into the *Belinda's* side—right between two fenders—and buried her anchor out of sight in the *Belinda's* hull.

The *Belinda* lurched at the impact. Sounds of ruptured steel plate and buckling frames momentarily drowned out din of bombarding cannon. Hardly knowing how he got there, MacDougall found himself two decks below the bridge, shouting to crowds of enlisted men on the two vessels. "Don't just stand there gaping! Get out your mooring lines and hang on. Do you want her to surge back and crash us again?" Not six feet from MacDougall the young junior lieutenant scrambled to his feet, laughing in the foolish, embarrassed manner of one who did not know what to do about the situation. Feeling himself being roughly thrust aside from behind, MacDougall turned angrily around, only to see that he was being pushed by Captain Gedney, whose face was livid with rage.

Gedney took MacDougall's place, hung out over the railing and shook his finger at the junior lieutenant of LST 627. "Laugh, you driveling idiot!" he screamed. "It's my ship you're wrecking!"

The junior lieutenant gaped back at Gedney, too overwhelmed by his rank and his anger to make any reply whatsoever. Now Gedney heard a respectfully urgent voice at his back, and turned to be confronted by Harrison. "The hull board, sir," suggested the navigator. "Shall we survey damage, sir?"

Swallowing, Gedney regained his composure. "Yes, by all

means. Then report to me." Gedney swung forward abruptly and, as his crew fell away before him, ran lightly back up the ladder to his bridge.

Searching methodically for damage, Harrison came to a crowd about the entrance to the troop officer's head on the deck below. Worming his way into this large compartment, he was startled to catch a glimpse of the LST through an anchor-shaped aperture punched in the side of the *Belinda* just above a toilet seat. The adjacent seat was occupied by an artillery major who sat quietly puffing on his pipe in calm detachment from the furor all about him. Fraser, the *Belinda's* first lieutenant, was on the scene with his damage control party. "Bring in the shoring, Chips," he yelled to his carpenter. Harrison walked to the hole in the ship's side and bent his lanky frame to peer more closely at the jagged edges.

Just then the artillery major poked his head around the thin partition to confront Harrison. "What caliber?" asked the major.

Harrison chuckled all the way to the bridge. Before reporting to Gedney he told Randall about the major in the troop officers' head.

"Wasn't he scared at all?" asked Randall.

"He didn't seem to be," Harrison said. "But if he was, he was in a good place for it."

Harrison began his report to Gedney, who was now concerned with other matters and waved him aside. Sitting tensely, one leg thrown over the metal arm of his high chair, Gedney aired his indignation in a loud voice. "Messages; thousands of messages filling the air—not a single one of the slightest use to me, or that can be understood for that matter. Such utter lack of discipline and order: everyone shouting at once! Meanwhile, where is Sherwood? Where is O'Bannion? Why have I not heard from them?"

Robinson, the communications officer, gave up trying to dig a hole in the steel deck with the toe of his right shoe. "I'm sure they're trying to get through, Captain. I have two Six-hundred Ws on their circuit—continuous watch kept on both of them."

"Can't you cut in another circuit?"

"No, sir. We're on the only bands authorized for ship-to-shore."

Gedney whirled around, jerked a thick, mimeographed volume from his bulkhead bookshelf and thumbed through the Communications Plan for the operation. "That's right," he conceded. "Well, do something, Robinson; don't just stand there. I must hear from the beachmaster and the boat group. Hundreds of men worked for years to design and build your equipment, the best communications procurable. I have told you

140

many times that the main battery of an attack transport consists of her boats. We must maintain control of our main battery at all times." Gedney's voice rose nearly to a scream. "Yet this is the best you can do! Listen!" Gedney pointed to the TBS speaker on the bulkhead just above his seat.

Above incessant roar of static and overlapping syllables, certain sounds rather than sentences could be identified: "Blah—zing babel bombard—proceed—pendently, form on guide eighteen thousand, I repeat eight—Sycamore, this is Spinach—twenty-five—raise your—blah—dangering own forces—itch Roger, Wilco, over and—"

"Just listen to that!" exclaimed Gedney. "All the wonders of modern science! They had all that racket thousands of years ago in the Tower of Babel. But can I get Sherwood? Can I get O'Bannion? No!"

Momentary silence from the TBS, then a crystal clear message: "Punchbag, this is Bounder. Reference your work request of zero five four eight dash seventeen, I say again repairs to dishwashing machines will be performed by ship's personnel Xray initial."

The babel took over again. MacDougall stirred. "Listen to that. Six weeks ago, back in Pearl, they ask to get a dishwasher repaired and some jackass waits until D Day to say, 'No.' Does he think they've been eating on the deck for a month, waiting for him to make up his mind?"

Gedney had regained his professional mask. He looked disapprovingly at MacDougall. "Perfectly in order," he said. "No doubt taken in correct sequence from the flag secretary's message board." Gedney considered his statement. It was logical; it was proper, but there was no comfort or help in it. "MacDougall," he said, the words blurting out suddenly, "I want you to get into the next shorebound landing craft. Go find Sherwood and O'Bannion. See what has happened, then report to me at once."

Sharp edges of the ammunition case made an uncomfortable seat. MacDougall scrambled back to the cockpit of the lurching LCVP and stood beside Tommy Jones, the coxswain. Cases of 37-mm ammunition, resting haphazardly in three large cargo nets, filled the boxlike compartment: three tons of ammunition, no doubt badly needed on shore. There was food for boat crews and beach party too; Shadow Rockwell had seen to that. Jones seemed indifferent to his cargo—stuff to sustain life or to take it. He peered anxiously ahead, seeking his way in rain and smoke, looking for the landing place. The *Belinda* was lost to him in a maze of anchored ships astern. Battle noise, smoke and stink grew as his craft closed the island. Murky lagoon water, once crystal pure, was cluttered with bits of flotsam: small wooden boxes—probably Japanese rifle-ammunition cases—rice tubs, shattered planks and strakes of wrecked small craft, bits of frame dwellings, here and there a corpse, floating face down in oily water.

Now they were in the midst of a vast flotilla of landing craft from many ships. Loose groups of LCVPs and LCMs wallowed shoreward with their loads. Singly and in strings empty craft raced back to their parent transports. Among them MacDougall saw boatloads of wounded, going out to the fleet for treatment and rest: the knife, the needle, clean sheets—perhaps a pair of those comical pajamas donated by the Red Cross: unmatched tops and bottoms of wild stripes and splashes of color in this regimented world of khaki and dungaree blue.

At last they reached an unbelievable mass of loaded landing craft, lying to, waiting for permission to land. Having no forward motion, these craft rose and fell with extreme sluggishness, motions of boats no more apathetic than their crews, who lay sprawled over varied cargoes of ammunition, gasoline, water, provisions and all manner of military weapons and equipment. It came as a shock to MacDougall. Out there on the *Belinda*, Pappy Moran and Chief Alvick were working the hearts out of their men, getting the stuff out, racing with crews of other ships to be unloaded first. Here the stuff lay, so near the beach, yet apparently unwanted.

MacDougall looked ahead once more. They were closing in on the beach now: smoke blacker, noise louder, shattered trees and high-piled rubble commanding attention. Out of the corner of his eye he saw a command boat, signal flags. Some extra noise added to thunder and crack of guns ahead. Jones poked him gently and pointed. MacDougall looked to starboard. A young naval officer was yelling something through a power megaphone. MacDougall nodded to Jones, who spun his wheel and closed in on the other craft.

"Where are you going?"

"Red Beach."

"You can't go in. You must wait your turn. Where is your traffic card?"

"Take it easy," said MacDougall as the two boats rubbed sides. "I'm on a special mission for commanding officer, *Belinda*."

"But you have to be assigned priority and wait until your boat is called."

MacDougall looked at the young traffic officer's collar. Single silver bars of a junior lieutenant, shiny new. Looked like a nice enough kid. "Listen, Bud," he said, "unless you shoot me first with that forty-five of yours, I'm going in."

"But you can't—"

"Now take it easy. Your orders concern combat cargo. My
142

orders are direct, from a captain U. S. Navy to our beachmaster. They don't concern you. I'm going to land, then I'll send the boat back to you, load and all. . . . Oh, say—you hungry?"

"Why—yes."

"Here. How about ham sandwiches? Take some for your boat crew. . . . So long, now." MacDougall prodded Jones and the LCVP lumbered towards the beach.

Markers of gay-colored bunting showed the limits of Red Beach One and indicated spots for loading various types of combat cargo. A helmeted but barefoot sailor with a carbine slung like a small toy across his broad back waved the boat in with a pair of semaphore flags. It was Boski, big signalman from the *Belinda* beach party. This was the right place. Jones ran his boat against Kwajalein sand and dropped the ramp, MacDougall waded ashore, waved Jones off the beach and turned to look for information. Boski was busy down the beach, directing another boat. MacDougall spotted Whitey McClintock, another of O'Bannion's men. "Hello, Whitey," he said. "Where's Mr. O'Bannion?"

"He's over on the other flank of the beach with Hatcher. They're blasting coral."

"I see. Where's Mr. Sherwood? I didn't see him out with boat traffic."

A shadow passed over McClintock's phlegmatic face. "He's up there, sir."

MacDougall followed the direction of McClintock's arm, which was aimed at a large khaki tent. Over the roof of the tent and in front of it were white bunting flags, each marked with a red cross. Perhaps he's visiting Bell, MacDougall thought. They're good friends. Hardly the time for a visit. Couldn't be . . . He pushed aside the canvas fly and stepped into the tent. Inside was a strong mixed odor of sweat, alcohol and ether. Dr. Bell was busy with a litter case. The stretcher rested upon two packing cases, forming a rough table near a fly, open to air circulation and daylight. A Coleman lamp cast strong light down upon the face of the wounded soldier. He was a little older than the average, probably a platoon sergeant. His leg was badly shattered. Bell worked without a false move. He's quick, MacDougall thought, standing to one side where Bell could see him and speak when he had a chance. After several minutes Bell looked around and saw MacDougall. "Yes, Mac," he said without hesitating in his work. "Want something?"

"Looking for Sherwood."

Bell worked on, taking clamps and forceps from his corpsman. At last he paused and jerked a thumb over his right shoulder. "He's over there," Bell said. His voice sounded a little unsteady. MacDougall looked sharply into Bell's face, but the

143

doctor was concentrating on the sergeant again. "More plasma, Jim," he said to his corpsman.

MacDougall looked around the tent at faces of wounded men lying on litters all about. Some looked apathetic, some were twisted with pain; all had that singularly patient look common to wounded men. But these faces were strange to MacDougall. They were wounded and he felt sympathy for them, but they were the anonymous wounded. There was just one more litter in the tent. The form of a tall man lay upon it, perfectly still, with a blanket over his face so that ankles and long feet were exposed. Dread fear, which had been slowly creeping upon MacDougall since he reached the shore, struck hard now. The feet were covered with stained canvas tennis shoes. His thoughts went back to the little alcove in the *Belinda's* wardroom: fellows gathered for supper; Sherwood's lanky form sprawled over a chair, legs reaching out towards the center of the group so that when Quigley arrived he could not fail to see those non-regulation tennis shoes. And then this morning—could it have been this same morning? Still dark, boat davits whining, mass of troops shuffling towards debarkation nets. Sherwood with one thin leg over the side of the command boat, singing at 4 A.M., "Oh, What a Beautiful Morning."

MacDougall pulled back the blanket carefully. Sherwood's face was pale. The eyes were closed and the facial expression was completely relaxed, as if he were back in his bunk on the *Belinda*, resting from a tough go in the boats. How that man could sleep! But there was something different here; a remoteness, a finality of repose. He's far away, thought MacDougall as a shudder worked its way up the tightness of his chest . . . so far away. He'll never kid me any more.

MacDougall stumbled outside the tent. While looking for Sherwood he had forgotten the noise, the coral dust. Now the endless concussions of bombs and shells pressed into his eardrums again. Here came McClintock, bringing five-gallon cans of water for the wounded. "What happened to Mr. Sherwood, Whitey?"

McClintock put down the two cans and wiped at the sweat which ran down his stolid face from under short-cropped hair. "I don't know, exactly. . . . It was just before we reached the beach. . . . Ain't quite sure what happened." McClintock wasn't a talker; give him time. MacDougall looked down at the stocky sailor intently, keeping his silence. "You see," McClintock continued, "we was back in the third wave with the beach-party boat, and Mr. Sherwood was up ahead with the first of the VPs. We was watching the beach mostly, but I saw Mr. Sherwood stand up in the boat and signal with his flags. 'Close up.' That's what it was. And then he just fell down in the boat real sudden. Hatcher says he saw splashes in the water: ma-

144

chine gun bullets . . . but I don't know for sure." McClintock paused in his slow account, dabbing at his face, though the sweat was gone. "I—well, we had to get our gear ashore. Doc Bell couldn't do nothing for him, I guess."

"Thanks, Whitey," said MacDougall. He patted McClintock's solid shoulder, harder than he had intended. "Mr. O'Bannion still up the beach?"

"Yes, sir. Right across that little point there. You go right that-a-way." McClintock pointed over a slight rise in the shell-pocked ground, then picked up his water cans again. Mac-Dougall nodded and scrambled up the loose sand.

At the top of the rise he gasped with astonishment. The tip of Kwajalein looked like a tremendously expanded child's sand-box after play. Scoopfuls of sand were tons of crushed coral and island soil, scoured out and thrown up in heaps by battleship projectiles. Little sticks were coconut trees, broken, shattered, lying this way and that. Blocks were pillboxes, lifted explosively from carefully prepared positions, tops off, sitting on corners as if tossed there by some disinterested hand. There were guns: broken, twisted, some pointing back from the sea, lifted bodily and twisted around by the bombardment; but they were not toys. They were guns from Yokosuku dockyard and guns captured at Singapore. There were soldiers too, not toys but discarded like broken toys. From a distance they did not seem like men or even things that had once been men. There was no question in MacDougall's mind but that they were dead. The only things to disturb the fantasy of the overgrown sandbox were dozens of shattered coconut stumps from which were suspended countless telephone wires, tangled, crisscrossing endlessly, yet eventually leading to various units up in battle line.

MacDougall took a step forward. His foot caught on a half-buried coconut log, tripping him so that he fell hard, face down. He put out his hands to get up, placing them on what seemed to be another log. Hands sank into something warm and yielding, like soft putty. He tried to take his hands away from the corpse and fell again, rolling sideways away from it. He got up and wiped his hands up and down against his thighs. He had rolled into a small shell crater. Erect now, he could see at his feet the sand-filled remains of a pillbox. Japanese here had evidently been dead since the first bombardment, several days before. Their bodies were seared and bloated; the stench was sickening. One was half-buried in sand. For a moment Mac-Dougall was not sure whether or not he had on any clothes. Then he realized that the body had neither clothes nor skin. All clothing and skin had been burned from his back, the remaining flesh was dark brown, dried in the sun. His head lay a few feet from his body. One of his mates reminded Mac-Dougall of a bronze statue in San Francisco's Golden Gate

Park. Helmet still on, he crouched face down, both hands holding to a coconut log of his pillbox. It was the sand which seemed merciful, MacDougall thought; it had done its best to cover these men. Then he went on, looking for O'Bannion, stepping over and around many other wrecked pillboxes and gun mounts, each with its pattern of death.

At last he came to the beach again, where he found Mike O'Bannion, vibrant and very much alive, working waist deep in sloshing water. Leaving Hatcher and other beach-party men, Mike lumbered up from the reef to greet him. "Well, well, Mac. Nice to see you." Then in explanation: "The stuff is rolling in over the left flank of my beach. Coral pinnacles on this side . . . good beach isn't wide enough . . . holding up the boats."

"Yes, I saw boats—hundreds of 'em—waiting turns out there. What are you doing here? Getting ready to blast?"

"That's right," said O'Bannion. "Some of those two hundred-ton LCTs are due here at high tide. I don't want trouble so I'm cutting the tops off the coral. My lads are well-organized now, with Mike O'Bannion to show the way."

MacDougall grinned. "I don't doubt that. . . . The Old Man was worried about you and Sherwood; couldn't raise you on those fouled-up radio circuits. He sent me in to find out the score."

"They tell you about Sherwood?"

"Yes, I saw him."

Mike sighed. "Well, we've got to get on with the job. . . . How did you come from the landing?"

"Across there. What a mess!"

"Yes. I want to show you something." Mike led the way to a shattered pillbox situated just above the battered revetment. It had no doorway; the entire entrance had been blown away by some tremendous explosion, exposing construction details of large coral blocks. "It's a big place," said Mike. "I found it while looking for a sheltered spot for Chuck Palmer's radio gear—all this rain, you know. We need a shelter for night work too: can't show a light—these snipers—"

"It is big! Looks like just the thing."

"Well, yes, but there's something about it don't sit well on Mike O'Bannion."

"What do you mean?"

"Come here. I'll show you." O'Bannion led the way down a rough slope into the dim interior of the pillbox. The place had a queer, musty smell, which to MacDougall was strangely reminiscent of the Orient. A broad shaft of light entering through the shell-blasted entrance was alive with dancing dust particles. Like one in a strange dream he tried to look through the light to O'Bannion, but all he could see was vague shadow. Then he climbed over the rubble to the inner dusk where O'Bannion now stood. "Look here, Mac." O'Bannion held up a bundle of clothing, clean and neatly folded: socks, underwear, white trousers and blouse of a Japanese Navy chief machinist's mate. "See. Here's his shoes, all shined up for Saturday inspection—even got his name cut in Jap characters at the back of the heels. . . . And look at this." O'Bannion reached into a small wooden box neatly lettered in characters. He handed MacDougall a bundle of letters from Japan, the top one looking as if it had been handled often. While MacDougall paused, weighing the letters thoughtfully in his hand, O'Bannion passed him some dog-eared photos, about post-card size. MacDougall held them up in the shaft of light and saw what evidently was a family group: a pudgy petty officer in wrinkled summer whites, with a rather young woman in a neat kimono at his left. In front of them sat two young daughters, each dressed in the shapeless middy blouse and short skirt of Japanese schoolgirls. MacDougall looked carefully at the family group, then glanced at the others. Some showed the same little man with shipmates, standing before a cheap backdrop simulating a battleship. Another showed the family bathing at some coast resort, the Inland Sea perhaps. MacDougall handed them back to O'Bannion without comment. There seemed to be nothing to say. O'Bannion put the stuff back in the boxes. "It's too bad," he said at last. "This is a snug spot for beachmaster's headquarters, but—well, you know I've got two little girls myself, back in Boston."

They looked around the place carefully. It seemed to have been a storeroom for provisions and spare parts and naval guns at the point. A number of plain-looking bunks, each with its small store of clothing and personal articles, indicated that the compartment had doubled as berthing space. There were no bodies; the occupants had either been on duty elsewhere or had been in that portion of the pillbox which had been destroyed.

As the two men stepped outside into sudden sunshine—once again louder gunfire, fresh sea breeze replacing musty Asiatic odors—Hatcher came running up the beach. "Mr. O'Bannion. Mr. O'Bannion. . . . That last charge didn't go off. I tested the battery—seems all right. . . . Think we ought to wait, sir?"

"No waiting today, lad. Those LCTs will be here any time now. How many sticks you got there this time?"

"Just one, sir—tied to a pinnacle, kind of small."

O'Bannion started down into the water. "Well, Mike O'Bannion's not waiting for one stick of dynamite this day."

"Mike," called MacDougall. "Wait a minute." O'Bannion was wading out to the coral and did not seem to hear. MacDougall ran to the detonating battery and jerked the wires from the binding posts. O'Bannion was beside the coral pinnacle. It looked like a small affair, just big enough to hang up a big,

147

flat-bottomed landing craft like an LCT. A wave swept past, swelling the water a little above O'Bannion's waist, then receded below his knees. O'Bannion drew back his right foot and kicked hard with his heavy beach shoe, trying to scatter the charge. Immediately there was a sharp explosion. O'Bannion collapsed in the water while smoke bubbled up and drifted up the beach.

Hatcher and MacDougall plunged into the water, followed by others of Hatcher's gang. They picked up O'Bannion and carried him to dry sand. MacDougall turned quickly from the welling blood, appraised Hatcher's men swiftly, picked a wiry youngster who looked as if he could run. "You go get Dr. Bell as fast as you can run. Get some corpsman and a litter. Now beat it."

O'Bannion's right boot was opened up like a half-peeled banana. His foot was bleeding profusely and appeared to be a hopeless mess of pulp and small, protruding bones. O'Bannion's face was white and sweat rolled down his face. "What did I do that for?" he groaned. "I must have hit the cap. . . . I must have hit the cap!"

MacDougall was down on his knees, twisting his large white handkerchief tightly around O'Bannion's ankle, using a bit of shell for a toggle, setting it tighter as blood flow stained white into crimson. "It's all right, Mike," he said. "We'll have you to Bell in a minute. Everything's all right, Mike." And his heart was telling him, what a lie that is. Everything is not all right. Everything is fouled up; the whole world is fouled up. Then he noticed that he was holding Mike's hand and Mike was squeezing it back hard, sweat still running down his face, jaw trembling now from pain and shock. Then O'Bannion grinned, a sickly grin, but that's what it was. "You gol darned old Irishman," said MacDougall. "What's so funny now?"

"I was thinking . . . about you—that last dry run." O'Bannion spoke slowly and with difficulty between clenched teeth that were beginning to chatter. "Careless of you to get caught—smashed up like you did . . . in that boat."

Time. It was time he must stall for. MacDougall continued to banter, to insult Mike O'Bannion, but all the time he held tightly to his hand and fought to hold back the tears. Then he looked up and there was Doc Bell, puffing from his run across the point. How good he looked!

Bell stooped over O'Bannion's shattered foot. "What's the matter with you guys?" he said. "You need a wet nurse around here; that's what you need!" Then he reached into his bag and began to work on O'Bannion's foot. He checked the bleeding at last, gave the beachmaster a syrette of morphine for the intense pain. Then Hatcher and his boys picked up the litter carefully and started along the beach towards the landing place. O'Bannion's eyes were closed.

Walking with Bell behind the litter, MacDougall said, "I think I know how he feels. After a while the waves of pain take over and you snuggle down inside them as if they were blankets."

"You don't want to get too cozy," said Bell. "I've seen more than one man slip away like that."

"Not old Mike. He's too full of fight."

"Yes, no doubt of that. The only trouble—" Bell looked out over the offshore reef for a few moments, watching busy destroyers and minesweepers without really seeing them. "The only trouble is . . . I'm afraid that Mike will have to do his fighting from now on without that foot."

MacDougall had feared this might be the answer, yet the actual words came as a shock. "What a hell of a day this has been," he said at last. "Of all the fellows on the ship, the two I've felt closest to were you and Sherwood. And Mike—you know how he is: bull of the woods, into everything. What a flat empty crate the *Belinda* will be without Mike O'Bannion!"

Bell put a friendly hand on MacDougall's shoulder. "Take it easy, Mac. You know how it is."

"You shut up!" said MacDougall suddenly, wrenching his shoulder away from Bell's hand. "Don't you go and feed me that crap about there's no indispensable man—not today; not you, Frank."

Bell stopped walking and looked directly at MacDougall. "You're a funny guy, Mac," he said quietly. "Let's get old Mike back to the *Belinda* as quick as we can—save him the shock of a second move later on. Perhaps Pat Flynn can save the foot."

They're just kind words, MacDougall thought. Bell's an orthopedic specialist. He knows there's no chance for that foot. But he ran on ahead, looking for a boat.

A VP was just retracting from Red One as MacDougall arrived. B-21 on the stern, Tommy Jones's boat. MacDougall tried to hail him back, but with his injured throat shouting was impossible. Boski came and bellowed, but Jones had his eyes set on the smoky horizon and his diesel engine exhaust thrust back at them as he made his turn and headed out, sound fading gradually until the craft was lost among thousands in the lagoon.

"Stop the next *Belinda* boat, Boski. If we put Mr. O'Bannion on some other ship's boat he may never get back to the *Belinda*." Boski nodded. He was busy signaling in one boat after another. O'Bannion was flat on a litter, but the organization he had set up was rolling smoothly. Boats slid in, touched sand, dropped ramps. Beach-party sailors held them from broach-

149

ing to. Shore-party soldiers ran down to unload package stuff, gasoline and ammunition. Bulldozers were there to haul out guns, drag palleted shells for the field artillery, cases of C rations and small arms ammunition to back up the line. Some of the lighter guns were attached to jeeps. The instant ramps dropped, jeep drivers wheeled up the sandy slope in four-wheel drive. If they stuck, a bulldozer waited with a towline. Nothing was allowed to stand still—motion everywhere on Red Beach. Thirty-six ton LCMs came splashing in to drop two-ton steel ramps with rattle and thud. Out of them rolled thirty-ton tanks, more bulldozers, chewing sand and riding with ease up and over everything on their way to the line.

Bell had returned to his wounded. MacDougall waited beside Mike O'Bannion, waited for any boat with the big *B* painted white on sea-gray ramp. MacDougall was concerned about replacements for O'Bannion and Sherwood. He wanted to stay on the beach and take over, but his orders from Gedney were to return and to report. "Ask Mr. Palmer to come here," he said to McClintock. Chuck Palmer came at once, grimy, mussed up in contrast to his customary well-shaven neatness aboard the *Belinda*. "Got the ship yet, Chuck?"

"Yes, sir. It was a communications madhouse the first few hours. I can get a message through in about fifteen minutes now, sometimes sooner."

"Report Sherwood and this accident to O'Bannion?"

"Yes, I did. Want me to send anything further?"

"The Old Man'll have to send somebody out to take over here on the beach. These boys are swell; they know their work, but they can't argue successfully with three stripers." MacDougall grinned. "I like to argue, but I have to go back aboard and report to Gedney."

"Oh, I should have reported to you—" Palmer hesitated.

"Yes?"

"I got word from the *Belinda:* Tony Brooks has been ordered to take over the boat group and Bosun Torgeson is on his way here to act as beachmaster."

"Fine," MacDougall said, thinking: boat commander number three, beachmaster number two. Who's next? He said, "Well, here comes a *Belinda* VP. Next time you raise the ship, tell them I'm on my way back with O'Bannion."

MacDougall felt a tug at his wet khaki pants—Mike O'Bannion, reaching from his litter. "I want Hatcher; want to talk to him." They got Hatcher. The sharp-eyed boy from Arkansas leaned down over O'Bannion's litter.

"Yes, Mr. O'Bannion."

O'Bannion was nearly under from drugs and from shock; his voice soft as the voice of a man coming from another room, yet as he filled his great lungs for each few words, inner fire of the man came with them. "Hatcher, lad . . . remember the things . . . Mike O'Bannion taught you. . . . Keep the beach clear. . . . Don't let the boats broach to. . . . Always keep the stuff movin' in."

"Yes, sir, Mr. O'Bannion. We'll take care of things."

O'Bannion closed his eyes. Later on, at the sound of an approaching boat he opened them again, saw Hatcher still waiting beside him. "You'd better . . . take care of things . . . or the back . . . of me hand . . . to you!"

The boat's ramp dropped and Hatcher sprang to attend to its unloading. Then they carried O'Bannion into the boat. As they retracted from Red Beach and headed out to find the *Belinda*, MacDougall chuckled for the first time since he had tossed ham sandwiches to the young junior lieutenant. That Mike O'Bannion, he thought, looking down at the silent, bulky form of the beachmaster, now quiet in the litter beside him. He's like that old Boston fire horse his father used to drive: crippled on an icy street, down but still breathing fight. Wouldn't surprise me at all if he comes around in a minute and starts telling the cox'n how to get his VP back to the ship!

Wash water was turned on that evening between seven and eight. MacDougall took a shower and lay down in his bunk. He felt very tired, but tossed restlessly, unable to sleep. He felt utterly miserable and depressed. His thoughts went back to Sherwood: singing before dawn of a beautiful morning, dead on a litter before noon. If it were only possible to live this day over with things perhaps turning out differently, the timing changed just enough to avoid— Perhaps they had botched it; perhaps he could have cautioned his friends: Sherwood not to expose himself, O'Bannion— Why, he'd had a lot of experience with underwater demolition in Hawaii before the war; he should not have let O'Bannion take such a—never, never. Never another chance in a war; each day final, finished like those Japs on Red Beach.

MacDougall lay on his back thinking about the landing beach on Kwajalein, thinking about Mike O'Bannion, his roommate, now in the sick bay waiting to have a foot off. The bunk beneath was empty, the room utterly still. The little head where O'Bannion used to do his needlework was empty, and so was Flynn's room next door—even "Body" Newth was sufficiently awake to be down in the wardroom. After considerable deliberation and consultation with Bell by radio, Dr. Flynn had decided to leave O'Bannion's foot until he gained strength after the heavy loss of blood. There was no hope for the foot.

151

It was dark in the room except for dim light from the red battle lantern in the passageway outside the room. MacDougall began to count rivets in the overhead, some two feet above his face as he lay in his bunk, staring upward. Thirty-six rivets, one for each year of his life, all tinged blood-red from the battle lantern. He shut his eyes, but still he saw the rows of red rivets. He wanted very much to cry; no one would see him here and it wouldn't matter, yet crying seemed somehow impossible. Crying was for thousands of miles away—at home. Then revulsion took charge. Somehow he got to the head and retched; his whole body shook with misery. He clung to the lintel over the door to the head until his swimming senses settled. Then he crawled back into the bunk and counted the rivets once more: still thirty-six, still blood-red. Sleep seemed impossible. "Oh, I wish I were home with Nadine—just for five minutes," he said softly to the empty room. Five minutes, ten, fifteen, a day, a week, soon gone, done like this day which could never be relived, redone, improved upon. MacDougall swung down from the bunk and moistened his dry mouth from a glass of water saved from water hours, then he snapped on the desk lamp, reached for paper and began to write to his wife. The sentences came tumbling out of him faster than he could scrawl them on paper. He wrote about the island, about O'Bannion and Sherwood. Then he wrote:

The war leaves a stamp on you. You take a bath and don't feel clean. You want a spiritual purge of the whole stinking business. You feel you'd like to be baptized and have communion. You want to lie on the grass and watch the cumulus swimming by in the blue of the sky. You want to have your arms around one very near and dear to you, and snuggle your head deep beside your beloved and feel the tenderness of her lips on yours and the clean warm living scent that is her. And then sleep, and there shall be no more war, no parting, no killing, no smell of death: just peace.

He had other things to tell her: cheerful little things. To-morrow would be soon enough for the rest of it. No chance to mail a letter for weeks anyway. Well, there it was, how he felt written on a bit of paper. Some of the bitterness seemed to have left him, bitterness and misery. It wasn't that he felt sorry for himself; she'd know better than that. He looked at his watch: two hours until midnight and the bridge once more. MacDougall climbed back into his bunk, and this time he slept.

CHAPTER 17

Sunrise battle stations aroused that minority of the *Belinda's* crew which had been allowed a few hours of uneasy sleep. An hour later Gedney left his station on the bridge wing and reentered the pilothouse.

"Randall," he called.

"Yes, sir."

"Secure from general quarters and set Condition One Able. Let the crew have breakfast one section at a time. Keep all the five-inch and half the anti-aircraft guns manned—and watch your lookouts. They have a tendency to look at the shore."

"Aye, aye, sir." Randall spun about and soon the PA passed the word and men of the first section ran whooping to form in the chow line, cheering not at the prospect of mush and beans but with relief at securing from the rigidity of general quarters.

Within half an hour, unloading of combat cargo resumed full swing. Ship's tackle clanged and quavered and voices of Pappy Moran and Alvick were heard fore and aft above the hum of winches. Landing craft splashed and bumped alongside, arms of boat's crews upraised to land slingloads without being crushed under them. Ammunition, gasoline for tanks and for flame throwers, provisions and drinking water in tins still rose from the deep holds, swung overside, then dropped down towards rocking landing craft beneath extended tackle. Most of the tanks, field artillery and bulldozers had been landed on Red Beach. Vehicle hatches now disgorged ambulances, communications jeeps and repair trucks to succor damaged tanks which were reported to be holding up the infantry advance on Kwajalein. The *Belinda* and her sister ships had launched the attack; now they sustained it and cared for the wounded.

Fortified with hotcakes and bad coffee, MacDougall relieved Randall on the bridge. "She's all yours, Mac," said Randall. "Doc Bell is coming out to the ship with sixty more casualties. He'll stay here and work with Flynn. Young Hardwick, the *Belinda's* new doctor, went in to take over. Everything's under control—Fraser's growling around the hatches as usual—permission just granted engine room to blow tubes and pump bilges. Boats are all accounted for—"

"Yes . . . yes," said MacDougall, half listening to the official spiel, regarding anchor chain, bearings and boilers in use. He was running down the list of landing craft, kept on a special blackboard outside the pilothouse bulkhead. He leaned out over the bridge wing and looked up. A light American plane, painted bright red—the sort of plywood craft you saw at home on Sunday afternoons—hovered in the air just off the tip of Kwajalein. Massed artillery on Enubuj still cracked out rapid fire in support of the infantry advancing on the main island. Shells were traveling towards targets some seven miles distant from the firing cannon. No tracers indicated the flight path of these shells, yet it seemed to MacDougall that the small red plane, carrying pilot and observer, must be circling dangerously close. Nothing happened, and Randall went down to get his breakfast.

Randall returned shortly and was first to spot returning *Belinda* LCVPs. At his call, MacDougall hurried over and put his binoculars on the boat. "Yes, that's Kruger all right—Boat Twenty-One," said MacDougall. "Bosun's mate. Pass the word to stand by to receive casualties, starboard side, number five hatch."

MacDougall lowered his binoculars and watched the approach of the wounded. The boats, led by Kruger in Twenty-One, were about a thousand yards from the ship when, from the corner of his vision, he saw a flash in the sky. Looking up, he saw the little red observation plane falling in a helpless sideslip towards the lagoon, wings and cockpit nearly enveloped in a growing mass of yellow flames which streamed away from the direction of fall. The small plane dropped towards cool, fresh air only to have new oxygen add to bright flames until very little red paint remained. MacDougall found himself praying under his breath: "Give him a chance, God, just a chance!" The plane was a small, flaming meteor now. Bits of wing fluttered loose, then a huddled body dropped straight down. MacDougall bit his lower lip, waiting for the parachute to open.

Ensign Kruger sat on the gunwale of LCVP 21, leading the group of six boats, all loaded with wounded on litters, back to the *Belinda*. These were the most seriously wounded, and Kruger had ordered Tommy Jones, his coxswain, to rev up the boat to full speed. Throaty roar of diesel exhaust submerged all other sound, even the cannonade from nearby Enubuj Island. It was a relief to get out of here, away from battle shock and stink of the main island. Kruger looked idly about the horizon and up to the sky. Wind hauling south, blowing the smoke back on Kwajalein. Nice to see clean blue sky again. Then he turned his attention to the *Belinda*, growing larger in his vision as the boat closed in, wondering if Fraser would be ready to hoist them in without delay—without this priority stuff for some tank or boatload of ammunition hanging from ship's tackle. Kruger looked down into the boat. Nine wounded infantrymen lay close together in three rows of three litters each.

Two more litters were lashed across the transom deck, abaft the cockpit, where the boat's motormac stood by to see that they did not roll overboard. The very young deckhand stood near the ramp. He had tried to make conversation with a red-headed sergeant with a shattered leg and wounded hip, but the sergeant just looked at him. The young deckhand shifted his feet between the crowded litters. He wished that they were unloaded and headed back to the beach with C rations. It wasn't the bloody bandages that made him so uneasy—those staring faces, looking at you, looking at you. He couldn't help it if he was all in one piece. Then something in the sky caught his attention: "Look!" he cried, pointing.

Kruger looked up. A ball of fire was dropping straight towards his boat. Pain shot down his back from sudden shock. "Left!" he screamed to Jones. Was that the right direction? Yes, the thing was moving downwind a little as it fell. All these wounded—helpless. Must be that spotting plane. Was it going to miss? Something falling out. A man—small black ball out of a big orange ball. Now the plane overhead, slithering off to starboard, dropping fast but clear of his craft. Black ball of man coming down. A man, not black; yes, black and smoking. "Right, Tommy, right rudder. . . . Now steady. Cut her." Kruger held up his hand. Jones twisted his throttle and the diesel roar died to a sputter, giving place to sharp crack of cannon: guns on Enubuj. Body catapulting down; now white silk of parachute trailing out but not billowing, not opening, not holding him: no good. Splash! That was the body, silk dropping over it like a shroud. "Go alongside, Tommy." Engine roaring at first sound of his voice: Jones right in there. . . . The plane! Where now? Kruger jerked his head around in time to see flame hit the lagoon a ship's length away. Hissing, then no more flames or hissing, just a few bits of stuff floating in the center of spreading ripples. Ripples lost now in slap of small waves; plane gone. Kruger looked ahead of his boat. Jones was drifting up to the floating parachute, backing down on his engine. Kruger took a boat hook from the young deckhand and got hold of the white silk. Then he put down the boat hook and hauled in the parachute, hand over hand. Drops of water from the wet silk splashed on the red-headed sergeant. The deckhand took out a soiled handkerchief and wiped the sergeant's face.

Kruger got hold of the body; yes, it must be just a body. It was limper than anyone could relax, as if every bone were broken. Shattered stubs of bone stuck through torn flesh. Clothes, hair, skin: all burned off. Kruger grasped the shroudlines tightly and dragged the body halfway over the gunwale. The head flopped loosely at the neck like a small door on hinges. Kruger looked at the wrists and around the neck for dog tags: no identification.

It seemed to him that somewhere there must be an order, what to do now. The pilot had been up there on orders, observing, spotting fire for the gun that had shot him down. The gun was fired on orders. Orders had brought him here with this boat. What's the matter with me? Kruger thought. Am I losing my grip? He heard sounds of retching in the boat; it was the red-headed sergeant, helpless on his litter a scant yard from the dead aviator. Something stronger than orders motivated Kruger now. He whipped out his sheath knife, cut the shroud-lines and gently tipped the broken body back into the lagoon. This guy was beyond any help. He must care for the living, get them to Flynn. The body sank slowly from sight. Kruger found himself staring at a few slowly rising bubbles and at a small wooden tub, probably something the Japs used for pickles. It drifted there; the man was gone. Kruger leaned far overside to grab the tub—just why, he was not sure. The parachute. Yes, that was it. He shoved the wet silk into the little tub, yard after yard, as if this in some measure compensated for deserting the remains, then looked Jones in the eye and jerked his thumb upward in signal to go ahead again. Jones shoved in his clutch and roared after the other boats which were already lying to off the *Belinda,* waiting to be hoisted in with their loads of wounded. Kruger's young deckhand bent over the red-headed sergeant, wetting the dirty handkerchief from a canteen, wiping his face again. He wondered if the sergeant would speak to him now.

When his wounded were safely aboard, Kruger went up to the bridge, where Captain Gedney was intently watching discharge of a heavy bulldozer which dangled overside at number three hatch. Kruger had nothing official to report, yet felt compelled to tell the captain what had happened and why he had let the pilot's body go. "I couldn't find his dog tags, Captain . . . and the wounded—"

Gedney found himself responding to Kruger's sincerity, his deep concern, his troubled spirit. Feeling to his surprise more father than commanding officer, Gedney held up a hand, halting any further painful explanations, reconstruction of something which had hit young Kruger hard. This was a good boy here; he had stuff in him; it was important to help him back to firm ground. To get his feet solidly on deck once more would be more in tradition, yet somehow Gedney was thinking not how he must preserve this young man for the Navy, rather for the boy himself. "That's all right, Kruger. Get something to eat; you must eat, you know. Then carry on with the transfer of wounded. Supervise your boat crews; see that wounded are handled gently but avoid every minute of wasted time. Our boats are needed to back up the landing. Wounded must be given every possible attention, but they are of no further use in the action."

"Aye, sir," said Kruger, thinking: he forgot to say that the boats are the *Belinda's* main battery. Kruger felt dull, depressed, all sucked out inside. Heading for the ladder he noticed the small wooden tub under his arm; he had been carrying it all this time without noticing. What to do with it? What good questions or answers about a parachute that hadn't opened? What good the parachute? It never occurred to him that anybody would ever willingly trust his life to that thing again. It had not opened; it was no good—yet here he was hanging on to it as the only tangible thing left from the whole experience. Kruger put the tub down in the after corner of the bridge wing, noticing as he did so that there was something snowy and nice about that white silk, glistening with drops of lagoon water.

Only one seat was vacant in the wardroom. Officers in sweat-stained khaki with sleeves rolled up from sunburned arms sat at the long tables. The usually cheerful wardroom seemed moody and oppressive; officers hunched over plates of lima beans and Spam, eating fast to get out of the humid wardroom and to get back on the job. Kruger took some beans, stared at them, then shoved back his plate and lit a cigarette. Shadow Rockwell, seated opposite, looked at him appraisingly but said nothing.

It was a relief to get out to the slightly cooler air of the open deck. Kruger took a turn aft to see how the wounded were being handled. One at a time boatloads of wounded were being hoisted to the rail and the wounded removed gently and swiftly. Like most other jobs about the ship, a technique had been evolved for handling casualties, like everything else, subject to constant revision, improvement. Satisfied, Kruger turned forward again, only to come face on with Lieutenant Fraser, dour ship's first lieutenant, busy as usual at expediting. Nothing ever quite suited Fraser, no man worked quite smartly enough, no cargo was ever stowed to suit him or unloaded properly. Fraser's red, weather-beaten face reflected disapproval wherever he went. O'Bannion, now helpless in the sick bay, was in charge of forward decks and spaces, MacDougall aft. All three were former masters from the Merchant Marine and provided the backbone of seamanship know-how aboard the *Belinda*. Quigley, even Gedney, gave them a free hand in the handling of cargo and boats. Yet, while these three lieutenants agreed basically, they often disagreed violently over details. MacDougall outranked Fraser and did about as he pleased, which added to Fraser's perpetual scowl. The junior

157

officers assisting MacDougall were the goats. Here was Fraser waiting for him, ready with the blast he'd like to give to MacDougall.

"Ensign Kruger," said Fraser in a loud, belligerent tone, "I want you to keep better check on your men."

"But I—"

"I'm telling *you*. I just caught a seaman from the second division smoking within ten feet of a slingload of gasoline. Three more are flaked out on the fantail asleep. . . . Where's your chief bosun's mate? Why aren't you fellows out here checking up? Want to blow up the ship?"

Kruger gulped. "I don't know, Mr. Fraser. I just—"

"You just attend to your duties. Where you been, loafing in the sack?"

"No, sir, I just got—"

"It doesn't matter. Excuses won't help. Now you go round up that chief of yours who's supposed to be so all-fired efficient. Tell him to knock off this smoking when the smoking light is out. Tell him to check up on the rope slings once in a while. They're using chafed rope slings on that gasoline. We can't have an accident here. Now get going."

"Yes, sir," said Kruger, shouting the words into Fraser's face. He was burning—this seemed so petty after his experience in the boat, but there wasn't any use in arguing with Fraser. The only remedy was to see him first and duck the other way. Kruger went down to the chief's quarters, found the place empty except for the chief watertender just up from the boiler room for a late meal. Kruger went aft again; at last he found Chief Alvick in the after gear locker, pouring with sweat as his nimble fingers tucked a splice into the last of a pile of new rope slings.

Kruger told Alvick about Fraser. Alvick had a temper too —Kruger often wondered what Alvick said from time to time down in the chiefs' quarters. It must be pretty good, but he knew just how far to go with officers. His face looked slightly redder but his voice was even, controlled as he said, "Well, here's his rope slings. . . . Those men on the fantail, sir: that's the first sleep they've had in twenty-four hours. They're handy there where I can get them when I need 'em. I'm not going to wake 'em up, sir."

"Why don't you just get them out of sight, Chief?"

"Yes, I can do that."

"There's no excuse for smoking near the gas."

"That's right, sir, but men get careless when they're tired."

"Maybe so." Kruger turned to climb topside, then paused while a slow grin stole over his earnest, homely face. "They get too tired and careless and we'll all get blown clear out of this lagoon."

Kruger soon forgot about Fraser. From the afterdeck he saw boatloads of wounded converging about the *Belinda*. Boats rose and fell in the gentle chop, engines sputtering idly, boat crews moving restlessly. Men on litters lay still; only occasionally apathetic movements showed life. These wounded aroused curiosity aboard the *Belinda*. Well men paused in their duties to lean over the rail; others thrust heads out portholes, eyes watching, little said. This was something different from routine, which grew dull even one mile from raging battle. Here was evidence of the fight most *Belinda* men had not seen: new exhibits joining with bomb and shell blast, blazing fire and star shell. Sympathy for men in pain, desire to help, yet also intense curiosity. For the moment these watching sailors became sidewalk superintendents at a war.

Alvick left the gear locker and climbed to the deck. "Snap into it, sailors," he called. "Bear a hand here." Heads jerked in; men surged around temporarily neglected slingloads of gasoline and rations, intent now on getting the casualties aboard. Davits whined and blocks slammed as boats were hoisted level with the deck.

Orders from junior petty officers. Cries of warning: "Watch out there, Mac. Steady that block. . . . Easy there, these guys are hurt bad enough already. . . . Watch out, Mac; you'll smash in his skull!" No word from Mac down in the boat, struggling silently with the dangling, swinging block. At last the boat was hooked on. Alvick jerked his thumb. The winchman moved his levers and the dripping boat rose smoothly to the rail, where it was lashed fast. Two pharmacist's mates got into the boat and handed the litters out one at a time to their fellows on deck. Each boat in turn was hoisted to the rail, unloaded quickly but smoothly, then dropped to the water to be replaced with another boatload of wounded. Kruger watched, making no comment, thinking, our own men are getting to look and act more and more like those fellows on the hospital ships. They handle wounded faster and smoother —more and more like so much ammunition, radio gear, bottles of plasma. And the wounded. They want to live. It's really more important to be efficient than just sympathetic.

CHAPTER 18

Shortly after midnight Gedney sent for Kruger.

"Do you know how to get to Ebeye Island, Kruger?"

"Yes, sir. I was there with Brooks yesterday morning."

"A platoon of our troops has been cut off at the tip of Ebeye. They are in danger of being wiped out. The chart shows considerable shoaling a hundred yards from the beach. We can't tell much from these obsolete charts. There should be a small boat passage somewhere; you'll have to look for it. Brooks is in at Red Beach. Do you think you can get the troops off?"

"Well, sir . . . I'd like to try, Capt'n."

"Very well. Take four boats and shove off. There's no time to lose."

"Aye, aye, sir."

Gedney hesitated a moment, then made what for him was a great concession.

"Kruger."

"Yes, Capt'n."

"Take your orders from the senior officer present, regardless of service."

Star shells burst above a thick blanket of smoke-contaminated cloud, lighting Ebeye Island with a ghostly tropical aurora. Kruger groped through black lagoon waters less than a hundred yards from the beach, leading his string of four LCVPs. A near collision with the superstructure of a sunken wreck had made him cautious. He moved along slowly, trying to ignore flash and sound of nearby action, concentrating on his search for the rendezvous with a boat expected to be waiting for him just outside the reef. He was near the north tip of Ebeye and by all appearances a sharp action was taking place on the small island. Where was that boat? One black shape proved to be the floating roof of a shattered dwelling, another just an empty box floating close at hand yet looking like a distant boat. At last he found a landing craft and, sighing with relief, he drifted alongside. Deckhands reached out and held the two boats together. Kruger faced two officers, silhouettes in dim light wearing helmets and kapok life jackets.

"I'm from the *Belinda*," said Kruger. "Understand there's trouble ashore. My orders are to help if possible."

"You the boat commander?" snapped the smaller of the two officers.

"No. He's at Red Beach. I'm Kruger, the assistant. Captain Gedney sent me in here."

"I'm Major Scott," said the larger of the two officers, a deep-chested man with an M-1 slung on his shoulder. "Do you know Lieutenant Chesney, here?"

Kruger took a deep breath. He wished he didn't know this little wise guy from the commodore's staff. He said, "Yes, sir, I know him."

"I'm from regimental HQ," said the major. "We're after two platoons—perhaps a whole company, or what's left of one. They're along the beach here somewhere. I'd like to take a try for them."

Chesney broke in. "I told you before, I tell you now, Major.

You can't get in there. There's a secondary reef between us and the shore. A boat'll just get hung up there until daylight, and you know what'll happen then."

Silence in both boats until Kruger drawled, "Well, we can't just sit here. The least thing we can do is to try."

Chesney exploded, "Oh you *Belinda* people! Wise guys, that's what you are! There's no passage through the reef." Chesney leaned out from his craft to wiggle his finger under Kruger's nose. "I got a Silver Star at Attu that says you can't make it!"

"This puts me on the spot," said the major. "You're the Navy. I can't order you in, but I need help."

"You got a flashlight in the boat, Cox?" Kruger asked.

"Yes, sir."

"Let me have it." Kruger squatted in the boat, covered the flashlight with his hands and tested it. Then he stood up. "Well, Major, I'm going in. Want to come along? My skipper told me to take orders from the senior officer present. Army or Navy. That's you, ain't it?"

"That's me," said the major. He waited until the two boats rubbed together again, then jumped into Kruger's craft.

"Well, I've got useful work to do," said Chesney in a sour, angry voice. "Open her up, Cox'n. Back to Red Two."

The roar of Chesney's boat faded away. Kruger called softly into the darkness, "Vinson."

A head bobbed up in the nearest of the three boats. "Yes, sir."

"Drop your hook, Vinson. Tie up the other two boats alongside. Let out a good scope of line. . . . Understand?"

"Yes, sir." Movement in the boat and an anchor splashing.

"All right. Keep everybody quiet. Keep blacked out. If you smoke, get down in the boat. Don't use your flashlight if you can help it. Don't come after me. If I'm not back when it begins to get light, go back to the *Belinda* and report. Got that now?"

"Y-yes, sir."

"Now listen, Vinson. What do you like to eat?"

"Me? Oh, pork chops, I guess."

"O.K. If I can't find you in the dark when I come back, I'll call, 'Vinson.' Then you yell, 'Pork chops,' just once. Well, so long."

"So long, Mr. Kruger. Good luck."

Kruger turned to the coxswain of his own boat. "All right, Jones, listen carefully now. I'm going to ease the ramp nearly flat, shade a light and try to find a channel through this coral. The major will pass the word along to you. O.K., Major?"

"You bet. Let's go."

"Don't gun your motor, Jones," Kruger said. "We don't want to rip out the bottom; don't want to be heard, either." Kruger scrambled forward in the boat. The deckhand released the ramp catch and Jones lowered the ramp carefully. Squatting beside

161

it, Kruger watched. "Hold it, now," he called softly. The top of the ramp was about two feet above calm lagoon water, forming a slanting platform. Kruger got the flashlight and crawled out on the ramp.

"You may draw fire if you show a light," said the major.

"Can't help it," said Kruger. "Five men for two hundred is a good gamble."

"That's right," agreed the major. "Here, shield it with his life jacket."

Kruger turned his back to shore. Leaning outboard where ramp hinged to hull, he lowered the kapok life jacket vertically to the water, put the tip of his watertight torch under the calm surface and turned it on. A new, beautiful world suddenly opened to his startled eyes. Green water, crystal clear in a great coral chalice. Coral nubbins reaching up within inches of the keel. Boat drifting over deep pothole now: graceful coral fan and sea grasses, flash of striped fish attracted by his light then frightened away to unseen hiding place. Kruger flicked off the light; as suddenly, black nothingness again. He called to Tommy Jones, "Shove in your clutch and ease ahead, Tommy." The boat moved ahead slowly, then drifted again. Once more the shaded light: crags of coral rising to the surface. "Back down," Kruger called in a hoarse whisper, passed along by Major Scott. Sound of propeller shaft grinding astern. "Easy now." Coral grinding under the bottom. The major and the deckhand shoved off with boat hooks. "Here's the reef line," said Kruger. "Come right, Tommy. Ahead easy. . . . Must be a hole somewhere along here."

"Should be," said the major. "Got to be. . . . You're heading south, safe direction: towards our lines. But no telling just where the Japs are."

The boat crawled along in darkness, now and then bumping the reef, sheering off, veering back to bump again. Then they stuck. Kruger kneeled on the offshore side of the ramp, carefully tried the light. Coral on both sides. "Back her down, Tommy. Keep backing. . . . Pole off, you fellows. That's good. Now come ahead easy on right rudder. . . . Let her coast." The light once again; once more the beauty of underwater stalagmites. Kruger found the lagoon side of the reef, followed along, bumping again, muttering to himself, hoping, praying for an entrance. He found a narrow gap and started in. "No. Back out, Tommy. No good."

"What's the matter?" asked the major.

"Too shallow for a loaded boat. We'd never get out through there with your men if we found them."

"Time's wasting."

"I know, Major, but we've got to do this right." More groping, then at last a boat passage, full fathom deep and wide

162

enough for the nine-foot beam of the landing craft, with a few inches to spare. Flares further south illuminated the shore line. Ahead it was dark, tall coconut trees overhanging the water. Kruger stretched face down across the ramp. He must be very careful this time with the light. Lowering one end of the life jacket until it trailed in the water, he dunked the flashlight and turned it on. So clear the water, the boat seemed to float in empty air. Sand now, beautiful pink and white coral sand, tiny particles gleaming in the light, shelving gently towards the beach. They were over the reef now; no more need of the light. Even as Kruger pulled the button back a nerve-chilling squeal sounded from under nearby trees. Kruger nearly dropped the torch, managed to get it off, then lay on his stomach across the ramp with fear clutching at him. Japs there; they often imitated animals. Was he too far north now—or too far south? His first thought was to stop the engine and drift away. No, too much noise starting that diesel engine again, and the boat was too big to pole along. Jones pulled his clutch to neutral, wondering through his fear what Kruger would do now. All five men in the boat listened, momentarily holding breath, mouths hanging open with the intensity of listening. The squeal again—gurgling squeal as through a cut throat. Kruger crawled back into the cockpit and ordered the ramp up.

"What do you make of it?" he asked the major.

"Japs or pigs; not sure which. Lots of Japs squeal like pigs in night action—not much sense to it, but they do."

"Let's go north a little," said Kruger. "About where we started in." He clambered past Jones and stepped up on the transom deck where the motor-mac trained a cocked machine gun towards deeper blackness of shore. "Don't get buck fever now, Hanson. Probably our own men in there. Hold fire unless I order you to fire. Understand?" Hanson grunted unhappily. He wanted to shoot at something, shoot at that squeal, that's what he wanted to do.

Kruger got down in the cockpit beside the major, both men peering over the gunwale towards shore. "Look's like the end of the island up there, Major. This must be about right. Want to try it?"

"Might as well."

"Head for the beach, Tommy." Kruger went forward to the ramp, followed by the major with his M-1. As the boat crawled shoreward they listened acutely. At last, in spite of battle noise, they were able to hear gentle lapping of lagoon water against the beach. Kruger had the feeling that he was running into a trap. No help for that now. "Hit the beach, Tommy." The boat slid up to shore and came to a final stop. Tommy Jones lowered the ramp quietly. Hanson stood by his gun. Then they waited, watched, listened. Nothing to see but dark shapes of shrub and

163

tree silhouetted against distant fires. Nothing to hear but far-away bombardment and semi-distant rifle fire. Nearby only the gentle wash against the beach; not even twigs snapping.

Major Scott took a deep breath. "Blanchard," he called. Kruger jumped: the called name more startling than the sudden crack of old Gun Two on the *Belinda*. They waited, wondering what to do now.

"Wonder where they are," Kruger said. The major said nothing. He was straining to hear the slightest sound, thumb on the safety of his M-I. "I don't know which way to go from here," said Kruger. "Do you think . . . ?" The major clapped a hand on his shoulder, silencing him. What was that? Underbrush rustling. Yes, somebody out there.

Then a clear voice in the night: "Ferry to Ashtabula?"

"That you, Blanchard?"

Tones of relief in the answer. "Yes. You Major Scott?"

"Right. Got your men? Let's go."

Suddenly he was there in front of them, this Captain Blanchard, a big man with the quick, light movements of a cat. He reached out and grasped Scott's forearm, squeezed it hard. "Man!" said Blanchard. "You don't know how . . . We were cut clean off; got ahead and lost contact with the right flank entirely. Radio haywire. Runners never got back—no contacts at all—Japs everywhere, crawling, sneaking, hiding. When they charged it wasn't so bad. You knew what was coming. You—"

"Sure, sure," said Scott. "Let's go now."

Blanchard sucked in a deep, uneven breath, then peered out into the empty blackness that was the lagoon. "Just one boat?"

"Three more outside the reef," said Kruger, stepping forward. "Fill her up. I'll bring the others in quick as I can." Blanchard spoke to a platoon sergeant and men streamed out from the cover of shrubbery, glancing nervously about before they crossed the ramp and crowded close in the boat. Kruger stood on the wet sand beside the ramp, watching these soldiers from out of the night, feeling their warmth and aliveness, sharing their sense of relief. For them the worry and fear, the anxious search—and now, because of them, the nearest thing to happiness he had experienced in days.

From the other side of the ramp Scott scanned the shrubbery, alert for Japs.

"Where the Japs now?" he asked Blanchard.

"Hard to tell, Major. All around, I think. We've been cut off from the battalion and HQ for hours. It's quiet now, but I lost men just a few minutes ago. Ever since the pigpen it's been fouled up."

"Pigpen? . . . Well, never mind now. How many men you got?"

164

"Hundred sixty—if I'm lucky."

"I'll keep coming 'til I get you all," Kruger said. "You staying with your men?"

"Yes," said Blanchard. "We'll take a defensive position right here."

"O.K. I'll try to make time," said Kruger, jumping aboard and crabbing along the gunwale to the controls. "Ramp up," he ordered. "All right, Tommy, back her off." Engine roared astern but the boat failed to move. "Rock her, you fellows," cried Kruger. "She's stuck. Everybody to the right . . . now to the left." Jones gunned his engine to full power. The boat began to slide back into the 'goon. "That's the stuff. Keep backing, Tommy. Work her clear of the sand. . . . Now you've got her. Open up and get out of here!"

Kruger ran south in a burst of full power, then slowed down to look for the reef passage. Finding it much easier than he had any reason to expect, he got through, checked his time and ran wide open towards the other three boats. Once again he stared for low shapes in the water. He must work fast: three more boat loads and daylight coming soon. This tension was not shared by his passengers. "What a safe feeling out here," one of the soldiers remarked.

"Yes," said the man next to him. "Cockeyed Navy giving round-trip rides. I thought they was on the way home already."

"Keep a'going, Cox!" yelled another. "Take me to Brooklyn."

"Pipe down, you fellows," said Kruger. "We got to find those boats and get the rest off." Then he thought, what difference does it make? You can hear the engine for a mile. . . . But I've got to find those boats. At last he made them out: darker spots in darkness. Forgetting his password he gunned alongside Vinson. Speed was the thing now. Kruger jumped into Vinson's boat. "Tommy, you follow me to the reef entrance with the other two boats. Anchor there and mark the spot for me."

"I'll go for the ride," said the major, jumping in beside Kruger. Restless from the long wait, Vinson opened up his engine and ran south to Kruger's directions. Kruger had his timing in hand now. He found the hole on the first try, left Jones and the other boats outside, slid inside the reef and ran back to the landing. Captain Blanchard filled the second boat with his men. Kruger got away and took them out through the reef.

Ten minutes later he was back with the last two boats; Jones at the wheel of one, having changed places with the regular coxswain. Kruger ran both craft up on the beach with the greatest confidence he had felt all night. Silence was his only greeting—no sign of Blanchard or any of his men.

"Now what's the matter?" said Kruger. "Must have run over the spot."

"Better wait," said the major. "Blanchard can correct easier

165

than you can." Kruger waited, listening for rustling in the bushes—or that squealing again. Then, without warning sound, Blanchard came out of the shadows with the last of his men. He was short of breath and had nothing to say. There was plenty of room in the two boats.

"That everybody?" asked the major.

"Far as I know."

"Shove off, Cox'n," said Kruger.

All four boats ran southward in deep lagoon water well outside the reef. Off to port, behind the Japanese seaplane ramp, artillery shells were exploding among already burning fuel storage dumps. Kruger picked out Blanchard from clustered helmets in the boat and jumped down beside him.

"Those Japs squealing"—Kruger said—"did you hear those Japs squealing like pigs?"

Blanchard turned from watching the fires. "Those weren't Japs—just pigs."

"Pigs! You mean to say—"

"Listen, brother," said Blanchard. "Plenty more besides you Navy guys got scared crapless by those pigs running loose. Japs chased them out of the pigpen and took over. When we got to the pigpen it wasn't pigs that shot us up!"

MacDougall completed the last entry in the midnight-to-four rough log, tossed the pencil on the chart table and pushed his way through blackout screens and men on watch to the open bridge wing. Here he gulped in fresh air and looked about: star shells hanging in the air three and four at a time, fires burning, boats churning the lagoon, heard but unseen. Kruger—where was Kruger? All *Belinda* landing craft accounted for except Kruger's little flotilla of four VPs. MacDougall searched the sector of black water towards Ebeye. He ought to be out there doing something. This waiting—one overwhelming sea on a fool practice run had smashed his life in the boats. All the trouble happened in shallow water. Ship always safe in deep water: dangers about but never harming, it seemed. The surf took its toll: Sherwood, O'Bannion . . . And now Kruger out there, and not a word from him since he left. MacDougall was tempted to wake up Jim Randall on his camp cot: somebody to talk to.

MacDougall paced back and forth. After several turns his foot struck something: that wooden bucket with the parachute Kruger had left in the corner of the bridge. Kruger still had a chance, but not this fellow. The chute hadn't opened for him. The chute—MacDougall bent down and picked it up, feeling the soft of wet nylon, noting the glow of dim light reflected in its snowy whiteness. Such an innocent, inanimate thing, but it hadn't opened. MacDougall had the odd feeling that the dead

166

pilot was very close to him. "I'm sorry, fellow," he said softly, thinking that it might have been either of two of his nephews who were fliers. "Just a nice kid," he said. Then he put the chute back in the bucket and went to check the ship's position.

While he hunched over the pelorus he heard a splashing alongside and a voice calling out, "On deck there: man the davits and hoist us in!" Kruger's voice, back safe from Kwajalein shallows.

CHAPTER 19

The PA again, jarring into the night. "Stand by to transfer casualties." MacDougall turned over the bridge to Randall and limped aft to take charge. The *Belinda* lay to her anchor, completely blacked out in Kwajalein Lagoon, yet moonlight washed the afterdeck with helpful light. MacDougall saw Dr. Flynn, just out from the sick bay.

"All ready, Pat?"

"Well, Mac, that depends on how you look at it. I'm still protesting this fool stunt of moving wounded men to the *Woodbridge* when it isn't necessary. But everything's ready—the wounded, that is. They're just as ready for moving as we can get them. . . . You going to take charge of the boats?"

"Yes, the Old Man sent me down to see they don't land on their heads in the bay. But this moving, Pat. What's the sense in it?"

"No sense at all that I can see. We're nearly full up, but there's still room for more. The seriously wounded have all had surgery or what special care they needed. What they need now is rest—time to recover from shock and gain strength. This little boat ride to the flagship isn't going to help."

"Why move them at all?"

"Orders."

"Whose orders?—I mean, whose idea?"

"Hard to tell. Facilities on the flagship are little if any better than ours. Gates swears the senior M.O. wants to hog credit for all the casualties he can get aboard."

"What do you think?"

"I really don't know. . . . I don't expect sense any more."

"Well," said MacDougall, "if we've got to move 'em, let's go."

"O.K. We should move them as quickly as possible without roughing them up. This one litter at a time stuff seems so slow, using that casualty davit. . . . It will jar the patients to pack litters up ladder to the boat davits up above. . . . These fellows shouldn't lie around all night on canvas litters."

"Don't need to, Pat. We can use the after cargo gear—swing

167

them overside a whole boatload at a time right from this deck."

"You can? . . . Fraser said it wasn't safe to lower them in loaded boats with the cargo tackle—said he wouldn't be responsible."

"He doesn't need to be. Perhaps that's why Gedney— I'll stay right here until they're all off."

"Good. I'll start the litters your way."

MacDougall went aft, calling over heads of men working in the moonlight. "Alvick . . . That you, Doyle? . . . Where's the chief? . . . Oh, here he is. Alvick, we have to get the wounded off fast and smooth. I want to rail-load the boats at the after hatch. Get the best men you have to handle winches, guys and slings."

Tall form of the chief boatswain's mate, visored cap held between thumb and forefinger while remaining fingers scratched the nape of his neck.

"Looks a little risky, sir," he said quietly.

"I know, Chief, but we can do it. I'll work with you. . . . Let's go."

After considerable discussion as to exact procedure, and two practice runs lowering a boat smoothly from the rail and unhooking without dropping heavy hooks or straps into the boat where they would almost surely injure further these badly wounded men now ordered to be transferred, MacDougall ordered the boat lashed to the rail. He was sweating and happy in the release of physical activity. Turning inboard he became aware of the wounded, lying quietly in their canvas stretchers on the covered hatch. Navy corpsmen had carried them out from the sick bay, were bringing more, yet it seemed to MacDougall that they had some suspended power of movement, as if they had come here to the boat by themselves. Moonlight playing tricks, he thought.

They got the first boat loaded. In spite of all efforts to be gentle, one fellow suffering a compound fracture of the humerus screamed with unbearable pain when his litter was jarred. Walking to the bulwarks, MacDougall looked down at the water; four-foot waves, stirred up in the great lagoon, slopped against the *Belinda's* hull. It would be a neat trick to get the seven-ton boat afloat without shock to wounded passengers. Worst danger was at moment of releasing the great hook which held the boat by its wire sling. The released boat would dance in the waves, great hooks swinging above it like a lethal pendulum. Helpless men could be crushed—would be if he didn't prevent it. He was responsible now. Well, time to try it. "Ready now, Alvick? . . . Lower away easy—don't stop now—keep her moving. . . ." Waves falling away, now surging up towards the boat. "There she is; land her!" So far, so good—now the hook. "Watch that hook, you in the boat! Watch your sling! Hold it

168

up, man! Easy, now. . . . All right, Vinson. Shove off for the *Woodbridge*."

With practice the *Belinda's* crew gained experience and confidence. Boat after boat was hooked on, hoisted to the rail, loaded with eight litters—each with its wounded burden—then lowered into the water again. Waiting to go, some wounded soldiers lay quiet, a few smoked and talked with the sailors about them, some groaned, some talked deliriously. One big fellow, head completely swathed in dressings except for nose and mouth, kept yelling over and over, "Get down! For God's sake get down! Get down, I tell you, get down! GET DOWN!" He started out slowly, then accelerated until the last words came out in a gush. Then, after breathing heavily for a minute or two, he started all over again, "Get down, I tell you—"

"Shut it off. Shut it off! SHUT IT OFF!" cried the soldier in the next litter, extreme irritation, almost hatred in his tone. After a pause he said in quieter tones to whoever would listen, "I'm sorry for the guy, but I been listening to that for two days and two nights."

The wounded endured pain. The well worked with all possible speed and gentleness, feeling sympathy, yet reticent to show it. At last Dr. Bell came out from the sick bay. "This is all of them," he told MacDougall. The last boat was being hooked on and hoisted to the rail for its load. MacDougall looked at the six litters on the hatch. Nearest him was a fine-looking young soldier, so tall that he extended over both ends of the stretcher. Something about his face compelled MacDougall to speak.

"Well. On your way home now, fellow?"

"Sure hope so."

"Where you from?"

"Little town near Ashland, Oregon."

"You are! My brother-in-law has a fox farm at Eagle Point. Know where that is?"

"Sure. Eagle Point. . . . Name's Dwight, ain't it?"

"That's right." Gentle moonlight flooding the lagoon, softening war and pain—mention of familiar faces and places—somehow home did not seem so far away. The last boat came up to the rail and was lashed in place. The last litters were carefully handed in. MacDougall got into the boat and took the head end of the Oregon boy's stretcher, lowering it carefully to the bottom boards. "Comfortable?" he asked, knowing well that a man with his right femur shattered by gunshot wounds could not possibly be comfortable.

"I'm O.K." The soldier from Oregon had a faraway smile on his good-looking face. He seemed no longer aware of MacDougall or the *Belinda;* even his pain seemed temporarily forgotten. "Yes, I know him," he repeated softly as if to himself. "Eagle Point Fox Farm. He sure has beautiful foxes."

Supper aboard the *Belinda* on the evening of the fifth day was the nearest to a normal meal since the fleet had closed in on Kwajalein. Chow lines wound from foredeck to steamy mess hall below decks. The wardroom, one deck below, was crowded with officers, tired-looking and unshaven but joshing and kidding each other with almost complete lack of tension. More somber were the doctors, still upset over loss of their patients to the flagship.

"That was the lousiest thing I ever heard of"—exploded Dr. Gates—"transferring wounded men like that!"

"You mean the lousiest thing since last time," said Flynn. "We worked night and day, day and night on battle casualties at Makin, then got orders to transfer them."

"Yes, but that was a hospital ship," said Bell. "At least it made sense officially. This time we get orders to transfer sixty-two litter cases to the *Woodbridge;* just another APA, even if she is the squadron flag. I'll bet old Splice Gut Bromley—"

"Old *what!*" said MacDougall with an amused twinkle in his eyes.

"Splice Gut Bromley," said Flynn. "That's what we all call the squadron medical officer: fellow who got so sore at his assistants for using his 'coffee water' from the surgery sterilizer for shaving. . . . His specialty in surgery is—well, never mind. As I was saying, he probably had exactly sixty-two empty bunks in his sick bay and, with his usual brilliance, seized upon this opportunity to turn in a glowing report on himself at this operation."

"I don't care about reports," blurted Gates. "I wouldn't give you a dirty sock for a report on the *Belinda's* medical performance. All I'm thinking about are those multiple fractures, the head and belly wounds; patients deep in shock who may die if moved. That Thomas kid: how we sweat over him after it seemed sure he was a goner, pulled him through and then, when he's hanging on the border line, in concussion delirium, we have to dump him in a boat. It's murder, that's what it is; organized, official, officious murder!"

"Well, Ez," said Bell quietly, "the damage is done now. No use rehashing it."

John Brown, Negro mess attendant, hovering within earshot, began to unhook the steel deadlights which reached across the forward bulkhead from their dangling chains. As he dropped each one with a bang, more and more daylight was excluded, and the stagnant air within the wardroom seemed at once more fetid and depressing. MacDougall, sitting quietly between Bell and Flynn, was startled from his thoughts. "Leave those backers open," he said irritably to Brown. "Won't be sunset for half an hour yet. Time enough then to live like sardines."

Brown looked inquiringly at Quigley, who sat at the head of

the table dressed in his customary fresh khaki, seeming at home in the wardroom, yet somehow detached from the wilted weariness about him. He rose gracefully from his seat, noted the inquiring glance of the mess attendant and chose to ignore it. "Well, settle the fate of the nation, boys," he said with a smile. "I'm going to write a few lines to Eva."

Dreading the next few minutes, MacDougall followed Gates to the sick bay. Early in the day the three surgeons had amputated Mike O'Bannion's right foot. He'd be lower than a skunk now. White paint on sick bay bulkheads somehow looked whiter than any other paint; sheets too—perhaps the laundry used extra bleach. Whiteness of everything in the place was unnerving. MacDougall passed down long lines of double-tiered bunks, each with a drawn face and the strangely common look as if a similar expression had been stamped on each man somewhere on the way back from the line. Individuality seemed to be marked rather by an elevated foot or a bandaged head. Quite a lot of casualties already—after that transfer only two nights ago. Had they moved Mike? No. There was his familiar bulk filling an upper bunk.

"Hello, Mike."

"Hello, Mac. How's tricks up on the bridge?"

"About the same, Mike. How—" Nearly put his foot in his mouth that time. Nearly asked Mike how things were. Things would never be the same again for Mike. . . . Something to say. What do you say to a fellow when you're standing on two feet?

It was Mike who spoke first. "They took the foot today, lad." MacDougall drew a deep breath. Mike's voice went on, quiet, almost casual for him. "It's funny, Mac. I don't feel so different without the foot. I don't miss it, at least not yet; I don't miss it much."

"You old son-of-a-gun!"

" 'Twill take more than the lack of a foot to keep Mike O'Bannion down on his back very long. Right thinking, Mac— You know." Now the first signs of tremor were in the words spilling slowly out of the big man. "Wasn't that a grand sight from the battleship the day before we landed?"

"I guess it was, Mike. I had to stay behind."

"That's right, so you did. My, that was a sight! I can shut my eyes now and see the great guns belching smoke and thunder at the shore . . . trees flying like sticks. . . . My old father, how he'd have loved it all! The fireworks at Boston were nothing to it at all."

"I'd rather be the garbage grinder on the ship," said Fauré.

"I'd rather clean oily bilges on my hands and knees. Why—I'd rather miss stateside liberty."

"What are you bitching about?" asked Fraser, coming into the wardroom where Fauré stood gulping a cup of black coffee. "You boat jockeys—you don't know what trouble is. You should be first lieutenant of this bucket." Fraser looked at Fauré. The kid had clammed up. "Well, what were you doing?" Fraser asked.

"Burying Japs and pieces of Japs. Taking them out four miles to sea and dumping them over the ramp like so much garbage—that's all."

"Why can't they bury them ashore?"

"No room. It'll be all one big airstrip, and besides men have to live there. The shallow soil—it isn't healthy with all those bodies, thousands of bodies—"

"I suppose," said Fraser, wiping the sweat from his reddened face and reaching for a coffee cup. . . . "I suppose."

Suddenly again, even as at Makin, the Army returned to the *Belinda*. One minute the ship lay quietly at anchor; then deep-laden craft sputtered and roared with short bursts of full throttle, getting alongside. Brooks was bringing the battalion aboard. Debarkation nets sagged with slowly climbing infantrymen, some burdened with packs and rifles, all with five days' beard, filthy clothing and bodies, hollow, staring eyes. It was like the tide coming in. First groups standing about the nets, looking about them; succeeding boatloads following them up the net, flowing about them, pressing them back. Jammed together on overcrowded decks individuality was lost in a slowly moving mass of sweat-stained khaki which soon concealed untidy odds and ends of combat cargo and misplaced gear about decks. Pushing patiently, almost gently, yet with an irresistible flowing, battle-worn soldiers covered decks, filled ladders and companionways, compartments, mess halls, latrines. The sickening-sweet, kerosenelike smell of modern battle: burning oil and human decomposition, sweat and shallow island earth which had hovered over the lagoon since the landing now penetrated darkest passageways and most remote compartments. Army and Navy, battleground and ship were bonded together with the stench. Wash water unlimited was the rule. During the next twenty-four hours fresh-water showers ran wide open; naked men pushed along in lines for the feel of the cleansing water and soap. Fraser grumbled that, in spite of evaporators running at full capacity, soundings of ship's tanks showed a net loss of forty-six thousand gallons, which nearly emptied them. Scuppers gurgled and ran with soapy water, yet the odor persisted. From now on it was part of the ship and would never entirely leave her. No orders from the bridge, no amount of compartment cleaning or angry inspection could completely erase that smell of island battlegrounds.

Waiting turns to bathe or to eat, soldiers read tattered comic books, played with battered and filthy cards, or slept. They slept anywhere they could find space to lie down where they were not likely to be trampled upon. Under nested landing craft, on top of force draft cowls, on raised hatches in spaces not occupied by nested boats, by men waiting in chow lines or by informal groups huddled over cards or souvenirs—they lay with mouths wide open, insensible to activity about them, to tropic sun or to downpours of rain.

Into one such tight grouping on number four hatch, Chief Alvick worked his way. All about him were conversational sounds:

"Fade me, Jug Head."

"Hey, Larry. Seen this one?—Sad Sack on KP?"

"No, it wasn't that way, I tell you, it was like this. . . ."

Alvick's faded dungarees, contrasting with khaki, attracted attention upon the tall boatswain's mate as he said, "Sorry, soldiers, I have to open this hatch. You'll have to move, soldiers." Cards and comic books were shoved into pockets. Pressure from the center was put on soldiers crowded around the hatch until they gave way slowly. Then Alvick moved in with his sailors, awakened heavy sleepers, stripped off tarpaulins and removed hatch covers. "All right, sailors, trim your boom. . . . Little more amidships. Hold that and set tight." Down into the ship's bowels went cargo hook and sling, returning shortly with bundles of white painted slats in two lengths.

"What's them for?" a soldier asked Alvick.

"Crosses."

"Huh. . . . They think of everything, don't they?"

═══ CHAPTER 20 ═══

Commodore Bowles was furious. Every breath angrily expelled from his thick chest, every gesture of his short, stocky body, choleric purple suffusing tan on his broad, weather-beaten face—all attested to his rage. Standing with feet wide apart on the miniature stage of his flagship's briefing room, he pounded the speaker's stand and shouted, "What you did was inexcusable: landing a hundred yards south of the grand-stand—all those Very Important People waiting to see a dem-onstration landing!" Bowles was looking over the heads in the first row of seats facing him, occupied by Captain Gedney, a classmate of his, and by other captains in his transport division —somewhat younger men, yet all Academy graduates, sea-

173

soned, experienced. The commodore's angry glances, gestures, shoutings were for the ten reserve officers seated behind their captains. "You navigators and boat commanders: I'm talking to you. Were you all born and raised high in the Rocky Mountains? Haven't you ever seen salt water before? What you did was utterly impossible for real sailormen. . . . Here, come with me!"

Jumping down from the stage, the commodore left the briefing room, followed by Gedney and the other captains, by the navigators and boat commanders, including MacDougall and Brooks from the *Belinda*. They followed Bowles to the open wing of his signal bridge, seventy feet above water, where he leveled his binoculars and re-examined the Coronado sand dunes, nine thousand yards away, then pointed angrily with them while he shouted, "Look! Just look for yourselves! It's all so simple; you can see it as plain as your face! There's the grandstand, right on your assigned landing beach. Just beyond it, among those trees, is a big red barn." The commodore took out a large white handkerchief, blew his nose loudly and glared at the lieutenants and *j.g.s* clustered on his bridge. "If you Rocky Mountain navigators could have put your ships anywhere near the station I assigned—kept them there while hoisting out boats—all you boat officers had to do was to head for that red-painted barn!"

Captains, navigators, boat group commanders—all were silent. After Kwajalein, instead of expected leave, there had been six seemingly endless weeks of practice landings in the surf of California and outlying islands for the benefit of boot marines and rookie soldiers practicing for war. During the first week Harrison was transferred to another ship and MacDougall became the navigator of the *Belinda*. It took some of the sting out of the fifteen dry runs at Morro Bay, Aliso Canyon, San Clemente Island and here at Coronado strand. When the last boat-weary marine stepped ashore with his pack, the *Belinda's* crew, like the rest of the division, expected a well-earned blow, no leave of course, but a seventy-two-hour liberty —at least a forty-eight each for port and starboard watches before returning to the South Pacific sweatbox to grab another island from the Japs.

No such luck. Dispatch from the Naval District: A demonstration landing will be made on Coronado strand by Task Unit Eleven dash Thirteen point Thirteen. . . . A dawn landing will be witnessed by the following members of planning staff . . . also by Mr. Garvin Wiggins, landing craft manufacturer. . . . The importance of an efficient demonstration will be stressed. . . . Landing will be made directly, repeat directly in front of bleachers constructed on Coronado strand. . . .

At three o'clock on the demonstration morning Bowles had

led his transport division to a spot exactly three sea miles from the bleachers on the sand. MacDougall and the other navigators had experienced no difficulty in keeping their ships precisely on station during hoisting out of boats in the dark: with radar, the sandy Coronado Peninsula stuck out like a sore thumb, with the landing beach at the knuckle. Out into the dark went Brooks with his boat group, steering a compass course at reduced speed while waiting for first dawn light and sight of the bleachers filled with VIPs. To his dismay, first light disclosed to him nothing more definite than a monotonous strip of sand dunes dotted here and there with clumps of trees—not a sign of the bleachers. His landing craft were lined up in five waves, each abreast of corresponding waves from the other four transports: strictly according to the landing manual, which was what they wanted at demonstrations. Nothing to do but push on for the surf. All too late, Brooks and the other boat commanders saw the low-lying bleachers two hundred yards north of the section of beach they faced. Instinctively, all boat commanders corrected as much as was possible until they reached the surf. The waves were sullen, heavier than usual, adding to the responsibility of five thousand lives in their hands. Remembering the nine soldiers drowned during the previous week's exercises, they prudently straightened out their lines of craft, rode through the surf and landed one hundred yards south of the bleachers. The Very Important People swung their necks to the left, witnessed the landing, expressed polite appreciation to officers conducting their tour, then hurried to the three busses waiting to take them back to San Diego and hot breakfast. Brooks and his fellow boat officers grumbled about the tidal current, which had swept their landing craft off course, and the general fortune of boat commanders, always handicapped in their low craft by foreshortened horizons with corresponding reduced visibility. Then they returned boatloads of water-soaked soldiers to their ships.

When the commodore had concluded his caustic remarks, Gedney, MacDougall and Brooks climbed down to the quarterdeck, got into the command boat and headed for the *Belinda*. Gedney sat alone in the stern sheets. MacDougall and Brooks stood inside the canopy beside Hatcher, the coxswain, talking loudly in order to hear each other above roaring of the boat engine.

Brooks spouted his indignation. "He should yell! Sure, he could see fine from that signal bridge of his. He could see the red barn easy—way up in the sky like that. . . . He should try a worm's-eye view like we get in the boats. I can take him out in this boat right now, all the way from his ship to the beach, and I defy him to see even a glimpse of that red barn— even when you get to the surf it's hid by that clump of trees. He doesn't know what he's talking about. It's an entirely different picture down in a boat like this."

"That's right," said MacDougall. "He forgot all about the earth's curvature—at least it was convenient for him to forget it this morning. You need a periscope." MacDougall laughed. "I know what you need, Tony. You know Robbie, my little boy?"

"Sure."

"Couple of weeks ago, between dry runs, I took him to Balboa Park to see the animals. The critters he got the biggest kick out of were the giraffes. He said, 'Daddy, look at that grandpa giraffe. Look at that funny long neck!' That's all you need, Tony. If you had a neck like a giraffe you could see the red barn just as easy as the commodore."

"Well," said Brooks, "I guess there's hope, even for me. My neck stretches a little more every time I make a landing."

MacDougall glanced aft in the command boat. Gedney still sat silent in the stern sheets—surely he had heard every word they said. MacDougall saw a gleam of amusement in those clear blue eyes. Yes, the Old Man had heard them all right. I wonder why he didn't say anything, MacDougall thought. In spite of all his tremendous respect for properly constituted authority, the old boy had a way of speaking out when a situation seemed unreasonable to him. When he did, it was always surprising, always to the point in a startling way, so that nobody had any effective answer. Take that time the week before when Chesney and the rest of the staff had been wrangling over exactly where the line of departure for a practice landing at Aliso Canyon should have been. Ship argued with ship; captains became involved until finally the simple point in question was completely forgotten. At last Gedney got to his feet, dusted a bit of lint from the four tarnished gold stripes on his seagoing blues and waited until the briefing room was quiet. Then he said, "Commodore Bowles, gentlemen: I see how it is. First comes me, then my ship, then the division, the squadron, the task force, then the United States Navy—and last of all, God help them, the people of the United States of America, whose servants we are." Then he sat down in a room which remained completely silent until the commodore cleared his throat and dismissed the critique.

Silent now, Gedney had forgotten the commodore, the critique and the red barn. He was expecting transfer to a nice berth ashore, much more important than the one held by Commodore Bowles: nothing less than command of a gigantic training station, where he would teach all that he knew about the ship-to-shore movement to thousands of young officers and enlisted men who would then swell the growing landing waves now sweeping westward across the vast Pacific. MacDougall and Brooks would have to take care of the red barns.

CHAPTER 21

"New captain comin' to the *Belinda!*"

"Yeah. You seen that man? Tall fellow, straight like a post, eye like a hawk—goin' to be no foolishness with him, I tell you."

"O.K. O.K. Get that table set up there, Davis. An' wash them forks again. Mr. Rockwell, he say got to be no food particles on them forks, especially today."

"Yeah, boy! Especially today—new captain comin' today!"

"Get all your men up here," said Pappy Moran to his first division boatswain's mates. "Break out the deck hoses and scrub her down, but good."

"O.K. Pappy. We know what to do."

"You'd better! When I say scrub, I mean scrub. Bear down on those handles. Change of command will be held right here on number three hatch. Whole crew will be mustered here on the foredeck—every inch of it must be spotless. If you want a happy life in the cruise ahead you'd better have a clean ship for the change of command. I've been in this Navy long enough to know that!"

"But can't you see, Mr. Kruger, there ain't time! Change of command this morning. I know they squawked about the new boats we got aboard just before inspection. I know the gear ain't stowed right or the numbers painted on. I got my men running around like crazy, and then all of a sudden they have to be clean and in dress blues like they just came from Sunday School."

"I'm sorry, Hatcher. They just have to be done, that's all. Mr. Fraser said you'll have to get every last boat ready—then clean up."

"Oh, there you are, Chief. Get your quartermasters busy on that new gear. Every last bit of it must be stowed away before ten hundred. We can't have any loose gear around the bridge today."

"Do my best, Mr. MacDougall. I'm trying to get the quarterdeck lined up. Alvick's picking side boys." Chief Scott allowed himself a chuckle. "You ought to see Pappy Moran, sir. That screwball garbage grinder found chicken guts in a G.I. can—they clog his gears, you know. Hubert threw the whole mess out on deck right at number three hatch. You should have heard Moran, sir! He really told him!"

MacDougall looked over the bridge rail at an unhappy group swabbing away the last traces of garbage. He grinned at Scott. "Better not have anything like that up here, Chief. You know the old saying, 'The bridge is the showplace of a ship.' This is spit-and-polish day—strictly regulation. Tomorrow we'll carry on with the war."

Chief Gunner's Mate Vandemeer stumbled into the chief's quarters to find most of his mates leaving the table.

"Any breakfast left?" he asked.

"Guess so," said Rinaldo. "What're you puffing about, Guns? Been running the four-minute mile?"

"Same thing as everybody else. Haven't stopped running for three days now, getting ready for this change of command."

"How do you like the idea of a new skipper?"

"You know me, Jerry. Love me, love my guns. I like skippers who like to shoot."

"Well, old Captain Gedney knows his gunnery."

"Sure, he's all right. Like I told you before, I was shipmates with him years ago on the old *Arizona* when he was navigator, and then on the *Colorado* when he was first lieutenant. Captains come and captains go. You get me a skipper that likes to shoot before breakfast. I'll go anywhere with him."

"Boy! He sure caught me flat," said Fauré. "You know how it is on the mid."

"Yeah," said Bud Foster, pulling his best blues out of the locker. "Everything that's going to happen—happens. Then it's quiet and you just wait out the clock."

Fauré got the last of the lather off his neck and reached for a white shirt. "That's right, only it didn't work out this time. MacDougall made the rounds—gave me a beef about slack breast lines. Then he turned in. No trouble with the liberty section: just a few good-natured drunks that weren't too hard to roll into the sack. Messenger and the bosun's mate taking slack out of the lines. I was just playing with the idea of sending the sentry for a pot of coffee—then thought I'd better wait: Gedney's had me in my room twice for stuff like that."

"And me once," said Bud. "Remember that time at Maui? The impossible always happens in this Navy!"

"Sure does. Well, here I was flaked out over the rail, yawning my head off. Then I saw something moving down on the dock. You know how those overhead lights beat down hard and bright so you can't be sure of a thing in the shadows? All of a sudden he pops out into the light—just a flash of white hat and scrambled eggs. That's all it took to send a shiver

178

through me: a four striper coming up that brow at me fast. And the way he moved: straight and easy but so quick. Before I could get my breath and my hand up at salute he was right on top of me."

Bud laughed. "You never miss, Fauré. You just couldn't be squared away to meet the new skipper. Not you!"

"Well, I'm just an ensign—at least I had my pants on. Did you hear about MacDougall?"

"No. What?"

"Well, the messenger told me . . ."

"Hello, Mac," said Flynn. "Come on in. Have the chair."

"Thanks, Pat. I'll sit on the bunk just a minute—little short for time today—all this fuss over change in command. I'll be glad when it's over."

"What's this about greeting the new captain? Barefoot they tell me. Is that Naval tradition too?"

"Well, I was tired: my work and Quigley's too—he's been on leave, you know. Repairs, the crew—all that stuff. I've been ashore with the family every night I could get away, but last night I got stuck with the duty. Things were quiet so I hit the hay. We were expecting the new skipper any day but not in the middle of the night. I was doing a real job of sleeping. Then came this banging on the door—Fauré's messenger—new captain down on the quarterdeck. I was fumbling for clothes, trying to think of a way to stall him off until I got my shoes on at least, but no luck. 'Here's the new captain, sir,' says the messenger. Then he left my door open and ran. That's how I met Captain Hawks: barefooted, shirt in one hand, no hat. . . . You can't salute in the Navy without a hat, you know."

"One good thing about the Navy," said Flynn. "Well, go on. What then?"

"He shook hands hard and quick as if he wanted to be just friendly enough. I was still half asleep, trying to greet him decently and at the same time trying to size him up. He looks like a man of action: hawk-like face—his name just fits him, except for the straight nose. He's much taller than Gedney: about six-one. Very neat blues with that corner of snow-white handkerchief peeking up at three rows of fruit salad on his chest."

"Yes, the white hankey, of course," said Flynn. "That's the Academy Old School Tie."

"Don't be bitter, Pat. He's probably a bang-up skipper. I like what I've seen of him so far, but he puzzles me too."

"Why?"

"Oh, not so much what he says—he seems pretty good at pinning you down with questions as far as that goes. What I mean is the way he acts: straight but not stiff; relaxed physically yet poised on the balls of his feet as if all set to spring into

179

action—all the time those eyes of his drill right into you while he talks. He seems almost casual outwardly, yet all wound up tight inside. I almost expected him to start shouting orders—heave up anchor, commence fire, something like that. But he just talked about Gedney being ashore—how he didn't need the cabin, the emergency cabin would be fine."

"Where did he sleep?"

"Gedney's bunk, don't worry. Gedney would have had a fit if I hadn't put him in the main cabin for the night. So there he was, standing in Gedney's doorway. 'Good night, Mr. Navigator,' he says. That's the way he came—without warning, without baggage—in the middle of the night."

"It's been a pleasure sailing with you, Capt'n," said MacDougall, poised halfway through the curtain which hung across the cabin door. Last time alone with Gedney, for all he knew. He couldn't just walk out—so these polite words in an empty phrase. Pleasure was a strange word for Makin and Kwajalein, for long, worried nights with Gedney on the bridge. Yet now that they were gone as finally as Sherwood, or O'Bannion's foot, in spite of the bitterness there was pleasure of sorts in the remembrance.

Gedney rose from his swivel chair and grasped MacDougall's hand warmly. "I will remember you, MacDougall," he said. "You are not an Academy officer, but you are a sailor and I am a sailor. In a way, we have shared the *Belinda* together."

Strange how quickly the stiff curtain draws aside, revealing warmth, acting like a trigger releasing something deep inside MacDougall which he had not thought of in many weeks.

"There's just one thing I can't forgive you for, Capt'n."

Gedney smiled serenely, not in the least disturbed. "Yes, what is it, MacDougall?"

"Taking me out of the boats. . . . And that reconnaissance trip at Kwajalein to sound the reef before the landing. I wanted very much to go. I wasn't navigator then; it seemed to me that you could have spared me for a few hours." Now MacDougall felt foolish, showing his feelings like this. Kwajalein was past and done; why rehash it now? But he had felt it and he had said it.

Still the smile on Gedney's face. "I considered the risks, MacDougall—the long view, that's all. You are the *Belinda's* navigator now and where is Sherwood? . . . You see?"

"This is really fun," Quigley said to Flynn. "The whole ship dressed up for once: crew in dress blues with neckerchief; officers in service dress blues, white hats, gray gloves. It's too bad we can't wear swords. They've done away with that for the duration, of course—I always wanted to wear a sword."

"Yes, it's too bad," said Flynn. "While we're busy playing war we ought to do a good job of it. Couldn't you get hold of a drum for someone to beat?"

They had been waiting a long time for the word. Now that the boatswain's pipe whistled dismally throughout the ship, divisions already mustered straightened out their lines again, scarcely listening to words blasting from the PA: "All hands to muster. All hands to muster."

"Stand by to wait," said Stanowski, radarman second, to his mate, Carlson. "What's the use of all this, anyway? I got my five days leave and that's that. Best thing I can do now is help get this war over with and get home for keeps. Bring on the new skipper so I can get back to the bridge and check my new gear. That A scope on the Sugar George seems out of calibration."

Beyond routine remarks and a little kidding back and forth, few of the crew had much to say. Change was in the air, and every man had his own thoughts. Vinson looked up at the shovel-nosed command boat, hanging from the bridge deck davit. He wished they'd hurry up. Just one more liberty, then good-by stateside again. Dry runs, then another pay run—that's what they'd get. That slick, fresh-painted boat up there, scooting over the water, riding herd on all the boat waves. It was a thrill to handle her. . . . I hope I still get to run that PL for Brooks; he's a swell guy, but golly I miss Mr. Sherwood!

Tommy Jones, another boat coxswain, was thinking about his bride. This was his home town, San Diego. One more night with Lorraine. I wonder how long we'll be gone this time. Hope I get back. I've just got to get back to Lorraine.

Different the thoughts of Sacktime Riley, landing craft motor-mac, known as best sleeper and poorest worker aboard. Skippers are trouble whoever they are. What difference does it make anyhow? Fellow ain't got a chance against four stripes—unless he sees 'em coming first. Let's get this funny business over with, then if the Chief don't find me—that nice dark hole in the gear locker—a little extra shut-eye on those spare life jackets will fix me up for liberty tomorrow.

"So there you have the picture," said Captain Gedney pushing aside stacks of fitness reports, requests for repairs and alterations, hull reports, lists of secret publications—these and many more forming bewildering heaps on the large cabin table in spite of orderly segregation. "Here is an itemized list of all official documents as required by regulations. Here are lists of blueprints of the ship, three hundred seventy-eight in all. Here is a list of damage control data, ship's characteristics, maneuvering data. Here are the unexecuted orders—I went over all of them with you yesterday. All records are now complete." Captain Gedney leaned back in his chair, took a deep, relaxing breath and beckoned to Johnson, his cabin boy, to bring on the coffee. "Cream and sugar, Captain?"

"Lots of both," said Captain Hawks.

Gedney reached out beyond the cups to finger a stack of the official papers reflectively. "As I have indicated, repair work is pretty well in hand," he said. "Some of the alterations to hull and machinery I requested—"

"I know about what to expect these days from a fast Navy Yard turn around: seven days availability after a year at sea. But what they've missed perhaps I can have performed by ship's force."

"That's the way we've been carrying on," said Gedney. "The shipfitters are outstanding. Rinaldo could build a new ship if he had to."

"Who's Rinaldo?"

"The chief shipfitter: good man; he was at Manila when the shooting war started—put out the red navigation light on La Monja with a boat hook."

"He did, eh? That's the kind of man I like to have in my crew. This Moran, now, I hear them talking a lot about him."

"Moran is chief boatswain's mate of the first division," said Gedney. "I consider him the most important enlisted man aboard—worth several of the officers put together."

"Officer material?"

"His formal education was limited; I think he shines as a chief. In some strange manner he holds the ship's company together, makes men do what seems impossible to them. Moran is an Old Navy man. I don't know what more I could say for him."

Captain Hawks swallowed his coffee at a gulp and banged the cup back on its saucer. "Depends on how you look at it," he said. "We've got power, speed and gear now we never dreamed of before."

"Yes, sir," said Gedney, his blue eyes shining, "that's exactly the point. What good is it all without men who have the right stuff in them?"

Captain Hawks frowned at his empty coffee cup and nodded abruptly to Johnson, who stood to one side, open-mouthed, holding the tall silver coffee pot with its long spout. There were things Hawks felt like saying. He'd take this ship to sea and then—but it wasn't his ship yet, not for another hour. "You've brought ship and crew a long ways, Captain," he said at last. "From here on it's up to me. I'll see what I can do."

Gedney chuckled. "You should have seen the beginnings:

fourteen minutes to report all guns manned and ready; one hour and forty-three minutes to hoist out boats, some of them launched one end at a time!"

"How long does it take now?"

"Two minutes, fifteen seconds for the guns—damage control stations are still a little slow in reporting; eighteen minutes to hoist out all boats. The thirty-six ton tank lighters on number three hatch are controlling factors there. I advise caution putting them overside when the ship is rolling badly; resolution of forces, calculations and stress tables give a strain of 86 per cent tackle-breaking strength during a heavy surge. It is all a matter of timing and balance—that's where Moran comes in."

"I see," said Hawks. "I like things moving. Nothing's so good it can't be better. Now the officers. Some of them you said . . ."

"Yes, the officers," said Gedney. He paused a moment, lingering over the matter of the boats. Pretty sure of himself, this man. He would learn—indeed he would learn some dark night with the ship wallowing in the trough—he would learn then that the man is more important than the machine. Now he spoke smoothly, calmly. "As I have outlined, some officers are outstanding while a few are not what they should be. Some reserve officers lack the slightest conception of naval and military duty, others have exceeded all that might reasonably be expected of them. In between are the average. The same might be said for the crew. In entirety I rate them above the average of the fleet as it stands today."

Captain Hawks drained his second cup of coffee. "I took a squadron of LSTs to Sicily last winter. Some foulup when I assumed command: no organization, almost no planning and a lot of seasick young skippers. Everything I did there had to be an improvement; I couldn't go wrong. But the best ships can be made even more efficient; every man can be made smarter; every officer can be made more incisive. I will see what I can do with your ship, sir."

A wistful smile played across old Gedney's weather-beaten face. He was leaving a lot of himself behind in this ship. In some respects command here had been the high spot of his naval career. He would have liked a cruiser, but the *Belinda* had been his ship, responding towards the last almost to his unspoken thoughts. Then a full smile crinkled his wide mouth, and his blue eyes twinkled. No matter what changes Hawks might initiate, the *Belinda* was pretty much what Winthrop Gedney had made of her. Hammered into the ship's hull like the ship's permanent magnetism, much of it would be hard to change. "Now, Captain," he said, pushing a neatly typed statement before Hawks, "here is a transfer receipt for your signature." Pen poised above the sheet, Hawks frowned as he read:

"Received from Winthrop H. Gedney the following . . ." At last the pen stabbed downward to splash the bold strokes of his signature.

Gedney reached for his cap and rose to go out on deck for the last time. He stepped forward to the row of cabin portholes and looked out on his crew, now mustered for change of command ceremonies. "I'll be over on the Atlantic side training crews for new attack transports," he said, turning back to look Hawks full in the eye. "I'll be reading the dispatches, following the *Belinda* from island to island. I know that you will find her a good ship."

Hawks glanced in the cabin mirror. He straightened the corner of white handkerchief peeping from his breast pocket towards the Distinguished Service Medal which presided over three rows of lesser ribbons on his breast. Then he made a quick face at himself in the mirror, took up his orders to command the *Belinda* and followed Gedney from the cabin.

MacDougall stood at the quarterdeck, web belt of his forty-five strapped outside his best blues, gray gloves uncomfortably tight. He could almost hear old Gedney saying, "The navigator always takes the deck during change of command." It would not be long now—all this frantic preparation over and done with. While the sweat of the effort still soaked into their clean skivies the officers and crew of the *Belinda* mustered in tight lines for the change-of-command ceremony. Men almost neat enough standing at attention in almost perfectly straight lines, packed so close together that the spotless exactitude of decks and gear was hidden by blue uniforms and white hats.

The only clear space on the two-hundred-fifty feet of foredeck was an area of about twenty by thirty feet to starboard of the foremast, reserved as quarterdeck. From here the brow led down to shore. Manropes on the brow were covered with canvas scrubbed snowy white. Boatswain's mate of the watch on this special occasion was Chief Alvick, straight and tall in spotless blues, fingering his silver pipe. Four well-scrubbed youngsters from his division stood two at each side of the gangway in honor of Captain Gedney, who would pass between them as he left the ship. Down on the wharf the sentry paraded stiffly with his carbine. On deck were two messengers and the watch quartermaster with his notebook. MacDougall looked from this small group to the six hundred officers and men packed in tight divisions on the rest of the foredeck. Except for Quigley, who paced nervously about on the upper deck waiting until all should be in readiness for the captains, and a few men on steam and signal watches, every officer and man of the *Belinda* waited at quarters to witness official greeting and farewell.

Time now for the change of command. Excitement rippled through the mustered crew like a breeze across a wheat field. Maxwell, chief master-at-arms, came to the hatchway and shouted, "Ten—shun!" Clack of heels, men straining to unnatural stiffness, then Quigley appeared, followed by the two captains. Once on the hatch, Quigley stood aside. MacDougall looked at Gedney—so soon to be gone, perhaps never to return. It was against tradition to wander back aboard after relinquishing command to another. All stiffness and form now at number three hatch. Captain Gedney standing before his crew reading dry as dust orders: date, from, to, via what authorities, references—read so that the humblest seaman on the *Belinda* should know that he had been ordered to be relieved of command by Captain Jebediah S. Hawks, United States Navy. Gedney read every word, then stepped back and handed the orders to Quigley, who handed them to Biggs, who put them carefully into Captain Gedney's briefcase, still unfolded. True to the Old Navy, thought MacDougall as Biggs scuttled past him, dived between unmoving side boys and placed Gedney's briefcase in the ship's jeep waiting on the wharf. MacDougall remembered the first of many lectures by old Gedney—way back in the shipyard he told them: "An officer never folds his orders." The yarn he told: ship sinking; captain calling out to his exec in the water, "There goes thirty years of orders." They'd be unfolded of course, and no endorsements in rubber stamps.

Captain Hawks was reading his orders now. Standing before the crew, harsh, monotonous voice reading down through the rigmarole and finally to the heart of the matter, ". . . to then take command, U.S.S. *Belinda*." He was doing it now! Folding the paper carelessly, jamming it into his pocket as if of no further importance, he stepped smartly up to Captain Gedney, saluted and said, "I relieve you, sir." These last words were not the dead-sounding things he read from the orders but live words, ringing out clear so that no man needed the aid of the PA to hear. Captain Hawks now commanded the *Belinda*. He shook hands with Captain Gedney, then swung about in an arc so that his sharp hazel eyes bored for a fleeting instant into those of each of his crew. "I am now your commanding officer," he said. "The orders and directives of my predecessor will remain in force for the time being." He paused, then continued in a lower tone that was difficult for MacDougall to hear: "There will be some changes later . . . but for the time being they all remain in force."

Was this a clue? MacDougall wondered. Old Navy due for a beating, maybe? Perhaps it was all routine. Here they came, Hawks escorting Gedney to the quarterdeck. MacDougall gave the nod to Alvick. The chief drew himself up another inch and called, "Ten–shun!" The four young side boys, already stiff almost beyond endurance, shuddered simultaneously from the shock of arms jerked suddenly from rigid sides to position of salute. Long wailing on Alvick's pipe, his own left hand at salute. It's like a funeral, MacDougall thought. Then, though his face was as rigid as the others, he smiled inside, for Flynn had told him about the drum. Yes, they should have a long roll on the drums, distant band playing "When Johnny Comes Marching Home." "Anchors Aweigh" didn't fit here. Gedney passing him now—surely he would say a word, at least nod. But no, he, MacDougall, and the other six hundred officers and enlisted men were so stiffly at attention they were part of the ship. Hawks and Gedney were quite alone, strolling casually, Gedney tossing a friendly salute to the colors as he stepped for the last time from the decks of the *Belinda* to the brow. Three steps down towards the wharf he stopped and turned back to smile up at Captain Hawks.

"Good-by, Captain," said Gedney. "I may see you again some day. After all, as they used to say, 'It's a small Navy.' "

"It's a bigger Navy than it used to be," said Captain Hawks. "Good-by, Captain."

CHAPTER 22

"Execute!" cried Captain Hawks, striking the palms of his hands together with a sharp crack. "Bang! Like that! Have your signalman rip the hoists down from that yardarm." The new commanding officer of the *Belinda* clapped MacDougall on the shoulder. "What's the matter, Mr. Navigator—afraid of the *Woodbridge* because they've been flag so long? The commodore flew to Pearl. We're running things from the *Belinda* now. Be incisive. Let 'em know who's boss. Now let's see you whip that ship around the *Belinda*."

"Aye, aye, sir."

Wearing a pained expression, the chief signalman stepped aft to the flag bag and rearranged his men. Then he returned to MacDougall's side, buttoning up his faded denim jumper. It was getting chilly on the unprotected signal bridge—no chance to break out the joe pot with the new skipper hanging around. Morgan wished he'd get done with this silly tactical drill—two ships waltzing around all alone. Why, the *Belinda* had maneuvered with a hundred other ships. He . . .

"Morgan," snapped Captain Hawks.

"Yes, sir."

"Where did you get that jumper?"

"At Pearl, Captain—seven years ago, sir."

Captain Hawks looked down from his six-foot-one at the stocky signalman. His lower lip jutted out to one side as he stared straight into Morgan's brown eyes. Then he snapped, "This is a combatant ship of the United States Navy, not a museum. That jumper is non-regulation. Take it off and don't wear it again."

"Aye, sir." There was surprise and hurt in Morgan's face. He peeled off the beloved faded jumper and tucked it in the flag bag.

MacDougall pulled a folded memo from his shirt pocket, glanced at his schedule of maneuvers, gave an order to Morgan and watched the signal gang pull the bright-colored bunting from the flag bag, snap them together and jerk them aloft to whip in the breeze from the yardarm—all in a matter of seconds. Then he walked to the wing of the signal bridge and trained his binoculars on the *Woodbridge*, now five hundred yards astern. By the time he raised his glasses, the same signal flew from the *Woodbridge*, indicating that his order was understood. "Execute," called MacDougall. Down came the flags. The *Woodbridge* heeled sharply to port, cutting a deep furrow of white froth in the cold blue sea as she maneuvered at full speed to take station close abeam of the *Belinda*. MacDougall lowered the heavy glasses back on the neck strap so that they rested against his chest, then turned to look again at the hawk-like features of his new commanding officer. The last ten minutes had disturbed a feeling of complacency quite natural on a simple passage of two ships between San Diego and Pearl Harbor, two thousand miles from active war. For the first time since he had taken command two days before, Captain Hawks had raised his voice. Could it be an omen of things to come, like the first clap of thunder before a storm? Was this the same man who had come aboard so unostentatiously, who had been so affable, friendly except for his way of keeping at a distance, asking questions, listening carefully, looking all about his new command? The crew welcomed a change. They had become a little tired of old Gedney's exactitudes. Now the new captain was beginning to take in the slack; MacDougall sensed something in him he had never seen in Gedney: love of power, perhaps—surely more driving force. Hawks seemed to have put aside his company manners with the spotless blue uniform. Soon, perhaps, they would see his khaki manners.

Hawks looked at the *Woodbridge*, now dancing along off the *Belinda's* beam. "What's her distance, MacDougall?"

MacDougall raised his binoculars again. From long practice he could estimate ranges quite closely by eye. "About six hundred forty yards, Capt'n."

"I didn't ask about how far," said Hawks, snapping out the word *about* as if the very sound of it were distasteful to him.

"I said, 'How far?' When I ask how far, I mean exactly how far."

MacDougall swallowed. "Range, radar," he called down the intercom.

"Range six-five-five, opening slowly, sir."

"You see," said Hawks, pleased tone in his voice now. "The range was not six-four-zero, it was six-five-five."

For once MacDougall let a crack regarding his seamanship pass almost unnoticed. He was deep in the Sailing Day Blues, his mind back in San Diego with Nadine and Robbie. All that happened here was just a bad dream. So he made no reply, thinking of San Diego, of all the U.S.A. over the curve of horizon far astern. These other fellows around him: ship's company and the load of cocky young marines just out of boot camp they were taking to Pearl—what part of the States did their thoughts go back to?

Only yesterday afternoon they had watched the mainland fade into empty haze—gone for how long they had no idea. No more stateside liberty for the boys. Another operation planning; where, they could only guess, but it would be soon and they would be in on it. Bigger than Kwajalein, scuttlebutt had it; bigger than anything they had seen yet.

MacDougall looked back at the wake, lifting binoculars slowly to where the trail was lost in restless, indifferent sea. Memories came filtering up through all the things around him, clouding any thought of the future. He could account for nearly every happy hour of the precious time he had shared with Nadine and Robbie, but the memories were fading already, losing freshness the more he clung with each of the five senses to each remembered word and picture. That trip to Balboa Park: so proud and happy with his wife and little boy, yet sweetness mixed with shadow of parting. The giraffes: that's what Robbie had liked best. "Look at that grandpa giraffe, Daddy!"

Then he thought of Tony Brooks, all mad from the commodore's dressing down. "That's all you need, Tony," he had said. "If you had a neck like a grandpa giraffe, you could see the red barn."

Now, if he himself had a neck long enough—could he see Robbie? . . . How long would it take to get back there in a plane? Two hours, perhaps. Well, Nadine and Robbie would be on the train for Berkeley now—looking out over the water, maybe. They were gone. And that little cottage they had rented: cold sheets in an empty bed. But they had been warm. They had known love—Nadine's arms tight around him while her lips whispered in his ear, "I will never be far." Oh, but she was far, so far! Further away than during the trips half-way around the world he made for a living before the war. There was a Thing between them now, something more binding than ship's articles, something almost as final as death.

But was she far? MacDougall reached into his pocket and pulled out one of her handkerchiefs. Faint perfume brought Nadine back close to him with a rush of warmth and feeling. Then he remembered the door to the front of the cottage—that confounded screen door. He was on the outside, shutting it between them, Nadine's tear-stained face dim through the screen—the most miserable little face, the dearest little face he had ever seen. They had said good-bys before. They were old-timers at this stuff. You kissed hard with your very souls communing through trembling lips, and you held each other hard as if it were possible to make up for the empty nights and days ahead—and then you broke it. That was the only way. You had to break it. But this time he couldn't. Oh, God, he couldn't! He had jerked that screen door open again and they had clung sobbing together, misery rising with each kiss. Finally he had done it: turned and walked away and not looked back until he got to the corner. Then he turned and waved. She looked so small—and they were just a block apart. One block or four hundred miles—four thousand miles for that matter. There was nothing you could do about it.

Pearl Harbor lay far astern. In the midst of a task force composed of over five hundred ships, the Belinda steamed southwest for newly captured Eniwetok Atoll in the Marshalls. She had finished another series of dry runs at Maalaea Bay, this time with a battalion landing team of the 4th Marine Division. Navy and Marines had had a chance to rub a few sparks off each other's shoulders and get acquainted. Urged by that stern taskmistress, battle to come, they learned to work together. Those few who knew actual combat destination kept close-lipped, yet every boat coxswain knew relative positions of transport areas, lines of departure, boat lanes and extent of beach. They had seen it all pictured on blank maps; they had practiced it at Maalaea like a water and shore ballet to the music of rehearsal bombardment. Somewhere in the Pacific was an island and a five-mile patch of water where they would do this all over again, only it wouldn't be rehearsal. Japs would be shooting back and there would be no Kehei village store with candy bars and soda pop.

At Eniwetok last supplies of fuel, food and ammunition were taken aboard. Time for a bum movie but no liberty for the crew or troops other than an hour's swim over the side. Then it was sailing time again—a blistering hot afternoon, the lagoon all highlights and no shadow. With MacDougall at his side and surrounded by plotters, quartermasters and signalmen, Captain Hawks stood on the flying bridge, where he had an unobstructed view in all directions. Clanking chain and groaning windlass sounded from the forecastle as Fraser and his men heaved around.

"Anchor's aweigh, sir," said the talker.

"Very good," said Captain Hawks. "Ahead standard." The *Belinda's* propeller beat a white froth from blue-green water in the lagoon, ship moving ahead towards battle officially unknown to her six-hundred crew or to the BLT of twelve hundred Marines embarked. Dead still air in the lagoon, tropic sun beating down upon glaring water and dazzling white sands of Parry and Eniwetok islands, now stripped naked of all vegetation. Shady coconut trees mowed down in recent battle, remaining stumps uprooted with bulldozers and the crushed coral smoothed into airstrips, island-long. As the *Belinda* gathered headway towards Deep Entrance, air began to circulate about weather decks. Men stepped clear of obstructions wherever possible to get a breath of moving air, just a suggestion of coolness, for the sun still beat down, radiating waves of ovenlike heat from steel decks too hot to touch with bare hands.

Eniwetok anchorage was alive: five hundred other ships getting underway. It was an orderly process—mimeographed copies of the admiral's movement order in the hands of every commanding officer and navigator. First out, the busy destroyers, scouring deep blue water outside for prowling enemy submarines; then divisions of carriers dashing into the wind while taking on planes; next, lines of ponderous old battleships and leopard-sleek cruisers, chunky attack transports with nested landing craft, their weather decks studded with thousands of marines, equally crowded with troops the low LSTs, yawing around coral heads to form in sloppy columns—everything headed seaward towards the attack.

Red-faced and sweat-soaked from raw heat, MacDougall bent over his charts, plotting the course. "Mid-channel now, Captain. One thousand yards to Buoy Baker. Next course zero-six-five true."

"Very good," said Captain Hawks. "How are we for time?"

Very good, very good, thought MacDougall. Everything is very good with this skipper or it's no good at all. Well, mid-channel is always good—all those reefs and coral heads around to rip your bottom off.

The ship moved along. Parry Island close aboard now so that Quonset huts, planes, jeeps and men stood out clearly upon the dazzling sand. Then the *Belinda* swung eastward, nicely in place next astern the *Woodbridge*, caught the long swell from open sea and swept out Deep Entrance with the honker calling all hands to the guns. "All troops may remain topside," announced the PA. Approving murmur rose to the bridge from tight-packed marines, watching the shore and other ships, wondering while half knowing what island lay ahead for them.

Captain Hawks looked astern, watching the channel range and estimating his distance from Parry Island. The moment he considered the ship's PA out of earshot to any listener on shore he made a quick grab for the portable mike. That harsh-speaking voice now reached out over his ship. "Attention all hands. Attention all United States Marines. The cook may have told you already, but now I'm telling you officially. We're going to head west for a thousand miles more, and then we're going to take Saipan away from the Japs."

The lid was off now. Cheers and whistles split the air with an electric vitality foreign to oppressive heat. Whether they knew already or thought they did, whether they were afraid of that beach ahead or thought that they were not afraid, they yelled, releasing almost unbearable tension. Then men began to think. Excited conversations died down. By the time the *Belinda* closed up astern of the *Woodbridge* at the head of the first squadron of attack transports, the decks were quiet again so that the swish and sigh of the bow wave could be heard from Captain Hawks's bridge.

Coxswain "Whitey" McClintock of the beach party stopped MacDougall in the passageway. "Are you still deck court officer, Mr. MacDougall?"

"Yes. Why?"

"I was overleave in Diego, sir. Will I get a deck court? I been overleave twice before now."

"I'm afraid so, Whitey. You shouldn't have tried to stretch a seventy-two into ten days leave. Why didn't you holler for some leave when we hit the coast? There's so much to look out for, it's hard to be fair. Some of you guys from way back East . . . You have to speak up for leave, Whitey, when time is short. I was gone on five days myself—I'd have done what I could."

"Oh, that's all right, Mr. MacDougall. I don't care. I got to see Mom and Pa. I can take what's comin' to me—only one thing—you won't take my crow, will you? I think a lot of that crow on my sleeve!"

"Well, son, if you lose your crow it won't be my idea. It's up to the skipper at mast, what happens to you. You know how it is in this Navy. Rules are strict and a P.O. is supposed to set a good example. I'll put in a good word for you. That's all I can do."

Mast was always nasty business, but the men were more nervous than usual today. This was the first time with the new skipper, and it was hard telling what he'd dish up. Chief Master-at-Arms Maxwell lined up the prisoners before the pulpitlike mast table where Chief Yeoman Barton stood with the mast book and a fist full of dog-eared service records, each with its rubber band holding together all the good and bad officially recorded in the records of each man awaiting the captain. Division officers and department heads stood a little to one side, ready to give a character reference for their men in trouble. A single spectator watched from the signal bridge, one tier of deck above. There stood Ensign Twitchell, the signal officer, his bulbous eyes gleaming in anticipation of punishment for these enlisted men. He hoped they all got brig time. That was the only way to handle men: treat 'em rough and they'll keep their places. He'd hoped to have his chief signalman up at mast this time. Morgan had been pretty snotty since leaving the States. It was time to get him back in line. If he could only trick him into some show of open rebellion. . . .

Quigley's nervous cough announced the captain's approach. Maxwell ordered the prisoners to attention and salute. Captain Hawks strode up to the mast table, swung his arm quickly in answering salute, took the mast book from Barton and loudly called the prisoners, one by one.

Two seamen were awarded loss of ten liberties each for being overleave. A cook-striker was confined in the brig on bread and water for being drunk and disorderly. Then the captain's voice snapped out at the line of trembling prisoners. "Next!" Ensign Twitchell felt a golden glow. He hadn't been so happy since the time he got Smith restricted for the whole time the ship was in San Diego. He hoped the next guy would get the brig too.

McClintock was next. Somehow he stepped forward in time to hear the captain read the charge against him. Then he was looking up at those piercing eyes.

"Well," said Hawks, "haven't you anything to say for yourself?"

McClintock lowered his eyes to the deck for a moment, then looked up at his captain again. "No, sir," he said.

Hawks looked hard at the stolid face. He saw sincerity there. This was no man for cheap alibis, but his record for overleave —just bad. "What's the trouble—girls?"

"No, sir."

Hawks turned to MacDougall who had stepped up beside the mast table. "What do you know about McClintock?"

"He's very quiet, Capt'n. Never has much to say, one of the best workers on board. He's been outstanding in the beach party."

"But he doesn't get back to the ship," said Captain Hawks.

MacDougall hesitated. What say now? How could he tell this Academy officer that McClintock came from the slopes of Sassafras Mountain, where a man was free to go wherever he wished whenever it pleased him. "Yes, sir," he said, "he has had trouble getting back. His home is back in South Carolina. He should have been given some leave."

"My home is back in Tennessee," snapped Hawks. "Can I go back to Tennessee when I feel like it? No," he said, looking back to McClintock, "I can't and you can't. I have no choice but to award you a deck court." It was quiet now, quiet enough to hear sounds of water overside. A movement on the deck above caught McClintock's eye. Looking up he met Ensign Twitchell's baleful stare. The little punk, he thought. Somebody's goin' to give him a push one of these nights. Then, as McClintock stepped back to the rank of prisoners, he heard Hawks saying to MacDougall, "You won't have to try him. Your new collateral duty will be senior member, summary court. I'll get another officer to handle deck courts."

Once again McClintock met MacDougall in the passageway. "You heard 'em read me off, sir?"

"Yes," said MacDougall. "I'm sorry. I—well, I will say it— I think it was a dirty trick to take your crow. They had five other kinds of punishment to choose from. But don't let it get you down, Whitey. You keep your nose clean and I'll see you get your rating back again, first chance."

"Thanks," said McClintock. He looked out to sea and blew his nose. "It's all right, sir. Anyhow, I got to see Ma."

"This Ensign Tuttle: what can he do?" Captain Hawks shoved aside the stack of operation plans, planted both elbows on the cabin table and frowned at the last page of the Roster of Officers, U.S.S. *Belinda*.

"I really don't know, sir," said Quigley.

"You don't know! You're my executive officer. You're supposed to know."

"He's new to the ship, sir. We're trying to fit him in. Somehow he—"

"Come, now," said Hawks, banging his empty coffee cup into its saucer. "He must be good for something. There are no passengers on the *Belinda*. We're going to capture Saipan. Every man aboard must fit into the team, and it's your job to find out just where."

Quigley sipped his coffee, put the cup down carefully and looked thoughtfully through the porthole at a patch of empty blue sky.

"Well, sir, he plays the trombone."

"He does! Why didn't you tell me?" Captain Hawks sat up

abruptly and rang for his orderly. A bell clanged outside the cabin and Biggs popped through the curtain as if propelled by its sound. "Find Ensign Tuttle," said Hawks.

Two minutes later Biggs returned. "Ensign Tuttle is on watch, sir."

"Well, tell the officer of the deck to have him relieved," said Hawks. He turned impatiently to Quigley. "Can't somebody relieve him?"

"Oh, yes, sir. Anybody can relieve Ensign Tuttle."

Biggs disappeared again. A few minutes later a stocky ensign with thin blond hair entered the cabin. Hawks waited for him to report. The ensign did not seem to know how but hesitated just inside the curtain.

"Ensign Tuttle?" Hawks asked.

"Yes, sir."

"Play the trombone?"

"Yes, sir."

"Go get it." Ensign Tuttle stood motionless, regarding his commanding officer with mouth half open. "I said, 'Go get it!' " roared Hawks. "Go get your trombone!"

Tuttle stumbled through the curtain, to return shortly carrying his instrument in a battered black case which he opened very carefully. Hawks looked at the long loops of highly polished brass tubing. "Very good. Very good," he said. "Play it."

Again the openmouthed stare. At last Tuttle found his voice. "What shall I play, sir?" he asked in the next thing to a squeak.

"Play the 'Beale Street Blues.' "

Tuttle put the instrument together and gave the slide an experimental thrust. Quigley ducked hastily out of the way and took a chair in the corner of the cabin. Face expressionless, Tuttle took a deep breath, puckered his lips and shattered the cabin with a very loud and fairly accurate rendition of the 'Beale Street Blues.'

"Very good," said Captain Hawks. "Go back to the bridge."

The *Belinda's* bridge was a busy place this afternoon, two days' steaming from Saipan. While Jim Randall busied the watch in the routine yet intricate business of zigzagging precisely in formation with five hundred other ships of the attack force, MacDougall, with his quartermasters, worked on the lee wing of the bridge, carefully fitting together sections of combat maps, pasting and stapling them upon four-by-eight foot sheets of waterproof plyboard borrowed from the boat repair shop. Brooks and Kruger stood at his shoulder, waiting impatiently for a large-scale look at landing beaches which would soon be their intimate concern.

"There," said MacDougall at last. "Now we can get the

picture. . . . See, fellows: there's the stack on the sugar mill at Charan Kanoa. That's where we land."

Brooks sucked in his breath. It was coming back to him—that feeling he had had at Kwajalein, at all the other beaches. Your belly just sucked up about six inches and stayed there until after H Hour. "You going to put in the boat lanes for us?" He hoped his voice sounded casual.

"Sure, Tony. You come back in about an hour and we'll have her all laid out for you. Then we can work out the boat schedules."

"Fine," Brooks said. "Come on Karl, let's go investigate the coffee situation. These people need room to work."

Captain Hawks came out on the bridge wing, looked at the cot which he had ordered welded to the bulkhead just outside the pilothouse door, where he could sleep in comfort, protected from rain squalls yet instantly available in case of trouble. How Gedney had ever managed to sleep in that chair of his was beyond belief—torture instrument, that's all it was. Hawks had ordered it unbolted from the deck and thrown overboard the first day at sea. The carpenter was building him a new captain's chair, not quite so high, because he was much taller than Gedney—a comfortable chair that a man could sit in and forget his back while concentrating on business. Well, he'd have a good chair now, and this bunk was wonderful, needing only a canvas windbreak at the head. Hawks considered taking a short nap, but restlessness carried him on to the wing where MacDougall worked with the battle maps.

"What have you got here, Mr. Navigator?"

"We're plotting the beach area: boat lanes, line of departure, rendezvous locations, transport areas."

"Very good. . . . What's that pile of stuff you have there?"

"More maps, Capt'n. Hundreds of sheets to make up dozens of maps. We'll never need 'em. I picked out those which will be most useful to us—"

"How do you know some of the others won't be more useful?"

"I checked them, sir. I—"

"Listen, Mr. Navigator." Hawks came over and bent over the temporary table where Willicut measured off yardage from Red Beach to the line of departure. Then he frowned at MacDougall. "We haven't got to Saipan yet. I like to see everything there is to see. We have lots of bulkhead space around this bridge. Use it."

"You mean, stick the maps up—"

"Certainly. Stick 'em up all around the place. Let's see what this Saipan looks like."

"Aye, aye, sir. . . . Willicut, send a couple of your men

aft to the boat repair shop. See if Rinaldo can spare about three more sheets of plyboard. We'll use them for plotting around our beach area. The rest go up on the bulkheads—as long as the space lasts."

"What you got here, Mac?" Tony Brooks, back from coffee with Kruger, gasped in amazement at the map-plastered bridge bulkheads. "Looks like a seagoing billboard. . . . And this plyboard? Belongs to my boats, doesn't it?"

"That's right. I borrowed it."

"Don't be surprised if Jerry comes screaming for a sheet of plyboard when the cox'ns start tearing out boat bottoms on reefs."

MacDougall laughed. "Well, if they get lost they can just look over the side and find Saipan stapled across the transom!"

Kruger and Brooks crowded behind Willicut, studying the boat lanes in relationship to the Saipan shore.

"This is a good map," said Brooks. Then he whistled. "Look at the buildings right back of our beach. Wonderful place for snipers."

"Don't forget the mortars and machine gun nests," added Kruger.

Brooks clamped his lower lip tight between his teeth. "Lots of houses there too," he said. "Wonder if there'll be any natives left there when the bombardment picks up."

"I suppose so," said Kruger. "Always seems to be some of 'em left around. Wonder how they feel—having their homes shot up."

"That's not our problem," said Captain Hawks, who had come up silently behind the two boat officers, unnoticed by them. "Our problem is to carry out the landing of our BLT of U. S. Marines—to do it better and faster than any other ship in the squadron." Hawks walked to the forward apron of the bridge and looked down over the foredeck where serious-faced marines huddled about their platoon officers, getting exact instructions as to how they would deploy from the beach. "They have their job cut out for them," said Hawks. "This is going to be a tough landing. A lot of those marines will be dead before this time next week." Hawks's jaw worked back and forth in an ugly movement, as if trying to cancel out inevitable death—as if finding it impossible to do so. Then he said with quiet intensity that electrified every officer and man within hearing upon his bridge, "I expect to break the *Belinda's* record for throwing a combat load of men and materiel on a Jap beachhead. . . . Gedney said something about this ship being a beachhead lady." The jaw worked again, across and back, then Hawks said, "Lady or no lady, this ship is going to produce for me. . . . You're all going to produce!"

CHAPTER 23

Feeling strangely uneasy, the elderly Chamorro rubbed sleep from his eyes and looked out the doorway of his cottage. Dawn light rimmed the peak of Mount Tapotchau, five miles to the northeast. Little bits of pink-white cumulus floated gently towards sunrise in the hands of night-cooled breeze—lovely June morning, yet something wrong. Had his sleep been disturbed by dreams after hearing words from radio Tokyo in the streets of Charan Kanoa the night before? War coming to Saipan, they said: Americans tricked into too deep an advance would be cut off and defeated by Japanese forces. Yes, perhaps he had dreamed of many planes in the sky, though he was not a man given to dreaming. He worked hard at his task of tallying sugar at the mill dock so that he grew tired enough to sleep well in spite of his sixty-seven years. Perhaps Japanese planes had awakened him; after all they had a large field at the south tip of Saipan. Ah, the strange sound—no dream at all—louder and louder now; strange roaring of airplanes, full-throated and not the high singing of Japanese planes to which he was accustomed. Power of many planes near now. Then a whistling growing to a scream, great shock of sound blotting out all other sounds, suction pulling at his body in the doorway; houses of neighbors turning in air, smoke and dust rising, small objects and broken pieces falling. Above the smoke, dark wings escaping; roaring of engines pressing down upon the wreckage and upon him.

Overwhelmed by these impressions it was difficult to think. Something he must do—yes, his wife, the grandchildren and the wife of his son: he must get them away from here. Flames sweeping through the village—cries of pain and cries for help. "Come with much water. . . . Come lift this beam." Others must do these things. He was an old man—his grown son off at Garapan working for the Japanese—all of his strength was needed here. He turned around to find the house still there, only the windows gone. His wife and the wife of his son were gathering half-dressed children together, looking to him for instructions, amazement rather than fear in their faces. That was good; fear would come soon enough. "Come," he said, "we will go quickly to the cave. No, do not wait for food and water. I will return for these things. Come now." His wife scooped up odd garments. He carried one small child; the wife of his son carried her baby. The others followed closely behind him, scrambling over wreckage, looking about with astonishment. "Come," he said. "Come." He got them to the cave which had been prepared for such a time: a large cave shared with other families, dug into the side of a small ravine so that the entrance was hidden from the air and at right angles to the shore. "Wait here," said the old man. "Do not leave until I return with food and water." So he left them, scrambling over rubble for food and a wooden bucket, then to the cistern for water. In anxiety to be with his family he hastened up the path toward the cave. Sounds: that roaring of planes again. They were returning. He must hurry. He felt inclined to drop the water and run; but that would not do, the water was needed. Louder the sound, so quickly from a whisper, here now with roaring and the shrill dropping that was explosion and dirt in his eyes and falling on his body as he lay face down in the path in spilled water.

He rose unhurt; only a strange stunned feeling and a singing in his ears. He ran to the cave, food and empty bucket left behind. It was bad; houses along the path smashed and burning. The cave! It must be all right! He must see; he was tired but he must run. Oh, trouble! Dirt tumbled down, blocking the entrance. Running back now. Some tool—anything! Ah, this old spade in the field of cabbage; quick now, dig, dig! More earth falling down; large stones falling down—the timber they had placed . . . Others now helping; he hardly noticed. He must dig faster. Then a foot, a man's foot. More digging and there were the people who had been inside. Not his wife. Not the children of his son, the wife of his son—yes, at last these too. His wife covering the two young children; the wife of his son with the baby hugged to her breast. There seemed to be no life. But surely—he had just left them to get water and food. . . . Hand of a neighbor on his shoulder, sad shake of head. Oh, surely—oh, no! Then the facts of the matter begin to seep into the mind.

Two days of wandering about in wreckage and hiding from bombers; two days in which to watch ships approaching Saipan Island. During this time the dream started: he saw all things as in a dream. In this haze he saw the ships: at first just a few bombarding the beach from Charan Kanoa, beyond Garapan to Tanapag Harbor. No Japanese were to be seen. They had withdrawn northward and into the hills eastward. This would have seemed strange a week ago, yet now that he had buried his wife and the family of his son it seemed more like early days on Saipan before Japanese came. In this thinking he found absence of pain until more planes came and shells of great battleships reminded him of change to Saipan. He had no fear now. It mattered little whether he lived or died. Something he did not understand pulled him down to hide from explosions. He did not run; he seemed to have nothing to do with it. After the bombs fell he would rise and look out once more.

Early the third morning, from a vantage point up the slope behind Charan Kanoa, he looked westward over ruins to waters beyond filled with ships as far as the eye could reach. In astonishment he began to count, practiced eyes of a tally clerk reaching out for small groups, adding these together into one total. He reached the sum of five hundred fifty, yet some were hidden behind others and still more came over the rim of the sea. For twenty years he had checked bags of sugar into the monthly steamers calling at Charan Kanoa, and all the ships he had seen in that time were fewer than this. Here were ships great and small; from pictures in old Japanese magazines passed from hand to hand about the village he knew them to be ships of war. Until today ships of war had not come to small Charan Kanoa.

With wife and grandchildren to care for he would have remained in the cave. Now there was no one to care for. He could not help his son—there seemed a strange convenience in not caring whether he lived or died—so that between explosions near at hand he could look out at this strange sight. Half interested, thoughts projecting out of a well of sorrow for his lost family, he looked out upon this great invasion fleet. Exact duties and purpose of various types of ships were not known to him. He understood clearly that the sum of their efforts would produce invasion. Groups of small steamers towing cables swept carefully along near shore. To left and to right, columns of warships both great and small moved slowly along, sudden flame and smoke from their gun barrels followed by great noise and shaking in Charan Kanoa. The compact town, dwelling place a few days earlier of nearly two thousand inhabitants, was a ruined shambles, nearly hidden by clouds of dust and smoke rising from burning dwellings. Molasses tanks at the sugar mill were on fire. Strangely the tall mill stack remained standing, but surely it could not long remain.

The old man's weary eyes, smarting now from smoke, looked again toward the invasion fleet. A new group of solid-looking ships had moved closer to shore. As he watched, each ship spawned many smaller craft until there was no counting of them. They were like sea gulls resting upon the moving sea. This needed no explaining; they would be filled with soldiers. In spite of anything the Japanese could do with their many hidden guns, some of these men would reach shore and a battle would follow. Chamorros visiting from Guam had told him that Americans were to be preferred to Japanese as rulers. Whether there would be any improvement of the situation at Saipan, he did not know. One thing he knew: no change could any longer improve his situation.

The smaller boats—they were not so small but that he

thought he saw the heads of many men in each—formed in groups and headed towards Charan Kanoa. Then bombing planes came as they had not come before, and battleships great and small poured exploding shells upon the shore like waves in a great storm—only waves of flame and death—such frightful explosions that even while he told himself that it did not matter, for he had no further desire to live, he found that he had run involuntarily to the mouth of another cave. A moment before watching, now face down in the earth, hands over head to shut out awful sound; but nothing could shut out this sound. The earth shuddered and heaved beneath him. He heard the screaming of shells passing overhead, great shock and explosion all about. Then suddenly there seemed to be quiet, a strange unreal quiet in which was no peace or rest. The trembling of the earth stopped, revealing the trembling of his own body. Then the shooting began again but with different sound: a slower pace with fewer explosions near and more shells screaming as they passed overhead. Now a new sound: pop and chatter from behind, small sharp explosions along the beach and in the water. Japanese mortars and machine guns—he knew these sounds. They had practiced much before Americans came.

There no longer seemed any reason to rise. He was very tired, beginning to feel the shock. So he lay, mind cushioned in nothingness—bees in the summertime buzzing. Voices now: strange voices. He looked up. First bayonets on rifletips poking into the cave. Then big men, tight faces reddened by sun, moving in cautiously, looking at him quickly then deeper into the cave as if for enemy Japanese. Without reasoning why he felt inclined to tell them that there was no danger within, but he could not speak the language of these men. He was not sure whether he could ever speak with men again: same sort of wall about him which had crushed his wife and grandsons, their mother also and perhaps his grown son, father of these children. Wall holding him in, shutting out the living, molding him to death and days past, all reality gone—what he saw before him unbelievable nightmare.

Evidently these soldiers meant him no harm—some strange thing one said, slapping his own chest as if in self praise: "Me American Marine, no hurt you, Joe." The words meant nothing, but the tones conveyed clumsy friendliness. They took him back to another of their comrades, who took him down to the beach, passing the street of his house. It was difficult to recognize anything familiar: house burned—goods scattered, smashed and ruined. It did not matter; nothing mattered.

Other Chamorros were on the beach; some he knew. He felt distant from them; what they said seemed part of the dream and he was not able to speak to them. It surprised him somewhat that even his own people were now without this wall which held him in. In a daze he looked out on all manner of strange craft: steel boats with wheels climbing dripping out of the sea and running along the beach. Boats with crawling feet like caterpillars moved out of the water, clanking over all things in their path. Boats ran against the reef with doors which dropped down, allowing strange mechanical beasts— larger and more gruesome than the land tanks of the Japanese —to wallow and clatter ashore. Some of them did not reach shore: they turned over on the edges of coral and fell into deep holes he could not see but knew to be there. Caterpillar feet turning like mad things and then stopping; the best of steel now dead. Some of the men on the beach were dead. Others were hurt and being helped to shelter. Mortar fire of the Japanese falling near now. Men were falling; others lay flat, then got up and ran towards higher land. One big man, kind but gruff and hurried, even perhaps somewhat in the fear he had felt before the loss of his family, took him to a boat having wheels. Two women and some children were put into the boat. Very quickly they ran into the water. Beyond the reef they were put into one of the boats having a door in front. The women chattered without pause, but the children seemed frightened into silence. Fast and powerful, this boat: throbbing of the motor like the quaking of the land when all the great guns spoke with one voice before the soldiers came. He was lost in thought of all which had happened. Suddenly the hull of a large ship—great steel wall of side and at the top many men running about and shouting down. Above were great davits such as he had never seen before. Hooks were lowered, then the boat was lifted like a small child in the arms of his mother.

Sailors looked down in astonishment from the *Belinda's* weather decks. "Look," one of them cried from the shadow of a boat davit. "There's Saipan Sam with his old lady and kids." The *Belinda's* crew had no way of knowing that the old Chamorro's family was dead, that these others were not related to him. As word of his arrival spread about the ship he was called Saipan Sam by everyone aboard, and so known until the day he died and was buried from the *Belinda's* fantail. He was tall, rather thin and by his general appearance must once have stood proudly erect. Now his shoulders were bent and bewilderment clouded his wrinkled brown face. He might have been fifty or a well-preserved seventy, it was hard to tell. Soft brown eyes seemed to express thanks to the sailors who helped him aboard from Kruger's boat. Otherwise nothing but sad, gentle dignity and the continuing cloud of bewilderment showed in his face. He gave no indication of understanding any English. He did not speak in his native Chamorro or in the Okinawa dialect of Japanese spoken by immigrants to his island. He did not speak at all, now or when refusing food with a gentle shake of his head, or at any time the rest of his life. So he became a mystery aboard the *Belinda*, an object of great curiosity—much more so than the two women and their children.

The women talked readily enough. The older one took charge; she was skinny and wrinkled, dressed in thin black jacket and pantaloons cut in the Chinese manner. With her sharp tongue she scolded the children, keeping them from under the rough boots and dangerous implements of these white men. Sensing that the Americans meant her no harm, she had nevertheless the suspicious manner of a quick, black bird; her manner implied that she had been fooled by men before. She took the food that was given without thanks. It is not necessary to thank men who have destroyed one's home and killed one's husband. Ayee, that was bad! Great explosions and fear in the village; the home suddenly gone with great sound; timbers, building stones and rubbish falling about their heads. Sudden pain in her arm, then numbness so that in fear for her family she forgot the pain. She crawled and hunted in the wreckage. First she found her husband, crushed under a heavy beam. Then with fear in her heart she looked for the children. She found the little one, screaming his head off but unharmed. Then the other, stunned by the falling roof . . .

Here on the ship, as she fed her children and the others, her mind returned to the fears of this morning. Shells still screamed into the village from great guns on the ships. Danger —more danger; she could expect nothing else. There would be a landing and fighting in the town. She was sure of that although she did not see the Japanese soldiers coming to repel the white men as the Japanese radio had promised these many days. She got the children into the cistern and crouched beside them until the Americans came and took them to the beach. She had not seen Americans before, excepting only the one who had visited Charan Kanoa before the war, escorted by the Japanese governor, no less. They said this American was harmless because he rode a bicycle in Japan. Only persons of small importance rode bicycles. These Americans today—they did not ride bicycles. They had more and larger of everything than the Japanese soldiers. They seemed to mean her no harm. It was evident that the Japanese had lied—but she would be cautious. For the present, the children seemed safer upon this ship than in the village. It was necessary to speak now, even though these Americans did not understand. It was necessary to explain about the death of her husband and the destruction of her home. It was necessary to speak to the children to keep them from mischief, and to that younger woman who complained aloud that her husband was gone and that she would not see him again. Husband, indeed! Concubine of the Japanese sub-lieutenant, with her fat baby. It was well that she came. The child had done no harm; his mother foolish and attracted by promises of a better house and a silk kimono. Great scorn in her feeling for this younger woman, yet she gave her a fair helping of food and one of the blankets for her sleeping child.

Her arm! Yes, it had been shattered by the falling roof. This seemed to be a doctor; she must go with him, it seemed. Very well, she would go, but the children must come with her; she lacked strength to search for them again.

"O.K. I relieve the watch."

"O.K. Still on One A. Here's the setup—"

"Has Saipan Sam had any chow yet?"

"No. He won't eat."

"Said anything?"

"No. Just sits lookin' at the beach."

"Maybe his guts are hurt. You know—internal injuries. That's bad. Sometimes they bleed inside."

"I dunno what's the matter. Maybe he's shell-shocked. Just sits there—don't seem to know we're around."

Kearns, boatswain's mate second, was very proud of his new assignment. Commander Quigley had put him in complete charge of the prisoners. Not that they were dangerous or wanted to escape—some said they were Japs and some said they were Chamorros: more like Chinks or Filipinos. He didn't know much about that stuff. Back in New Hampshire they didn't have folk like these. It didn't matter; they were harmless and the kids were cute. The old lady was no trouble. He knew how to handle her: just look her in the eye and talk a little rough. She'd keep the rest of them in line. The old man, though —that Saipan Sam. He just didn't look good. Staring that way at the beach it gave you the willies to watch him, and the worst of it was he never said a word.

Clean 'em up, the exec said. Get 'em in the uniform of the day. Was he kidding? . . . "Come on, Mary. Shower bath: you savee? All make clean." Kearns went through a vigorous pantomime of scrubbing himself. The old lady jabbered something to the children and to the younger woman. They all followed Kearns down the deck towards the head belonging to berthing compartment three-ten. Kearns hesitated a moment over Saipan Sam, then shrugged his shoulders and went on without him. "Guess he ain't interested in water hours," Kearns said to the compartment master-at-arms.

An hour later, passing on his way to the bridge, MacDougall noticed the oldest boy of the Chamorro woman naked and shivering in the shade and early morning breeze of the weather deck. Kearns must have thrown away the child's dirty rags. All hands were busy about the *Belinda*—no time to fit clothes to a native orphan. Impulsively MacDougall went to his room, pulled a clean undershirt from a drawer and returned to the mother. "Here, Mary," he said, pointing to the child, then swung back up the ladder to the bridge.

Later still, entering the wardroom for breakfast, he heard the teasing voice of Dr. Pat Flynn: "I see Mrs. MacDougall is taking the morning air." MacDougall went to the forward porthole where Flynn was looking out over the foredeck. "See, she looks spiffy this morning." MacDougall pushed Flynn out of the way and looked. The boy was still naked, warm now in the sun. His mother wore the undershirt, which looked startlingly white with her dark and wrinkled neck protruding. The shirt hung loosely between skinny shoulder blades like a sail becalmed, and stenciled plainly upon it were the words: LIEUT. DAVID MacDOUGALL. "You got your brand on her in a hurry," said Flynn. MacDougall smiled weakly. There did not seem much point in explaining.

Saipan Sam sat quietly upon a gray Navy blanket which Pappy Moran had spread for him in a quiet spot on the *Belinda's* forecastle head. From this vantage point the elderly Chamorro watched the destruction of Charan Kanoa, which had been his home for sixty-seven years. In spite of the busy sugar mill, it had been a quiet village which seemed to sleep on sunny afternoons, watched over by nearby Mount Tapotchau. Old Sam loved the springtime best, bright flame trees blooming in the valleys and the pathway to the mountain lookout bordered here and there with wild flowers. Some of his neighbors did not care for such things, saying they had no practical value. But something there just for the sake of being made such casual blooms of importance to him. Cabbages do not grow along a mountain path of their own choice. Sam used to climb the winding path up the western slope of the mountain and look down over terraced cliffs to the sun-rise sea. When he was young, the first Japanese had come, humble immigrants, almost unnoticed except for their remarkable industry. Then more arrived, bringing women who bore them very many children. A time came when there were more Japanese than Chamorros and it became noticeable that the Japanese now tilled the largest and best farms, built most of the new houses and excelled in shopkeeping and in beginning new industries. Ships from Kobe called more and more frequently, a change which had made possible his position as tally clerk at the mill dock so that he need no longer work in the fields.

One day great excitement ran through the village: the ship from Japan was bringing persons of importance. This disturbed him little; visitors were welcome, new faces interesting. All Japanese settlers gathered at the water's edge dressed in holiday clothing and holding the small Japanese flags of which they seemed so fond, waiting to greet the arrival of some person of importance. At last a boat was rowed from the ship to the shore. Deference was made to one Japanese dressed in white, much bowing performed after the Japanese custom. Only then was it disclosed to the Chamorros that this gentleman was the new governor, sent to Saipan by the Emperor of Japan. First years of Japanese rule were moderate; growth and improvements came to Charan Kanoa. But there was a loss of free feeling, new sensation of being pushed, slowly but irrevocably. Chamorros were now of the lesser importance. There came to be doubtings upon the island regarding the nature of true religion. In nearby Garapan, near ruins of a pagan temple left by some prehistoric civilization, the bell tower of an old Spanish mission still rose through dense, neglected foliage. In his youth there had been talk of the Christo in the village, somehow good-humoredly mixed with local superstitions and folklore. Sam was not certain how his particular race came to be on Saipan or where they would go after life. Being a thoughtful man, he pondered upon these things. He did not attend the church, but he enjoyed listening to the church bells which brought a feeling of joyous assurance to the countryside. Then, adding to the confusion, a new Japanese Shinto shrine was built and well attended by the now preponderant Japanese. Here fish fresh from the sea, well-scrubbed carrots and bundles of unthreshed rice were offered to gods of the Japanese. There was no joyous assurance in the dull sound of gongs struck by Shinto priests. Other changes came quickly now: Japanese real estate offices doing a thriving business with immigrants arriving by OSK from Japan; sounds of wooden clogs in the streets; places of moving pictures, where for a price one saw and heard samurai tales of early Japan and pictures of war in China, where it was said the Japanese brought peace and a thousand years of prosperity. Smell of fish in the streets, sounds of women gossiping, laughter of playing children: these things remained about the same, though there was now another language in the talk. Japanese soldiers arrived at Saipan; they passed through the streets on patrol or during maneuvers. On days off they were good customers at the shops, many were kind to children, some took Chamorro girls into their quarters. There was little of the military regimentation of nearby Iwo Jima; this they learned from the soldiers, who were happy to be stationed at Saipan. Defense of the island was mobile, and though troops and small tanks rattled through Charan Kanoa they were stationed for the most part in the hills and caves.

Recently there had been little of general information in the news from Tokyo that blared from radio loudspeakers. War, war, all the time news of war. At first all was strength and victory for Japan. America, the new enemy, was at the point of surrender. Sam knew little about these Americans—the lone visitor years before, the reports from Guam. There was uneasiness in his mind regarding all these things, but he thrust them from his mind and looked to the slopes of Mount Tapotchau for peaceful reassurance. Then more and more the Tokyo radio spoke of strategic withdrawals, a phrase repeated so many times that many Chamorros believed that the Americans were increasingly victorious and some day might come to Saipan. He had considered these things, yet his principal concern had been that a young Japanese—polite to him, well educated—had replaced him as chief tally clerk at the sugar mill. Once more he sat beside open cargo hatches, counting bags in slingloads of sugar. His resentment to changes in Saipan centered about this loss in prestige and salary. Now he understood that the problem had been one of greater significance. It would be good to sit beside a clattering winch once more, counting sugar bags, knowing that his wife, his son and the children of his son were safe at home. Knowing full well that these things could never be returned to his life, Saipan Sam sat quietly upon the gray Navy blanket, watching from the *Belinda's* forecastle head the completion of the destruction of Charan Kanoa.

CHAPTER 24

Kruger looked left along his line of amtracks—line wasn't the name for this tangle of nearly submerged amphibious tractors, treads thrashing at heaving swell, blunt bows yawing from one side to the other. Set faces under the helmets studding the square tubs: marines quiet in all this racket, waiting for their moment. He knew they were quiet: no lips moved, no expression changed. They might as well be frozen, in spite of cold sweat running down their faces. Only the paddle tracks spun relentlessly around while the Army sergeants plucked savagely at their controls, trying to keep formation. Kruger's guide boat was hard enough to handle at this slow four knots necessary for lumbering amtracks. His green coxswain was white and expressionless now as he spun his wheel and over-gunned his throttle, then jerked his clutch to neutral until the lumbering amtracks caught up. Kruger hovered over his coxswain. "Close in on 'em, Cox. Don't be afraid of 'em. . . . Shove 'em over."

Somehow time and distance were running out; somehow it must come out even, time and reef. Last savage diving of carrier planes over the beach strip; sudden easing of bombardment shock pumped over their heads all the way in. Frightening quiet now so that the mere roar of amtrack and boat engines, the clatter of treads stood out sharply. Hillside now a smoky haze with full sun in his face. Smoke blowing along shore, clearing enough so that the stack showed plain. They had been pushed out of position by five miles of amtracks spreading out a yard here and a yard there. Brooks was beckoning Kruger frantically to close up to the left. Kruger shouted to his coxswain, then shook his head, grasped the wheel and spun left, shoved his boat against the nearest amtrack and waved northward with his helmet. Here and there an amtrack got the idea and cut left, followed by others. The line grew more ragged than ever, but it was sliding up into range. Time was running out but they had a chance to make it. The landing had to be in the right spot for each platoon in that five-mile line: each one was briefed for an exact sector on the beach. This was more important than getting in front of a bleachers filled with VIPs; life and death now to get to the proper place, leaving no holes in the advance inland, no costly redeployment along an exposed beach raked by Jap mortars. Smoke filled Kruger's nostrils now. Whether smoke from bombardment or smoke from enemy fire splashing just ahead he could not tell. He only knew that it was acrid, somehow stimulating, challenging. Two minutes to go; Brooks's arm pointed to the beach. Straight in now, and by some miracle, after two minutes of jockeying, for the first time all morning the long line of amtracks copied the wavy line of shore and reef.

Little flags stuck up in the water ahead, dipping under the swells, then showing wet but clear: white flags, red flags, not bobbing up and down like buoys. Markers on the reef! Jap target markers! That was the reef, close ahead, and Jap mortars were registered upon them. That's why the mortars plopped in that harmless looking way just ahead. They're waiting—waiting for us! Tightening of muscles at the back of your neck and that clay-baked feeling on your face. Jagged line of white reef showing close ahead as high tide slopped over it. His ramp boat could not cross that reef; the amtracks would have to go it alone from there. Through the smoke, hills and trees, a bit of white sand and a lot of brush; mill stack and ruined town to the left. Leave it, leave it; time and place were settled now. Right or wrong, this was the place and the time of landing. Herd in the amtracks; shove them at that reef! Bayonets reflecting early sunlight, dots of camouflaged helmets covered with netting, tanned faces toward the beach—man in the nearest tub swallowing and swallowing at nothing. Then up, those screwball amtracks, up from almost awash, exposing bulky armored sides. Tracks gripping and sliding at reef edge, rising bow first, some level, some at a forty-degree list, quivering there then leveling off and grinding over the reef—all but one in his wave of eighteen. This fellow rising only on one side, up and up, then flipping over on its back, spilling marines, helmets, bayonets. A swell blocked them from view, then up on the next swell with his VP to see heads bobbing and arms thrashing water, marines weighted with packs, grenades, portions of machine guns they carried. That cruel line of reef formed a wall between them so that he could do nothing to help—might as well be miles away. Up again on a swell—glimpse of the rest of them clattering up the beach now, land creatures again, lumbering into battle—those that weren't hit by mortars, those that didn't fall into deep potholes to drown their engines and leave more marines swimming.

No time to gape around now; time to put over the marker buoys at the flanks of the boat lane and right at the reef line. Kruger looked along the reef to Brooks, who was dropping his buoy now, a few yards from the reef. Brooks was in a hurry; he had to go back and guide in the second wave. Kruger had time to do a careful job—if the mortars would let him. His boat was about ten yards from the reef. He motioned his white-faced coxswain to take the boat closer, then turned his attention to the buoy. It was a cumbersome affair of sheet metal, with a large orange-colored flag at the top to show up against water and reef. Ten fathoms of new line connected it to the anchor, a two-hundred pound tub-shaped chunk of concrete. The buoy had to be dropped close to the reef. Water shelved off deeply; if he dropped too far from the reef, that anchor would pull buoy and all beneath the surface. Brooks had been lucky—like some of the amtracks. He must take no unnecessary chances with this marker. The other waves must have a guide to follow. "Here, you fellows," Kruger called to deckhand and motor-mac, "give me a hand." Together the three of them dragged buoy and heavy anchor up to the bow and lowered the ramp nearly horizontal. Kruger looked about him, then motioned to the coxswain to correct position a few yards further south. Something plomped into the water near the boat, followed by a sharp explosion. Water cascaded upon them all, gallons of it washing about in the open cockpit. Jap mortar fire! They had the reef registered all right; knew just what to do with those nasty little guns to hit any spot along this reef. "They're zeroed in on us all right. Let's hurry up and get out of here!" Another geyser of water nearly swamped their boat. Before spray quit falling, Kruger raised his hand in signal for the coxswain to hold position. No time to lose; the next one might be a direct hit. "All right, boys. Let's put her over." A quietness behind him. He turned around to see his two helpers flat on their faces in the bilge—in a funk, no use bothering with them now. He struggled alone with the concrete anchor, shoving, edging, rocking it. At last the thing teetered over the edge of the ramp and splashed down, bights of line flying wild and at last the buoy jerking out, nearly taking him along with it. Well, it was out there, just at the reef edge—but those greenhorns! "Hey, you two," he yelled, angry now. "Crank up that ramp! Get up off your faces; you aren't in the sack!" No response. He lunged at the two, slapping one across the rump and kicking the other. Deckhand and motormac shivered a moment, then rose sheepishly, faces gray-green, looking around them just in time to see another near miss.

Grinding sound under the skeg: the coxswain had let the boat broach to and drift upon the reef. Quick look overside. They couldn't back the engine; that would rip off prop and rudder. Here came Brooks with the second wave. No use shouting for help; battleships now sending a rolling barrage into the hills, drowning out all human sound. Voice radio was useless, channels overcrowded and nothing decipherable in this din. Kruger grabbed up his semaphore flags and wigwagged violently. Almost at once Brooks held up an answering hand; help coming, things could be worse. Down the line some fifty yards two amtracks of the second wave were hit. One faltered, then floundered up on the reef ledge, lurched ahead a few yards, then stopped dead, nearly high and dry. The other amtrack was running out of control in tight circles, one track shut off. At last it dropped into a pothole, sank halfway down and stopped. Marines clambered overside, picking their way around potholes as they waded shoreward. The rest of the second wave swept over the reef unharmed and lurched up the beach.

Here came Brooks, with Larson gunning the speedy command boat wide open. Another mortar shell threw up water just astern. Speed helped that time. Boat alongside now; help at last.

"What's the trouble?" yelled Brooks.

"I'm hung up on a reef. Give me a tow."

Brooks was laughing at him, yes, laughing! "I've got to go bring in the third wave. You're on salvage duty now, Karl. Get yourself off." Larson gunned the command boat motor and Kruger was left alone with his reef. He was frightened and angry, but he put his emotions to work.

"Come on, you guys, if you want to live! We'll get out and shove her off." Two feet of water on the reef here. They got onto it carefully, Kruger grabbing a stern fast as he jumped. I'm not going to let this green cox'n run off and leave me standing here, he thought. They couldn't rock her loose, not just three of them sloshing about on slimy coral. All they could do was to wait for each swell and then push together as she lifted. The third swell did the trick; the boat floated free, and somehow they floundered aboard, dripping and short of breath. "Open her up, Cox'n. We'll go out a piece first. Keep the boat moving. We're going to live through today if I have to brain the whole lot of you."

First minutes after H Hour had always been a letdown on the *Belinda*. It was a long grind from first plans to the enemy beach: exhausting rehearsal landings were followed up with more training and study during the anxious approach deep into enemy territory. The last night at sea was a sleepless one for almost all hands: maneuvering with the squadron, lookouts alert and all guns manned against enemy reprisals, breaking formation on signal to take assigned station in the transport area four miles west of the landing beaches, launching boats in black night, debarking marines, guiding boat waves to the rendezvous area by radar—bridge and weather decks a mad whirl of comings and goings, orders and counter orders—orders of boatswain's mates drowned out by screaming boat davits, orders of Captain Hawks outshouted by PA and TBS. Then all hands remaining aboard sweat out the timed waves while bombardment crescendo reached its ear-shattering climax. Until Saipan this mad activity had been followed by a half hour of near quiet, waiting for boats to return. Later, much later than the excited crew liked, orders came to stand in close to the beach.

Saipan was different. Before the seventh wave hit the beach, orders came to proceed to the unloading area off the reef as soon as boat lanes were clear. Hawks reacted immediately with, "Ahead, full speed. Take her in there, Mr. Navigator. Looks clear enough to me right now. Let's get in there first and show the squadron how to unload an APA."

Seventh and eighth timed waves of LCVPs and tank lighters were still on the way in. Minesweepers, patrol craft and thousands of landing craft just retracted from the beach dotted blue water off the reef. Surging along at full power, white lace of bow wave curling from her bow, the *Belinda* swept past anchored destroyers still marking the line of departure.

"Here comes the ninth wave," said MacDougall to Jim Randall, who had the deck.

"Sure enough," Randall grinned. "But don't forget to get me stopped before we hit the beach. I don't think the *Belinda* could retract!" Hawks seemed content to leave the direction of the ship to these two. After a glance at *Belinda* boats from alongside, now trying to catch up, and a satisfying check on the other ships in the squadron which still remained in the outer transport area, he trained his glasses on the beach, watching amtracks crawling from reef to shore, watching marines deploying around the outskirts of Charan Kanoa. MacDougall noticed that Hawks's nostrils were quivering as if pleasurably excited by the sight of beach and battle, the shooting and getting shot at. The *Belinda* would soon identify herself with this close-range action, and her ship's boats would make three trips for every one possible from the outer transport area. As the *Belinda* threaded her way past boat waves, LSTs and self-propelled barges, MacDougall and Randall shared something of this feeling. Here, on this high bridge of exactitudes, they longed for the boats again, for intimacy with salt water and reef, the uncertainties, changes of scene, excitement of danger. Unable to go in the *Belinda's* landing craft, like two small boys they played boats with the mother ship for the fleeting moments of this swift run in to the reef. Then planned regulation would take over again.

Saipan loomed up at them, scrubby trees on Tapotchau and lesser peaks protruding above billowing smoke. Mountains here instead of coconut trees, yet sameness of acrid smoke and barking guns, of dive bombers plunging down. Closer still to the reef—*Belinda* poking ahead on a one-third bell. Other differences from Kwajalein: instead of tottering radio towers, big mill stack shot through with holes yet still erect, forming an accurate visual marker for plotting of ships, boat lanes, gunnery. With radar and a visual marker like that there was little guess work for the invading navy. That mill stack was now a worse enemy to the Japanese than any single unit now hammering at Charan Kanoa. No time for gazing from the *Belinda's* bridge now as she swept up to the white coral wall of the outlying reef. MacDougall stopped engines, coasted ahead then backed down with the ship's bow poking within five hundred yards of the reef. "Five fathoms under the bottom, Capt'n."

"Very good. Just give me room to swing the stern, Mr. Navigator."

"Aye, aye, sir. . . . Three-eight-zero yards now, sir. Four fathoms under the bottom. I can't be sure of the bottom closer to the reef. I'd suggest—"

"Oh, you would, would you? Very well. . . . Let go the

starboard anchor," shouted Hawks. "Hold her at short stay now; we may have to get out of here in a hurry. . . . And keep the engineers on their toes. When I order speed ahead, I want power right now!"

"Aye, aye, sir."

"Get your boats alongside now and get that combat cargo to the beach. I want the ship completely unloaded by sunset."

Mouth open with astonishment, MacDougall stared at Hawks. Could the man be serious? It was impossible to land nine hundred tons of ammunition and supplies on the reef in her own boats between now and sunset. Perhaps one more day —MacDougall closed his mouth, waited until Hawks's hazel eyes stopped boring into his own, then reached for his binoculars and went to the wing to check up on the ship's boats. Small blue-green wavelets slapped the ship's side playfully as loaded craft from transports still out in deep water churned past on their way to the reef, where everything going ashore had to be transferred by hand to amtracks. Tide was ebbing, and amtracks lumbering across the reef were high out of water now as they picked their way around deadly potholes. The reef line was dotted with wrecked amtracks, some lying on one side, some capsized, others submerged in deep potholes. Small red and white flags, set along the reef by the Japanese for mortar registration seemed now like gravestones for these dead mechanical monsters. Randall came up beside MacDougall.

"That's a dirty looking reef, Mac. Look at that mess of junked amtracks—just enough reef to tip 'em over, just enough hole to drown everyone aboard. I wonder how many men . . . ? I wonder why . . . ? Here we stand, you and I up on this cockeyed bridge when we ought to be down there with the salvage boat, pulling them out from under."

"Take it easy, Jim, take it easy. It's too late now. Anybody still pinned under those things is past help."

"I know, I know," said Randall. "But just standing here. . . . Well, here comes our boats. Time to pass the ammunition."

Humming electric winches dragged ammunition out of cargo holds far below the *Belinda's* waterline and lifted it to her weather decks. There it hung, slingloads of all caliber, badly needed in the fight. Eleven boats bobbed alongside, each flying the Victor flag of diagonal red cross on white background, signal of boats carrying wounded. Chief Alvick took a quick look overside. "Belay the ammo, boys," he said. "Set your loads down on deck, easy now. We'll have to unload the casualties first. . . . Ned, scamper up to the bridge and tell Mr. Mac-Dougall."

Captain Hawks looked very displeased. "What's the delay, MacDougall? We've got to get that ammunition ashore. Here's three dispatches in the last ten minutes. Thirty caliber, fifty caliber, thirty-seven millimeter, seventy-fives, one-oh-fives—they want everything!"

"Mr. MacDougall. Mr. MacDougall, sir."

The navigator looked around. Ned Strange, that naïve kid from the second division. "Tell it to me later, son. Run back to Chief Alvick. Tell him to get those boats loaded and headed for the beach. They're running out of ammo ashore. We can't hang the hook now."

"But Mr. MacDougall, sir. I was trying to tell you. Them boats are loaded."

"What's this?" roared Hawks, leaning over MacDougall's shoulder to glare at Strange. "What are the boats loaded with?"

"Wounded, Captain. One marine's got his balls shot off! He's bleeding something—"

"All right, all right," snapped Hawks. "Go back with your message." Hawks jumped to the PA, pushing the watch boatswain's mate out of his way so hard the youngster crashed into the bulkhead. Hawks flipped on all groups and stuck his face into the microphone. "Attention all hands concerned with casualties. Expedite hoisting in casualties; get the wounded to the sick bay. Reload boats with ammunition, you deck divisions; shove them off for the beach. Keep things moving. This is the *Beachhead Belinda* where we do everything better and faster than any other ship." Hawks snapped off the PA, walked out to the port wing and looked down at the waiting boats, each with its burden of litters. He had seen the same thing at Guadalcanal, at Sicily: sallow faces of wounded men, shivering under gray blankets in this hot morning sun—the blood-soaked bandages. It had to be that way. Get the troops ashore. Send them ammunition, guns, bulldozers. . . . The *Belinda* had to be the first unloaded, she had to be! They would be the first, and at the same time they would take efficient care of every casualty that came alongside. There were always better ways, faster ways. His mind flashed back to the morning he had taken over command of the *Belinda,* telling Gedney, "Everything can be made more efficient. . . ." Now he swung around and grabbed MacDougall by the shoulder. "Go down to the after-deck and loosen up the bottlenecks. Try to take worst casualties aboard first, but remember, our primary job now is to get that ammunition ashore. Understand?"

"Yes, sir," said MacDougall and shot down the ladder railing on the sweaty palms of his hands, thinking as he hurried aft, that fellow with his balls shot off is merely secondary.

Kruger shoved off from the *Belinda* with a light load: blanket-wrapped bodies of five marines who had died of their wounds notwithstanding the combined efforts of Flynn, Gates and Bell. Five litters did not fill his boat, but other VPs waited alongside and it seemed out of place to carry ammunition with the dead. This was the same boat and crew he had used to guide in the first wave earlier in the day. All three youngsters, still shaken from their introduction to mortar fire, looked uneasily from corpses to shore. They looked to Kruger for reassurance, but gloom reflected in his face only added to their discomfiture. Kruger stared at smoke billowing beyond the reef. Remembrance filtered through its murk so that he found no cheer in the brightly impersonal sunshine dancing on the water about his craft. Makin, Kwajalein, now here. Hit the beach with men in helmets; bring sallow faced wounded men back on litters—sometimes a helmet rolling about in the bilge; finally, these completely quiet ones, blankets over heads obliterating face and personality. One of them he knew about: husky blond fellow, his groin a mass of bloody compresses. Kruger had nearly burned up the engine, revving him out to the ship. Back in the boat now in less than two hours—straw stubble of cropped head covered, but that was him: the forward litter in the starboard bilge.

Amtracks lay to just outside the reef, waiting for cargo. Kruger headed for the nearest one. When within hail, a bulky marine called out, "Got a load for us?"

"Yes," said Kruger, "I've got a load."

"What you got?"

Kruger did not answer but motioned his coxswain alongside the LVT. He noticed sergeant's stripes daubed on the big man's fatigues, and that his face, naturally florid, was further inflamed by heat and exertion.

"What kind of ammo you got, Lieutenant?" he asked.

"No ammo," said Kruger. "Five dead for burial ashore."

As the VP bumped gently alongside the amtrack, the red-faced sergeant stood on the prow of his armored craft and looked at the litters in Kruger's boat. "Stiffs!" he said, contemptuously. "We don't need stiffs. We need live men—ammunition." The sergeant nodded to his driver who clashed gears and headed for another VP.

Kruger tried three other amtracks, but the answer was the same, though more gently spoken. No one wanted these dead. On the last amtrack he noticed a marine corporal, obviously a passenger for he hopped about nervously and looked anxiously up and down the reef.

"What're you looking for?" Kruger asked him.

"I'm looking for Sergeant Pitzer. He had the phones and radios for our outfit. Didn't show up. The captain thinks he may be stalled out here. Can you help me?" The corporal looked at the blanket-covered stretchers, then back to Kruger.

"I'll help you," said Kruger. "Might as well be doing something." He thought about his orders from Captain Hawks—the Old Man would be very angry about this delay. But here at the reef, only half a mile from the *Belinda* and Navy regs, he was in a different world—the sergeant wanted ammunition. "Know the number of the amtrack?" Kruger asked.

They poked along the reef, climbing out of the boat to scramble up and look into one amtrack after another, some stalled more or less upright, some tipped over on boxlike sides. One of these was shattered by mortar fire. It was not the one they looked for. Within they found three mutilated bodies which they put in the bottom of the VP beside those from the *Belinda*. The seventh amtrack was completely capsized. Screwing his head around to make out the number, the corporal showed immediate excitement.

"That's it!" he cried out. "That's the one!" Then his voice trailed off in—"But they couldn't be. They just couldn't be."

Something was tightening up in Kruger, but he shoved it back within himself, tried to keep his voice calm. "Let's have a look," he said. "Tide's going out—perhaps we can get into it."

They scrambled up on the reef again and splashed around the LVT. One corner on the far side rested on a small hummock of coral, allowing sea water to slosh in and out. Kruger held his flashlight while the corporal carefully thrust head and shoulders into the capsized cockpit. After a long minute the corporal withdrew his head slowly. "They're in there," he said simply. "Sergeant Pitzer and Gowan and Charles; two other guys too."

I knew it, thought Kruger. "We might as well take them too," he said. "I'll hand 'em out to you. Be real careful when you pull them through. Don't push against the side; I don't want to be bottled up in this thing." Then he tossed his helmet into the boat and crawled under the gunwale of the capsized amtrack.

Dark and nearly suffocating-hot dampness inside. Kruger had the feeling of being imprisoned here; waiting for the tide to come in again and shut off the air. Hollow sound to the barrage; now and then between reverberations he heard musical sloshing of water over the reef. Soft, warm and limp, these bodies. No way to move them but to put his arms around and struggle in the dark to the small hole of light. He had to take off packs from two so that they would go through. All five bodies out at last; Kruger turned for a last careful look. Startled by movement—what, life in this thing? It was the corporal, after equipment. "They're all smashed," he said, putting down the last of the battered radios very carefully, as if afraid to shock a tube. They got out of the thing, the corporal dragging a reel of telephone wire. The hole was not quite large enough for the reel. A shell burst nearby.

"Come on," yelled Kruger. "Let's get out of here!" The coxswain shoved his clutch in reverse and gunned the motor. Water boiled around the propeller but failed to move the boat. "We're hung up on the reef," said Kruger. "You stay there, Cox. Rest of us out on the reef and shove her off. Come on now. Get hot!" They strained against the ramp, waiting for the next explosion, wondering if they were stuck for good. "Heave-ho, boys. The tide's going out. You want to stay here?" At last the boat came free—no more Jap fire. "Get her out to deep water, Cox. Let's take a blow!"

A hundred yards off the reef Kruger stopped the boat. They were reasonably safe here. He looked at his watch: 1430. The boys hadn't had any chow since midnight. "You fellows hungry?" he asked.

The coxswain looked at his mates, who shook their heads. "No," he said, "we ain't hungry."

Kruger thought of eggs, toast and coffee, hastily gulped before boats were away—his stomach uneasy ever since, but he did not feel hungry. "Here," he said, reaching behind kapok life jackets stowed along the bulwarks, "I got some pineapple juice—lots of it." He pulled out a tall can, punctured it with his sheath knife and passed it around. Each man took a mouthful or two. The stuff was warm, sickening sweet in this heat, but it moistened dry mouths. The sun had charge of the boat now, beating nearly straight down into it. No breeze, no shade, only this craft rising with its corkscrew motion over the chopped-up swell. They were dazed and frustrated; sound and sight of battle so close, just a shocking thing that pounded into their eardrums and flesh without any particular significance. Clothes soaked from salt water and salt sweat now nearly dry again, salt showing white on jungle-green fatigues. Kruger's clothes were torn and stained with dried blood from nasty coral cuts. He noticed this casually; none of it seemed important. "Go back to the reef off Red," he said to the coxswain. "Perhaps they'll take the bodies now."

Sliding up to the nearest amtrack Kruger found himself facing the red-faced sergeant once more. "Got any ammo?" asked the sergeant. "Oh, it's the floating mortuary. . . . I got my orders, Lieutenant: nothing but live marines and ammunition."

"Then you don't want us," said Kruger bitterly. His lips curled into an ugly snarl as he fairly spat out at the sergeant, "I've got thirteen stiffs now." Then weariness crept into his tone. "Shove off, Cox," he said.

"There's another of our boats shot up, Captain," reported Jim Randall. Hawks strode across his bridge and glared down at Boat Twenty-two, under tow of another VP. Ramp askew, plyboard sides splintered, thin steel sheathing, jokingly referred to by shipfitters as armor plate, riddled with holes. Down by the head and nearly awash, this craft; the man at the wheel evidently not the regular coxswain, clumsy and excited as he struggled to get alongside. Second division sailors swung overside on the cargo whip at number five, sloshed down into the boat, got out the sling and hooked on. Winches hummed: up went the boat, water gushing from holes; motor-mac wounded, coxswain dead.

"We've had enough of that!" cried Hawks angrily. "Robinson. Oh, Robinson." Then turning impatiently to his orderly: "Get the communications officer." Robinson came running from Radio One. "Call Checkerbox," said Hawks. "How many times have we asked for call fire this morning with negative results? Five times?"

"Yes, sir. Still negative answer: no priority available. When DDs return to targets of opportunity—"

"Forget the destroyers," shouted Hawks. "I've got guns. I'll handle my own target of opportunity."

Art Hall, the *Belinda's* gunnery officer, slid down the ladder from his control station atop the signal bridge. "I've got those Jap guns spotted, Captain. We can give the range when we ask for call—"

"I'm all through asking," Hawks interrupted. "Go get Gun One ready—H.E. and fragmentation."

Hall's face brightened. "You mean you're going to let me take a crack at 'em, Captain?"

"Why not?" said Hawks. "Guns are to shoot with." He swung around to MacDougall. "Get out that Army grid map and plot the *Belinda's* position on it accurately."

"Aye, aye, sir." Quartermasters ran up with a sheet of four-by-eight foot plyboard upon which the pieces of the huge grid map covering Charan Kanoa were carefully pasted together. The crew of Gun One busied with ammunition.

Somehow word got around the ship. Feet clattering up steel ladder to bridge—a major and captain of artillery, on stand by orders to go ashore with their division. The major saluted Captain Hawks. "Understand you're going to take on that shore battery, Captain. We've made a study of the terrain— glad to assist in spotting fire."

"Fine," said Hawks. "I want to get that fellow out of there. Here's my gunner and navigator . . ."

Mount Tapotchau dominated lesser hills which clustered about her so that part way up her side were many small valley-like depressions. From one of these, green and pretty as a golf course, came the mortar fire so deadly on the *Belinda's* beach and along the reef line where her boats worked. Hidden from view in that hollow, the Japanese guns lobbed their shells over a five-hundred foot hillock and dropped them with deadly accuracy on registered positions on beach and reef. Judging from puffs of smoke there were two emplacements of two or more guns each. "Initial azimuth zero-six-seven; range five-zero-two-five yards," said Hawks to the bridge orderly, who stared back in a startled way at his captain, wondering if any action was expected of him. Hawks laughed aloud at the blank look. "Commence fire," he shouted to his talker, just five feet away. Three seconds later the five-inch bow gun cracked sharply, barrel recoiling abruptly with a quick flash of muzzle blast. While the shell sailed through the air all hands watched the green hill intently. "There she is," cried Hawks as a neat puff of smoke blossomed on the high side of the small green valley. "Over." The next shot landed short. Corrections passed through the phone lines from the gun spotters: ". . . up. Left two minims."

"Two shots more and we'll be on 'em," said Hawks in a conversational tone to the bridge messenger. The boy swallowed. He couldn't make this skipper out—ignore you like a stick; then sometimes . . . "She's on; dead on!" shouted Hawks, dancing happily in a circle, then slapping his binoculars on target once more.

"Jap fire along the reef getting heavier, Captain," said Mac-Dougall anxiously. "Another boat hit."

"All right, all right," said Hawks. "We've got 'em under the barrel now." His voice rose commandingly, "Rapid fire. Pour it in on 'em!" Smoke billowing up in the little valley now, gradually blotting it from view. During all this time no enemy had been seen, nor had the *Belinda* herself been menaced by the Japanese fire which killed her boat crews along the reef just over the bow. It all seemed a most impersonal business.

Ten minutes later Hawks gave orders to cease fire. No more puffs of smoke came from the high green valley, and all the rest of that afternoon not one *Belinda* boat was shattered by Japanese mortar fire.

Before the empty shell cases had been gathered up, Hawks sent for the ship's painter. "Paint two Jap field pieces in white, six inches high, outboard of both wings of the bridge. Paint a small Jap flag over each gun. Have it done in thirty minutes. Then stand by with your paintbrush. I may find another target of opportunity."

"By any reasonable standards the man should be dead now," said Dr. Bell to Chaplain Hughes. "Shattered leg: compound fractures to fibula, tibia, femur—the works. Broken wing: that one is just a simple fracture of the humerus. Seven ribs fractured: don't see how he can breathe. But those are mere scratches to this: he's got a horrible skull fracture—brains exposed from a blow on the side of his head that should have killed a mule, let alone a CB. But look at him over there—

won't even lie down! Wants to see what's going on, he says."

"Think he'll pull through?"

"He hasn't got a chance to live 'til morning. Don't let that bright look fool you. . . . Well, Chappie, I've got to go back to surgery now. Plenty more of them waiting there." Bell placed his hand on the little dark-eyed chaplain's shoulder for a moment. "We sure appreciate what you are doing here."

"I'm only doing my job."

"So you joined the Navy to empty bedpans!"

Hughes smiled. He was thinking of One who washed the feet of His disciples, but he only said, "I don't have trained hands like yours, Doc, but I can give your hospital apprentices a good run for their money."

"Those little extra things you do make a lot of difference around this place." Bell turned to leave, then added with a grin, "Better put on your ear muffs before you visit that CB. His language! . . ."

Chaplain Hughes had been at it for over thirty hours, ever since the first casualties had been lifted aboard. At first he had confined help to spiritual aid and to the writing of letters. But the flow of wounded marines increased, boatload after boatload, filling the sick bay, over-flowing into the troop officers' mess hall here and now to the after hatch and to the better ventilated of the troop compartments belowdecks. Twenty-five hundred casualties had been sent out from the beach in the last twenty-four hours. There were no hospital ships; the full burden fell upon ships like the *Belinda*, which herself had now over two-hundred-sixty, some deep in shock, some recovered sufficiently to joke about their experiences, others slipped beyond the last shadow. The *Belinda's* doctors worked almost continually in surgery; corpsmen did work which normally would be done by a surgeon, so Chaplain Hughes fetched water and carried bedpans. Sometimes there was time to read from the Testament in his sweaty shirt pocket, always as he did little helpful things, he found time and made opportunity to speak of eternal life and to repeat words he knew and loved so well: *"In my Father's house are many mansions . . . I go to prepare a place for you . . . Greater love hath no man than this, that a man lay down his life for his friends. . . ."* Hughes could talk with a bedpan or a tattered comic book in his hand; he could talk gently, reassuringly while holding fingers soon to stiffen in death; he could joke and kid along with those who seemed to need some of that. An overhead blower puffed hot air into the fetid mess hall. The after part of the compartment, near the entrance, was used for space to diagnose wounds, to remove tattered and filthy combat fatigues and to scrub up for surgery while litters were suspended by their handles between two long mess tables. In the forward half of the compartment tables were covered with mattresses brought up from the troop officers' quarters. Here lay some of the more seriously wounded, screened off from the others where they could be quiet and have as much ventilation as possible. The CB referred to by Dr. Bell reclined against a half sheet of plyboard set at an angle under his mattress. Dark eyes twinkled from beneath a mass of bandage about his head. Left leg and right arm were immobilized in Dr. Bell's orthopedic casts and he breathed with difficulty, ribs heavily encased with adhesive wrappings. Lanky, heavy-boned, he waved his good arm in greeting.

"Hi there, Padre. Need a little help from me today? You been awful busy."

Shivering inwardly from impact of the good-natured nickname alien to his Methodist background, Hughes grinned back. "Sure," he said. "You give me a little moral support. I need it."

"Oh, I never been much good at morals, Padre, but I'll cheer you up with a funny story about what happened to me today."

"You shouldn't tire yourself talking too much."

"Oh, that's all right, Padre. I'm just restin' here—just taking a few days off. Some of my brains is leaking out, but I've never had much need of 'em."

"Anything I can do for you?" Hughes asked solicitously—this man was marked for death. *He hasn't got a chance to live 'til morning. Don't let that bright look fool you.* Perhaps a letter to write for him. "I'd like to be some help."

"Then listen to my story, Padre. I got to tell somebody what happened to me. Most of 'em think I got shot in the head. Doc was even X raying me for shrapnel. Truth of it was I got hit on the head with a crank—just like life on the farm."

"You got hurt like this and you weren't shot at all?"

"Oh, sure. I got shot—at first, that is. Just a little mortar in this here leg. If they'd left me there I'd have been all right, like as not. But they was so busy rescuing me I durn near got killed."

"What do you mean?"

"Well, my outfit was boltin' on jewelry—that's the steel straps that hold sections of a pontoon together. You start with a few sections side-launched from an LST, tow it to the beach, secure one end to shore and work out through the water from there, boltin' on sections as you go along. We pushed in there while them marines was still going ashore in ramp boats, got one end of the pontoon on the beach and three sections of it anchored out. One more and we'd be ready for them big LCT barges with tanks and stuff—so they could just run along our pontoon to shore. Japs was shootin' out of the hills. I don't say I liked that either. They got Johnny Walters and hit Sam

Peters, he's to another ship I guess. If you find him here, tell him old Josh Blackburn got tired of workin'."

"You're lying," said Chaplain Hughes with a smile of admiration.

"Sure. I like to work. We practiced long enough, puttin' them fool pontoons together. I wanted to see the job through when it counted, but it didn't work out that way. Just 'Bang!' real loud and there was a bunch of holes in the pontoon, Johnny and Sam down and my leg in a helluva mess, if you'll pardon the expression, Padre. Chief Nelson, he put on a tourniquet and then splinted her the best he could, but he had to go on with that pontoon. After a while some fellows came with a litter and lifted me out to the end of that pontoon and onto one of them power barges fitted with an overgrown outboard motor. You know how they are. They pull up anchor with some kind of hand windlass, kind of crude rig with a big crank to wind. Well, sir, they just set me down there nice and easy and another shell landed on that thing. There was men flying every which way and something or somebody hit that windlass so the pawl got released and the anchor started lettin' out with a rush, and that fool crank spun around and gave me the gol durndest lickin' I ever took in my life. I felt the ribs go and held up my arms to protect my face. The next time around got my arm and the time after that lay my scalp right open. The brain's exposed. They don't think I'm goin' to live—I heard 'em whispering. My ears is real good. But I ain't goin' to die. You can feel it when your time's come. My time ain't yet."

Hughes found himself smiling back into the twinkling dark eyes. He'd seen nine of them die during the last day and night; he'd felt like crying over every one of them and here he was, laughing with the tenth. It troubled him; he was failing his God and his fellow man. He ought to give words of warning and of hope, but how warn a man who threw death aside like a blanket, how give hope to one already having it so abundantly —hope for this life at any rate. Hughes prayed silently. He'd try again later in the day. "I'll be seeing you," he said.

Hughes turned now to a husky youngster on the adjacent table—the stomach case Flynn expected to recover without complications. The kid looked glum.

"How are you son? Can I do anything for you?"

"No."

"How about a little fruit juice?"

"No."

"Write a letter for you, maybe?"

"No, thanks. I have nobody to write to. It doesn't matter anyway. I'm going to die."

Chill swept through Hughes. Come, man! Here's a lad in a funk. Help him out of it. "I'm sure you'll feel better tomorrow," he said. "You've been through a lot. It's just shock—gets everybody for a while."

"It's got me for good." Words from deep within this boy; some problem, some deep trouble rooted here long before today.

Hughes felt tired, futile. Help me, God, he prayed. Then he pulled the dog-eared Testament from his pocket and read little snatches he knew by heart, taking comfort himself from the words: *"I will never leave thee nor forsake thee. . . . You have a heavenly Father, son; one who will never let you down."*

The young marine lay very still on his mattress, blue eyes looking troubled, unsure. "I wish I could believe that, but there isn't any use, not for me. Oh, God, my guts hurt! Why don't He do something about that?"

"I'm sure He will, but you've got to help too, son. You've got to have faith that He can."

"Oh, buck up, kid," cried the CB. "We'll be playin' checkers tomorrow."

Hughes rose. He'd better go; perhaps he'd talked too much as it was. The boy needed sleep. "So long, son," he said. "I'll come back soon."

The young marine said nothing—only those blue eyes looking up at him miserably. Hughes turned to the CB. What a strange situation: lad on the mend preoccupied with death and a dying man on the next mattress talking about a game of checkers tomorrow.

"Good-by, Josh," he said. "You've helped me a lot."

"You helped me too, Padre. My Ma used to read the Book when I was knee high. Lots I done would be a shock to Ma, but what you read now puts me in mind of them days. It was real nice."

Chaplain Hughes smiled through sudden tears, picked up the young marine's bedpan and headed for the door.

CHAPTER 25

By sunset two Marine divisions, together with their reserves and sufficient artillery, tanks, ammunition and supplies to sustain them for twenty-four hours, had been carried across the reef to Charan Kanoa beaches. These marines held a narrow beachhead, at some spots extending in just a few yards from salt water. They were well dug in, had annihilated a spectacular but unsuccessful counterattack by Japanese tanks and were carrying the fight steadily to a nearly hidden enemy in the face of increasing mortar and machine gun fire.

Hove to, ships of the invasion fleet were sitting ducks. It was considered that the landed force would be able to get along without them during the night. Danger of Japanese attack by sea or air was greatest then. Orders were received for all attack transports to retire for the night on prearranged courses, as had been done earlier at Makin. Difference here was in number of ships. When sunset was in its red glory, flag hoists which could scarcely be distinguished snapped from flagship yardarms. Smothering out babel of voices on the TBS came authoritative sounds, equally difficult to understand. Mad rush about decks of the *Belinda* and her sister ships, hoisting in what boats were at hand. Hawks ordered Brooks and Kruger to take charge of all other *Belinda* craft and to lie off the reef until morning. Many of these boats were loaded with supplies prescribed by battle plans to be landed on D Day, but in heat of action bypassed for needed ammunition and reserves. Waters directly west of Saipan were cluttered with ships of all types, some surging along with boats still crawling up their gray sides, some secured for sea and running out at full speed to form up further offshore. There seemed no order or observance of rule in their confused rushing, which resembled a string of wild horses breaking for range. The battleship *Pennsylvania* led the way, several attack transports, *Belinda* included, hot after her. The amphibious flagship *Rocky Mount,* with seeming dignity, remained off the reef, watching operations along the beaches as long as possible.

While sunset dimmed to pale yellow, first squadrons of Japanese planes were picked up on air search radars. TBS called the warning and gave permission to fire at the enemy when in range. There was tenseness in men at the *Belinda's* guns. After months of practice, they were about to get a crack at enemy planes, anticipated danger still sufficiently remote to be exciting—almost pleasant. Jap planes had searched them out at Makin, but there a heavy rain squall provided cover, preventing enemy afloat and enemy aloft from seeing or destroying each other.

Radar now reported many Japanese planes, flying at ten thousand feet, probably medium bombers. Scattered clouds would never hide five hundred ships from these, so while those on the bridge strained to get the ship out to sea and into formation without colliding with sister ships, the gunners waited, watching northern sky.

Now gunfire announcing arrival of Japanese planes was starting, first from a few northernmost ships, then heavy explosions increasing as more of the closer ships opened fire. Flat trajectory of flaming tracers, reaching up, pointing out. There they were, neat formation sky high, steadily closing, seeming afloat in pale light, held aloft by continuous mushrooms of exploding five-inch shells. Like a sudden thunderstorm approaching, crash of thousands of elevated gun barrels swept across the maneuvering fleet. Captain Hawks stood tall and still at the conn, buckles of his helmet straps banging against his cheeks as he swept binoculars across the sky. When the neat Vs of buzzing bees came in range he snapped out word to commence fire. Sudden sharp crescendo of gun barks blotted out all other sounds: high whine of racing turbines, rushing waters, all speech and never-ending orders from the TBS. Hawks sniffed and tweaked his nostrils as if his senses were pleased at struggle and sound. He buckled his helmet quickly, bent down to shout close into MacDougall's ear, "You've got her," and rushed up the ladder to control his guns.

It pleased MacDougall to be left at the conn. He too felt exhilaration after strain and waiting. He was racing to catch the division flagship, eighteen hundred yards ahead. The enemy formation now was directly overhead. Bombs dropping soon— well, there was more water than ships to hit. Nevertheless, this was a dangerous threat, best avoided by rapid emergency turns left and right to throw off the bombardiers. Now a sudden flicker from the *Pennsylvania* yardarm, emergency turn to the right, how much MacDougall could not read in the pale glare of fading sunset; could not hear from the signal bridge; could not hear from the TBS, though he expected that the ir formation was being called out even as he wondered. Time to guess and try. "Right, full rudder," he shouted. The helmsman gazed straight ahead, giving some minor correction to the left. These idiots: were they mesmerized by the guns? Couldn't they hear? That was it; they couldn't hear. All this in a flash, with a rush into the pilothouse, knocking over the messenger en route. MacDougall waved his hand violently to the right several times. Chief Scott at the wheel nodded and spun spokes. The *Belinda* heeled over to port and swung right. MacDougall ran to the starboard wing of the bridge to see if all was clear there. Jim Randall watching for him. Good old Jim, never worry about him. Back to the port wing. Ship going too fast, too far. What was the order—turn seven, turn five? All a guess. Steady sign to Scott, hand cutting up and down. Nod from the chief quartermaster. Now they were rushing up on the port quarter of the division flag. "Down five turns," MacDougall shouted to the petty officer at the engine annunciator. The man looked at him blankly. These people must be excited, thought Mac-Dougall. He shoved the man aside, stabbed five times on the lower push button. "Make seventy-three turns," he shouted. At that moment there was a split-second pause of the *Belinda's* guns, just enough to reveal to him a strange voice fairly screaming words from his own mouth. That was all it took to settle him. Who's excited now? he thought. Then explosion of bombs all about, sea pitted with salt water craters; ships pushing through, apparently none hit yet. Emergency turn to left and again to right; all a guess as far as MacDougall was concerned, for he could not see color of signal flags or hear shouted radio orders. Excitement on every bridge, he felt sure: some still trying to get boats hoisted in, others steaming fast to seaward among clutter of sister ships to form up in squadrons, each ship in its appointed place; at the same time wriggling this way and that to avoid dropping bombs; at the same time shooting at fast moving targets from speeding, swaying gun platforms. The fancy flashed through his mind of the time he took Robbie to see the Western movie in San Diego: six-gun shooting from a bouncing stagecoach at fast-riding Indians. No benefit here of the niceties of fiction to contrive hits.

A second wave of enemy planes, then a third; more sticks of bombs falling and more emergency turns. The *Belinda* steamed along unharmed, her crew deafened from sound, her decks littered with expended shell cases. Still high and level, those Jap planes. Were the devils going to get clean away? What was that? One leaving formation now, faltering, smoke trailing from wing tips and nacelles; bursting into flame now, bright flame of high-test gasoline, bombs not yet dropped exploding, bits of plane skittering like great maple leaves in fall wind, main part plummeting down in smoke and yellow flame; another crater in the sea, larger than the others, then waters closing over, ships steaming on with another waltz to the right to avoid more sticks of bombs from more planes. Far out to sea two more planes coming down, smoking. Then things quieted somewhat. The *Belinda's* shooting slowed and stopped, so that MacDougall could hear methodical, unimpassioned orders from the TBS; once again whine of turbine and slosh of running sea alongside.

It was nearly dark on the surface of the sea; high in the sky still yellow and pale-pink cloud. Captain Hawks reappeared suddenly, followed by Ensign Twitchell, the recognition officer, whose duty it was to advise the captain as to identity of all planes seen. Intent on conning the ship, MacDougall turned to see Hawks and Twitchell watching a small flight of fighter planes flying at about eight thousand feet on a course roughly parallel with the fleet but off to port. Gunfire again: ships of the fleet firing at the planes. MacDougall felt doubt stab up through his preoccupation with maneuvering the *Belinda*. This shooting not right, not right at all. Hawks had not commenced fire. "What do you make them?" he asked Twitchell. The ensign stared at the planes through his binoculars without reply. Hawks's voice snapped out at Twitchell as gunfire rolled at them again, ships closer and closer to the *Belinda* opening fire. "Are they Japs or friendlies?"

Twitchell licked his lips, lowered his binoculars, blinked the lids rapidly over his bulging eyes. He raised his binoculars for another look, then glanced about at blazing naval guns. Planes looked like F6Fs but they must be Japs: the others were shooting. At last he faltered, "They must be Jills."

Hawks did not look back to the planes. He swung to Mac-Dougall, just completing another emergency turn. "Identify those planes, MacDougall."

MacDougall was irritated, all his mental faculties straining to keep the *Belinda* in formation. That pop-eyed Twitchell, so superior and sure of himself while giving identification lectures down in the wardroom: one twenty-fifth of a second should be enough, Mr. MacDougall. Let him do his own identifying. Now MacDougall's first uneasy feeling about those planes returned. He swung his binoculars up at the formation. They were climbing in a slow turn now at an altitude of some ten thousand feet. Pale rose light flashed from their wings, shells burst all about them, red tracers surging up like myriad pointing fingers—it didn't look right. All this in quick flashes of impression. "Friendly Hellcats, Captain," said MacDougall. Perhaps he was wrong. He turned back to the urgent business of handling the ship.

Captain Hawks said nothing. He withheld fire of his own guns. Fire from other ships wavered and ceased. Then from the TBS an admiral's indignant voice, "Cease fire! I say again, cease fire immediately! Planes fired on are friendly. Planes fired on are friendly."

Hawks spun around to glare at Twitchell. A nasty curl came to the captain's lips. He spoke softly but as if spitting out the words, "Ensign Twitchell, go to your room and study your recognition manual. Draw twenty-five freehand silhouettes of F6Fs, all three angles, and bring them to me. While you are doing it remember that you advised me to shoot down Americans."

By ten in the morning of the second day, sun beat hot on dry sands of Red Beach. Capsized and disabled amtracks, casualties of D Day assault landings, lay at all angles on the dry white reef, high above low tide, perfectly still as if frozen in motion. Lieutenant Gettman, the *Belinda's* new beachmaster, had dispersed his beach party against further mortar fire: part of the radio here, part there; the same with his hydrographic and cargo control sections. Only the medical aid station was together. Dr. Hardwick, *Belinda* junior medical officer, was set up under the trees where there was shade for the wounded. Gettman still felt concerned about Japanese mortar fire. A battery of artillery set up just above the beach line was throwing a rolling barrage ahead of advancing marines. The racket must be rough on the wounded waiting for transportation to the *Be-*

linda—good thing they were soon carried across the reef in amtracks and taken in VPs to the nearest transport flying the signal indicating that she could still handle more casualties. The *Belinda* was nearest, her stern just clear of the reef. She must be crowded with wounded.

Gettman's train of thought was interrupted by Hatcher, his leading boatswain's mate, who came running up the beach from the direction of Charan Kanoa, calling out, "There's some wounded marines in trouble."

"Where?" Gettman asked.

"Our corpsmen found them in a shell crater over there, but some Japs sneaked in and shot two of the corpsmen—Spencer and Langren, I think. Ain't no marines around the beach now to help. Can Boski, Whitey and me go get them wounded to Hardwick?"

This was a new situation for Gettman, still strange to this work on the beach. His mind reverted to rules, training manuals, planes—no help there. "You may run into trouble," he said. "You'd better wait for some of the shore-party marines. This is a job for somebody with basic training in infantry tactics."

"Listen, sir. Those guys can't wait for basic training. They're in trouble. We're all mountain boys—raised with guns. We'll be all right."

"But I can't afford to lose you boys; you're my key men on this beach."

"Don't you worry, sir. We been up in the line lots of times. Most of our free time at Kwajalein we was up in the line, us three—rabbit hunting, that's what we called it but Mr. O'Bannion raised Ned with us when he found out. . . . These guys can't wait, sir. They need help. Let us go, won't you?"

The new beachmaster hesitated—after all . . . "All right, Hatcher. Go to it. I'll see if I can round up some help. Now watch it. I need you three men on this beach. I'll—"

Hatcher was gone on the run to meet Foots Boski and Whitey McClintock, who came from the beachmaster's HQ carrying two carbines and an automatic rifle. Gettman watched the three disappear over a hillock of sand. There were many details to attend to and, for the time being, all thought of his three hillbillies slipped from mind.

Hatcher and his pals found a hospital apprentice from the *Belinda* tending five wounded marines in the shell crater. Two other marines had died of their wounds and lay huddled beside the bodies of Spencer and Langren, who had tried to get them to safety. Obviously the shell which had made this crater had landed near the end of a slit trench leading inland from the

227

beach. Looking it over, Hatcher said, "The Japs must have come down that trench there." All three boys hit the sand as a grenade exploded nearby.

"They're still in there," said Whitey McClintock.

"Wish we had some grenades," said Boski.

Hatcher got to his knees, saw that one of the wounded marines had been hit again: fresh blood oozing from his sweat-stained jungle greens—the apprentice corpsman crawling over to help. "Japs are up that trench all right," said Hatcher softly. "Not far in either; those Japs can't throw a grenade too good." He bit his lip, remembering uncomfortably something he had read about Jap kids taking to baseball. "Anyway, there's no time to fool around. One of us should work up that slit trench and smoke him out. He'll probably jump out or run; then maybe the other two of us can pot him."

"May be more'n one," said Boski. "I sure wish we had some grenades."

"You guys go along the top," said Whitey. "I'll go up the trench."

"I'd better go," said Boski.

"No, you're too big. They'd get you right off in that little trench."

"Well, O.K.," said Hatcher, who usually decided things for the three. "Take it easy, Whitey. If you need help, holler." Hatcher and Boski crawled out of the shall crater and moved cautiously along, one on each side of the slit trench.

Whitey crawled across the crater and looked into the trench. It was about five feet deep, so a short Jap could duck along without being seen outside. Nothing in the trench as far as he could see; no movement, just empty rifle cartridges scattered on the dirty gray sand. About fifty feet ahead was a jog in the trench. That was the way most of them were; he'd have to be careful. Whitey dropped down into the trench, snapped his carbine off safety and moved cautiously forward. He did not feel particularly excited; he was a calm fellow. What he felt rather was the alertness of the hunter. This very alertness brought Sassafras Mountain to mind, no day or place in particular, just that sharp feeling in early morning, looking for a quick shot at a rabbit, his dog Blackie sniffing in the brush. Getting close to the jog now; Hatcher and Boski must be all set. He glanced up quickly but couldn't see them. He'd have to keep his eyes ahead now. This was kind of bad, this dogleg. You never could trust them Japs.

Whitey came up to the jog. He could feel nervousness now: if there was a Jap in there he'd have to be quick—should have a grenade to heave in there. He raised the muzzle of his carbine closer to his chest, took a careful step up to his side of the jog, then he leveled the gun and shoved chest and shoulders through the slot. Quick look up the trench: empty, just like the first part. He looked sharply at the end of the trench: one more jog about seventy feet further along. It was in shadow there, hard to see. What was that? Beady dark eyes looking at him! Sight the gun, fingers squeezing trigger. Sound not of his gun; shock crashing against his chest, driving him back against the side of the trench. Here was Hatcher now, jumping down beside him, arms around him, holding him. Pain now, so much pain. He had to tell Hatcher what happened; how he had things all straight, only that shadow foxed him up. Hard for him to talk. He gulped and at last words came out, quiet in this new weakness, without passion. "That Jap bastard got me," he said.

"Jap's dead, Whitey," said Hatcher. "Boski drilled him full. You're hurt bad. . . . We got to get you out of here, fella."

Whitey tried to tell him how it was—somehow it didn't matter. Nothing was going to matter. His lungs were filling up with something like water; blood maybe. Yes, it was blood; he was coughing up blood now. Then he was too weak to cough any more. He could feel life running out of him and it was so hard to breathe. He closed his eyes and slumped back in Hatcher's arms. Bright sunlight filtered through closed lids, kind of smoky like mid-morning on Sassafras Mountain. Blackie; he wondered about Blackie. Hatcher got to see Blackie that time they went back to Carolina overleave. Hatcher; that was the last thing Whitey ever heard: Hatcher crying like a baby, holding him. Just like drowning only kind of nice, softlike. Nothing mattered anymore.

CHAPTER 26

"There's the boss admiral out there in that flashy looking cruiser," said Hubert, the garbage grinder, to Brown, Cook Second Class. "Now they say that admiral is boss of all the big carriers and new battleships, and all these ships here are just a sideline with him. What I want to know is: where is this Jap fleet they talk about that's coming out to get us? And this boss admiral, is he going to do something about it, or just stay here looking around?"

"Why ask me? I don't mess around with admirals much and I been too busy cooking beans to pay much attention to the Jap fleet."

Hubert looked most disappointed. "You mean it ain't so what they say: that you cooks know the score?"

"Oh, I know which mess cooks were corking off in the bake shop this afternoon instead of peeling spuds. Want any more secret information?"

"No," said Hubert. "I just want to know about that boss admiral."

Up on the bridge they didn't know much more than Hubert. Something was brewing and it lay uneasily in the air. Men in clusters aboard every ship talked in low tones, rumor and conjecture swallowing small bits of fact; everywhere unanswered questions. Where were the Japs? Where was Task Force 58? What chance did APAs have against battleships and carriers? Threaded through this was a wistful desire to go out and take on those Japs.

Not interested in rumor, Captain Hawks was trying to put small bits together: noncommittal position reports of Jap fleet units sighted northeast of Luzon and of others further east, steaming to join. "It looks like fleet action," Hawks said to MacDougall and Randall. Complete radio silence guarded whereabouts of the Fifth Fleet's powerful task force. Of course the Fleet admiral knew. Just arrived in his flagship he was now in conference with the amphibious force and Marine commanders. At such times admirals do not give out news bulletins. Hawks was doing his own reasoning. "The task force must be somewhere between us and the Japs. We're juicy bait and perhaps they can get the Nips out to fight. That's fine, but I don't like to be bait. I like to get out and fight too, but you can't throw a lot of landing craft at a Jap battleship, so I guess we'll just sit here."

"It's queer we haven't had more air attacks," said Randall.

Hawks looked over at Japanese-held Tinian Island, just south of Saipan and only three miles away from the anchored *Belinda*. "There's a Jap airstrip on Tinian, one minute from us by air. Most of what planes they had were destroyed before D Day. I think Jap carriers will try to fly in more planes to Tinian, Rota and Guam, probably at night. Then our evenings will be more exciting." Hawks's eyes gleamed suddenly, "Lead the target! Lead the target!" he shouted, clapping his hands and spinning around on one heel. Then the sparkle faded; once more he was the serious commanding officer, watching his decks with critical eyes.

Within an hour sudden orders came to hoist in boats alongside and to steam to sea on indefinite retirement. There was barely time to get messages to Gettman on the beach and to Brooks in his radio-equipped boat, telling them that they would be on their own. Then the *Belinda* stood out once more from Saipan, leaving half her boats behind to exist and subsist, orphan fashion, until she was ordered to return.

Leaving vessels assigned to bombardment and a handful of supply vessels to sustain landing craft and supply emergencies, the bulk of the attack force formed up and steamed around the northern tip of Saipan until out of sight of land. Then for several days they carried out a strange and monotonous maneuver, marching in columns, back and forth over their own wake at an eight-knot crawl so as not to expend precious fuel unnecessarily. Completely blacked out during the night, these ships, yet huddled close in such vast numbers that oil, steam and sweat lying heavy in starless air gave proof to those on each ship that they were not alone. Rain squalls swept over during the night, but there was no refreshment in this torrential water, just suffocation, feeling of oblivion and repression, added fear of collision with others while the fleet turned about. Then daylight coming to weary watchers standing behind more than twenty thousand guns, looking for Jap planes or surface craft which did not come, waiting for signs of enemy submarines known to be lurking about. An hour perhaps of lovely tropical early morning, then clouds drifting downwind towards the horizon, ships panting along at half speed under scorching sun.

During the first afternoon came the distraction of fueling at sea. For months these ships would never touch land, never go alongside a wharf. All their provisioning came in their own boats from supply ships sent out to the forward area. All their fuel oil, life blood of a ship, came through snakelike bights of black six-inch hose hung yard and stay between oiler and carrier, oiler and battleship, oiler and attack transport. Fleet oilers steamed along on both flanks of the main body of ships. Each ship was assigned to a certain oiler in ordered priority, so as to avoid confusion. "Watch HAYMAKER, now, Randall," said Hawks. "As soon as he disconnects his hose I want to get over there . . . fast! MacDougall, get out your maneuvering board and compute course from fleet at eight knots, *Belinda* at sixteen knots to station alongside HAYMAKER. I want to slide in smartly."

They swept through and across column after column, cutting astern and ahead of other ships in a manner threatening imminent collision, yet by geometric law assured that at the exact moment there would be an opening ahead—always the variations between the simplicities of theory and the imperfections of actuality, needing course adjustments here and there. Fast-beating navigator's heart; Hawks's darting glances, jaw out; ship finally slipping up to HAYMAKER, slowing gradually, sliding up to her port hand just sixty feet away.

"Hose out," called Hawks, though no orders were needed. The oiler now took the lead, steaming steady while the *Belinda* wiggled in and out, fishlike, trying to keep between fifty and seventy feet away; helmsman sweating at the wheel—MacDougall sweating even more at the conn. Friendly now this sight of another hull, scuppers gurgling, overboard discharge pouring hot water into warm sea, graceful arc of masts and yards swinging towards and away.

Shouts from Pappy Moran on the foredeck: "Look out for the shot line now . . . Grab it man, grab it! . . . No, not that chock; further aft like I showed you. . . . Now lead her up to the bitts. . . . Get your backs into it, sailors!" Black hose dangling from the oiler's yard amidships; Machinist Campbell and his men reaching far from *Belinda's* side, getting hold of the end of it. Word to the bridge, "Come ahead ten feet." Fine changes in relative positions of two ships moving side by side at eight knots. Oiler crew heaving on great spring line until at last the hose lined up and was coupled to filling line. Black hose bulging, thrusting oil into *Belinda's* double-bottom tanks deep under water. Constant alertness on the bridge, yet chances to glimpse quickly into the intimate life of another ship: fresh bread coming from the bake shop; two men, hidden from their own petty officer, laughingly playing cribbage under a boat; others busy with the never-ending task of scraping off rusted paintwork and daubing on fresh gray. Two hours of this, men striking up casual conversations from rail to rail shouted across fifty feet of water—then fueling completed. Hose and lines taken back to the oiler; *Belinda* sheering off, dropping back, cutting over through the fleet to take place in formation again.

While the *Belinda* was taking on fuel oil, three wounded marines died. Standing beside the body of the last to die, Bell spoke bitterly to Flynn, "It's this heat; they don't have a chance, the critical ones. We begged for more blowers down in this deck so we could take decent care of casualties in the tropics."

"Well, you all done the best you could, Doc." Both doctors looked up from the still corpse to meet calm, dark eyes of Josh Blackburn, the CB so terribly wounded that they had felt positively that he had no chance at all for life. There he sat, propped up by pillows and plyboard, confounding medical judgment, playing solitaire with a pack of greasy cards. "Sure sorry about that poor feller," continued Josh. "Somehow he just let slip and went, didn't he?"

"That was about it," said Bell. "By the books you should have died instead of him, and there you are. Nobody'll play cribbage with you any more: you beat them every time—and you're not only alive but getting stronger every day. . . . This kid here just didn't have the will to live—perhaps it was more that he didn't feel there was anything to live *for*." Bell went to the nearest porthole and looked out, blinking back the tears a doctor shouldn't show. Then he felt a hand on his shoulder, turned back to face little Chaplain Hughes.

"I'm sorry, Frank," the chaplain said. "Perhaps I was the one who failed there. I came in to see that kid a dozen times a day, talked with him, offered to write letters, read from the New Testament—sometimes just sat holding his hand. I couldn't get next to him at all: he had a remoteness about him as if he had

232

already declared himself a goner. . . . Like they say in this Navy: 'Results negative.' "

"Well, no use moping here," said Bell. "Plenty more wounded marines waiting. I've got to get back to surgery. . . ." The doctor turned to Alvick, entering the compartment with two litter carriers. "Right here, Chief. This is the man, right here." Bell watched Alvick's men carry away the body of the young marine, then he followed Flynn out of the place for a gulp of fresh air before the next round of cutting and sewing.

On the following morning, immediately after sunrise battle stations, screening destroyers dropped back by turn from their fanlike formation ahead to take on fuel from attack transports. Once again hose winged out overside from the *Belinda*—some of the oil received the day before pumped out again to the short-ranged, sleek destroyer fishtailing alongside, drinking liquid fuel so necessary to her flashing speed.

Keeping an eye on the fueling operation, Captain Hawks called Quigley to the bridge. "Get ready for burial at sea this morning," he said. "There's nothing else to do with those three marines who died yesterday—no chance to send the bodies ashore. All refrigerator boxes are being used for provisions. No telling how long we'll have to stay out here—and in this heat, you see."

"Aye, aye, sir," said Quigley. "I'll get the men busy on it right away." The prospect interested Quigley. A little gruesome, but surely a very colorful ceremony. As quickly as possible he went below to bone up on regulations covering burial at sea and to dip into Captain Lovette's *Naval Customs, Traditions, and Usages*. Then he went to the wardroom where the officers were finishing breakfast. "Gentlemen," he announced, "we are going to hold sea burial at ten hundred. I need an officer to command the honor guard. Who will volunteer?" Quigley scanned the faces looking up from fried potatoes and spam hash. "I would like the most military officer available."

"That lets me out," said Fraser, the salty first lieutenant, getting up and heading for the door.

"Just a minute, Fraser," said Quigley. "I would like you to have the foredeck clean and some kind of platform provided for the corpses."

"My decks are always clean," growled Fraser. "I'll rig the rest of it for you."

As Quigley looked around the wardroom, Ensign Twitchell pushed his way through rows of chairs, calling out, "Let me take charge of the guard."

Quigley looked down at this short, stocky ensign: hard, calculating face with its protuberant eyes in the oversize head. Twitchell wasn't exactly military—he looked more like the punchboard salesman which he had been in civilian life—but he was neat, his loud voice would carry and no show of emotion would fluster him when it came time to order volleys fired over the dead. "All right, Twitchell," said Quigley. "Get up a squad of men who know which end of a rifle to hold and put them through a few dry runs of three smart volleys. Be sure you don't muff your lines, now."

After Quigley left the wardroom, Lieutenant Dan Hill, the Marine Corps officer permanently assigned to the *Belinda* as transport quartermaster, dug his thumb into Jim Randall's ribs. "I know this is no time to be funny, Jim, but I just can't help laughing," he said.

"You mean about Twitchell?"

"Yes. Of course it really doesn't matter one bit to me—I'm much happier handling debarkation and combat cargo than drilling men. It's just that I had five years of close order drill and combat infantry training: four at college ROTC and a year at Quantico. Then one day they take me down to a dock and say, 'See that thing floating there, Lieutenant? That's a ship.' So I blinked twice and there I was, an expert on cargo and troop loading. Now they pick Twitchell for military smartness!"

"That wasn't like Quigley," said Randall. "He must've slipped up on you. Want me to remind him?"

"Course not. I'd rather keep out of it. I'd feel different if we had a Marine contingent aboard. This is all Navy."

Randall grinned and a teasing look stole across his face. "So Quigley passed you up for Twitchell! Just shows that you've been accepted here as part of the ship. Why, we never think of you as a gyrene."

"Yeah, I guess they had things figured out right: it only takes one U.S. marine to keep a Navy ship in line."

After the bustle of the bridge, MacDougall found the fantail peacefully quiet. Gun Two pointed over a warm slosh of sea towards the next ship astern. The gun pointer's shirt, soaked in a recent squall, hung over the barrel to dry. In the shade of the ready box Chief Alvick bent over three still forms wrapped in gray blankets. "How about the weights, sir?" he asked.

"Got some old shackles? Lash them around the blanket near the feet so they won't come adrift through the canvas." MacDougall squatted down beside Alvick and put his hand gently on the largest blanket-wrapped body, feeling surprising warmth and softness. Here we talk of shackles, he thought—as if we were rigging tackle. These fellows walked these decks, waited in the chow line, probably bitched about cramped quarters and water hours.

Alvick seemed to be pondering something but his face was that expressionless mask which had so often puzzled MacDougall. "How much weight do we need on the shackles, sir?"

"Oh, fifty, maybe sixty pounds, I'd say." MacDougall looked down at the blanket again, in imagination following this man down the net, clumsy with full pack and rifle, swaying out over dark shape of the boat below. What had happened to him? What was his story until he was brought back in a litter? Of the rest Bell had told him some; Chaplain Hughes a little more. This was the husky young fellow with the stomach wound, the one Flynn and Bell were so sure ought to live. Even dead and wrapped in a blanket like the others you could tell: big guy, tall, broad shouldered—anybody would 'have picked him to outlive that lanky CB. Yet here he is, thought MacDougall, perfectly still on this hot deck while we collect shackles.

It took all the old shackles and a few shiny new ones. MacDougall helped them with the lashing and the fitting of canvas, which Alvick then sewed. Limpness and weight in these three mute figures roughly silhouetted in their canvas shrouds, having the slight individuality remaining to them of difference in size. They were now carefully placed on hatch boards; faces covered —blond and dark hair covered alike—even identifying dog tags inside blanket and canvas. Tommy Jones came down from the bridge with three new flags which he helped Alvick to drape over the bodies. Then Alvick grasped one of his men by the arm as he passed and swung him around. "Here, Smitty," he said. "Go tell the exec we're ready."

Fueling hoses were barely stowed away when the PA blasted out call to quarters to witness burial. Not since change in command ceremonies had the entire ship's company, excepting watch standers, been mustered together on the foredeck. In less than two months Captain Gedney had been nearly forgotten; now, in new thunder and fresh death, Makin and Kwajalein nearly forgotten. Dressed in working dungarees, the crew waited quietly in tight divisional ranks, some staring out to sea, some looking aft to half-masted colors, the majority looking curiously at the group of carpenter's sawhorses supporting freshly scrubbed hatch covers, ready at the rail. Forward and aft of the sawhorses Alvick had placed side boys. Grouped forward and to one side was a squad of twelve sailors with carbines at parade rest, Ensign Twitchell strutting before them, impatient for his moment. Captain Hawks remained on his bridge, looking down on the scene. Quigley stood on the upper deck, just above the mustered crew, checking details against his recent study of regulations.

Then, without announcement, Chaplain Hughes stepped from the bulkhead door leading out from sick bay country. Behind him moved three flag-draped figures, each carefully carried by six bareheaded sailors. The little procession headed for the platform at the rail. Here the bodies were gently placed, feet outboard; then the pallbearers stepped aside. Though no order had been given, the ship's company stood at attention, heads uncovered.

Chaplain Hughes looked out over the faces of his shipmates. A young man, he was nevertheless well familiar with death, and had learned to accept it. Today his sympathetic nature was unusually touched by the sadness of this scene; strange manner of death and burial far from green grass of homeland cemetery plots. Above all this, he was moved and disturbed by the death of the husky young marine, who in spite of every medical aid and his own pleading seemed to have set life aside as if something no longer important enough to struggle for. With this emotion surging up within him, Hughes stepped up to the flag-draped forms, opened his Bible and began to read.

Dr. Bell stood outboard of the mustered three pharmacist's mates, his eyes on the center one of the three flag-draped bodies—that big strapping lad who had insisted that he was going to die. Well, there he was. Chaplain's voice breaking into his thought: *"Lord, now lettest thou thy servants depart in peace, according to thy word . . . It is appointed unto men once to die."* Appointed to die, but why like this? And why did this kid give up—nothing to live for? *Give the plasma to some other guy, Doc.* No family to write to, he said; nobody cared about him. . . . *". . . though I walk through the valley of the shadow of death, I will fear no evil: for thou art with me . . ."* Bell searched himself; perhaps he had failed in some way. That would be easy, with three hundred wounded all needing attention at once. But no, he could think of nothing. How he had worked on this boy!—tried to breathe life into him, will him back! But all the time he was slipping, slipping. . . . *"In my Father's house are many mansions . . ."* Many ships running along at half speed in dead air. Dead men —more dying in spite of all the modern helps: plasma, penicillin, sulpha, whole blood given gladly by some of these men standing behind him. Still they die, and this is just a small corner of the war.

Quiet now for a moment at the close of the chaplain's prayer, then Captain Hawks's voice, clear and loud. "Stop the ship." The engine room annunciator jangled to STOP. Reply jangled on the bridge, yet in accordance with the captain's previous instructions, the propeller maintained its even beat, for in spite of Naval custom the *Belinda* could not break formation to bury dead.

The chaplain nodded to Alvick. Pallbearers lifted outboard ends of the hatch boards to the solid bulwarks. Ensign Twitchell stiffened, threw out his chest and shouted, "Order Arms!" Then, one at a time, the bodies were consigned to the deep; the flag was lifted a few inches above each canvas shroud as the hatch was gently tipped. Slowly, as if reluctantly, each body in turn began to move, then slid smoothly over the side, dropping down feet first, landing with a surprisingly loud splash in the dancing blue sea to sink steadily downward into fathomless darkness, soon forever lost to all human sight.

"Ready!" snapped Twitchell to his squad. "Aim! . . . Fire!" Flat cracking sound of carbines: first volley, second, then third. Three flags lay flat on the hatch boards. The ceremony was over.

"May I have a position for the log, sir?" asked Ensign Fauré, puzzling over the morning's official entry.

"Sure," said MacDougall. "Got the names there? Let's see now. Entry for ten-thirteen: The remains of George R. Waskowitz, P/Sgt. USMC, died of wounds; Antonio J. Perez, Pfc. USMC, died of wounds; John C. Stanton, Pfc. USMC, died of wounds. Buried at sea with military honors, lat. 15° 27' N, long. 146° 13' E.

The admiral felt depressed. Taking his constitutional walk to clear his brain of nearly overwhelming operational details, he had noticed all too many attack transports with colors at half-mast, indicating that they were burying casualties. His mind went back to another war: that time they maneuvered all day at reversing order of ships in the battle line. They buried a man at sea that day too: fell from aloft still hanging on to his marlinspike—how the years flew by! The admiral was a young officer of the deck then; responsibility of handling his ship had driven away from his mind the depressing picture of a body sinking into the depths. Yes: reversing the order of ships, a fine old maneuver—good then, good now. The admiral took a last gulp of fresh air, then went to the cabin and sent for his flag lieutenant.

Aboard the *Belinda*, two thousand yards astern, Captain Hawks sat in his new high seat and looked critically about his decks; things were entirely too quiet, the crew moping around after burying dead. He'd have to do something about this.

"Orderly," he bellowed.

Biggs came from the shadow of the pilothouse door. "Yes, sir."

"Get the chaplain."

Chaplain Hughes was in the sick bay, writing a letter for a marine with a shattered arm. "I'll be back, fella," he said, and followed Biggs to the bridge.

Hawks swung around in his chair and looked down at Hughes. "You did very well with that service this morning, Chaplain." Hughes made no reply. He wanted to forget the whole business.

"Yes," continued Hawks, "you did such a good job the crew haven't gotten over it. Look at 'em pussyfooting around down there."

The chaplain stepped forward and looked over the weather cloth. Down on the foredeck men looked glumly out across the water or talked quietly in little groups; no card games, no singing at work. "I guess you're right, Captain. They're numb."

"That's easy fixed," said Hawks. "Just break out that record player of yours, set it up on the hatch down there. Put on a record with some pepper in it and turn it up good and loud. There's nothing like a lively tune when the men start dragging their tails."

A few minutes later electronic crackles indicated to Hawks that Hughes was on the job. Then the apathetic silence was shattered by twelve-tube amplification of the "Tiger Rag." Hawks swung a long leg back and forth, keeping time with the insistent beat. He swished the spoon around in his coffee cup, draining it in three gulps. Then, waving cup and spoon, he croaked in an off-key voice, "Oh, hold that tiger. Hold that tiger!" The blast of recorded sound carried though the decks to cooks at work, to wounded in the sick bay and to men drinking unofficially brewed coffee in obscure corners of the ship. Hawks watched a red-headed coxswain stamping about the anchor windlass, clapping his hands, while in the pilothouse he could hear the helmsman tapping time on the oak grating as he turned the spokes. Then the captain looked to the bridge wing where MacDougall, squinting through the pelorus, winced at the syncopated screech.

Hawks laughed. "What's the matter, Mr. Navigator—can't you take it?"

MacDougall grinned. "It's got power all right," he said.

"That's what we need—make 'em pick it up and set it down. I'll tell you something. The chaplain's in charge of morals but I'm in charge of morale; and boy, I'm charging their batteries!"

"Signals!"—the voice of the watch signalman alerting his assistants: flags were blossoming from flagship signal halyards.

Two minutes later, Captain Hawks read the penciled message. "Good," he said to anybody within hearing. "Very good. Just what we need." Hawks swung around in his chair and handed his empty coffee cup to Biggs. "Tell Commander Quigley to assemble all line officers on the bridge at fourteen hundred for tactical fleet maneuvers."

Nervous expectancy throughout the invasion fleet at fourteen hundred: ships six hundred yards apart nearly to the horizon. On every bridge were young officers from inland states, among them former druggists, doctors of economics, farm boys from state colleges, all waiting nervously to take

238

part in the marching and countermarching of five hundred ships. In the group with Quigley on the *Belinda's* bridge were Hall, the gunnery officer, a Baltimore pharmacist; young Fauré from Pomona College; Marty, the tank lighter officer, a Vermont farmer's son having a master's degree in romance languages; Robinson, the communications officer, a Missouri highschool teacher; Cooper, ship's secretary, a C.P.A. from Denver; and Twitchell, signal officer and former punchboard salesman. Jim Randall had the conn, keeping ship on station with casual competence. MacDougall came out from his chart room, glanced at the group of tactics students with a hint of condescension and strolled over to take his place near Hawks. Chance for a little relaxation, perhaps fun, watching these landlubbers maneuver ship.

Tropic sun beat down on the fleet, crawling along at eight knots to preserve precious fuel. Men below decks roasted in ovenlike compartments; those on weather decks broiled in solar radiation. Even Pappy Moran's voice calling to his men on the foredeck sounded muffled, as if muted by heat. Slight following breeze canceled out by eight-knot speed ahead over warm sea: dead air about these ships, dead and stale in compartments where overtaxed blowers weakly puffed hot breath upon half-naked, sweat-streaked firemen in the deep bowels, upon cooks stewing in galley steam, upon listless wounded, waiting, waiting in their sick bay cots.

Signal flags hung limp from every yardarm: flagship originating each order; all others acknowledging and passing the word along. Limp rags of flag difficult to read until the signal executed: two seconds of energetic motion as a thousand signalmen jerked downhauls; five thousand flags flapping downward revealing identifying color and design. Then lassitude again on these ships moving slowly hull down off Saipan, sucking in warm sea water to cool turbines then spewing it out again hot enough to burn a man's hand. Ships retiring during battle, out of the fight now: crawling ships with dispirited crews.

The admiral's preliminary signals were over now. Limp flag hoist and TBS gave out the first tactical signal, "All divisions simultaneously reverse order of ships."

Captain Hawks jumped out of his chair. "All right, MacDougall. You're the tactical expert. How do we do this?"

MacDougall hurried into the pilothouse and snatched up the manual on naval tactics, hunting in the index for Reverse Order of Ships. "This is something new to me," he said to Randall. "Ah, here it is. Hmm."

Captain Hawks leaned over MacDougall's shoulder, eyes stabbing at the print, following the diagrams of maneuver. Back in the dim past somewhere he had done it. Not much use in a disposition like this—just an exercise. It was Hawks's policy to question and search but never to admit ignorance of any procedure. Reading fast now he said nothing. Check, check—always check. They had their finger on your number all the time. Drive your subordinates, drive yourself—but never foul up. Reverse order of ships . . . now the details were coming back.

"We used to do this with the old batdivs before the war," he said to MacDougall. "Let's see now. Number One hauls out to starboard from column, slows to four knots and drops back."

"That's right, sir." MacDougall consulted his tables for a moment. "When eighteen hundred yards astern she sheers in and goes to eight knots. When she comes to fleet speed she should be in position. . . ." They discussed each detail of the maneuver hurriedly: order to execute the signal would be given at any moment now. "I've got it all straight now, Captain," said MacDougall. "Shall I explain it to—"

"No, don't explain it to the others," said Hawks. "Take the conn and show them. Gedney said you were good at tactics. I want to see for myself."

MacDougall felt his scalp tingling. This had better be good. Then he shoved his head through the loop of his binocular strap and stepped up on the grating beside Randall. "O.K., Jim, I relieve you," he said, adding in an undertone, "I thought you and I were going to have a rest cure this afternoon."

Randall chuckled, pointing his thumb at Hawks, now on the bridge wing lecturing Quigley and the other officers. "Never a rest cure with him around. Now if he was the admiral, wouldn't we have fun this afternoon!"

Clatter on the signal bridge. MacDougall caught a brief glance of signals whipped down from all ships ahead; then an unsynchronized duet between chief signalman and TBS: "Execute the signal, sir. I say again, execute Roger How Baker Queen. Execute. . . . Execute."

Squadron flagship swinging right and dropping back close enough for MacDougall to see two men in faded dungarees hastily hauling up a bundle of rinsing deck swabs from her propeller wash. Now it was his turn. "Right full rudder," he ordered. "All engines ahead one third."

Dr. Bell closed the surgery door and climbed to the upper deck for a smoke and what fresh air he could find. He looked about, expecting the familiar pattern of ships. Something different now: flag hoists, ships heading this way and that at varying speeds. Bell leaned against a stanchion, resting from surgery and his particular sphere of exactitudes, watching these fleet maneuvers. He saw the *Belinda* floating idly like a stick adrift while columns of other ships flowed past very close aboard. Exact speed and tactics of each group mattered little to him; it was a study in relative movement, interesting to watch after monotony of eternal columns and zigzag. Pulse of accelerating engines as the *Belinda* speeded up and cut back into line. Other ships now hauling out, then darting in, performing a gigantic square dance in this column and all columns of this squadron: in countless other columns of squadrons. Curtsy and bow. We cannot help the marines up in the line. We threw them ashore across the reef, gave them guns, ammunition and rations, attended their wounded, buried their dead. Now we dance a minuet for the dead in the sea, for the Old Navy also dead. . . . All ships swinging together now like "squads right" in the infantry, yet different, these pivoting ships crowded together in a warm sea. Line of masts changing, bows dishing up white foam: a *danse macabre*, that's what it was: a dance of death. Bell flicked his cigarette overboard, watched it drop and quench in the foaming wash alongside. Then he returned to the sick bay.

Quiet in the pilothouse again after order of ships reversed, then normal order restored by two ninety-degree turns to starboard. The *Belinda* slogged along next astern the squadron flagship.

Captain Hawks came in from the wing. "Very good, MacDougall," he said.

"Thanks, Captain, but it was really very simple," said MacDougall.

Frown on Hawks's face as he came close to MacDougall; eyes stabbing deep while he snapped, "When I say something is very good, Mr. Navigator, it *is* very good!" MacDougall gave Hawks back his stare, but internally he winced from the penetrating eyes, from the accented *is*. I am the captain in command and my saying makes things so: that's what he meant. Relief from uncomfortable feeling to hear Hawks say, "Now, Mr. Cooper, let's see what the ship's secretary can do at conn."

With a little help from Jim Randall, Cooper made two sixty-degree column turns. Intelligent, methodical, self-possessed, he followed along mechanically, not having the feel of the ship yet managing to bring her through this second dance on the admiral's card.

"Very good, Mr. Cooper," said Hawks. "You got a little outside the guide's water; but very good for a ship's secretary. Now, Commander Quigley—you're second in command— let's see what the executive officer can do at conning ship."

Quigley tried to hide his nervousness. He had spent a lot of time on the bridge watching others but had never handled the *Belinda* in even the simplest maneuver. On his last ship he had

241

tried it once and nearly rammed a carrier. Smooth talking had kept him from the *Belinda* conn until today. Now he was on the spot. If he fouled up it would be all over the ship in ten minutes. As Quigley stepped onto the grating at the pilothouse window he assumed an artificial smile, like a circus acrobat about to perform on a slack wire. He was scared but he wasn't going to show it. "Free ride on the merry-go-round," he said to Cooper. "I relieve you."

Hawks beckoned to Randall. "Stand by all officers-in-training at conn. Observe them closely and keep them out of trouble." Randall knew that Hawks really meant: keep me out of trouble. The captain felt his responsibility while unsure hands guided his ship. Randall stepped up on the grating and put his binoculars on the flagship. Some of the tension went out of Quigley for a moment. Hawks stood a few feet back, balanced easily on the balls of his feet, yet alert to spring into action. Officers must be trained, even Quigley, but he had to be careful with his ship.

Simultaneously, a string of flags jerked up to flagship yardarm and sharp-voiced TBS ordered: "Emergency turn nine." Having interpreted the flags, the chief signalman shouted the same words down his brass tube—words crashing into Quigley's ears; words requiring action now.

"What's that?" he asked.

"Emergency turn nine, sir," repeated the chief signalman with more than a hint of scorn discoloring respectful words.

"Yes," said Quigley, "but left, right . . . on execute? What is the meaning of the signal?" This was maddening. Hawks insisted that signalmen give first the signal and then its exact meaning, even if this was obvious. Yet here was the signalman disregarding the captain's orders and the captain standing by without protest.

Then Randall nudged him. "Come right full rudder. Turn the ship like 'squads right.' Emergency signals are executed when understood: that means right now!" Quigley glanced ahead. Every ship in sight was swinging right; quick now or he'd ram somebody. The helm! He must get it over! He turned to see the helmsman casually chewing gum, leaning on the spokes with an elbow and standing on one leg while he scratched the other. It was Willicut, an old hand at the wheel who knew what the score was and often started the wheel over when the O.O.D. was confused, or at least got set on the proper side of the wheel for a fast whirl.

At last Quigley got it out: "Right full rudder!"

"Right full rudder, sir," replied Willicut without enthusiasm. The quartermaster pulled at the spokes as if they were almost too much for him—this fellow who had spun them around like

242

a top for little Cooper. Sluggishly the *Belinda* began to swing to starboard, then, as the rudder reached full right, she spun as fast as the other ships, but hopelessly behind them, late and outside, like an awkward rookie.

Suddenly Quigley remembered something else: "Bearing on Number Five," he called.

The man watching bearings was on the wrong wing of the bridge for Number Five, the last ship in column, so that he had to dash through the pilothouse and to the other wing for his bearing. At last he called out, "Two-two-five, sir."

Quigley looked to Randall. "What should it be?"

"Should be two-one-five," said Randall. "You were slow turning. But Five isn't guide any more. Flag is guide again: should bear zero-three-five."

"Bearing on the guide," called Quigley. The man watching bearings came through the pilothouse again, walking at a speed he estimated barely sufficient to avoid a reprimand from Captain Hawks. Had he known the captain's thoughts he would have walked even slower. Quigley tried to keep his head and choke back anger.

Then Randall's pleasant smile and steadying advice: "Never mind bearings now, just keep coming."

Quigley kept coming. Very decent fellow, this Randall, helping him in a quiet way without attracting attention. But the others seemed all against him, acting as if they wanted him to foul up. All these ships looked so strange and out of place. It must be time to take off the wheel now; he'd have to take a chance. "Ease the wheel, quartermaster. Come to one-two-five." Willicut shifted his gum, repeated the order and obeyed it with such alacrity that the ship was steady on course within less than ten seconds. Then Quigley saw why. He was too far left and Willicut knew it; it was part of this unorganized conspiracy against him. He must come right again—but there wasn't any room. Number Three had closed up on him.

"Goose her up!" yelled Hawks suddenly. "Get her in there, Quigley, you're dragging back." Speed! Quigley had forgotten the speed which must be regulated from moment to moment. He began to sweat. That ship closing in to starboard; it seemed like they were all closing in, even other ships conspiring against him, yet he must get in there. Quartermasters gave him bearings from both sides now and so fast that they had no meaning for him. He looked to Randall in silent supplication.

Randall reached for the speed adjuster and punched up ten more revolutions. "If your bearing's too far right, just steer to the right," he said cheerfully. "Just shove Three over. He'll move when he gets nervous."

Before Quigley got on station the admiral signaled another

243

sharp turn. Bells were ringing in Quigley's head and nothing made much sense any more, but he stuck it out and somehow made the turn without further help.

"All right, Robinson," said Hawks, "you take over now." Quigley stepped down from the grating and wiped his face with a clean handkerchief. The shirt he had put on fresh at noon was limp with perspiration. He thought of the wardroom as a mariner in storm thinks of safe harbor; this bridge was no place for him. Then he noticed the captain looking appraisingly at him. I didn't fool him any, Quigley thought. Then a twinkle lighted Hawks's eyes. "Very good, Quigley. Very good," he said. "You must take the conn more often."

Half an hour later, Hawks went down to his cabin, officers returned to their regular duties, leaving Randall and MacDougall alone with the bridge watch. Zigzagging was ineffective at the fuel-conserving speed of eight knots. Protected merely by scouting destroyers, the fleet plowed ahead in straight columns. For the moment the *Belinda's* bridge was quiet. Randall left the station keeping to his junior watch officer and strolled out to the bridge wing, where MacDougall was taking an azimuth of the sun.

"What a circus!" said Randall. "Quigley sure had a ride for himself. He was just hanging on to her tail all the way through those emergency turns."

"Well, you have to give him credit for staying in there," said MacDougall. "You give a man two point five for trying in this wartime Navy."

"Yeah, but that's just a passing mark, and in this case it would be a little generous."

MacDougall played with the prism of his instrument, flashing a sharp sliver of sunlight back and forth across the compass card.

"Jim," he said after a pause, "did you ever think what would happen to this ship if you and Fraser and I were in a huddle with the Old Man on this bridge and a bomb should get us all?"

"I wouldn't like that," said Randall grinning.

MacDougall was serious. "You know what I mean, Jim. Can you feature the executive officer actually handling this ship in a desperate emergency?"

Randall's grin only widened. Snapping to attention and giving MacDougall a mocking salute, he said, "Sir, I beg to report that this ship has no executive officer."

CHAPTER 27

Early morning sunlight and shadow filtered through wardroom portholes opened after dawn battle stations and the end of blackout. Although the wardroom was already uncomfortably warm there was a suggestion of chill in long shadows deliberately reaching out, then drawing back with each slow roll of the ship. Battery officers down from their guns came in one at a time, tossed their helmets on the settee and headed for hot coffee on the sideboard. Bantering good-naturedly as they entered, each in turn fell silent as he saw Dr. Gates leaning against the bulkhead by the coffee maker. Dressed in crumpled surgery white flecked with blood, the big Irishman slumped against the warm steel, heavy shoulders sagging, dejection etched in deep lines on his ashen, weary face.

Uncomfortable silence settled upon these men cheered by early morning fresh air and prospect of coffee. Then Gates spoke, words coming slow and colorless from this big man usually so ready and sure. "I just lost another marine—his name was Jones and he didn't want to die. . . . It shouldn't bother me like this; I'm an old hand at this sort of thing. They carried broken men to me from nasty factory accidents—brought them up from coal mine shafts. I've watched men die all the way from Guadalcanal to here. But this fellow got me—he wanted to live so much."

Gates's words surprised Ensign Cooper, who, without reasoning about it, felt disappointed. He had always thought of doctors as competent, professional—friendly without being emotional. And here was Gates, grieving as if for the loss of a brother. "It isn't your fault, Doc," he said. "You can't have a war without people dying."

Gates looked slowly at Cooper. At last he asked, "But why did this lad have to die? That's what he kept asking me: 'Why do I have to die, Doc? Why do I have to die? I don't want to die; I've got so much to live for.' He'd told me about his wife in Kentucky and the baby expected." A great sigh shuddered up from Gates's deep chest. "That's what he said, voice growing weaker—fading out with the last gasps of breath. 'I don't want to die, Doc.' But there was nothing more I could do." Sudden anger flushed Gates's face. He turned and slapped the bulkhead hard with his open palm. Then he looked slowly over the men about him, his gaze finally resting on Cooper, who noticed with some shock the glaze in blue eyes usually so clear and confident. Gates trembled for a few moments while the flush faded from his face, leaving it sallow, lined with fatigue and frustration. Flat, emotionless his voice once more as he said, "We do what we can." Then he left the wardroom.

Paged by Biggs, Quigley reported to Captain Hawks in the cabin. Hawks sat at his large worktable, which was already cluttered with maps, reports and operation plans. Quigley recognized the weather-beaten man of average size sitting in a corner chair as Lloyd Brown, prominent photographer and correspondent for *Life* magazine. They nodded to each other.

"Mr. Brown, I see you have met my executive officer," said Hawks. "Good. Now, Quigley, we have another casualty to bury at sea and Mr. Brown would like to take photographs for his publication. We should select a graphic location for the ceremony. I want you to exercise care in selection, and in supervising dress of personnel involved in order to reflect favorably upon the United States Navy and the U.S.S. *Belinda*. What suggestions do you have?"

Relief flowed warm within Quigley, glad to be on safe ground again after the perils of the bridge. Into his mind flashed a sparkling halftone in *Life:* flags, men at attention and a nice profile of himself—it would please his wife no end. A gun in the background . . . Yes, Gun Two on the fantail: that would be the best place.

"I would suggest the fantail, Captain; Gun Two in the background."

"Good," said Hawks. "Excellent. Nothing very secret about the breech of a five-inch gun. We will have all the department heads lined up behind the commanding officer and yourself. Pick the smartest looking seamen aboard for bearers and honor guard."

"I would also suggest fresh khakis with neckties, Captain."

"Fine," said Hawks. "Very good. You attend to the details. Work things out with Mr. Brown here. I must get back to the bridge now. Oh, another thing. Put Marine Lieutenant Hill in command of the guard. His appearance and performance are much smarter than Twitchell's."

During this exchange Mr. Brown slouched in his chair, looking at the over head with a bored expression. Then he roused himself somewhat to ask, "How about the rest of the crew? Where will they muster? There isn't much room back on the fantail, is there?"

"That's true," said Quigley, "but the details of the guns and so forth are more interesting there than on the roomier foredeck."

"That's right," agreed Hawks.

"You see," said Quigley, "you photograph the captain and his key officers with the corpse laid out before them and the guard in the background against the five-inch gun. Just assume the crew are at quarters behind the camera."

Brown slumped into his chair until he rested on his spine. Then he squirmed about, rummaging in a back pocket for a crumpled cigarette. He worked carefully at the battered cigarette, smoothing it gently. At last he said quietly, "It's your show. You stage it and I'll shoot it."

On his way to the shower, Flynn looked in on MacDougall, who was hunting in one of the drawers under his bunk for a presentable shirt. MacDougall threw the shirt on his bunk, reached into his locker and jerked out the black tie he had last worn on sailing day from San Diego.

"A necktie!" he exclaimed indignantly. "Can you feature wearing a necktie out here?"

"It's being featured today," said Flynn, reaching into his pocket. "Allow me to read the executive officer's memorandum: 'All department heads will assemble on the fantail at fourteen hundred for burial ceremonies. Uniform will be khakis with necktie and garrison (overseas) cap. Due to the presence of a photographer from *Life* magazine neatness in dress is emphasized.' "

"It's a wonder they invited the guy who died," said MacDougall. "He isn't wearing a tie—I know that. I just helped the boys sew him up in blanket and canvas."

"Yes, I'm afraid he doesn't quite belong in this show," said Flynn. "Private Lester Jones, U. S. Marine Corps—he isn't even an officer. But there's one little matter they can't do anything about: he's dead."

At 1400 the fantail was a crowded place, gun crew pushed aside by officers and men specifically assembled to witness burial of Private Lester Jones. In the space to port of Gun Two, Quigley stood before a line of the ship's senior officers. Like him, they were dressed in starched khakis, choked in oppressive heat by black neckties; but there was uneasiness in their manner reaching beyond physical discomfort, a burden of spirit which seemed to rest upon all present except Quigley and Hawks. Assembled in two perfect lines against the long barrel of Gun Two was the honor guard of twelve dungaree-clad sailors with their carbines, in charge of Lieutenant Hill. Between these groups stood six sailors, acting as pallbearers. Resting on carpenter's sawhorses, the canvas-wrapped and flag-draped body of Private Lester Jones. Captain Hawks moved about, active in adusting positions of all about the corpse. Brown, the news photographer, stood on the gun platform taking no active part.

Captain Hawks frowningly considered the positions of his department heads. "Move your officers further outboard,

Quigley. Now, boatswain's mate, move the corpse two feet further aft. Lieutenant Hill, bring your men into the picture a bit; they look like they were plastered against that gun." Shuffling of men, light scraping of sawhorses, flag slipping askew and being adjusted again by a dozen hands. Rumble of steering engines two decks below, moving rudder in response to the helmsman. Steady vibration of thrusting screw, pushing ship, men, corpse—all along in this aimless eight-knot crawl over the sea. A moment of awkward quiet, then Chaplain Hughes pushed gently through the crowd of spectators about the antiaircraft gun tubs, climbed the short ladder to the fantail and took his place beside the flag-draped figure.

Quigley stirred and looked about him. "How's the sun?" he asked the photographer.

"Doesn't matter," said Brown in a flat voice. "Sun's straight up any way you turn."

Now Hawks gave a last check. The guard was in exact position, faces expressionless. Not so his senior officers: nothing he could exactly identify, but resentment—they were not with him in this thing. Well, he was the captain who decided such matters. He would show them. "Quigley, move the officers another pace outboard . . . Officers, attenSHUN! Right DRESS! . . . Front!" Now let them stand there and sweat!

Chaplain Hughes was uncomfortable amid this military stiffness. He knew about Lester Jones, had heard his cry for another chance with life while Gates worked with all possible skill to keep the feeble spark alive. Hughes had heard the last despairing words, "I don't want to die," fading away as life ebbed out for Private Jones. Somehow he must try to preserve decency for this body, so unwillingly separated from its spirit. He opened his Testament and drew a deep breath to commence reading.

"Wait," commanded Captain Hawks. "The corpse doesn't show up well. Move one pace aft, Chaplain. Alvick, move the corpse a little further forward. Now turn it more nearly perpendicular to the camera. Not too much. There; that will do."

MacDougall stood in line between Gates and Flynn. No jokes now from Flynn, the doctor who found some humor in nearly every situation; his face set, he stared over the draped flag at a ship in the next column. On the other side, Dr. Gates, face unnaturally pale, deep shuddering sigh working up from the big frame. Chaplain Hughes raised his Testament, then paused, uncertain as to whether to go on. Quigley stood directly in front of MacDougall, his usually rounded shoulders straining back in a posture of military correctness. Quigley's shirt beautifully laundered—where did that come from? Surely not from the *Belinda* wear and tear laundry. Look at him, afraid to expel much breath for fear he would not look his best in

248

Life magazine. In perfect immobility the corpse of Private Lester Jones, who wanted to live, but died, who wore no tie this tropic afternoon, but overcoats of blanket and canvas. Hoarse whisper: MacDougall speaking to Flynn and Gates but aiming for Quigley's ear, "The corpse is just a prop."

At last the chaplain's words, spoken slowly, interspersed with moments of quiet except for clattering steering engine and beating screw. Brown moved about unobtrusively, sighting his camera with competent assurance, setting and snapping the shutter, peeling off film pack. Then the final salute; the body of Lester Jones committed to the sea, splashing into froth of wake; the triple volley. Once again the empty flag, another sea burial over, another name for the log. Gates pulled off his tie, crumpled it into a pocket and opened his collar. Then he pushed his way through the crowd, heading back to his work in the sick bay.

CHAPTER 28

The *Belinda's* command boat was anchored off the reef at Charan Kanoa. Brooks and Kruger, in charge of *Belinda* boats left behind during retirement of the attack force, were resting from routine trips out to the few supply ships which had been left behind. Brooks put down the earphones and turned from the boat's voice radio. "Another little errand, Karl," he said to Kruger. "I think you'd better go along—combat fatigue case for LST 1021."

Kruger crawled off the bow, where he had been watching night bombardment, and reached into the cockpit for his gun and helmet. "Why LST 1021?" he asked. "They're not hospital-equipped. Isn't that floating headquarters for Army shore parties?"

"That's just the idea. This is the colonel's son."

"Oh. . . . Well, I'll take Boat Twenty-one and shove."

An amtrack, splashing and clattering out from Red Beach to the edge of the reef, brought Kruger his passenger, a very young second lieutenant of infantry. Huddled on the bow of the amphibious tractor, he clasped both arms around bent knees.

"Can you make it into the boat, fellow?" asked Kruger.

A convulsive shudder ran through the young lieutenant. Then he tried to straighten his shoulders and to raise his neck. "I'm . . . I'm . . . I'm all . . ." He took a deep breath and tried again, "I'm all . . . right." He started to clamber into the boat but was overcome by a severe chill, his entire body quivering, outstretched legs beating a quick tattoo on the amtrack's steel deck.

Kruger's boat crew and the soldiers in the amtrack looked away uncomfortably—all but one, evidently a medic, who watched the young lieutenant with clinical interest. "We got him chock full of phenobarb," he said, "but he's still goosey."

Kruger felt a flood of embarrassment and anger. Anger that a man should show weakness; anger at the medic's crudity. "Come on, fella," he said, reaching up a hand. "Let's get out to your old man. Maybe that'll help."

The young lieutenant made it into the boat. After they had shoved off for the LST, Kruger sat beside him on the stern transom. The boy was crying silently now and wiping the tears away with angry fists. Kruger put an arm across his shoulders for a moment, then looked back to Saipan, thinking, I wish I could cry. Things hit me and I just feel dried up inside. Then he watched the bombardment trajectory: red hot shells moving in fast low arcs from the south end of the island to drop out of sight and explode unseen far to the north. There was the feeling of men crawling around in the dark, maneuvering to see but not to be seen, to shoot first, to move forward yet to live. Incessant gunfire, cracking and snapping of small stuff, deep booming of heavy caliber artillery beat into his ears. It was mixed now with the roar of his boat motor and the vibrations coming up through him from the deck. This is no time to give in, he thought. We can't all sit down and cry.

Towards Garapan a terrific flashing light was followed by an explosion which for the moment drowned out all other sound. Then multiple flashes radiated up and out in all directions from an ignited ammunition dump, followed by sounds like the multi-impact shock of an H Hour barrage; above all a pink cloud mushroomed towards the sky, reflecting flickers of bright light much as a distant lighted neon sign. The coxswain looked over his shoulder. He was the same youngster who had steered Kruger's first-wave guide boat on D Day. "Fireworks," he said. "Looks like the Fourth of July in Philadelphia." The motormac and the bow hook were standing near the ramp, watching the scene with interest. They had calmed down a lot, but sometimes it seemed to Kruger that their nonchalance was studied, as if they were trying hard to make up for their funk under mortar fire, to show him that they weren't scared any more.

At last the blacked-out LST loomed out of the murk, and Kruger scrambled aboard with his passenger. A gray-haired officer in clean fatigues stepped forward. Kruger noted the eagle on one tab of the open collar and the engineer's castle on the other—this must be the father. He didn't look much like the young lieutenant—frame bigger, face stronger.

The colonel hesitated a moment, then stepped forward and put an arm around the boy. "It's all right, son. You just need rest. You'll be right as rain in the morning." He stood still, looking down at his son, fatherly love struggling with the disappointment and desire for military restraint plainly showing in his face.

The young lieutenant stiffened half to attention. "Sir," he began, then his voice faltered and he crumpled against the bigger man. "Oh, Dad," he sobbed. "I tried to make it. I—I—I tried. I tried to make it. . . . But I was so scared. It was that damned hand that did it!" he screamed suddenly, all traces of stuttering gone for the moment. "That bloody hand hit me in the face—and nobody hitched to it—just a hand!" He clutched his father and sobbed convulsively, "Oh, Dad. Oh, Dad!"

Feeling that this was no place for him, Kruger nodded to others on the LST, hardly noticing who they were, and got back into his boat. "Shove off, Cox'n," he ordered, thinking: The colonel wanted to see his son make a showing and this is what he got—a boy perfectly normal one day coming back with the shakes, stuttering and scared to death—you just can't expect much bravery. . . .

On the way back to the reef Kruger saw an indistinct shape lying in his path. He cut throttle and began to swerve clear when a voice hailed him across the water. "In the boat, there . . . Will you give us a hand?"

"Go alongside, Cox'n," said Kruger. It was a large barge loaded high with gasoline in drums, rising and falling deliberately in the chop while the light VP bounced alongside. Kruger saw shapes of three men crawling around the drums to his side of the barge. "What's the trouble?" he asked.

"Engine conked," said one of the three. "Can't get her started. We've been drifting for hours—wind's shoving us to sea now."

"These overgrown outboards are nothing but trouble," said another. "They can take it and—"

"Well, Sam can always get it to run."

"Sure, sure, but he had to go ashore scrounging for chow."

Kruger felt impatient. He really had nothing much to do, but uncomfortable after the experience on the LST, he wanted to get back to the reef. Then he shook off the thought. "I haven't got much boat here, but I guess we can shove you along. Here—take a line."

The loaded pontoon barge weighed nearly two hundred tons. It wallowed sluggishly from side to side while the thirty-six foot landing craft struggled against an offshore wind. Kruger considered letting go and running in for more help, but the night was very dark; he might not be able to find it again. The motor-mac frowned professionally over the VP's diesel. "She's going to burn up on us, Mr. Kruger."

"Oh, I don't think so. Just watch your oil. . . . And watch

your revs, Cox'n. Keep her below twenty-one hundred." The night wore away, first hint of light to eastward outlining Mount Tapotchau. The beach seemed as far away as ever. The coxswain started to light a cigarette, squatting down in the boat so that the light should not be seen. In a flicker of amusement Kruger recalled old Captain Gedney saying, "The light of one match may be seen by an enemy submarine at a distance of two miles." He was so tired now after a week of bouncing around the reef that it didn't seem to matter much any more.

"Hey, you! Put out that cigarette! Do you want to blow us sky high?" It was one of the men on the barge. Kruger started guiltily, conscious for the first time of the reek of gasoline fumes. Some of the drums must be leaking.

"No, Cox, don't throw it overboard. Grind it out. There's gas on the water all around us." More light; soon it would be day again. Kruger longed for the day though he knew that the heat would soon blister them again and then they would long once more for night. Now suddenly, towards Garapan, he saw antiaircraft fire like sparks flying upward. "Japs," he said. The gunfire increased, coming closer and closer.

A man who had been sitting on top of the gasoline drums pointed suddenly, "There's two of 'em, coming in low!" He slid down the pile of drums as if feeling less exposed at one end of the load.

Then Kruger saw them, and three others: five planes buzzing the boats and barges lying between them and the reef. Most of the boats were firing now. The motor-mac and the bow hook scrambled up to the two machine guns mounted at the VP's stern. "Hold your fire," yelled Kruger. "Those thirties are no good unless they make a pass right at us. This gas here—" Small caliber stuff was good mostly for moral support. There was strong desire to fire at the strafing planes now darting across the water, firing bursts at anything ahead of them, zooming, diving, twisting. It was hard to tell if anything was hit, but how could they miss? Now they were crossing about a mile ahead. Kruger wondered if they would turn his way; if so they would be on him in about fifteen seconds.

A spatter of lead showered down upon the boat. Before they could hit the deck it was all over. Everybody got up again except the bow hook. He lay in much the same position as at the reef on D Day, overcome by fear of mortar fire when he should have helped set the buoy. Kruger bent over the lad. He was out cold, just a little blood oozing from around a scrap of spent slug imbedded in his scalp. "Probably some of our own stuff," Kruger said. "Don't bandage it or put on any pressure. He isn't bleeding enough to hurt."

A staccato of explosions brought his attention back to the strafing: drums of gasoline in another barge similar to this one burning and spurting flame. Planes fading fast towards Tinian a few miles southward. "Glad that's over with," said the man who had been sitting on top of the gas. "Hey! There's another one; coming this way!"

Kruger jerked his head about. Down from the north came one more, flying faster than the others, dipping, zooming, weaving to avoid fire from a half dozen LST's, but his mean course right for them. They wouldn't have a chance this time. Without looking he could visualize this barge burning like the other. They'd better all jump overboard—even then they might— "Hey, you guys," he yelled, "all of you—"

A bargeman cut in, yelling, "Look! They got him! They got him!"

Kruger looked, saw the plane slung over on one wing, spinning down in flame, crashing with a sharp detonation in the water five hundred yards away. "Shall we cast off and go over there?" asked the young coxswain excitedly.

"No. Keep on shoving gas for the reef. There's no prisoners to pick up over there—just an oil slick."

The bow hook had regained consciousness. He sat on the transom holding his head and looking about in a bewildered way. "What happened?" he asked. Everybody laughed.

"It's just the sun," said the bargeman, who had climbed up on the drums once more.

The bow hook looked up at the sky, turning slowly through all points of the compass. "The sun ain't up yet," he said. Then he felt his head carefully, touched the scrap of metal, looked at the blood on his fingers. "Oh," he said, and lay down again.

"You're O.K." said Kruger, not sure whether he was or not. "Just leave your head alone. We'll let Doc Hardwick fix you up." He was wondering, what's a man's skull like, anyway? Hope that slug isn't in his brain.

The sun was high before they reached the reef. All amtracks still in working order were in use near Garapan. Brooks commandeered a rubber raft to float the bow hook in to Dr. Hardwick. Then he came with help to get the gas drums ashore. "The tanks are running out of gas," he said. "We can't wait for amtracks."

"I don't think I can get through the reef," said Kruger. It was low tide and the reef line stuck up like a breakwater of white coral. Within were lower spots, even deep pools, but no channel large enough for a landing craft. It was getting hot already. Kruger looked around at the overturned amtracks and wrecked tanks strung out along the reef. Discouragement swept over him.

"The drums are sealed," said Brooks. "I think we can roll and float 'em ashore. It's worth a good try anyway." They tied the barge alongside the reef, made a wooden ramp and started the drums ashore. Kruger and Brooks tied all their landing craft together, leaving them in charge of a few boatkeepers. Then they took the rest of their boat crews onto the reef and began to roll and float the drums towards shore. Gettman, the beachmaster, sent some of his men in rafts and waded out with others to receive the drums and drag them ashore. He had radioed to beach headquarters for more machinery, but it seemed doubtful that any would come. He was learning to go ahead with whatever help was at hand.

Kruger floundered around on the sharp reef, directing his men as they rolled the drums over rough coral, shoved them into the pools and then pulled them out at the inshore side. At one place he slid into the water to help boost out a drum. Refreshed by its coolness, he swam a few leisurely strokes. Something soft bumped gently against him. He scrambled out of the pool and looked down into the water. A pale something drifted slowly under the surface. He climbed over the coral to a spot where he could look straight down. It was the naked body of a drowned man, face down, hanging limp from the hips. Kruger walked further around the rim of the pool, looking down. He found two others. Evidently the roiling of the water by the drums had brought them up from some underwater crevasse. Forgetting the gas drums for the moment, he waded to the next pool and peered down into the water. It was the same story here, white bodies suspended gently, some coming to the surface. One had no head; a fish nibbled at another. Some looked as if sharks had been at them: it all seemed so unreal. Kruger thought of burial, of leaving the gasoline while they gathered these dead. Then he shook his head and began floundering back to the working party, saying aloud to the reef, "Nobody wants a stiff."

Late in the afternoon they got the last of the drums ashore and went back to their boats. Kruger's throat was dry; he longed for a drink of cold water. They had no water or food left. It was time to go scrounging again. Then he remembered the pineapple juice, reached behind the life jackets and pulled out a half-used can. He looked at the faces of his motor-mac and coxswain as he extended it in a little half-circle gesture. They shook their heads. He put the jagged hole to his lips and took a swig. The stuff was sickening sweet—even warmer than the last time he had tried it. He thought of Shadow Rockwell, who had conserved it for the boat crews, refusing it to others in the face of insistent demands so it could come cold and refreshing out of the refrigerator into the boats, to be heated like this in the sun and spurned by men who had little stomach for sweetness. Kruger made a face, the sweet taste sticking to his palate. "Everybody wants pineapple juice when it's cold," he said. "But this stuff! . . . Clear, cold water, that's what we need.

It's time to round up the boat crews and go out to the supply ship to fill our water kegs and get a decent meal. . . . Start her up, Cox. I want to talk to Mr. Brooks."

As Kruger's craft came alongside the AKA, he noticed the O.O.D. of the big supply ship looking down at his tattered crew with critical eye. "Ahoy in the boat," hailed the O.O.D. "Are you one of those orphaned boat groups?"

Just a hint of patronage in his tone, thought Kruger. Well, the *Belinda's* boat group didn't have to take their hats off to a supply bucket. "Yes," he said. "We're from an APA, the *Belinda*. I don't want to bother you. . . . We'd just like to fill our water kegs—and if you could just feed my men—"

"Certainly, certainly. Tie up alongside and bring them aboard—chow's nearly finished. After they eat, we'll take care of the water."

They were very decent about everything. The supply officer sent the men down to the mess hall for a regular meal, and promised to make up plenty of lunches to take back to the reef. Yet there was something here that irritated Kruger. He didn't quite understand it, though it seemed to have something to do with the clean decks, the clean dungarees and khakis, the casual, business-as-usual tone of everything—even the PA announcing that small stores would be open for the crew at 1700. Here was the supply officer again, smiling and saying, "Come on down to the wardroom for chow. We've got something special tonight: a real good stew made with stateside beef. Perhaps you'd like to wash up first."

Kruger filled the wash basin with cool fresh water and stuck his face in it, tasting the freshness of it, and then the salt as dried sweat and sea water sluiced away. When he raised his face from the water he saw reflected light dancing in the small bowl. In a flash he was back looking down into the reef pool. Then he shook off the remembrance and dried his face.

The wardroom was hot, like all others in the area, but it was clean and restful after the constant bouncing and rocking in the boats, alternately burning in the sun and freezing in the chill of passing rain squalls. Someone in a clean shirt smiled and pushed a plate in front of him. A tidy young Negro with a pleasant face brought a loaded platter of stew. The scent of perfectly cooked meat and vegetables drowned out the constant odor of diesel fumes in Kruger's head. He filled his plate and took a mouthful. The stuff seemed to gag in his throat. After a struggle he swallowed it, toyed with another forkful, then put it back on the plate, looking about to see if his actions were attracting any attention. Light conversation buzzed all around, but the supply officer was watching him with a quizzical smile. Kruger blushed a little, then thought, he thinks I'm reef-happy, and blushed furiously. He remembered the young lieutenant he had taken out to the LST—after all, what was so different about him? I'm just lucky, he thought. I'm just luckier than he was, but will I always be lucky?

"I guess I'm not very hungry," he said apologetically. "Could I have some coffee?"

"Sure thing," said the supply officer. "Say!" he exclaimed. "We've got a special treat in the icebox—been saving it for our boat jockeys. . . . Oh, Johnny," he called to the mess attendant. "Bring this officer some of that pineapple juice."

Anchored once more off the reef at Red Beach, the *Belinda* stirred with intense activity. All five hatches were wide open, exposing steel caverns far below the waterline. Soldiers and sailors worked together in these lower holds, dragging out and slinging up last loads of gasoline, ammunition and rations. Pappy Moran went from hatch to hatch, his gravel voice rising above the hum of winches, calling, "Get it out, sailors. All of it! We haven't got 'til Christmas!" And to a winch driver, "Watch that coaming, Bugeye. That's high explosive ammo, not scrap iron you're banging around." Landing craft buzzed like flies about the anchored ship: loading alongside, gunning it for the reef, returning for another load.

Lieutenant Hill, the ship's lone marine, smoothly co-ordinated this movement of supplies from ship-to-shore. Using his hatch network of phone talkers, calling boats alongside with his bull horn, talking to the beachmaster on shore by voice radio, he cleared bottlenecks and kept things moving. Red-faced Lieutenant Fraser, in charge of unloading ship, growled his approval to Hill: "For a fellow who never saw a ship before, you do all right!"

Captain Hawks watched from the bridge. He left details of unloading to Fraser and Hill. MacDougall would keep the ship off the reef. Hall would supervise the guns. Brooks and Kruger would run the boats. Responsible for all of these things, the captain's eyes swung constantly from place to place, probing for any oversight or weak spot in the ship's operation and defense. He looked up at the search radar antennae to see if they still swept the horizon from their masttop perches. Intermittently he looked to the flagship for any sudden signal. Seeing none now, he called for his communications officer.

"Oh, Robinson."

"Yes, sir," answered Robinson, running out from the pilothouse, where he kept watch over the TBS.

"Did the beachmaster get his amtracks?"

"Yes, sir. The message is coming in now." Robinson ducked back into the pilothouse. Hawks lifted the binoculars from his chest strap and looked towards Red Beach. The reef gleamed like a white ribbon, separating reef and shore. Landing craft bobbed along the seaward side while amtracks scuttled, antlike, over the coral between boats and shore. Hundreds of soldiers and marines hurried the stuff up the beach into the tangle of trees and shrubs above high-water mark.

During this time fourteen lookouts scanned assigned sectors of sea and sky. Gun pointers and trainers swung their gleaming barrels, ready for the sudden enemy plane or torpedo. These were business-like precautions; there was little apprehension. The battle for the island still raged in nearby hills and towns of Saipan, but that no longer directly concerned these sailors. They worked with the intense energy and enthusiasm of boys playing a game, trying to beat the flagship at unloading. During the night they had watched the continuing bombardment: red tracers of artillery shooting northward in low arcs; great flames from burning oil dumps leaping upward towards ever-hovering star shells. Now in daylight much of the island was obscured by smoke. Signalmen, peering through the ship's telescope, followed movements of tanks and mechanized artillery towards the line. Day and night battle din sounded in their ears, and the concussion of gunfire ashore shook the ship, yet most of the crew went at their work with snatches of song, with friendly jeers and catcalls. Captain Hawks had no morale problem now. By some miracle a lumbering patrol bomber had dropped down to the bay with mail. Nearly every man had a letter or two poking from a dungaree pocket: letters from home to be carried about and reread until sweat, creases and dirt nearly obliterated the memorized sentences.

During the afternoon white-hulled hospital ships and planes arrived at Saipan. Most of the wounded aboard the *Belinda* were transferred for return to Pearl Harbor hospitals. Word passed around the ship from man to man: "We're leaving Saipan. We're sailing tonight!" It was unofficial but everybody knew it. Where they might go did not seem important; just to get away, to make a liberty somewhere if possible—to get going on another operation, get the war over and go home. Anything for a change.

Orders came to send all natives ashore. Reluctantly Kearns, the burly boatswain's mate, got the Chamorro women and children together and put them in a boat. Many of the crew gathered around to say their good-bys.

"Here, Mary, here's your skivies—all washee. . . . Here's candy for the kids. . . . Here's chow—can milk for babies, C ration, rice." The younger woman laughed her silly laugh, nodding and grinning, showing her gold teeth. The thin older woman they called Mary remained poker-faced, taking everything offered without hesitation, as a mother cat takes food for her young. Laughing and carefree, the children played about with some of the sailors until they were lifted into the boat. Then, with a whine of davit gear, the boat was quickly lowered away and the decks of the *Belinda* seemed strangely empty without them.

Saipan Sam remained aboard. During the entire four-day retirement he had remained on a blanket in some out of the way spot on the weather deck. Regardless of the course or position of the ship he had always known the approximate direction of Saipan and kept watch for any sight of his island. On the fourth day he saw the misty peak of Mount Tapotchau lifting from the horizon. While the ship rounded Marpi Point and came to anchor close to the reef off Charan Kanoa he watched the mountain. He was weak and ill, yet something in his manner made it quite plain that he wanted to sit and watch. Dr. Flynn was much concerned as he said to Bell, "He's very weak. He should be down in the sick bay, but—well, he may be a simple native and ragged from his experiences, but he's got more dignity than an admiral. You just don't tell a man like that to come down to your sick bay."

The old man sat and watched the mountain until swift tropic darkness blotted it out. Then, by a nod, for he seemed to understand that these people meant well and wished to take him somewhere, he consented to be put on a litter and carried below. He lay still and listless while the three doctors examined him.

"There's nothing you can put your finger on," said Bell. "No fractures, no definite evidence of internal injury."

"He's still in shock," said Flynn. "Just how much was caused by concussion and how much by mental stress is hard to tell."

Big Ezra Gates held the old man's wrist, feeling the feeble pulse. The eyes were closed now, holding in the vision of Mount Tapotchau at sunset. "I think it's wounding of the spirit," he said. "An old man like him would have a family. He came on board alone. If he thought they were alive he would have been at us to take him ashore."

"I think you're right," said Bell. "I've been watching him day after day. He doesn't seem to be living in this world any more."

During the last afternoon they carried him up on deck very carefully. He was extremely weak, having eaten nothing since coming aboard. Intravenous injections of glucose and plasma failed to rally him. His tired brown eyes found the mountain, then he sighed and leaned back against the bulkhead. The last of the ammunition was unloaded. The wounded were transferred and the other Chamorros were taken ashore. The old man paid no attention to any activity about him. Just before sunset battle stations Dr. Bell came to visit him. "Well, Sam," he said, looking into the old man's face. There had always been a hint of recognition, sometimes a trace of a smile. Now his eyes

258

seemed to see only the mountain. After battle stations, Bell began to work forward through the crowd of sailors scrambling down from their guns. He wanted to have another look at Sam before the corpsmen carried him below.

Working up the last passageway he collided with Nelson, one of the pharmacist's mates. "Oh, Doctor. Old Sam—he's died on us. . . . Will you come and—?"

"Sure," said Bell, "I'll come. . . . I'll come."

Captain Hawks tried to make official arrangements for burial of the old man ashore, but sailing time came and no reply had been received. Brooks and Kruger were back with their men. All boats were hoisted in and all hatches closed. The anchor was hove short and the bridge bustled with preparations to sortie.

As Hawks took his place at conn, Quigley found him in the dark. "This Saipan Sam, Captain. Is he to go ashore, or shall we give him the deep six?"

Hawks's mind was filled with details of departure, but at this he swung around and peered directly into Quigley's face. "Where did you learn that expression?" he asked. "You've never heaved the lead, have you?"

"Why, no, sir. Nowadays we have—"

Hawks cut him off sharp, scorn in his voice now as he said to Quigley, "A sailorman gives the deep six to old shackles and rubbish. He gives his dead sea burial. . . . Have the chaplain take charge. I'll send word as soon as the ship is in deep water."

Quigley left the bridge and sent for Chaplain Hughes. "We are to bury the old native at sea," he said. "Will you do the necessary?"

Anchor aweigh, the *Belinda* steamed away from the island, forming up with other ships of her squadron, using radar for eyes in the darkness. Three small flights of Japanese torpedo planes appeared on the radar screen from the north. They circled about like wolves around a flock of sheep, darting in to attack, then banking off. Ships on the fringe fired rapidly; the *Belinda* and others in the center of the disposition could only stand by the guns and wait, tracking the enemy by radar: "Bearing zero-eight-five; range two-six-zero-zero." Formed up, the fleet set course for Eniwetok. The *Belinda's* crew remained at battle stations, waiting for combat air patrol to chase the Japs, waiting for dawn.

First daylight showed ships all about, plowing steadily along, and the dimming outline of Mount Tapotchau, mist-blue in the distance. The remains of Saipan Sam, neatly sewn in canvas, rested on hatch boards at the fantail rail, ready for burial. While Chaplain Hughes read from his Bible, six bareheaded seamen stood by to slide the body overside. Nearby gun crews and ammunition handlers edged as close as possible from the limits of their battle stations to witness the last journey of this old man they had liked as well.

Then a voice cried, "Wait a minute. Wait a minute!" Kearns panted up the ladder from the flag locker with the *Belinda's* holiday ensign under his arm. Hands reached out to spread this enormous American flag over the still form. So they buried Saipan Sam in deep water off his native island. Kearns folded the flag again just as the PA sounded: *"Secure from battle stations. Set Condition Three. On deck, the First Section."*

Then Doyle, pointer of Gun Two, gazed towards land. "Look!" he cried. "It's gone: the mountain—Saipan—everything."

CHAPTER 29

Anchored at the foot of The Slot, off jungle-tangled Guadalcanal, the *Belinda* shimmered in early morning sunlight. This was a rare day of rest in the endless pattern of invasion, recovery from wear and damage of invasion and preparation for the next invasion. After Saipan the *Belinda* had returned to Pearl Harbor for repairs. Then her propellers churned familiar water in Maalaea Bay, Maui. Once again her boats landed untried combat teams on the sands at Kihei and her antiaircraft guns fired at red sleeves towed overhead by yellow-painted bombers. Anchored now some three thousand miles southwest of the Kihei village store, the *Belinda* had joined a task force preparing to attack some secret target far to the west. Tomorrow she would embark troops and begin another series of exhausting and exasperating dry runs in preparation for actual assault. Today one fourth of the crew were to have liberty at the Guadalcanal fleet recreation area.

Lieutenant Commander Quigley strolled out on the bridge wing where MacDougall hunched over the rail, gazing morosely towards shore.

"Hello, Mac. Looking the beach over?"

"Yes," said MacDougall sarcastically. "There's some coconut trees along the beach. Always wondered what they looked like."

"What's eating you?"

"Mail boat just got back: one half sack of overage periodicals; no letters."

"We'll have to disrate the mail clerk."

"Might be better to give him a crystal ball," said MacDougall. "Somewhere there's a big pile of mail for this ship, probably out in the rain on some island without a name. Back in 'Frisco they must have a top secret list: 'Places where the

U.S.S. *Belinda* never goes.' The dispatcher shuts his eyes and puts his finger on a name. Then he puts our mail on a ship that isn't going there, just to make sure."

"You're in a bad way," said Quigley. "You need a little run ashore."

"You mean sit on a coconut log and stare back at the ship? No thanks. I have to make up charts for the dry run tomorrow."

"Oh, forget your work for one day. Let the hired help do it. I want you to take a party ashore to the target range."

"What's the matter with the gunnery officer? It's his pigeon."

"Hall is ashore lining up ammunition. The chief gunner's mate will do the instructing. All I want you to do is to arrange transportation—Army truck or something like that—and keep them from shooting each other or getting in fights with marines."

As MacDougall reached the quarterdeck the PA shouted, "Liberty for the fourth section will commence in five minutes. Uniform for liberty will be clean dungarees and white hats." The quarterdeck swarmed with sailors, some holding yellow liberty cars, others carrying rifles. Under the watchful eyes of Jackson and Shadow Rockwell, recreation beer was being loaded into a tank lighter.

"Are you sure it's all here, Shadow?" asked Jackson.

"Yes, it's all here now. One case was missing for a while. I should have known better than to use restricted men to pack it up from the reefer. Couple fellows haven't been ashore for three months—this Navy prohibition is a little rough on 'em."

The chaplain elbowed his way into the crowd. "Where's the supply officer, Mr. Rockwell? . . . Oh, there you are, Jackson. How about substituting Coke for some of this beer?"

"Anybody want Coke instead of beer?"

"Yes—you think it's funny, I know—but we have over a dozen seventeen-year-olds in this section. They go ashore in this heat, and there's no water, nothing but beer to drink. I feel responsible for them."

"Well, it's certainly O.K. with me," said Jackson. "Though personally I wouldn't go ashore and hike a mile to drink a bottle of Coke I could buy for a nickel right on board. Only trouble is the authorization for expenditure of welfare funds. You'd have to see the exec about it."

Chaplain Hughes looked around, saw MacDougall. He rushed over to the navigator. "Would you do me a favor, Mac? Go ask Commander Quigley if we may substitute Coke for some of this beer? I'd be glad to go myself, but somehow he always gives me the polite brushoff."

"I could," said MacDougall, "but why bother? We can buy beer for liberty with welfare funds, why not Coke? Let's just do it and tell Quigley about it afterwards. After the thing is

done he won't have to make a decision. . . . Say, Jackson
. . ." Amid loud protests from a few of the liberty party, the
exchange was made. MacDougall followed the liberty and rifle
parties into the tank lighter, which shoved off for the beach.

War had not disturbed the jungle very much. Rusting landing
craft, casualties of the assault two years before, lay half buried
in the sand. Here and there a boat landing, with its collection
of huts crowded about a bamboo signal tower, stuck out from
the fringe of rank tropical growth. The tank lighter landed at
one of these. MacDougall went to the hut which served as
headquarters for an Army motor pool and requested transportation. There would be a truck in about an hour, he was told.
Thanking the major, MacDougall went back to the landing.
"We're due for a wait, Vandemeer," he told the tubby chief
gunner's mate. "Could you keep track of your men in the
recreation area?"

"With a case of beer, I could," said Vandemeer with a grin.

The recreation area consisted of a five-acre grove of battered
coconut trees, bordered by a dusty road at one end and a narrow beach of black sand at the other. Sailors dumped armloads
of baseball bats, mitts, balls and sundry athletic equipment as if
they had thus completed a job. Two of them climbed trees for
coconuts, which already littered the ground in profusion. Two
others played catch. A few walked the beach or went swimming.
Most of them sat down in the coarse grass or upon trunks of
coconut trees felled during assault landings two years earlier.
MacDougall sat down on one of the logs next to Russ Secor, a
boatswain's mate from the second division. Before them lay a
panorama of ships at anchor in a bay churned by hundreds of
landing craft.

"Isn't it funny," said MacDougall; "this morning we were on
the ship staring at the beach. Now we're on the beach staring
at the ship."

"One thing about it," said Secor with a grin. "There's no PA
to get you off your tail every time you sit down for a blow."
Welcoming shouts and wisecracks announced arrival of the
beer and Coke. The two tree climbers slid down in such haste
that their legs were scratched and bleeding. The place came to
life as men crowded about the cartons.

MacDougall went to see about transportation to the rifle
range for his men. "I'm sorry," said the major. "The truck I had
lined up for you has been rerouted. You'll have to wait another
hour." When MacDougall got back to the recreation area he
found much more life in the party. Encouraged by the beer, a
ball game had been started between *Belinda* sailors and a contingent of marines from a battleship.

Grandy and Lubiski, from the boat repair gang, were keeping
close to the beer supply.

"Drink up, Lubiski," said Grandy. "Better drink it up before it gets too warm."

"Sure, Grand, sure. Warm suds is bad for you."

Now the ball game broke up and both sides crowded around Ensign "Junior" Barbey, who was umpiring.

A burly marine protested violently, "I was safe, I tell you. I was safe. He never touched me."

"Oh, yes I did," said Secor, who had been catching for the *Belinda* team. "Want me to knock you out when I tag you?"

"Try it now," said the marine. "I dare you."

"Come on, boys," said Junior. "Break it up now. . . . You were out at the plate, fella."

The big marine had sampled enough *Belinda* beer to reveal his personal opinion of ensigns. He towered over Junior, shaking a mitt-sized fist in his face as he pressed against him and forced him back from the playing field. "No little ninety-day wonder is going to call me out when I ain't out."

Now Secor pushed Junior aside. "You can't hit him, sir. I can." Instantly the fight was on, a free-swinging affair which both teams joined. Sometimes sailor hit sailor and marine knocked down marine. MacDougall rushed in, picked up the bat, considered trying to quell the riot with it, then threw it out of reach. In the end, heat won the fight, which stopped almost as quickly as it started. The marines left for their own recreation area and the sailors sat down to rest. There was no more baseball; it was getting too hot for that. MacDougall went back to the landing to see about his truck.

Ensign Twitchell tossed aside his empty beer can and walked over to two struggling sailors, both young and very angry. One of the two, with scratches down the inside of forearms and calves, was trying to take a green coconut away from the other. Before Twitchell reached them negotiations broke down completely, and they began to exchange punches. Twitchell tried to force his way between them. "Stop it, you two. Attention! Listen to me; I'm an officer!"

Both youngsters continued to struggle for the coconut, each hugging it with one arm and punching with the other. Then, gasping, they paused to argue.

"It's my coconut," said one. "I got all scratched up climbin' that tree—gimme that coconut, I tell you!"

"It's my coconut," said the other. "I picked it up. Anybody can pick up a coconut: finders keepers."

"It's mine, I tell ya. It's my coconut. Give it to me!" He jabbed again with the free fist.

"You dirty baboon!" said the other, letting go the coconut and pummeling the scratched-up sailor with both fists. "We'll settle this right now."

"Attention, men!" cried Twitchell again. "Attention, I tell you; attention!" Twitchell's voice rose to a scream. The coconut lay on the ground and the two young sailors slugged it out: sweaty, shirttails flapping, dungarees torn. Twitchell stepped forward and grabbed the scratched-up sailor from behind. The sailor, who had started a wild haymaker, spun around and without recognizing his target, landed it on Twitchell's jaw. Twitchell staggered back, holding his jaw. Then he advanced again, crying in a voice hoarse with emotion, "You're under arrest—striking an officer!"

"Oh, shut up!" snapped a deep voice behind him. The tone and the words triggered off the last of Twitchell's control. Thought of bringing these sailors before the captain was replaced by blind rage. About the same height as the scratched sailor, but much heavier, Twitchell shoved him close to a coconut tree and began to punch his head against its trunk.

A gathering murmur sounded at Twitchell's back. "Aw!" cried a spectator, anger and disapproval in his tone. Boos, now; more boos than at the short ball game. Twitchell grew even angrier. He held the young sailor by the front of his shirt and punched him in the face with all his strength.

Sudden pain of a sharp blow behind the ear spun Twitchell around in time to see Secor with his fist still cocked, to hear the same deep voice now saying, "Here's one for your yellow guts, you little tin horn!" The second blow doubled Twitchell up and knocked him backwards over a coconut log, where he fell in a heap.

Returning once more without the truck, MacDougall pushed and wormed his way through the crowd just in time to see a fist rammed hard into Twitchell's midriff. "All right, fellows," he called out. "Break it up; break it up; break it up." Momentum seemed to have run out. The crowd was quiet, startled at the sight of Ensign Twitchell squirming in the dust. Secor stood over Twitchell, rubbing his right fist against the palm of his left hand. Secor had been in trouble before and now he was in trouble again, but he pushed aside thoughts of inevitable punishment, glowing with the pleasure of this fleeting moment.

Twitchell struggled to his feet, dusted at his khakis, felt his jaw. His large, protuberant eyeballs seemed ready to pop out of their sockets. His whole face radiated hatred and desire for revenge. "You saw it, Mr. MacDougall. You're a witness. He hit me. He struck an officer!" Twitchell's voice dropped to a hoarse whisper. "I'll break you for this, Secor. I'll break you for this!"

MacDougall shoved both hands deep into his pockets. He looked from Twitchell to Secor and back to Twitchell. He looked at the two young sailors, leaning together against the tree, the forgotten coconut at their feet. Why didn't I stay at the truck pool? thought MacDougall. Me witness for Twitchell!

I'd just love to pop him one myself. . . . But he is an officer and I did see Secor hit him: Secor with a service record like a comic strip. It didn't matter if he was one of the best workers in the crew; he'd probably be disrated for this.

"Mr. MacDougall, sir." Chief Boatswain's Mate Alvick stepped forward to speak to his old division officer. Alvick stood his six-foot-two as straight as a ramrod. His khakis were spotted with sweat but otherwise clean, and still showed the laundry press. It was quite clear that he had not been involved in any brawling.

MacDougall was stalling for time. Surely there must be some way to get Secor out of this, to avoid taking Twitchell's part. Alvick was regular Navy and proud of it; strong on regulations. He liked Secor and hated Twitchell, but he'd go by "Rocks and Shoals," MacDougall was sure of that.

"What is it, Chief?" MacDougall said irritably.

"Perhaps you didn't see exactly what happened, sir," said Alvick in level, self-possessed tones. "These two seamen, Jenkins and Flint, were wrestling for a coconut. Mr. Twitchell must have thought they were fighting. He pushed in between them and they dropped the coconut. Mr. Twitchell tripped over the coconut, hit his head against that tree trunk and fell down, sir. Nobody laid a finger on him."

Relief flooded through MacDougall. He remembered the time during one of Captain Gedney's inspections when a bundle of dirty swabs had been left on deck. Alvick had spun a seaman out of division ranks, shoved the swabs into his arms and kept him circulating around the deckhouse, always on the opposite side from the captain. Now he had done it again. "Thank you, Chief," said MacDougall. Then he looked around at the crowd. "Did anybody else see exactly what happened," he said, exaggerating the word *exactly* as if officially converting fable into fact. Then MacDougall spotted Hatcher, leading petty officer of the beach party. "How about it, Hatcher: what did you see?"

"Oh, Mr. Twitchell tripped over that coconut, sir. I was standing right behind him. Nobody hit Mr. Twitchell."

"How about the rest of you men—what did you see—exactly?"

"Just like Chief Alvick said, sir."

"He tripped all right."

"Nobody hit him."

Twitchell glared at MacDougall. "It's all a pack of lies. I'll get witnesses. You'll all pay for this!"

MacDougall laughed and walked away. He got his truck at last and loaded the rifle party aboard. An Army driver familiar with the terrain whirled the truck over a narrow dirt road. They passed a military cemetery: rows of neat white crosses under wider-spaced rows of coconut trees, with a small, thatched chapel to one side. After skirting the west bank of the Lunga River, they suddenly darted into the jungle. Overspreading tangle shut out sunlight and sky. Rank ferns and lush tropical undergrowth grew in deep shade between matted trees. Every inch between them was covered with wild morning glory vines, festooned like gigantic spider webs. Here and there a snag of rotting log protruded, as did occasional neat piles of poison gas shells, half covered with vines. The truck stopped suddenly at a check point. Damp smell of jungle decay overpowered gasoline fumes. Weird calls of strange birds came from somewhere in the tangle where Americans and Japanese had crawled about, hunting each other. Continuing on, the truck entered the lower end of a small, steep valley and stopped again at the edge of a clearing. Intermittent small-arms fire broke into the silence. "All out for the rifle range," said the driver. The sailors jumped down; the driver spun his truck around and disappeared into the jungle.

"A combat BLT is using the main range," the Army captain in charge told MacDougall. "There's another range further up the valley. You'll have to pass through the line of fire to get there. A field telephone is strung between the two ranges. When your men are all clear on the other side, let me know and we'll commence fire again. When you're ready to come out, give us another ring and we'll cease fire."

"Thanks," said MacDougall. "We'll do that."

"And say," the captain added, "hurry it up past my line of fire, will you? My company is due—well, I guess you know. We've got to have the best shooting possible."

"Sure," said MacDougall. "I get you." When the fire ceased he took his men down the valley. In about three hundred yards they came to the secondary range, called back, "All clear," to the Army and started practice. Vandemeer, the chunky chief gunner's mate, took over as instructor.

MacDougall and Kruger worked in the pistol range with their forty-fives. The spattering bullets seemed to have a casual sound. "It's funny," said Kruger. "Same guns, same ammunition, but they don't sound mean when you're just practicing."

At last, tiring from the heavy kick of the forty-fives, they sat down with Vandemeer to share a canteen of warm water. A tech sergeant in dusty fatigues appeared from somewhere and watched Hatcher firing a submachine gun into the center of a target. "Pretty good shooting, Joe," said the sergeant, "but that ain't always enough. Look here." He took the gun from Hatcher, shoved the butt against his stomach, squatted in a crouch and frog leaped around, back and forth as if on a pivot, menacing the Navy men about him.

"Say, that thing's loaded," said Vandemeer.

"Sure, it's loaded. In the Army we use loaded guns. You sailors—"

"Listen, you short-time soldier," said Vandemeer. "I've done time in the Army, the Marines and the Navy. You ain't holding that gun right. Now the Army manual says—"

The sergeant laughed. There was braggadocio and bitterness and a hint of madness in his laugh. His eyes glittered hard as he snapped a fresh clip in the gun. "They taught us the book," he said, "but it was here in this valley . . . The Japs—they taught us how to shoot." Then he laughed again, leaping about with the gun butt against his belly while the muzzle made a dry run on MacDougall, Kruger, the fat gunner's mate and every sailor in sight. Then the sergeant spun about with his back towards them and his weird laugh was drowned out by gun chatter as he ripped the clip of bullets back and forth across the target. "See?" he said. Calm once more, he handed the gun back to Hatcher and disappeared into the jungle.

When they were ready to leave, MacDougall went to the field telephone and tried to phone the captain, but the line was dead. He jiggled the hook, turned the crank, followed the wire as close to the shooting as he dared. He could find no break in it, but there was no response. There was nothing to do but wait; the trail out was directly in the line of fire. There was no shade in this part of the valley and the sun beat into them, cooking out enough sweat to drench their clothing. They were thirsty, but the canteens were empty.

"I guess one of us had better crawl around and contact that captain," MacDougall said to Kruger.

"Want me to go?"

All at once the firing stopped completely. "Wait a minute," said MacDougall. Perhaps the company was through practice. "It's time for the truck to meet us. We can't expect the driver to wait."

"We'll have lots of fun hiking through the jungle after dark," said Kruger. "There isn't a flashlight in the crowd."

"The trail runs below the line of fire—I don't know how much below. Think it's safe to try?"

"Oh, I think it's all right—if they keep on the target."

MacDougall grinned. "They'd better," he said. "O.K. You and the chief start ahead with the men. Make it fast. I'll come behind with Hatcher to round up any stragglers." Kruger started up the trail with the heavyweight chief rolling along beside him. "Get in there, fellows," said MacDougall to the others. "Keep moving right along; this may not be healthy. If they start firing again, hit the dirt fast. Then we'll see how much ceiling we've got." When everyone was on the trail, Hatcher and MacDougall followed. Hurrying along they soon saw thick trees ahead. "Won't be long now," said MacDougall.

A volley of rifle fire cracked over their heads, close. The whole crowd hit the dirt. MacDougall looked up. The tallest bushes were about four feet high, and though the whining bullets seemed to be passing lower than their tops, there was no indication of it. Hatcher crawled ahead with MacDougall following. Soon they came up with the chief gunner's mate, who had dropped back. His faded dungarees were muddy with a mixture of sweat and dust, and his shirt had been torn by a brush snag. He puffed along on all fours, face brick red from exertion. "Anything in the manual about this, Chief?" MacDougall asked.

Past the line of fire at last, they reached the fringe of trees and got to their feet. "Reminded me of Kwajalein," Hatcher said. "Foots Boski, McClintock and me up in the line, rabbit hunting. Poor old Whitey—he'd a got a kick out of Vandemeer dragging his belly back there."

The company commander smiled when he noticed the dust on MacDougall's khakis. "Did you try to call us, Navy?" he asked.

"Yes. Line was dead."

The captain chuckled. "Just splicing a bad spot in the line," he said. "Well, here's your truck."

The driver stopped at the bank of the Lunga River. The area was dotted with small piles of clothing and the river was dotted with bobbing heads of swimming soldiers. The driver looked questioningly at MacDougall. "Nice fresh water," he said. "Most of the fellows have a swim before they go back."

MacDougall looked at the water, running swift and smooth. After water hours aboard ship—washing six times over in the same quart of water—here was a chance to swim in the stuff again. "Good idea," he said. "Want to go swimming, boys?"

"Oh, boy! Hey, fellows; swimming!"

"Let's go. Beat you in!" Piles of faded blue joined the khaki. Bodies tanned to the waist, white below, dashed to the bank and dove in. The truck driver was the first in. He coasted downstream with his toes sticking out of the water, flashed upstream in a strong crawl, then floated down again. The sailors splashed, laughed and ducked each other.

"It's just like the old swimming hole back at Woodstock."

"No it ain't. It's more like Spring River, Arkansas—except for the girls."

"Girls! What's them?"

"Wish I could show you, boy!"

The call of the water was irresistible; MacDougall tucked strap watch into folded khakis and dived into the stream. The water was just cool enough to be refreshing: product of tropic squalls, running quickly down mountainside to the sea. MacDougall swam under water with his eyes open, blowing air bubbles and watching them dart upward in filtered light, reveling in velvet-smooth comfort of unlimited water. Some distance downstream he came to the surface, worked his way towards shore where the current was less swift and began to swim upstream with lazy strokes. Brakes squealed as a Navy jeep stopped suddenly at the river bank. A Naval captain and a commander, both wearing medical corps insignia, sat in the back seat.

"See, Commander Phillips," said the captain, indignantly. "I've mentioned this before. Why this continued violation of my directive? Five days ago I posted the Lunga River as contaminated and out of bounds to Naval personnel. Look at those dungarees there! The Army may do as they please, but I expect my directives to—"

"Yes, sir. Quite right," said the commander. "I'll send a tracer."

"Make it strong," blustered the captain, rising to get out of the jeep. "I think I'll take some names here—make an example."

"Yes, sir. Of course, they're expecting us at the club, you know."

"That's right," said the medical captain. "Let 'em scratch their fungus. . . . Go on, driver."

Kruger had drifted downstream beside MacDougall. Hanging on to lower branches of an overhanging bush which concealed them from the jeep, they had heard the conversation.

"Stuffy old goat," said MacDougall.

"The old Senior Officer Present stuff," said Kruger. "Well, you're S.O.P. now. What're you going to do?"

"Sop your head," said MacDougall, suddenly rising up, then shoving Kruger underwater with both hands. Kruger came up sputtering and laughing. MacDougall swam away but Kruger caught and ducked him. MacDougall had gulped a lungful of air. He stroked down, then coasted along underwater, enjoying this rare luxury of a river full of fresh water. Fungus! They were always fussing about something, a shot in the arm for this or that. He'd take a chance on the fungus. Then he remembered something the captain had said: "I have posted the Lunga River. . . ." The Lunga River—fall of 'Forty-Two—that time he sailed his ship to the Canal from Vila with six tons of combat boots. They were fighting across the Lunga River—this river. Bodies of Japs and Americans floated downstream together, lay bloating in the shadows. Shivering as if with chill, MacDougall swam to the bank and climbed out. He pulled on his clothes and raked his wet hair back with his fingers, then walked to the bank. Most of his men were getting out; a few strong swimmers flashed back and forth. The fat chief floated slowly in a quiet pool, both hands resting on his stomach. "All right, men," said MacDougall. "Time to go now. Everybody out."

The boat landing was almost as hot as the target range. Sun glinted on salt water all the way across to Tulagi on nearby Florida Island. Landing craft from many ships churned in and out from the boat landing, but no tank lighter from the *Belinda* was in sight. MacDougall turned back to the cluster of Quonset huts and thatched shacks grouped behind the pontoon dock. Kruger came up to ask, "Want some coffee? There's a lady in the Red Cross shack over there, giving out free coffee."

MacDougall followed Kruger to a small portable hut, where they got in line with soldiers, sailors and marines. Reaching the open counter, they saw a neat but plain-looking woman of about thirty-five, with a tired, kindly face, wearing the pale blue Red Cross working uniform. She paused now and then to wipe perspiration from her forehead with the back of her hand, then continued to ladle out steaming coffee. At last it was Kruger's turn. "Will you have sugar and cream?" she asked in a pleasant, matter-of-fact voice.

"I . . . I . . . I . . ." said Kruger. He tried again but no sound came out. He looked at the Red Cross lady. She looked at him, holding out the cream and sugar. At last Kruger moved away with his paper cup of black coffee.

MacDougall joined him, stirring his coffee. "What's the matter, Karl?" he asked. "You aren't a black-coffee man."

Kruger's face, red from the heat, turned still redder. "It was the queerest thing—I haven't talked to a woman in over three months—I couldn't even ask her for sugar."

Those of the *Belinda's* crew who were off duty assembled for movies after supper, an early meal finished before tropic sunset. For the first time in weeks they were in an anchorage considered safe enough to dispense with sunset battle stations. After sunset they would have to wait for darkness and then for the captain before movies could start. Darkness was swift and sure here at Guadalcanal—Captain Hawks would come when ready, possibly hours after sunset. Movies must not start without the captain. Meanwhile the crew sat in the open air anticipating, talking to each other against the din of the chaplain's record player, watching the shore.

"Hey, fellows," called a signalman from the after part of the signal bridge, "there's Bob Hope and a dame on the beach!" This announcement was greeted with catcalls and whistles. Men left precious vantage points they had been holding for a better view of the movies and rushed to the rail for a look. Quartermasters and signalmen who had binoculars instantly became the most popular men aboard.

"Hey, Willicut, lemme look."

"Naw, I'm next."

"What's she look like?"

"What's she got on?"

"Oh, boy, look at that chest!"

"Say, that's Frances Langford." The speaker took a long look, then handed back the binoculars reverently. "You can have my place at the movies, bub. I'm goin' to the sack and sleep on this."

By eight o'clock Captain Hawks had worked almost to the bottom of the stack of papers on his desk. Jackson, the supply officer, waited impatiently. He hoped the captain would quit now so they could cool off at the movies. Any old movie would do—just to sit in the dark and look at some different face, some face he didn't have to feed.

Captain Hawks picked up the last sheet. "Welfare Fund Expenditure," he read aloud. "Item one: sixteen cases of beer. Item two: ten cases of Coca-Cola. Is that correct?"

"Yes, sir."

"Who authorized the Coca-Cola?"

"No one, sir. The chaplain suggested to MacDougall that we ask the executive officer. MacDougall thought it would be all right to go ahead—he didn't want to bother you at the time."

"Oh, he didn't," said Hawks. "How about you? Aren't you the supply officer?" He took off his spectacles and glared experimentally at Jackson. When Jackson showed no change in expression, Hawks turned the glare into a grin. "Very good. Very good," he said. "Beer if they want it. Coke if they want it—of course, they can get Coke aboard most any day." Hawks picked up his pen to sign, then poked it towards the supply officer. "Tell me this, Jackson. Was it beer or Coca-Cola that Ensign Twitchell had been drinking when he stumbled over that coconut?"

CHAPTER 30

"What's the matter with you, Grandy—you slipping? Scared of that new warrant, that's what you are. You and the chief and the whole boat repair gang—all except me. He ain't going to bull me around—at least not very long. He'll wear down like all them new brooms. Just let him eat a few weevils in the bread we're getting these days. Just let him get up for battle stations three times a night and then do a twelve-hour day. Just let him—"

"Oh, shut your trap, Lubiski. Start shoving up the mahogany. We got work to do here. This boat looks like a battleship leaned on it."

"O.K. O.K. Here, Mr. Apple Polisher, here's your lumber. You whittle on it: fit her in there nice and pretty for Long John. Maybe you'll make first class one of these days."

Grandy mounted the portable scaffold rigged around *Belinda's* Boat Seventeen, nested at number four davit above a similar craft. He reached down for the plank and continued his repair job with practiced, if unhurried skill. "It ain't that at all, Lubiski. I'm no speed ball, but things look different than when we commissioned this bucket. There's something about working together, doing things that can't be done and then doing 'em faster. It's getting so I like it."

Lubiski leaned against the davit and scratched his heat rash. Looking with distaste at both scaffold and boat to be repaired, he failed to notice a tall, rawboned figure with a candid but aggressive face which now approached along the line of nested VPs. "You're getting sentimental, Grand," Lubiski continued. "Won't get you anywhere. Now I've got the system. I know when to loaf and when to—"

A deep authoritative voice close behind Lubiski interrupted him: Warrant Carpenter John Long saying, "Get up on that scaffold, Lubiski, and start repairing boats before I lift you up there with my boot. I'll teach you my system. Work, work and more work—that's my system. Now get up there!" Lubiski had no need to turn around to see the speaker. With the back of his head he could feel the towering figure of the new warrant carpenter. Buttocks quivering in expectancy of a kick which did not come, he swung up on the scaffold as if propelled by Long's foot.

Long had moved to the forward end of the boat, where he frowned at a jagged hole punched through the side, just abaft the ramp. "Now, Grandy, when you get to your plyboard patch, use less glue than you did yesterday and set your clamps tighter."

When Long swung down the ladder to inspect other landing craft on the foredeck, Lubiski said defiantly, "It's still like I said, Grand. He's a new broom here—trying to make a show for Hawks. I don't care how much noise he makes; these mustangs are all scared of four stripes."

Grandy laughed as he balanced the plank across one knee and reached for his folding rule. "You got him all wrong, Lubiski. Long came aboard at Pearl with one sea bag and twelve thousand board feet of hardwood from Waimanalo Boat Pool."

"Sure. What of it?"

"Well, he just wants to use all of it up on our boats before some other ship bums it away from him. That's all."

Captain Hawks leaned far back in his swivel chair, yawning and stretching. Upright once more, he frowned at the vast mass of official paperwork spread over his cabin table. Then he swept a section of the table clear with his left forearm and rang for the orderly.

"Biggs."

"Yes, sir."

"Get Mr. Long."

The tall warrant carpenter knocked at the open door, then hesitated outside. "Come in, Long, come in," said Hawks. Long pulled aside the hanging curtain, ducked under the door frame and entered, hat in hand. "Sit down, Long. Have a cup of coffee—I'll ring for fresh."

"Thank you, Captain." Long sat down on the edge of his chair and looked about nervously, like a pheasant in a clearing during hunting season.

Smiling disarmingly, Hawks shoved a copy of *Yachting* under the carpenter's nose. It was opened at a double-page description of a twenty-four foot knockabout sloop, complete with transverse and longitudinal sketches, dimensions and specifications. "Nice little boat, isn't it?" asked Hawks.

"Yes, sir. It's a nice boat." The carpenter's voice carried faint overtones of annoyance. Sure it was a nice boat, but what did it have to do with repairing thirty-two landing craft for action. His mind was wrestling with detailed problems connected with battered LCVPs.

"Could you make one?" asked Hawks.

"One of those, sir?" Long's thoughts were on ramps now. Seven of the boat ramps were out of alignment. He'd see Rinaldo, the chief shipfitter. Ramps had to fit.

"Yes. One exactly like this."

Long's mind jarred away from ramps. He looked at the plans again: some fine faraway, peaceful day—"Why, yes, sir. I could make one. I'd need blueprints, of course."

"The specifications are there," said Captain Hawks, his voice casual, almost dreamy. "Could you dope them out and build the boat without blueprints?"

Long's puzzlement gave way to relief. Skippers were pretty much alike. This man was trying him out, seeing what he would say—putting him on the spot professionally. "Yes, Capt'n," he said. "I could build the boat, with blueprints or without."

Hawks jerked forward abruptly in his swivel chair and
273

slapped the palm of his hand upon the yacht plans. "Very good," he said in incisive tones, "take this along and start building my sailboat."

"Build her now, sir?" Astonishment and dismay showed in Long's rugged face. "Surely you don't mean——"

Hawks volleyed the words back at him. "Yes, build her now! I certainly do mean just that. You have the plans, the men to assist and the materials. I've seen your lumber pile: beautiful stuff. It will make a little dandy for me to sail when the *Belinda* is at anchor." Then, with a note of scorn in his voice, Hawks said, "If you get bogged down—the navigator and the first lieutenant both consider themselves to be very superior seamen: you can ask their advice." Hawks reached into his pocket and brought out his ocarina. Leaning back in his chair and resting his feet on a heavy volume labeled ComSouWesPac Oplan Ninety-Two dash Forty-Four, he performed with flourishes a few inaccurate measures of H.M.S. *Pinafore*. Then, noting Long's startled and confused expression, he beat time with the ocarina and hummed in an off-key voice, "La-la-la-la, la-la-la-la. That now I am the ruler of the Queen's Navee."

Long realized that he had been dismissed. Picking up the magazine and his cap he left the coffee untouched and walked slowly aft towards the boat repair shop.

During midafternoon, "Scuttlebutt" Barbaroli, shipfitter third, wandered into the starboard mess hall, burning with news.

"Heard the scuttlebutt?"

"What? No mail again?"

"No. This is good. You won't believe it until you see for yourselves. Just skip aft to number five hatch, just forward of the tank lighters, and take a look!"

"Take a look at what? Frances Langford come aboard?"

"No, this is straight dope. They're laying the keel for a mahogany sailboat, and the Old Man is right there, standing over 'em while they do it. Almost all repair work on the ship's boats is knocked off. Chips is down on his hands and knees studying a copy of *Yachting Magazine*."

"Save your applesauce. Who do you think you're sucking in?"

Barbaroli was quite offended. "I'm not kidding at all. Go back and take a look. You'll see. Well, I got to go tell 'em down in the fire room—a cute little sailboat for the skipper!"

This little redhead must be new, thought Boatswain's Mate Doyle. Strange he hadn't noticed him before. All the new draft had been assigned to divisions, and he had personally checked in the Second Division hands for Chief Alvick. The kid was looking at Gun Two as if it were something wonderful; he couldn't have been around much.

"Where you from, Buddy?" Doyle asked.

Not seeming to hear, the boy kept staring at the gun. Then noticing Doyle's eyes on him he asked, "How far will it shoot?"

"Oh, about seven miles; but closer is better. . . . I said, 'Where you from?' What's your division?"

"Me? I'm not in any division here—I was stationed at Tulagi."

"Then what you doing here?"

"I guess I'm what you call a stowaway."

Doyle snorted with disbelief. "Aw, go on! Nobody would jump duty on a peaceful little island with beer and liberty every other night. Nobody would leave that to stow away on this bucket."

"I've got my reasons," said the boy.

"You couldn't dream up a reason good enough. Do you realize what they can do to you now?"

"Oh, I suppose I'll get a court."

"No suppose about it. Your C.O. will send form letters to your commandant, to your folks—even to your county sheriff back home. They'll search until they find you and then you'll get a general court: probably a dishonorable discharge with two to ten years brig time to think it over."

The boy bit his lip, trying to stop its trembling, quiet stubbornness in his tone as he insisted, "I've got my reasons, I tell you. I know what I'm doing."

Doyle shook his head. "You've been out in the sun too long without your hat."

Ignoring Doyle's remark, the boy looked out over the rest of the task force, steaming westward. Then he turned back to Doyle at Gun Two. "Well, who do I report to?" he asked.

Doyle looked down from his six feet at this little fellow, so unimpressive physically, yet with intense blue eyes regarding him steadily from under mussed-up carroty hair. "Better come down to chow first," Doyle said, "then I'll take you to Chief Alvick."

"I'd like to speak to the captain," said the stowaway to Alvick.

"Don't worry," said Alvick. "You'll see him. Come up on the bridge with me." Alvick led the way forward and upward, elbowing with practiced skill through groups of soldiers in passageways, ladder scuttles and deck spaces between winches and landing craft. Only the bridge deck was clear of troops. Alvick stepped up to Kruger, who was conning the ship. "Mr. Kruger, I have a stowaway here."

"What's that?" roared Captain Hawks from his high seat beside Kruger. "A stowaway?"

"Yes, sir," said Alvick, stepping back a pace, leaving the stranger to face the captain alone.

"Name?" barked Hawks, glaring down at the lad.

"John Ryan, sir."

"Rating?"

"Pharmacist's Mate, Third Class."

"Duty station?"

"Naval Station, Tulagi, sir."

With wrinkled chin and lips twisted into a leer, Hawks leaned well forward in his chair and peered down at Ryan. "So you were running away—but you ran the wrong way when you got on my ship. We have no room for cowards here aboard the *Beachhead Belinda*. We fight Japs and we fix people like you. What've you got to say to *that?*"

Ryan looked steadily at the captain. "I wasn't running away, sir."

Hawks opened his mouth to crush all alibis, but something in Ryan's blue eyes stopped him. Hawks closed his mouth and stared down at Ryan. Ryan stared back at him with a steady gaze which showed neither defiance nor fear. Hawks waited for the blue eyes to drop, but they remained focused on him. "You don't look like a coward," said Hawks at last. "Why did you run away? Did you think we were bound for Pearl Harbor or the States?"

"No, sir," said Ryan. "I don't know exactly where you're going: that's secret, of course. But you aren't going back to 'Frisco with all these infantry soldiers and tanks. You're going somewhere after Japs, and that's where I want to go. I want to fight Japs too."

"What's that?" Hawks asked sharply.

Now Ryan's voice rose with feeling. "They got my brother, George, at Pearl Harbor. He was quartermaster second on the *Oklahoma* and he didn't have a chance. They got him quick and dirty, without any warning. So I joined the Navy to fight Japs. I volunteered to fight, but they made me a bandage wrapper and stuck me on a captured island without a Jap in sight. I worked with the wounded: fellows who'd been up in the line or out with the fleet—where I wanted to be. The more I saw of them the more I wanted to get combat duty myself. I asked for a transfer but they wouldn't give me one. I asked and asked. Yesterday they sent me out here with a boatload of medical supplies. I just stayed on board. I know I did wrong, Captain. I'll take what's coming, but please give me one crack at those Japs before you turn me in."

Then Ryan dropped his eyes from Captain Hawks's and stared at his own shoes. Hawks looked off into space and the

Belinda's bridge was very quiet. Then he addressed the stowaway directly. "Ryan, I believe your story and I'm going to give you a chance to prove it. You are a prisoner at large, of course, but you need not muster with the prisoners. You will not leave this ship at any time unless properly ordered to do so. You are assigned for temporary duty with the beach party under Lieutenant Gettman, here. You will land in the third wave on Red Beach at Angaur, Palau Islands, now held by the Japanese. That will be just seven minutes after H Hour. Does that suit you?"

"Yes, sir. Thank you, Captain."

"Don't thank me. You may be killed. If not, I will review the beachmaster's report on your performance of duty, which will determine whether my own report on you will be favorable when I return you to your commanding officer at Tulagi." Hawks wrinkled his chin, thrust his lower jaw to one side and wriggled his protruding lower lip in an ugly grimace. "You're in a lot of trouble, Ryan. It will take a very good report to help you at all."

"Yes, sir. Thank you—"

Hawks held up a hand for silence. "You have already disobeyed one of the cardinal Rules for the Government of the Navy: deserting duty station in time of war. Remember, you are in the Navy. You will obey orders. If you disobey orders on the beach you will be shot. Is that clear?"

"Yes, sir. Thank you, Captain. Thank you, Captain."

Tony Brooks, the *Belinda's* boat commander, strode into the first lieutenant's office, where Stuart Fraser struggled with weekly hull reports. "Listen, Mr. Fraser. Got a few minutes to look at some of my babies?"

"Time?" said Fraser, his ruddy face scowling up from the stacked paper work. "I never have time. What's the matter now?"

"Same thing as yesterday—and last week. We're six days from a pay run on a rough beach and my boats look like junk from a boneyard. We took an awful beating on all those practice runs."

Fraser dropped his pencil and got up from the desk. "O.K. I'll come; but I don't promise you a thing. In a fouled up situation like this I'm lucky to keep the *Belinda* floating, let alone repair your boats." Brooks had gone, so Fraser followed him, muttering to himself as he climbed to the boat deck.

Brooks was waiting at the nearest davit. "Look here, Mr. Fraser. Look at this beat up VP! That's average, maybe a little better than average. The hull leaks like a wicker basket. She needs new planking, lots of it—but all the mahogany is back at number five hatch, going into the Old Man's sailboat. What's worse, I can't even get a patch slapped on: all the carpenter's mates are back aft, building that toy boat!"

Fraser blew his nose loudly into a bandanna handkerchief. "Sure, sure. I know, but what can I do?"

"You've got to do something, Fraser. Look at this boat here. Ramp's frozen, won't drop when released. Then when you pry it open you can't close it when you retract. . . . Now, wait a minute, that's just the start. The prop shaft's out of line: motor only revs up twelve hundred when it should sing along at twenty-six. She might as well not have an engine. Even if it was in shape it wouldn't do any good: the prop blades are all out of line so they just stir up foam astern. I'm ready to swap the whole thing for a sail."

"That's out," said Fraser. "The Old Man's called for all the duck. We're going to start cutting sail this afternoon."

"Sailboat, sailboat! That's all I hear. Carpenters cutting frames; shipfitters busy on fancy ironwork—'Gudgeons for the sailboat, Mr. Brooks.' Motor-macs are turning out brass running gear. Sailboat or no sailboat, you've got to do something about these landing craft!"

Fraser colored several shades deeper than his usual ruddy tan. "Don't blame me, Brooks," he said angrily. "You don't think all this is my idea, do you?"

"No, of course not. But you're the ship's first lieutenant. These repair gangs are under you. Surely you can get something—"

"Listen," Fraser said loudly, "I do what I can. I like to see things done: you know that. How do you think I like this? I just get me a bang-up warrant carpenter who keeps things humming—handles men without any foolishness and even brings his own hardwood lumber; then the Old Man grabs him for a little private job and takes the hardwood! Chips is so burned up I don't think he'll ever settle down. He hasn't been aboard a month and he's yelling for a transfer to another ship. Same thing with the rest of my key men. Take Jerry Rinaldo, my chief shipfitter, a man who could build another *Belinda* if he had time and material. . . . And Campbell in the boat shop: he loves engines—I think he sleeps with 'em. They're close to mutiny!"

"Sure, Fraser. That's what I'm getting at. We've got to do something about this. Why don't you keep the best of the gang out to repair boats; let the others build the skipper's toy!"

Brooks looked around at his broken-down boats and then back to Fraser. "I don't get it; I just don't get it. I know how strong-willed the Old Man is, but he's always been for the ship. A sailboat: that's just for recreation. I'm looking D Day right in the eye—without a single landing craft in what you'd call first class shape."

Hint of twinkle in his eye, Fraser asked, "Why don't you go sing the blues to Quigley? He's the exec. He's got rank."

"Who're you kidding? He'd send me to the chaplain for a sympathy chit." Brooks punched his fist through a hole in the side of Boat Twenty-two. "I guess I'll have to go fight it out with the Old Man."

"Good luck," said Fraser. "I'll come visit you in the brig."

"Mr. Fraser. Mr. Brooks." It was Biggs, the stubby orderly, short of breath from hurrying. "The captain wants both of you right away. He's back at number five."

"The sailboat," groaned Brooks. "I suppose he wants us to turn to on it with the rest of the gang!"

They found Captain Hawks standing beside the hatch, glowering at a laminated keel and a few naked oak ribs which pointed upwards like curved fingers. The chief carpenter's mate and his men stood beside the keel, but Hawks seemed to ignore them. Looking about, Brooks saw the usual tight pack of soldiers who had no other place to go. A ring of sailors, many belonging in other parts of the ship, crowded between soldiers and carpenters. They had the interested look of a spectator group, mysteriously formed the instant anything unusual was going on. Brooks knew that look. It could mean only one thing: trouble. They gather like sharks around a slop chute, he thought. Brooks looked closely at the carpenter's mates, saw in their set faces doors closed against any communication with their shipmates. He looked directly from face to face, but none showed him any recognition, nor gave hint of inner thought, nor seemed to ask for help. They looked as wooden as the stark ribs to the sailboat. Then Brooks saw the impassive face of Maxwell, chief master-at-arms, pushing into the circle. Following him came Barton, good-natured chief yeoman. Brooks had no need to ask any questions. There could be only one answer.

Captain Hawks gave that answer now as he roared, "This is Mast! Grandy, Carpenter's Mate, Second Class; Lubiski, Carpenter's Mate, Third Class. Step forward." Grandy and Lubiski whipped off their hats, stepped forward smartly and stood at stiff attention two paces from Captain Hawks. They seemed to know exactly what to do. After all, thought Brooks, they've had plenty of practice. For a few silent moments Hawks gave Grandy and Lubiski the glare, then intoned, "You are charged with dereliction of duty in that while under direct orders to work diligently at the construction of a boat, you neglected your duty and were found by your commanding officer playing cribbage under the shade of LCM Number Four, the United States then being in a state of war. Furthermore, you falsely represented to your commanding officer that you were ill." Hawks pointed his finger at Grandy. "You did lie to me, didn't you? Shall I send for the medical officer and have you examined? Answer me, now. Speak up in your own defense. Did you perform duty as ordered? Did you tell the truth to your commanding officer?"

Grandy and Lubiski stared at the captain's shoes. They know they're licked, thought Brooks. They're wondering about the punishment.

Hawks's voice cut into Brooks's contemplation, speaking quietly, almost kindly: "I'm going to make things easy for you men. You know I could punish you severely, make examples of you both." Glancing at Fraser and Brooks as if noticing for the first time their presence on the hatch, Hawks turned to face the yeoman and the master-at-arms. "To solitary confinement on bread and water for two days," he pronounced. "And as for the rest of you," he shouted to the other carpenter's mates, "just remember that there is plenty of room left in the brig!" Then he spun about and headed for the cabin.

Barton made the entries in the mast book. Maxwell, still expressionless, led Lubiski and Grandy away to the brig. The chief carpenter's mate looked after them without comment, then shook his head, wiped the sweat from his face and stared at Long's working sketch of the sloop without seeing any of the details. "Come on, fellows," he said to his mates. "Turn to."

Hawks was out of earshot now. Working forward with Fraser through the dense crowd, Brooks was conscious of a vast wave of murmuring, distinguishable only in that it was profane. Just one remark he heard clearly: a smart-looking young private saying to his buddy, "Just who does he think he is?" Before Brooks could make any comment of his own, Biggs returned. The captain wanted Brooks and Fraser again; this time in the cabin.

Hawks was already busy with the stacks of operations plans on the cabin worktable. Laying down his pen he smiled in greeting. "Come in, gentlemen. Sit down." Up went Hawks's arm to the steward's buzzer over the table. He pressed the button twice. That meant, bring fresh coffee, Brooks knew. Hawks discussed the damage control plan with Fraser, and certain details of the ship-to-shore plan with Brooks. He seemed to have forgotten the incident on the hatch. His manner was businesslike but pleasant, until they rose to leave, when he gave each in turn a cold, penetrating stare. "Mr. Fraser. Mr. Brooks," he said in his official tone. "I hold you two officers strictly responsible for the expeditious construction of my sloop. No other work must be allowed to interfere. Any further lack of zeal on the part of carpenters or any others concerned—such as I found this morning—will be reflected in your next fitness reports."

"Fitness reports!" growled Fraser as the two went down the
280

ladder. "Trying to throw a scare into us with that Regular Navy stuff."

"He doesn't understand this little Okie," said Brooks. "I don't care what kind of fitness reports they give me in this wartime Navy. All I want is landing craft that float."

"Hurry up, Chief," said Warrant Carpenter Long. "Find the right key and let my men out; we've got work to do." When the key turned, Long pulled open the steel door impatiently. Lubiski and Grandy dropped dog-eared comic books and stepped out. They looked as if they had just come from the showers. Long noted with surprise the clean dungarees and damp hair neatly combed. Those funny books—regulations allowed only the Bible to be read by brig prisoners—well, it was nothing to him.

"You fellows go eat a good breakfast and then turn to. We've got so much to do, I—"

"We've had breakfast, Mr. Long—all we could eat."

"Unofficial, you understand, don't you?" said the master-at-arms with a trace of anxiety.

"Sure," said Long. "That's fine. You boys can turn to right away." He led them up the ladder and out the scuttle at number five hatch.

Grandy and Lubiski looked at the sailboat with amazement. In place of naked ribs they saw mahogany planking perfectly steamed into place in flowing lines from stem to transom. "Well, what d'ya know!" exclaimed Lubiski. "She's pretty." Grandy walked over to the boat, examined smoothly cut knees and breast hooks.

"Come on, you two," said Long. "You don't need to work here anymore. I've got plenty of VPs to patch."

Grandy ran his fingers over the smooth mahogany. "Would it be all right, Mr. Long, if I worked here in this boat?"

"You mean you really want to work on her?"

"Yes, I really do."

Long shook his head. "O.K. You can turn to on the centerboard trunk. Here: I'll show you the dimensions." A few minutes later he asked, "Got it now?"

"Yes, sir," said Grandy.

"Good. Well, come on, Lubiski. I'll put you to work on something useful."

Captain Hawks left the bridge and headed aft in the moonlight. Weird shadows from nested landing craft moved back and forth across the narrow boat deck passageway. He stumbled against a carpenter's sawhorse, sent it sliding out of his way with a quick kick and made a mental note for Fraser regarding securing working gear while at sea. Hawks looked up at the craft beside him. A raw wood patch showed next to sea-stained gray side. His carpenter's mates were working with accelerating haste from sunrise battle stations to sunset battle stations. He had them now; they knew that only forty-eight hours remained before the fleet stood in to Palau. Landing craft must be ready, and they would be ready. Men did what they had to do. Hawks descended one steel ladder after another until he reached the afterdeck, then worked through the crowd of chatting soldiers, hunching his left shoulder sideways to break space. At last he reached the roped-off area where his sloop was cradled. Parts of it were darkened by moving shadows of overhanging tank lighter ramps, but moonlight flowed over the rest of its varnished perfection. Hawks fondled the gudgeons and worked the tiller experimentally. He had caused this boat to be built. His crew had rebelled against it, but here she was, sleek and beautiful, ready for launching. As for the landing craft: he had known all the time that repairs could be completed under the deadline. This was his organization he had built up. Gedney's crew would never have been able to build this boat and repair landing craft too. Men worked best under pressure: they found ways to do what they had to do. Yet none of them bore a load equal to his. He liked the load—he was king here. He would always see to it that the things which had to be done were done. He would see that they were done better and faster, so that the *Belinda* would be outstanding in squadron and fleet. Yes, he could carry the load—but to bear it all there were some things he must have; it was right for him to have them; he must have them. This boat was one of the things he needed. He might not be able to sail it for weeks. Some day in a snug anchorage—until then he had it here on his ship; something warm and intimate, all his. He ran his hand along the gunwale and rested his cheek against the boat's cool smoothness. Some of the unbearable tension ran out of him, as if the boat had taken it to herself. Drawing a deep breath, Hawks turned and worked his way forward towards the bridge.

CHAPTER 31

Ryan, the stowaway corpsman, groped in the predawn blackout towards his debarkation station, stumbling, colliding with one mass of moving bodies after another. The boat at last; check in, crawl over the side with heavy pack of beach gear; then the long wait. Sharp commands from the PA at last. The landing craft fell from under him in its plunge into black nothing with whirr of davits; silent men hanging tight to the boat. With sudden splash they were waterborne. The engine roared and the vibrating boat surged forward. Complete darkness was broken only by blinks from faint signal lamps, yet in some manner beyond Ryan's understanding, his boat and others which dimly appeared from time to time were formed together in waves and headed towards thunder and flash of bombardment, towards this Red Beach they talked about.

Gun flashes and sledge hammering of naval shells increased until all the world seemed shaken. Rough water tossed the boat in a dizzy, corkscrew motion. Ryan felt sick and frightened, weakened enough in his resolve to wonder why he had risked so much for a chance to be killed so miserably. Then rain fell, and while it added to his chill it also washed his face and steadied him. Over the ramp, as the bow dipped down between swells, he saw rough shoreline of Angaur Island ahead: two small coves separated by a steep knoll which rose about a hundred feet above water.

The boat wave bore to the right, passed the wreckage of a small shattered dock and entered the deeper of the two coves. White surf beat against a steep beach of gray sand, but Ryan heard only thousands of exploding shells and rockets pock-marking every square yard of beach and bluff. He saw sheer cliff topped with leaning trees, gouged with shell craters which had started slides here and there. At one spot he thought he saw the entrance to a cave and the glint of gun barrels, but of that he was not sure. The boat had reached the surf. Thunder of naval barrage swept over his head. Enemy mortar shells splashed and exploded in the wild foam all about. The nearest boat was hit. Ryan saw it yaw drunkenly away from shore but all other craft in the wave kept on. Then the planking beneath him lifted violently. His boat rose on a foaming crest and hurtled forward to hit the beach with a grinding jolt which threw him forward against his mates. The ramp splashed open. Half pushed, half running, he staggered out of the boat, plunged into shallow water and floundered up the loose sand of Red Beach, wondering why he was still alive.

Battle din drummed confusion into Ryan. Infantrymen crossed the beach, heading for the line. Sergeants and boatswain's mates shouted unfamiliar orders. Soldiers and sailors milled around him. Ryan looked about, wondering what to do and spotted Dr. Hardwick putting emergency splints on a soldier's leg. Two experienced corpsmen assisted the doctor. Ryan wasn't needed here. Then someone called, "Here, Red. Come lend a hand with this canvas." Ryan helped set up the medical aid station under partial cover of a tree which overhung the bluff. Next he helped to carry in those who had been wounded during the landing. These were given first aid and returned to the *Belinda* in unloaded landing craft. The other corpsmen were decent enough to Ryan, but, while they seemed to know exactly what to do, he felt like an extra cog.

Walking wounded came back from the line. Later an Army jeep rigged for litters began to shuttle between line and beach with more serious cases. All those were given prompt and expert attention by Hardwick and his regular corpsmen. Once again Ryan found himself out of a job.

"What'll I do now?" he asked the leading corpsman.

"You?" said the corpsman. "Oh, go down and rustle up the rest of our medical supplies."

Ryan ran down the beach to the pile of cases stacked about a red cross marker. He picked up two cases and started back to the aid station. As he panted up the beach he noticed the stencil. These were sterile compresses from Tulagi, the same cases he had brought aboard the *Belinda* when he stowed away. Here he was, a thousand yards or so from the fight, still stuck with bandages. Resentment welled up within him. There had been plenty of wounded fellows to help back in Tulagi. He had stowed away to fight, not to pass bandages. Now that he had overcome the stark fear he had felt when landing through the surf he felt strangely stimulated by sound and shock of gunfire, smell of burned powder. Perhaps he could get a gun and sneak up to the line, get just one Jap to square it for his brother. With a guilty start he noticed sentries around the beach, armed with bayoneted rifles. He remembered what the captain on the *Belinda* had said: "If you disobey orders on the beach you will be shot." Ryan estimated his chances to escape from the beach. Perhaps the beach sentries were just looking for Japs and would pay no attention to him. But Ryan could not forget the penetrating eyes of Captain Hawks boring into him as he said, "Remember, you are in the Navy. You will obey orders. . . ." Ryan moved on towards the medical aid station, carrying the Tulagi bandages.

Order began to show in the confusion. Ryan could see that this beach party worked in a smooth team. Different types of combat supplies were neatly formed in ever-growing piles on the beach. Radio men were talking with the Army command post, with the *Belinda* and with radio-equipped boats off the beach. Wounded soldiers were given prompt attention. If he could only stay with an outfit like this, perhaps there would come a chance—he must have a chance! Just one Jap—then he'd go back to bandages!

About noon an Army officer came down to the beach, red faced from running. He yelled orders very insistently until soldiers in the working party picked up their rifles and followed him into the brush. Gettman, the beachmaster, ran after them, remonstrating, demanding explanation—but he came back alone and went at once to the radio tent. A few minutes later the beachmaster called the entire beach party into a huddle. "That nervous colonel has gone and done it," he said angrily. "He's committed all his reserves and now he's called up the Army shore party. He's got all three of our bulldozers up in the line. There's just us with our bare hands to unload the boats. Until we get help I want every man who isn't doing essential work to unload boats. The Army will run out of ammunition soon, and then they'll have to come for it. Now get going, fellows!"

Ryan went down with three other corpsmen and began unloading stores, water and gasoline from the boats. The rest of the beach party were working on the ammunition. Ryan noticed that there were about three loads of ammunition to every one of anything else. He saw Hatcher, leading boatswain's mate of the beach party, struggling with a heavy clover leaf of artillery ammunition. Ryan dropped a case of rations and ran to help him.

"Good boy," said Hatcher. "This ammo is really heavy. You better stay here and work with us."

"Say, Hatcher," protested one of the corpsmen, "you send him back. Corpsmen ain't supposed to handle ammo. You know, that Geneva Convention, or something?"

Hatcher looked at the corpsman contemptuously. "This ain't Geneva," he said. "I bet them Japs ain't thinking about Geneva, either. I sure can use Red for a while."

"O.K. O.K.," said the corpsman. "But you'd better take off that medical brassard, kid."

Ryan untied the red cross brassard from the arm of his jungle-green fatigues and shoved it in his pocket. Then he stayed close to Hatcher, trying to lift his full share; after all, ammunition was better than bandages. After several trips from boats to ammunition dump they slumped down beside a rock to take a blow. This Hatcher was a quiet fellow, didn't say much. Near him Ryan felt safer and more useful. Hatcher had killed Japs, too; the other fellows had told him that. Tarawa, Kwajalein, Saipan: he'd been on all those beaches and up in the line on every one of them. If he stuck close, there might be a chance to go with him here. Ryan wondered what Hatcher was thinking about now. Perhaps he was planning how to get away from passing ammunition, how to sneak up in the line and kill Japs. Ryan opened his mouth to ask about the chances when Hatcher spat carefully at a small lizard and said, "This is the most snafu beach I ever did see."

"What do you mean?" asked Ryan. "I thought—why everything seems awful smooth to me. Just look at that ammunition dump: enough to fill a good-sized barn—all that stuff off the ship since we landed!"

Hatcher was watching a crevice in the rock. At last the lizard stuck his head out cautiously. Hatcher spat again, chasing the lizard back with a near miss. Then he said, "That's just the trouble. Ammo ain't supposed to pile up on a beach. It's supposed to move up into the line and get a ride up a gun barrel."

"Why don't they come and get it?"

"You go ask the colonel. I don't savvee this little operation —I'm watching for mortar fire now. Japs fired on us when we first landed, then kept quiet. They're foxy with mortars—got 'em hid good some place."

"Where do you think?"

"Hard to tell. Mebbe those caves up the bluff between this beach and the other one. They're watching us, don't you worry. We can't see any signs of them but they know what the score is."

Hatcher rallied his gang and they went back to packing clover leaves. It was heavy work; some of the big ones weighed nearly three hundred pounds. The flooding water rose until the narrow beach disappeared and they were forced to pass supplies straight up the bluff from the ramps of jouncing landing craft. Some loads slipped and fell back into the boats. Sun beat down on them vertically from a cloudless sky. Sailors were getting tired and angry. "Where's them gol durned bulldozers? They could give us a wire and drag this stuff up in no time! What a dumb situation! Let them soldiers hustle their own ammo."

Only Hatcher and Boski seemed to have heart left for the job. Hatcher set a good example, hiding his weariness behind wisecracks: "Come on, boys. Pass me another pillow!" Big Foots Boski's stolid face showed a trace of pleasure as he swung the heavy shell cases up six vertical feet of sun-baked dirt. Ryan nearly forgot the Japs, forgot about danger on the beach. His small body was one consolidated ache, his arms felt like lead weights and his jungle greens were soaked with sweat. He couldn't keep up with a fellow like Boski. He was wondering how much longer he could last when the first Jap mortar shell landed near the dump.

It did not seem like much at first, merely the annoyance of a few shells exploding in the beach area. Everyone hit the dirt. Hatcher looked around cautiously. Flames shot skyward from a pile of five-gallon gasoline tins.

"Come on!" yelled Hatcher. "The fire-fighting gear's at the CP. Come on, you guys!"

Before Hatcher reached the fire, Kruger landed in the *Belinda's* salvage boat, followed by his men with CO_2 bottles.

"We'll handle this, Hatcher," he said. "You'd better take your men back. We've got to get the boats unloaded."

Hatcher started back with his gang, Ryan keeping beside him like a small tug waiting to assist a deep-water ship.

"I don't like this," Hatcher said to Boski, "but we've got to keep that ammo moving."

"Can't we look for those Japs first?" asked Ryan.

"Nope," said Hatcher. "Ever hear of orders?"

Ryan looked with dismay at the number of landing craft bobbing under the bluff again, waiting to be unloaded. Occasional Japanese mortar shells fell in the beach area, well spaced, moving further away as if deliberately searching for something. Ryan looked out across the six-mile stretch of water between Angaur and smoke-covered Peleliu Island, where unloading transports lay. Here and there cascades of water rose like geysers. The Japs were trying to shell the ships.

"Come on. Come on," said Boski, impatiently. "Here's another one, Red." Ryan reached down for his end of the heavy clover leaf. It was all he could do to hang on. Hatcher had to do most of the lifting. As soon as the boat was emptied another took its place. Boski grabbed up a clover leaf singlehanded and swung it up to Hatcher and Ryan. Ryan, near the end of his endurance, played with the thought of just one more Jap shell landing near the dump—not too close, just close enough so that they could hit the beach again for another short rest.

Almost instantly a deafening explosion blasted out just over the bluff from Ryan's head. Before his eardrums stopped singing he heard metal scraps slam against the steel hulk of a tank lighter. There were startled cries in the boats; men sliding and swearing; then Hatcher's voice, loud and insistent. "Run and hit the dirt, boys. Run and hit the dirt. They got the dump. The whole works'll go up now!" Hatcher's voice was drowned by frightful sound. Then Ryan heard him again, yelling, "No. No. Not there! Jump down in the water and hug the bluff." All hands scrambled to leave the area. Boat engines gunned in short spurts. Ryan slid down the bluff. Someone knocked him into the water and stepped on him. Someone else yanked him to his feet. Splashing frantically along the flooded beach Ryan saw a huge back working along ahead. Boski had stopped to help him. Ryan floundered ashore and stumbled to a large, sunbaked rock. As he started to crawl behind it, an earth-convulsing explosion froze him. Brain paralyzed with shock, he clung to the exposed surface of the rock, which seemed warm and comforting. Something yanked his leg: Hatcher pulling and yelling against detonating thunder, "Get down, you little fool! Get behind the rock; it don't need protection from you!"

Still he could not move. Hatcher dragged him to cover in the lee of the rock. Vast sections of the dump exploded now in relentless succession, flinging deadly shell fragments and burning white phosphorus in all directions. A crescendo of horror pinned Ryan down so that he saw nothing more. Seared by heat, nearly suffocated by phosphorus smoke, forced down into the sand more snugly by each hammerlike detonation, he became mere shrinking flesh, incapable of movement or thought.

Ryan lost all sense of time as he cringed under the overhanging rock. It seemed to him that he had always been there, that there was no hope of ever getting out. This was how his brother George must have felt before they got him at Pearl Harbor. Now it was John Ryan's turn, his personal turn—and then he wouldn't be able to say anything or do anything about it.

After a time it seemed that the force of the explosions was somewhat less. He thought: you can get used to anything, I guess. His eardrums continued to sing and his head felt crushed in, but he found that he was able to move his muscles again. Experimentally he moved first one leg, then the other. Once more he became conscious of Hatcher's presence. Hatcher was peering out cautiously from his side. He seemed calm enough but concentrating on dangers without so that he paid no further attention to Ryan. Crawling slowly towards his side of the rock, Ryan took off his helmet and pushed it out carefully into an exposed position. Nothing happened. He put on his helmet, inched his head out and looked around the edge of the rock towards the ammunition dump. A tremendous exploding pattern of phosphorus shot out huge, spreading flower petals, like Fourth of July fireworks, expanded fantastically here in this hot sunlight so far from home. Then a shell fragment ricocheted from the rock just above his head. Ryan got back in a hurry. For a time he lay flat on his face, trying to avoid the choking fumes by gulping air through a crevice beneath him. Then he crawled over and tugged at Hatcher's leg. Hatcher looked at him with a trace of amusement crinkled in the corners of his mouth.

"Having fun, Ryan?"

"I'd like to kill the Jap that started this."

"Well, you asked for it, didn't you? You volunteered. You could be back in Tulagi, waiting to go on liberty."

Ryan let the remark go. "What set this all off?" he asked.

"Jap shell. It only takes one."

"Yes, I know. But where from?"

"Probably from that cliff over on our left flank—just the opposite direction from the dump. Look!" Hatcher worked carefully around the back of the rock and pulled Ryan beside him. "See the sandy patches in that cliff there. There's some caves—don't look good to me. Probably full of Japs with their nasty little mortars."

"I thought I saw something just before we hit the beach. But the bombardment! How could the Japs live through that? Isn't this beach all cleaned out now?"

"Takes more than a bombardment to clean out a beach," said Hatcher. "You have to get in there and weed 'em out by hand."

"I don't see how there could be any Japs left on this beach. Why did they let us walk around?"

"That's an old Jap trick. They let you land and unload. They hole up and wait their chances to cut you down. They know they've got to die. They just lie there real quiet and wait for chances to take as many of us along with them as they can. Sometimes they crack up and act crazy, but never sell a Jap short. Watch out all the time!"

"I just want to see one of them," said Ryan, standing up. "I want to shoot a Jap; take a bayonet and stab him in the belly." His voice rose to a scream. "I hate 'em! I hate 'em! I'd like to blow them all up, burn 'em, kill 'em!" A bullet whined close over Ryan's head and splattered against the rock. As he dropped to the sand again, shaking with mingled fear and rage, he heard the vicious chatter of an automatic weapon, and a shower of bullets landed a little short and towards the water from his position. Then he saw Hatcher calmly checking his rifle and ammunition.

"What you going to do?" Ryan asked.

"Check on snipers—those caves. Think I got them spotted now." Watching his cover carefully, Hatcher crawled around rocks and brush, heading for the left flank. Ryan looked around, saw a rifle deserted in the confusion. He picked it up and started after Hatcher.

Hatcher stopped and shook his head. "Better put down that gun," he said. "Corpsmen aren't supposed to bear arms. That's just inviting atrocities from the Japs."

"You were willing enough for me to pass ammunition," said Ryan. "Anyhow, how'll they know I'm a corpsman? I got my red cross in my pocket."

"O.K., Red. You been spoiling for this for a long time. Might as well come along and settle it one way or the other. But keep low and don't jump up again. I don't want to get shot because a damfool medic gives my position away." Hatcher crawled forward. Ryan watched him for a moment. Another bullet whined a little above and behind Ryan. He ducked, then got back to his knees and crawled after Hatcher.

As they worked past the beachmaster's CP, Gettman called out, "No, Hatcher, no! Don't expose yourself. You won't have a chance out in the open."

"I'll be careful," said Hatcher. "We can't do a thing on this beach until somebody cleans them out up there."

"Wait a minute, now," insisted Gettman. "We'll find a way. I'm requesting call fire. You're my key P.O. I can't afford to lose you like we lost McClintock."

Hatcher fingered his rifle and looked towards the bluff. Boski, armed with a BAR, crawled up beside him and peered ahead. "Look," said Boski. "Tanks coming around the bluff from inshore—must've landed at Purple Beach."

Gettman looked relieved. "That'll put the heat on 'em," he said. "It was about time. We lost men in the boats and they're bringing in a lot of work for Doc Hardwick right now." Ryan brushed aside the thought of carrying wounded. The beachmaster hadn't seen him. He'd lie low and sneak past the CP when Gettman's back was turned.

Three tanks roared around the high land reaching inshore from the cliff between Red and Purple Beaches. They clanked down towards Red Beach and, without hesitation, wheeled to the heavy wooden door at the mouth of the first cave and opened fire. An infantry platoon followed the tanks and deployed among the rocks and shrub. There was no more sniping. "They're buttoned up again," said Hatcher to Boski. "Let's go!" Followed by Ryan, they crawled closer to the cave. The tanks were firing point blank. Ryan saw the heavy door to the first cave splinter and fall apart, disclosing the dark, gaping entrance. The platoon closed in with flame throwers and automatic weapons. Everyone was quiet, waiting to see if the Japs would make the next move. From a vantage point just above and behind them, Hatcher, Boski and Ryan looked over the infantrymen into the cave mouth. Ryan could hear the Japanese within, squealing and yelling to each other.

"Last minute saki party," said Boski.

"Not much time for a party," said Hatcher. Ryan held his rifle ready. He snapped off the safety. Let them come out. He was ready. This was what he had been waiting for. He raised up for a better look. Hatcher frowned and said, "Keep your head down, Red. They may come charging out, and then anything can happen." After several minutes of quiet Ryan began to wind up with tension. Perhaps they'd stay in there like rats in a hole. He shivered at the thought of going in there after them. Staring into the cave's dark entrance until his eyes watered, still he saw no movement. At last Hatcher stiffened. "Something there," he said quietly. Ryan looked more intently than ever, but he had been staring so long that his vision was blurred and he saw nothing. "There he is again," said Hatcher. "He's coming out!"

Then Ryan saw something too—a dark body moving slowly out into the light. He drew a bead with his rifle; his fingers began to squeeze down on the trigger. Somebody shouted in a clear, authoritative voice, "Hold fire! Hold fire!" Hearing the order, something triggered off inside Ryan. He would not be cheated. He would shoot, now! Directive force almost apart from himself curled his trigger finger back so that he was surprised at the sudden crack of his rifle and at its kick against his shoulder. Instantly he saw what he had shot at: a naked little Japanese boy not more than ten years old, walking uncertainly out of the cave with both hands high over his head. The little boy sat down quickly and pressed his hands to his stomach. Soon he rolled over, face down in the dark sand, kicked convulsively, then lay still.

The first thing Ryan heard was Hatcher's voice, contemptuous, cold, saying, "Hair-trigger medic!" Half defiant, half ashamed, he tried to meet Hatcher's eye. Hatcher said nothing more, just glared at him and spat in the sand. Ryan's eyes dropped. A shock far greater than any caused by the exploding ammunition dump now hammered in his head. It was not this little boy that he had fired at, but at the *thing* which had brought him to this beach after revenge, which had frightened him and worn him down and set his mind awhirl with the lust for killing. Now shame and remorse swept away the last of his hatred. He looked at the small body in the loose sand. Remembering the red cross brassard in his pocket, he got up and started to go to the boy.

"Get down, you fool!" yelled Hatcher. "Here they come!"

A compact group of more than a dozen Japanese soldiers charged out of the cave entrance, shouting, "Banzai," and uttering piercing screams. Their leader waved a sword, the others fired rifles as they ran. An efficient hail of BAR and machine gun fire cut most of them down, but three continued on until met by expertly directed bursts from flame throwers. Ryan saw flaming creatures, once men who had also taken life, now running forward a few unbelievable steps, then falling in charred ruin.

When all was quiet again a squad carefully explored the cave, found mortars and machine guns, no more Japanese. There was a general stirring and easing in the cautious movements of all about the cave. Ryan began to stand erect, but had trouble with his trembling legs. At last he found courage to look at Hatcher again.

"You just as good as killed the whole caboodle of 'em," said Hatcher. "They must have shoved out that little kid to see what would happen. You shot him, so they made the best show of it they could. Maybe they'd have surrendered—maybe not. We'll never know now."

The team of tanks, men and weapons moved on towards the next cave. Ryan reached into his pocket, pulled out his crumpled brassard and slipped it on his arm again. Then he moved carefully through the huddled bodies of Japanese from the cave and knelt down beside the little boy. He rolled the limp body over. Dark eyes stared at him unseeing; there was no pulse, no life. Someone called, "Nothing you can do for them things,

Medic. Here's a man needs help." Ryan ran to the speaker, a soldier leaning over a wounded buddy. "You take care of him," said the soldier, and ran on after the tanks.

Ryan saw at a glance that the wounded American had lost a lot of blood. He unbuttoned the flaps of his fatigue pockets and pulled out his nearly forgotten first-aid gear: first a morphine syrette, then compresses. "Hey, soldier, don't pass out on me yet. You hurt anyplace except that arm?" The soldier looked at him but made no answer; he was fainting away. Looking about for help, Ryan found himself alone: no other corpsmen, no litter. He must get this man to Doc Hardwick without delay. After a struggle he got him over his shoulder in carry position and started back to the medical aid station. The soldier was considerably heavier than Ryan, but the little fellow struggled along. That Jap kid, now: he wouldn't have weighed much. Nothing he could do for him . . . nothing . . . nothing. This guy was heavy but he'd make it somehow; he'd have to make it. He'd fouled up enough on this beach. His arms and legs were dead-tired lumps of ache but somehow he'd make it; he had to make it.

At last he spotted the red cross flying over the medical aid station. Then big Boski saw him and came lumbering over. "Let me help, Red. I can carry him easy."

"No, I got him," said Ryan, blinking back tears he didn't want Boski to see. "He shouldn't be shifted around much. Besides, this is corpsman's work." Stumbling and lurching onward, Ryan carried his man the last few yards to Dr. Hardwick.

CHAPTER 32

"Say, Mac. Here's something you'll be interested in." Gene Cooper, ship's secretary, pushed a neatly typed letter across his desk in the ship's office.

MacDougall skimmed down the From: To: Via: rigmarole and got into the meat of the thing, noting Captain Hawks's bold signature slashed across the bottom. "Recommendation for Hatcher and Boski: Silver Star . . . beyond the call of duty . . . assault and capture of Saipan . . ." MacDougall scratched the nape of his neck. "Swell, but how about Whitey McClintock?"

Cooper glanced over his shoulder at curious yeomen with listening ears. He gave MacDougall a knowing look and asked, "Why don't you go see Commander Quigley? After all, I can't do much about these things but smooth up the dictation. If Quigley will listen to anybody, he'll listen to you."

MacDougall stepped out the door and jerked his head, motioning Cooper to follow. "Let me get this straight, Cooper.

Are you trying to tell me that after all that kid did—and got killed doing—they're not going to recommend him for a medal?"

"That's the way it looks," said Cooper. "I mentioned McClintock's name when Quigley and I started on the rough draft of this thing."

"What did he say?"

"He just gave me his best senior-officer's-club look; said McClintock had been out of line, that he had discussed it with the Old Man and that it was a closed issue." Cooper paused, slight figure resting against the bulkhead. Then he straightened up on the balls of his feet, dark eyes flashing with unspoken disagreement. "But it isn't! As far as the rest of us . . . Well, I thought you'd like to know, Mac."

"Thanks," said MacDougall. He started forward towards the executive officer's quarters, walking fast as anger boiled up within him—Quigley giving the brushoff to this kid who had volunteered and given his life trying to rescue wounded marines on Saipan's Red Beach. Then MacDougall slowed his step and paused. I've got to keep my shirt on, he thought. Quigley's a smooth operator. If I blow my top there won't be a chance for the kid to be recognized.

Quigley looked up from his stateroom desk to see MacDougall at the door. "Oh, hello Mac," he said in a friendly way. "You're just in time for coffee. I'll ring for another cup."

"Thanks," said MacDougall. "Believe I will. I'm still strong enough to go to the wardroom and pour my own, but I guess it's nice to sit and be fetched for."

"You're always sounding off, Mac. Why don't you enjoy your rank and relax a little more?"

"Not the type," said MacDougall, then waited until the orderly served his coffee. "I came to see you about a little inconsistency in the fruit salad and medal department."

"Didn't know you cared about that stuff," said Quigley. "I thought you hard-bitten marines wanted nothing but salt on your uniforms."

"Oh, it's not for me," said MacDougall. "I'm representing a fellow who can't speak for himself—you see, he's dead."

"Who do you mean?"

"McClintock from the beach party. I understand that Hatcher and Boski have been recommended for the Silver Star for their part in rescuing those wounded marines on the beach—something they surely deserve. McClintock was with them, volunteered to take the hot spot and got a Jap slug in his chest. Somehow his name was left out of the recommendation for an award. Perhaps it was an oversight."

"No," said Quigley, smiling urbanely, "it wasn't an oversight. You forget that McClintock was on probation after being disrated. Furthermore, he failed in what he was trying to do, didn't he?"

MacDougall stared at Quigley in amazement. Quigley looked back at him, quite unperturbed. "But a bullet can stop anybody!" MacDougall protested. "McClintock was a loyal kid, a hard worker. I know he was disrated: a pretty stiff sentence if you ask me, for being overleave."

"But he was ten days overleave, not just a few hours," said Quigley. "I granted him a seventy-two hour liberty and he stretched it to ten days."

"That's just the point," said MacDougall. "All your yeomen got ten days leave. The apple polishers and the smooth talkers got ten days leave. Biggs, the orderly, got ten days and he lives in Santa Ana, one hour's travel time from the ship."

"All leave must be requested through proper channels," said Quigley stiffly. "Such requests are then given consideration in the priority in which they are received."

MacDougall snorted, "Yeah, who stacked 'em? I suppose the yeomen put theirs at the bottom!"

"You touch me deeply," said Quigley. "I didn't make the rules, regulations and customs of the service. I simply carry them out."

"Yes, I know," said MacDougall. "So McClintock, who was a worker and not a talker, had a low priority on his request for ten days leave. Why he had a low priority I don't know and you don't seem to care. He should have had top priority: his home is in the South Carolina hill country, off the main line. It takes eight or nine days just to come and go. The best he could get was a seventy-two, so he just stretched it to ten days, went back to Carolina, saw his Mom and his dog, then came back to San Diego and turned himself in."

"He broke the regulations," said Quigley. "Dead or alive, he doesn't rate a medal. There's nothing I can do about it."

"Yes, there is," insisted MacDougall. "You can go to the Old Man and ask him to reconsider. Listen—the same spark that took Mac over the hill to see his Ma and his dog took him down into that slit trench on Saipan, ferreting out a Jap he knew was dangerous, who might kill him. McClintock knew he was taking a chance when he went overleave. He took his medicine without sulking—and it meant a lot to him to lose that cox'n's crow. Nobody ordered him to go down into that slit trench. No rule or regulation said he had to go; he volunteered. It just didn't work out for him, so he's under the sand there on Saipan, and here we are sipping coffee. Surely the least thing we can do is to send his mother a medal to hold in her lap."

"You're breaking my heart," said Quigley with a sardonic

smile. "I have to maintain discipline, and to do that I have to abide by regulations."

Blood rushed to MacDougall's head. He measured the distance to Quigley's face. How he would love to wipe off that superior smile with a good punch in the nose! He gripped his coffee cup, restraining the impulse to throw it. How nice those spotless khakis would look dripping with coffee!

When he had calmed somewhat, he said, "Well, sir, there's nothing else for me to do but to go over your head. I'll go see the Old Man about this myself. He'd ask the Congressional Medal for the garbage grinder if he thought he rated it. Perhaps nobody's told him about Whitey McClintock."

"But you can't do that," protested Quigley. "I realize that you are next to me in the chain of command, but all department heads—even you—must obtain my permission before speaking officially to the captain."

MacDougall laughed in his face—a nasty, bitter laugh. "So I can't, huh? You're the guy who knows all the rules. All that's important to you is a lot of rules: who sits where in the wardroom—that officers wear black socks and enlisted men wear white socks and how everybody wears their hats. It's about time you squared *your* hat! Why don't you read the book again? Read who's supposed to conn the ship frequently in and out of port—the executive officer. Read who's supposed to be the Old Man's right bower in operations—the executive officer. You know that I've been doing your job for you—the tough part of it. I'm going to see the Old Man now and there's even a rule for it: the little bit there in Navy Regs that says the navigator shall have direct access to the commanding officer at all times. What are you going to do about that?"

Quigley colored slightly, but otherwise maintained his composure. "You're just tired, Mac," he said. "You need a run ashore: perhaps the officers' club at Tulagi—"

"Now don't sidetrack me," said MacDougall. He struggled for control over his feelings, swallowing to overcome the dryness in his throat. "I want to remind you about another of your rules," he continued in a quieter tone. "A man who has been disrated by a summary court is on probation for three months, during which time he may not be promoted. But there's nothing in regulations to prevent giving him a medal for outstanding bravery in the face of the enemy, above and beyond the call of duty."

Quigley relaxed in his chair. Once again he had full control of the situation. It really was splendid to be second in command of a ship like the *Belinda*. He stirred his lukewarm coffee and sipped experimentally. "You're so impulsive, Mac," he said at last. "After all, it's very simple. You won't need to see

295

the captain at all. A case like this may always be reexamined when new evidence is available. . . . Now don't rush off. I'll ring for fresh coffee. Just relax and let your neck fur down— I'll see the captain about medals for mothers."

CHAPTER 33

Captain Hawks removed his slippered feet from the cabin table and thrust his ocarina into a shirt pocket.

"Come in, Fraser, come in," he said genially. "Sit down and have some coffee." Breathing heavily from his rush up ladders to answer the captain's call, ruddy-faced Fraser looked suspiciously at Hawks, who continued light-heartedly, "Here we are, anchored safely among the reefs and plantations of Lorengau in the Admiralty Islands. Wasn't sure we'd make it all the way in last night: pitch black and that downpour of rain! Port's officially closed after sunset, you know, but we entered anyway—then MacDougall nearly hung me up on a coral head as we felt our way in. He thinks he's pretty good with his navigation and piloting. . . . As a matter of fact, he is—but now and then I make him sweat: keeps him on his toes." Hawks reached out over the table, pulled the ever-present coffee cup closer, peered frowningly into it, drained the lukewarm remains and set the cup back into its saucer with a bang. "As you know, Fraser, we made it in here without hitting shoal or ship so you could drop the pick for me. Here we are with the fleet, snug at anchor on a bright, sunny morning. This is the day I've been waiting for. What a wonderful day!"

Fraser stared at Hawks. Up to this morning their personal relationship had been strictly businesslike. Fraser preferred it that way; things were less complicated. This sudden, unexplained friendliness made him cautious. Puzzled face loosened by a mere hint of a smile, Fraser wondered: what's he up to now?

Hawks did not enlighten him. "We have plenty of time, Fraser," he said. "I'll serenade you on my little sweet potato while you drink your coffee." Hawks whipped out his ocarina and, after a few flourishes, played the opening bars of an old sea chantey. "Remember this one, Fraser?" Hawks cleared his throat, rocked his chair back on two legs and sang in his harsh, unmelodious baritone:

> "A Yankee ship came down the river;
>   Blow, boys, blow—
> With her masts all white and her sails
>   all silver . . ."

Hawks broke off the chantey abruptly, brought his chair solidly onto four legs, slapped the table with his open palm as he rose and kicked the chair against the bulkhead. "Come on, Fraser," he cried. "We'll go launch my sailboat!"

Launching a twenty-four foot sloop was no problem to men accustomed to hoisting out thirty-six ton tank lighters in rough water with the ship blacked out. Yet Hawks fussed about, testing slings, inspecting shackles and pins, calling for more chafing gear. Abundant help was available; half the ship's crew crowded as close as possible to the captain's gleaming toy. At last the graceful hull was lifted from its cradle, swung gently overside and held carefully at the rail. Hawks gazed at it with loving pride, then noticed the stern swing six inches towards the ship's side. "Watch that steadying line, you fool!" he snapped at the sailor holding the bow line. "Watch out for my boat. D'you want to wreck her before she's waterborne?" Then Hawks jumped lightly aboard, crooked an arm around the mast and looked appraisingly at the crowd around the hatch. "I need a crew," he announced. "Quigley—where is Commander Quigley? . . . Ah, there you are, Quigley: you shall tend jib for me. Now, let's see: MacDougall, you tend mainsheet. Brooks, Kruger: you come along in my crew. I want some good boatmen on the maiden cruise. . . . No, no! You can't wear those shoes. Don't you know any better? Go get tennis sneakers—borrow 'em, steal 'em, but get 'em. Nobody's going to scuff up my sloop."

MacDougall was disturbed by mixed emotions. What a strange experience, he thought. Here we are, surrounded by the Seventh Fleet in one of the wildest spots on earth, getting set for our biggest assault landing by taking a nice little sail. Yet what a beauty this was, so gay and carefree against the background of dingy gray paint and sullen-looking guns! The very name, *Albatross*, carved across her gleaming transom and lettered with gold leaf, belonged far to the southeast, beyond the reach of war, in that lonely open sea where the great, white-winged gulls were free as the wind.

"Well, MacDougall, are you coming?" snapped Hawks. "Get aboard, man. We're ready to lower away." Down went the sloop to meet water. They cast off the slings, lowered the centerboard, hoisted sail and shoved off. She floated like a graceful swan. Breeze filled the white sails and she stood out on her first tack.

They were hardly clear of the anchored *Belinda* when Hawks shouted, "Ready about." Putting the tiller down, he cried, "Hard alee!" The sloop came about swiftly. Brooks and Kruger ducked under the swinging main boom while MacDougall hauled the sheet flat. Surprise and baffled, Quigley hung on up in the bow with the loose jib slapping him in the face.

"Let her fill away, Quigley," shouted Hawks.

"Fill away, sir?"

"Yes. Jerk your head out of the way. The sail knows what to do. Then haul in the slack." The *Albatross* was heeled over now and cutting the water smartly, but there were wrinkles along the foot of the sail. "MacDougall," Hawks ordered, "let Kruger take the mainsheet. Go over the lacing and get the wrinkles out of my sail. . . . Ah, she's a smart craft—no racer perhaps, but she handles beautifully. Ready about. . . . Hard alee!" They sailed past clusters of moored destroyers, under the shadow of carrier flight decks, past battleship quarterdecks. Everywhere amazed spectators gathered at ships' rails. Hawks returned their gaze impassively, then looked up at the small ensign which flapped at the mainsail peak. "They're jealous," he said, more to the *Albatross* than to his officers. Then he looked sharply at their faces, searching for signs of pride in the boat. This was his sloop! He shared it with nobody else! "Ready about," he called, more sharply than the first time. "Hard alee! Sheet her home!"

CHAPTER 34

Captain Hawks stood on his bridge, peering into midnight blackness which hid the Philippine Islands from sight. Boats hung overside from winged-out davits, waiting to load assault troops and plunge down to the water off Leyte, now less than a hundred miles ahead. About him were the islands hemming in Surigao Strait and ships of all kinds by the hundreds. The long Pacific swell which deliberately raised his ship and thrust it towards waiting beaches seemed to come from nowhere. Hawks could see only one thing from the wing of his bridge: the phosphorescent glow where his port paravane cable cut the waterline and extended outward and down to the submerged, torpedo-shaped paravane with its fins and cutter, waiting to sheer adrift any moored enemy mines. The *Belinda* was halfway through this Jap minefield: so far, so good. The minesweepers preceding the fleet had done a good job, but there had been little time to sweep thoroughly and this was the largest enemy field so far discovered. There was no way around it, no way to the beachhead at Leyte except right through the middle. Each ship carried her own paravanes for protection against stray mines. Hawks's crew were well trained. He had personally examined the paravane cutters before they were lifted overside. Towed from the bow by taut cables, they now rode wing-and-wing abreast his bridge. The anchor cable of any Jap mine moored in the ship's path should be dragged outboard to the cutter which would sever it and allow the mine to surface. The ship's boatswain and his most dependable mates kept watch over the paravanes and would report any unusual strain. Riflemen stood by to detonate the mines. The possibilities of hitting a drifting mine head on or of getting one fouled in the cutter where it might explode against the ship's side and flood the engine room were calculated risks which had to be faced.

Hawks had radar and a multitude of other electronic and mechanical aids to help him carry out each detailed instruction outlined in those dog-eared battle plans down on his cabin table and the orders coming in moment by moment over voice radio. He had capable assistants whose hands and brains were at his disposal like so much well-regulated machinery. He stepped into the pilothouse, saw the dim outline of Jim Randall, busy and capable at conn. "I'm going into the chartroom, Randall," he said. "Want to see where MacDougall's got us on his charts."

Captain Hawks blinked as he entered the chartroom. Contrasted with complete blackout on the bridge, the well-shaded lamps seemed to blaze at him with shocking intensity. "Got a fresh plot there, MacDougall?" he asked.

"Yes, sir," answered the navigator, shoving back the long arm of the drafting machine from the chart. "Here's our position now, just inside Surigao Strait. The nearest Leyte beaches are forty miles ahead. It's sixty-five miles to our transport area off Tacloban."

"Very good. How's our timing?"

"We passed Control Point X ray three minutes ahead of schedule, but ebb tide is stronger than predicted and the current very confused." MacDougall traced the channels twisting between islands with his finger tip. "This place has always been a mad whirlpool during strong spring tides—all that water trying to get out at once."

"Yes, yes," said Hawks, "the tide has always been here, but the mines haven't. We have this twelve-mile patch of anchored mines to pass through, and the sweepers always miss a few. Torgeson, Alvick and Moran are tending paravanes, but I am relying heavily on your radar watch. Keep them constantly alert. They should be able to spot and identify floating mines at one thousand yards. That gives me a minute and a half to avoid them if you report at once. Report any target smaller than a ship. I don't care if it proves to be a floating box or a man overboard from some ship ahead; keep me informed. We can't take chances on mines." Hawks turned from the chart table. "Who's on surface radar? Ah, Stanowski and Carlson. Good." The captain moved to the surface radar and peered over Stanowski's shoulder. "Keep alert for mines."

"Yes, sir," answered Stanowski without looking up. ."Do you want to see the full picture, Captain?"

"Yes. I want to see everything. Quick, now. You must get back on watch for mines."

Stanowski snapped the range switch. The close-up picture faded from the screen and a smaller-scale projection took its place, painted on fresh with each rotation of the antennae. Here was everything on the surface for seventy-five-thousand yards in all directions: Leyte, Samar and the invading armada flowing into Surigao Strait.

"All those hundreds of ships," said Stanowski—"like a stream of white ants crawling over the screen."

Hawks ignored the remark. "MacDougall," he called sharply, "show me the beaches."

MacDougall touched the screen with his pencil tip. "There's Taytay Point at the south end of the beaches: doesn't show up very well yet. Our beach at Tacloban, thirty-five miles north, should be about here. This is the line of hills behind the landing beaches; the villages: Tolosa, Dulag, Tarragona, Abuyog —they're all strung along here. This is San Pedro Bay area: reefs—"

"We'll handle reefs later," said Hawks. "I'm concerned with mines now." Stanowski snapped the range switch. Distant beaches faded; ships and nearer islands showed up once more in the larger scale. Stanowski stood up, rubbing his eyes, while Carlson sat down in the chair and took over radar control without one moment's loss of time.

Captain Hawks returned to the bridge wing, where he stood erect, peering ahead through his binoculars. At last he said crisply, "Alert the lookouts once more. Lookouts will report at once any object seen in the water. They will not wait to positively identify objects."

When this word had been passed through the talker's phones, MacDougall started over to the starboard wing where he would keep an eye out while Hawks remained on the port side. The captain's talker flipped his long phone cord and began to step casually out of the way. Then he stiffened, evidently excited at what he heard over his phone. "Captain," he shouted, "Bosun Torgeson reports mine fouled in starboard paravane."

Automatic reactions of training and experience clashed instantly in MacDougall's brain. The *Belinda* was second ship in her column. Tactical regulations required second ship to haul out of column to the left. Hauling left would bang the mine against the ship's starboard side.

"Captain," he shouted. "Right! We must come right: the mine!"

"Yes. Right full rudder," Hawks cried sharply. "That's right." Hawks shoved lookouts and messengers from his path as he charged for the starboard wing. "Reports. Continue reports," he cried to the talker who ran behind him.

In rapid succession, the *Belinda* sent out her warning message, HIGHTOWER ordered her out of formation, the rest of the column wriggled and squirmed past, leaving the *Belinda* to her fate while the PA cried for a crew to man and launch the salvage boat. The annunciator jangled engines to a stop. The foredeck thudded with running feet. Instructions and reports were shouted in the dark. These were further complicated by orders scheduled long before to direct the precise debarkation at Leyte. Passages were clogged with patient infantrymen, intent on the transfer from ship to beach, on the battle to be fought when they reached shore. "A mine . . . are you kidding? Ain't we got troubles enough today?" . . . "No fooling, a mine?—caught in that wire they tow? Navy all fouled up again. . . ."

"We can't carry on any further," said Hawks. "We'll run into the next column."

"We can't lie here, Captain," said MacDougall. "Wind and tide are setting us down on the mine. . . . We're closing on it a little faster every minute."

"There isn't turning space between the two columns," said Hawks. Then he shouted down to the foredeck, "Hurry up with that line, Bosun. Pass a bight of it around the paravane cable; get the boat halfway out to the mine with it and have them tow straight out from the ship."

"Bosun reports troops in his way, Captain."

"Pass the word, 'All troops on foredeck move to portside. All troops on afterdeck move to starboard side. All others stand fast.' That'll get 'em away from the mine up there and keep the ship from listing. . . . Now send word to Fraser at damage control: 'Stand by with shores and fire-fighting equipment. Check closure of watertight bulkheads. Keep away from starboard side amidships until ordered to proceed.' . . . No use to the ship if they get blown up first! . . . Get all troops out of that area. Pass word to suspend all movement towards debarkation stations until further notice."

MacDougall leaned over the wing of the bridge. It was in the dark of the moon: the landing had been planned that way. Silhouettes of nearby land and blacked-out ships were faintly visible. He could make out the salvage boat, carefully exploring the tidal water, could hear Brooks's anxious instructions as he tried to locate the mine, bobbing around out there a few yards from the ship's side, chemically impassive, but ready. How quickly these things could go off! They were more deadly than a bomb: you could always fight fire, but a ship compartmented like the *Belinda* could not take a mine amidships. That was her most vulnerable spot and that was just where this mine would hit. They dared not haul in on the paravane cable: that might bring the mine surging against ship's side. He looked down from the bridge at the steep side of the ship. Inside that dark hull were light and life: hundreds of men to blow up with one false move here on the bridge. A puff of wind from the opposite bow hit MacDougall's cheek, cleared his brain.

"Capt'n," he called, "the bow is setting down. . . . We can back a few seconds to get way off her, then come ahead strong on right rudder enough to get her swinging. Perhaps she'll back into the wind for us."

Hawks jumped out beside him. "She'll have to. I'll make her come around. . . . Alert the engine room: smart attention to bells. . . . Have Brooks ready to slip. . . . Radar ranges to columns on either side . . . Rudder amidships; back full . . ."

The *Belinda* seemed sulky, reluctant to obey laws of seamanship or will of man. "I'll turn her if it's the last thing I do," muttered Hawks. "Why couldn't Buships provide twin screw ships for this close work? . . . Now mind your helm, quartermaster. Right full rudder; ahead standard . . . Stop all. . . . Where's that mine now, Brooks?"

Brooks's voice drifted up out of the dark. "Fifty feet off the bridge, Captain . . . Drifting in slowly."

"Back full!" cried Hawks. "Ranges, radar? . . . Stop engines. . . . Report, Brooks."

"She's—she's steady, Captain. . . . I think she's coming clear!"

"You think?" bellowed Hawks. "I don't care what you think. I want to know what that mine is doing."

Brooks called back loud and clear, all hesitation gone. "The ship's pulling clear, Captain, but the vanes on that paravane are canting the mine first one way and then the other. . . . Look out, Cox! You're letting the boat drift down."

"How's the wind, MacDougall?" asked Hawks.

"It's on the port quarter now. Tide's pushing her too."

"Can you hold her like this for five minutes?"

"I think so—" *You don't just think in the Navy.* "Yes, sir. I can hold her."

"Very good. Hold her. . . . Brooks, get out of there, now. Hoist in your boat. . . . Below on the foredeck . . . Have you got Hatcher there, with his rifle?"

"Yes, sir."

"Very good. . . . Hatcher!"

"Yes, Capt'n."

"You're a mountain boy, the best shot in the crew, aren't you?"

"Well, sir. I'm pretty lucky at hittin' rabbits."

"Very good. Get up in the forward gun tub. I'm going to get that mine close on the starboard bow—the bosun will let you

302

know how the paravane leads ahead. I'm going to turn on the searchlight. You have to hit one of the horns on that mine to detonate it. Just plugging it with holes won't do any good—it's fouled in the paravane cutter. If you can avoid puncturing the paravane, do so, but the mine *must* be detonated. We have a date with Purple Beach, paravanes or no paravanes."

Two minutes later the captain's talker reported, "All ready on the foc'sle, Captain."

"Turn on the main searchlight."

A sharp beam of light cut into black nothing ahead, swept back and forth ahead of the bow, raised several degrees and came to rest on the mine. Nearly awash, it wallowed sluggishly in the light chop, reflecting searchlight from wet sides. Two stubby horns, like overgrown cow's teats, protruded from the thing, waving slowly from side to side as the mine rolled. Hatcher's rifle cracked out, the first shot falling two or three yards short and ricocheting over the flat target. "That searchlight is poor light to shoot by," said MacDougall. Hawks said nothing; his glasses were trained carefully on the exposed portion of the mine. Hatcher's rifle cracked again. Hawks saw a quick splash just over and between the two horns.

From the pilothouse TBS a bellicose voice blasted: "BASKETFUL to unknown ship violating blackout: Put out that searchlight immediately!"

"Who's BASKETFUL?" asked Hawks quietly, without taking his glasses from the mine.

"Commander, First LST Squadron: Fifty-seven, point seven, point one," answered MacDougall.

"That's Stu Masterson, class of Twenty-six; he's junior to me." Hawks walked into the pilothouse, took the hand microphone of the TBS from the hook and, without any formal preliminaries, said, "Stick around, Stu. You haven't seen anything yet."

"BASKETFUL to unknown ship: Identify yourself. I say again, identify yourself."

Hawks ignored this transmission and concentrated on the mine.

"Hatcher hit it twice now," said MacDougall.

"Hit one of the horns?"

"I couldn't tell, sir. Perhaps it's a dud." Hatcher fired again. A brilliant flash of light shot up from the sea and the *Belinda* shuddered as if slapped by a giant hand.

"Turn out the searchlight. Ahead all engines, flank speed. Left, full rudder," barked Hawks. "Course and distance to the guide . . . Take her back there, MacDougall. What did you say about a dud?" Hawks chuckled. "Some dud!" After listening to reassuring reports from damage control and ordering the spare paravane streamed and debarkation preparations re-

303

sumed, Hawks rested his chin on the rim of the steel wind-break and stared ahead in silence while MacDougall ran the ship up column and into station next astern the squadron flag-ship. At last he spoke, half to MacDougall, half to the black night, "That Stu Masterson always goes by the book. That's all he knows. . . . Well, how's the tide, MacDougall?"

"Just turning, Capt'n: beginning to flood."

"Well, we had our ebb and our horned mine. Now it's our turn to dish it out. . . . H Hour at zero-six-hundred. There'll be a whale of a flood tide at Leyte this morning!"

The Leyte beaches lay astern, half hidden in battle smoke. High in the sunset-tinged haze the last of an attacking force of Jap dive bombers plummeted down through heavy flak to-wards the retiring attack force. Captain Hawks conned the *Belinda* away from Purple Beach. "Flank speed," he ordered. "I want to get away from these shoals before dark if possible—get formed up so we can stream paravanes again." Hawks sagged against the steel bridge apron. Three days and nights without sleep had seamed his face with fatigue. His voice was thick and slow, lacking the usual confident ring. With an ef-fort he shoved against the weather cloth and turned around to watch the flurry of red tracers streaming up from the *Belinda's* guns. Far astern a Jap bomber fell in flames, hit by some rear-guard destroyer. Several others streaked towards Samar and safety: Slight chance of hitting them at this range. "Cease fire," he shouted. "Cease fire." The guns stopped their racket but his ears still rang; his body felt as if shaken by some giant machine. Hawks looked ahead to the gap along the darkening eastern horizon. Out there beyond the mine field was the en-trance to Surigao Strait. Once out and in the clear, he could flop on his cot beside the pilothouse and sleep for a few hours —if they could just get out there without fouling another mine.

"Reef ahead, Capt'n," said MacDougall. "We should haul right fifteen degrees at once."

"Very good, Mr. Navigator, haul right. What does that make the course?"

"One-nine-seven, sir."

"Very good. Make it so. . . . Now you keep me clear of these reefs, MacDougall. I don't want to rip the double bottom out of her. . . . Got some coffee handy?"

Hawks gulped the coffee. It was hot but it seemed to do no good. His stomach sloshed with countless cups of coffee. His mouth tasted sour and his tongue was coated from chain smok-ing and from endless sandwiches eaten standing up. He set down the cup and turned to look at the smoke-filled dusk astern. Purple Beach back there—they had done well at Pur-ple Beach today: assault waves landed precisely on time; over five hundred tons of combat cargo unloaded and landed on the beach in less than twelve hours—the *Belinda* a shade ahead of any other transport in the squadron.

"Ship on collision bearing to starboard, Capt'n!" cried Randall.

Hawks jerked alert, calling, "Can we swing to starboard, MacDougall?"

"No, sir—coral head."

"Stop the engines, Randall." Darkness was falling. Everywhere about the *Belinda* were gray shapes of transports, battleships, destroyers, all racing through the reef-studded waters of San Pedro Bay. Until ships could be formed into divisions and divisions into squadrons, it was every captain for himself. "Keep those radar ranges coming," said Hawks. "I want to get out of here into deep water and stream paravanes. . . . What's that? Bearing altering ahead now? . . . Good. Ahead flank speed, Randall—and send somebody for more coffee; make it black and strong."

"Mr. MacDougall . . . Hey, Mac! Wake up, will you? I'm in a jam and I can't get the Old Man out of the sack."

MacDougall groaned, threw off Brooks's arm from his shoulder and sat up on his camp cot, which was placed in the starboard wing of the bridge.

"What time is it?" he asked.

"Two twenty-five. I'm sorry you only had an hour's shuteye, but the Old Man's down for the count. He lay down for a short nap. 'Call me in twenty minutes,' he said; but I can't wake him up. I've tried everything but blowing the bugle in his ear."

"O.K. I'll get up. What's doing?"

"We're still on our own: all alone and setting all over this bay. We're going to hit something sure: mine or ship or beach!"

MacDougall shook his head to clear it. "Got some coffee?"

"Sure; right here. I know better than to wake you up without coffee."

MacDougall gulped the bitter stuff, got up yawning and looked around. Nothing but blackness to see, yet he could feel land, mines and ships all pressing in on him. He stepped into the pilothouse where the helmsman grasped wheelspokes and gazed impassively into dimlit compass. From the bulkhead speaker came mixed voices; orders to form up, requests for instructions, warnings of submarine outside. MacDougall went into the chartroom, where he found Willicut, his bright young quartermaster second, bending over a plot.

"She's right here, sir," said Willicut. "Setting twenty-five degrees off course. Could that be right, sir? I can hardly believe it."

"Could be," said MacDougall. "Currents are crazy in this strait. I'll check it." He went to the radar. Carlson and Stanowski were on watch again; good. "Give me a round of bearings, Oscar," he said, taking a scratch pad over to the PPI scope where he peered over Carlson's shoulders. There were the islands, plain enough, but ships were everywhere—hundreds of them, some in division columns, but most of them steaming independently, crowding each other as they headed for the swept passage through the mine field. "Hurry up, Oscar; this is a nasty situation. We've got to watch the traffic."

The plot showed Willicut's estimate of the set to be conservative. The *Belinda* was dragging southward. She might clear Dinigat Island, but she would never make the swept channel on this course. MacDougall jumped for the pilothouse.

"Oh, Tony," he called.

"Right here," answered Brooks, coming up to grip his arm. "Say, there's a ship squeezing me in to starboard, I can see him."

"Come left, forty degrees," said MacDougall. "We're setting down on the mines. This is the worst set I've ever seen this side of the Yangtze River." Brooks changed course immediately. MacDougall went out on the starboard wing and stared into the gloom. At last he made out the dark shape of the other ship and beyond it the silhouette of Dinigat Island. Some of the pressure drained away. A man could contend with things he could see. Radar was wonderful, but somehow unreal and mysterious, especially at two in the morning after one hour's sleep. MacDougall went back into the pilothouse.

"What's this about the Old Man, Tony? You say you couldn't wake him?"

"No. I hollered and shook him—he lies there like he was dead."

"He's all beat in."

"Well, I don't feel so good myself," said Brooks. "I was up all last night and out herding boat waves all day. Hasn't he been getting any sleep?"

"None that I know of; not for three days. He generally naps in the daytime and then wakes me up for a little planning about midnight—you know what a night hawk he is. But I guess this time old Leyte's got him. . . ."

MacDougall went out on the port wing. Captain Hawks slept in his folding cot, which was welded to the pilothouse bulkhead. "Capt'n . . . Capt'n Hawks!" MacDougall watched the prone figure, listened to the slow, deep breathing. Mac-

Dougall was fully awake now and getting the feel of things. He hoped that Hawks wouldn't wake up, but to ease his conscience he shouted again in his ear, quite loudly, "Captain Hawks!" There was no answer from Hawks, no movement—only the deep breathing. MacDougall sighed, half with relief, half with the chill of responsibility settling upon him. The *Belinda* was his baby now; he hoped the Old Man would stay there in his bunk.

After another round of bearings, look at the chart, brief conference with Brooks and resulting change in course, MacDougall went out on the bridge wing and climbed into Hawks's high seat. A dim star showed through soft mist above the rocky shore of Dinigat Island. MacDougall could feel the ships about him; he had their timing now: the constantly changing pattern of their relative movements. Paravanes swam on each side of the *Belinda* at the ends of taut wire cables. Remembering the experience with mines while entering, he shivered, then yawned up at a star. It was up to the paravanes now. Relaxed in the chair, he enjoyed the feeling of command. There was just enough danger to be stimulating, yet not enough for him to lose the sensation of having control of the situation.

Brooks came tumbling out of the pilothouse, crying out, "Lookout reports floating object close on starboard bow. . . . Looks like another mine!"

"Left full rudder . . . Have lookout report when the bow is up to it." MacDougall vaulted from the chair and peered over the side of the bridge.

"Even with the bow . . . close! Looks like a mine, he says."

"Right full rudder. Quick now!" MacDougall watched the wing repeater, saw the ship steady, then swing to starboard. "I'm swinging her stern away; she'll pivot now."

"There's something in the water," said Brooks, pointing. "Hard to make anything out."

"Steady," called MacDougall. He stared down where a stream of live phosphorescence divided the equal blackness of hull and water. At last he saw something bogging around, and at the same instant Brooks began to laugh. "Well, that's that," said MacDougall. "You'd better report it for ships astern of us. Everybody is excited enough as it is."

Brooks took down the TBS microphone and broadcast to the fleet: "SOYBEAN to GALAXY. Floating object close aboard SOYBEAN at zero-three-zero-five identified as orange crate. Over and out." Brooks hung up the microphone and came out beside MacDougall, who was steadying the ship back on course. "That's the kind of mine I like," he said.

After passing through the swept channel into the broad reaches of the Philippine Sea, they located the squadron flagship together with two other transports of their division. While they were sliding the *Belinda* into her station next astern the flagship, Jim Randall came up to relieve Brooks.

"You missed some fun," said Brooks. "All you have to do now is to play follow the leader."

"I'm going to hit the cot for an hour or so," said Mac-Dougall. "I'll try reporting to the Old Man first." MacDougall crossed the bridge to Hawks's cot, high against the bridge bulk-head. "Capt'n," he called. "Oh, Capt'n." Hawks did not respond, heavy breathing the only sign of life. Looking at him, MacDougall thought, what if he died? It would be up to me then. Quigley—second in command—what could he do? He couldn't do a thing up here except watch the rest of us and make clever remarks.

MacDougall returned to his cot on the opposite wing of the bridge. He seemed to have just fallen asleep when Biggs, the captain's orderly, shook him awake again. MacDougall sat up and squinted around the horizon: signs of dawn light to eastward and diagonal lines of indistinct gray hulls. They were formed up with the fleet again and busy with the endless zig-zag. Biggs coughed politely to remind him that Captain Hawks was waiting. MacDougall was tired to the point of being dispirited. It was not likely that Hawks would express any appreciation for his having looked out for the ship during the night—that was just part of his job. *The Naval officer shall consider himself to be on duty twenty-four hours a day.* After all, there had been a certain amount of satisfaction in it, yet somehow in pale dawn the humor of the orange crate was lost.

Captain Hawks was freshly shaven and dressed in clean khakis. He looked rested and wide awake as his piercing eyes stabbed into MacDougall, taking in his unshaven and crumpled appearance.

"Mr. Navigator," said Hawks sharply, "I would like an explanation from you." Hawks paused for a moment, staring MacDougall down, then continued, "Why didn't you call me last night?"

"I did call you, Capt'n," said MacDougall. "I yelled and shook you."

"You couldn't have," Hawks snapped. "I wake up easily enough. It should not be necessary for me to remind you that Naval Regulations require the navigator to obtain captain's permission to alter course. If you changed course in emergency—as you well may have done—it was your duty to inform me immediately what action you took and why."

This is all the thanks I get, MacDougall thought. Many a time I've maneuvered this bucket around by the hour while he blissfully pounded his ear in that cot, and now, when I try to give him a little rest, he throws the book at me. Resentment flooded through MacDougall until his scalp tingled, but he said nothing.

Hawks looked steadily at MacDougall, then smiled and continued in a softer tone, "It doesn't make any difference how competent you are, Mr. Navigator. It is your duty to consult me. Do you understand?"

"Yes, sir," said MacDougall. He was beginning to understand all right. Hawks's tone belied his words. He's glad I let him sleep, thought MacDougall, but he won't admit it. The Regular Navy never lowers its personal guard. This is just his way of saying, "Thanks."

▬▬ CHAPTER 35 ▬▬

Rising swiftly in blue tropic sky, the sun blazed down on the *Belinda,* now steaming across the Coral Sea. Up on the boat deck, beside nested landing craft, a soldier in faded fatigues sprawled in sleep across the passageway, equally unmindful of the changing pattern of sunlight and shadow which played across his face as the ship rolled and of the constant stream of soldiers and sailors who stepped over him. He looked quite comfortable without pillow or blanket, completely relaxed on the warm steel deck—muscles slack, mouth open in a deep-tanned face sallowed by constant doses of atabrine.

A buddy came down the deck, weaving from side to side against the ship's roll. "Hey, Joe," he called, "wake up and hear all the dope."

The sleeper stirred but did not open his eyes. "No," he said. "Don't tell me nothing. I've heard all the stories about French girls in Noumea. I'll wait 'til I see 'em."

"You ain't going to see 'em."

"Why?" said Joe with a note of sarcasm. "We goin' right up in those Caledonia hills to get hardened again?"

"No. We're going to stay soft—back in the line."

"Quit your kidding. This is a good spot; I want to sleep."

"I'm not kidding. We're going back, I tell you."

"Back to Guam? We captured that place."

"No. We're going to Leyte—Ormoc, they say. Things are tough here; Japs counterattacking and punching the Eighth Army full of holes. We're going to back up the line."

The sleeper sat up and rubbed his eyes. "I don't believe it," he said. "They wouldn't bring us way down here in the Coral Sea, then send us right back to the Philippines. We're being rested."

"You don't believe me, huh? Just look at the sun before it gets too high—rises in the east, don't it? What's the sun doing back over the stern?"

"We could be zigzagging."

"We're zigzagging all right—zigzagging back to dig two little foxholes, one for you and one for me. Just relax, Joe. You can forget all about the French girls now."

Leyte palms leaned over blue water towards the *Belinda*, now anchored as close as possible to shore off Abuyog. Sister ships of her squadron were anchored nearby, and the water between ships and dark sandy shore was thickly pockmarked with landing craft. All hands were busy getting the 77th Division ashore on its way to reenforce the line at Ormoc, where the Japanese were counterattacking violently. A mood of urgency had settled over the ship. A steady flow of infantrymen climbed down debarkation nets to waiting boats. Tanks and artillery pieces swung overside and decks were piled with ammunition. Men worked fast at the accustomed task of debarkation without the usual wisecracks and incidental horseplay. Captain Hawks watched from his bridge, standing quietly, little worry lines crinkling the corners of his mouth. Every man not busy with debarkation and unloading stood at the guns. The *Belinda* had arrived early this same morning during final minutes of a heavy Japanese air raid. At any minute the enemy might return.

"Captain!" called a voice through the radar intercom. "Bandit, bearing three-zero-zero, five miles, closing fast."

"Alert gunnery," snapped Hawks. "Keep the information coming." While all guns tracked towards shore, Hawks talked over the phones to Art Hall, the gunnery officer. "Track your target, Hall, but do not open fire unless you get word from me —do you understand? The Army's flying CAP over us. We can't shoot down our own air cover; but keep tracking. The situation may change without warning."

The PA crackled with flagship orders: "Flash Red, Control Green." Enemy planes closing on anchorage; all fleet units hold fire.

"There he is!" someone shouted. A single-engine plane of unmistakable Japanese silhouette appeared suddenly over the shore line and headed directly for the *Belinda*.

"Track the target but hold fire," shouted Hawks, jostling MacDougall aside and training his binoculars on the plane. "It's a meat ball all right. Where's the Army Air Force?" The lone plane closed rapidly on the *Belinda* in a shallow power dive; then when a few hundred yards short, pulled into a steep climbing turn. Hawks groaned, "What a target; we could chew him to bits with a few Buck Rogerses." The plane climbed out of line of sight from the covered bridge. "Keep an eye on him," ordered Hawks. "Keep tracking, but keep a sharp lookout for others."

Constant reports droned in from radar plot. The plane was circling at five thousand feet. Now a sharper tone from radar: "Three friendlies losing altitude fast, closing bandit rapidly!" Hawks and MacDougall craned their necks, searching the indicated sector of the sky. On the open deck just above their heads a battery of four twin-barreled antiaircraft guns tracked the Jap, their crews intent, gun pointers eager for permission to open fire.

At last the Jap came into view from the navigation bridge, diving steeper and faster, weaving from side to side, but his mean course directly towards the *Belinda*. Hawks bit his lips. Kamikaze—that's what he was! Explosive-laden suicide plane, coming in to crash! Those decks piled high with ammunition! If only he could shoot—the fellow was a perfect target now— blast him to bits! Time to shoot; they had to shoot! But the orders were to hold fire. It was up to the CAP. Well, where was the air cover? What were they doing up there? Why were they so slow? Then into his line of vision came three P-38s, flying close formation, closing fast on the Jap. That Jap would hit the *Belinda* in a few seconds now. Why didn't they shoot? Then Hawks saw that the Jap was discolored by more than rust. Flames from her engine streamed back past the nacelle and licked her wings: she had been hit already. Sharp pain stabbed in Hawks's head—that would make it worse—being hit by a flaming plane. If only he could give that Jap one five-inch burst, he'd splatter her!

The P-38s were close to the kamikaze now, trying to herd him down to water between ships. One by one they crossed a few yards from his tail, gave him a short, deadly burst, then zoomed up and away. The Jap was losing speed and altitude, wavering crazily from side to side. Flames enveloped him as he pointed first for the *Scanlon,* anchored nearby, then back to the *Belinda*. He was seconds from a flaming crash now, but where? Hawks estimated the kamikaze's glide. He might hit short; yes, perhaps he would, for a rip of machine gun bullets from his nose was striking a path in the water. He could see the pilot's head; making a last desperate try—or perhaps slumped dead over the stick.

Then a startling, frightening clatter of automatic fire shook the bridge. Plane's nose was up again: his fire must be hitting the bridge.

"Duck!" somebody shouted, "He's firing at us!"

"Get out of here," yelled somebody else.

Hawks tried to look at the plane but was pushed inboard by a group of panicked sailors. The awful chatter of bullets was upon him. He saw MacDougall in his way—queer, puzzled look on the man's face. In some strange manner, as if in a dream, Hawks found himself also pushing inboard, angrily

311

shoving MacDougall. Now MacDougall stopped resisting, was running with him—arms and legs from all directions, men shoving, pushing, fear in their eyes. Now they were falling in a heap under the bridge ladder; many underneath him, more on top. Hawks felt himself giving in as if some overpowering mechanical force outside himself had momentarily taken charge and propelled him away from sudden death. Then his sense of responsibility flashed back, sweeping his mind of this demoralizing terror. He must look out for his ship! Angrily he threw off arms, legs, torsos which lay upon him. He felt MacDougall struggling beneath him. Somehow the two got free, stumbled over the pile of prostrate bodies and got back to the bridge wing just in time to see an exploding geyser of water and smoke shooting up within fifty feet of the bridge. The light tank which had been hanging overside from number three yardarm was gone and the tackle was a broken tangle. The plane had come close enough to take the tank along with it.

All this had happened in a matter of seconds, and in a flash Hawks realized several things. The Jap had been firing all right. His gunfire might or might not have hit the bridge, but the overpowering crash of gunfire which had triggered off the panic had come from the *Belinda* flak battery just above his head. The gun crew had fired without orders from him. Furthermore, he seemed to recall the unmistakable sound of two or three five-inch bursts from Gun Two on the fantail. There might be dead or wounded on the bridge if the Jap's fire had got close enough—he looked about, saw all hands back on their feet, looking shaken and bruised, but not one wounded. Perhaps on the signal bridge—shame flooded through Hawks. He had been robbed of dignity and firm control of the situation at the very moment he most wished to set an example and exercise his proper authority. He noticed MacDougall standing at the rail with a mixture of embarrassment and anger on his face. It triggered off Hawks's own smoldering temper. "Biggs," he shouted to his orderly, "get the master-at-arms." He swung up the bridge ladder, rage taking further possession of him at each step. Lower jaw working, he glared at the crew of the antiaircraft battery; they had evidently been enjoying a joke about something. Smiles faded from startled faces, all except that of Ensign Tuttle, the battery officer, who retained a frozen, vacuous grin.

"Which of these guns fired?" demanded Hawks.

Tuttle gulped. "They all fired, sir."

"They all fired, did they?" Hawks's lower lip curled into a cruel leer. "Did you order them to fire?"

"N-no, sir. I guess my phones weren't working properly."

"You guess! *Officers* do not guess. If you didn't order the guns to fire, who did?"

"Well, sir, I didn't hear any order. But Lubiski here heard something about commence fire on his phone—he's pointer on Seventeen. So he fired and everybody fired and, gee, Captain, that Jap almost hit us. I've never been so scared in my life. That's what we were laughing about; I guess some guy on the line made some crack about commence fire. It really seemed like somebody ought to shoot, Captain. I thought—"

"Shut up!" Hawks shouted. He'd punish him; he'd punish them all. They'd pay for this. Lubiski—yes, Lubiski, that troublemaker who had stolen medicinal whisky and then shirked duty on his sailboat. The brig: that's where he'd put Tuttle and Lubiski and the whole lot of them. Bread and water; that would change their tune. They could have their jokes down in the brig. Ah, here was the master-at-arms.

"Maxwell," said Hawks, his voice shaking as he tried to conceal his lack of emotional control, "this entire gun crew is under arrest. Ensign Tuttle, the battery officer, is under arrest. Confine them all in the brig on bread and water."

Maxwell looked unblinkingly at Hawks. "Yes, sir," he said, then nodded to the gun crew to follow him. The sailors climbed out of the gun tub and followed Maxwell. Lubiski, after making sure that Hawks was not looking, put on an air of comic tragedy. The others, including Tuttle, looked stunned and confused; they had no more jokes and made no protest, just followed Maxwell obediently down to the brig.

Back on the navigation bridge, Hawks took a look around the decks. Pappy Moran and his men were repairing the damaged tackle. Boats were coming alongside again; the normal pattern of debarkation had resumed without a word from him. Turning to look aft, Hawks remembered Gun Two and sent for Chief Alvick, its gun captain.

Alvick looked impassively at the captain's orderly. "You say the Old Man wants me? O.K. Go on back to the bridge; I'll be along in a minute." As soon as Biggs was gone, Alvick stepped quickly to the breech end of the gun and scuffed two empty brass shell cases towards the scupper. Then he stepped to the scupper and kicked them over the side. "That was pretty close shooting," he said. "We almost took the corner off the bridge, but we got the Jap. . . . Now listen, you men. There was some foulup about the order to fire—from the chitchat over the phones, it sounds like the word may have come from some other gun, not from control. Unless you get word from me, we just didn't fire this gun. Savvy?"

Captain Hawks drained his coffee cup, set it down on the pilothouse log desk and made a face at the TBS loudspeaker. That monotonous, scolding voice—he'd shut the thing off but for the danger of losing some vital message. He walked to the wing of the bridge, yet snatches of the message still reached out to him: "This command has previously stressed necessity for not, I repeat, not endangering own combat air patrol and nearby fleet units. . . . Commanding officers will be held strictly responsible for gunnery discipline. . . ." Hawks slumped over the rail. He was tired; he wondered why he was so tired. He'd had little sleep, but enough. The decks were humming with activity, yet it seemed difficult to keep up with details of what was going on. Well, he had built up a good organization here; let it run by itself for awhile. If no more Japs showed up the ship should be unloaded in record time. At last the TBS was quiet. Hawks sighed. He thought, I've trained these men to shoot Japs. If I punish them too much for overdoing what I teach them they won't be any good in a pinch—but I've got to keep control. He looked up and saw Alvick waiting quietly. Hawks stood up straight so that his eyes were nearly level with those of his tall chief boatswain's mate.

"Alvick," he asked, "did you fire Gun Two at that kamikaze?"

Alvick looked steadily back at Hawks. "No, sir," he said.

Hawks gazed back at Alvick for a long time. At last a crooked smile crinkled his mouth as he said, "You're lying, aren't you? You look too proud; you knocked that Jap off, didn't you? . . . No, don't answer me. As far as I am concerned, you didn't shoot. Go back to your gun now." Hawks leaned over the bridge again, thinking about Ensign Tuttle and his gun crew. They would have to be lectured; a trigger-happy gunner had no place on the *Belinda*—not unless he was an artist at it like Alvick—but Hawks did not feel like scolding now.

"Biggs," he called, "go find the chief master-at-arms. Tell him to let the prisoners out of the brig."

A few hours later the *Belinda's* tackle fell silent as her crew scrambled to battle stations to repel a Japanese air raid. Again the order came to hold fire. While lookouts peered skyward looking for the combat air patrol, a squadron of Japanese bombers in formation made a horizontal bombing run. Hawks bit his lip until it bled, but said nothing. Sticks of bombs fell from open bomb bays. Like so many tossed potatoes they fell into the anchorage. Smoke and flame rose from the stern of one transport, but most of the bombs exploded harmlessly in the water between the anchored ships. While the bombers continued in formation as if on parade, the TBS continued to admonish all ships to hold fire. The enemy bombers headed for sea; it looked as if they would make a clean getaway.

"They're gone free!" exclaimed Hawks bitterly. "No use giving us permission to shoot now: we could shoot all day without hitting them, at this range and position angle."

"Flash Red, Control Yellow," said the TBS.

"Commence fire!" shouted Hawks. It was a useless expenditure of ammunition, but some of the crew's tension was released with the futile barrage. Battleships and destroyers poured thousands of rounds after the Jap bombers, now low over the horizon, some six miles away. The air vibrated with tremendous multiple explosions, red tracers and black pocks of exploding shells clouted the sky. As if sure of their safety, the flight turned south and flew perpendicular to the line of fire, skirting the perimeter of exploding flak.

Then the TBS spoke again. "Cease fire. Cease fire. CAP vectoring."

Hawks gave orders to cease fire. One by one the ships of the fleet fell silent. Smoke still pocked the sky and the bombers continued to circle the fleet.

Then a hum of engines, growing to full-throated roar: three P-38s screaming low over the fleet. In what seemed like a matter of seconds they came up on the Japanese bombers and methodically splashed them in flames, one by one. Hawks wrinkled his chin at the P-38s. "Showoffs," he said scornfully. "If they'd just stay clear we could take care of these Japs."

Unloading continued once more. Shortly afterwards Hawks was summoned ashore for a conference of commanding officers. Just before dusk he returned aboard with a small, dark-gray monkey perched upon his shoulder. Hawks sent for his cook, took two brown native eggs from his pocket and ordered them soft-boiled. Then he sent for Dr. Flynn.

Ten minutes later, Flynn banged on Dr. Bell's stateroom door. "Come down to the dispensary with me, Frank," he said. "We have a passenger—a very interesting specimen of *Macaca philippinensis*, belonging to the commanding officer. I'm going to treat him for fleas."

"Treat whom?" asked Bell yawning.

"Just the monkey, Frank. Just the monkey."

=== **CHAPTER 36** ===

Tightly packed about number four hatch, the *Belinda's* crew crowded every cranny three decks high and perched in every landing craft nested in the area. Officers and chiefs sat in folding chairs around the incinerator, where they had an unobstructed view of a canvas movie screen hoisted between mainmast kingposts. Sun had set and eastern sky beyond the movie screen glowed brilliant crimson. Concluding a series of rompish square dances, played as usual at full volume, the chaplain's record player began "Red Sails in the Sunset." Then the master-at-arms called, "Attention!" The music stopped abruptly. Officers and chiefs jumped to their feet while the crew remained seated in their crowded or precarious positions, enjoying this one moment in the ship's routine when only officers rendered obeisance to the commanding officer. Quigley escorted Hawks to his seat, then sat down between the captain and MacDougall.

"Shall we start the movies, Captain?" asked the electrician's mate standing by the projector.

"Not yet," said Hawks. "Play the sunset piece again." When the record resumed, Hawks slouched low in his seat, absorbing song and sunset, watching brilliant cloud color fade into night. "You know, Quigley," he said, "that's a nice tune." When the song ended, Hawks rose quickly and nodded to Quigley, who produced official-looking papers and three small medal boxes. Standing ramrod straight, Hawks intoned in his harsh, dry voice, "Lieutenant, junior grade, Karl Herbert Kruger. Albert Hatcher, Boatswain's Mate First Class. John Boski, Signalman Second Class."

MacDougall reached back and gave Kruger a friendly yank. "Come on, fella; come and get it," he whispered. Kruger felt blood rush to his face as he pushed through closely packed chairs, followed by Hatcher and Boski, and stood before the captain.

While Quigley held a flashlight, Hawks cleared his throat and read the official citations. Then, reaching into the small boxes, he pinned a Silver Star medal on each of the three, shaking hands as he did so. Then he said, "Turn around, you men, so everybody can see your medals. Put the flashlight on their breasts, Quigley." Light reflected from the simple lines of the medals: small silver star on large bronze star; it rippled on the clean red, white and blue stripes of ribbon; it played across backgrounds of faded blue and crumpled khaki shirting, the whole effect given life and movement with each breath. "Look at these men," said Hawks proudly. "They're heroes. Kruger found a narrow pass through the reef at Kwajalein; went in there in pitch dark while under enemy fire and rescued a company of infantrymen isolated by the Japanese, without losing a man. Hatcher and Boski risked their lives above the call of duty to save lives of wounded marines, under enemy counterattack. . . . Wouldn't you like to be heroes? Let's make this *Beachhead Belinda* a heroic ship. We'll do everything faster and better than the rest of them. One day we'll sail her up Tokyo Bay!"

The crew broke into cheers and catcalls. There were shouts of "Free beer! . . . Will we find our mail there? . . . Will we all get thirty days leave? . . . I want a transfer!"

The clamor quieted. Standing uncomfortably, Quigley still played his flashlight upon the chests of Kruger, Hatcher and

316

Boski. Inadvertently, he moved his hand a bit, so that the flashlight pointed at a higher angle. From his seat close at hand, MacDougall noticed the peculiar effect the light gave to the faces of these three men. Above shadowed flare of opened shirts a glowing V highlighted each throat, giving the dimlighted heads the appearance of floating in air. Noses, chins, ears stood out as if from sunken cheeks. Eyes glistened from deep in shadowed sockets. MacDougall thought: It's as if they had died too, along with Whitey and the rest we've buried —along with all the thousands who never got medals. McClintock, back in his sandy grave at Saipan—would his Ma ever get a medal to hold in her lap?

Hawks cleared his throat again; he was rustling another sheet of paper. Kruger and the two others faded back into darkness and Quigley held his flashlight over the official communication. Hawks waved off Quigley and flashlight, spoke from the dark to his crew. "I have a letter here which states that a Silver Star medal has been awarded posthumously to Stuart McClintock, Seaman First Class, killed in action on Saipan while rescuing wounded marines from a Japanese counterattack—he was with Boski and Hatcher, as you know. The medal will be sent to his widowed mother in South Carolina." Hawks heard a restless stirring and low murmur of approving conversations in the solid mass below him. "Now men," he said, "we will soon return to the forward area. I promise you'll see excitement up there. Enjoy yourselves tonight; there's work to be done tomorrow. Start the movie."

Gleaming curves of thirty technicolor violins in a row; thirty bows moving as one. Warmth of softly glowing wood and flowing sound, then brassy blare of Harry James. Smooth-skinned graceful legs, knotty comedian's legs—familiar gags in a pretty package; soft total of nothings which could be automatically absorbed, leaving the mind free to travel. Medals for Mothers . . . Listening now to the Heifetz "Hora Staccato," MacDougall wondered who was feeding Whitey's dog, Blackie, back there in the Carolina foothills of Sassafras Mountain. He pictured blue smoke penciling upward from some cabin chimney; then a dissonant blare from the sound track brushed Sassafras Mountain away. In its place he saw the shell-pocked stack at Charan Kanoa, thick battle smoke over Saipan's Mount Tapotchau. MacDougall shook off the image and looked clearly once more at the movie screen. The smoke's blown clear from Saipan now, he thought. Whitey is resting quietly, back of Red Beach. I wonder if he ever dreams about Blackie.

Returning to his cabin after the movie, Hawks felt restless and wide awake. He unlocked his safe, considered a stack of voluminous operations plans, shoved them back in the safe and locked the door. He ordered a pot of coffee, toyed with the litter of outgoing correspondence on his desk, then got up to look for his monkey. Chipchee was curled in a ball on the corner of his bunk, fast asleep; Hawks left him there. He picked up his ocarina and tried a few random bars of music remembered from the movie. Harry James played the trumpet with smooth, effortless competence—Hawks seemed to remember that the chaplain had a trumpet in his collection of instruments. He called his orderly and sent for the chaplain.

Chaplain Hughes, who was just turning in for the night, pulled on his shoes again and reported.

"Chaplain," said Hawks, "do you have a trumpet down in your locker?"

"Yes, sir. We have one but it's not very good—not that it matters: nobody aboard can play one, excepting Ensign Tuttle, and he has his own trombone."

Hawks glared at Hughes. "I played trumpet at the Academy; I may be a little rusty but I play the trumpet." He thrust his jaw towards the chaplain, wordlessly daring him to argue the matter. "Are you going to get that trumpet?"

"Oh, yes, Captain. I thought perhaps you wanted to say more about the Academy—the trumpet, of course—"

"The Academy!" A pained and bitter look came into Hawks's face, worked through and around it in grotesque grimaces. "I hated the Academy; it was a fight, nothing but a fight!" Hawks's voice rose to unnatural height; he spat out the words bitterly: "A barefoot country boy: that's what they called me. That's what I was but it was none of their business. What did they know about the hill country of Tennessee, or what struggles a barefoot boy and his kinfolk went through to get him entered? But I fooled 'em. I swallowed my pride and pretended to like it when I obeyed, and now I'm captain of this ship and I can rise like this from my captain's seat and order you to bring me a trumpet, so I can wake up the navigator and wake up Quigley—wake 'em all up!"

The chaplain, who had been in unusual situations before, sat quietly. Hawks paused, shook his head as if astonished to find himself crouching over the table shaking a pointed finger in the chaplain's face. He sat down slowly, took out a clean handkerchief and wiped his face.

Then, in his normal voice, he said, "Just forget it, Chaplain. I'm tired."

"But the trumpet, Captain: would you like it?"

"Certainly I'd like it. Didn't I say so?"

When the trumpet arrived and the chaplain had gone to bed, Hawks took the battered instrument carefully from the case, fingered the stops and tried the mouthpiece. Then he blew a long, loud blast which finally settled on a single note. Next he tried a few bars of the "Beale Street Blues." The rendition was not accurate; but that did not matter to him, for in his own mind the tune ran perfectly and there was strong feeling of satisfaction in the sheer volume and lung power he was achieving. Hawks got up, parted the gray curtains at the doorway and blew a loud, raucous blast in the direction of MacDougall's door, which was on the hook. He heard MacDougall strike up the hook, watched the door slam. That's good, he thought. I got his goat—now let him sweat without cross ventilation. Hawks sat down again and rang for the cabin boy. He rang several times without response. Then he went to the pantry, turned on the light and saw his boy sprawled on the floor, fast asleep. He pushed the Negro gently with his foot. "Make me some more coffee, Jenkins," he said quietly, "then you may go turn in." Hawks sat silently until the coffee came; he fingered the trumpet, hearing in his mind the quick, accurate notes of Harry James. He thought about his monkey and his boat; he would take Chipchee for a sail one of these days. Let's see, what was that piece they played before the movie? Yes, "Red Sails in the Sunset." Hawks raised the trumpet and managed to get through the chorus; he played softer now and some of the notes were sweet and true. Then he rang for his orderly. Biggs came gladly, expecting to be dismissed for the night, but Hawks said, "Go get the supply officer."

Jackson was still awake; he had been writing a long letter to his wife. Used to sudden calls to the cabin, he combed his hair and came up the ladder quickly.

"Yes, Captain," he reported cheerfully.

"Jackson, how much red ink do you have?"

"Red ink, sir? Oh, I think I have a couple of bottles."

"You think?"

Jackson chuckled unconcernedly. "We don't have much need for red ink, Captain. I just keep track of where things come from and where they go. I guess Congress takes care of the red ink."

Hawks gave Jackson the glare. Jackson was used to it. He returned Hawks's stare as long as it was comfortable to do so, then gazed at the porthole, waiting for Hawks to speak.

"I am quite familiar with the duties of a supply officer and with Congressional appropriations for the Navy. Approximately how many bottles of red ink are now on board?"

"I really have no idea, Captain—two or three, perhaps."

"Go get them."

"Now, sir?"

"Now."

Forty minutes later, Jackson returned with seven small bottles of red ink. It had been a strenuous interval: going through offices and storerooms, waking grumbling sleepers. He wondered what possible use Hawks could have for red ink, but knew better than to ask. Hawks glared at the bottles, picked up one and examined the label.

"Two ounces," he said contemptuously. "Seven two-ounce bottles. Is that the best you can do?"

"I'm sorry, Captain. I searched general stores, executive office, first lieutenant and supply offices, log room, medical office, chart room. Frankly, sir, I don't know where else to look."

"Did you try the chaplain?"

"Why no, sir. I can't imagine what he'd do with red ink."

"What the chaplain would do with red ink has nothing to do with it. He is the only man aboard who does not have to account for his gear: most of it was donated to him. When we were out of soap, he had soap. When you let us get out of toilet paper on the return from Saipan, he saved your neck with seven cases of Kleenex, didn't he?"

"Yes, sir. But red ink—"

"We're not talking about logic; we're talking about the best place to look for red ink. This evening I wanted a trumpet. You are my supply officer but I didn't ask you for a trumpet; I asked the chaplain and here it is." Hawks lifted the trumpet from the table and blew a loud blast at Jackson. "Go see if the chaplain's got some red ink."

Ten minutes later Jackson returned with a full quart bottle of red ink. Hawks put down the trumpet and reached for the ink. "That's better, Jackson," he said. "Good night." Hawks rang for his orderly. When there was no answer he stepped to the passageway. Biggs was slumped in his folding stool, fast asleep but still clutching a comic book. "Biggs," the captain shouted. When Biggs shook himself and stood up, Hawks said, "Go get Karako, my gig cox'n. Then you may secure for the night."

Shortly before four in the morning, Lubiski, carpenter's mate, passed forward along the second deck alleyway on the way to his berthing compartment after an illicit dice game just concluded in the after boatswain's mate's storeroom. He paused at the door of the bakery issue room; perhaps he could promote a little cake or pie.

Thomas, the night baker, returned Lubiski's gaze coldly. "Scram out of here, Lubiski. No chow on the cuff tonight."

"Come on. Give with a slab of that pie—what's in it?"

"Dried apples, Noisy; none for you."

Lubiski kept his eyes on the pie. "Ya wantta hear the latest scuttlebutt?" he asked disarmingly.

"Listen, wood butcher, I hear everything first hand on my secret radio. You ain't getting no pie tonight."

Lubiski squeezed past a stack of fresh-baked bread and whispered hoarsely in the baker's ear, "I gotta tell you, even if you don't give me no pie. Know what I just seen down in the sail locker? Charlie Karako is dipping the sails to the Old Man's boat in red ink! 'Captain's orders,' he says. I tell you, the Old Man's finally gone nuts!"

"You're kidding!" said Thomas.

"No, I ain't. Give me that slab of pie."

Absent-mindedly Thomas handed the pie to Lubiski, locked the issue room and headed aft for the sail locker.

From his high seat on the bridge, Captain Hawks glared about the Sansapor anchorage at the western tip of New Guinea. Faintly spiced sea breeze from the Indies only added to his peeve. He wanted to sail his little *Albatross* in this pleasant anchorage, but time was running out; the advance party of jungle-sallow troops he would take to Luzon for the attack on Manila were already aboard. He needed more red ink badly. How could he sail a boat with half the jib dyed red? Jackson had failed him. Quigley had failed him. He was surrounded by incompetents: intensively trained people who could not round up a few quarts of red ink.

Somebody behind him was coughing for attention: it must be Quigley. "What is it?" Hawks snapped.

"Shall we give the crew liberty, Captain—just a few at a time?"

Hawks did not turn around. "No," he snapped. "Look at those sailors down there on the foredeck: fat and lazy, leaning over the rail. You should have smarter organization, keep them employed. A busy man has high morale. You are my executive officer. Put the crew to work, all of them—hold a field day. I'll teach you how to handle morale on this ship!"

"Aye, aye, sir. Is there anything else, Captain?"

"No."

When Quigley had gone, Hawks looked about until he spotted his monkey sitting in the chartroom porthole. "Here, Chipchee," he called. "Come here, little fellow." The monkey jumped from the porthole to Hawks's outdoor cot; then Hawks lifted him to his shoulder. He petted the monkey and said, "We're going to put a little life in this ship, Chipchee—six hundred men under my command and they can't find a few quarts of red ink. We'll show 'em!"

Quigley went down to the wardroom deck where a number of officers were leaning over the rail, enjoying the rare breeze and looking for the mail boat, which was due to return from shore. Going up to Bell and MacDougall, who were busy kidding the chaplain, Quigley said, "I'm sorry, gentlemen. The captain turned thumbs down on your suggestion of liberty for the crew."

"I wonder why," said Bell. "Surely they'd be more efficient after a little change of scenery."

"They'll get a change," said Quigley. "We're going to hold field day. Where's Fraser? We've got to rouse all hands off watch and turn them to scrubbing paintwork."

MacDougall spat over the side. "What's the sense in scrubbing paintwork when we're loading mud-caked troops and equipment. We'll have to clean up all over again when the ship's loaded."

"Sorry, sorry. Captain's orders, Mac. The chaplain will provide crying towels."

Bell was looking intently towards shore. "Isn't that the mail boat coming?"

His question was answered by glad cries from the signal bridge. Word passed from group to group: "The mail boat! Mail boat's coming! That's Larson all right; wonder what they've got."

"Parcel post."

"Naw, airmail. I want airmail."

"I'll settle for anything I can read or eat."

"Hey, look. The boat's loaded! Look at them bags! Hot dog! Hey, fellows: mail, lots of mail!"

The salvage boat closed with the ship. Excitement grew as more of the crew crowded the rails to gloat over the heap of fat canvas bags, yet MacDougall felt the sudden lift to his spirits checked by growing doubt. There was something wrong about those bags: they were too fat, and instead of a dirty, uncolored canvas they were a drab olive. As he looked, a signalman with binoculars exclaimed, "I'll be a low-down, dirty, suffering skunk! They're just Army duffle bags. No mail, fellows; no mail!"

Rain pelted down on the crew at sunset battle stations that evening. Out of the squall a boat came within hail and swept alongside. Jackson came up the ladder to the quarterdeck, shirt plastered to his back, shoes sloshing, water streaming down his trousers. Mumbling to Kruger, who had the deck, he headed for the bridge, clutching a small bottle of red ink. Stiff as a stanchion at his command post, Hawks turned about, eyes peering down at Jackson from under his dripping helmet rim.

"Well, Jackson?"

"Just a pint, sir. I tried the whole attack force, Captain. No one has the stuff."

Hawks snapped, "Take your battle station."

"Aye, aye, sir."

Hawks turned to his talker. "Get me the executive officer.
. . . Quigley, we will maintain Readiness Condition Two
throughout the night: half the crew at battle stations with no
exceptions. Tomorrow at eight hundred we will continue field
day. I will inspect lower decks at fifteen hundred."

Kruger groaned and sat up in his bunk, automatically motivated by insistent honking of the battle call. He glanced at his
watch: forty minutes sleep seemed like nothing at all. He'd be
lucky to get back in the bunk before four, when he would be
due on gun watch again. Battle stations before breakfast and
then he had the deck until noon. After lunch he would have to
scurry around second division territory getting the place ready
for inspection. Pulling on his shoes, he anticipated the familiar
scene in the after troop berthing compartments below the
waterline: sweating sailors scrubbing newly smeared bulkheads
and cursing the Army; tired, atabrine-stained soldiers stowing
duffle and rifles into hard canvas bunks tiered four high and
cursing the Navy. With this picture still in his mind, Kruger
stood up, yanked the sheet from Brooks, his groaning roommate, struck the floor from the hook and stumbled down the
dim, red-lighted passage towards Gun Two. Portside aft and
down. At last the gun—clatter of helmets and shadows of the
crew getting set, tall shape of Alvick, his gun captain. Without
a word, Kruger pulled on his phone headset and listened. Alvick reported, "Manned and ready, sir. Ammo ready."

"Control: Gun Two manned and ready." Kruger waited for
acknowledgment, then shoved one earphone up on his head
and said to his men, "One bogey, a snooper, circling out of
range."

Doyle sat steady on his pointer's seat. "Hope he comes in
range so we can knock him off; my sack's waiting for me."

"He won't," said Alvick. "Just forget about sleep." Alvick
was right; the enemy snooper circled about the anchorage,
keeping barely out of five-inch range. Three hours later he
veered off towards some Japanese base to the westward. Hawks
kept the entire crew at battle stations for another hour; then,
feeling that the snooper was gone for the night, he returned to
Condition Two: watch and watch. Kruger looked at his strap
watch; it was nearly time to take over the duty again. He sat
down on a mooring bitt and rested his chin in his hands.

CHAPTER 37

Chaplain Hughes got out of the boat, crossed the Sansapor
beach and walked along the jungle trail to Air Force HQ. Ned
Strange, his assistant, stumbled along behind him, carrying two
battered cans of movie film. Within the hut, three perspiring

sergeants worked at makeshift desks built with packing cases. The nearest sergeant rose to greet Hughes: "Movies, Padre! You weren't kidding. . . . Hey, you guys! Movies!"

Hughes smiled. "It's only a stinker, but you're welcome to it; we've seen it three times and no other ship will swap anything for it."

"That's O.K., Chaplain," said the heaviest sergeant. "Anything's better than staring at the wall or betting on the number of lice on a bush."

A mud-spattered jeep rolled up from the runway and a heavy-set major squeezed out from behind the wheel. Glancing at the movie cans he said, "Thanks, Chaplain. You've been pretty good to us: books, magazines, ice cream and now a movie. I don't know why you do it? We're sort of forgotten out here, you know. Our only contact is with Hollandia by air, and everything there is pretty well picked over before we get to it. I wish we could do something for your boys."

Hughes looked at a weather-worn C-47 on the runway. "Say!" he exclaimed. "No, I don't suppose it would be possible . . ."

"What's on your mind?"

"Well, Major, it's our mail. Our Christmas mail has been fouled up for weeks, always arriving just behind us. We were going to get it at last, back in Hollandia; then we sailed the day before the mail boat arrived. . . . I was thinking: if you just had some room in a plane for a sack or two . . ."

"Why, certainly. We're making a flight early in the morning, if the weather holds; be back before dark. Would you like to go along?"

"They'll want the mail clerk to go. Thanks, so much! I'm sure he'll show up this evening and wait all night for flight time! We wouldn't miss a chance like this. What a wonderful break!"

On Christmas Eve the *Belinda* stirred uneasily at her anchors. Once more the equatorial weather front had pushed south against the New Guinea coast. Dark squalls rushed across a leaden sky while humid gusts of wind whistled an ever-changing tune in the rigging. Sailors waiting for the call to battle stations lined the rail and gazed towards shore. Some were quiet; some shouted: "Where's our Christmas mail? . . . What's the matter with Larson? Where's he gone with that boat? . . . Boy, he'd better have that mailman aboard!"

"We ought to get fifty bags."

"I'll settle for three. All I want is just one letter from my girl."

The husbands, the lovers, the homesick of all ages and ranks stood quiet and watched for the boat. They had seen the plane circle the strip, then head into the wind with wheels down. That was ten minutes ago—ten hours! Where was that mail boat?

Kruger sighted it first from his post on the bridge. It was past time to sound the alarm for sunset battle stations, but in his excitement he leaned out from the bridge rail and looked down over the heads on lower decks to the darkening water between ship and shore. The boat was hard to make out in failing light. Kruger thought of mail: stacks and piles of it which would take all night to sort. Then, remembering routine, but with a happy lift in his voice, he called for the boatswain's pipe and pulled the battle honker.

Anxious for letters from his wife, Quigley waited at the quarterdeck for Larson's boat. Now and then he could make out the thrust of white bow wave as the boat dropped into the chop. The roar of engine grew louder; the boat swept alongside. At once Quigley sensed that something was wrong. Even in the dark, so quickly settled about the ship, the boat's shadowy bulk should not seem so void.

"Ahoy in the boat," Quigley cried. "Is the mail clerk there?"

Larson's voice answered, "Aye, sir. He's here."

"How many bags of mail?" There was no answer. Quigley cried again, impatience and anxiety in his voice, "How many bags of mail?" The only answer was a silent one: the mail clerk coming up the ladder with his leather mail pouch sagging empty. "Speak up, Shepherd," demanded Quigley. "The mail! Where is the mail?"

The mail clerk answered at last, his voice dull, beaten. "No mail, sir."

"But our Christmas mail—you mean it wasn't at Hollandia?"

"Yes, sir, it was there, but they turned the plane around. We landed and I just fixed up a jeep ride from the field to Hollandia and then they came running after me. Storm coming, they said. We had to come right back."

Late that night the Jap sniper returned and circled the ship for over three hours. He was careful to keep just out of range while the crew stood at their guns, cursing him and waiting for Christmas morning.

Other units of the attack force entered the bay on Christmas Day, anchoring about a mile to westward of the *Belinda*. Signals from Hawks regarding possibility of mail brought negative replies. It was a dreary day of equatorial storm.

Jackson, Rockwell and Hughes took an LCVP on a scrounging trip to the newly arrived flagship. They returned in a tropical downpour, the craft rolling and yawing in a nasty chop. Jackson had another quart of red ink, the chaplain had two

325

battered movie canisters and Rockwell kept close to several cases which were covered with a streaming tarpaulin. A thin line of hardy watchers at the rail welcomed them with: "How's the wine business, Mr. Jackson? . . . Got some mail there, Rockwell? . . . What's the movie, Chaplain?"

Only the chaplain answered, "I've got a Four-O picture."

"Baloney! That's what you always say."

Quigley met Rockwell in the passageway and stood aside to avoid water streaming from the rotund commissary officer. "What are you going to do about Christmas dinner, Rockwell?"

Rockwell looked at Quigley appraisingly, then sensing his mellow mood he ventured, "I pulled a fast one on the admiral, sir. You'll keep it confidential, won't you?"

"Why sure. What are you looking so guilty about?"

"I was in the 'flag' storeroom, making a dicker with the admiral's steward. I swapped two sacks of fresh spuds for five cases of spam. Then I noticed a dozen cases of tinned whole Virginia ham. A dozen cases, mind you! I had my boys waiting outside the door to the issue room and when the admiral's steward went to the galley about something I handed out five cases of ham real quick like, put the spam in its place and threw a tarp over it. There's enough baked ham for all hands if we're careful."

"Wonderful," said Quigley. "But the fresh potatoes—where did you get them? Have you been holding out on the wardroom? We've been choking down that desiccated stuff—"

"Oh, the spuds?" Rockwell grinned. "I got them from the supply ship that came in with 'em this morning—got enough left to go with the ham today. The admiral's steward was glad to get 'em. I forgot to tell him where they came from."

The weather improved, and two days after Christmas Shepherd was given another flight to Hollandia. This time he reached the fleet post office, where the ensign on duty said brightly, "*Belinda?* Oh, yes, we sent off your mail on an LCI. It should be there by now. Here's the portion of the dispatch covering you."

The happiness rising in Shepherd's breast choked into a lump as he read, *U.S.S.* Belinda, *five bags airmail, four bags periodicals, thirteen bags parcel post, dispatched LCI 965, destination Guam.*

Shepherd fairly screamed, "But you sent it to Guam! We're at Sansapor. You've got us all fouled up again!"

The ensign bristled. "Oh, no indeed; I have it straight. See, here's the top secret location of fleet units, Western Pacific. Look here." He pointed angrily with a stubby forefinger:

U.S.S. Belinda, *APA 15: Guam.* "If you shifted ship to some other anchorage, you can send a boat, can't you?"

Swallowing hard, Shepherd took an angry swing around the mail office, his eyes sweeping over hundreds of mud-caked bags of mail, all for other ships. Then he said in a low voice, "My ship is at the western tip of this stinking New Guinea, twelve hundred miles from our mail at Guam."

"That's very unfortunate," said the ensign. "However, there's nothing I can do about it. I followed instructions to the letter."

Tony Brooks turned from watching the last of six PBMs wing over the coconut trees and settle with a foaming splash into the waters of Sansapor anchorage. Miller, the chief signalman, was jumping up and down beside Captain Hawks's empty high chair, excitedly waving a pencil-scrawled message blank. "Mail, Mr. Brooks! Those planes have mail from Guam!"

"O.K.," said Brooks. "What are we waiting for?" Five seconds later the boatswain's pipe shrilled out, calling a boat crew. Fifteen seconds later, Larson and his crew ripped the lashings from the salvage boat. The boat was swung out while they were still clambering aboard, the davit crew shouting at them to hurry. Shepherd came on the run with his leather mail pouch, which served as badge of office rather than expected receptacle for mail, for his mind was calculating in terms of bags stuffed full of airmail.

Before Shepherd could swing his leg over the boat's gunwale, Tommy Jones, quartermaster third, rushed up to Brooks with pleading written in his brown eyes: "May I go, Mr. Brooks? They'll need help, sir. . . . I'm off watch. I know there's a letter from Lorraine. She promised; she promised—"

"Go on; get going," said Brooks. "You're holding up the boat, Tommy. . . . Lower away boys. Lower away." No one heard the order; the boat was already screaming downwards towards the water with Tommy Jones, who had jumped at the last second, still scrambling to his feet. As the blocks were hastily cast off, the engine coughed and broke into a roar. Larson whipped the craft away from the *Belinda* and churned up the anchorage towards the anchored seaplanes.

As other ships were anchored closer than the *Belinda* to the seaplane mooring, Larson's boat was not the first to arrive. Gigs and salvage boats cruised about the moored seaplanes while their crews shouted the names of their ships and inquired for mail. One anxious pilot stood on the snubby nose of his plane, shouting, "Sure, we got Christmas mail. So what! You don't have to ram us with your boats. Stand clear. We'll call out the names of your ships as we get the mail out. Stand clear, all of you!"

Despite this warning, landing craft in increasing numbers surged about the moored seaplanes like sharks around a fresh wreck. A self-propelled barge was shovelling up a square bow wave as it labored out from base landing, but there was no waiting here for such orderly process as sorting mail on a barge. When the plane crews shouted the name of a ship, the boat concerned darted in alongside, amid renewed protests and warnings from worried pilots. Boat crews whooped and yelled as each fat, grimy bag was tossed from plane hatch to boat. Each lucky boat would then draw reluctantly back and wait hopefully for another call. One after another, the names of cruisers, attack transports and destroyers were called out: "*Custer . . . H. A. Ford . . . Monacacy. . . .*"

The *Belinda* had not yet been called. Larson, Shepherd and Jones looked at each other for reassurance. "This waiting's tough," said Larson. "They'd better hurry up a bag for us— I'm ready to blow a gasket—waiting like this."

Shepherd took a few steps around the cockpit, then sat down once more on the engine box. "That's all I do; wait for mail," he said.

"It's there, all right," said Tommy Jones earnestly. "It's got to be there."

The calling of ship's names and the tossing of mail bags slowed down and at last stopped completely. After a minute or two of further waiting, all other boats started up their engines and roared back towards the cluster of anchored ships, each boat having at least one fat bag of mail. Only Larson's boat remained. Shepherd jumped out on the covered bow deck and shouted towards the nearest seaplane, "Got any mail for the *Belinda?*"

A head popped out of a hatchway. "No, not us. Why don't you ask the mail clerk? He came along from Guam; he's aboard six-oh-five."

Larson nosed alongside the indicated plane where a dungaree-clad sailor worked with a stub of pencil at a long checksheet. "Hello, George," said Shepherd. "Where's our mail— the *Belinda*—remember me?"

"Ye-ah," said the mail clerk thoughtfully. "Yeah, I remember you. *Belinda!* Say, you guys aren't here, are you? I had seven bags of airmail for you. Got orders last night just before we left—sent yours back to Hollandia."

Late on the Saturday night between Christmas and New Year's Day, MacDougall sat on the railing outside the *Belinda's* wardroom together with Flynn and Brooks. The night was sultry and their sweaty clothing stuck to skins raw from tropical heat rash and, in MacDougall's case, also aggravated by fungus. The anchored ship was blacked out, her decks quiet. Hawks and Quigley had gone ashore to the small officers' club shared by all services. The three officers on the railing were discussing the dry run made early that morning a few miles up the New Guinea coast, the last before the pay run on Luzon.

"I've lost count of the dry runs I've been in," said Brooks. "There are always surprises—somehow dry runs always get more fouled up than pay runs on Jap territory. But what happened to the first wave this morning tops them all as far as I'm concerned. Of course, after what happened to our mail yesterday, I shouldn't be surprised at anything any more."

"Yes," said Flynn, going off on a tangent, "that mail business. Now who do you think is deliberately fouling up our mail? It's all too cleverly diabolical to happen by accident. Some lousy brass hat is mad at the *Belinda*."

"Sure, sure," said Brooks. "Now, as I was saying, this dry run was the screwiest yet. The *Belinda* comes sweeping up with the squadron all in nice formation while cruisers and cans bombard the beach. At four hundred we debark troops and form up boat waves in the dark, and for the first dry run I can remember, every boat got into the proper wave and every wave hit the line of departure at the exact minute. Even Ensign Tuttle was ten seconds ahead of schedule—it was all too smooth. I took the right flank of the combined first wave. Just at dawn we swept up on that empty beach with the coconut trees staring back at us. It was too perfect: smooth black sand, not a bit of coral or rock. It was like those fake landings we used to make back at Coronado."

MacDougall stirred and scratched a patch of fungus on his chest. "Yes. Remember the red-painted barn? I can still hear the old commodore howling. Wish we were back there—one night with mama would take care of a lot of this lost mail!"

"Shut up!" said Brooks. "I feel bad enough without you reminding me about it—I'm talking about dry runs. So we made the landing—just dropped our ramps on that smooth black sand, right on the button according to my watch, when we heard the awfulest yelling I've heard this side of Kwajalein. Out from under the trees came forty or fifty Japs, screaming and yelling and shooting a few stray shots—wounded two dogfaces."

"No!" said Flynn. "You mean this actually happened? Why didn't you say something about it before?"

"Well, I had my mind on that mail deal, I guess. I thought maybe they'd fly it here from Hollandia today. I know Betty—it's just getting me down—"

"Yes, but the Japs," said Flynn. "What about the Japs?"

"Well, we've got a lot of old-timers in this Army outfit; I'm glad of that. They just hit sand wherever they were, in the water or out of it—rifles cracking all along the beach. They mowed those Japs down like wheat—every last one. We looked 'em over afterwards—you should have seen what they had to fight with: rifle here and there—machetes—bayonets tied to sticks. Some bypassed outfit lost in the jungle—none of 'em lived to know it was just a dry run."

MacDougall sucked in his breath. Fitful stirring of breeze had cooled his wet shirt. He shivered, then looked off into the night. "I think the gig's coming, Tony. You'd better alert the watch."

It was the gig. Captain Hawks stood in the open cockpit, holding on to the canopy. When the gig came alongside he climbed carefully from gunwale to accommodation ladder without a hint of his usual speed or smartness. Quigley followed behind, looking carefully at Hawks as if ready to offer assistance. MacDougall looked at Hawks's face; there was something strange about it, perhaps the harsh spotlight recklessly turned on from the bridge wing above to assist the commanding officer aboard. No, it was something more than that: a look of strain or shock. Then MacDougall saw a trickle of blood running from the side of Hawks's mouth. For a moment they faced each other as Hawks stepped aboard, neglecting to give his usual smart return to the salute of official greeting. What was wrong with the Old Man's mouth? Teeth missing? The top incisors gone!

"What happened?" MacDougall asked Quigley as Hawks followed Flynn down to sick bay.

"That blacked-out landing," said Quigley. "We had to cross one of those steel pontoon barges to get to the gig. He stumbled and fell—it happened just like that! There he was, flat on his face with all those teeth gone! I surely sympathize . . ." Quigley felt his own jaw appraisingly as he added, "Strange thing is, we had been talking about my teeth at the club. Perhaps you haven't heard—I have a pretty advanced case of pyorrhea. The skipper was just telling me that I should go back to Pearl for treatment. That would be wonderful, of course, but it looks as if he is going to need fancy dental care more than I will."

Two pain-filled hours later, Hawks walked into his cabin. Shaw, the dental officer, had managed to extract the stumps of broken teeth—said a good bridge would fill the gap. Hawks was still under shock; it had all happened so quickly. Striding towards his gig he had tripped over that confounded crossbar—then this in a flash of sudden pain: the surprising grit of broken teeth in his mouth. Hawks stepped up to his bathroom mirror and examined his bloody gums. What a hole! he thought. They'll swear I was drunk. Let 'em; it's my teeth that matter. He returned to his cabin; the long table was bare except for his trumpet. Without further thought he picked up the instrument, put it to his lips and blew. His lips, still numb from novocaine, felt like thick slabs of leather. Air rushed through the toothless gap; the trumpet made no sound at all. Sudden anger at the pain and frustration surged up from within. With a fast overhanded sweep he flung the trumpet crashing against the steel bulkhead. Then he turned in his bunk but could not sleep.

Captain Hawks paced restlessly in his quarters, back and forth from stateroom to cabin. As he turned swiftly at the bulkheads without breaking step, he looked about the place like a lion behind bars in a zoo. He looked at his bunk: he would see very little of that bunk in the days ahead, but somehow he could not bring himself to lie down upon it now. He glanced at the safe, crammed with the detailed operations plans which he could almost quote by section and paragraph. Pacing, pacing, pacing, he glanced resentfully at the stack of official correspondence in his action basket; back into the cabin with three long steps to the bulkhead, he looked at the photo of his wife over the bunk. She had an understanding face—he'd like to sit beside her now, hold his cheek against hers, tell her about things: the way they were. He hadn't written to her for several days; writing to her just now seemed out of the question. If she were here things would pour out of him, but they didn't look right on paper. Back into the cabin, four paces to the pantry door—the row of emptied coffee cups—too much coffee, no help in the stuff any more. He glanced at the clock; time soon for early supper and then battle stations. That snooper would probably come back again after midnight—just as soon as he was finally asleep. The lousy little Jap! Somehow he was losing his impersonal attitude towards the enemy. They were doing something to him, wearing down his skin to the tender nerve ends. Pace back and forth, back and forth—if he only had some outlet! This stuff boiling inside him! The ocarina on his desk—some other time, not now; at least he could play that. Feeling the empty gap in his teeth, he looked over to the corner of the cabin: there lay the trumpet with the dent in its brassy mouth. He had thrown it hard against the bulkhead. How could a man play his trumpet without four front uppers—play a trumpet, eat that confounded Australian mutton, speak incisively on his bridge?

Chipchee: where was his monkey? Hawks lengthened his swift pacing to enter the pantry. No signs of Chipchee there, he must be gone for one of his runs about the ship. The crew had better be kind to that monkey. If he ever caught anybody—! It was lonely here without Chipchee. It was lonely to be captain; beyond pride and feeling of power it was lonely. Something seemed to be pressing upon Hawks. He walked back and forth as if in a groove, like the animated monkey on little tracked wheels he had seen when a lad in a Memphis store. Round and round that monkey went. You put a penny in his cup as he whizzed past; he'd dive into a tunnel, then come around again and pop out with a bit of chocolate. If he could only reach back in time and toss a penny in that monkey's cup again . . . that little mechanical monkey—pile of rusted junk God knew where; gone and dead like the carefree barefoot days. Something was pressing on him, pressing him down, filling his head and body with strange and unfamiliar pain. There was a queer throb to it too, something outside of himself; what was it? Not the steady hum of the auxiliaries in the engine room; not the intermittent whine and whirr of mechanical davits; it was an unceasing vibration with a particular meaning. Hawks stopped pacing and listened: it was the troops coming aboard from the last exercise on shore, troops coming aboard for the pay run to Luzon. Tramp of footsteps pressing in all around the cabin—you had no freedom on your own quarterdeck; you had to pace in your cabin. Thought flashed that the business of assault troops was the basis of his command; for the moment he rejected it in a surge of resentment against the Army: they spoiled a ship—this tramp of feet and clanking of equipment. And why wasn't there enough red ink? That's why he was here; that's why he couldn't be out sailing the *Albatross!* Only three quarts of red ink, enough for the jib perhaps. He'd get ink for the mainsail, from peak to clew. He'd sail into the sunset with red sails—but when? Troops to take into action, days on the bridge with air and submarine attacks sure, mines, shore batteries on Bolinao— there might not ever be a quiet evening to sail his boat; time might be running out. Well, what are you standing there for, Hawks? You're a man of action, aren't you? Yes or no? I don't care what you think, what anybody thinks; get some action, man!

Was this his arm reaching for the bell, ringing for the orderly, shouting for the chaplain, for Fraser, for Quigley and MacDougall? No, it was someone else. He was just a spectator, watching the mechanical monkey and waiting for the bit of chocolate.

"Chaplain, rig your record turntable on number three hatch. Commence playing 'Red Sails in the Sunset' at full volume, and continue playing it until I order you to stop!"

Chaplain Hughes looked at Hawks with astonishment. Could he be serious?—right in the middle of embarkation? Troops in full pack jammed the hatch, waiting for a chance at the scuttles leading to berthing compartments below. That fragile turntable would be trampled flat. Yet he had never heard the captain's voice so incisive, so sure of himself, in such perfect command, it seemed. It would be futile to remonstrate; the sailors would help to rope off a space, and the soldiers might like the tune at that. Hughes left the cabin to carry out his instructions, but in his mind there lingered a disturbing impression of something very odd about Hawks's eyes: they had not really looked at him but seemed focused on some distant horizon, and they had had the glazed look of enameled pottery.

Fraser roused out his anchor watch and began heaving short. Dropping an anchor or heaving up were all in the day's work to him. Day or night, he could pick up the hook with his eyes shut, know by the particular clank what instant to look overside for the fluke. . . . There she showed in the clear blue-green, still below the surface. "Anchor aweigh, sir. Clear anchor."

Quigley stood back out of the way on the bridge, feeling the surge of power as the *Belinda* gathered momentum through mirror-calm water. Gusts of artificial breeze made by the ship's forward motion breathed refreshingly into his face. He wondered where Hawks was taking the ship and why. Hawks was keeping his intentions more and more to himself these days; it was embarrassing to be executive officer, yet in the dark as to what was going on. Quigley turned and strolled over to Robinson, the communications officer, who stood by the flag bag.

"Is this trip necessary?" quipped Quigley.

"I don't know," said Robinson. "All I know is, we'll be late for chow again."

MacDougall spun from the topside pelorus to his chart board and slapped down a three way cut. Strange, the Old Man getting under way like this without a word of explanation; he could remember no other time when Hawks had failed to tell him where he intended to take the ship and what he intended to do. Hawks was always the commander, difficult and even unreasonable about many things, but in matters of handling the ship they worked together in a partnership which allowed MacDougall full share in responsibility, if not in authority. This gave him an edge over Quigley which allowed him to be quite rude in perfect safety; but more than that, it strengthened MacDougall's secret feeling that the ship was in his care. Now, in ignorance as to Hawks's intentions, he felt growing uneasiness, for Hawks had merely said: "Have Fraser heave up. Set standard speed at seventeen knots. Ahead standard . . . Steady her into the sun and keep her there, Quartermaster."

Ahead lay the sun, setting in Oriental splendor of the first magnitude amid an intricate pattern of blazing cirrus, alto-cumulus and stratus cloud. Dead ahead and much closer were grouped fifty-three anchored ships of the attack group. The *Belinda,* first of the lot to arrive at Sansapor, had been anchored alone, reasonably safe from submarines, for the narrow entrance to the roadstead was constantly patrolled by three destroyers. MacDougall wondered if the *Belinda* had been ordered to anchor closer to the squadron flagship. If so, it would still be strange that Hawks had said nothing about it, for he was fussy to a fault about anchoring on the precise pinpoint assigned, a maneuver which required coaching from the navigator. How many times Hawks had glared at him and ordered Fraser to pick up anchor again? Times without number they had made a circle to seaward, approached and anchored again because the ship had brought up with the hook a mere twenty-five yards from exact center of the assigned five-hundred-yard ring. Hawks gripped the rail, staring steadily ahead. Not once had he looked around or said another word since ordering speed ahead and course into the sunset.

MacDougall stepped up beside Hawks and asked quietly, as he usually did when working on the bridge with him, "Have we instructions to change anchorage, Capt'n? I'll need bearings—a range on something . . ." Staring ahead, Hawks did not seem to hear. The *Belinda* was up to the full seventeen knots now, cutting a foaming wedge in calm, pink-tinted water as she headed into the sunset and bore down upon the three squadrons of ships anchored together in close formation. MacDougall glanced down at the close-packed infantrymen on the foredeck. Apparently enjoying the breeze, they seemed in no hurry to find their stuffy quarters below. Some of them faced a small roped-off area on the hatch where Chaplain Hughes's record player obediently continued to play "Red Sails in the Sunset." "Captain!" called MacDougall as loudly as he could manage. "I'll need anchor bearings, sir."

Hawks did not answer. MacDougall shrugged; perhaps the Old Man was going to pull this one off the cuff: run her up on a close approximation of bearing, jump to the compass at the last moment to line her up precisely, back engines full, judge his distance by seaman's eye and drop the hook on the run. It could be done; good seamen did it every now and then, but it was not like Hawks. Gyro true bearings, radar and stadimeter ranges, constant soundings and mooring-board plots: Hawks was a man to calculate his seamanship mathematically and then express resentment at any discrepancy resulting from wind, tide or the ship's turning circle. Something queer about all this: even four-stripe skippers didn't just go for a little evening sail with a combatant ship of the United States Navy. MacDougall reached out to pluck at Hawks's shirt sleeve, but drew back from such familiarity. It was then that he noticed Hawks's eyes.

334

They were full on the setting sun, now a mere diameter above the horizon. Some of the sunset seemed to reflect from the usual hazel-blue of his eyes, but what startled MacDougall was their glazed look. Hawks seemed hypnotized: perhaps he had had a heart attack. MacDougall looked ahead once more; they were within a thousand yards of the flagship. Her masts seemed to rise ever higher from the sea, beckoning the *Belinda* to collision. In less than two minutes they would crash into her and cut her in two unless something decisive was done at once! MacDougall's hands gripping the rail were clammy with nervous perspiration. He looked around, saw Quigley staring open-mouthed at the clutter of shipping ahead. Willicut, the ship's best helmsman, even as he kept the sun a perfect bull's-eye, dead ahead, wore a look of alarm on his usually imperturbable face as his eyes begged MacDougall for instructions. MacDougall gave him a quick shrug of the shoulders and then shouted to Hawks, "Capt'n, Capt'n Hawks! Oh, *Captain!*" Now as before there was no answer. But there must be an answer! MacDougall grasped Hawks's khaki shirt sleeve and jerked hard.

These moments since deciding to weigh anchor were the happiest and most carefree that Hawks had known for months. His little sailboat was stowed on the afterdeck, her sails not yet red, but the *Belinda* was much bigger and he was also captain of the *Belinda*. He remembered rust-red sails of Portuguese fishermen sailing out into the sunset; he was doing the same with his ship, carefree as they. Sunset filled his vision; sun, sky, sea and ship all rosy now. In this soft-tinted mist he saw great red sails billowing in a fair breeze, drawing his ship gently onward. It did not matter that the *Belinda* cut through mirror-like waters and stagnant air; he had no problems, large or small—only the sunset beckoned. Later he would have to go by those war plans in his safe, obey flag hoists from admirals, be slave to dispatch boards and the TBS, but now for a little time he was free—he'd see how close to the sun he could get. His face remained expressionless; this was something deep inside he would not share with any other man about him. He was captain to them: their commanding officer. He'd never tell them he was really a barefoot boy in Tennessee, waiting for a monkey to bring him a penny's worth of chocolate. He'd fool them! He'd show them! He'd make them do things they thought impossible—even for *Beachhead Belinda!* Some day he'd be an admiral and free from orders, orders, orders. . . . What was that? MacDougall jerking his sleeve, shouting almost incoherently. What's wrong with the fellow?—why should he get jittery now? Everything was fine. "Anchoring instructions? What anchoring instructions? We aren't anchoring out here. The sun's set now. Take her back and anchor as before."

MacDougall jumped back to the helmsman's side. Take her back! Anchor as before! What was Hawks up to? Well, he had the conn now; no time to ponder. "Right rudder," he called to Willicut and waved a violent gesture for haste with his right hand. "Right full rudder." The current was setting her to starboard—he had been watching that. The flagship was dead ahead, only eight hundred yards off: bare turning circle for the *Belinda*. He'd back her in a few seconds, get her swinging fast to starboard, then hook her on ahead and get out fast. It was the only chance to avoid sure collision! It was going to be close; too close. Now was the time. MacDougall opened his mouth to order engines astern.

Suddenly Hawks spun around, leaped up on the pelorus stand and brushed MacDougall aside. "All engines back full," Hawks called in a clear, confident voice. "Keep full right rudder, Quartermaster." The *Belinda's* stern was swinging rapidly towards the flagship while the bow clawed ineffectually at the narrowing bit of water between the two ships. "Stand by the starboard anchor," cried Hawks. "Let go anchor. Just touch bottom to hold the bow and hang on. I'm coming ahead." Every man on the signal bridge stood frozen in electrified tension, only Barton, the captain's talker, moved after Hawks, dragging his phone cord and firing Hawks's orders over his phones. The *Belinda* was parallel to the flagship now and her davits, which were swung out and held suspended landing craft, seemed like clawing fingers, poised to rip and tear. Startled faces showed all along the flagship's rails; then her collision siren screamed in warning and they broke for comparative safety inboard. Others rushed up with fenders which they hung overside.

MacDougall stood by the pelorus stand, lining up the two ships, considering ever-changing factors of pivot point, stern swing, tide and suction. Now was the time to go ahead: throw a well of water between the two ships and get clear if possible. It was now or never! At the instant these thoughts were resolved, Hawks barked, "Ahead, flank speed! Steady your helm." Whine of the turbines dropped down the scale into silence; then, after an incredibly short interval, they went ahead in anguished sound rising from a low, insistent moan to a high scream. The *Belinda* continued to surge beam on towards the flagship while her propeller thrust back tons of churning white water.

MacDougall spoke up: "We should come right, Capt'n—get the wash against her side and shove us apart." Hawks nodded, and before he could give the order the alert Willicut had the wheel over. Slowly, as if reluctantly, the *Belinda's* bow pointed away from the flagship; then, as her propeller clawed ahead, the boiling wake thrust the flagship away and the *Belinda* ahead. In a matter of seconds, eighteen thousand tons of steel, explosives and men had been diverted from deadly collision. The *Belinda* withdrew and hastened under darkening skies toward her former anchorage.

Hardly had the flagship recoiled to the limits of her anchor chain before a signalman sprang to his platform and vigorously signaled a message of indignant inquiry to the *Belinda*. Hawks stood imperturbable, relaxed, watching MacDougall return the *Belinda* to solitary anchorage. Signalmen behind him were laughing and exclaiming. Hawks turned around casually just in time to see Chipchee performing antics around the top of the smokestack. "Chipchee," he called. "Oh, Chipchee!" The monkey came down the stays, swinging, scrambling, sliding in comic pretense of falling, until with a last happy jump he landed on Hawks's shoulder and snuggled against his neck, and from this safe position made faces at the crew. Fondling the monkey, Hawks glanced at the flagship's dispatch, handed him by Robinson, and asked for a message blank. Resting the clipboard on the bridge rail, he dashed off a reply to the admiral with vigorous strokes of his soft pencil:

> While swinging ship in order to calibrate effect of recent gun installations by ship's force on magnetic compasses, casualty to steering gear responsible our unintentional close approach your command.

Hawks handed the message board to Robinson. "Send him that," he said. "What's he fussing about? We didn't hurt him."

After battle stations that evening, Quigley went to MacDougall's tiny stateroom and knocked on the door. Entering, he was relieved to see Flynn sitting on the bunk, evidently joking with MacDougall about something; trust Flynn to find the light side of things. Quigley was worried, but he nodded pleasantly and said, "Glad to see you both here; I want to talk to you about something."

MacDougall got up from the only chair, offered it to Quigley and joined Flynn on the bunk. "Shoot," he said. "I've got plenty of time now; we're anchored as before—all secure for the night."

Quigley sat on the edge of the chair, shuddered as he drew in a breath and exhaled it sharply. "Yes, we're all secure now. That was too close for me: what happened this afternoon. I want to get your slant and Flynn's. You two fellows: you won't blurt all around the ship—I wanted to see what you thought . . ."

MacDougall looked sharply at Quigley. Where was that smooth line of chatter? This was the first time he had seen Quigley really concerned—must be worried about Hawks. MacDougall thought: now is the time to draw him out, see what he really thinks.

"Perhaps you want Pat to take your blood pressure," said MacDougall, sliding off the bunk. "I'll leave you two—need a little fresh air anyway."

"Oh, no, Mac, don't go. I want to talk to both of you—something very confidential."

"Something's eating you," said Flynn. "Why don't you spill it? We won't spread it around. For all you know, we're thinking pretty much the same thing you are."

"So you were talking about him too, when I came in; weren't you?"

MacDougall looked appraisingly at Quigley. After all, in spite of his superficiality, the man was straightforward, and no fool. "You mean, the Old Man?"

"Yes," said Quigley, "I'm worried about him. I certainly don't need to tell you that he nearly wrecked the ship this evening. For some time I've been observing—well, I don't have your salty background, Mac, but several times I've noticed that he—that he—"

Astonished at seeing Quigley in this mood, MacDougall blurted, "Take it easy. Don't look so guilty. No one's plotting against authority here; we're just talking things over." MacDougall leaned back in the bunk and glanced at Flynn before continuing: "Sure, for a long time now I've been watching a gradual change in the Old Man. It works both ways: sometimes he's more brilliant than is normal even for him, makes perfect decisions with split-second timing. Sometimes he's eccentric to the point of danger; you never know what he's going to come up with. The trouble is, there isn't much time up there on the bridge to decide which is which, to promptly obey the good orders and tactfully argue against the bad. I'm beginning to feel the pressure myself. . . . How about you—away from the bridge? Have you noticed anything?"

More relaxed now, Quigley tipped the chair back on two legs and lighted a cigarette. "That's just the trouble," he said. "It all seems to be coming out on the bridge. His paper work is better than ever; he really writes forceful correspondence. Of course he's always shoving a lot of controversial letters up through the channels to higher levels of command, trying to get things which have been refused by immediate superiors: more guns, ventilation blowers, medals—all kinds of stuff."

"Medals for him?" asked Flynn.

"Oh, no—of course he likes to wear them too. I mean for the crew. He's beating his brains out trying to get the Unit Citation for the ship. He keeps up a steady stream of letters all the time, and you have to admit, he gets some results." Quigley leaned the chair far back, blew smoke and watched it drift out the shuttered porthole, then continued: "It's driving the yeomen nuts, but there's nothing you could call irrational about any of that. Some things about the sailboat of course—that red ink—harmless enough. But on the bridge—"

"Like that little excursion we took this evening," said Mac-Dougall. "Do you realize how close we came to disaster? It doesn't matter how good you are; even then it's a matter of luck to get out of a situation like that. We were just lucky. What worries me is that this happened in a period of quiet. What's likely to happen next time we get into action? Suppose he blows his marbles in the middle of an air attack!"

"What are you smiling about, Flynn?" Quigley asked. "What do you think about all this?"

"What's so different about a couple of red sails or a little trip around the anchorage? A war is supposed to be dangerous, isn't it?" Quigley banged the chair back on four legs and stared at his well-shined shoes. Flynn winked at MacDougall, then added, "I'm just the medical officer. I'm perfectly willing to go on record that in my opinion Captain Hawks is overtired, that the strain is beginning to show. You're the executive officer, second in command here. Any action is up to you."

Quigley raised his head and looked from Flynn to Mac-Dougall. "Do you think we should report Hawks's condition to the commodore? Give him some warning—go on record now so if we ever have to do anything drastic, there'll be some basis for it."

"Listen," said MacDougall. "I'd rather sweat it out with Hawks up on the bridge; he's not a bad guy."

"Perhaps you're right," said Quigley. "It might take some time to send a relief."

"Send a relief?" Flynn was channeling a roguish grin straight at Quigley. "I thought that when a captain was incapacitated the executive officer took over; isn't that what you're here for?"

"Now listen," said Quigley. "Don't get me wrong. I was merely asking for an opinion. It's my duty to weigh all sides of this thing. It looks to me as if we'd better go slow for a bit. Well, thanks for your opinions and remember"—he waved a hand in a quick negative gesture—"this is all very confidential. Good night, gentlemen."

It was New Year's Eve, though few of the *Belinda's* crew remembered. To them it was the last night in anchorage before sailing on the long, dangerous run through the Philippine Archipelago for assault landings in Lingayen Gulf. Inadequate blowers struggled with fetid air in berthing compartments crowded with the embarked landing battalion and ship's company not on night watches. Shortly after midnight, call to battle stations roused out all Navy sleepers. MacDougall found him-
339

self in the chartroom alternately rubbing his eyes and tying his shoes while at the same time peering over Stanowski's shoulder into the air-search radar screen.

"What you got there?" he asked.

"Bogey and a friendly—friendly right on bogey's tail. This won't last long, sir. We'll soon be back in the sack."

MacDougall got shoes and eyes attended to and concentrated fully on the radar screen. Then he said, "Must be two friendlies, Stan. Sure that one ahead doesn't show friendly?"

"Oh, yes, sir. I checked them both before they closed."

"Could be something wrong with his IFF signal?"

"I don't think so," said the radarman. "You know those radar night fighters they have on night patrol—?"

"Sure, but if he's on his tail, why doesn't he shoot?"

"Oh, they've got to ask permission, sir. We've been listening."

As the usual clatter incident to manning battle stations died away, the sound of an anxious voice came from the TBS speaker: "Base Tizzy, Base Tizzy, this is Black Five. Good contact on bandit at two hundred yards. Request permission to splash. Over."

Stanowski pointed out the two nearly merged pips on his air-search screen. "See, sir. There they are. Old Black Cat's got on that snooper's tail at last. Boy, will we be glad to see the last of him!"

MacDougall held up a hand for silence as another voice came through the TBS crackle: "Black Five: this is Base Tizzy. Do not splash; repeat, do not splash. Our screen clear. Your bogey must be friendly; do not splash."

Then came the pilot's exasperated voice: "Black Five to Base Tizzy: Bogey is not friendly: Bogey is 'Zeke' float snooper, identified visually. I have him in my gunsights at one hundred yards. Request permission to fire. Request permission to fire."

"Base Tizzy to Black Five: Our screen clear over base. Do not splash. Do not splash. Vector three-zero-zero, thirty miles; investigate bogey there. Over and out."

The chartroom door crashed back against the bulkhead and Captain Hawks burst through the doorway, his helmet strap swinging violently from side to side. "Did you hear that idiot, MacDougall? These shore-base people never know what the score is. The pilot saw a float plane, identified him visually and had him in his sights at a hundred yards. That's the snooper we've had around here every night. They'd never chase me away from a spot like that. I'd splash the little yellow belly— then they could ask me all the questions they liked." Hawks brushed his way past others in the chartroom and looked over Stanowski's shoulder. "What do you have here?" he demanded.

"Bogey, sir: that's him right there. Range seven miles, bearing two-two-five, closing very slowly. That's our night fighter there, sir, he's opening on the snooper and vectoring after that other contact."

"What contact?"

"The one shore base was talking about, sir. There he is: you can just barely make him out at thirty-seven miles—must be flying low over the water. I can't understand, Captain, why—"

Hawks jerked erect and said to MacDougall, "We'll stay at battle stations. That snooper may get bold now and come within range." Then Hawks shoved his way out into the passage, where he collided with a messenger carrying a huge pot of coffee to the bridge. "What are you doing away from battle stations?" Hawks demanded. Then, before the startled youngster could answer: "What you got there—coffee?"

"Yes, sir."

"Is it hot?"

"Yes, sir."

"Well, give me some. Where's a cup?" Hawks took the mug of steaming coffee and went out to the wing of the bridge where Jim Randall was scanning the starlit sky with his binoculars. "See anything?"

"No, Captain. Guns One and Two are tracking with radar."

"Very good." Hawks stepped under the intercom speaker and called in: "Radar, keep me informed on that snooper."

"Radar, aye. He's closing slowly, bearing . . ."

Suddenly *Belinda's* gun crews were electrified by a sight new and amazing to them. From a dozen spots about the land-locked harbor, and from two small islands near the anchorage, sharp searchlight beams stabbed into night sky. At first they crossed and recrossed each other like so many gigantic straws, then they settled into a pinpoint and stayed there, tracking together. At the point of intersection there seemed to be a small round nub of reflected light. Hawks trained his binoculars on the spot, took a careful look, then shouted, "There he is! They've got him caught in the lights. There's our snooper! Come on, little yellow boy; just keep coming and I'll take care of you."

Word from the flagship, the first since battle stations were called: "ARISTOCRACY to PLEBS: Flash Red, Control Green. Firing at present angle will endanger own side."

"Oh, brother!" groaned Hawks. "Shore base sends away the night fighter; now the OTC won't let us shoot!"

Similar orders had not been given to the shore batteries, whose flak shook the anchorage with concussion or rapid fire as they laid a carpet of bursting shells under the snooper. Their fire fell short; high above the bursts, the snooper moved slowly and deliberately across the anchorage. "Good," said Hawks.

"They can't reach him. If he keeps on three miles more like this, he'll be ours." Hawks looked around the ship and anchorage. Ebb tide held the *Belinda's* stern out towards sea; her bow pointed inland and away from other ships. Then he sent orders to control: "Keep tracking target with your five-inch guns. Watch your windage settings. Stand by for instantaneous action if I order you to fire one or both guns."

The snooper was almost directly overhead now. Shore batteries had ceased fire; the snooper seemed supported at ten thousand feet by angled shafts of searchlight. Hawks could plainly see that it was a single-engine fighter type with one large pontoon: Zero converted into float plane for observation work —a type which could be dragged under the coconut trees and easily hidden by day. "That's the little boy who's been keeping us awake," said Hawks conversationally to the shadows of his bridge. "He thinks he's safe now, but in just a minute more they'll be giving us permission to fire." Hawks pulled on a phone set and handed the cord to his talker to plug in so that he could speak directly with the gunnery officer at control. Passing steadily over the *Belinda*, the snooper continued on an easterly course which brought him somewhat on the *Belinda's* port bow, all clear but at a very high position angle. Hawks spoke sharply into his phones: "Control, stand by for orders." Thirty seconds of silence followed while every man on *Belinda's* weather decks stared open-mouthed at the Japanese snooper. There was something mothlike about his appearance as he moved in the bright pinpoint of converged searchlight beams. He seemed to have cast a spell over the Sansapor anchorage: rounding it just out of range for seven sleepless nights, entering it now just above range of shoreside antiaircraft. Watching him, there seemed no reason to believe that any gun could reach him; he lived a charmed life so that sailors might not sleep.

Then from the TBS came first words of an order to all ships at anchor. Anticipating their content, Hawks shouted, "Gun One, commence fire!" Instantly, Gun One cracked out three rapid shots: three red-hot shells reaching skyward. Before the second and third shells had time to reach the target, a bright flash paled all searchlight. A few seconds later, sounds of a tremendous explosion came down from the sky. Still lighted by searchlights, the blazing snooper began his fluttering descent. Too late, guns from the rest of the squadron barked out, then stopped abruptly. The Jap was falling faster now, bits of wings skittered out like flaming autumn leaves. After a moment of awed silence, the *Belinda's* crew broke into tumultuous cheering.

Above this shouting, one clear voice exclaimed loudly, "One shot! Boy, oh boy! . . . One shot: one Jap!" After a pause, the same sailor added with exaggerated self-commiseration, "Them other two shots was wasted!"

Hawks stood silent, watching intently, feasting his eyes on flaming wreckage. Leaking gasoline mixed with oxygen encountered during the fall increased the intensity of fire. A long tail of flame seemed to remain motionless in the sky while the brighter head of burning aircraft rushed cometlike to water beneath. With a sound of roaring flames it splashed into the anchorage a hundred yards from the *Belinda* and lighted the water in a flaming pool of gasoline. The comet-like tail was gone. The float kept the wreckage above water while gasoline from fuel tanks fed this fantastic bonfire.

Randall stepped up beside Hawks. "Shall I lower a boat, sir?"

Hawks did not turn his head from watching the fire. "No," he said at last. "There will be no survivors." He felt impersonal about the snooper now. One shot: one Jap! Remembering thousands of futile rounds fired by *Belinda's* guns at other times, he felt a warm glowing sensation within. The tightly wound spring he carried in his breast eased a turn or two as he thought: you always pay your penny and wait for the monkey; only once in a long while you get your chocolate.

CHAPTER 38

Hunched over the wing of his bridge, Captain Hawks watched the flaming wreckage of three sinking Japanese men-of-war. Nothing else remained of the handful of Japanese cruisers and destroyers which had sailed out past Corregidor to challenge the great invading armada as it steamed toward Lingayen Gulf. Excitement, which had flared up so suddenly in the night, was dying with the flames—even the TBS was quiet. American cruisers and destroyers released from rigid formation had boiled across his bow to close with the enemy and take him under accurate, radar-directed fire. For ten minutes it was a two-way fight: flat trajectory of red hot shells exchanged. Then one by one the Japanese cruisers were straddled, hit and set ablaze. Flames mounted; their gunfire weakened and lost accuracy; now they were sinking infernos, helpless and doomed. MacDougall stood at the pelorus, coaching radar plot on the burning targets. One by one the fires went out until the horizon was black again. Hawks lowered his binoculars and climbed back into his high seat. He looked at the luminous face of his strap watch; the entire action had taken less than fifteen minutes, during which the invasion fleet had kept on without the slightest pause or deviation from course.

Hawks leaned back in his seat and closed his eyes. This was the night of 7 January 1945; his ship had been underway for a week as a unit of the great invading parade through the Philippines, passing island after island still held by the Japanese. Lost in reflection, he saw a continuous picture moving slowly across the soft emptiness of night: a river of ships flowing with equal deliberation in dazzling sunshine and in pitch black of squally night. There had been sorties from many ports, a few ships here, a group there. At no particular staging area had ever-watchful Japanese snoopers found warning of large-scale invasion. The *Belinda* had left lonely Sansapor in a group of fifty-six ships: attack transports, cruisers, jeep carriers and screening destroyers. Hawks could look back in the darkness through time and space, remembering what he had seen through his binoculars by day and in the radar screen by night: impressions burned into his senses until, though he knew each unit by number and commander, they seemed more like so many logs floating down river. Groups joined and flowed on together across the southwest corner of the Pacific to the Philippines. Fully united in the greatest task force of Pacific history, twelve hundred ships of all types poured into Surigao Strait, carrying the Army towards Manila by way of the same Lingayen landing beaches used by invading Japanese in December 1941.

As if from a distance, Hawks heard all the normal sounds of his ship's bridge while underway. At the slightest variation from a normal pattern of sound he would come jumping out of his chair, wide awake and ready to take active control. Now that he was free to rest he wished that he could blank out the pictures flowing before his eyes. It made absolutely no difference whether he opened or closed them to the warm darkness; he had tried that. It was like the experience of a drunkard trying to steady a room whirling madly around him by alternately opening and shutting his eyes—it was no use, he must watch to the end; it was stamped into his brain, into his being. Fleet speed of advance was maddeningly slow. He chafed at this ridiculous eight knots made necessary since the joining on astern of a huge appendage of LSTs and LCIs. He longed to order full speed and get on to the waiting beachhead at Lingayen, but the armada plowed stolidly ahead with radar antennae sweeping the sky. Each group of ships was preceded by a fan of protecting destroyers which probed waters beneath and at first sign of danger closed in protectingly. Whether attacked or not, by day and by night this procession moved steadily onward. Hawks felt them about him—from miles astern they seemed to pass right through his ship, across his radar screen, through his eyeballs to project into darkness ahead, steaming four abreast; there was no possible escape from their relentless crawl.

Hawks rubbed his eyes, eased the chafing binocular strap

from the raw, sunburned spot at the back of his neck and remembered the enemy. The Japanese knew perfectly well what was up: they held all the land which the fleet passed close aboard, day after day. This meant invasion on grand scale and they threw everything possible against it. The operation was a gamble that protection of naval guns, of destroyers and carrier-based planes would enable the fleet to continue to the inevitable beachhead.

Hawks got down from his chair and went into the chartroom to have another look at the radar screen. There it was again: long line of ants crawling along the Pacific shore of Bataan. He went to the chart: there was MacDougall's careful plot of the long winding track ahead and astern. He went out again into the dark of the bridge, waiting until the silhouettes of nearby ships showed with the return of night vision. He felt the ceaseless throbbing of engines at half throttle. Hawks looked about the bridge.

"MacDougall," he called.

"Right here, Capt'n."

"Sit in my chair and look out for her. Keep an eye on Fauré. I'm going to turn in my cot—be sure to call me if there's anything at all."

"Aye, aye, sir."

Hawks removed his shoes, swung up to the chest-high cot and pulled the light blanket over him. Happily chattering, Chipchee dropped out of the shadows and landed on the cot. Hawks pushed the monkey gently away from his feet and closed his eyes. It was no good: the picture was there before his eyes again; wherever he turned, opening or shutting his eyes he saw the slow panorama of countless ships. He remembered the Jap planes. Gone now, back to base or into the sea; some, after crashing, had burned with their victims in the superstructures of ships near the *Belinda*. One had scorched past his bridge close enough to be hit with a heaving line. Their images still tormented him. Hawks poked around with a foot until he found Chipchee, then sat up on the cot and stroked the monkey between the ears while it chattered contentedly. Gradually cold reason cleared his mind. Then he drew the blanket up again and fell into quiet sleep.

MacDougall sat in Hawks's high seat, drinking a cup of over-brewed coffee. A low bank of strato-cumulus formed a barrier between Jap-held Bataan Peninsula and the invading fleet. Except for this solid wall to starboard, the sky was clear. Starlight shimmered and danced on the mirrored surface among black silhouettes of darkened ships steaming northward. MacDougall finished his coffee and placed the mug in Hawks's dispatch box, then leaned back in the seat and looked out again into the clear night. Following the line of the next column he could make out as far as five ships ahead. The rest were swallowed up by night and distance, yet he knew that the *Belinda* was near the middle of a line of ships four abreast and eighty-nine miles long. It seemed incredible, but he had measured it by radar.

Minutes ticked into hours while the ships forged slowly and steadily into darkness and silence ahead. A deceiving feeling of peace and security lulled his watchfulness. The submarine attacks off Cebu, the air attacks all along the route seemed remote, things met with and overcome—just entries in the logbook now. Sitting erect again, he stretched and yawned, then stirred about in the seat, listening to all the sounds, peering at nearest ships on all sides. It was then that he first heard a foreign sound: a quiet, distant clatter which was no part of the *Belinda* or her crew. MacDougall tilted his ear to listen, alert, awake, somehow uneasy. Could it be an approaching plane, it sounded . . . Say! It could be a Jap! He vaulted out of the high seat calling out, "Possible bogey, Fauré; I can hear it. Alert control and radar. . . . Call the captain." There was no need to sound the general alarm; the crew was at battle stations, half the men alert. Guns were loaded and ready, but one had to be very careful about popping off in the middle of the fleet; after all he might be wrong—it could be one of the night patrol. The plane approached steadily yet unhurriedly. The sound of it, growing louder, was unlike any American engine he had ever heard. A voice from the TBS now confirmed the plane as Japanese, yet cautioned ships not to fire unless directly attacked.

Moments later *Belinda's* gun crews saw a dim shape crossing close astern about a hundred feet above water, and Captain Hawks appeared, asking, "Where's he now, MacDougall?"

"Flying low off the port quarter, Captain; position angle about ten—no chance to shoot without hitting our own ships. . . . You can still hear him."

Hawks strode to the bridge wing and looked out. He saw only vague silhouettes of other ships, no sign of the strange aircraft; but he heard its peculiar clatter, not a Zero, but Japanese. "Kamikaze," he said. "Keep on him with radar; he may bank around and head for us."

"Aye, aye, sir," answered MacDougall, nearly adding: *some poor little lost Jap looking for a place to crash*. He kept the thought to himself; Hawks didn't like whimsy. It seemed unlikely to MacDougall that the Jap would swing around and crash into the *Belinda*. Pondering this, he thought that perhaps the preceding hour of quiet calm had given him a false sense of security. Some ship was due for trouble: the Jap must have sighted the fleet.

Voice of the radarman over the intercom: "Bridge: Radar. Bogey now turned and closing in, four thousand yards astern."

Hawks and MacDougall looked aft along the shadowy line of ships astern. They heard a sudden burst of naval gunfire climaxed by a loud explosion and the brilliant flash of burning gasoline. Over the TBS an excited young voice reported serious damage to an LST. The lost Jap had found a place to roost.

The following noon MacDougall was preparing his position report when Flynn stuck his head into the chartroom. "Come on, Mac," he said. "You're missing the minstrel show."

MacDougall made a face. "You mean that racket . . . ? I like it nice and quiet."

"You really should come look see," said Flynn. "I came up to answer some questions about the binnacle list: the Old Man wants all the lame and lazy cleared out of the sick bay before D Day, all set for casualties. I waited out by his chair for nearly five minutes but he doesn't even know I'm around."

MacDougall followed Flynn to the bridge wing. Hawks sat in his high seat playing loud skirls on his ocarina while Chipchee shifted nervously from shoulder to shoulder. Three short Mexicans from the second division stood beside the engine room annunciator, grinning with friendly pleasure. One of them held a guitar and the other two were tuning up odd-looking banjos. They had come to the ship recently in a new draft of recruits; this was the first time they had been on the bridge or within speaking distance of their captain. MacDougall liked them personally and censored their colorful letters with a tolerance which would have shocked the junior officers; they were good workers at ship's routine back in the second division, but they did not belong here on the bridge. The monkey and the sweet potato were bad enough.

Captain Hawks was enjoying himself; he played the chorus of "Red Sails in the Sunset" once more for the benefit of this, the first truly appreciative audience he had had on his bridge. The bridge crew kept straight enough faces and then went around the corner to laugh. Sensing this, Hawks blew a squeal of contempt for any smirkers around corners, then put the ocarina in his pocket and coaxed Chipchee onto his lap. He gave the three Mexicans an affirmative nod: down and up again as if to say, *That'll show 'em!*

"There," he said. "How did you like that?"

"Bueno. Bueno, Capitán."

"Very good. Now it's your turn. Play 'Red Sails' for me; sing it, all of you."

The Mexicans looked puzzled. After a pause during which all three grinned at Hawks in polite incomprehension, one of them stepped forward.

"We do not have American words, 'Red Sails,' Capitán."

347

"Sing it in Spanish."

"Not have Spanish words, Mexican words, any kind words this 'Red Sails,' Capitán."

Hawks stroked Chipchee thoughtfully. "You there with the guitar; come here!"

The man stared at Hawks, his soft, dark eyes filled with wonderment. The Mexican who had spoken to Hawks poured out a voluminous explanation in his native tongue. The man with the guitar nodded in understanding and stepped forward, grinning afresh and removing his dirty white hat.

"You play 'Red Sails,'" said Hawks. "I'll sing it."

Flynn walked around the corner of the pilothouse, past a smirking group of the bridge watch, and looked over towards the transport closest abeam. Her ensign was at half-mast; she was having sea burial for twenty-two men killed by a kamikaze the day before. Flynn thought, I wonder what we'll have down in the sick bay this time tomorrow. Then he walked back to wait for a chance to give his report. The three Mexicans were relaxed and at ease now, playing and singing one of the innumerable variations of *La Cucaracha*:

> *El Capitán se pasa plata:*
> *Marinero mucho rico . . .*

At three in the morning on *D Day*, amid almost overpowering noise, Hawks, MacDougall and Randall worked to keep the *Belinda* moving in precise station with her squadron, yet ready to break away on order and rush to the exact spot assigned to her by the operation plan for debarkation. From minute to minute, by PA loudspeakers, by phones and by messengers, they set into motion the various complicated details of debarkation. Meanwhile they strained to recognize orders intended for the *Belinda* among the constant stream of coded gobbledegook now pouring from the TBS. In the darkness ahead, the bombardment group of battleships, cruisers, destroyers and rocket-throwing LCIs stretched along seven miles of shore while they poured a flood of high explosive into the marshy beachhead area. At the same time they fired their antiaircraft batteries skyward, trying to protect themselves from the most determined Jap air attack yet experienced. Standing on his bridge, Hawks looked all about him, sizing up the situation and wondering exactly where he was with reference to his assigned debarkation spot. The plans and diagrams he knew by heart; this was the real thing, gigantic and confusing even to a man with his training and experience. Land was near at hand on three sides, but hidden from sight by darkness and smoke. Silhouettes of countless ships appeared and disappeared, now lighted by the flashes of ten thousand muzzle blasts, now obscured by drifting smoke or lost once more in

348

the night. He saw wave after wave of Jap dive bombers and suicide planes diving and weaving into the vortex of tracer bullets, some to rise again miraculously safe, others to drop all the way like great flaming torches which were only slowly extinguished as they sank in the gulf. Some of the ships were burning too. It was a crazy world, Hawks thought, impossible but true, in which it was his duty to keep order within his own command. At any moment this flaming tide might sweep over the *Belinda* as well as these others now burning. His jaw set at the thought; the *Belinda* would continue on, no matter what—even in a screaming nightmare of flames he would have to comply with every directive so unemotionally assigned to him in that stack of operations plans locked in his cabin safe. As details of what he must carry out with his ship flicked through his consciousness his ship moved steadily toward flames and thunder. His scalp tingled; his mouth was dry. The loose skin at the back of his neck grew tighter, like a shirt wrung out by hand. Of all his senses, only that of smell liked this hour. His nostrils quivered with the exciting smell of burned powder: like pepper on flat-tasting food, it had the effect of sharpening all other sensibilities so that together with fear and anxiety were mixed the thrill of dangers all about, impending but not yet specifically threatening him.

Hawks turned the *Belinda* this way and that, slowed down and then speeded up in compliance with the staccato of TBS orders from the flagship. It must be nearly time to proceed independently—Hawks called to Randall, "Get MacDougall on the squawk box; get course and distance to station in Area Able. . . . Oh, there you are, MacDougall. Where are we now? Are you all set up to proceed independently?"

"I'm having trouble, Capt'n: lost Bolinao astern . . . the only high land. This beach ahead is nothing but a swampy delta of river mouths, too low to show on the screen yet. The hills behind the beach show, but nothing definite; I'm getting a contour of hills instead of the beach line. Screen looks like two beaches: the hills and that mass of bombardment ships all melted together on the scope."

"Listen, Mr. Navigator, I don't want excuses; I want answers, accurate answers right now."

"I'll do the best I can, Capt'n. I can give you a general course and distance; then before we get there the beach will show on the screen and I can do accurate work."

Hawks turned briefly from watching the horizon and fixed MacDougall with a glare. "I said I didn't want excuses. I want answers. Go get me answers."

"Aye, aye, sir," said MacDougall, just a shade of surliness in his tone. He thrust his way through the crowded bridge to his chartroom, muttering, "Answers, answers." Chipchee was perched on the chart hopping nervously about and smudging carefully drawn boat lanes with his dirty feet. MacDougall lifted him off the chart and made a face at him; then noticing the little animal's fear and confusion, he scratched him between the ears and went back to Stanowski and the radar screen. Three minutes later he flicked the intercom switch and called, "Capt'n, I've got the beach now, eight thousand yards ahead. Course to our debarkation station is one-nine-three, distance, twenty-three hundred yards."

Moments later orders came to proceed independently. Mac-Dougall coached Hawks through the smoke-enveloped mass of shipping, working carefully between little pips on the radar screen which Hawks saw as fire-blackened cruisers with smoke-stacks bashed and bent like crooked fingers. At last MacDougall dropped his pencil on the chart and called into the intercom, "On station, Capt'n—right on the button!"

Then engines shuddered astern and the boatswain's mate's pipe blasted from PA speakers with Hawks's order, "Away all boats, away!"

Captain Hawks mopped at his face with a sweat-soaked handkerchief and looked at his watch. It was fourteen hundred, eight and one-half hours after the landing of the first wave. With the exception of the Army working party, his ship was clear of all troops and three quarters unloaded. *Belinda's* boats shuttled busily between ship and shore, landing ammunition, gasoline, drinking water and provisions on the black sand. The landing had gone off well—no coral heads here and the bombardment had been exceptionally thorough. Infantrymen were now well beyond the beach, working inland beyond the nipa villages of the swampy Lingayen delta. From the sounds of increasing artillery, they must be finding the main Jap positions.

In a practical departure from the rigid geography of operation plans, transports and bombarding ships now crowded together, close to shore. While a new flurry of Navy call fire broke out all around the *Belinda*, the old battleship *California* cut across her bow and anchored, too close for comfort.

"How far off is she, MacDougall?" Hawks asked.

"Three-hundred-ten yards, sir. She's bringing up now, won't get much closer."

While Hawks watched, the old battleship's stern swung past his bridge with deliberate dignity. Then he went over to the starboard wing of the bridge to watch a crippled destroyer which was coming alongside the *Belinda* to fuel. MacDougall stayed on the port wing watching the *California's* stern. Undoubtedly the old battleship had her hook barely on the bottom so that she could get under way immediately in an emergency. It seemed to MacDougall that she was setting down on the

Belinda, and as she was too close to measure by radar, he called for a stadimeter. While he watched, a gun spotter walked out on the *California's* number two turret top carrying a camp stool. He sat down on the camp stool and trained his binoculars carefully ashore. Soon a secondary battery began to fire carefully towards the hills beyond the left flank of the landing beaches. MacDougall's attention was directed towards the silhouette of these hills; he was not concerned with the spotter's ground target but with the possibility of low-flying Japanese planes which might approach undetected by radar, then burst from cover and swoop down upon the anchorage. Things were too quiet: the landing had gone off without a hitch and Japanese surface craft were pretty well accounted for. Danger here was from the air. It was easy to be lulled into drowsiness by tropic heat and the atmosphere of success. In spite of intermittent call fire and the rapid cracking of distant artillery it seemed peaceful in the anchorage, yet MacDougall had only to look about him to see what the Japs could do from the air.

On the opposite wing of the bridge, Captain Hawks sucked on a toothpick while he looked over the destroyer now coming alongside the *Belinda* to take on fuel. Her bridge was gone; it just wasn't there at all. There were no smokestacks, no after conning station; the kamikaze had sheared off her topsides in a second or two, as neatly as a gang of wreckers with cutting tools could have done in a week. Incongruously enough, a gyro compass repeater remained at the end of some twisted wiring and Hawks could see that it was still functioning. There was also a portion of brass speaking tube, evidently leading somewhere, for a young lieutenant was using it to maneuver the crippled destroyer alongside the *Belinda*.

"Where's your commanding officer?" Hawks asked.

The lieutenant looked up to the *Belinda's* bridge. "I'm the commanding officer," he said in a dull, matter-of-fact voice without a sign of either pride or self-consciousness. "I was first lieutenant until this morning."

"I see," said Hawks. Irritation swept through him: this youngster, so coolly in command—and the object lesson of what one Jap plane could do just as easily to the *Belinda*. He looked two decks below where a fueling hose was being passed from the *Belinda* to the destroyer. There was considerable bustle, then the hose hung slack. Hawks looked at number three hatch, which was blocked off by the destroyer's bow, then noticed a 105-mm howitzer waiting in the slings while Pappy Moran urged his men at shifting cargo tackle to the other side. Hawks looked back at the fueling station; still delay down there. Rinaldo, the chief shipfitter, who had been working with the fuel hose, was sitting on the rail, looking at the damaged destroyer.

"Rinaldo," yelled Hawks, "come here!" When Rinaldo reported, Hawks asked, "What's the delay on that hose?"

"The oil king is hunting up a new fitting, sir."

"You should have had a spare fitting handy."

"It was the destroyer's fitting, Capt'n."

"What difference does that make? You should have been prepared for that too. Now get back there; get the fuel into that can and get her away! I want to finish unloading before sunset."

"Aye, aye, sir," said Rinaldo easily and ran down the ladder. There was nothing in Rinaldo's manner to give Hawks the slightest hint of his feelings. He was an old Navy man who knew when to keep his mouth shut. When he reached the lower deck he spat over the side. Fueling a destroyer was not a shipfitter's job; he had just been helping out. Rinaldo thought, when I was building those new gun platforms I was the fair-haired boy. Ever since he gave me the job of making all that fancy ironwork for that sailboat, he's been snapping my head off. Give me the men and materials and I can build a ship, but I couldn't make him a brass mermaid for a figurehead—he's never gotten over that. Some of the black gang were hurrying up the deck with another fitting. Rinaldo spat again, carefully this time so that the spit drifted midway between the two gray-painted hulls; then he gave them a hand with the fuel connection.

Satisfied that the *California* was not drifting down, MacDougall headed for the chartroom to eat a long-delayed plate of lunch. It would be cold, he knew, but better late than never; he had not eaten since three in the morning.

The captain's monkey had beaten him to the lunch. Gravy, mashed potatoes, excrement and spilled coffee were smeared all over the carefully prepared chart of the landing area. MacDougall swore. Hearing an answering chatter, he looked up above the chart table. Chipchee was perched on a conduit a few inches below the overhead. He spat out a chunk of gravy-soaked bread and leered at the navigator. MacDougall felt the blood rushing to his head; anything but this. The chart had taken hours to prepare and there was no other on board. He scrambled up on the chart table, lunged for the monkey and missed. Chipchee screamed insanely, jumping about on the conduit, just out of reach. At last MacDougall cornered the monkey, grabbed him by the tail and flung him out the chartroom door. Panting for breath, vexed yet ashamed of what he had done to Chipchee, MacDougall walked to the port bridge rail to collect himself. He watched Boat Seven return from the beach and come alongside for refueling. When the two-inch hose snaked out from the *Belinda,* MacDougall noticed that the boat's coxswain got hold of the end and stuck it in the fuel tank. Riley, the craft's motormac, who was responsible for the job, was sound asleep on the engine box. Still wearing his kapok life jacket, he used those of his two boatmates for a pillow. MacDougall grunted, "There's Sacktime Riley, flaked out as usual." Smith, the coxswain, was a clean-cut, intelligent youngster. MacDougall had recently picked him out for one of the three condition watch bridge talkers. MacDougall waved to Smith, then returned to the chart table, where he found Willicut cleaning up what he could of the mess. The quartermaster was grinning from ear to ear and whistling "La Cucaracha." The chart was a permanent ruin; they would have to make it do somehow. "You'd better dry it in the sun, Willicut," he said.

After Willicut had gone, MacDougall stood in the chart-room door looking out. He sagged against the door frame, his mind momentarily vacant except for his resentment of the lost lunch and ruined chart. The sun beat full into his face and he relaxed in its radiation. Then he heard an unfamiliar sound, a strange engine. Three seconds later the hum had deepened into a roar. Frozen there, MacDougall stared into the dazzling sky but saw nothing except the sun. It was a Jap, he realized—diving out of the sun. It had to be but he couldn't see a thing. Dive bomber—that open hatch: gasoline! In another second the roar overwhelmed all other sound and pressed into his brain. Then the *Belinda* rocked as if slapped by a giant hand, followed rapidly by the sound of a tremendous explosion. MacDougall saw a geyser of water shoot up alongside, mast-head high. Then, right over Gun Two, he saw the plane, a twin-engine Mitsubishi bomber with the red meat ball on each wing, sitting on its tail and climbing away out of there with her unsynchronized engines roaring wide open. Now the crew of Gun Two opened fire on the escaping plane. A few seconds later the *California's* antiaircraft batteries blackened the sky with rapid fire, as if to make up for having been caught napping by a single plane. The Mitsubishi continued his weaving climb and soon disappeared over the hills. The firing stopped and Art Hall, the gunnery officer, came on the run from control.

"He caught us flat!" Hall exclaimed excitedly to MacDougall. "First thing I knew was the bomb. It's almost impossible to hit a fast plane running away. . . . Golly! One second earlier on dropping that thing and he'd have hit the *California;* one second later he'd have dropped it right down number five hatch into that gasoline—hatch wide open like that, he durn near splashed salt water into it! Was his timing ever perfect . . . for us!"

Suddenly MacDougall remembered Boat Seven. He jumped to the rail and looked down. The boat was gone; only bits of wreckage floated about, none of them larger than an opened newspaper. In the midst of the wreckage a single head bobbed around, supported by a life jacket. As MacDougall opened his mouth to call out the standby boat, it shot around the stern and closed in on the flotsam. Out of the water they pulled a limp figure. One of the men in the boat shouted, "It's Sacktime Riley. He's passed out cold."

"Where's Smith and the deckhand? See anybody else down there?"

"No, sir. No sign of them."

"Bring Riley around to the quarterdeck, then get back there fast and keep looking for the other two. Look under the surface and work aft with the tide; keep looking around that wreckage as it drifts—there's just a chance . . ."

Captain Hawks appeared. He seemed very calm; ordered a thorough inspection of the *Belinda's* hull for damage from the near miss. Word soon came from sick bay that Riley was unhurt except for shock. MacDougall was waiting for Hawks to ask why the *Belinda's* radar had failed to pick up the bogey. She was assigned to a different search sector than the one from which the Mitsubishi had appeared, but Hawks would be unlikely to accept that as sufficient excuse for not keeping an all around watch in a place like this. Hawks, however, seemed to have something else on his mind; he walked restlessly about the bridge deck, poking into lockers and peering into portholes, but had nothing further of importance to say to anyone.

When the bomb exploded, Chipchee was stealing food in the wardroom pantry. Frightened, he ran into the wardroom, jumped upon a table and from there sprang aloft and clung to the wire guard of a large electric fan which was fastened to the bulkhead. It was here that Jackson found him. Noticing that the monkey's tail lay foul across the fan blades, Jackson started the fan. The monkey screeched with pain and dashed into Quigley's stateroom, which adjoined the wardroom. Jackson hurried from the wardroom to investigate the explosion. It seemed to him that the whole ship had shaken as if struck by an earthquake shock. He had stopped to tease the monkey almost automatically; only after Chipchee had run out screaming with pain did the explosion register in his mind. It was such an odd sensation; something new to him. At the wardroom door he saw Quigley angrily kicking the monkey out of his stateroom. Chipchee emitted sharp cries and ran across the passageway to starboard.

"The dirty little devil!" Quigley exclaimed. "Look at my room: the bunk, my clean linen, the wash basin covered with his dirty paw marks! I don't see why the Old Man puts up with him. What has happened out there!"

When the bomb exploded, Rinaldo ran across the ship to the port side in time to see the last of the salt-water geyser splash back to the surface. He was the one who called out first for the rescue boat. When they had picked up Riley he went back to starboard to see if the fuel line to the destroyer was undamaged, and found the six-inch hose still throbbing regularly with a steady flow. Just then some oil bubbled out of a gooseneck vent and spread over the deck: they must be gravitating down below, getting a little nervous about bombs. Rinaldo decided that he had better go down to damage control; they'd be sure to check the ship for damage now. He leaned down to see if any more oil was overflowing from the gooseneck vent. At that moment a small, dirty ball of fur dashed out of the officers' quarters, skidded in the oil, brought up hard against his face, then regaining balance, streaked down the passageway and out of sight. Rinaldo straightened up, cursing the captain's monkey, while he dabbed at the fuel oil now streaked all over his face and shirt.

"Dirty little kamikaze," he muttered. "It's a good thing he hasn't got wings."

Captain Hawks could not find Chipchee. At first realization of the absence of his monkey lay nearly dormant in the back of his mind, disturbing, but not clearly felt. When Fraser, the first lieutenant, made his damage report—two buckled plates, a sprung bulkhead and sundry leaks in fire and steam lines— Hawks ordered immediate repairs to be made. Fraser reported that Chief Rinaldo was already at work with his shipfitters, and continued to give Hawks a solemn recital of steps taken to assure quick action in case of further damage or fire. Satisfied, Hawks told Fraser to carry on. Accustomed to being cross examined on fine points, Fraser was astonished at the captain's complacency. When Dan Hill, the debarkation officer, jubilantly reported the ship unloaded, Hawks merely nodded. MacDougall looked sharply at Hawks. What could be eating the man? The *Belinda* had beat the division again and not a word out of him. Then Hawks called Biggs, his orderly. "Go look for Chipchee and bring him to me."

An hour later, Biggs returned without Chipchee. The anchorage was under mass air attack and Hawks was maneuvering the *Belinda* evasively amid a constant roar of antiaircraft fire. He passed the conn to MacDougall and turned sharply upon the stocky Biggs. "I want my monkey. Go find him; don't come back until you do."

The situation was confused: some ships were unloaded, others not; some continued to attempt unloading priority tanks while the disposition was under fire, while others cast off all landing craft and performed evasive maneuvers together with the ships already unloaded. Some of the bombardment ships continued to give call fire, others concentrated on the Jap planes, arriving singly and in pairs from almost every conceivable direction and altitude. No definite orders came from higher authority. The landing had been orderly and most successful, yet now, at D Day's end, the hundreds of ships which had marched into the gulf so precisely, seemed to mill about without plan or co-ordination. This indecision added to the strain and weariness so evident about the *Belinda's* bridge, where Hawks failed to bring his usual air of incisiveness to every bewildering situation. Officers and men on duty there seemed unsettled by this unusual lack of concern or even interest in what was going on. This evening he slumped against the splinter shield, staring into the void ahead and apparently lost in contemplation. Whenever it was absolutely necessary for him to do so, Hawks lifted his head and gave the proper order in a clear but uninspired monotone, then retreated within himself once more. The *Belinda* seemed to be steaming about without command: it was an odd feeling, MacDougall thought, in which the smoke and mist of overcast twilight seemed an integral part. Voices in authority discussed the disposition of destroyers for antiaircraft or anti-submarine deployment and the uncomfortable situation of unloaded transports —whether the use of boats belonging to unloaded transports warranted their remaining in the gulf any longer. Snatches of the voice of old Commodore Towne could be heard suggesting that these ships form up together and steam from the gulf until a decision could be reached. More gobbledegook, but no intelligible decision from key admirals concerning this or anything else which concerned the *Belinda*. During this phase, she groped through a maze of shipping: anchored, drifting and underway. Shortly after midnight the *Belinda* rounded Cape Bolinao at the entrance to Lingayen Gulf. As her bow rose and fell to the cadence of South China Sea swells, the men on her bridge began to relax. Some enlisted men clustered together in the shadows, chaffing and kidding each other. Holding a long-delayed cup of coffee, MacDougall walked out to the bridge wing, where he stumbled over the short figure of Biggs.

"Did you find the monk?"

"No, sir. I looked everywhere."

"What did the Old Man say?"

"Nothing; I haven't reported. I don't know what to say. He told me not to come back without the monkey."

MacDougall placed a hand on Biggs's shoulder. "I guess you're in for a rough deal," he said. "You know, Biggs, sometimes when I've been beating my brains out on this bridge, I've envied you, leaning against the bulkhead. But I wouldn't swap places with you now."

Hawks stared ahead from the opposite wing of the bridge. The squadron was not yet formed up, nor his monkey found.

Something would have to be done about both. Right now he might as well get a little sleep.

The next morning, Biggs got help from all hands. Hawks had the crew mustered and questioned man by man to gather together all possible information regarding the whereabouts of his monkey. Hawks usually remained aloof while Quigley received reports from department heads on the bridge, but this morning he strode up and listened to every word said. Reports on Chipchee were meager but pointed up to one thing: about a dozen men had seen the monkey just before or immediately after the Mitsubishi had dropped his bomb on Boat Seven. Nobody reported seeing him since that time.

Hawks listened in person to Quigley, MacDougall and Jackson. He sent for Chief Rinaldo and listened to his story. Then Hawks beat his right fist savagely into his open left palm. His eyes were wide awake with the alertness of a man in a fight as they stabbed into one man, then the next—searching, demanding this news he must have. He paced back and forth before the line of officers, then stopped suddenly, spun about and faced them once more. "Running, running; you all saw him running. You all sound so innocent. . . . Somebody started him running—he's never gone off like this before . . . and where did he go to? Where is he? Where is my monkey?"

A geyser of water shot up around the stern of the *Herkimer*, transport abeam in the next column of the formed-up squadron. "Submarine!" exclaimed MacDougall as the blast of a detonating torpedo reached across a thousand yards of water to the *Belinda*. Hawks spun around to watch the *Herkimer* swing out of control and drop astern. He said nothing while the TBS blared out queries, reports of damage, orders to two destroyers to drop depth charges and assist the *Herkimer*.

When the explosive patterns were completed and the roiled waters lay still once more about the disabled transport, Hawks spoke again.

"Quigley, conduct a thorough, organized search of the ship for my monkey. Open up every compartment and locker. Chipchee must be found!"

Two hours later Flynn and MacDougall climbed out of the manhole from the last of the cargo spaces they had been searching. Just to make sure, MacDougall took another turn around the steering engine room, then climbed to the fantail and joined the doctor for a short rest while the sun dried their sweat-soaked shirts.

"If that monk is still alive he's more than one jump ahead of us," said Flynn. "Can't say just why, but I have the feeling that we've seen the last of little *Macaca philippinensis*. . . . I wonder where he is."

357

"What I'm wondering," said MacDougall, "is what effect it will have on the skipper. Not good, I'll bet you. That monk seemed to keep him steady on his rocker. I really would like to see the dirty little brat again . . . think I'd even let him mess up another chart."

"Oh, I wouldn't worry too much," said Flynn. "The skipper is pretty tough; he took the teeth business very well. He'll find something else to play with. . . . Well, I've got to get back now and finish my paper work. I think I'll take Riley off the binnacle list; there's nothing wrong with him."

"It was amazing, the way he got out of that mess with hardly a scratch."

"MacDougall, you can take a fellow as relaxed as Riley and fire him out of a gun barrel without the slightest harm."

"You take him. He's been in my hair for two years: lazy, doping off every chance—while kids like Smith—"

"That's life," said Flynn. "Well, I'll leave you the little job of reporting, 'No monkey.' "

"Not me," said MacDougall. "I'm going to stay clear of the bridge for at least half an hour. Quigley can do the reporting; this time I'm going to follow Navy Regs to the letter and go up the channels."

CHAPTER 39

While unlimited torrents of rain fell without let up from an ugly sky, the dismal day wore on. By midafternoon, the first unofficial watchers for the mail boat began to reinforce quartermasters and signalmen on the bridge. A gradually increasing crowd of firemen, motor-macs, bakers and steward's mates gathered in the lee of deck houses or huddled under nested landing craft, all peering northward into shapeless murk. When Bundy, ship's bugler, blew the chow call, few responded. The crew kept a better watch for the mail boat than they ever had for Japanese periscopes or planes. A nasty chop from eastward made identification of boats in the failing light increasingly difficult. Tension mounted; would Larson never get back from Tacloban?

Gray sky darkened to black as night fell over the huge Leyte Gulf anchorage without sight of Larson's boat or any mail. The watching crowds thinned out; yet down in the mess hall over acey-ducey boards, or gathered about unofficial coffee pots in obscure crannies of the ship, they still discussed the chances for mail. Despite past experiences, until Larson should actually return emptyhanded, there was always that warm glow of hope.

Long after he had been relieved of the watch, Tommy Jones, quartermaster third, kept his binoculars trained northward from the bridge. Others of his shipmates skylarked around the binnacle or read tattered comic books. Jones did not feel like sharing this moment or his feelings with others. Cold, distant, aching loneliness after learning that there was to be no mail: that was one thing. When it was like that he seemed to bleed inside, and every mile of the seven thousand between him and his wife, Lorraine, seemed stretched into ten. But while he waited, while there was the least chance, his heart sang a happy-sad little tune and the miles seemed softened, not so long. He thought about the small white bungalow in San Diego, the neat fence he'd built around it, though as yet they had neither children nor dogs. Inside the light would glow over the kitchen sink and from far down the sidewalk he could see Lorraine's soft brown hair that glowed with lights and made her look somehow like a kid. Yes, there were things about waiting for the mail boat—even the chill of water running down inside your shirt felt good; it would warm up there while there was hope of mail.

So Jones was first to spot Larson's boat, barely visible in the squall as it rose on the crest of a whitecap, then fell from sight into the trough. He didn't know how he knew it, but that was Larson's boat: something he instinctively noted in the dim silhouette or in the particular sound of its engine, subtly different from hundreds of other boats. Nobody else had seen it and he was off watch; he would nurse to himself his glowing hope for mail. He could see the heaped load under the streaming tarp. When at last he could no longer bear the secret alone he shouted at the top of his voice, "Mail, fellows, mail! It's Larson. We got mail; mail from home! The boat's lousy with mail!" Then Jones went over to the opposite wing of the bridge where he was all alone and nobody would hear his sobbing.

Pacing restlessly in his cabin, Captain Hawks paused at the open porthole to hear the excited comments of sailors preparing to hoist in the salvage boat. Mail at last! he thought, resenting in a very personal way the Navy's complete failure to deliver his wife's letters to him. There was no excuse for this asininity; it was unreasonable and unfair. Well, here was mail at last; at the very least there would be five or six letters from Louise. He needed those letters; they steadied him like her hand on his forehead. "Biggs," he called, "go down to the mail room and stand by to bring up my letters. Tell the mail clerk to hurry."

Larson's boat was indeed loaded to the guards with fat, overstuffed mail bags. Shouting and dancing with joy, the crew nearly hauled the boat from the water by hand. Alarmed by their overeagerness, Shepherd, the mail clerk, shouted, "Easy, boys, easy. For the love of mud, take it easy! You'll drop it all in the bay!" If any had fallen, sailors would have dived overboard after it; but none did. In the miraculous manner of ants carrying their eggs from a flood, they passed the heavy load of mail over the heads of the crowd, down jammed scuttles and ladders, and within five minutes it lay in a huge, dripping pile before the mail room door. A crowd of sailors milled around the mail bags shouting and catcalling, but with that wondering look of men who were now thinking of mail in individual terms. Already mail messengers and their unauthorized helpers from every division, clamored and stormed at Shepherd for their division's mail. "Get back, you guys," he yelled in a voice hoarse from shouting and from the chill of his fifty-mile ride in a cloudburst. "If you want mail, just give me a chance. You'll have to wait too, Biggs. Even the skipper will have to wait until I get the bags open."

Pappy Moran appeared with a coil of light line, which he lashed from stanchion to stanchion enclosing both mail room and the stack of mail bags. Shepherd chose a few helpers at random, then while the crowd outside the ropes watched his every movement with extreme concentration, he began to open the bags. In rapid succession he opened a dozen of them, peered intently into each, then without comment reached for the next. Shepherd's face was white and his hands trembled, but the excitement in the place was so extreme that nobody noticed. Suddenly, and with a burst of all his energy, for he was a small man, Shepherd began to empty out bags onto the steel deck. He turned over sack after sack, tugged savagely at the bottom ears and dumped the contents into a growing pile. There were no letters. There were home town papers and magazines six months old, with pages damp, musty, stuck together, blurred, torn, insect infested. There were parcel post packages: Christmas packages three months too late—forever too late. Not one parcel retained its original shape; sodden, crushed parcels with half-obliterated addresses, alive with crawling insects from New Guinea jungles, the beaches at Guam, Kwajalein, Eniwetok, Saipan, Manus and Palau, where they had rotted while waiting for a westward-moving *Belinda* which never returned for them. Sack after sack of scattered paper puzzles, photos of loved ones crumpled, torn and smeared with the contents of broken bottles of homemade jam and melted peanut brittle. Jungle stench rose from the lot, from bits of wrapping and twine, shreds of Christmas wrappings, infested candy and spoiled preserves—all the pitiful little things that could be spared from a wartime economy, made of paper and wood, wrapped with love, half consumed by the insects of Micronesia.

A shocked hush fell over the crowd, quickly followed by muttering, bitter swearing and a few weak jokes. Shepherd bent over the stinking wreckage, salvaging what he could from the mess, calling out name and division when able to identify them, handing out the larger fragments across the ropes. Now for a time the swearing mellowed and the jokes grew less bitter as

360

packages were opened. After some time of this Shepherd straightened up with a faint smile. "Here, Doyle; here's one for you—looks in good shape."

The boatswain's mate caught a compact package and eagerly unwrapped several protecting layers of stout corrugated pasteboard. "Boy! I'm in luck: all in one piece . . . Holy cow! Spam! . . . I wonder how many red ration points my Mom give for it? She should of got her some good chewing meat." Doyle held the Spam up for all to see. "It's from home, anyway," he said. "I'll bet it tastes better than that junk we get out here." Doyle sighed. "Boy, oh boy, them steaks we used to have at home!"

Others less fortunate than Doyle held smelly messes of ruined jigsaw puzzles against their faded blue shirts; things they would never use, which they would throw away, but for the moment they clutched them tightly, remembering the loved ones who had sent them, squeezing the long miles from Abuyog to Pine Bluff or Reedsville a little closer together.

Still pacing in his cabin, Hawks felt worlds apart from Sweetwater, near the Little Tennessee. For all he knew, Louise might be out on the Coast, waiting for his return. Wherever she was, he liked to think of her in sight of the old Smokies. Home! A sailor's ship is his home—he'd said that lots of times and almost believed it; but it was a lie, a bitter lie. The *Belinda* was his ship and he was proud of her, but she was hard steel; she was no home to him. He slapped the hot bulkhead so that his open palm stung with pain. "Biggs," he called. "Biggs, go back to the mail room; tell the clerk to see immediately if there is not a letter for me."

Weariness and frustration showed in Shepherd's eyes as he looked up from the ruined parcel post. "Listen, Biggs," he said. "He can send you down here as many times as he likes: if there isn't any mail for the captain, there just isn't any mail for the captain, that's all."

The rain stopped shortly after two in the morning. It was quiet about the decks, all hands not actually on watch having obeyed the admonition of the PA: "Turn in your bunks and keep silence about the decks." Only the watch stirred: firemen, watertenders and electricians tending boilers and the main switchboard, keeping up steam and auxiliary services. On the bridge, Jim Randall and his watchkeepers moved dimly in the shadows. He had placed Neilson and Jones in the bridge wings to keep lookout. "I'm going to write up the log," he said. "You boys keep a sharp lookout for me. Ships all round: watch we don't drag down on 'em. Watch for bumboats drifting down alongside. The Japs are still thick a few miles inland—you know what one mine secured to our rudder post could do."

361

"Yes, sir," they said. "Yes, sir." Their minds were not on dragging anchors or Japanese saboteurs. In the semi-independence of the midwatch they thought about the mail bags, and wished they were home. Yes, they would watch out, but their hearts were not here on the bridge.

Randall went into the pilothouse and began to write up his log. The place was blacked out except for a small pencil flashlight he used. Reflecting dimly from white pages, its light glowed softly on Randall's strong, good-natured face. Jones, his thoughts dwelling in the San Diego bungalow, turned from searching the black water in his sector and looked into the pilothouse. It was not Randall he saw there but the sweet face of Lorraine, his wife, with soft brown hair flowing down about her shoulders. He saw the hollow of her throat where lamplight gathered, almost heard her whisper, "I love you, Tommy. You'll get a letter tomorrow." Then Randall moved; the floating bust took on a definition of square lines. Jones saw clearly the highlights of Randall's strong chin and turned-up Irish nose, the tiny beads of perspiration on his balding forehead. Strong shoulders moved on heavy legs towards him; the illusion was broken. A sense of futility and aggravation swept through Jones as he tried to hold on to the dream; then the mood dropped away and warm man-to-man companionship took its place. Like most of the crew, Jones was very fond of Jim Randall.

"No mail, eh, Tommy?" said Randall, placing a hand on his shoulder. "Well, never mind. Maybe we'll get a whole boatload of letters today. You'll get so many you won't be able to read 'em all in one watch below—probably catch Old Billy from the O.O.D. for reading letters while on duty—eh Tom? . . . I might even get one myself."

Pappy Moran beat on the post office door until the weary Shepherd crawled down from his cot and opened up. "Listen," said Moran. "We've got to clean up this mess now; it's the only dirty spot in my whole division."

Pulling on his dungarees, Shepherd looked unhappily at the rubble cluttering the deck outside the post office. All identifiable packages had been claimed. A few fragments of use or interest had been carried away; the vast bulk remained.

"Rubbish!" said Moran. "That's all it is: rubbish."

"O.K.," said Shepherd, "I'll check it just once more."

While Moran's men picked up the trash and dumped it in G.I. cans, he watched carefully. Somehow it seemed to him he was betraying his trust as mail clerk. Near the end of the job, Shepherd noticed a grimy airmail stamp sticking out from under a shovel full of torn pasteboard. Shepherd grabbed it quickly as it hovered over the trash can. It was a letter: dirty, torn, crumpled, but a letter—over six months on the way, placed by error in a bag of parcel post.

"Who's it for?" asked Moran.

"Let's see; I can hardly make it out." Shepherd wiped off the tattered envelope carefully. "I got it," he said: "Thomas Jones, Quartermaster Third Class."

CHAPTER 40

His face shining with relief and pleasure, Jackson climbed the ladder to the cabin. Behind him a storekeeper carried an open carton containing dozens of odd-sized bottles of red ink which totaled well over two gallons. This collection represented sixty miles of traveling from ship to ship in Leyte Gulf, begging red ink, making endless explanations as to why ink was needed. It marked the end of an epoch to Jackson, who felt that for the rest of his life whenever he looked at a map of the South Pacific area he would see, not tropical atolls but hundreds of red ink bottles of various sizes and shapes. Hawks would be pleased— he'd get a grin out of the Old Man, probably the first since D Day at Lingayen—he'd never been the same since losing Chipchee. Jackson almost regretted having turned the fan on the monkey's tail.

Jackson's knock was answered by a sharp, almost savage command to enter. He parted the curtain to find Hawks glaring down at him, lower jaw to one side in its ugliest set. "Well, Mr. Supply Officer, what's your excuse this morning? How many months do I have to wait—?" Then Hawks noticed the storekeeper, the large carton bulging with bottles of red ink. Instantly the jaw, the face, the whole man relaxed. "Well, Jackson," he said, his voice now warm, friendly, "you've done it at last! True to best traditions of the Navy: the difficult we will do at once; the impossible will take a little longer. . . . Sit down, Jackson; we'll have a cup of coffee. . . . Put down the carton, son. . . . Oh, Orderly, Orderly. Get my sailmaker on the double." Hawks stirred sugar into the hastily brought coffee and beamed at Jackson. "We'll dye sails this morning—dry them in the fiddley. This afternoon you may have the pleasure of going for a sail as my guest."

Biggs, the captain's orderly, shouted down the scuttle leading to the rope locker, his voice respectful yet urgent: "Mr. MacDougall . . . Mr. Fraser . . . Mr. Randall! The captain wants you gentlemen at once. . . . Please report to the quarterdeck on the double. The sailboat—" There was a sudden clatter of shoes on steel deck, the slamming of a watertight door—no other reply. They're taking a powder, thought Biggs. I've got to get them, the Old Man'll fry me. Biggs panted down the ladder, opened the steel door, ran on his short legs through the troop berthing compartment, oppressed by the heat of a tropical afternoon and by his awkward situation. For weeks as he sat outside the cabin on his camp stool, he had witnessed Hawks's fury at not getting red ink, and not having a chance to sail the *Albatross*. Everything was set now, the Old Man ready to shove off for a sail, and he wanted the three best seamen in the wardroom to go with him. Here they were running for cover. If he failed to find them he'd get it from Hawks. If he did find them against their will—officers had nasty ways of getting even with captain's orderlies. Biggs hesitated at the next ladder, wondering whether to run up or down in pursuit of the three officers. Then he ran up towards the quarterdeck, hoping against hope to find them in the boat. Biggs reached the ship's side just in time to see the *Albatross* shoving off. No sign of MacDougall, Fraser or Randall. Hawks had a full crew: Quigley, Robinson, Twitchell, Tuttle and the old man's special guest, poor old Jackson. The situation had straightened itself out. Hawks's full attention was now centered upon making sail.

While Hawks sailed the *Albatross* through the fleet under sunny skies, an ugly mass of black nimbus formed over Samar. Hawks noticed it casually while listening to Ensign Tuttle playing his trombone; then he gave tiller and main sheet to Quigley, who by now had learned to handle the sloop quite well in a moderate breeze. Quigley tacked well away from the long line of fleet anchorages, for he wished to avoid the catcalls and shouted wisecracks to which Hawks seemed impervious. Jackson sprawled to leeward of the centerboard; he had been up most of the previous night concluding the long search for red ink in one final burst of energy. Very tired and stretched out face down on the grating, he was fast asleep. Tuttle finished the "Missouri Waltz" and looked to Hawks as if asking permission for an intermission. Ignoring Tuttle for the moment, Hawks looked about his craft. Robinson lay over the decked bow, watching flying fish take off across the wind. Twitchell, stationed at the jibsheets, sat on an opened case of beer fondling the ship's camera and glaring at the sun, which had been in the wrong position for a good shot of Hawks at the tiller. Nothing like keeping in good with the Old Man! Ordinarily he'd ask him to turn the boat around, but there was something funny about today; he could sense it. Perhaps it was the screwy red sails; they looked raw, but he guessed they'd photograph well enough—somehow or other they meant a lot to the captain. He'd heard talk enough to make him very careful not to offend today. Play it safe; give them what they want: that was the system. Now that fool MacDougall: what would he get out of this deal? Wouldn't even go for a sail with the captain. He'd get chopped down to size one of these days.

Hawks was thinking: Twitchell is a dope, he'll always be a dope, but convenient to have around. Then Hawks flopped down on the grating to windward of the centerboard and rolled over on his back.

"Tuttle."

"Yes, sir."

"Play 'Red Sails.' Play it sweet and don't be in too much of a hurry to get done: at least three good choruses."

"Yes, sir."

Hawks looked up at the bright red canvas which was drawing nicely in the steady breeze. Satisfying, satisfying; there was ease in it, healing in the red-red of sunset, red of blood. Was it the beer? Couldn't be, he'd only had two cans. It took the pressure off somehow; he hesitated to ask Flynn for nightcaps from the store of medicinal whisky. He was the commander, the example; he was the resolute officer who had court-martialed Lubiski and Grandy for breaking into medicinal whisky stores. The whisky was more rightly his; he was the one carrying the load. But now, but now—if he could only get rest. Something was missing, something that would really bring contentment now. Out of a kaleidoscopic whirl of frustrations popped a clear picture of Chipchee. Misery flooded over Hawks again; nothing was ever right. He got a trumpet and lost his front teeth; he had a sloop with red sails and no little Chipchee to share it with. His relationship with Chipchee had required no stiff front, no distance; he could be completely himself with that little monkey. Where was the little devil? Had it been an accident: jumping and sliding in his carefree way, losing his grip and falling overboard? It did not seem possible, but of course Chipchee was raised in the jungle; there was a vast difference between the jungle and a steel ship in deep water. Had there been foul play? He feared so, knew he couldn't prove it. If he could have proved anything, there'd have been some suffering; he'd have fixed 'em! But it was all so futile, a blank wall —you pushed here and it gave, but the nothing, the absence of any trace or clue flowed back all around. There was just nothing he could do. Another monkey? He had thought of that but rejected the idea: the things he had told Chipchee could not be confided to a stranger.

The very monotony of the sloop's motions, the deliberate movement of the sail's red peak under blue sky lulled Hawks against his will, pushed his resentments and anxieties back into the deep well of unconsciousness. Creak and lift. It was like time, endless time; they said time healed—he didn't know about that, but at this moment it seemed hard to rebel against lethargy. . . . "Red Sails in the Sunset" . . . Hawks sighed deeply, breathed in the warm salt tang, absorbed the soothing tune—who'd ever think a dumb bunny could handle a trombone like that Tuttle? Why, he'd give a leg if he . . . Oh, let it go, let it go. Sun and shadow on that red sail, come and go, like most everything, monkey, teeth—no, let it go, let it go—in the sunset, way out on the sea . . . Red sail moving against blue sky, then sleep.

"Captain, oh, Captain!" Quigley's voice; what was Quigley . . . ? Oh, yes, rush of water and that cold press of air which came before a squall; the *Albatross* heeled over.

Hawks sat up beside the centerboard. No sun, no blue sky; dirty black squall bearing down on them; white steam of rain beating the gulf to a froth, nearly upon them. "Put down your helm, Quigley; spill the wind," he yelled. Before Hawks could get to his knees in the lurching craft, the first of the rain beat against his face. It was much more refreshing than the tepid water in his cabin washbasin. "All right, Quigley," he said. "I'll take her now. Stand by your sheets, I'm going to wear ship and run before the squall back to the *Belinda*." Quigley looked sharply at Hawks; the words sounded like a pronouncement. Remembering the trip into the sunset at Sansapor, Quigley shuddered. A collision on a big ship; you had a chance. This cockleshell . . . He hoped Hawks was all right. That's all he could do: hope.

Long had done a fine job on the *Albatross;* she took the gale and the cutting downpour like the wild sea-bird for which she was named. Quigley was beginning to feel better; they would make the *Belinda* somehow or other. The sailboat was lost in the squall, she seemed alone, but the great anchorage lay ahead. For the first time, Quigley began to wonder how his boatmates were taking it. Jackson, who had the only slicker, was sitting up, hanging on to the mast. Robinson had crawled opposite Jackson while Tuttle and Twitchell were jammed together for warmth and protection in the cramped space forward of the mast. The trombone rolled back and forth on the bottom boards; Tuttle must be pretty unsettled to neglect his precious instrument like that. There was something odd about all of them, perhaps it was the light. It wasn't the water cascading down them all—none of them could have gotten any wetter by jumping overboard—something about the color, that was it: color of this streaming water splashing on them from the dyed sails—that disgusting red ink! Their khakis were dyed with splotches of red ink! Quigley looked at his own uniform; it was splotched and stained like the rest. He looked up at the mainsail again; it was blotched from uneven running of the makeshift ink dye, like a crude native block print of hibiscus pattern on tapa cloth. The wind was flinging the stuff down upon him; the red rain was running down his face; his clothes were ruined. Quigley shivered from chill and distaste. For a long time he hung onto the centerboard well, feeling miserable; then he looked over his shoulder at Hawks.

The northern edge of the squall was passing overhead. The sky was clearing and sunlight shone full on Hawks's face as he held the lively tiller in one hand and the straining mainsheet in the other. Apparently unaware of Quigley or the others, Hawks sat in the dripping sternsheets with the proud and distant look of some ancient Viking sea lord, his gaze on the sunset and the red sails of the *Albatross*.

===== **CHAPTER 41** =====

Willicut looked at the pilothouse clock, then walked to the bridge wing where the ship's bugler dozed in the shade. "Wake up, Bundy. Ten hundred: time for sick call."

Bundy opened his eyes slowly, yawned, stretched, then strolled into the pilothouse and took his bugle from its hook. "Call for the lame and lazy," he said, then snapped on the PA and raised his bugle.

Down in the sick bay, Dr. Bell was busy with the usual lineup: colds, stomach flu, heat rash and sunburn. During a slack period, Bell sat at the desk and began entering names of the sick on a binnacle list for the officer of the deck. Noticing that the usual medicinal odors of the sick bay were being over-powered by a strong smell of stale sweat and greasy table scraps, he knew without looking up that the garbage grinder was back again.

"Don't you ever take a shower, Hubert?" he asked.

"My feet hurt," said the garbage grinder, ignoring reference to bathing. He wiped beads of sweat from his pale face with a grimy shirt sleeve. "My feet hurt all the time, Doc. I soaked 'em in a bucket of water like you said. I rub 'em good and wear heavy socks. I sit down once in a while when I get a chance, which ain't often—them mess cooks don't fix the slops right and I always—"

"Yes, I know," said Bell. "You told me several times before: chicken guts in the gears; but we haven't had chicken for months. Let's get back to your feet."

"My feet hurt; they hurt all the time. I soaked 'em in a bucket, like you said . . ."

"All right, all right. Just a minute now." Bell rose from the white stool. The man's feet were as flat as the deck; he would get Flynn's opinion. Perhaps special treatment could be arranged.

"Don't brush me off, Doc." Hubert pressed a soiled palm against Bell's white jacket. "I been here six times about my feet, Doc. You got to do something about it. My feet hurt all the time, I tell you."

"You sent for me, Captain?" asked Flynn, entering the cabin, where Hawks and Quigley sat at the worktable.

"Yes, Doctor," said Hawks. "The executive officer informs me you recommend sending Hubert, Seaman Second Class, to Naval Hospital, Guam, where the services of a chiropodist are available." Hawks savored the word once more. "Chiropodist," he repeated, rocking back on the hind legs of his chair and making a face at Flynn.

"That's right, Captain; Hubert has extremely flat feet. There is very little we can do for him here; he needs special shoes."

Hawks cleared his throat loudly. "He's been grinding *Belinda* garbage for eighteen months, hasn't he?"

"That's true, Captain," said Flynn. "But broken-down arches can be very painful. If the condition becomes worse we may have Hubert in the sick bay."

"That's your problem," said Hawks. "Hubert is not military and he is not sanitary but he is important to the safety of the ship. Hubert is the only man on board who likes to grind garbage. If I gave the job permanently to anyone but Hubert, I'd have to assign a master-at-arms to see that nothing was sloughed off over side. Hubert is the only man available for the duty who can be trusted to grind garbage properly day after day."

Flynn smiled. "I didn't realize that Hubert was so important," he said, "but I still feel it my duty to recommend special treatment for him at Guam."

"You're breaking my heart, Pat," Quigley said. "Are you sure I don't have flat feet or something equally lethal? You know that my teeth need attention. I should have orders to San Diego for extraction and dentures."

Quigley's tone irritated Hawks beyond any consideration of garbage grinding. "There is no indispensable man in the Navy," he said. "Haven't you somebody in training for the duties of garbage grinder?"

"No, sir; that is, nothing worked out well. I tried Troske; later on I put Kemp in there for two weeks. Hubert is really the only—"

"Nonsense," said Hawks. "I can find and train a man right aboard this ship to replace any other man." He gave Quigley a long, sharp stare, then cut him up and down with a glance which seemed to say, "I could rip the buttons off your shirt with my eyes." Hawks got up from his seat and looked at the chart of the Pacific Ocean which was taped to the bulkhead. "Let's see now," he said. "It's about twelve hundred miles to

Guam: three days each way. How much time would they need to treat this fellow, Flynn?"

"It shouldn't take them more than a week to fit him with special shoes, Captain."

Hawks's glance rested briefly on his safe, where secret plans for the next two operations were stowed. "Fine," he said. "We'll send him to Guam by first available transportation. Quigley, put another man in training for garbage grinder; start him in today. You and Flynn make arrangements for Hubert. We'll pick him up here after the next operation."

A homeward-bound supply ship carried Hubert to Guam. Upon arrival there he was given a bunk on a hospital LST and forgotten. A steady stream of badly wounded arriving from the Philippines and Iwo Jima kept all the doctors busy from early morning to late at night. After ten days had passed, pharmacist's mates, driven by Hubert's insistence, persuaded the chiropodist to have a look at him.

"Hmm," the chiropodist said thoughtfully, after a careful examination, "you have extremely flat feet, son. Were you drafted?" Hubert nodded. The chiropodist walked to the clinic washbasin and scrubbed his hands, then returned and flicked back through the pages of Hubert's health record. "They shouldn't have drafted you with feet like that—but of course that's out of our hands now. . . . Ever have special shoes?"

"No," said Hubert, "I never had a fitting of shoes that felt good. I used to go barefoot mostly, back in Tennessee. My people have a farm there and the soil is kindly to my feet."

"You ought to have special shoes," said the chiropodist, "but we don't have any facilities for them out here, at least not yet."

"My feet hurt when I stand," said Hubert. "I'm garbage grinder on a big boat and I have to stand for hours; them mess cooks liable to put anything in the garbage."

The chiropodist smiled. "I'll tell you what we'll do," he said. "We'll give you a pair of heavy field shoes—the best fit we can find. You put 'em on, go down to the beach and stand in the water as much as you can during the rest of the day. Then come back and we'll dry your shoes in the mold of your feet. That should give you some relief."

Hubert got his shoes and stood in the lukewarm water of Apra Harbor. While he soaked his feet, an LST stood in to shore, dropped her stern anchor and shoved her bow into shallow water close beside him. Her great bow port yawed open, the ramp was lowered and, with a great deal of good-natured shouting, her crew began loading light tanks aboard. Hubert watched these tanks, which had recently helped capture Guam from the Japs, splashing past him and clattering up the ramp. He supposed that they were bound for fighting somewhere else; but tanks were outside his sphere of interest and the soldiers who ran them were to him merely men who crowded aboard transports, thus complicating the work of a garbage grinder. In return, nobody paid any particular attention to Hubert or asked him why he stood in the water. Salt water was refreshing, but at last he tired of standing up. Wading out to the bow of the LST, he sat on the edge of the ramp. A sailor dragging a coil of lashings looked at Hubert.

"You new here?"

"No. I'm soaking my feet: they hurt all the time."

"On liberty?"

"No."

"Where's your ship?"

"Leyte."

"Leyte! That's where we're going. How'd you get here?"

"Come to get my feet bettered. Say! You going to Leyte?"

"Sure. Why?"

"They never tell nobody where the ship's going."

"You ain't sailed on an LST, mate. We know everything."

"They told me the cooks knowed everything, but they don't. In one of these here wars, nobody knows everything."

Hubert heard a clanging sound from under the coconut trees where a mess cook was beating the commissary triangle. It was time for chow. He waded ashore and got in line with over a hundred other out-patients. The ground was very muddy from frequent passing rain squalls. From time to time Hubert took plodding steps in this deep mud, moving slowly towards the food. Then a large group of men in dungarees wedged in at the head of the line. Grumbling worked back towards Hubert. "Lousy politicians," said the man ahead of him. The line seemed to have lost all forward motion. Hubert squished his feet in their sopping field shoes deeper and deeper into the soft and comfortable mud.

Suddenly the drowsy noontime peace with its slow hum of idle conversation was shattered by ear-piercing screams, followed by hoarse shouting. Startled, Hubert looked up from the mud to see three naked Japs, stragglers from recently defeated Japanese forces, coming out of the jungle. They were armed with wicked-looking machetes which they swung in front of them in vicious, cutting arcs. Screaming and squealing like pigs, they bore down upon the chow line. Men ahead and behind Hubert broke from the line and ran for their lives. One paused briefly to beat a few rapid strokes on the triangle; several shouted for the guard. Impulse told Hubert to run, but his feet were so deeply imbedded in the mud that he could not move. All the men in the chow line were gone. The nearest Jap, some fifty feet away and coming fast, held his machete with its heavy curved blade in a competent two-handed grip, and his eyes were on Hubert.

With desperate energy, Hubert leaped upward and out of his bogged-down shoes. Barefooted, he ran towards the beach. After a few rapid steps he came abreast of several marines armed with bayoneted rifles. Hubert pushed between them, deflecting the aim of one who was about to fire. He heard shots behind him but did not pause or look around. At last he reached the water; blind fear drove him deep into it until only his head remained above the surface. Gasping for breath, he looked around. The LST which had been loading tanks was retracting slowly from the beach—she was going to Leyte, the fellow had said. Leyte, anywhere was better than this! Hubert floundered to shore, ran along the sand until opposite the gaping mouth of the retracting LST, then plunged back into the water and managed to clutch the end of the ramp. A soldier reached out a hand and helped him aboard, saying, "You almost missed your ship, Bub."

Hubert crawled up the ramp and lay in the corner of the tank deck, gasping for breath and dripping water. At last he looked around: the crew was busy securing the ramp while a group of soldiers sat around a spread blanket, playing with dog-eared cards. Once again Hubert had the feeling that nobody cared whether or not he was here. Crawling deeper into the shadows, he found a temporary bunk in a coil of mooring line and went to sleep.

When he awoke, the big landing craft was rolling in a quick, jerky fashion much different from the steadier *Belinda*. Loose ends of gear banged and clattered against the steel bulwarks of the tank deck. Hubert heard voices. Going aft, he saw soldiers and sailors standing in line together. Smell of gasoline was overcome by the pleasant odor of hot food.

"Hello, mate," one of them called. "Get your feet fixed up? I told you we was going back to Leyte."

"I ain't got no papers," said Hubert. "I guess I'm AWOL."

"Nobody cares about papers here," said another sailor. "Ain't you been on an LST before?"

When the LST shoved her nose into the sand at Dulag, in Leyte Gulf, Hubert waded ashore and hitchhiked fifteen miles down the beach to Abuyog. There was the *Belinda*, less than a mile from shore. Within an hour he found a *Belinda* boat and went out to the ship. Tony Brooks had the deck. He was chewing on a stub of pencil, writing notes for his log. "All these two-bit notes," he muttered to Willicut. "Stores received: every cockeyed case and bag. 'Five hundred tins, Australian mutton; satisfactory as to quantity, questionable as to quality.' Have you got the names of all the men in that new draft from the States?"

371

."Yes, sir. Say, here's the garbage grinder coming aboard. Why, he's barefoot, Mr. Brooks!"

"Hello, Hubert," said Brooks. "You back from Guam?"

"Yes."

"Fine; give me your orders. . . . Hurry, man, I've got a whale of a log to write up at twelve hundred; I'll never get to chow."

"I ain't got no orders."

"You haven't! What's the matter—lose 'em?"

"They never give me none."

Brooks looked sharply at Hubert, thinking: everybody has orders. I wonder if he took a powder—but no, couldn't be that. Nobody would ever come back to this bucket unless he was sent. This should be reported to Quigley; then mast, questions and explanations, written reports. "Aw, nuts!" he said aloud. "I've got boats to get ready." As soon as Kruger relieved him of the deck, Brooks wrote up his long log, ending with the entry:

> At 1155, Hubert, Gilbert R., S 2/c, returned to this command pursuant instructions AdComPhipPacMed, Guam, upon completion of medical treatment.

Two hours later, Dr. Flynn left the sick bay to make an informal inspection of the garbage room. He was beginning to regret ever having requested treatment at Guam for Hubert. The man was personally filthy—no amount of naval regulation, supervision or moral persuasion would ever succeed in keeping his person clean—yet his zeal for cleanliness of the garbage room and its grinding machinery was amazing. Since Hubert had left for treatment, a succession of disgruntled seamen had been assigned to the garbage room. Not one of them ever kept up with the rapid accumulation of garbage incidental to feeding the twenty-five hundred officers and men aboard. These temporary garbage grinders hated the duty, and their attitude towards it was just short of mutinous. Whether or not they obeyed orders was no concern of Flynn's; his responsibility was the health of all on board. Since Hubert's departure, Flynn had become increasingly anxious about the garbage room. He opened the door now, his mind prepared with appropriate phrases of disapproval, then blinked with astonishment. There was Hubert, muttering to himself as he furiously scrubbed the gears of his beloved garbage grinder. Flynn looked down at Hubert's feet—the fellow was barefoot.

"Hello, Hubert," he said. "I didn't know you were back. What did they do for you at Guam?"

"Nothing."

"Didn't they fit you with special shoes?"

372

"No," said Hubert, sloshing a bucket of suds down the grinder.

"Surely they did something. . . . You mean to tell me you didn't get any shoes? What happened there anyway?"

Hubert reached carefully into the business end of the garbage grinder. After considerable struggle he extracted a long strip of tough gristle and threw it into a clean G.I. can; then he wiped his hands on his shirt and looked steadily at Flynn. "It ain't no use trying to explain," he said at last. "Nobody would ever believe me. . . . I'm satisfied to get back here and straighten out this garbage business."

"We're very happy to have you back, Hubert."

Ignoring the compliment, Hubert looked about his garbage room, taking note of bulkheads to be scrubbed and a rusty G.I. can which should be replaced. He did this automatically. His mind was back in Tennessee: Nell Clark, that dark-eyed mountain gal, swishing her skirt and stamping her feet, asking him, "How do you expect me to square dance with a man fitted out with paddles for feet? . . ." Scorn in her voice—in every curve of her as she said, "Just move along with those duck feet, Mr. Hubert, and look for another gal! . . ."

One hand on the grinder, Hubert looked down at his feet: they were flat as paddles all right. There'd been times when he'd felt the music fairly bursting in him . . . but these feet . . . Without a trace of smile, Hubert looked accusingly at Flynn as he said, "Doc, my feet still hurt."

CHAPTER 42

The roof of the Tacloban church had been blown off, making it easier to read the faded tags on thousands of travel-stained mail bags piled there for sorting. With his working party of the mail clerk and twenty seamen, MacDougall attacked a corner of the huge pile. Working parties from other ships were spotted around the periphery of this tremendous mound, yanking bags down, looking eagerly at the tags and then throwing all but the very few marked for their own ships into a series of smaller but still unsorted piles.

MacDougall looked up the officer in charge, a stocky and bored-looking junior lieutenant, past middle age, who leaned against the crumbling masonry wall of the ruin, drinking warm beer from a can.

"Haven't you any system for sorting this mail?" MacDougall asked. "You know—alphabetize by first letter of ship's name or something like that. This mail will be pawed over five hundred times before it's sorted this way. It'll take days. It rains here every day, you know. The whole thing will be a stinking mess like the last batch we got."

The j.g. finished his beer, threw the empty can through a broken window, reached for another can and fumbled for his knife. "Listen," he said, fastening bloodshot eyes on Mac-Dougall. "I was sent all around the Pacific to straighten out the snafu mail situation. When I started out the mail was three months late; six months is about average now. I been everywhere, taking loads of mail from one island to the other. I got a foot locker with a change of socks and ten thousand directives about mail—most of 'em fouled up. Everybody's got a system . . . I had a system. . . ." He poked MacDougall in the chest with a stubby thumb. "You wouldn't believe it, but I worked fifteen years in the Chicago Post Office before I joined the Navy. If I ever get home again, I'll never go near a post office as long as I live. Mail: I hate the stuff. I got a new system now." The j.g. finished opening the can and gulped at the warm, foaming beer. "I'm going to lean right here and work on this beer and watch you and your sailors race the termites for what's left of that mail."

Late returning in the *Albatross,* Hawks ate a leisurely supper with Quigley as his guest. After the meal, Hawks called for mail and dispatches. He thumbed carefully through the thick stack of pink message blanks on the board, circling various department heads for action or information. Then, handing the board to Quigley, he turned to the official mail which had come over from the flagship during his absence. Quigley played a bored glance over each message while he hastily scrawled his initials and turned to the next. Floating mines in latitude thirty-seven south; decision of the Deputy Commander, Western Sea Frontier regarding the Treasure Island Degaussing Range: one entrance buoy to be moved . . . Quigley wondered what movie they had for the evening; a musical, he hoped. He was halfway through a message concerning collection and return of all winter clothing issued to the crew when Hawks whistled and said, "Here, Quigley; I have another surprise for you."

What, more ribbons? thought Quigley. But he said, "Yes, Captain?"

His indifference was shattered as Hawks said, "Here are orders for you: 'Proceed immediately, Pearl Harbor . . .'"

Orders at last! Quigley wondered if he could have the orders endorsed at Pearl, get back to San Francisco . . . He'd work things somehow—take Eva to the Top-of-the-Mark. A revulsion for pink message blanks welled up within him. He rose and said, "Do you need me any longer, Captain? May I be excused?"

"Certainly," said Hawks. "But what's your hurry? What are you going to do?"

"Pack, sir."

Hawks grinned at Quigley, the toothless gap showing in his upper jaw. "Very good; very good," he said. "But first have my yeoman draw up all necessary papers for turning over your duties as executive officer to MacDougall. . . . Biggs!"

"Yes, sir."

"Tell Mr. MacDougall and Mr. Randall I want to see them."

Every inch of space around number four hatch was crowded: sailors waiting for Hawks to come and movies to start. It was a calm dark night and, after heavy rain during the afternoon, the atmosphere was crystal clear so that overhead stars seemed intimate and friendly. The movie screen with its mended tear and the marks of oily winch runners not quite scrubbed away hung between the two mainmast kingposts. The crew was gathered in a familiar and settled pattern, product of no rule but one of custom and habit. Across the hatch from the screen, decks tiered three high. On the top were signalmen, radio and radarmen. On the next deck, beside the incinerator house, the officers sat on chairs carried from the wardroom. To one side of the officers were Negro cooks and stewards, to the other side men from the first division, who worked in the forepart of the ship. Directly beneath the officers were the chiefs, seated with casual arrogance in chairs carried up from their quarters. So it went: firemen and oilers here, gunner's mates and shipfitters there, corpsmen at the edge of the hatch corner handy to the sick bay. The boxes of this outdoor theater were the ship's boats nested about the hatch and in the two after sets of gravity davits. Perched in these exclusive but uncomfortable positions on the sharp edges in plyboard coamings were the boats' crews, who looked down with lofty superiority upon their mates crowded below. The second division men took care of this after part of the ship and were custodians of the movie screen, which they regarded as their own. They were gathered on the fueling hoses stowed immediately before it, from which close-up position their necks grew stiff from looking up sharply at a picture so near that the motion strained their eyes. Yet this very nearness—the greatly enlarged and blurred images of faces and bosoms they saw here—had a special intimacy with which they had become identified.

Six hundred men were crowded together in this restricted space; they sat on cradled cargo booms, they hung suspended in bights of rope from topping lift cables or sat precariously on light planks spanning empty space between boats and lowered booms. All petty frictions as to exact placement had been long settled. Time and tropic enervation had contrived negotiated truce even between hotheads; like fowls in a barnyard, minute priorities had been established among them. It was for this reason and not because of any service provincialism that the sharing of movie space with soldiers or marines was so upsetting to them. Movie time and the waiting for movies had become a growing social factor in the more relaxed routine between operations. Crumpled letters were taken out, carefully smoothed and reread, then homey news items were exchanged and girl friends discussed. When there was no mail, tattered packs of cards came out and the dice for acey-ducey games were thrown in spaces too small for a man to sit. Boatswain's mates worked on square-knot belts, carpenters polished bits of fancy woodwork and machinist's mates finished the handwork on metal trinkets.

During these periods the crew often listened to recordings played on Chaplain Hughes's turntable; from time to time they saw still one more showing of that perennial favorite, the last half of *Bathing Beauty*, reported lost overboard and therefore theirs forever, and to be played with or without the presence of Captain Hawks. Tonight as a special treat, they were being entertained during the wait for the captain by Karl Kruger and his visiting brother, Ed. As Biggs, the captain's orderly, approached the area, the Kruger brothers were singing and playing "Leave the Pretty Girls Alone," learned during their college days from an old Carson Robison recording. Sailors whooped and whistled as they listened to the melodramatic adventures of a traveler, fleeced by cuddly gold diggers in London, Memphis, Spain and Hawaii. MacDougall and Randall sat together with their backs to a kingpost, enjoying the Hawaiian section:

> *Then I went to Honolulu*
> *Just to see what I could see*
> *Saw the hula girls ashakin'*
> *On the beach at Waikiki.*
> *Thought that they were fair young maidens*
> *Gee, but they were nice and brown.*
> *I learned a lot about their shakin'*
> *When they went and shook me down.*

MacDougall fingered a packet of letters from his wife. Tattered and impregnated with earthy jungle smell, they evoked precious memories, fresh impressions, reassurances of faith and love. Little flashes of home flicked through his mind: the broken rung on Robbie's highchair waiting to be fixed; the big stone fireplace which smoked with a strong south wind; the fat robin who sat on the fence waiting for the strawberries to ripen . . . Nadine's sweet face and trim figure, moving about the house, glancing out the window, perhaps with a silent prayer that some day he would be walking up that path with eager steps, throwing open the door, engulfing them in his arms. . . .

Biggs wormed his way into the group of officers, looking over the figures he had learned to identify in dim light.

"Mr. MacDougall. Mr. Randall. Captain wants to see you."

"All right, Biggs."

"He wants you right away, sir."

"All right, I said. I'll be coming; the ship won't sink." MacDougall leaned back against the warm kingpost, half hearing the song—hanging on to his moment at home while Karl and Ed sang the last chorus:

> *Oh, don't forget my lesson:*
> *A woman's heart is made of stone*
> *And don't forget my warning*
> *And leave the pretty girls alone.*

While the uproar of tumultuous applause rose above the *Belinda's* topmasts, MacDougall got to his feet and nudged Randall. "Well, Jim, we'd better go see what the Old Man wants."

It was half an hour before MacDougall returned with Captain Hawks and sat beside the captain in Quigley's regular seat. Quigley was belowdecks, busy with his packing—herewith detached for dental treatment—dreaming of San Francisco's Top-of-the-Mark. MacDougall—now the *Belinda's* executive officer—was dreaming too, dreaming strangely of this ship about him: the things he wanted to do with her—with these men crowded so closely together before the weather-beaten movie screen. The feeling was very different from anything he had expected; perhaps it was the mood of the moment, he did not know. He only knew that he felt closer than ever to these men—to the many he liked and even to the few he despised—they were all in his care now. Somehow he felt welded together with them and with the *Belinda,* as if there would never be any other life for any of them.

Captain Hawks stepped from his cabin door and intercepted MacDougall, who was transferring a double armload of books and directives from the navigator's cubicle to his new and larger quarters. "When you stow that gear, Mr. Executive Officer, turn the ship over to Randall for a few hours. I want you to go for a sail with me."

"A sail?" MacDougall's face clouded with a puzzled frown. Sure, it was a great day for a sail, nice cooling breeze out there in Leyte Gulf—but tomorrow they'd start loading ship for the assault, getting ready for the BLT, fifteen hundred strong. Surely this was no time for recreation.

Hawks flashed a quick smile, then worked his facial muscles back and forth like so much modeling clay. When he was finished the smile had changed into a pouty frown that clearly meant: you'd better come willingly or I'll make you come; I'm asking you but this is a command. Aloud he said, "I think the two of us can handle her. I want to talk to you alone."

The air was dry for Leyte; banks of strato-cumulus moved westward, leaving a clear dome of blue which promised noonday heat. The *Albatross's* red sails were no longer spectacular —heavy rain squalls had faded the ink. Regardless of color, they filled nicely in the breeze, heeling the sloop well over and skimming her along to windward and away from the anchored fleet.

Hawks talked at length about the operation ahead, the route they would take, the weather, fuel, gunnery, the crew and the pattern of ship-to-shore movement. "This is the biggest operation we've been on," he said. "We had more ships of smaller types at Lingayen, but Okinawa is more important than the Philippines; it's got to go off right." Hawks stood up carefully, hanging on to the mast and looking out at the clusters of APAs which reached to the horizon. "The *Belinda* is a good ship," he said. "We've always beat the division—usually the whole squadron—in performance: gunnery, ship-to-shore movement, combat cargo unloading, prompt and efficient care of battle casualties." Holding the tiller with his left hand and the main sheet with his right, MacDougall looked appraisingly at Hawks, as if he had never seen him before: tall figure, straight as a ramrod for a naval rifle, hawklike face with eyes that were so penetrating when clear, cloudy now with a dreamlike quality as he said, "This is it, MacDougall. Here's where we shoot the works! We're going right up into the Japs's back yard and take it away from them." Hawks sat down beside the centerboard and trimmed the jibsheets to his liking. At last he continued. "We've smashed the Jap surface fleet, MacDougall. If only we can handle their submarines; that's what's got me worried."

MacDougall stirred uneasily at the tiller. "Yes, sir. They'll come at us from the air too—everything they can throw at us: dive bombers, torpedo planes—what they have left—and those dirty little kamis."

Lost in thought, Hawks did not seem to hear. At last he burst out, "They'll try to crash us, to set fire to us and sink us, that's sure! We must be alert, constantly alert. Our gunnery is very good now but we can't afford to get caught flat again like we were by that dive bomber at Lingayen."

MacDougall had been half listening, mind filled with details of his new job and preparations for troop embarkation. Mention of the near miss sent a shiver down his spine. "Yes, sir, we'll have to keep awake this time. . . . Trouble is, the Japs know we're coming."

"What do you mean?" asked Hawks sharply.

"They must know, Capt'n. When I was ashore at Tacloban after mail—well, sir, that afternoon I bumped into a little Filipino boy with a fighting cock under his arm."

"What's that got to do with it?"

"He asked me if I was going to Okinawa with the rest of them."

Hawks dropped the jibsheet and sat upright. He looked at the Leyte shore line for a long time, then he said half to MacDougall, half to himself, "There really is no such thing as a secret." Hawks fumbled in his hip pocket and brought out a four-ounce medicine bottle, half filled with whisky. He drained the bottle and tossed it overboard. "Medicine," he said. "Dr. Flynn has been prescribing—"

MacDougall nodded and smiled. Flynn had been telling him about the medicinal whisky, how Hawks hounded him for it these days. "I don't know just what to do," Flynn had said. "If I say, 'No,' he may blow his top in the middle of this next operation. If I give in more than a third of the time, he'll be on a howling bender come D Day." What am I sympathizing with him for? MacDougall wondered. Hawks had been mean enough about the summary court when Grandy and Lubiski broke into the medicinal whisky stores back in Palau—made life miserable for me when I wanted to let 'em off with a fine. It's different when he's doing it. Yet somehow it seemed to fit into this picture, this queer picture with its air of unreality: that coast of Leyte over there, hundreds of ships, thousands of gun barrels, waiting troops, fighting cock, these confounded sails, dyed with half the red ink in the Pacific Fleet and now Captain Hawks taking off his shoes and wiggling his toes.

"I think better barefooted," said Hawks. "I envy that Hubert, going barefoot in his garbage room. Sometimes on inspection . . . That's the trouble with this world; nobody understands the need of going barefoot. You fight back and take on stiff ways and pretty soon you're keeping the little boys in line yourself." Hawks stopped abruptly as if embarrassed at having expressed his feelings. MacDougall said nothing; he was embarrassed, too, and kept his eye on the sail, wondering how many quarts of ink were left in it and how many had been washed into Leyte Gulf by rain squalls. Then Hawks roared out at Mac-

Dougall, at the faded red sail and at Leyte Gulf, "I can be stiff as any of 'em! I can make my crew jump through hoops and I can take the *Belinda* anywhere from Truk to Tokyo. Nobody will ever get a chance to call me soft. . . . You know, Mac-Dougall, I love it, I've never been so happy in my life as in command of the *Belinda*. I feel free—when they leave my ship alone, that is—feel like nothing is too hard for Jebediah Hawks. I feel as high as that bedspring of an air-search antenna."

MacDougall brought the sloop closer on the wind until the jib shivered, then eased off the sheet and let her skim free. This is a dandy little boat, he thought, but no rest cure with this wild man aboard. I should have hid in the rope locker again. No, he would never be able to hide in the rope locker again. From now on it was up to him to be a cork fender between Hawks and his ship. Hawks had fallen silent and was busy feeling the sloop's ribs with his bare toes. "We've got a good ship, Capt'n," said MacDougall suddenly. "We'll take her there O.K., and we'll give the rest of them a good run for their money." Then he thought, what am I getting chummy with Hawks for? Almost a year now we've got along fine with a little distance between us; this may be a big mistake.

As if he had been reading MacDougall's thoughts, Hawks said, "You've been a good man, MacDougall, stubborn and proud but you're a good man. You really love that *Belinda*, don't you?"

"Yes, sir, I do."

"I'm getting tired. I should have had more leave after Guadalcanal and those fouled-up Mediterranean landings; a man can take so much, you know. I have a singing in my head which bothers me: sickness and headaches that nobody knows about. I'm going to have to lean on you. When I'm on the beam nobody can improve on my performance of duty; but there are times when you've got to say, 'No,' to me, tell me when an order is wrong." Hawks got on his knees, scrambled aft beside MacDougall and pounded MacDougall's knee until the muscles ached. "You've got to say, 'No,' Mac; you've got to say, 'No.' I've tried three times to get you a promotion and I'm recommending you for a naval command of your own, but your duty now is to stick by me and I expect you to do your duty."

MacDougall moved his knee out of the range of Hawks's fist. For months he'd stewed about that promotion, yet somehow it didn't seem so important now. Ashore perhaps, but the *Belinda* was a family, a strange gathering; not always a happy family, one with resentments and frictions, but a family. You didn't need gold braid in a family. "Hadn't we better get back to the ship, Capt'n?" he asked, but there was no answer. Hawks had

380

crawled alongside the centerboard and seemed asleep, his bare toes cooling under the shade of the faded red sail.

══ CHAPTER 43 ══

These moonlight nights were dangerous but beautiful, MacDougall thought as he leaned over the bridge rail watching the great invasion fleet perform a waltzing zigzag towards Okinawa. Even on a dark night one could see nearby ships. Tonight was cloudy-clear, with full moon illuminating fleet units from horizon to horizon. Whipped by freshening trade winds, the lively sea formed a constantly moving pattern: black valleys of shadowy trough separated row upon row of breaking seas which spilled snow-white froth upon rolling wave slopes of velvet-smooth metal. The zigzagging ships appeared as silver-gray shapes on the moonside, as black silhouettes on the other: clear targets for any waiting Jap sub. How could they miss hitting something in such a mass of ships? The Jap fleet was staggering now, but the sea path from Leyte to Okinawa was within range of land-based planes from Japanese-held islands. This peaceful scene . . . Looks could be deceiving; how quickly the *Liscome Bay* had turned from a boxy-black shape to the blazing funeral pyre of seven hundred men, with bright orange flames shooting up half a mile into the sky! MacDougall looked aft: next astern of *Belinda,* the *O'Keefe's* bow wave shoveled up white snow out of liquid silver while the loaded transport danced a measured waltz, rising and falling with the waves and zigzagging with her sister ships. Every change in course produced a different pattern, compass bearings remaining constant but relative positions suddenly changing every few minutes like a kaleidoscope all black, white and silver. With these changes in pattern the movement changed: on one course all ships cut to windward, heaving and tossing, each with intricate variations in pitch and roll according to individual stability and trim, while on another course they steamed along the trough with a measured rolling motion. MacDougall looked out at the different ships; old battleships steady as churches when compared with the rest; cruisers pitching with slow deliberation, indifferent to tons of sea water cascading from their bows; small lively destroyers, watchdogs of the attack force. He saw line upon line of attack transports: old familiar liners long since converted to APAs, their names and customs changed before Guadalcanal, Attu, Tarawa; the majority built for this duty since Pearl Harbor, some of them like the *Belinda* veterans of many beachheads, others in green divisions a little ragged in executing the zigzag, as yet untried by enemy fire.

The sky was nearly clear and the general impression was one

of peace. Yet to the trained eye there were signs of possible trouble ahead—little wisps of frozen cirrus, perhaps merely indicating a gale far to the north, perhaps the first visual warning of the typhoon now reported to be nearing Leyte. Fleet meteorologists aboard the flagship felt certain it would intercept the attack force, perhaps demolish it before it reached Okinawa's beaches. MacDougall looked out at these ships loaded with troops and fighting gear, these ships festooned with landing craft. It was impossible to snug them down for a typhoon: the treacherous blasts of shifting wind and the confused seas slapping bridge high from several directions at once would smash landing craft to matchwood, shift tanks and bulldozers in transport's holds, listing the ships, wrecking indispensable gear and sickening battalion landing teams to the point of combat ineffectiveness. Looking at those wisps of cloud, MacDougall lifted off his cap and scratched his head, wondering; then he went in to look at the barometer. It was following a normal pattern, a little on the low side; no sign of the deceptive rise which he knew so often went before a sudden drop of pressure and increase of wind and sea. He went out on the wing once more and looked at the ships again. The beauty of the scene cut into him so that he sucked in his breath, thinking of Nadine and longing to share with her this beauty of clean sea and wind, of stars and moonlight.

MacDougall turned to see Captain Hawks at his elbow. Feet braced against the sea motion, Hawks looked out at the ships but not at the overhead sky, then asked, "This typhoon they're forecasting: what's your opinion, MacDougall?"

MacDougall remembered his new responsibility: Hawks in the sailboat saying, "I'm going to have to lean on you." There was no sense in burdening Hawks with his own doubts; he would have to stall for time until he could give a definite answer. Hawks broke into his thoughts, saying impatiently, "I want your opinion about this typhoon, MacDougall."

"Yes, sir. I'd like to plot the reports first." He moved away before Hawks could say more, plunged through the blackout screen into the chart room, sorted out all reported positions of the typhoon and plotted them on Randall's navigation chart. Before MacDougall was done, Hawks followed him inside and stood breathing against the back of his neck. MacDougall plotted the typhoon's course, small crosses represented its position as reported at six-hour intervals. From the vicinity of Yap Island they formed a path curving down across Kossol anchorage, north of Palau, thence slightly north of west right through Tacloban.

"It's sure to cross Leyte," said MacDougall. "When they hit land like this they always run across. This one should end up off Indo-China."

"How do you know?" demanded Hawks. "Okinawa gets a pasting from typhoons several times a year—how about that?"

"That's later in the season, Capt'n. These March and April storms either curve up around Guam and get out of the way or else they run west across the Philippines. As far as I know, only one on record ever came up this way in March or April."

"All right," said Hawks. "You admit it now. One of them did come up this way. How can you prove to me that this fellow won't do the same thing: move right up on our tail at three times fleet speed and wreck the whole task force?"

"No, sir. We just extend the plot curve and—"

"How is it that you're so cocksure? All these trained meteorologists—how can they all be wrong?"

"I can't prove a thing about it, Capt'n, but I'd stake the *Belinda* on what I've learned out here— This typhoon will be as close to us by morning as it will ever get." MacDougall ran his finger across the chart ahead of the storm plot. "It should speed up now and be way over here in the China Sea by morning. From then on we'll be gradually drawing away from it—get a little swell, that's all."

"But these meteorologists—?"

MacDougall bristled. "I don't think these half-baked meteorologists they have here with the fleet know their business." Hawks gave MacDougall the changing frown which started with raised eyebrows and ended with a wrinkled nose, but MacDougall did not falter. "I've spent half my life in this part of the world, Capt'n. At this time of the year there isn't a chance in a thousand of a typhoon coming within three hundred miles of here, and it's five hundred more to Okinawa."

"How do you know this isn't the thousandth time? Here's the admiral's report."

"Maybe the typhoon doesn't know about the admiral, sir."

Hawks glared at MacDougall, took another long look at the chart, then threw it back on top of Randall's plotting sheet. "O.K. O.K., Mr. Half-your-life. Get me the signalman." Hawks reached for a signal blank and wrote swiftly with bold pencil strokes: "In my opinion, typhoon will not, repeat not close within three hundred miles of disposition." Handing the message to the signalman, Hawks blew his nose noisily. "There," he said. "That'll show 'em!" He looked at the clock. "Two hundred already; go get some sleep. I'll want you in the cabin after morning G.Q. We've got to work out better defensive measures against Jap attacks. That's one kind of typhoon we can depend on meeting head on."

The *Belinda* wallowed and yawed before an ugly swell rolling in a threatening manner from the direction of Luzon Strait. Hawks and MacDougall sat across from each other at the cabin worktable, piled high with operation plans, boat-wave schedules, debarkation outlines, unloading priorities forming islands between trickles of spilled coffee which had slopped from a number of cups during the four hours the two had been at work. Hawks reached up for the bell button, pointed to the mess and waited for his Filipino steward to mop up the coffee. Clearing his throat loudly he looked out the porthole at fast-scudding nimbus cloud, black with rain. "You and your typhoon, Mac-Dougall—so this is as close as it gets to us. Hmm—you'd better be right."

MacDougall got up and stepped to the porthole. Marines on the weather deck who preferred salt water to stagnant air belowdecks were soaked to the skin by seas which broke along the deck after each exceptional downward swoop of the loaded transport. Automatically MacDougall's glance took in all boat gripes and lashings within view. So far they all held securely and not a single landing craft was stove in. His experience indicated that at this point the fleet should begin to draw away from the typhoon, yet he longed for more definite assurance: a brightening of the rain-filled sky, an easing in the ship's tortured movements. He knew that one great wave thrown by a ninety-mile wind would smash every landing craft aboard to kindling wood and render the *Belinda* useless to the expedition. What if the fleet meteorologists were right after all? The task force was sandwiched between the typhoon and the Japanese waiting up ahead. MacDougall wondered if they would see Okinawa as scheduled on Easter Sunday morning.

When the steward had gone, Hawks rearranged the papers before him. "Very good, MacDougall; let's wind up here. We have to get the *Belinda's* Oplan together and mimeographed today. We've checked reports from all department heads. Let's see now; Medical, Engineering, Navigation and Communications, Boat Group, Damage Control, Cargo and Debarkation Plans, Supply. Get out your check sheet and let's go over required items for each department. . . ."

After another hour all plans were ready except for some of the details of cargo unloading.

"This gasoline setup doesn't make sense to me," said Mac-Dougall.

"Why?" asked Hawks. "What's the matter with it? Here's AdComSouWesPac's Shore Sustaining Plan." Hawks licked his forefinger and worked down through the volume. "Here it is: Zebra thirty-seven, paragraph two, section Charlie: 'The following APAs will provide fuel alongside to dukws and amtracks as required from 1 April through 7 April: *Doyen, Monrovia, Belinda* . . .' It's all in order."

"It's ordered all right," said MacDougall, "but it doesn't make sense to me. There's no need to jeopardize a ship of this size with a crew of more than six hundred, plus whatever wounded we have aboard—say two hundred of them—just to be a floating service station."

"Everything's expendable in combat."

"Yes, sir, but not that expendable. An LCT weighing two hundred tons or so would do the job just as well, probably better. They're lower in the water, they're just suited to handling gas drums."

"This is an order from an admiral. Do you think you know better than an admiral?"

"In this small detail, Capt'n, it is quite likely that I do. I've had more experience with gas drums than most admirals."

Hawks's face grew red. He rose from his seat and pounded the table with his fist. "Just last week I promote you and already you're getting too big for your britches! You lousy reserves—just who do you think you are, anyway?"

MacDougall's face was nearly as red as Hawks's. "Captain, I was merely pointing out—"

"You don't need to point out anything to me. I give the orders on this ship; you obey them. Now I want you to hoist out gas drums at every opportunity during debarkation. Get them all on deck as soon as possible; I want to get them clear above that waterline, in case of submarine attack."

MacDougall sat down and looked carefully through the admiral's plan for fueling amtracks and dukws. Not a word there about stowing explosive gasoline on deck. I'm into this now, he thought; I might as well go all the way.

"Wouldn't that be jumping from the frying pan to the fire, Capt'n?"

"What do you mean?" demanded Hawks with an ugly jaw.

"I think our main danger off Hagushi Beach will be from the air and not from subs."

"There you go again—expert on tactics now. You may be a good ship handler and know something about mercantile cargoes. This is a military question. I'm not just your commanding officer, I happen to be a graduate of the United States Naval Academy and a graduate of the War College with twenty-four years of training and experience in the Navy. Now you're giving me lessons! All right, go ahead, Mr. Executive Officer. I'm listening, but it had better be good!"

"I didn't mean it that way, Capt'n. I was just trying to say—"

"Well, say it then."

"The Japs have never done much to us with their subs: a ship here and there, but nothing like what the Germans would have done to us with the same setup. I don't think they've got it under the water."

"Oh, yes they have!" said Hawks. "They've got hundreds of short range subs saved up for this very thing. They have better torpedoes than ours; their fish run cool and straight. . . . If we take Okinawa, they've lost the war. They know it and they're going to hit us with everything they've got!"

"Yes, sir, but I'm sure it's going to be from the air."

"Shows what you don't know. We've got their fleet; their carrier divs are no longer operational. We'll have the air: hundreds of our own aircraft flying CAP over us. Submarines are something else. Even two hundred DDs can't stop a determined attack by five hundred submarines. You get that gasoline up on deck, mister."

"Is that an order, Capt'n?"

Hawks's lower jaw jerked to the left. "That's an order. Get those drums up on deck."

"Aye, aye, sir—but I'm afraid we're going to be sorry."

Hawks rose so abruptly that his chair clattered backwards to the deck. While his lower jaw worked angrily from side to side he poked MacDougall's chest. "What d'ya mean, we're going to be sorry? You don't have to be sorry at all; you just have to obey my orders. I'm running this ship!" Hawks sat down suddenly and wiped beads of perspiration from his forehead. "All right, MacDougall," he said in a quieter tone, "what *do* you mean?"

MacDougall's voice was quieter too as he said, "I mean the kamikazes, Capt'n, the Divine Wind boys. I suppose you're right about those submarines, but after what we saw in Leyte and at Lingayen, it seems to me that the crash-plane idea is the biggest threat the Japs can cook up against us. As you say, they know that Okinawa is the last island. They must have several thousand planes still operational. It wouldn't matter whether they were Army or Navy, they could fly 'em off Kyushu—any idiot could fly a compass course to Okinawa from there. If they mean to come in and crash I don't see how we can stop 'em all, we just can't. . . . Why that fellow at Lingayen—just three seconds out of the sun from a little hum to a bomb splashing in your face! I just don't see how they can miss."

Hawks put his head down on the table, cradled in his arms. After a long pause he lifted it again and gave MacDougall a steady look. "All right, I'm asking you," he said. "If you were in my shoes, what would you do about that gasoline?"

"Why, I'd—I'd—"

"See? It's different when you carry the load. You wise guys can advise me all you like, but I have to carry the load!" Hawks's voice rose almost hysterically as he repeated, "I have to carry the load, not you. I have to carry the load!"

"I'd leave the gas in troop gasoline compartment. We've got steam-smothering line, sprinkler system and CO_2 there; it's the safest place, sir. I'd bring it on deck as needed—and then get rid of it quick."

Hawks was staring at the bulkhead just in back of Mac-Dougall, who thought, he's looking right through me; I don't think he even sees me. Those eyes, glassy, almost opaque. I hope he gets through this one. I don't think I'd want the load —not that way at least, not from a skipper cracking in the middle of a landing. Hawks shook his head quickly from side to side as if to clear it.

"What did you say? Get rid of what?"

"The gasoline, sir—the storage."

Hawks stepped into his bathroom, took a full four-ounce bottle of medicinal whisky from the cabinet and drained it in rapid gulps. "O.K., O.K.," he said, wiping his mouth with the back of a hand. "You take care of it, Mac."

CHAPTER 44

On the morning of Easter Sunday there was no evidence of the fury of Japanese defense: no clouds of counterattacking paratroopers reported waiting in Kyushu; no hornetlike buzzing of fast suicide boats with built-in warheads, known to be hiding by the hundreds in small coves, ready for the sudden rush to thunderous, glorious death; not a shot from Okinawa's well-placed coastal artillery; most surprising of all, no fury of Divine Wind Special Attack Force suicide planes diving from the skies. Desperate counter measures on a scale not yet seen must surely come as Japanese died hard in defense of Okinawa, their homeland's last remaining island outpost, but there was no evidence yet as the great invasion fleet approached the main landing beaches at Hagushi on the southwest coast. Okinawa had been bombarded for seven days and nights while minesweepers protected by fast battleships swept all waters about Hagushi. Transport squadrons now steamed unmolested past Kerama Retto, a group of small islands within sight of Hagushi which had been captured during the previous week by the 77th Division. Now was the hour of testing: H Hour at 0830. One hundred twenty thousand Japanese waited behind carefully prepared defenses while over half a million American soldiers, marines and sailors closed in for the kill. Hearts beat fast and lumps refused to be swallowed in countless throats while men wondered, each in his own way, what was to be the grim joke-of-the-day this Easter Sunday—this April Fool's Day, 1945. And, at day's end, whom would the joke be on?

The sun rose bright in a sky that was clear except for great clouds of bombardment smoke rolling in from the sea. Standing tense but quiet on his bridge, Captain Hawks got his first glimpses of land through occasional gaps in drifting smoke; saw stony little hills of Naha, Yonabaru and the ancient fortress, Shuri. His crew was keyed up from long practice and overwaiting, eager to get into action. At the first indications of commands long since familiar, they sprang into landing craft, to boat davits, to cargo winches and to landing nets. Before the ending of the boatswain's mate's pipe: *Away All Boats,* winch-drums screamed and smoked with uncoiling wire cables while helmet-studded landing craft plunged down to the water carrying John, Dick, Joe, Carl to Okinawa this Easter Sunday. Others moved up to take their places, moved with a deliberate tramp, tramp, tramp—loaded with fighting packs, inflated life belts and rifles in Pliofilm—up the scuttles, along the decks and overside for the one-way ride. Davit boats dropped six at a time to upper-deck railings, paused long enough to load thirty-six marines in each, then dropped with the speed of elevators to dancing water, forty feet below. Winches hummed, steel cargo blocks slammed against hollow steel booms groaning with weight, yet Pappy Moran's hoarse shouts rose above all mechanical din as the rest of the landing craft were hoisted out yard and stay. "Hit that steadying line, Red. Take a turn now; take a turn. . . . Drop her now; DROP HER! . . . Unhook, down there. Pick up another one." Down the nets went human ants in jungle green: men, guns, ammo boxes, heavy machine guns in four pieces, in an unbroken flow like molasses from the lip of a man. During this process of debarkation the *Belinda's* rudder moved from side to side, like a fish's tail in a riffle, and her propeller moved ahead in short kicks, maintaining the exact geographical relation between ship and shore so that landing craft might hit the precise sector of beach. No red barn to head for here, only ancient Okinawan tombs, unidentified on plan or chart but plain in white splendor when seen through ragged gaps in gunsmoke.

Hawks moved quietly about his bridge, remaining motionless for minutes on end. His nostrils quivered with excitement as acrid smoke drifted past; nerves taut as overtuned fiddle strings but outwardly quiet, his manner seemed almost casual to the enlisted men at his elbow. Anxiety showed clearly on Jim Randall's pleasant face as he plotted the *Belinda's* position and kept her on station, "Things ought to pop any minute now," he remarked to Willicut, his quartermaster first.

Down in the *Belinda* command boat, anxiety clouded Brooks's face too as he cruised slowly around the ship, forming his boat waves, alert for any deviation from carefully worked out plans. Things were clicking this morning. He'd never seen it so fast, so smooth: thirty-two landing craft, four of them thirty-six ton LCM's, plus four extra dukws launched in thirteen minutes. The *Belinda* davit tenders dropped their fully loaded boats with the casual competence of office-building elevator operators. Moran and Alvick had practically tossed the rest of them overside with cargo tackle. Boat officers were sharp today: all waves were formed up exactly as planned with the right boat in the right wave circle carrying the right landing unit; even Ensign Tuttle was on station. When Brooks came alongside Kruger's first-wave guide boat he grinned and yelled, "We might as well have stayed in the sack, Karl. They don't need us at all this morning." Kruger grinned back briefly, but his tanned face was serious again almost instantly and his gaze was directed skyward, rather than towards the smoke-obscured shore line. Brooks could feel his face tightening once more—that sky: best place to look for trouble. Then he shrugged his shoulders. "Take her around the other side again, Cox," he said to Larson. "We'd better check up on those other waves; it's nearly time to shove off."

Aboard the *Belinda*, some of the crew looked anxious, perhaps because of the intent quiet of these veteran marines climbing down the nets for another one-way ride into battle. More than half of the sailors went about their well-rehearsed duties with considerable pleasure. During the passage from Leyte they had thought quite a lot about their chances of being killed this morning, but everything was humming now, winches, boat davits, the steady throbbing turbines and auxiliaries below-decks, and the motion was reassuring. After midnight reveille, two o'clock breakfast and the long wait at the guns while the attack force stood in to the transport area, the mingled feeling of warm sun, no Japs and familiar work to do was most welcome.

Around number five hatch they whistled as they rigged slings to hoist out gasoline drums, and stocky Ned Strange paused to ask his boatswain's mate, "Where is them Japs?"

"Don't you worry, little boy," said Doyle. "There's Japs in them hills over there."

"But why ain't they shooting at us? They got big guns; you told me so yourself. Why ain't they shootin' at us—and where's them kami planes? Ain't nobody's been crashed; this here's a picnic, sort of."

"Cut the chitchat, you two," ordered Chief Alvick. "Let the gun crews worry about the Japs. All you have to do is to run those winches smooth and fast and keep your eye on the hatch tender; we can't muff any signals or drop any loads today."

MacDougall, busy prowling the ship looking for bottlenecks in debarkation and finding none, had time to wonder about Japs. Why were they so quiet? What was the matter with the shore batteries? How about the hundreds of suicide crash boats; the kamikaze planes—were the Japs saving them for tonight, tomorrow? Or would they come tearing out of noth-

389

ing, like that dive bomber at Lingayen, only this time from all directions at once? This was like the phony war in France in 1939. Notwithstanding all the unearthly thunder of battleship salvos and rocket barrages, he had the odd sensation of being in a vast vacuum of silence.

During midafternoon, MacDougall slid down the ladders from the bridge and strode into the wardroom for a quick cup of coffee. He found Dr. Flynn standing under the radio speaker listening to a propaganda broadcast in English from Radio Tokyo.

"Business must be light, Pat," remarked MacDougall. "It's really something; you listening to Tokyo Rose on D Day—L Day, that is."

"Yes, just three casualties aboard so far, and they're not bad. But you must listen to this dame: she's the limit!"

By the time MacDougall had filled his mug and walked over to the speaker, a man with a pseudo-Oxford accent had taken over the mike at Tokyo: "American forces . . . landing at Hagushi . . . repulsed with terrific losses. . . . Reef strewn with bodies of these foolish ones. . . . Japanese soldiers defending to the glory of the Emperor . . ." There was quite a lot of this sort of thing. Bored and remembering that it was time to get up to the bridge and relieve Randall for a few minutes, he started for the door, only to be stopped short by the following: "It has now been positively determined that if Okinawa is lost to the American forces, Japan will be lost. Therefore this is the hour of Japanese opportunity to exercise glorious defense."

Flynn was shaking his head. "The guy must be nuts, admitting something like that. No matter what they do we'll take this island somehow or other."

"We'll take it all right, but we haven't seen the last of our little Jap friends. I can feel it in my bones. We're going to get it—somebody is. It isn't possible for them to give up this place without giving us the works first. You just wait—"

Flynn held up his hand. "Listen, Mac. Listen to this."

The phony accent from Tokyo was getting worked up now as he gave an English version of a pep talk to Jap suicide pilots:

"The faithful kamikaze special attack plane units—divine eagles, bombs composed of men and planes which plunge down on enemy ships—young, ruddy-faced men—are ever seeking the glorious road, again and again dealing crushing blows to the enemy. Each man ties scarf of white silk about his head, symbol of glorious death, rejoicing forever with ancestors at Yasukuni Shrine. Friends wave sad farewells to these broad-shouldered youths who are without even parachutes. The skies are slowly brightening for the Imperial Forces, brightening with the flaming ruins of American warships!"

"Trying to scare us," said MacDougall.

"Trying to!" exclaimed Flynn, wiping his face with his handkerchief. "As far as I'm concerned, he's succeeded very well!"

MacDougall laughed, yet as he climbed back to the bridge to relieve Randall, his face sobered while he thought: what a repulsive proposition! There was a nice breeze on the bridge wing and the sunlight cheered away his misgivings. It was time to run to the reef in order to cut running time for the boats unloading tanks, guns and ammunition.

Hawks was standing beside his high seat, eating a late lunch from a tray placed upon it.

"You take her in, MacDougall," he said. "Randall will plot her along for you."

"Aye, aye, sir," answered MacDougall, then to the O.O.D., "Ahead standard; right twenty degrees rudder." Listening to Jim Randall's voice giving efficient directions through the chart room intercom, MacDougall stood on the bridge wing, conning the *Belinda* in to the reef, cutting left and right to dodge drifting transports and to avoid line of fire of destroyers providing call fire to marines in the battle line. At the beginning of the run in, a dense cloud of battle smoke rolled along shore, obscuring most of Okinawa from sight. Now and then he saw the peak at Naha, always the combat air patrol droning high and American dive bombers plunging down into the smoke, adding to the fires, rising again and streaking back to the carriers. Then off-shore breeze worked at battle smoke, rolling it inland so that here and there little hills stood clear—hills and lovely green valleys, slopes ridged with storm-warped pines, tile-roofed houses nestling together in small groups, white tombs shaped like tremendous easy chairs with oval backs and arms set into the contours. At last he picked out the mouth of the Hagushi River, water gleaming clear in the sunshine, cooler than the Lunga River, he thought. *The Lunga River. "I have posted the Lunga River—"* Cool, satin-smooth, drifting with the current—death had been there; now Okinawa on Easter Sunday. MacDougall scratched the rash on his chest.

There was the *Belinda's* beach just south of the river mouth: beach flags, little dots of men moving about the sand, bobbing landing craft—all this popped into view through his binoculars. He had the *Belinda* moving slowly now, inching towards the clusters of landing craft until there was no further need of binoculars to see landing beach and white reef bare now at ebb tide.

"This is about it, Capt'n."

Hawks, who had been leaning over the weather cloth, watching the shore but making no comment, raised his head sufficiently to nod. "Very good," he said at last, his voice sounding as if it came from far away.

"Shall we anchor at short stay, sir?"

"No, just drift around, keep close to our beach." Hawks turned slowly in a complete circle, looking all about the ship, then leaned over the weather cloth again. "Keep lookouts alert, especially surface—submarine—" Hawks's voice drifted off and he seemed lost in contemplation once more. MacDougall felt his scalp tingling. I get it, he thought. He's letting me handle things while he rests. He never does that unless he's expecting trouble.

MacDougall looked about the water, feeling foolish at the relief he felt that there were merely landing craft all about, no sign of sneaking periscope. Then he shivered and all sense of relief left; that broadcast—that stupid, damnable propaganda— "divine eagles, bombs composed of men and planes, which plunge down on enemy ships." MacDougall walked over to the bridge talker. "Alert all sky lookouts," he said. "Tell 'em to keep sharp; get in the reports; don't wait to be sure." Then he headed for the charthouse to shake up the radar crew.

Debarkation continued with increasing acceleration. The tide was low, yet battalion after battalion was carried to the reef in LCVPs, transferred to amtracks and dukws which landed them dry feet on the banks of the Hagushi River mouth. Further north the same operation was being performed by other transport squadrons. Divisional command posts were set up ashore together with reinforcements not yet needed. The line was everywhere two miles deep—already beyond the point previously planned a reasonable for three days of fighting. LSTs with pickaback pontoons moved close to the reef and side launched them for use as cargo barges and floating docks. Bulldozers were already at work on Yontan and Kadena airfields, which had been captured within the hour. Casualties thus far were surprisingly light; to the astonishment of all, no Jap mortar fire had fallen upon the boat waves, no coast artillery had yet opened fire upon the mass of ships off Hagushi. Things were humming. Jubilant sailors slapped each other on the back, asking, "Where's them Japs?"

On the signal bridge there was a happy commotion as a message to all ships was hoisted to the flagship's yardarm. Moments later MacDougall handed a message to Hawks, who raised his head from his elbows long enough to read, *"Well Done to all hands."* Hawks grunted, handed the message back, and retreated within himself once again.

MacDougall carried the message to Randall on the opposite wing of the bridge. "The Old Man is really in a stupe," he said.

Randall raised up from the pelorus stand. "What now?"

"We got a 'Well Done' and he just grunted. In this Navy a skipper will stand on his head all day for those two little words. At Leyte he pranced around the bridge like a wild man, yelling, 'Well done; well done, *Belinda!*' He even sang us a ditty about it; now he grunts. And this has been something to get excited about: over twice the number of men have been landed here already today than were landed on D Day at Normandy!"

"That was twenty-one thousand, wasn't it?"

"That's right; Hawks told us all about it. Now we land fifty thousand before sunset and he's sad and weary about it all."

Looking tensely about, MacDougall still saw no evidence of the full fury of Japanese defense. The first hint came with sunset. All ships except a few retained for bombardment, for screening and for the mothering of landing craft remaining at the beach had been ordered to sea for night retirement, the most sensible defense against air and submarine attack. More supplies and troops had been landed than could be used during the night. Underway and clear of land, ships could maneuver at high speed together as a team and mass their combined fire-power against air attack, while screening destroyers could be deployed most profitably against submarines known to be lurking in the area. But the dipping of the sun seemed to signal Japanese planes. While the fleet was still disorganized in a vast traffic jam of hundreds of ships rushing out independently to rendezvous beyond Keise Shima, five miles offshore, American radar picked up unidentified planes, closing in from north, east and south. The time for hot gun barrels and uneasy stomachs had arrived.

Captain Hawks was anxious to get the *Belinda* out to sea and formed up. "Flank speed," he ordered, from his position at conn, just forward of the pilothouse. Jim Randall answered from within the steel shutters, clanged shut across the windows at call to battle stations.

MacDougall stood beside Hawks, sweeping the sky with his binoculars. He saw no planes, not even the friendly combat air patrol. He supposed that they had been vectored out to intercept the Japs, but there were no reports of friendly planes from radar. The voice of Gene Cooper, the radar officer, came with a brisk confidence which MacDougall did not share, "Bogeys, three; zero-five-five, twenty miles, closing. Bogeys many, desig Raid Two, zero-one-zero, twenty-five miles, closing rapidly." On and on went Cooper's voice. Would he never stop? MacDougall wondered. Gun barrels were trained in the direction of the nearest raid. Distant ships began firing; still MacDougall's glasses revealed nothing but crimson and gold cloud forms swimming in a shimmering, empty sky, blue deepening towards black with overtones of yellow smoke haze.

MacDougall looked at Hawks, wondered what the skipper

was thinking about. All this time, both had been looking left and right at dozens of nearby ships which had broken clear of the central mass and, like the *Belinda,* were steaming in a general westerly direction. The trouble lay, MacDougall saw, in that squadron flagships were widely separated so that individual ships were steaming at intersecting angles, each trying to get formed up in proper column. A large attack transport was bearing down upon the *Belinda* from starboard. MacDougall jumped to the pelorus, squinted through the sight vane for a few seconds, then hurried back to Hawks's side. "Ship zero-three-five, relative, Capt'n; on collision course. Shall we swing astern of her or slow down?"

Hawks continued to stare straight ahead. "What's her name?" he asked.

"PA 79, sir."

"That's the *Riverside.* Carry on. Hold course and speed."

"But Capt'n, she's got the right of way."

"That doesn't matter."

"But Capt'n, directives clearly require—"

"I said, 'Hold course and speed.' "

"We'll hit her."

"No we won't. Carruthers Johnson has her. I'm senior to him."

MacDougall jumped to the pelorus and took another bearing of the *Riverside's* bow. He rushed back and broke into another of Cooper's bogey reports.

"Bearing hasn't changed, Capt'n. We'll hit him!"

"We won't hit Carruthers," said Hawks. "I shoved him naked the length of a soapy deck at Annapolis. He'll give way."

The fool! MacDougall fumed inwardly. Here we go on another trip into the sunset; well I'm not going to wait so long this time. I'm not going to ruin my career and drown six hundred men for a crazy man's notion. He ran over to the wing. Radar was too busy with Japs; he'd have to estimate distance by eye. About nine hundred yards—he'd swing right, stop engines and fight it out with Hawks later. Then to his amazement he saw the *Riverside* sheer away and let the *Belinda* pass clear. Still Hawks had not turned his head to look at her after the first quick glance.

The thunder of gunfire rolled nearer. Out of the yellow battle smoke, high up in the darkening sky, MacDougall saw a small black shape darting down, a second, then a third: Japs for sure! Down they came out of scarlet and gold sunset into the darker nether air, twisting and turning, but ever downward, lighted now by exploding flak. Cooper was reporting something about bogies but his voice was drowned out by gunfire, rolling closer. Hawks swept the sky with his binoculars, paused to watch the diving enemy, then swept on. He looked briefly at MacDougall and shouted, "He's after the Northern Group."

MacDougall nodded, swallowing as he searched for closer planes. Hawks was not sightseeing; was not interested in anything which did not menace his ship. A steadily increasing mass of ships was milling, surging, rushing all about, the mass movement was seaward, yet as involved as a large school of fish. Worst traffic mess I ever saw, thought MacDougall. The *Belinda* seemed about to draw into a comparatively clear spot when another attack transport, carrying a squadron flag, suddenly bore across her bow from port. It looked like a dead heat; if each ship maintained course and speed they were bound to collide.

MacDougall pressed Hawks's elbow. "Look, Capt'n—look at those fools! We have the right of way; they're supposed to stay clear."

Hawks dropped his binoculars to horizon level and swung around for a quick look at the converging transport. "Sheer off and back her down," he ordered.

"But Capt'n—Rules of the Road require us to hold course and speed. They must take the action; we're not allowed to alter course or speed until they—"

Hawks grabbed MacDougall roughly by the shoulder and spun him around. "Stop engines, I say! Back full!"

Angry and apprehensive, MacDougall complied. This is going to be a mess, he thought. What in the world?—in this Navy you never know! Hawks was shouting at him again while Cooper's voice, no longer calm and methodical, yelled from the squawk box something about bandits closing, collision course; but Hawks's words mixed in with and overpowered Cooper's. "The Commodore," Hawks was shouting. "Much senior to me . . . Always give clear passage to flagships." Then something in Cooper's report registered with Hawks. Looking aloft, he sighted another diving plane, much closer than the others. "You watch the ship!" he yelled to MacDougall; then to his talker, "Control, get on that fellow! Commence firing; Commence firing! Lead the target, you fools, lead the target!" Hawks began jumping up and down with excitement, striking his right fist savagely into his left palm. "Hit the dirty black bastard! Lead the target; lead the target!"

Belinda's guns reacted so suddenly and savagely it seemed as if the ship herself was exploding. MacDougall took one split-second glance upward at a tremendously exciting movement of exploding color ringed about a single-engined Jap fighter now plummeting down towards a point a few hundred yards ahead of the *Belinda's* bow. He ran to the engine annunciator and swung the handle once more to emphasize the full astern signal to the engine room. A scant seventy-five yards away, the flagship APA, head of another squadron, swept majestically past. Torque of backing engines was swinging the *Belinda's* bow away from the reckless advance of this other ship. MacDougall felt a slacking in the tension caused by this near collision, yet at the same time an increase in his awareness of that black plane diving closer. He stole another glance upward around the rim of his helmet: gun barrels pointed lower, exploding shells blasted nearer, while the plane still dropped. She was in a flaming sideslip now, heading toward the exact spot the *Belinda* would soon have occupied had her engines not been backed. All the flagship's guns were belching and chattering. MacDougall saw figures of men running excitedly across her upper bridge, upturned faces on lower decks; everywhere clusters of guns with men in helmets hanging back in the firing straps or thrusting in fresh clips of ammunition. The flagship was passing fast, uncomfortably close and still converging but she should pass clear. MacDougall watched the relative movement of these masses of gray steel, caught a glimpse of a tall man in a gray helmet standing stiff and proud in the center of the flagship's bridge—her captain no doubt, standing motionless in command while lesser men ran busily about him. Now the crashing of guns and nearing flames pulled MacDougall's gaze away from all else. The flaming ball of shattered kamikaze dropped at a steep angle. One wing was shot away, then the other caught in the flagship's rigging. The plane spun around like a crippled windmill. What looked like an engine—perhaps a warhead—dropped out and fell into the open hatch just forward of the bridge, while the flaming wreckage crashed into the bridge itself. Tremendous double explosion, bridge gone, captain gone—guns silent now while white-hot flames seethed upward like writhing snakes of fire. Bridge, captain, helmsman gone; the flagship's propeller nevertheless maintained an even beat, thrusting a boiling white wake astern as she swept on in flaming dignity across the *Belinda's* bow. They got her instead of us, thought MacDougall. That Hawks! . . . Breaks two Rules of the Road in three minutes and saves his ship!

MacDougall ordered speed ahead and left rudder to avoid the burning flagship. She would have to help herself for the time being; salvage tugs might be available but a ship could easily sink or burn to the water's edge while waiting for help. It was the duty of other transports to get to sea and avoid a similar fate. The *Belinda* shook violently as she gathered headway and left the burning transport astern. MacDougall heard intermittent bursts of gunfire towards the south, but the battle sound was moving away. Here and there towering flames shot up from the darkening waters, showing where other ships had been hit and set afire. Hawks was over on the starboard wing now, both elbows on the railing, chin cupped in the palms of his hands, silently watching the flaming hull of the flagship to which he had given right of way and, unintentionally, the privilege of being crashed by a Jap suicide plane. He waited until he saw streams of water from a dozen fire hoses playing on the blaze, then walked amidships and stood beside Mac-Dougall. "All right, Mac," he said. "I'll take the conn now." Hawks looked ahead, ordered a small change in course, then poked MacDougall sharply in the ribs, leering into his face as he said, "So you wanted me to take the right of way, did you?"

MacDougall grinned and sighed with relief. How glad I am to be wrong this time! he thought as he walked to the bridge wing and looked about. Gun crews still stood tense and alert while their loaders refilled ready boxes from fore and after magazines. All around the horizon he saw ships plowing seaward, eager now to form up and to be lost in the darkness. Sea and lower sky were fading into deep shadow now, but skies high aloft to westward glowed pale yellow and gold where an invection of cooling battle smoke floated among islands of rose-tinted alto-cumulus. A new rash of gunfire brought MacDougall's attention back to the surface. A single-engine Jap "Zeke" had come out from Okinawa, flying low over the water, unseen and unheard in the confusion. Unlike his fellows, he chose no crash to flaming death but flew brilliantly about, banking sharply, zooming to masthead heights then swooping down until his propeller fanned a wake in the darkening sea. Ship after ship opened fire, cautiously getting in a few bursts whenever possible to shoot without hitting other ships. While Hawks watched for his chance, the *Belinda's* guns followed the "Zeke's" movements. The little Jap seemed to live a charmed life, streaking back and forth in the middle of this compact group of ships, any one of which could have downed him easily, had he been in the clear. At last, as if realizing that luck was running out, he streaked between two old battleships, his wings turret-high, then, gunning his motor, zoomed aloft for his life. At once all hell broke out in the fleet as half a million dollars worth of high explosive was thrown at him. They'll get him now, MacDougall thought; just a matter of seconds now. Amazingly the Jap still climbed, until the set-fused 40-mm flak peppered far beneath him. Still far from clear, he continued his weaving climb while proximity-fused five-inch shells passed by on either side to explode high in the clouds. Up he went, seeming gradually smaller to MacDougall's watching eyes, until at last he was a tiny black silhouette against that fading patch of yellow and gold.

Evidently feeling safe at last, he began a wild display of acrobatics, utterly without practical purpose. He seemed to be saying: *Here am I, brave Japanese gentleman. I do not lose face*

*with you. I fly close to your biggest guns. I am afraid to die and
I am not afraid to die. I perform most difficult acrobatics for
you. I observe the sunset. I bow to the Emperor, Son of Heaven.
Tomorrow I die: Divine Wind blow hot breath against your
ships: all destroy. Tonight I am Japanese boy going home to rice
and saki. Good night, sank you.* Ending his mad display with a
lightning quick snap roll, he climbed steeply still higher until
dying sunlight glowed faintly against his distant wings, and then
he was gone.

Captain Hawks spat over the side, the first time MacDougall
ever remembered him doing so. "Jap carrier pilot," he said
shortly. "Their Army men can't fly like that."

CHAPTER 45

Shortly after two in the morning of 6 April, Dr. Flynn climbed
the inside ladder which ran up from the passage next the captain's cabin to the chart room and bridge. Passing close to the
door of his own small stateroom, Flynn had looked at his
bunk—he longed to stretch out on that sweat-dampened mattress, just for two hours or so! He had been on the job steadily
now for three days and nights. Wounded were arriving as fast
as medics could pack them out of the deadly ravines or down
the brutal little hills and get them into the boats. No time for
sleep now. Flynn coughed, a dry, hacking cough, and opened
the door into the chart room. Here he came suddenly face to
face with MacDougall, who was hurrying out of the place.

"Have you got a minute, Mac? Something important I—"

MacDougall spun around on the ball of a foot and faced
Flynn from the other side. "Sure, Pat," he said. "Just a minute.
I got to see the Old Man; then I'll come back. . . . Hey, you
look corked, you old butcher! There's a pot of hot joe over
there by Stanowski. . . . You guys get the doctor some
coffee."

Flynn waved away an offered chair, took the coffee mug
with a nod of appreciation to Stanowski and leaned against the
chart table. The radarman looked sharply at Flynn. It wasn't
like the doctor to be quiet. They must be dying on him again,
Stanowski thought. At last Flynn sighed away a little of his
tension and managed a grin. "Afraid to sit down," he said.
"Wouldn't be able to get up any more if I did." He coughed
again, looked up at the ventilation pipe over the chart table.
It was silent like all the others aboard: turned off by routine
order whenever general battle stations were called. The air in
the chart room was not only stifling, but acrid with caustic
smoke, which he could see filtering into the place through the
galvanized louvers bolted over the porthole so as to permit en-

trance of a little air from without while preserving the blackout.

The inside door opened again and MacDougall returned, pulling off his steel helmet and loosening the straps on his kapok life jacket.

"What can I do for you, Pat?" he asked.

"The blowers," said Flynn. "I came to see you about the blowers. Can't you have some ventilation turned on in the sick bay?"

"I'd sure like to, Pat. Must be pretty ripe down there. . . . We just don't dare. The Japs are really after us now—reports coming in—they're pasting hell out of the picket boats now—attacking in force—it's just a matter of time—"

"Yes, but I've got to have air, Mac. Those patients—" Flynn doubled over with another spasm of coughing.

"I wish I could give it to you, Pat. I just can't. Don't you see what would happen. Boom! They hit you, and just like that one part of the ship is in flames and the ventilation ducts are shattered. Fire gets sucked in the hole—there's enough dust in those things to carry it through hundreds of feet of pipe in a matter of seconds—then the whole ship's on fire."

"Couldn't you have a man standing by to throw the switch. A man's life depends on it. We have a marine with shrapnel in his lung: have to enter the thoracic cavity. This oil smoke you're making to hide the ship—it's got down into surgery like a heavy fog. We can hardly see what we're doing. . . . And the patient. Even with an oxygen tent, I don't see . . . He's so weak, Mac. He can't fight that stuff."

In a flash MacDougall remembered the night he had been stretched out on that operating table—Flynn's first case. It had been something of a joke in the surgery then, but it hadn't been funny to him. He remembered the trembling chill of shock, the gasping for breath—and there had been no artificial fog, no question of survival. He'd have to get around the Old Man some way. Those blowers made so much noise they were easily heard from the bridge. Hawks was in no mood for any trifling with his orders today; he'd explode if he heard the slightest sound of a blower running. . . .

"Say! You couldn't use the blowers anyway, Pat. They'd only suck in more of this smoke—there's no provision for filtering it."

"Filter? You give me an idea. I can put wet muslin over the pipe. That should catch the smoke."

"Sure, and it'll keep all the air out too. There isn't enough poop in these blowers to turn over a feather. . . . Of course —if it was all concentrated in one pipeline . . . O.K., Pat, I'll go ask the Old Man anyway. You come along and give him your Mammy act."

"Fine," said Flynn. "Let's go. I should be back in the sick

399

bay. Bell and Gates will be ready." Flynn started hastily towards the pilot-house door.

MacDougall reached out, grabbed Flynn by the arm and spun him around. "Just a minute, Pat. We've got to rig you for the bridge. The Old Man's suddenly gone nuts on this flash-proof gear, helmets and life jackets. I don't dare poke my nose out there without at least a kapok jacket—that beekeeper's gear is just too much. I just say, 'Yes, sir,' every time he tells me to wear it, and keep on going. This smoke is suffocating enough." Flynn got into a spare helmet and life jacket and followed MacDougall into the pilothouse.

It's like going back to the coal mines, thought Flynn. Aside from the dim glow from the compass bezel, the place was pitch dark. He sensed, rather than saw, the men on duty who were crowded into the place. He could hear them coughing, smell their sweaty bodies; he bumped into some of them as he followed MacDougall's more familiar progress the best he could. The smoke had penetrated into this inner nest of steel, this so-called brain of the ship—a term he sometimes took exception to. He coughed again, stumbled over the wheel gratings and found himself out on the port bridge wing. As his eyes became adjusted to the darkness, Flynn became aware of masses of steel superstructure about him, of murky silhouettes of raised flak-gun barrels on the deck above, the ever-present men in helmets waiting in silence behind them. He knew that the ship was still anchored close to the reef off Hagushi, but all he could see was smoke, drifting and whirling from the gasoline-driven fog machines on bow and stern of every ship in the anchorage. Dirty stuff. Well, if it would hide them from the Japs . . . God knew he had trouble enough in the sick bay without a suicide plane blowing up the bridge here. His night vision was improving further now. He could see a row of heads on the bridge wing. That short sturdy figure, Jim Randall—the man never seemed to sleep—none of them did. There must be a new regulation against sleep, thought Flynn with a flicker of his old humor. That short fellow sagging half asleep between upright shoulder blades: that would be Biggs, the captain's orderly. But what was that out there—tall man from Mars? Hawks?—why it couldn't be! Yet there was no mistaking that erect figure, the square-cut shoulders. Nose and mouth were covered with a sort of veil which draped down from beneath his helmet—what had MacDougall said?—"Beekeeper's gear?"—that's what it looked like all right. The face was smeared with some of that gray-colored flash cream they'd sent aboard at Leyte but nobody would use. The Old Man's arms were covered with long, loose-fitting gauntlets. He looked so strange—it hardly seemed possible . . . Now Hawks turned around and shoved his face down to Flynn's. There was no mistaking those penetrating eyes.

"Well, Flynn," said Hawks. His tone sounded pleased, relieved at any rate. "You're just the man I wanted to see. Come down in the cabin for a minute. MacDougall, you watch those radar reports. Inform me at once if any bogey gets inside twenty miles."

"Aye, sir, but Flynn has a problem, sir. He's—"

Hawks cut MacDougall off abruptly. "I'll take care of Flynn," he said. "Watch out for her now. Continue to make smoke on all generators." Followed by Flynn, Hawks left the bridge.

MacDougall paced the open bridge wing, peering into the billowing clouds of mechanical fog which surged about him heavily in the feeble breeze. It seemed as if the fleet were trying to choke itself to death; the stuff stung his eyes and irritated his lungs. It was bothering the crew; from the foredeck and up on the signal bridge he heard dry coughing. I wonder if an ostrich enjoys sticking his head in the sand, MacDougall thought. More bogey reports from the intercom speaker in the bridge wing overhead: Stanowski's voice calling off positions of whole groups of attacking Jap planes as calmly as if he were giving a range on the guide ship. Day after day the Japs had been attacking the picket boats, swarming like flies around a jam pot. Every now and then a few broke through the picket line, ran the gauntlet of the combat air patrol and ended up crashing into some ship in the transport area. For three days the *Belinda's* crew had slept only beside their guns. After watch in the engine room, on the bridge, down in damage control, or wherever their special duties were, they stood four hours at the guns, after which they had four hours to eat or sleep beside the guns provided general quarters were not sounded. This endless rotation continued watch after watch, day and night. So far the *Belinda* had been lucky. Ships had been hit close about her; even the old battleship *Tennessee* had taken a kamikaze aboard. The long waiting, the frequent alerts, sudden bursts of firing followed by more long waiting —all had been nerve-racking at first. By now the crew were settled into a state of alert indifference. They slumped at their posts, talking about the same casual, monotonous things; yet the instant an alert sounded, they would snap wide awake, ready to take on Japs from any angle. They were worn and raw inside, but few of them noticed it; they were just sweating it out.

MacDougall listened to another bogey report: raid of six Japs swinging around the picket area. Reports of another destroyer out there in sinking condition. He walked over to

Randall, who sagged against the steel bridge apron with crossed elbows supporting his chin. "Those cans out on the picket line are sure taking it: warning us of Japs coming and then taking them on."

Randall raised his head. "Nothing much we can do about it now," he said. "Give 'em gas when they want it—the rest of the time stand by to wait."

"Reminds me of New Year's Eve at Sansapor. Remember the Jap snooper?"

"Yep," said Randall. "Good old Sansapor: nice peaceful place. Wish I was there again, waiting for mail."

"Wonder when the next bunch of Japs will break through."

"I don't know—tired of figuring it out. Like I said, nothing we can do about it."

"Nothing but make smoke. Those three fog generators are sure putting it out!"

"Yeah. I hope it's fooling the Japs," said Randall. "My throat's as dry as a piece of asbestos."

"It's worse on the wounded," said MacDougall. "Flynn wants me to turn on the blowers in the sick bay. He's got to saw through some guy's ribs. I was just going to ask the Old Man about it when he dragged Flynn down below."

"May be just as well," said Randall. "The skipper's been so touchy recently . . . But Flynn has a way with him; it's been weeks since I've heard Hawks make a single crack about doctors. Everybody else on the ship's been catching it; there must be some reason."

"Yes," said MacDougall, who felt strongly inclined to tell his friend Randall just what the reason was, "there must be."

Having set aside his flashproof headdress and washed off the protective cream, Hawks sat on the edge of his bunk, carefully nursing the last swallow from a four-ounce bottle of medicinal whisky.

"You'll bring me another bottle, Flynn, before you get involved again in surgery? . . . You'll bring it yourself, won't you?"

"Yes, sir. I'll get it right away." Flynn started out the door, then paused as if he had just remembered something. "Captain?"

"Yes," said Hawks, thirsting for more whisky.

"I know you've organized a very efficient damage control system—"

"Damage control, yes, sure; but that's not in your line. Why bring up damage control?"

"Well, sir, I have a problem in the sick bay. MacDougall has explained the regulations to me—he seems bound to go by them. But you have such an efficient organization down there with Fraser and his men, I thought that perhaps you would be

402

able to figure out some way to improve ventilation in the sick bay area during these prolonged G.Q.s. The surgery especially —this chemical fog is making survival difficult. We have such a fine record so far. Not even the flagship has—"

"Ventilation!" cried Hawks. "Is that all you need?"

"Yes, sir. I thought Fraser could have a man standing by to shut it off. I'm not trying to tell you—"

"Go on and get my whisky," said Hawks. "I'll have the ventilation straightened out before you get back. MacDougall is getting so he's afraid to break a rule. I'll show him—I'll show the commodore that old *Beachhead Belinda* can provide more gasoline and rehabilitate more wounded than that overgrown hulk he sails on!"

Flynn knew when it was time to go. "Thank you, Captain," he said. "I'll be back in a minute."

Flynn hurried down to the sick bay. Before he got the double-locked medical safe open, the welcome sound of blowers came from the vent pipe. Waving to Frank Bell, who stood impatiently at the surgery door, Flynn ran back up the ladder to the cabin. Hawks was midway through one of the quick shower-shave-and-change-of-khakis routines he did to freshen up after sleepless nights on the bridge. He put down his razor, reached for and opened the small bottle and took a long pull. Then he turned around, half sitting on the edge of his wash basin, and exhaled deeply.

"There's life in that stuff, Dr. Flynn."

"Yes, sir. As long as you don't overdo it."

"I won't. . . . We've got a long pull ahead before we get out of here."

"Oh," said Flynn. "I thought we'd be leaving soon—most of the gasoline has been sent ashore, MacDougall told me, and the sick bay is nearly full—of course nothing like we had at Saipan."

Hawks finished shaving with a few rapid strokes, washed and dried his face. Flynn noticed that he seemed like his old self: confident, eyes clear and penetrating as he said, "I mean a long pull in the next day or two, Flynn. A day can seem like a year. I found that out at North Africa, way back in this war. . . . I get my cryptic reports, you know. Well, I'll just tell you. Yesterday Marc Mitscher gave the Japs a pasting on the ground at Kyushu. Carrier planes shot down and destroyed over a hundred Jap aircraft. They're dispersed on fields all over the place. The Japs are clever at hiding planes, making dummies—that sort of thing. But they aren't that active unless they're planning something. I've thought all along that we'd really get it from the air when we got to Okinawa. Now Mitscher's stirred up a hornet's nest. They won't be able to wait any longer for fear of losing all their planes on the ground. There's only one thing a Jap does when he's cornered: he fights with everything he's got. That's why I'm changing my pants now. It's going to be a long day, Dr. Flynn."

Twenty minutes after Hawks returned to the bridge there was another urgent alert, and he set general quarters at once. Five Jap planes had veered off from the attack on the picket line, thirty-five miles at sea, found a break clear of the combat air patrol, which was busy fighting in a different vector, and swooped low over the transport area. TBS blared anew with reports and orders: fire only upon sight; it would be unwise to give away the location of fleet units; optimum camouflage required maximum use of mechanical fog by all ships. Here and there firing burst out.

"I'll bet they all can't see what they're shooting at," said Randall.

Engines roared close: a low horizontal attack. There was a tremendous explosion close to port, the ship anchored nearest to the *Belinda* had been badly hit. Flames glowed through the thick, choking smoke.

"Must've been a torpedo attack," said MacDougall.

"We'll never know," said Hawks. "But there's something more important. How do they know exactly where the ships are? That was no accident." Hawks looked aloft at the layer of billowing smoke. No human eye could penetrate it, but how high was it effective? After all, fog generators were down on main-deck level. Attack was coming from the air.

"MacDougall," Hawks called sharply.

"Yes, sir."

"Climb aloft and see how high this mechanical fog is going. Go yourself, then report to me at once."

"Aye, aye, sir." The radar mast reaching aloft from the signal bridge would do. MacDougall ran up the ladder, threw his helmet and life jacket under the tower and began to climb. It was like going into a no man's land: except for steel rungs and nearby framework, he could see nothing but thick, choking cloud: horrible emulsion compounded of diesel and vegetable oils, heated in a red-hot chamber and forced out under pressure of a gasoline pump. Adding to ship-made fog, Fauré was out there with his two smoke boats, dumping smoldering carbide into the water to windward of the anchorage. It was hard to climb, breathing the stuff. MacDougall was up four sections of framework; two more and he would reach the great bedspring antenna of the air-search radar, a machine which could see through this smoke, locate Jap planes a hundred miles out over the sea. He hitched at his belt and clambered up one more section. From there on up was nothing but naked steel mast with foot cleats welded on either side. Halfway up this MacDougall paused in surprise, breathing deeply of the clear air, yet not noticing it in his astonishment. He might have been on top of ten thousand foot Mt. Haleakala, back at Maui, or flying in a plane over a heavy layer of cloud—except for one thing: all about him were the tips of a hundred masts, poking up through the manmade fog. A hundred masts in neat little pairs of two which showed the location and even the heading of every ship anchored off Okinawa. Clouds of nature were five or six thousand feet above manmade fog: rolls of strato-cumulus with wide chinks between, enough to allow intermittent peeks at the gibbous moon which was giving the fleet away to the Japs.

MacDougall caught one swift look at Okinawa hills, clearly visible over choking billow of mechanical fog: gun flashes by the thousands, red-hot tracers and shells going up and down the slopes below Naha. Then he clambered down as fast as he could go, through the hundred-foot layer of fog into the secret little world of the *Belinda*.

Breathlessly he made his report to Hawks, who snorted: "Just what I thought. Who's kidding whom around here? Robinson," he shouted.

"Yes, sir," answered the communications officer.

"Got your TBS transmitter red hot?"

"Yes, sir—all ready to go."

"Very good." Hawks rushed into the pilothouse, sending enlisted men and junior officers sprawling left and right. "Here's where I tell the admiral what the score is! If the Japs can see us, we might as well have a look at them."

"Secure all mechanical fog," the admiral's order said. "Smoke boats will cease making smoke until further notice." One by one the ships closed down their fog generators. A short distance north of the *Belinda* flames burst out from the stern of another transport the second she showed clear of the fog. Moments later another burst into flames on forecastle and fantail: long gray shape burning brightly at both ends.

"The fools," exclaimed Hawks. "Fantail; foc'sle: be alert to prevent fires to fog generators. Remember to blow out fuel lines before shutting off—"

"Captain!" shouted a messenger. "Fire on the fantail!"

"What!" roared Hawks. "On my ship! Put it out! Put it out, you idiots! The sky is full of Jap suicide planes looking for targets. Go aft, MacDougall. Get that fire out at once!" Mac-Dougall was already gone, jumping over tackle and cargo gear. They must get that fire out!

His run was needless. Before he could reach the fantail, Rinaldo's shipfitters had the fire smothered and Rinaldo was saying things to the gunner's mate in charge of the generator which must be burning him hotter than the flames which had blistered the man's hands.

"Anybody else hurt?" asked MacDougall.

"No, sir."

"You go to the sick bay, fellow. . . . You boys going to remember about shutting off that fuel line?"

The usual obedient chorus of ayes was interrupted by a shout. "Say! . . . Lookut! Lookut!" Arms were pointing towards the transport outlined by fires fore and aft. Tracers were shooting over her stern. Following this, MacDougall saw a flaming plane—what looked like a two-engined bomber, coming in on low, shallow dive, heading for the vessel's bridge. Suddenly the plane burst into exploding flame and dropped on the transport's fantail. At once flames shot hundreds of feet up in surges like a tremendous Roman candle.

"Look at that!" said Rinaldo in a disgusted tone. "All because some lunkhead can't remember which way to turn a valve!"

CHAPTER 46

At first dawn light the two LCVPs acting as smoke boats were recalled. Fauré's boat, emptied of the smoke pots which had filled it the previous evening, but apparently unharmed, had the other in tow, stern first. The crew of the second boat, which was nearly awash, rode with Fauré, but Bud Foster, now one of the *Belinda's* more experienced boat officers, stood near the ramp of the damaged craft, tending a portable gasoline pump which was throwing out water almost as quickly as it was leaking in. Calling to his men for fast work, Chief Alvick lowered heavy-lift tackle overside. The sinking landing craft was hoisted clear of the bay and held alongside while cascades of water spouted from holes of various sizes which had been plugged with wadded life jackets and with strips of shredded blue shirt. The interior of the boat was a blackened mess: engine gutted by fire, sooty gear awash or sloshing about Bud Foster's feet. Most of the *Belinda's* men seemed speechless, but Chief Alvick spoke for them. "What happened, Mr. Foster? Get strafed by a plane?"

Bud Foster wiped the back of a blistered, soot-blackened hand across his face, which was a pattern of black soot streaked with sweat rivulets. "No," he said in a disgusted voice. "Some jackass of an LCI shot us up. Our friends! Dirty little greenhorns fresh from Chesapeake Bay! Thought we were Jap suicide boats, I suppose—and us out there protecting them from Japs with our smoke run."

Jerry Rinaldo, who seemed to be able to smell a crippled

boat, arrived at the rail now and looked down into the VP. "Kind of wild party you fellows had, Mr. Foster!"

Two mess cooks struggled down the deck with a large washtub filled with sandwiches. A second pair of mess cooks went the rounds, one with a three-gallon pot filled with steaming coffee, the other with a ladle and a large carton of coffee mugs. Cheers greeted the coffee everywhere: a long war and a coffee-drinking captain had modified the old Navy rule that all galley fires should be doused during general quarters. Rockwell kept a coffee watch busy in the galley. From time to time he personally doled out carefully hoarded cheese, butter, eggs—even chicken: items he had purchased, begged or stolen long before and stowed carefully away for mornings like this.

Even with full bellies the morning gloom hung on—all hands tired from a night of intermittent alarms. As so often happened after a few days of concentrated bombardment and artillery barrages, moisture-laden clouds gathered over Okinawa and adjacent waters. The day was surly and threatening, affecting the spirits of the crew, so that even though unloading neared completion, few voices were raised in the usual snatches of song or improvised wisecracks. Men working on deck looked up from slinging gasoline drums and cases of small-arms ammunition to watch carrier planes swarming like angry bees over Okinawa's rugged little hills and ravines. Down darted the planes, their guns chattering to Japs dying on the ground beneath them; down they went to the tops of storm-bent trees; then up they zoomed as elongated napalm bombs of jellied gasoline dropped from their bomb bays. Up went the planes, streaking for safety. Down went the jelly bombs, end over end until they struck and slopped about the ground, bursting instantly into searing flames which consumed buildings, living trees and men as if in fierce hunger. These planes working over Okinawa were friendly to the *Belinda*. Lew Doyle, Boatswain's Mate Second, who had charge of work at the gasoline hatch, looked suspiciously about the gloomy overcast. "Wonder where the Japs are," he said. "This stuff here will burn as good as jelly bombs."

The gasoline drums were heavy, unheroic, yet dangerous to handle under a sky dotted with planes, any of which might suddenly prove to be kamikazes boring in for the kill. Gonzales, Sanchez and Martinez, the second division's three little Mexicans, worked with American-born shipmates down in the gasoline space deep in number five hold. Ovenlike heat swept in an updraft of reeking gasoline fumes. The Mexicans worked on with vacant faces—pushing loaded gasoline drums with extended hands and arms, sometimes throwing heads far back for a look at the sky, then looking to each other with upturned palms. They spoke in Mexican of how to get out of the hatch if it caught fire. They agreed: chances of escaping through exploding flames—very slight. They had been drilled by Alvick and Doyle not to smoke the twisted cigars they liked so well. They were scared of striking a single spark: heavy steel cargo hook against steel stanchion. They found the native Americans working with them this morning tired and untalkative, so they kept to themselves, rolling out the heavy drums from a far corner of the deep stowage vault, setting the slings, steadying the loads as three drums at a time were hoisted out of the place.

At last Sanchez, leader of the three and the guitar player, scratched his sweaty dark locks and said, "Gasolina not so hot, pals. Play 'Estrellita' por El Capitán mas bueno."

Epstein, a sailor from Brooklyn, laughed at that. "Gasolina better *not* get hot! . . . *You* get hot, Sanchez: whoop it up a little. Come on, boy; give out with that 'Cucaracha.' "

Sanchez grinned but shook his head. "Singing is for be happy. Today not for singing, today for gasolina."

Epstein puckered his lips and gave Sanchez a raucous cheer. "I betcha you'd skin up that ladder quick enough to play for the Old Man!" Sanchez grinned sheepishly and turned back for another gasoline drum.

Captain Hawks was not thinking about songs this morning. For the moment he had forgotten the Mexicans, forgotten even his battered, unplayed trumpet, his sailboat cradled on the afterdeck; not once this morning had he remembered Chipchee, his little lost monkey. Hawks paced restlessly between bridge and chart room, watching water and sky, listening to the TBS, reading dispatches which told of the air war slowly closing in from the north, where the destroyers stationed between Kyushu and Okinawa on radar picket duty were fighting off wave after wave of suicide planes. It was just a matter of time until they ran the gauntlet of the American combat air patrol and came screaming down on the transport area. Each time he came into the chart room, Hawks swung past the chart table, refreshed his memory of details of the area, then went to the air-search radar and peered over the operator's shoulder at the circular screen with its green-luminous picture of surrounding skies and mountain peaks.

"Watch for those unidentified planes—watch for 'em every minute without fail," he said to Stanowski and Carlson. "There's a hornet's nest stirred up this morning. Keep watch for the swarm."

Harsh bright light glared down upon the white operating table in the *Belinda's* surgery. Every hour now, they brought more and more infantrymen and marines down the stony little hills and out of the cave-pocked ravines, down to Red Beach near Hagushi, then out to the ships. Most of the attack transports had returned to Leyte or Eniwetok. Ships like the *Belinda,* with four experienced surgeons and equipment to work with, were getting litter-filled LCMs alongside this morning. Bourassa, Chief Pharmacist's Mate, stuck his head cautiously through the half-opened surgery door, wanting to catch Dr. Flynn's eye. Dr. Flynn stepped back from the operating table, where he had been watching Bell and Gates skillfully work on a leg fracture, and went to the door. "We got another load, Doctor. They're overdoing it, sir. Shall I send them to the *Parkhurst?"*

Flynn nodded to Dr. Gates and left the surgery. Passing the sick bay, he looked in the door at the tiers of cots, already filled with wounded. There was room for about twenty more litters in the vacated troop officers' mess, one deck down. In an emergency he could use the most forward of the two troop compartments on the second deck at number five hatch; ventilation was fairly good there now that the hatchway, which passed through the after compartment, was open while unloading gasoline. Flynn hated to send wounded away; with Gates and Bell he had protested bitterly any unnecessary transfer of wounded men. He walked to the side and looked over. One of the *Belinda's* fifty-six foot LCMs bumped gently alongside. The large steel craft seemed empty at first glance, her cargo was so flat in the bottom: thirty men lying quietly in their blankets in the neatly placed litters: five across and head to foot six deep from the heavy ramp to the engine bulkhead. Thirty more patients, most of them needing surgery, careful cleaning and splinting. Fatigue burned around Flynn's eyeballs and stretched the skin tight over his cheek bones. "Load them aboard, Chief," he said, and walked away. If he waited, these anonymous wounded would have faces and eyes looking inquiringly into his in that silent way of the wounded. Flynn had a little more endurance left for cases: belly wounds, fractures, hemorrhages; he felt that he had nothing left for the personalities of wounded men. If they could only laugh or manage a wisecrack—but those patient, questioning, pain-filled eyes got a man down when his reflexes must be quick and certain, his judgment correct in professional decisions of life and death. Turning back to the sick bay, Flynn came face to face with MacDougall.

"Can you handle these people, Pat?"

Flynn grinned. "Why sure, you lunkhead. Did you ever see me duck a little work?"

MacDougall reflected just the suggestion of a smile, then his face went dead serious. "It looks as if we're in for a heavy air attack within an hour or so, perhaps sooner. The picket boats are catching hell just thirty-five miles from here. It's just a matter of time before they break through. They outnumber our CAP three to one, so we'll have to defend ourselves. You'd better get those litter cases under cover as quick as you can. Never mind your regular battle dressing stations. Fraser is running a phone line to the medical office. If you doctors can avoid crowding all together, I'd advise you to spread out: never know where you'll be needed and," MacDougall managed a wry grin now, "it would be rough on the rest of us if all of you pill peddlers were rubbed out at once."

Flynn laughed. "So you line officers do break down once in a while and admit that you need a doctor now and then! What's the matter, Mac, getting scared?"

"Perhaps. Say, Pat, have you seen the Old Man today?"

"Just long enough to give him his four ounces."

"What do you think of him?"

"He seemed all right to me—for him, that is. Why?"

"I don't know, Pat. He's awfully sharp this morning—got it all figured out what Halsey should be doing, why Randall's plotting isn't exactly perfect, what to do with that forty millimeter that's always jamming. What I mean, he isn't finding fault, he's just sharp. Everything he says makes sense. He showed me a better way to sling up ammunition, and you know both Fraser and I've forgotten more about cargo handling than anything he's ever seen—yet the man was right this morning. When he gets efficient like that, I start to worry; next thing you know, we'll be making another trip into the sunset."

"That's your headache," said Flynn.

"Yep," said MacDougall. "I'd better get back to the bridge."

There had been no time in Kyushu that morning for a last ceremonial dinner and traditional drinking of saki. Mitscher's carrier planes flew strike after strike over the numerous, well-dispersed fields where planes of Divine Wind squadrons were based. Two hundred Jap planes destroyed on the ground, the pilots reported; at least one hundred, said the coldly evaluating intelligence people. Whatever it was, more damage was sure to come. In desperation the Japanese made their own evaluation and did what all Japanese warriors do when there is no road left but the last road: they ordered the attack. Quickly the engines sputtered to last life; the undamaged wings were airborne. Formations were ragged, organization below par; many experienced lead planes had been cut to bits so that green young corporals and naval cadets would have to bunch it out the best they could. Thus, while fast carrier planes returned to Mitscher's great task force, the scooting little kamikazes winged south from their Kyushu fields, past Miyazaki and Kagoshima, past the rugged white cliffs which reached from Toi to Satano Misaki, out over the swirling warm currents of Osumi Kaikyo—homeland fading forever behind the pilots of over six hundred kamikaze planes. There were islands to guide them: long stretch of Tanega Shima, mile-high Yaku Shima, the twin two-thousand-foot-high hats of Kuchino and Kuchinoerabu Jima, and a continuing string of jewel-like islands having musical sounding names: Nakano Shima, Suwanose Shima, Ko Takara and Takara—little and big. The Divine Wind Special Attack Force flew low over the water to avoid radar detection. Thus they often looked up to green peaks of these Northern Ryukyus on the way to Okinawa to carry out the orders of their commander, Vice Admiral Ugaki: *Your brother pilots have sunk or damaged twenty carriers and battleships. The way is clear for you. Sink the transports!*

In addition to the destroyers on radar picket duty north of Okinawa, fifteen destroyers formed a rough semicircle around the beachhead, thirty-five or more miles to Hagushi anchorage. It was of these ships Hawks spoke to MacDougall as he strode from the radar scope and out to his bridge, tossing a message board back to the anxious communications officer. "The pickets and the CAPs are shooting down Japs like flies, but they're coming through. *Taussig* has been hit; *Jacinto* hit twice; the *Harmsworth* is still floating, but a wreck. There's another report, carrier *Hancock* under heavy attack, badly damaged already. . . . Now!" Hawks slapped the palms of his hands sharply together. "They'll be over our screen in a minute; watch for firing out there. Don't let the lookouts get excited and get out of sector. We must maintain lookout— here, give me the portable mike." Hawks grabbed the microphone on its long black cord, blew sharply in the way he had, which angered the electricians so, and called out to his crew in a loud, confident voice which was amplified and carried to the utmost recesses of the *Belinda*:

"Now hear this. This is your captain speaking. In a couple of minutes you're going to get the chance of your lives to shoot down Japs. A swarm of kamikazes is coming in to get the transports here at Nagushi, but they're not going to get old *Beachhead Belinda*; not if you all keep your heads and carry out my orders. Now listen, men; listen to me. Listen to your captain now before it gets too noisy; listen and save your lives and your shipmates' lives and your ship." MacDougall looked anxiously at Hawks. The Old Man's voice was getting up the scale; was he going to crack now? But Hawks made a face at his executive officer as if sensing this and rejecting it as ridiculous. His voice was controlled now as he said, "All you have to do is to obey orders and do what you have been trained to do. Loaders load; don't look around the sky. Load those clips and pass the five-inch:thirty-eight to the ready boxes. Lookouts: keep a lookout. Not in the other fellow's

411

sector where there's a plane to watch—look out for your own sector, NO MATTER WHAT!" Hawks took a deep breath and said, "Pointers, point; trainers, train. Do it easy, just like a dry run, and do it fast. Keep on the target, you five-inch gun crews; let the gun captain take care of windage. The rest of you trust your mark fourteen sights and lead the target. Gun talkers, listen carefully for orders from control. Some of you fouled up at Leyte. Can't afford to do that now. You battery officers: if communications are broken off for any reason so that you cannot get word from control, fall back on experience and training. Use your heads. That is all. Carry on."

Hawks let go the speaking button on the portable mike and held out his hand for somebody to take the thing. His eyes were back in the sky, watching for little black specks.

Reports came from radar and TBS in a steady flow: seven distinct raids were being reported. "Raid Five, many, mixed with friendlies, zero-four-zero, twenty; closing."

MacDougall came across the bridge to report, "Anchor at short stay, Capt'n. Engines ready to get underway; standard speed set."

"Everything ready to go?"

"Yes, sir. We can get underway in less than a minute."

"How about watertight integrity?"

"Watertight bulkhead doors and manhole covers dogged down securely." MacDougall reflected briefly on the men locked within these compartments: engine men ready at throttles, beside the superheated boilers far below the waterline; damage control parties standing by with fog nozzles, CO_2 and oxygen breathing apparatus; corpsmen standing by the wounded and ready for more; powder monkeys waiting deep down in the vaultlike magazines, ready to run ammunition up the elevators. The ship was terribly alive; the ship and her people . . .

"Raid three closing rapidly on transport area. Ten to fifteen planes; no CAP in vicinity."

Suddenly MacDougall remembered the gasoline drums at number five hatch. In answer to a request from shore, the last dozen drums were being sent off in an LCM. Fraser would be down belowdecks supervising his damage control parties; that hatch should be covered and the drums got away before the Japs closed in. MacDougall remembered the kamikaze he had seen on L Day, dropping in flames end over end into the open hatch of that flag transport. Leaving the bridge, he hurried aft to the gasoline hatch. Alvick stood beside the sailboat, which was cradled to port of the hatch coaming, nearly covered with snowy canvas.

"How much more gas left in that hatch, Alvick?"

"Six drums, sir. The other six are over there on deck."

412

"But I told you not to stack gas on deck—to put it overside right away. Thought you had an LCM."

"Yes, sir, but it came back with a load of casualties. I'm getting the gas up while I'm waiting for the boat."

"Good." MacDougall glanced at the four heavy steel pontoon-type hatch covers stacked neatly beside the open hatchway. "Get those covers on as quick as you can. I want to seal the ship up tight everywhere."

"Yes, sir. I'd like to get back to Gun Two. Will it be all right to put Doyle here? He knows what to do."

"Sure, but he's your pointer, isn't he? We've got to have the best men on point today."

"Hatcher's back from the beach, sir. He's pointing Gun Two for Doyle."

"That deadeye; O.K. Alvick. You keep the boys on their toes now and keep 'em cool." MacDougall looked at this steady boatswain's mate and thought, if they're all like him, we'll get by. Then he ran over to the starboard rail and looked down into the fifty-six foot LCM. Still half filled with litters—more than a dozen to go. The man next to MacDougall turned; it was Flynn.

"This is sure slow," said MacDougall, "this hoisting litters one at a time. I told 'em to use VPs—we can heave the whole boatload to the rail. I want to get this gas off, Pat. It's nasty stuff to have around on days like this."

"Many Japs?"

"More than you've ever seen at one time. You'd better get these people in fast, Pat."

"I'll get 'em in, Mac. No use in jerking their arms and legs off; they look tough enough as it is."

"You're the doctor, Pat—but let's keep her rolling." MacDougall ran up ladders to the bridge. The TBS was still barking out locations of the various raids. One thing struck MacDougall's attention before he could get up the last ladder: distances to the various raids of Jap planes were no longer twenty miles and over; they were five miles, six miles, four miles.

Hawks strode forward to MacDougall. "I was just going to call you," he said. "You take care of the bridge. Keep in contact with me by headphones. I'm going up to control and shoot down some Japs." Hawks swung around the railing of the ladder to the signal bridge, took the steps three at a time, then pushed his way past antiaircraft gunners and sky lookouts to the steel-lined breastworks abaft the stack, where Art Hall, the alert little gunnery officer, stood in a maze of communications jacks with his five talkers. "Give me a headset and plug it in on the JV line," said Hawks. "I'm going to stay here awhile and knock down Japs." Hawks took the offered head-

413

set, snapped the receivers over his ears and put on the over-sized, scooplike helmet which fit over the phones. Then he looked skyward. The afternoon breeze blew in from seaward, holding the *Belinda's* bow steadily heading out from land. Ugly cloud forms obscured the sky; it would be raining soon. Dark clouds, moving in from the sea. Something else was moving up there—little black specks boring in fast. Planes: Raid Three! Several of the dozen destroyers screening the transport area opened a sharp cracking fire with their five-inch:thirty-eights. A deeploaded fleet oiler just coming in from sea took up the battle, followed one after another by attack transports and supply ships anchored offshore from the *Belinda*. "Track the target with all your forward batteries," Hawks told Hall. "If they close, each battery will choose a target of opportunity and stay with it." Hawks listened to the ranges coming in from radar. No use wasting ammunition today. Track the target, watch the range; it would soon be time to let them have it.

Doyle, tall boatswain's mate from Texas and regular pointer of Gun Two, stuck his head down into number five hatch and yelled to one of the three Mexicans below: "How many drums, Sanchez?"

"Three drums gasolina remaining. You pick her up now, bose? We get out this place?"

"Yep, just a minute now. They've got all the wounded aboard out of that LCM. I'll give 'em the drums from on deck first; then you three boys ride the net up with that last sling-load. We got to close the rest of this hatch in a hurry."

"O.K. bose. Finish gasolina; finish—" Sanchez's voice was drowned out by a sudden burst of gunfire from forward.

Doyle looked across the hatch. Dr. Flynn and his corpsmen were hurrying the last half-dozen litters into the sick bay. Doyle had managed to set two of the heavy hatch pontoons in place from side to side across the forward half of the gaping hatch and it was across this smooth, gray-painted surface that Flynn's men were carrying the litters. Nine drums filled with gasoline were resting in their net slings just to starboard of the hatch coaming. Flynn was backed up against the drums, bending over a sallow-faced young marine in the last litter. Flynn read the chart tag which had been filled out on the beach by young Dr. Hardwick: morphine syrette, plasma . . . Flynn read on; a nasty belly wound, he was thinking. This is one for me to work on. Then Gun Two on the nearby fantail cracked into rapid fire, followed by the four supporting twin-forties. There was a sound of urgency in the long-continued burst of firing. Flynn dropped the tag and looked up. The gun barrels were pointed nearly straight up, belching muzzle blast with each rapid recoil, and from this cornucopia of flame and smoke shot streams of tracers interlarded with lethal antiaircraft

414

shells. Flynn followed along the line of tracers. Up they went, like pointing fingers against a background sky no longer leaden dull but lighted with crisscrossing tracers and exploding shells fired by the thousands from other ships. It was the *Belinda's* tracers Flynn followed; up they went, several thousand feet skyward, and there he got his answer. A dozen unfamiliar looking planes dove down in a weaving, scattering, crisscrossing pattern. As he watched, one burst into brilliant flame, exploded into a bright yellow comet which plunged in a steep glide across the sky directly over the *Belinda* and was lost to view behind the landing craft nested in the davit to port. Flynn gulped and looked up again. Gunfire had not slackened in the slightest. He must get his wounded to cover. "Shake it up, Brown," he called. "Can't you get the litters through the door a little faster?" Flynn's knee was braced against the litter beside him. He felt the marine with the belly wound stir. Flynn bent down again. "Just take it easy, fellow," he said. "You won't have to get up and walk for awhile yet—just a minute more and we'll have you moved inside." There was a faint sign of recognition on the marine's face. He probably couldn't hear a word in all this racket. The others were moving on now. Time to go. Flynn motioned to the waiting corpsman to lift up the forward end of the litter while he stooped to pick up the after handles. No use waiting for more corpsmen. Time to get these people under cover; they'd had enough shock. Then he'd have to scrub up again and get busy.

There was a slight pause in the *Belinda's* gunfire, then the guns burst out again. Flynn got a glance into the half-covered hatch as he climbed onto the pontoon with his end of the litter, saw the three Mexicans huddled on the last three drums of gasoline looking up at him with inquiring brown eyes. Flynn got his footing, raised up carefully until the litter was level and started forward towards the sick bay. The sound of gunfire had a frantic quality, five-inch, 40-mm, every one of the twin-barreled twenties, clustered as they were all over the ship's topsides—everything going all out. The ship was shaking. The vacuum sucked at his belly; it seemed as if he would stumble with the litter. Flynn came to a stop and leaned his shoulder against the winch drum to steady himself. The flames and shuddering concussions drew his eyes away from the litter and upward. Then he saw the object of all the gunfire: a twin-engine plane with rusty-looking meatballs on both wings. The thing was trailing flames but climbing as if to pass over the *Belinda*. Then it did a sickening, lurching wingover and began to drop rapidly. Flynn's eyes were glued on the burning kamikaze in horrified fascination. The flames trailed out more brightly, seemed to grow larger before his eyes. The flaming mass did not move from right to left—just grew larger with a terrible screaming of wind against flaming surfaces in all the hell of gunfire. He forgot the litter clutched tightly in his hands, forgot the hatch, the ship, all else save this flaming, screaming thing. It filled his vision, was upon him with hot breath and sudden shoutings that drowned out everything else in time and space and feeling as, with merciful swiftness, the war ended for Pat Flynn.

Hawks had seen the bomber sneaking in low from the land while Hall's gunners still poured their fire on two of the group diving in from seaward. Even as the first group of planes came tumbling down to port and starboard, hit by guns of a number of ships—sky and sea in unbelievable confusion of movement and flame: planes falling in flames; ships sitting in flames—even as these first planes came tumbling down, Hawks had seen the twin-engined bomber scooting out from shore not ten feet above the water.

Hawks got Hall by the shoulders, pointing out the plane just before the first report came in from after surface lookouts. "Gun Two," Hawks yelled. "All the forties; everything aft! Change target; commence fire; commence fire!" Round came the gun barrels to open fire in flat trajectory—surely those Buck Rogerses would hit him. They had to hit him! Thirty feet from him and the proximity fuse would do it. What was the matter? The bomber came on, weaving from side to side. The gunners hadn't had time to get settled; that was it. Next shot would have to do it. There was the Jap zooming up over the ship, hanging there. "Hit him! Hit him! Hit him!" Hawks was jumping up and down behind Hall, shouting a frantic admonition to gunners who heard nothing but thunder, saw nothing but the crazily moving pair of flaming wings which moved faster than they could crank their handles, faster than the complicated motor system could move five-inch gun barrels. Hall was sweating. Of all the times for his Mark 51 radar fire control to go out on him. Handwork now: pointers and trainers with eyes glued to their telescopes, cranking like mad. Blood pounded in Alvick's head as he whipped in his loads on rapid fire. Gun Two spun this way and that, the barrel higher, higher, away around now. He lost track of the ship; he was riding in space behind a gun, firing rapid shots at a burning devil which would not crash. Then the target seemed to hold still, pouring with flames from the forties. A split second later old Buck Rogers found him. There was an ear-shattering explosion and the thing began to drop, with Alvick pouring more shells into him. Only when the gun came up against the stops and ceased fire automatically did Alvick see what was happening. The Jap wasn't dropping into the sea; he was falling at a steep glide from the starboard quarter and was going to end up right at the gasoline hatch. Horrified, Alvick opened his mouth to shout to the forties. They must keep on firing up there; perhaps they could dump him before he hit. Then Alvick saw that it was too late for anything but damage control. While he turned the gun over to Hatcher, with a sharply shouted warning to keep an eye out for another one, Alvick jumped from the gun carriage and ran around the hatch just in time to see the bomber hit the hatch right where Dr. Flynn stood holding on to the litter. Things happened with incredible speed: left wing low, poking down into the gaping half of the hatch, sheering off together with the port engine and dropping in flames upon the three Mexicans with their last sling of gasoline. All of the rest of that flaming mass right on top of Flynn, shoving him, the litter—all the litters, all the corpsmen, all the wounded—crushing, burning, sweeping all before with irresistible power. Flames leaping up out of the empty hatch. Resistor house bashed flat with its ton of steel and electric switchboard. Topping lift released, boom crashing down, the whole stove-in house at the sick bay entrance shattered and burning fiercely.

Somehow there were men already on the run with snaking hoses stiff with a hundred pounds of water pressure. Alvick grabbed one from somebody, opened the fog nozzle and advanced upon the flaming ruin. Something rushed towards him from the fire: a man—Doyle! Face blackened, shirt burning with gasoline from a ruptured drum, arms outstretched. Alvick turned the hose on Doyle, knocked him down with it, watched the flames die out from the shirt. Then, with teeth gritted and a dry sob in his throat, Alvick left his closest friend to live or die while he moved in on these flames that were well on their way to consuming not only the *Belinda* but every man on board.

Hawks stood rigid at gunnery control, feet braced apart, arms outstretched as he clutched the steel splinter shield until his knuckles were white. He had made every study and preparation possible and yet it had happened to his ship. His ship had been hit—his ship! It seemed as if his own body had taken the shock and was now being consumed by flames. In a few nightmare seconds of dream he had seen the plane explode over his ship and drop, fiercely burning. Then movement returned to his body; his brain thrust off the shock.

"There'll be others," he told Hall. "Alert your lookouts again. Check all guns; keep me informed. I'm going back to the bridge."

Hawks found MacDougall receiving rapid reports of damage and ordering emergency counter measures. "Fire's the worst thing, Capt'n. If we can knock off the fire before it gets away from us, I think we can restore watertight integrity."

"*If* my eye! We *shall* put out the fire!" shouted Hawks. "Go down and take charge. Is Fraser still at central damage control?"

"Yes, sir. I told him to stay there and co-ordinate all damage control. We might get hit again—"

Hawks gave MacDougall a silencing glare which seemed to say: I won't let any dirty Jap hit my ship. MacDougall ran down the deck, considering the situation. Main engines and pumps were O.K. That was the most important thing. Yet when he got to the afterdeck the sickening actualities were almost unbelievable. Everywhere was blackened, twisted wreckage—an incredible, shocking transformation from the well-ordered deck where a short ten minutes before he had been talking with Pat Flynn. Boatswain Torgeson and a group of men were pumping liquid foam through a proportioner and smothering the fire in the gasoline hatch, which seemed to be nearly extinguished—that could wait. One of the jumbo booms at number five, used there to lift thirty-six ton LCMs and equally heavy medium tanks from the hold, was draped like a bent arm across wreckage of number six gravity davit and three VPs which had nested there. The resistor house, a small and strongly built deckhouse at the base of the mainmast which controlled electric power for the afterdeck, was bashed in like a cardboard carton which had been jumped upon. Crackling flames still poured from the sick bay where the remaining wreckage of the Japanese bomber had come to the exploding end of its journey. The place reeked with strong combined odors of burned gasoline, paint and flesh. There was a small hole in the wreckage where entrance to the sick bay passage should have been. It was plugged nearly full with heavy canvas fire hoses, leading to fog nozzles within the burning sick bay. MacDougall ducked his head, ran past flaming wreckage and entered the place. He heard Alvick's voice, loud and clear: "Bring up another fog nozzle, Nelson. Cool down the bulkheads and keep us wet as we move in on the fire." MacDougall's first sensation was of intense heat and suffocating steam; queer, brilliant, flowing light in the place, and salt water hissing against red-hot steel plating. Yet there was something else in the difference of this once familiar place. Then he saw that the steel overhead to the sick bay had been blown upward: great jagged area blown out of the deck above.

Concerned about the wounded who had been here, MacDougall ran back through the hole, calling for foam to smother the oil fire still burning in the corner of the sick bay. Then he ducked in again and made his way forward. He soon caught sight of Dr. Frank Bell. Bell's face was blistered, his hair singed, his clothing blackened and torn.

"How about the sick bay?" MacDougall asked.

"I'd just moved most of them over to the other side to make room for the new lot. About five of 'em killed in there; three more severely burned. We lost about the last dozen of them coming out of the boat."

"Where's Flynn?"

"Dead. He was bringing them in here."

MacDougall swore bitterly. Bell reached out and gripped his shoulder hard. He said not a word, but something of his strength and spirit flowed into MacDougall. "O.K., Frank. O.K. We'll patch her up." He choked up and, spinning around on his heel, worked back through the fire hoses to check on vital damage.

Hawks stood straight as a ramrod on his bridge receiving MacDougall's damage report. Now that the fires were out, he had the *Belinda* underway, crawling along off Hagushi at bare steerageway, but ready to leap ahead and make evasive maneuvers should there be another attack. After some decision arrived at privately, Hawks had discarded the beekeeperlike flash protection veiling, but his shirt was streaked with sweat and soot and the black stains on his face emphasized the look of fatigue.

"Go on, MacDougall," he said, "let's hear the rest of it."

MacDougall leaned against the bulkhead for support; it seemed difficult to stand straight. As if to refresh his memory, he held out dirty fingers of his right hand and counted off the items with his left thumb and forefinger: "We have watertight integrity in all compartments except number five hatch. Some part of that Jap went through the skin of the ship just below the waterline near frame one-forty-one. From what I could see the port engine must have done it—hole big enough to throw a jeep through. As soon as the fire was out I closed the troop gasoline space and dogged it down—strange, but it didn't seem damaged. The gas in those drums there must have exploded mostly upward—three Mexicans killed there. . . . Fraser is shoring down the lids on that gas storage space. We can pump it out later—build a coffer dam."

"Other watertight integrity losses?"

"Only above the main deck, Capt'n. The port after corner of the deckhouse is pretty well shot."

"Casualties?"

"As far as I know, sir, seventeen of the wounded were killed by the crash and two more died of burns. We lost seven of our crew: the three sailors in the troop gas space, three corpsmen and Dr. Flynn."

"Dr. Flynn!"

MacDougall swallowed. "Yes, sir. He was getting the

wounded in during the attack." MacDougall watched Hawks's face: his eyes seemed to dilate and a slight frown deepened into his forehead and stayed there. "Bell and Gates are busy with the worst casualties now. Doyle, bosun's mate first—very badly burned."

More bogey reports came in on the TBS. Hawks broke off his conversation with MacDougall to go to the PA speaker and alert his gun crews and lookouts, then returned to hear the rest.

At last he asked, "Is that all, MacDougall?"

"I think so, Capt'n—oh, there was one other thing."

"Yes?"

"The *Albatross,* Capt'n . . . completely demolished and burned."

Hawks's face showed not the slightest reaction. "My sailboat gone: demolished and burned," he said reflectively. Then his voice rose somewhat as he said incisively, "Very good. Very good. I don't need it now."

There was very little time between rounds. Before Fraser had the ruptured and flooded gasoline hatch sealed off, the next wave of kamikazes swept over the anchorage. It soon became evident that this second kamikaze raid of the afternoon was not only stronger but better organized than the first. Hawks did not know that it had come from further north in Kyushu so that during the longer run to Hagushi there had been more time for it to organize after Mitscher's strike over Japanese home fields. What Hawks could see at once was that these planes were skillfully deployed in such a manner as to strike suddenly at the crippled transports from many directions and levels of flight at once. TBS gave official warning, the *Belinda's* own radar showed them ringed about the area and closing in to crash. Maneuvering above the sullen cloud deck, the planes could not be seen. Other ships opened fire, operating by radar. The *Belinda's* radar fire control apparatus was still out of commission.

Hawks sent for Hall. "Listen," he said. "You're my gunnery officer; you must get that Mark 51 control operating at once."

"I'm doing all I can, Captain," said Hall, pulling nervously at his right ear. He was anxious to get back to his gunnery control; things were sure to bust loose now. "I've got both the radar and radio technicians working on it—I'd give anything to have that thing operational again, Captain."

"Keep them at it," said Hawks. "Meanwhile, get back to control. Keep me informed—I may join you up there but my intentions at present are to remain here and conn the ship at high speed. Watch your sectors of fire and have your battery groups rehearsed so that they can exchange targets when necessary. I'll be swinging ship in radical turns: what starts out to be a run for a starboard battery may have to be finished by portside guns and vice versa."

Hall started to edge for the ladder. "Yes, sir. I understand."

Hawks fixed Hall with his gaze. "You be ready. When I give the word, pour it to them. Knock down every last Jap that dares come near the *Belinda,* understand?"

"Yes, sir. I'll do my best."

While Hall ran back to gunnery control, Hawks looked about. Only seventeen ships of the five hundred remained in the immediate area off Hagushi. No other ship of his own squadron was left and he had not been assigned to any other tactical group. The senior officer afloat in the area exercised temporary command for administrative purposes only. The kamikaze had exploded the last of the *Belinda's* cargo; her gas-delivery mission was now completed. Hawks's own repair force was working furiously at the difficult job of temporary repairs to damage below the waterline at number five hatch. As soon as that could be done, his orders were to sail for Guam with the wounded. He would need to do something about the dead as there was not enough refrigerated space to care for them: probably have to hold sea burial again. That would have to wait; in a few moments he would have more urgent decisions to make. Streaming back and forth between Hagushi and Naha, Hawks waited for the little black specks to tumble out of the overcast and come at him. It was just a matter of time, and not much time at that.

MacDougall climbed the ladder to the bridge and walked over to Hawks's side. Hawks recognized his presence without turning his eyes away from the sky. "How's the repair work going? Got that collision mat rigged yet?"

"Almost, Capt'n. However, I'm afraid that the gasoline storage space is completely flooded by now. I'm rigging the after emergency pump; she's a good one. If the patch is any good at all, we should be able to keep up with the water."

"Who's on the job?"

"Fraser, Bos'n Torgeson and Machinist Campbell."

"Good. You stay here with me. Randall is handling radar and plot. A heavy raid is closing. Hall will handle the guns from control; I'm going to make fifty- and seventy-degree emergency turns. I want you to keep track of the relative bearing of the various raids as they close the ship."

"Yes, sir. Won't C.I.C.—the radar reports—?"

"Radar's fine," said Hawks shortly. "This thing is going to be too close and too fast for radar. We'll use our eyes."

MacDougall looked sharply at Hawks. The captain spoke in a conversational voice, yet there was an effect of finality in what he said; there would be no equivocation. He, Hawks, said that the *Belinda* was in for the fight of her life as if he knew. Whether he knows or not, MacDougall thought, what he says may be all too true. As Hawks was on the starboard wing of the bridge, MacDougall went quickly to the port wing and scanned the darkening sky. It was past the time of sunset but there had been no sight of the sun all afternoon. The murky cloud scudding across the horizon to westward was merely less dark than the rest of it. The sky looked empty; no sign of a plane, friendly or enemy. MacDougall listened to the TBS: nothing but some operational message referring to a pontoon needed at Purple Beach. Usually at such a time the air would vibrate with urgent messages from admirals, commodores, division commanders. It all sounded so routine now, like after the big game, he thought. Most of the crowd has gone, leaving a few of us behind to clean up the grounds. It was a silly thought; he knew that three hundred thousand men were fighting for possession of those nearby hills. Even this nearly empty anchorage would soon be crowded again when the train of supply ships arrived in a day or two. Yet the sensation of being nearly alone persisted: surely this was all a make-believe business; there couldn't be another strong attack tonight. As soon as it was dark they would grope over to nearby Kerama Retto, where temporary repair facilities had been set up. There they could bury their dead and patch their wounds. In another day or two they should be on their way: good-by, Okinawa, and good riddance.

The TBS knocked off routine messages long enough to report, "Five strong raids closing the transport area from all sides; now inside the CAP and closing. Repeat: now inside CAP."

Randall came out of the chartroom, exchanged glances with MacDougall. "You hear that?"

"Yes. I heard it. Here we go again!"

"I'll stand by the squawk box," said Randall, "call the raids for you."

"Keep it simple, Jim. Concentrate on planes that are closing in on us, never mind about the wolf packs out on the rim."

"Check." Randall ducked back into his chart room to hover over Stanowski and Carlson at the air-search radar.

There was no more talk of pontoons or gasoline over the TBS. "Raids One, Two and Three closing transport area. No friendlies within area at present. Repeat: Flash Red, Control Yellow."

"Good," said Hawks. "We're free to shoot now. The fly boys are out of the way. One or two Hellcats can't catch all these people now. I'd rather have the sky clear to shoot in!" For a moment it was quiet on the *Belinda's* bridge; men looked outward and upward, mouths open as they searched gray skies for bogies.

At last Jim Randall's voice came from the intercom: "Raid Two closing gradually; now three-zero-zero, nine miles. All three raids circling transport area."

Hawks said nothing; he stood up very straight, helmet tilted back on his head so that he could see better. Not only the bridge but the entire ship was quiet; everywhere blue-gray helmets clustered behind guns whose barrels searched the sky nervously. The only sounds heard were the steady singing of turbines, the soughing wash of sea water, and the occasional sound of rapid hammering on steel by the shipfitters at number five hatch. On the opposite wing from Hawks, MacDougall took off his helmet and scratched his sweaty head. Would those Japs never come? Why didn't they come on in and get it over with? Willicut turned the wheelspokes deliberately, but now and then he drummed his fingers impatiently on the compass bezel until Kruger, who had the deck, felt like yelling at him to be quiet. Even the bridge messengers, usually carefree and talkative when sufficiently far away from officers, stood out of the way on the bridge wings, watching the sky in silence.

Now a few vibrations of droning hum were heard. One by one the waiting men jerked straight and turned their heads from side to side, trying to authenticate sound so faint it seemed imagined. Now definite engine sounds were heard, faint but distinct. Heads still moved slowly back and forth, trying to judge direction. On the bridge and at the guns tension mounted, yet with something of relief that at last there was something tangible to be nervous about. There was no doubt about it, the Japs were out there—but where? The high, unsynchronized drone of engines seemed to come from everywhere at once, yet nothing was in sight, everywhere the gray murk of overcast beginning to fade into darkness. After ten minutes of this, Randall's voice came sharply from the intercom: "Captain. Planes closing now . . . several directions. The groups are splitting up. . . . Here's one coming in at three-one-five; six miles now and closing fast."

Suddenly Hawks started into motion, moving around the heavy machine gun bolted to the bridge wing so fast that he tramped hard on his talker's instep. "Control: visible target, zero-seven-zero relative, position angle thirty. Track target." There it was, a little black spot moving slowly against the background of dark gray cloud. Reports began to come in, from Randall, from lookouts; the TBS added its warning; the sound of engines grew louder, only to be drowned out as ships on the group's perimeter opened fire. "All engines ahead, flank speed," ordered Hawks. "Left, twenty degrees rudder."

With gunfire all about, the tempo of pounding hearts aboard the *Belinda* built up. As yet her guns were silently tracking, each group intent on the nearest plane in its sector of fire. There were about thirty Jap planes, all high, darting in, banking off, circling, still keeping outside the rough-formed group of ships. The *Belinda* was up to speed, humming from Hagushi towards Naha, far enough outside the reef to permit maneuvering either way. Hawks looked over his stern at the rest of the ships. Most of them were underway now; a few remained at anchor, though water splashing from their hawse pipes showed that they were heaving in. "This is a poorly handled situation," he told MacDougall. "If we were all in formation now we could concentrate firepower and give these Japs a run; as it is, it is every man for himself. . . . Well, they're not going to catch me if I can help it. You watch to port: ships and planes—keep me informed. I'll be watching to starboard. I'll take the conn now—may give it to you later. Watch her now!"

All at once, as if from a prearranged signal, the Jap planes were over the transports and the air was filled with gun thunder. Lookout reports were coming in to control, where Hall supervised his gun batteries. Hawks and MacDougall were watching the over-all picture, alert for the plane or group of planes sneaking in unnoticed or boring in despite the hell of flak whose tracers now crisscrossed the sky like a flurry of burning straw. Hawks kept his station on the starboard wings, using his phones to talk with Hall and MacDougall, calling changes in course to Kruger by means of the squawk box on the bridge wing. The action was still a general one; the *Belinda* was firing at four different planes, coming in at four different angles, yet all seemed bound for other targets.

The crew of Gun One on the bow broke into cheering as a twin-engined "Betty" came streaking down in flames. Moran shut them up and sent a few rapid bursts at the thing as it veered crazily toward the *Belinda's* bow. It hung on one wing some five hundred feet directly above Gun One while Hawks put the helm hard over and ran upwind to starboard. The "Betty" grew larger in his vision; she was closing. "The forties!" Hawks instructed Hall. "Hit the bastard! Knock him down!" Flame shot up from all over the *Belinda's* foredeck and bridge. The "Betty" hovered in air, shaking from the hammering, flames curling back as she dropped; then the left wing came off and skittered down to splash alongside number two hatch to port, while the rest of the aircraft sideslipped downward to starboard and crashed into the sea about a hundred yards from where Hawks stood on his bridge. Hawks ignored the floating pool of burning gasoline. The fire was sure to attract other planes; these crazed Japs were like moths, crashing down wherever there was flame. He wished he had more speed; forty-five knots would really let him maneuver, but the *Belinda* was shaking violently as her engines strained their utmost and it was doubtful if she was doing a knot over twenty. Left again with the rudder—land ahead now; Randall would have to watch that. Others doing the same sort of thing and darkness falling—avoid collision, avoid reefs, duck those dirty kamis and shoot 'em down, down, down! Over again with the rudder, get her around back towards Hagushi. Tracers everywhere; getting dark now, harder and harder to see. Ship on fire up ahead. How did that happen? So quick, no time. Left again; zigzag—zigzag. Screaming sound of an engine racing madly past him, bridge high. Plane on fire, oh God! Keep him away! Left again, now; hard over with the wheel. Crash and flame right ahead! Say, a ship there; he hadn't seen it. Randall yelling into the squawk box—MacDougall running over. Yes, I know, I know! Is the rudder hard over? Why doesn't she answer? I said, HARD LEFT! Now she comes. We'll make it—got to make it. Steady the helm—there we slide by. Those flames!—how could such a fire . . . ! Another plane coming in high; position angle eighty: concentrate fire. Get her, Hall, get her! Come on, there, lead that target! Five hundred feet overhead; why didn't they hit him? There was the small stuff licking his wings; flames showing him for the bigger guns: a "Val" with the big greenhouse. Oh, no! Winging over now, coming down. Get that bastard! GET HIM! Over on his side . . . now which way would he go? Right rudder, hard over, let's get out from under. Sideslipping, down, down. Knock him out, burn him, splash him! Shove him away with gunblast! TAKE YOUR FILTHY ANCESTOR WORSHIP AWAY FROM MY SHIP! Ah, the five-inch— both of them on him, nice, nice. Buck Rogers, got to fuse right. Got to hit him; got to shove him off, but how big he looks! Bigger and bigger—not sliding away. Can't do a thing with the rudder—ship can't outmaneuver plane. That flaming greenhouse, see the pilot's head. Alive or dead what difference—hit him hit him hit him! . . . He'd miss; close but miss. Hit the devil again! That's it—hit him again, smash him, keep him away! What's the matter now? What's he doing? Can't be, yes, swinging this way, bigger, hotter, scream past in flame! Hawks rushed across the bridge to port. Get out of the way you men —can't even feel the contact when you knock them down out of the way. Look at that Jap! Will he miss? Will he miss? Hands on the port rail, grip tight. Squeeze him away, shove, push, shoot! There he goes past my face—BUT HE'S COMING IN!

There was an ear-shattering explosion as the kamikaze crashed its warhead against the *Belinda's* port side, just above the waterline at number three hatch. Hawks and MacDougall, leaning over the port wing of the bridge together, nearly singed by the sudden flaming updraft, were knocked backwards by the blast. Parts of the burning "Val" were caught in what was left of the scramble net. Both men jumped to their feet and got back to the wing. MacDougall could see by the light of leaping flames that both deck and shell plating were bulged. Leaning overside he could see that a huge hole had been blasted into the ship's side, and from the reflection of flames from within the gaping hole which showed on the water alongside he knew that fire raged within number three hold. He sent a quick report to Fraser at main damage control. Then he remembered the engines.

"The engines, Capt'n! She must be strained badly. And the fire—draft, you know."

"Stop the engines!" said Hawks. "Leave the fire to Fraser. The Japs will really bear down on us now. Alert all the gun crews. Can't let them get distracted by the fire—leave that to damage control until we beat off this attack."

"Aye, sir," said MacDougall, wondering just how you went about preventing the distraction of flames shooting higher than the bridge, reflecting in the water alongside and lighting up anxious faces of the gun crews. MacDougall called control and passed the warning along to Hall. "Jerk the lookouts again, Art. Keep 'em boring out into that dark."

"You watch this side, MacDougall," said Hawks. "I'm going back to starboard. We mustn't let 'em get in again. I don't think the ship can take any more." Hawks rushed back across his bridge, once more knocking down all the bridge personnel in his way. Would they never learn that a captain has to get around his bridge?

Steam whistled from the stack as the overburdened safety valve popped off high-pressure steam suddenly denied the turbines. Otherwise there was a slackening in noise. The attack seemed to have eased off, at least for the time being. The only antiaircraft fire now came from the direction of Hagushi, further north. Thus the surface lookout, stationed inside his small steel tower on the after starboard corner of the poop deckhouse, was able to hear an approaching engine. By the time he had phoned in a warning to control and to the bridge, the sound was growing louder.

Unknown to the lookout, Jim Randall was watching a pip which showed on the surface radar but not on the air-search screen. It was coming too fast for any of those speedy suicide motorboats they had been warned about. It must be almost in the water to show only on surface radar. This flashed through Jim's mind as he jumped to the intercom and called urgently, "Captain; another kamikaze sneaking up from astern, just off the starboard quarter—must be very low. . . . Two

426

thousand yards now . . . fifteen hundred yards, Captain!"
Randall thought: he's coming at over a hundred yards a second; that plane can get to the bridge faster than I can run
there from this chart room!

Hawks had a number of things on his mind when Randall's
report came out to the bridge. These flames, his ship afire
with God knew what damage to her hull. MacDougall, get a
report. . . . What happened down there? Find out if I can
get underway. All these things he thought, but there was no
time to get the words out. He was shouting orders for the
after battery. "Gun Two, get on that fellow! Splash him!
Guns Five and Six, get on him. GET ON HIM!"

Back on the fantail, Alvick crouched over the breech of Gun
Two while his loaders slammed in powder bags and proximity-
fused Buck Rogers shells. Hatcher and Smith were straining
to get on the target, but it was all guesswork now. The radar
director was fouled up and it was black dark; a lousy combination when a kamikaze is coming in low across the water.

"Star shell," yelled Alvick. A loader swung over, threw up
a different type of shell, already set with a short fuse by the
canny Alvick. "Elevate," Alvick yelled to Hatcher. Up went
the gun barrel; crack went the gun. Almost immediately a brilliant greenish light hung under the clouds, clearly illuminating
other ships nearby, clearly outlining a Japanese "Zeke" flying
low and fast on a course which, in a few seconds, would take
him right past the muzzle of Gun Two and the two forties that
backed him up.

Hawks saw the Jap coming. For once, he had the feeling
that the situation was out of his hands. He had given all the
orders—anything more would only confuse. He had the feeling that if he had a gun in his hands he could knock the fellow
down, yet there he came, a seemingly irresistible object swooping, banking, slowing and speeding up in comparatively slight
but unrhythmical maneuvers which made it almost impossible
for the gunners to get on him. He was coming up so fast a
heavy gun could hardly be tracked around fast enough to keep
ahead of his flight path. Tracers from the two twin-forties
seemed to spray a shower of red-hot lead in his path, but on he
came. Now a wing lifted—there were flames trickling back
as if from ruptured and ignited gas tanks. Why didn't he explode? If he had a warhead—they all did—that proximity fuse
should get him, blow him up. Hawks opened his mouth to
shout, *Lead the target. Hit him! Hit him! You've GOT to hit
him!* No sound came out. He gripped the bridge railing with
all his strength. It seemed to him as if he had become a part
of the *Belinda*. Steel couldn't shout. Steel couldn't move. He
was steel; he was part of it. All hell was firing now: twenties
all over the ship. The sky was fire. Tracers by the thousands.

It seemed as if his guts were being sucked out and thrown at that weaving Jap. Now the "Zeke" came leaping out of the darkness, out of the fiery curtain of tracers, up on one wing, coming in on the bridge, and he was HERE NOW! Boat davit next the bridge and Japanese plane became one, slammed across the bridge and crashed with exploding flame into the radio room adjoining the pilothouse. The bridge was lifting all about him, torn apart like a huge giant of fire ripping a wishbone. His vision was filled with fire; his eyeballs were filled with fire. Flame leaped at his face, wave shock and concussion leaped at him, thrusting back every part of his body; his brain was wrung tight as a snapping fiddle string. Something hit him a sharp blow on the head, and with shattering eardrums he found release in unconsciousness from all his unbearable problems.

CHAPTER 47

Stunned and bewildered, MacDougall found himself face down on deck in the extreme port wing of the bridge, where he had been flung by the explosion on the other side of the pilothouse. Shaking his head and rubbing his eyes, he scrambled to his feet and looked around. Over to starboard flames leaped skyward, flames so brilliant and frightening he knew they must be gasoline fed. There was plenty of light to see, but what he saw was unfamiliar and unreal; the bridge did not seem the same place. The entire starboard portion, deck, house, bulkheads, was raised unevenly at an angle of some thirty degrees above horizontal. Everything had an expanded look. MacDougall's first thought was that the ship must be irrevocably lost, holed as she was below the waterline forward and aft, on fire from keel to bridge. Yet as he scrambled up the unnatural slope of wreckage which had been the familiar bridge, some automatic quality took hold of him. *Proceed in compliance with . . . Standard speed is 78 rpm; make standard speed. Turbines throbbing day after day —you don't just shut that stuff off.* The *Belinda* couldn't sink; this was some nightmare from which the battle honker would wake him. He'd find everything the same up here on the bridge, the captain sitting in his chair . . . But it wasn't a dream; it was a nightmare of actuality. Somewhere below he heard steam escaping from a shattered line, and the shrill sound thrust the urgency of the *Belinda's* distress upon him. Where was Hawks? He must find the Old Man and carry on with the fight.

It seemed strange to be able to cross the bridge without bumping into anybody. In the flamelight he could see why: men lay this way and that upon the slanting deck—some scrambling to their feet now, others remaining still. Instinct took MacDougall to a particular one of the motionless forms: tall man with helmet knocked off, sprawled in the wreckage of his bridge, one knee doubled up and hands clasped over the nape of his neck. There was the skipper. He couldn't be dead—a ship has to have a captain! MacDougall clambered rapidly over a crumbled stanchion and wreckage of the bridge-wing machine gun, knelt down beside Hawks and looked him over carefully. Blood ran down Hawks's face from a scalp wound—no telling how serious. Otherwise he seemed unhurt.

"Capt'n," MacDougall called. "Oh, Capt'n . . . Capt'n Hawks!" Remembrance flashed back to the first Leyte landing: the time he tried to wake up Hawks that night in the mine fields. Before Hawks there had been Old Gedney sitting in his high chair at Kwajalein: *The Captain never sleeps; he just rests his eyes.* MacDougall put his arm around Hawks's shoulder and rolled him over carefully. There was no time to worry about his spine; he'd have to come out of it and take over, or else lie there until the corpsmen came. I can't wait any longer, thought MacDougall; somebody's got to run this bucket. If he doesn't come out of it, I'm elected. Once more he tried: "Captain . . . Captain Hawks! The ship's on fire! . . ." Oh, leave him. Half a minute gone already; a ship can sink in half a minute.

MacDougall began to get up. Then Hawks's arm thrashed around and gripped him by the wrist; his eyes were opened but had a vacant unfocused look. "Fire? . . . Fire?"

I'm still elected, thought MacDougall. He fumbled at his belt for the snap-on first aid kit, got out a morphine syrette, ripped Hawks's torn shirt clear from his shoulder and stuck the needle in. Hawks lay still while MacDougall squeezed the contents of the small tube into the muscle. MacDougall got up to take a look at the situation. The starboard wing was a shambles, but the main force of the crashing kamikaze had been a few feet further aft, sparing Hawks's life. The starboard side of the radio shack was stove in. The remains of the crashed plane were so mixed with the ruin of radio transmitters, receivers, typewriters, desks and chairs that it was difficult to tell which was which. Everything inflammable in the place was afire; wherever there was paint or gasoline, flames licked over steel, giving even it the appearance of burning. There was a sharp explosion as another of the wrecked plane's gas tanks went up in a geyser of flame. This was followed by a sputter and crackle of improperly exploded flak as a sixty-round cylinder of 20-mm ammunition fell into the flames from the deck above and went off like a string of giant firecrackers. Somebody screamed with pain. There were men moving in on the fire, not waiting for a captain's orders. Machinist Campbell, battery officer on the signal bridge, had taken charge of survivors in the area. One group was throwing ready ammunition overboard before it could detonate in all directions and kill everybody within reach. Three other groups were moving in on the flame with three-inch diameter firehoses, stiff with one hundred pounds of pressure now spraying thirty-foot wide curtains of salt water on the fire. MacDougall ducked through the curtain of spray, ran around and into the pilothouse. The bulkhead between radio room and pilothouse was buckled and red hot in one spot, but it was holding. Kruger was not in sight, but Willicut, still holding the wheelspokes, looked to him for instructions.

"Rudder working, Willicut?"

"Yes, sir. Full rudder both ways. I called the engine room. No serious damage, they think. Except they said water coming out of the shaft alley."

"Shaft alley?" Must be from that first hit at number five. The shaft alley tunnel ran through the gasoline storage space in number five hatch. Well— "Did they say anything about pumps?"

"Yes, sir. All pumps operational."

"Good; we're going to need 'em." MacDougall went to the phone to call Fraser, see how it was at damage control central station. Fraser had sense enough to stay at central station and direct all his various damage control parties from there.

"Mr. MacDougall." It was Willicut, peering at him across the brass binnacle.

"Yes?"

"Things are kind of serious, aren't they, sir?"

MacDougall managed a grin. "Yes, just a little. We may sink." Then he got Fraser. "Hello, Stuart. What's the story?"

Willicut watched MacDougall, who slumped against the bulkhead until the heat got through his shirt and stood him straight in a hurry. The exec was grunting and swallowing as he listened to Fraser's report. At last he said, "Let's see, now. Number three lower hold flooded, first and second platforms on fire and spreading forward. I got the dope on aft. . . . Yes, the shaft alley; we may have more trouble back there . . . emergency pumps . . . shores for that panting bulkhead . . . foam . . . Yes, let's cut those wires. . . . Use jumpers from the forward emergency pump. . . . O.K., Stu, I'll get down as soon as I can. The Old Man's got a crack over the head. Lot of men hurt up here; get word to Frank Bell. Check those soundings. We've got to work fast now. O.K."

MacDougall went out the undamaged portside door to the pilothouse, doubled back around the bridge wreckage and went to have another look at the captain. Flames from the radio room were lessening; most of the gasoline was consumed now and Campbell's volunteer fire brigade was discouraging the rest.

Hawks was sitting up, hugging his knees with both arms, staring at the fire. He faced MacDougall but seemed unaware of his presence. MacDougall got down on one knee and looked into Hawks's face. Those glassy eyes, looking right through him but no longer keen, penetrating, disconcerting. He doesn't even see me, thought MacDougall. "Capt'n. Capt'n Hawks!" The man must have a serious concussion. Have to get him down to sick bay. MacDougall looked around again. He needed someone to take over up here on the bridge while he had a good look around belowdecks. He jumped to the railing and looked about. It was pitch black; no ship nor land in sight, no moon, nothing but some other ship burning far away—a ship, he knew, because he saw the flames reflected in the water. Then he looked down from the *Belinda's* bridge and saw his own crude shadow dancing grotesquely in a reddish pool of sea water and oil. He looked skyward, thinking of planes. Surely they weren't all gone. There must be some Japs left and, if so, they could not fail to see the flaming *Belinda*. Well, guns were still manned and ready. Time would tell about the Japs. . . . No use shouting to Campbell and the rest; they were doing all anybody could do with fog nozzles and CO_2.

MacDougall went back to Hawks. Still hugging his knees, he had not moved. MacDougall bent down again, then put his hand gently over the cut on Hawks's head. Hawks moved his head back and forth. MacDougall took away his hand and wiped the trickle of blood from his hand on his trouser leg and got out a compress from his first aid kit.

For the first time, Hawks seemed to notice him. He started back and his eyes focused somewhat upon him, still with that glassy look. "I know you," he said slowly. His speech was thick, drunken-sounding. MacDougall reached out again with the compress. Hawks ducked his head away. "I'm all right," he said. "I'm fine." There was another spurt of flame as something highly inflammable ignited in the wrecked radio space. Hawks seemed to be trying to remember something. He got up, staggered to the sooty bridge rail and looked out over the foredeck. Flames glowed from a scuttle door which had not yet been closed against the fire. Hawks turned around again and looked at the ruin of his bridge. Then he clutched MacDougall's arm in a vicelike squeeze. "Where's my monkey?" he asked hoarsely. "Where's Chipchee?" His glassy eyes were fixed on MacDougall. "I know you, Mr. Executive Officer," he said. "You're the answer man. Now tell me, where is my monkey?"

MacDougall opened his mouth to make reply; but what could he say? He shut his mouth again, looked at Hawks, hoping that smoky veil would leave his eyes.

Hawks slapped the bridge rail. "You know, don't you? You know where my monkey is. You're holding out on me."

"No, Captain. I don't know where he is."

"Well, do something about it. Don't be so slack. Be incisive,

Mr. Executive Officer. I'll tell you." Hawks put his mouth to MacDougall's ear and whispered hoarsely, "It's the Japs. They killed Chipchee." He raised up straight again and yelled into the flames, "The Japs killed my monkey! Call all hands to quarters! Search the ship for my monkey!" Once more his voice dropped to a whisper. "That's why we didn't find him before; there wasn't light enough. There's plenty of light now; you'll be able to find him. Search the ship; search the ship! You must find Chipchee for me!"

MacDougall looked around for help. That was Kruger leading the work with the nearest fog nozzle. "Karl," he called, "give me a hand over here." Kruger relinquished the fog nozzle to the man behind him and came over to MacDougall and Hawks. Kruger's face was blistered, his hair and eyebrows singed. "Get me a corpsman, Karl, then come back."

The pharmacist's mates and their apprentices had been busy all over the ship, crawling low along smoke-filled alleyways looking for wounded shipmates. Some of them had been working around the bridge. In less than a minute, Kruger returned with two of them carrying a litter. The corpsmen set the litter down and looked uncertainly at their captain, who was sitting on the deck again, staring at the fire in the radio room. Then Hawks noticed the litter. "Take that thing away," he said scornfully, "Dr. Flynn will prescribe for me." Startled at mention of the dead medical officer, the corpsmen looked uneasily to MacDougall, who waved them on. They picked up the litter at once and went around the corner to look for a more tractable patient. Then Hawks got to his feet, leaning heavily on MacDougall, for the morphine was beginning to affect him. "We will go down to the cabin now," he said slowly.

"Aye, sir," said MacDougall, then called to Kruger. "Get Randall out here from the charthouse. The squawk box is shot, you'll have to go for him. Tell him to turn the ship around easy, get the wind aft and head on slow bell for Kerama Retto. Then you get some men and cover up all ventilation around that fire in the hold. . . . I'll be back as soon as I can."

"Yes, sir," said Kruger, and went off briskly to get Randall.

MacDougall called after him, "And yell down the cabin speaking tube if there're any more bogies. Jerk up those lookouts."

Hawks seemed relaxed and unconcerned. When MacDougall was ready he started down the ladder to his quarters, leaning on him so heavily that MacDougall nearly carried him the last few feet. Things were knocked around in the cabin. The bell-striking ship's clock of which Hawks was so proud had come down from the bulkhead and smashed on the deck. The ship was taking a noticeable list to port, warning MacDougall that he could ill afford to spend much time as captain's nurse. He got Hawks

432

through the cabin and into his stateroom. Hawks leaned heavily against the edge of his bunk. "MacDougall," he said slowly. "As you know, Dr. Flynn has been prescribing for me. I haven't seen him for a long time. He must be . . . delayed. Mac-Dougall, look in the medicine cabinet." Hawks's speech was becoming very thick now. "I feel the need of a little stimulant." MacDougall stepped into the bathroom, got a four-ounce medicine bottle of whisky from the cabinet and handed it to Hawks, who sighed heavily, took off the metal cap and drained it down. "That's a good . . . You're a good man, Mr. Mac-Dougall. I'll just shut my eyes for a bit." MacDougall eased the captain up into his bunk, pulled off his shoes, covered him with a blanket and headed back for the bridge.

Machinist Campbell had got the fire out on the bridge deck. Randall had the ship half turned around; his familiar stocky frame was draped over the rail of the undamaged port wing. MacDougall went over beside him.

"Any bogies, Jim?"

"Not now. Sky's clear."

"Our CAP back yet?"

"No. . . . Screen shows a flock of friendlies north of the island. There must be another heavy Jap raid vectoring down this way."

"Well, we'll have to get these fires out. Look at that red-hot glow out the side of number three. There must be a hole in the ship's side big enough to sail an LCM into number three hatch. I'm going down to that hatch and see if anything else can be done. We're caught between fire and flood; either one may finish her off."

"If the Japs don't get to her first," said Randall.

"That's right." MacDougall looked out into the darkness. "Gyro operational?"

"Yes, gyro and radar. Chief Appelmann is rigging a temporary radio transmitter in the ship-to-shore shack. We'll get by up here as long as there's a hull floating under us."

"Good. Now listen, Jim. You keep in touch with Fraser. He can tell you about the bulkheads. You keep fudging along for Kerama Retto. We don't dare open her up; it'll fan the fire and spring the bulkheads. But I want to get her over where we can beach her if we have to. . . . Give me a toot on the steam whistle if the kamikazes start closing in again."

MacDougall ran down a series of steel ladders to the main-deck. The ship was developing a nasty list to port, so that it was difficult to walk in the dark over the disordered deck. He found the starboard scuttle leading down into number three hatch and looked about for a hatch wedge to knock the dogs loose about the watertight door, so that he could get down and have

433

a look. He put his hand on the door and took it away quickly; the door was blistering hot to the touch. MacDougall went aft into the deckhouse, turned forward again and tried to get down by a different way. As soon as he opened the WT door on the second deck and started through the deserted crew mess compartment, which was built above number three hold, he found himself in a different and more fearsome world than even the fire and confusion of the burning bridge deck. Smoke and an ovenlike blast of heated air drove him down to his knees. The place was jet black except for reflections on a distant bulkhead of some fire burning around a corner. The lights were out and the deck was cluttered with snaking fire hoses. MacDougall had forgotten to bring a flashlight. He crawled by dead reckoning to a place on the nearby bulkhead where he knew one of the many battle lanterns was placed for just such emergencies as this. Standing up, coughing in the smoke, he ran the flat of his hand about and found the lantern. Quickly he took it from its hook and snapped the switch. Blessed light poured in a strong beam from the lantern, though swirling smoke cut its effectiveness considerably. At once MacDougall remembered the countless captain's inspections made about these decks. A dozen times he had seen Hawks reach out and snap the switch to that lantern, bellowing for a new battery if it did not work. MacDougall could hear Hawks roar at the nearest enlisted man: "Been reading comic books again after lights out, ehhh? Fix this lantern and keep it fixed. It's for EMERGENCIES!"

This part of the ship seemed deserted, but MacDougall could hear commotion around on the low port side. He crouched down, pulled the open neck of his shirt over his nose and ran forward. There was more smoke on the other side: more hoses, water ankle deep, paintwork burned from the bulkheads. MacDougall worked aft, past watersoaked and sooty sailors tending hose. He brushed past these men and went down another ladder to the first platform, occupied by the *Belinda's* main refrigerator machinery, the largest of the cold-storage boxes and some crew shower stalls. This area seemed cooler than the deck above, but the slight feeling of security was a false one, he knew. It was just the draft from fire burning below. Draft meant more oxygen for the flames. But men had to breathe; men must stay down there fighting fire or the ship was lost, so there was no use in trying to batten her down against draft just now. MacDougall got on the next ladder and started down. He didn't need his lantern to find the way now. The vast cavern of number three hold, where medium tanks, field artillery and bulldozers had been combat loaded, was brightly lighted by flames leaping from fiercely burning material on the platform built over the freshwater tanks in the after part of the hold. The forward two thirds of the space was not afire; it was flooded to a depth he judged must be fifteen feet deep, for water was sloshing up to the level of the platform, where Pappy Moran and his men were driving solid streams of water into a huge pile of kapok life jackets, hundreds of cases of toilet paper and other combustible stores. Behind Moran, another crew sprayed him continually with a fog nozzle, while a third crew cooled down the blistering bulkheads with another stream. The smoke from the kapok jackets was nearly overwhelming. Some of the men wore oxygen breathing apparatus, but those in key positions were working with faces exposed. A tall man came over from a corner where he had been digging into the pile of kapok jackets to expose the heart of the fire there. It was Boatswain Torgeson. He leaned over from the platform, dipped his handkerchief into the surging water and splashed his face. "Kinda silly, trying to fight fire down here," he said. "We're goin' to get drowned any minute!" He pointed off to port. "Look at that! That's where the Jap came through. The plane's down in the hold there, under the water somewhere. Did he ever rip her skin open!"

MacDougall turned his torch towards the ship's side. He could see about three feet of jagged, triangular gash above the level of water rising in the hold. The sea welled in like water entering a nearly filled lock; less spectacular than it must have been at first, but more ominous to an experienced eye. That was the waterline, six feet above where it ought to be. MacDougall made a mental calculation. Fifty tons per inch immersion, six hundred tons per foot. Without bothering for the moment with the fore and aft trim of the ship—something he would certainly have to consider soon—the *Belinda* must have thirty-six hundred tons of sea water in her already, and more coming in fast.

"We tried to stop it," said Torgeson. "We shoved mattresses into the hole, backed 'em with crew bunk springs and shored the lot up with hatch boards and timber. It kept busting out and throwing the stuff back in our faces. Fitzgerald and three others got badly hurt. Now it seems like it's slowed down, but there's a gash in the ship's side about ten feet below what you can see. Fraser told me to try once more. I'm getting this fire out and then we'll go at it again." Torgeson coughed until he was doubled over.

"You'd better get up on deck awhile," said MacDougall.

"I'm all right. But we got to get this fire out, sir. Men can't work in this smoke with those heavy shores; we've tried it three times."

MacDougall was looking at the welling flow of sea water flooding into the hold. It looked like storm water coming out of a culvert.

"What pumps you got working in this space, Boats?"

"We've got four hose lines from forward emergency and three from the engine room on jumper lines."

"Good work. . . . But that won't do it. Just look at it coming in!"

"They're pumping the bilge line—if it isn't plugged with some of this litter."

MacDougall waved a hand dismissing the bilge pump. "That's no better than a tin cup to bail with," he said. "We're sinking!"

Boatswain Torgeson looked as if he were ready to give up number three hold. "What'll we do? Can she float without it, sir?"

"We've got to do something about this space, Boats." MacDougall knelt down on the fire-stained ledge and peered down into the submerged lower hold. "Shaft alley is flooded and dogged down, but there's some leakage back there and it may get a lot worse any time, so we can't count on number five space for flotation. What's worse, the bulkhead between that ruptured gas stowage space and the engine room is quivering like an autumn leaf. If that lets go, there'll be nothing we can do. Black gang's shoring it now and we'll just have to assume that it'll hold."

Torgeson was getting his breath again. He got to his feet to carry on again. "If the engine room bulkhead holds, then what's our chances if we lose out here?"

MacDougall scratched at the paste of soot and salt water in his hair. "If it weren't for the twenty-five hundred tons of ballast and all that top weight of guns and gun mounts, heavy davits—all that tackle and extra gear we've got topside—she'd float without this space here. As it is she'll have just about negative stability, like a submarine ready to dive."

"Can't we pump out the double bottoms and this fresh water tank here?"

"No. She'll capsize if we do. We've got to keep the weight down low, but she can't stand much more flooding here."

"If we could just stop that leak!"

"I tell you—let's make an old fashioned collision mat and haul it overside. Just weight the bottom of a tarp—there isn't time to run lines under the keel. She ought to suck in some while the pumps keep up with her. . . . You get started on the mat. I'm going aft to see Fraser, get the rest of the picture." MacDougall scrambled across a gap of water and went up the ladder to the first platform. There he came face to face with the refrigeration machinery. The pumps were no longer performing their normal duty of compressing saturated gases drawn from the evaporator. Compression—pumping air in. Salvage people raised shattered wrecks by pumping huge air bubbles into the tops of ruptured submerged compartments. That mat wasn't likely to be very successful. Perhaps it would be easier to keep air in than water out. "It's worth a try," said MacDougall out loud.

"What's that, sir?" asked Torgeson, right behind him on the ladder rungs.

"That compressor. I wish I knew a little more engineering. Let's get Ingalls and see if that— Well, we can't stand here while the ship sinks. I'll explain later. You've got the fire licked down below here. Get Pappy out of there. Forget the collision mat. Seal off the hold here right at the second platform. Run your hoses down in a solid block; use pipe if you can—get some shipfitters. Get Pappy to cover the hatch here, put down a couple of tarps and paint it with tar or anything to hold air inside, then weight the whole business down. I'm going to promote an air pump somewhere!"

MacDougall scrambled out of number three and got back to the maindeck passageway running aft through the main house. Here to his surprise, he ran into more snaking fire hoses, more smoke and reflection of flames. There were a lot of men here, for the most part mess cooks and bakers—more than were needed. One hose had a dozen men dragging it along—at least their hearts were in it. Shadow Rockwell came running past with a heavy CO_2 fire extinguisher.

"What's burning here, Shadow?"

"Didn't you know? Hole in the side—blew in dentist's office —forward end of sick bay country afire—all those wounded men—!" Shadow panted off down the passage.

MacDougall opened the WT door, stepped through and slammed it shut behind him. He found the place frighteningly hot; smoke stung his eyes—astonishing for he had passed here a few minutes before on his way to the hold. Some new disaster. More hoses, men and shouting. Voice of Hubert, the garbage grinder, shouting directions in a very authoritative manner: "Bring up that hose! Get me a short fog nozzle, I can't use that long pipe in my garbage room. Hey you, mess cooks; go get another CO_2. This one's empty!" Garbage room afire! No wonder Hubert was excited. MacDougall pushed through the crowd to have a look. It was a nasty fire, but a small one. Not much left in the place that would burn. What had caused these new fires? That was important to know. He crawled up beside Hubert, who was squirting cold white froth of CO_2 over a pile of 20-mm shell drums.

Suddenly MacDougall realized what had happened: the ready box on the deck above had caught fire, exploded the thin deck, perhaps melted it; anyway, fantastic as it seemed, here was ammunition exploding and burning up the garbage room and

Hubert. "Say, you fool!" yelled MacDougall. "Get out of here! Those shells will blast you to bits!" He grasped Hubert from behind by his belt and tried to drag him out of the place.

With all his reserve strength, Hubert flung MacDougall off. "This is my garbage room," he shouted. "They ain't going to burn up my garbage grinder!" Hubert tossed aside the empty CO_2 cylinder and reached for another, cut the sealing disk with a quick twist, opened the valve and turned the roaring stream on the pile of ammunition and burning grease in the corner.

MacDougall flung himself upon the fog nozzle being brought through the door, slammed on solid stream and turned the stabbing, cooling pressure on the fire. "Cool the place down!" he yelled. "Get out of there, Hubert. That ammo'll go off in your face! Anyway, that CO_2 will kill you in this closed-up place!"

"This is my garbage room," panted Hubert. "My garbage room! Nobody's going to wreck my garbage grinder!"

The flames reached a shell and the drums went off with a shattering fusillade of explosions which cleared the garbage room of all but Hubert. MacDougall, the last out the door, started in again as soon as the racket subsided. That's the end of Hubert, he was thinking, when he heard the garbage grinding machine start up. Hubert, unmindful of a bloody flesh wound in his left forearm, was staring intently into his machine. "It works," he said. "By golly, it still works!" Shaking his head, MacDougall backed out of the garbage room and headed for the other side.

MacDougall did not get to the sick bay; halfway down the passage he bumped into Walter Ingalls, the engineering officer. Ingalls would know about that compressor. MacDougall explained the situation; he had to have some kind of low-pressure compressor to pump a bubble of air into number three hold. Would the refrigerating machinery do the trick?

Ingalls scratched his head with an oil-stained hand. "It might have done it; we'd of had to break some pipes. But the refrigerator machine is wrecked, all our frozen stores will spoil if we don't get it going soon."

"Forget the stores. If we don't plug the holes in this bucket we'll all be swimming. I've got to have a compressor!"

Ingalls thought a moment. "There's a portable compressor in after boat repair—that small salvage rig."

"Why of course," said MacDougall. "What's the matter with me? We'll drag it right through here and get it going at number three."

"But it weighs half a ton. How'll you move it? The deck gear is wrecked back aft."

MacDougall considered for a moment. Then suddenly his richest resource came to mind—not machinery, but three human dynamos from the chiefs' quarters. "We'll get that compressor moved, Walt. You keep the pumps going." MacDougall ran forward, got hold of a first division coxswain and said, "Go get Pappy Moran. Tell him to round up five of his huskiest men and lay aft to the boat repair shop on the double. I'll see him there. Get going, now!"

Alvick was back at Gun Two, standing by for the next Jap. "Turn the gun over to Hatcher again," MacDougall said. "We've got a job. Where's Rinaldo?"

"Jerry's shoring up bulkheads in number five."

"Send for him to lay up to boat repair immediately. No time to explain now. I'll see you all there."

The pump was as large and heavy as the main engine of a good-sized ferry boat. Alvick, Moran and Rinaldo gathered about it. MacDougall looked at the machine with a sick feeling in the pit of his stomach. How would they ever get that behemoth across the listing deck, along the passageway and down the ladder to number three hatch? It was an eight-hour job for an expert rigger with a heavy overhead crane. These men had little but their hands to work with. MacDougall could not stay; he had the whole ship to look out for. Then he looked at the three chiefs and reassurance flowed into him. Alvick, fine marlinspike sailor, the most intelligent fellow in the three deck divisions; Jerry Rinaldo, dry-humored mechanical genius who could build a ship all by himself; and Pappy Moran, the most persuasive personality on the *Belinda*. He had the jackpot here; if anybody could move that compressor from one end of the ship to the other, they could. MacDougall left them there and headed for the central damage control station to confer with Fraser.

MacDougall found Fraser sitting on a stool at his long work desk in damage control central station. The place was littered with blueprints, capacity tables and oil-stained sounding reports. Puffing on his pipe, Fraser was adding another small brass weight to a working model of the ship's compartments.

"I think she's going to sink," Fraser said in a matter-of-fact voice. "I've checked and double checked my tables; damn near worn out my slide rule. I can't pump out any more double bottoms; she'll capsize on us for sure." Fraser reached over to his model, which hung in gimbals, added another small weight to the port side and watched her roll over on her side.

"We've got to keep this port list in her, Stu. If you can pump anything out of the high side, go ahead."

"I've done that already," said Fraser.

MacDougall looked at Fraser. They hadn't always got along too well; Fraser was a seaman of the old school, stubborn and cantankerous, but everything he had was for the ship. Here he sat on a stool, shut up in a room, getting his reports by telephone and messenger, working his slide rule and co-ordinating the entire effort of saving the *Belinda*. Fraser was no quitter, yet he thought she would sink.

MacDougall took a phone from the bulkhead and called the bridge. "Randall? How's it going? Bogies within twenty miles . . . CAP? . . . Hope the Hellcats can hold 'em. Remember the steam whistle if they get within ten miles. . . . Keise Shima abeam soon? . . . That's that small reef halfway to Kerama, isn't it? Well, ease down there and pass close aboard. We're still losing flotation; I may have to open up the engines and run her ashore there. Hate to do it; try to make Kerama if we can. There's a decent beach there where we can get her off again if she goes down on us. . . . Well, keep plugging along. I'll come to the bridge as soon as I can."

MacDougall explained to Fraser what he was doing with the air compressor. Fraser listened silently, worked his slide rule and removed two small weights from the forward half of his model. "I think that would do it," he said. "Only trouble is, you'll never get that compressor from the fantail to number three. I'm still wearing my life jacket."

MacDougall gave Fraser a half smile, then left damage control and started forward again. Remembering the fire in the sick bay—now extinguished, according to Fraser—he went by way of the port-side alleyway, which would take him past the sick bay. Kamikazes had hit forward and aft of the place; most of the wounded lying helpless between the two crash spots had been spared. Bell, Gates and young Dr. Hardwick were busy with survivors from battle ashore and disaster here afloat. Mac-Dougall found Bell in the dressing room adjoining surgery; he was leaning wearily against a bulkhead smoking a crumpled cigarette.

"Hello, Frank."

"Hello, Mac. Where you been, down in the bilges?"

"Just checking the sieve holes."

"Is it bad?"

MacDougall nodded. "Small river flowing into number three. I can't do much with it until the men move up a compressor. . . . Say, Frank, have you seen the Old Man?"

"No, I haven't. I got your message, but we were operating. Just sent a pharmacist's mate up to have a look. Hawks is tossing around. . . . You say you gave him a syrette?"

"Yes. Shouldn't he still be sleeping?"

"He should. Say—I've got to have a blow from this endless surgery or I'll be cutting somebody's throat by mistake. Let's go have a look. Can you spare the time?"

"Sure. Let's go."

Bell paused on the ladder. "He may have a concussion, you know. You say he was irrational?"

440

"Well, he was back monkey hunting."

"I see." Bell went rapidly up two decks and led the way into the cabin. Hawks was moving convulsively in his bunk, striking the bulkhead with both fists. Embarrassed, MacDougall hesitated in the doorway between cabin and stateroom, but Bell went in and took the captain's wrist in his hand.

For a moment Hawks lay still, then with a sudden wrench he jerked his hand away, turned on his stomach and began to sob. "Get away, get away. Leave me alone."

Bell did not attempt to take Hawks's hand again but remained quietly beside the bunk. At last he said in a matter-of-fact voice, "It's just Bell, Captain. I came to see if you needed anything."

Hawks lay for a time with his elbow over his face, then he flung himself over in the bunk until he faced Bell, exposing a face clouded by misery and frustration. "Those dirty yellow bellies got my ship," he said between sobs. "They wore me out and beat me down and wrecked my ship!"

"Yes, Captain. It's tough—but it can't be helped. You did all any man could. It was just one of those things."

"One of those things? One of those things! It was DELIBERATE! Everything was deliberate. They wrecked my ship, wrecked my sailboat, killed my monkey and they took Louise away. Why did they take her away? I need her. I need her to find Chipchee. She'll fix my teeth. . . . I had to show her the boat. I HAD to show her the boat, don't you see? Don't you see what they've done to me? And you aren't helping me, Flynn—Bell—whoever you are, you aren't helping me one little bit." Hawks closed his clouded eyes, rolled over on his stomach again and continued his sobs.

Bell went into the backroom, took a needle and some bottles from a pocket kit. Quickly he lit a match, set afire a teaspoonful of alcohol and sterilized a needle; then, upending another bottle, he plunged in the needle and filled the syringe. Motioning MacDougall to the bedside to help hold Hawks, should this be necessary, Bell swabbed Hawks's shoulder, stuck the needle in and pressed home the hypo. Hawks paid no attention but continued to shake with dry sobs. MacDougall stepped back again. Bell massaged Hawks between the shoulder blades, up and down his spine, kneaded the rocklike muscles in the nape of his neck until they slackened. In a few minutes Hawks was asleep again.

MacDougall looked admiringly at Bell. "Got to hand it to you, Frank, you sure—" A sharp toot of the *Belinda's* steam whistle startled MacDougall in his shoes. Randall calling him: Japs coming!

"What's that?" asked Bell.

"Randall calling me. More Japs. Keep your fingers crossed." MacDougall took a last look at Hawks in the bunk and bolted out of the door for the bridge.

"What's the matter, Jim? Bogies? How close?"

"Sorry, Mac. No Japs, not yet anyhow, but bad news just the same. Torgeson sent word that number three hold has cracked open more. She may be weakened—breaking her back. I thought you'd want to know."

MacDougall hung on to the bridge railing. For a moment he just looked out into the darkness. How peaceful it used to feel on this bridge, steaming along in formation with hundreds of other ships; feeling the strength of numbers, fretting at the rigid discipline, but feeling as secure as a person can in war. Now he was alone with a whole ship to play with: a leaky bucket, all his. The *Belinda* took a sickening, sullen lurch to port, ending several degrees further on her side.

"Read the clinometer," called MacDougall, still braced motionless so that he could feel any further list with his feet.

"Twenty-three degrees port list, sir."

Twenty-three. Like a shifted deckload in the old days. "I'm glad she didn't shift over," he said to Randall. "She'd have gone; nothing could have stopped her. . . . Say, Randall; call Fraser. Tell him we *must* keep that port list. You watch out for her. I'll go down and have another swim in number three hold."

═══════ **CHAPTER 48** ═══════

MacDougall skinned down inside ladders from the bridge deck, past Hawks's cabin, past the empty wardroom and down to the maindeck. The starboard alleyway was still suffocating with smoke which curled lazily above the dim red battle lanterns glowing ankle high at intervals down the hot steel passage. Firehoses had been cleared away from this space to make way for pipe rollers. At the far end MacDougall heard shouts and profane exclamations from a group of men gathered like ants about the bulky compressor, which they had succeeded in moving the length of the shattered afterdeck. Running aft to have a look, he could see that the machine would fill the alleyway, leaving no space for men to work on each side. The ship still listed heavily to port, adding to the difficulties of moving, difficulties which might prove fatal to the ship. Unless they could somehow get this compressor close enough to pump air into the shattered forward hold, the *Belinda* would probably sink in spite of anything else they might attempt to prevent it. Rinaldo and Alvick were flat on the deck, ready to replace a fouled roller while Moran, assisted by some of the ship's heavyweights, struggled to prize up the compressor's forward end and to slide it over the watertight washplate separating the wrecked afterdeck from the passageway.

"All right, men," Moran was saying. "We'll try again. I'll count to three and on *three* you lay your guts on the line there all together. . . . Ready, now: one . . . two . . . THREE!" Moran's sailors strained down on the heavy steel stanchion they were using for a lever, but failed to move the compressor even a fraction of an inch. Moran's voice rasped out at them like a file across the end of a bit of sheet metal. "Together! I said, 'Together!' You ain't going to move nothing one man at a time."

"We're all pulling together, Chief." That would be Lubiski's voice protesting. "Like I said before, Pappy, we can't move this thing with Norwegian steam. We might as well break out the life rafts."

"You overgrown baby!" Moran's tongue lashed into Lubiski. "You ain't got any steam in your useless carcass. Your mother bottle fed you right up to the day the Navy got you."

"Oh, no," Lubiski protested. "I tell ya—"

"Shut up. You don't tell me nothing. Now get hold of that pipe again with the rest of them. You ready, Alvick?"

"Yes. For Pete's sake hurry up!"

Pappy moved up to the end of the lever, braced his feet against the listed bulkhead and called out, "All right, men. This time we move her. On three, now—all together now. Lay your guts into it, all of your guts! One, two, and THREE!" In the dim red light MacDougall saw the forward end of the half-ton compressor move imperceptibly; heard the clank of pipe rollers underneath. None of these men had noticed him, not even Lubiski. Feeling a surging thrill of pride that his men were carrying on without any direction, MacDougall turned about without another word and groped forward towards the shattered compartment in number three hold.

Heat waves blasted at him as he opened the last bulkhead door into the place. The air was filled with acrid smoke, heavy with a saturation of condensed steam so that breathing and movement required unusual effort. Weariness flowed over MacDougall; he was tired, so tired. Well, what of it? They were all tired. Pappy was tired back with that compressor. It was better to be dead tired than dead. But what chance was there any longer to save the ship? It wasn't just heat and weariness; it was a sense of futility that was weighing down on his head and shoulders, the backs of his legs. He seemed to be swimming along without effort; if you just got tired enough you couldn't feel anything. Then he came to another washplate and the effort of lifting a leg once more seemed over-powering. That old damage from the boat accident was bothering again. Come on; get going, man. Get down there and find out the worst. Do something!

Halfway down the last short ladder, he paused to look about. The place had something of the atmosphere of a barn on fire. Where had he seen a barn on fire? Somewhere way back—no time now for such thought. The place seemed strangely unreal; perhaps it was the queer, flickering light: reflected flames dancing blood red on the white-painted overhead—fire and water down below on this devil's cave. Perhaps it was the stifling air: mixture of expended gun powder, fuel oil and the sickening-sweet odor of burned human flesh that by now permeated the entire ship belowdecks. Perhaps it was the agonizing pause in that squeaking reciprocating pump he could hear through an overhead air duct. Every stroke seemed like the last, like it would quit forever, like all pumps would quit. It had a distant sound, probably coming from the engine room—hollow sound like something coming from a cave, sinking, smothering. Other sounds now: voices that he recognized. Boatswain Torgeson and Shadow Rockwell. What was Rockwell doing down here?

MacDougall went down the last few steps into the first platform of number three hold. There were men working here in the dim light. The hatchway to the flooded lower hold was covered but for one small section on the starboard side. It was here that the reflection of flames on floodwater danced upward to the white-painted overhead of the second deck. Boatswain Torgeson came towards him from a group of men busy at covering and sealing over the hatchway.

"She's still on fire down there," he said. "Flashback just a few minutes ago. Shadow Rockwell climbed down there with CO_2. . . . Hello, below. You there, Shadow?"

"Yep?"

"Getting her?"

"I get her out, but she keeps flashing back in my face. This is all my toilet paper. There ain't no more in the ship."

MacDougall got down on his knees and peered into the hold. Shadow Rockwell stood at the edge of the fresh-water tank top poking into the flaming mass of tissue and smothering it periodically with bursts of CO_2. "Get him a hose. . . . Here, Shadow, give her a burst of solid stream."

Rockwell took the heavy brass nozzle and grasped the canvas hose, stiff with water pressure. He opened the nozzle, shoving it forward to solid stream. With a hissing sound the crimson flame was extinguished and the flickering light died from the overhead.

"There," said Rockwell. "Maybe I can save a little of it some time."

"Not now, Shadow," said MacDougall. "Come on up. We've got to seal in this place and get ready for the compressor." A sharp crack of rending steel sent a chill through MacDougall. How much could a ship crack without breaking in two?

"There she goes again, sir," said Torgeson. "That's what I sent word to the bridge about. If a couple of those frames let go—"

"Oh, it couldn't be a frame," said MacDougall, thinking as he spoke, it just can't be a frame! It mustn't be a frame! "Shell plating makes a terrific noise when it lets go, Boats. It's probably just the skin of the ship." But doubt gnawed within him. He must know right now. If the ship was about to render apart, this was the time to get the wounded off and into the landing craft. They could rail load the VPs from undamaged davits—number four was probably O.K. still. The LCMs were still at the beach somewhere. Marty hadn't shown up with them when the first attack came and the *Belinda* took off suddenly from anchorage—have to find the ship at dawn. What was he bothering with landing craft for? The ship breaking in two—he must know—indecision. Oh, yes, he'd been so complacent criticizing other commanders who lost their ships—didn't do this or that. *What are you doing, MacDougall?* Squatting here on your duff while the ship breaks in two in front of your nose!

Shadow Rockwell settled it for MacDougall. Turning off his firehose, he stepped back to help get the hose up through the uncovered space above him—stepped back too far and fell with a splash into the flooded lower hold. There was a sudden roar of laughter from men in the second deck. Flashlights played into the water below. There was the bulky form of Rockwell, head and shoulders emerging, water streaming from the wide and placid face with its short stump of unlit cigar clamped between right molars.

"Hey, Shadow," called the boatswain, "want a light for that cigar?"

A flicker of a smile crossed MacDougall's face as he regarded the grinning Rockwell. Then, as the commissary officer paddled towards the ladder, MacDougall said, "Hold the hatch open for a minute, Boats. I'm going to go down have a look where that Jap came in." Rockwell moved deliberately up to the ladder rungs. There was no time to wait. Impatiently MacDougall jumped into the flooded lower hold, hearing as he dropped the boatswain's shouted warning that there was a bulldozer right below him. He lit with a splash—water surprisingly cool—down under to sharp pain in his bad right leg.

445

Steel—he had his hands on it now, cool steel blade of the giant bulldozer. MacDougall shoved down hard and shot up to the top of the water. Light was dancing all about him now, rippling pools of light in the water, dancing reflections of light on the overhead: Torgeson and his men were shining down their flashlights and battle lanterns. MacDougall struck out first for the starboard side of the ship. If she was going to crack apart, there would be some sign of it here—should be. Reaching the side, he saw nothing but vertical lines of frames with the white-painted inner skin of the ship stretched tight and shipshape between. Perhaps the damage was below. While he pondered, he looked across seventy feet of water to the port side of the flooded hold. There was a blank space in the reflected white: empty and black except for a faint light, strangely distant, moving gently up and down. No, it was the ship moving down and up; he was looking out through the hole in the *Belinda's* side. That was a ship burning. Even as he looked, red tracers streamed skyward at some unseen enemy. He must hurry.

He took a deep breath, grasped one of the starboard frames which stood out some eight inches from the ship's skin, forced down as far as he could go, feeling the skin of the ship for the crack which would spell out disaster to the *Belinda*. Down ten feet, possibly fifteen—blood was pounding in his eardrums, he was out of practice at this sort of thing. Down a little more; the hull might be cracking from the keel upward. Nothing but the humps of rivet heads. Up he shot, gasping for breath, up to the queer dancing light of battle lanterns reflected in flood. Twice more at other frames with similar results—up at last to gulp awhile.

"Find anything, sir?" asked Torgeson.

"Seems all right. I'm going over to see how bad the other side is."

MacDougall worked over towards the tank top where Shadow Rockwell had been standing just a few minutes before. To his dismay he found the tank top awash: the ship had gone down by the head at least two feet in the last few minutes. That water tank rose seventeen feet above the double bottoms and now it was awash. Fighting off the sensation of being smothered and shoved down to the bottom of the strait inside this steel prison, MacDougall struggled to think clearly. If they could just get that compressor forward in time . . . He must see how bad the damage was on the other side of the compartment. If the ship's side continued to tear open until the fracture reached the top, there would be no help from the compressor. Pumped air would just bubble out at the top while the ship went down unhindered. He must see and see quickly. If there was a chance, they would have to seal up this com-

partment without delay and get that pump operating. Mac-
Dougall scrambled to his feet on top of the tank, scrambling
and splashing towards the *Belinda's* port side. His bad leg
dragged but there was no time to fool around here. Over into
the water again, cool shock of water and surprising draft and
suck of fresh air through the great ragged tear in the ship's
side; how much of a hole above this water? "Show a light!"
Lantern beams crossing each other in the ripples—jagged top
of the gash showing just a foot above the water now. Mac-
Dougall looked up: six or seven feet of sound metal to hold
the bubble of air. Would it tear open before he could get the
Belinda to Kerama Retto? That was the question. The answer
might be in how badly the side was torn below water. Mac-
Dougall kicked across to the forward side of the tear, gulped
air and clawed down a frame, feeling the jagged edge of torn
steel side as he went. As far as he could force himself down it
was torn. How wide now? He let go the frame and reached
across for the other side of the tear. His outstretched hand
waved back and forth, meeting only water. He went down a bit
lower and tried again, found nothing. It was as if the ship were
already broken in two and he were hanging to the trailing edge
of the forward part. He opened his eyes in the stinging, oil-
polluted salt; nothing but pale unearthly gleam twinkling
down, revealing not the slightest hint of the other edge. All
this in a matter of seconds, yet he was beginning to feel the
lack of oxygen. Time to go on up and get some air. Something
moved beneath him, something heavy, bulky. There had been
some sound, like heavy steel scraping on steel. Now for the
first time he recognized the pulsation of pumps; the far-off
sound of voices, as if coming through a long, cavernous passage, muffled, having no meaning, like sounds experienced
while under anesthesia. Then he was startled by something
pressing against his body, shoving him against the side; an
octopus—no, the blade of that bulldozer! The ship was listing
over more to port and the bulldozer was drifting down on him,
must be caught up on something. Better get out of here! Now
the bulldozer blade moved again. MacDougall tried to kick
against the ship's side and shoot up to the surface. His foot
went through the hole; perhaps this thing had shoved him out
the hole and overboard. Whatever happened, he must have
air. He shoved down on the blade and breasted down both
palms—still no top. Down with the palms once again, while
lack of air and fear of being imprisoned or lost overside
pressed in from all sides. At last he broke water; blessed light
of battle lanterns; blessed acrid air! He was still in the hold.
What business had he with this stuff anyway? He could have
been lost. His duty was on the bridge. Command is on the
bridge not under fifteen feet of water in a flooded hold. He

had younger and stronger bodies to explore for him. The team must work together; there was no time and this was no place for the individual. All this while gasping in air, gulping in air, hanging to the *Belinda's* fractured shell plating. She was cracked all the way down. There was less overhead than ever in this hold; he was sure of that. There wasn't a chance to save her now. Fraser and his slide rule had been right: she would sink.

Torgeson was calling, "You all right, sir?"

"Yes—get my breath here. Start covering the hatch; I'll be out." He had to rest a second more, leaned his head against the *Belinda's* skin. New sound now. What was that wonderful rumbling, like distant thunder, like far-off voices! Voices? No, the ship was tearing apart; that's what it was. Here we go, after all the grief; here we go down, down. Something strange in the sound; not ominous, not frightening. Voice of Moses; something reassuring. Baloney! What's reassuring about a ship blown apart, burned out and sinking? Listen to it. *She's a good ship, lad. A fortunate ship. She'll go far, this ship—and she'll come home again.* Voices? There were no voices. A ship talk? Well, they call it a ship talking. He knew what it was: stresses locked in the welded hull since the day of launching, released now by this shearing and shattering of side plates. Balaam's ass speaking to his betters at last. Well, that *was* talking, wasn't it? Hadn't he heard it? No, just a rumbling. I'm getting punchy, he thought, shoving across the water in the hold to the vertical iron ladder leaning up the manhole and out of the place. *A good ship. A fortunate ship. She'll come home again.* Why it was that little old man back in the shipyard at Alameda the night before they launched the *Belinda*. *She's a good ship and a tight ship . . . a lucky ship and fortunate.* A lot of water under the keel since then: Makin, Kwajalein—Come on, MacDougall. Get the lead out!

MacDougall glanced about the first platform of the hold. Boatswain Torgeson and his men had the hatch covered with tarps and were smearing the top canvas with hot asphaltum, strapping down the tarred canvas with locking bars.

"We can put the hose down the manhole," said Torgeson. "Then I'll seal her up all around."

"Good. Where's the compressor?"

"Coming down the scuttle from the main deck. There's a couple of ringbolts in the overhead there—chain tackle. Wasn't bad."

MacDougall could hear clanging of pipe rollers on the next deck up. He started for the ladder up to the crew mess hall, leaning away from perpendicular—they were all leaning. The *Belinda* had a dangerous list now: at least twenty-five degrees. He heard Moran shouting, "Come on, Lubiski. Slap a roller down. Put that dunnage against the bulkhead; keep her from rolling down hill. All right, boys, all together again . . ."

MacDougall stumbled up the ladder, favoring his injured leg. "That's wonderful, fellows," he said. "Drag her over to the scuttle now and we'll run the hose down two decks and start her up."

"Can't do it that way; hose isn't long enough." Rinaldo, sweaty and soot smeared, came from behind the behemoth.

"What do you mean? We've got plenty of hose. You can couple on some more."

"No, sir. Not on this rig."

"Why?"

"Well, this is a bit of gear Pappy and I lifted off the dockyard at Noumea. It's got French threads; our hose won't fit."

"Can't you burn it off with a cutting torch and spot on a standard flange?"

"Guess I could. It's a bad spot to work."

"How long would it take?"

"At least an hour, time I got set up and everything."

MacDougall looked at Rinaldo. He knew that if Rinaldo said a job was tough, it was well nigh impossible under the circumstances. "We haven't got any hour, Jerry." He looked from the bulk of the compressor to Alvick and Moran. "Think you boys can get her down another ladder?"

Moran spat on the deck and rubbed the palms of his hands together. "What are we waiting for?" he said.

The scuttle leading down from the mess hall to the first platform was small and steeper than the one already negotiated with the compressor. There were no ringbolts in the overhead and, again, to weld any into place would have consumed time which was not available while sea water crept up steadily against the pumps laboring in shattered number three hold just below. Alvick rigged a makeshift shear legs. They used watch tackles, barrel burtons, more rollers—none of it any good. Gasping for breath and defeated, they got out from under just in time as the thousand-pound compressor slithered out of control and jammed at the turn of the ladder.

"It's the list that has us stymied," said Alvick. "Nothing's up and down any more in this cockeyed ship. We ought to yank this ladder out."

MacDougall looked upward and shook his head. "No good. No pad eyes. Besides, we're stuck with it now. How'd we lift her back up again?"

Torgeson wiped the streaming sweat from his face with the back of a greasy hand. "If she was a mule we could light a fire under her," he said.

"Try the hose from here," said MacDougall.

"No use, sir. Won't reach."

Moran rose from the corner where he had been catching his breath. "There's only one way to lick this. Pick her up and walk her down there. Come on, fellows. Gather around. We'll just pick her up."

There were groans from some of the men, but they all circled the compressor, reaching uneasily about for a footing on the tilting ladder.

"You call out, Pappy," said Torgeson. "Now all at once, boys. Move with Pappy."

Three times they tried it. Human flesh could do only so much, no matter how urgently called upon with all Moran's practiced persuasiveness. The men sank back more exhausted than ever. The compressor still remained jammed at the turn of the ladder. Then MacDougall remembered something: Chinese coolies at Shanghai; sixty of them walking off with a five-ton propeller shaft. They did it with ropes and poles—and a good singsong. "Lubiski, go get half a dozen bunk stanchions from the troop berthing forward. Take Grandy with you and make it snappy!" Then he turned to Torgeson. "Look, Boats; it's a matter of getting more men around the thing. We'll rig a bunch of yokes. Get some more men down here. Get some lashing. We've got to get this thing down and start her up."

They got the men, the stanchions, the lashings. Yokes were rigged. Where there was no foothold for men to stand, stout lashings were passed up to the deck above. Then Moran, who had put many a tank lighter, howitzer and careening bulldozer overside in pitch black darkness, took over direction. "Come on, boys. Take a brace, now. I'll count slow to three and on three you tighten up your guts and heave together. . . . Ready now? . . . All right, here we go. One . . . two . . . and THREE." Nothing moved; the compressor was jammed firmly in place. MacDougall ducked down to peer into the manhole. The water had risen another foot. Time was running out. He watched while Moran tried again. There was one place, right at the bottom step of the first ladder; she was hung up there. Just as he noticed this, Moran came around and put his hand on the spot. Moran looked about, sizing up the strength and courage of the men around him. At last he spotted Foots Boski, the hulking signalman from the beach party. "I can use you, Foots; right here." Without the slightest hesitation, Boski worked through the crowd and took his place beside Moran. "We'll get our fingers around here and all of us heave her out together," Moran explained.

"But your fingers," MacDougall protested. "If anybody loses his grip, you two will lose your fingers!"

"They'd better not lose their grip," said Moran. "Come on, now. We're just going to pick her up now. Alvick, you watch the manropes; slack just when needed. Everybody set? Well, let's walk her around now. UP, YOU LAZY SONS! WALK HER NOW; WALK HER NOW. WALK HER, WALK HER! COME AROUND THERE; COME AROUND!"

As if it had suddenly decided to co-operate, the compressor moved up, around the congested turn, then down the second flight of steel ladder to the platform below. With practiced speed, Rinaldo and his mates rigged the short length of French hose and started the engine into roaring life. Soon the air pump settled down to a smooth, workmanlike throbbing. Torgeson sealed the manhole around the hose. The air bubble was started at last.

"Keep her going, no matter what happens," said MacDougall to the warrant boatswain. "If anything can keep the old gal afloat, this is it."

"We'll keep her going, sir."

"Good. Report to Fraser what we are doing here. I'm going back to the bridge." On the way up at the turn of the ladder, MacDougall found Moran slumped in a corner, both hands pressed against his groin.

"What's the matter, Pappy? Haven't ruptured yourself, have you?"

"I'm fine, sir. Just resting."

MacDougall looked at the pain-filled eyes. "You're lying," he said. "Better go see Dr. Bell for a check."

"No, sir. He's busy. I'm fine."

"O.K.," said MacDougall, making a mental note to speak to Bell about Moran, "but take it easy the rest of the day. Tell the kids what to do."

"Yes, sir, I'll tell 'em."

MacDougall looked at Moran's squarish, open face. Moran wasn't a talker; he was a hard man to thank. This man was the living soul of the *Belinda*, but who could tell him so? "That was a nice bit of work you did with that compressor, Pappy. Only, knowing you, it surprised me that you needed any help from Foots and the others." A slow grin stole across Moran's face. MacDougall left him there and went on up the ladders.

Biggs sat asleep on his camp stool outside Hawks's cabin. MacDougall entered, noticed the clock, still on the deck and now slid across to the lower port bulkhead by the increased list. Hawks was still asleep in his stateroom bunk, mouth open, face muscles utterly relaxed, snoring loudly. No use trying to wake him, MacDougall thought; at last the captain really sleeps. He picked up the shattered clock, just why he did not know, stowed it carefully in Hawks's easy chair and walked out.

From the bridge, there were stars after rain to be seen twinkling dewlike in a predawn sky. The bridge was a good place to get back to; even this twisted wreckage of what had

451

once been the *Belinda's* showplace seemed homelike after the awesome cavern of the flooded hold. MacDougall looked about the horizon for tracers and saw none; no gunfire, no shouting TBS. It was quiet enough on the bridge to hear the leisurely movement of sea wash along the tortured ship's side as she crawled for the haven of Kerama Retto. He got across the twisted deck and found the familiar silhouette of Jim Randall slumped over the forward splinter shield.

"Hello, Jim. What's the word up here?"

"Still afloat and making five knots on course two-four-seven. That's Tokashiki Shima showing up dead ahead, five miles; eight-hundred foot peaks near the north tangent. . . . Fraser reports the compressor started in number three."

"Yes, I was down there. How about gasoline stowage?"

"Bulkheads holding so far. Engine room reports a lot of water leaking from the flooded shaft alley; the watertight door is sprung. Chief's worried about the shaft."

"It should be all right; it's water cooled and shouldn't have to be lubricated in an emergency at this speed."

"That isn't it. The shaft is sprung. Nobody can get into the shaft alley to inspect it, but Ingalls reports a heavy strain on the shaft at a damaged bearing. He thinks the main shaft itself is sprung."

"Isn't that lovely!" said MacDougall. "We haven't had enough trouble; now we're going to have a frozen shaft. . . . How's the radar screen?"

"Clear for the first time all night. Our CAP chased them all out."

"Well, that's good news, but keep a careful watch on that radar screen. They may come back."

"Aye, aye. Say, here's a pot of joe, not too bad. Want some?"

MacDougall sent a messenger down to his room for some dry clothes. He had gulped down half the mug of coffee when the pilot-house phone rang. Fraser down at damage control central station reporting, "She's still losing flotation; not so fast but still losing. Bulkhead forward of number five is panting."

"Shore her up some more, Fraser. Those bulkheads ought to hold on a dead slow bell; we're only making five knots. One more hour should see us to Kerama Retto. . . . How about that water tank in flooded number three? . . . Yes, pump it all out. We can make more water, any time. . . . It's up to you, now. Keep her floating!"

Another shadow moved out from the captain's deck. Dr. Bell, up from surgery to have a look at Captain Hawks, now climbed towards the bridge with a sheet of memo paper in one hand. Just as his head reached bridge level he heard whispering voices followed by derisive chuckles.

"Come on, Grandy. What's the matter—chicken?"

"Naw. I been on report enough. You go right ahead, Riley."

"Aw, come on, you dumb wood-butcher. We'll sneak in that flak locker and sack out. They'd never look for us there."

"Nope. You're nothing but trouble for me or anyone else. I'm going up to my gun."

"Chicken."

"O.K. I'm chicken. Want to make something out of it?"

"No, course not, Grandy. Don't beat your gums about it, though."

"Don't worry, Sacktime. Go get your beauty sleep."

Bell waited on the steps. Quirks of human nature fascinated him. This Riley, now: Flynn always used to say that nothing could ever kill Riley; he was too relaxed. Just a useless hunk of boy, unless that relaxed attitude of his could be possibly construed as aiding ship's morale. Shaking his head, Bell continued up the ladder and crossed the bridge to MacDougall's side.

"Here's a preliminary casualty report, Mac. Thought I'd bring it up myself and get a bit of fresh air."

MacDougall turned a shaded flashlight on Bell's neat handwritten memo, glanced down the impersonal notations and whistled.

"Is it that bad!"

"It may be even worse. Except for a miracle, some of those fellows listed in the right-hand column aren't going to make it. This has been especially rough on those wounded marines who got smeared the second time: They'd lost a lot of blood and were in shock already before that flaming kamikaze bashed in their faces."

MacDougall gulped down a queasy sensation which had been fooling around somewhere between his stomach and gullet, then looked carefully at the memo, which read:

Battle Casualties, *USS Belinda*, 6 April 1945

Wounded marines in sick bay:	Killed 13	Further wounded 5
Ship's personnel:	Killed 28	Wounded 23

Additional casualties to ship's personnel fighting fire:

Dead by asphyxiation	1
Seriously injured	17
Ambulatory	48

Total Killed, 42; Wounded, 93

"Who's the one asphyxiated?"

"Ned Strange."

"Poor little guy; he's all through 'working' for Alvick."

"A lot of them are all through work."

"That's a hundred-seventeen of the crew out of commission, not counting wounded marines," said MacDougall. Three closely type sheets were clipped to Bell's pen-and-ink memo: names of dead and wounded. MacDougall looked over the list, exclaiming and sucking air between his teeth as he came to familiar names: Bud Foster, who had narrowly escaped in the smoke boat—he hadn't made it this time. Happy-go-lucky Doyle, second division leading P.O., burned almost beyond recognition and blinded for life! Scooter Larson would never rev up the salvage boat, heading for mail: killed at his gun on the bridge deck. Larry Jordan, blond kid from 'Frisco just promoted to boatswain's mate second: killed at the winch handles; Blackwell, the fireman, had begged a transfer of battle station from after magazine far below the waterline to the gun tub high on the signal bridge where the kamikaze had hit him. These and many more: Sparky Hatch; Chief Scott, who had been recommended for warrant; Tillman; Wilks; and the others—every name a face, a personality, a type or degree of skill lost to the ship.

MacDougall's mind whirled with memories of these men, but all he said was, "We'll have to draw up a new watch bill."

Bell nodded. "Yes, and there's something else, Mac. Most of the crew is near the point of exhaustion. I hate to mention it to you now . . . of course some of them can take it much better than others. The weak just get crushed; you can't blame them for folding up."

"That's only too true, Frank. We can't keep this up indefinitely; there's only so much juice in an orange. When you squeeze it all out . . . Some of the rugged ones are folding too." MacDougall told Bell about Moran, then continued, "If we can only make it to safe anchorage."

"How far we got to go?"

"See the hills ahead. That's the largest island at Kerama. We should slide in there within an hour, if we keep afloat and if we can hold off the kamis. One more crash would sink her like a rock."

Randall, who had been watching out for the ship with one ear cocked towards the conversation, stepped back beside them. "The screen's still clear," he said.

"Good. . . . As soon as we make it to Kerama, I'll cut down on the gun watches; right now I don't dare. The crew are so corked—once asleep the general alarm wouldn't mean a thing. I'd never get the guns properly manned. It only takes two minutes for a kamikaze to sneak out here from land cover at Okinawa."

"Speaking of sleep," said Bell, "Hawks is getting his, all right."

"Did you look in on him?"

"Yes. He's really going at it—best thing in the world just now. I'm quite concerned about his condition. His heart isn't good at all: this prolonged strain. More trouble there besides his overtired mind out hunting for the monkey."

MacDougall turned from gazing over the bow at Kerama Retto ahead. "I didn't know about the heart. Ever since Sansapor I've been worried about him: wound up like an eight-day clock. The way he threw himself into things . . . There were times when I wasn't sure where Hawks stopped and the *Belinda* began."

"It takes time to get to the bottom of things," said Bell. "I haven't got the time now: all those people waiting down below . . . The Old Man needs a long rest; that's certain enough. I wish I could feel more sure about him."

"I could do with some sleep myself," said MacDougall. "Just think of eight solid hours in the sack! It would be—"

He never finished the sentence. The low hum of turbines at one-third speed rose rapidly to a high, agonizing scream. At the same time sharp, grinding sounds of fracturing steel came up from the shaft alley and the *Belinda* shuddered from stem to stern with a violent, completely unnatural vibration. Then all was quiet; the engine revolution counter in the pilothouse had come to a complete stop. Randall and MacDougall looked at each other. They needed no report; the great steel shaft joining engines to eighteen-foot propeller had snapped at the damaged bearing. The main engines, themselves unharmed, were useless. Feeling as if he had at last been hit below the belt, MacDougall listened to the lap of sea water alongside slow and die out completely as the *Belinda* drifted helplessly.

"What's the tide doing, Randall?"

Randall consulted tables on the log desk. "Flood tide—sets north about one knot."

"That'll drift us away from land."

"That's right."

"Alert the signal bridge and radio. Have them increase efforts to contact those tank lighters. Marty will find us by dawn, but that may be too late. And Jim?"

"Yes, sir."

"Get Brooks. Break out all the VPs and start towing the ship towards Kerama. They aren't much account but they'll hold her 'til the LCMs get back."

Bell had been leaning over the bridge railing, drinking in

the sweet air from first puffs of morning breeze. In a minute he would go back to the sick bay and relieve Gates for a spell. Telephones were ringing on the bridge, messengers dashing in and out of the pilothouse, reporting to MacDougall, then going off on new errands. Bell felt detached from this activity, though he appreciated the technical significance of what had happened. After the endless series of crises he had experienced in surgery during the last forty-eight hours, it was almost pleasant to watch the difficulties of others. I can be sympathetic, he thought, but I don't have to do anything.

Sacktime Riley had not seen Bell on the ladder. Leaving Grandy, Riley walked aft on the undamaged port side of the bridge house, stopping at the steel door to the flak magazine where reserve ammunition for the antiaircraft ready boxes was stowed. Riley knocked back the dogs and opened the door. With eyes well adjusted to darkness he could see hundreds of drum-shaped cylinders, each containing sixty 20-mm shells. They'd make hard pillows. Out on deck Riley found a pile of foul-weather jackets and oilskin slickers beside the battery of portable radio transmitters used for communicating with the beach party. He picked up an armload; they were nice and dry, just the thing. Returning to the magazine, he moved aside several gallons of commercial alcohol used by radar and radio technicians in cleaning parts, spread oilskins and jackets on the deck and stretched out upon them. Riley sighed luxuriously, lighted a cigarette and puffed slowly. Then he allowed his eyes to close and drifted off to sleep.

Bell was sipping a mug of coffee handed to him by one of Randall's sailors. He really should be getting down to the sick bay, but the bridge was an interesting change. He had been up here before during quiet periods, but this was his first opportunity to see the bridge at work. Boats had been hoisted out and Tony Brooks had the *Belinda* in tow with twelve small landing craft, whose diesel engines roared simultaneously somewhere just beyond the bow. There had been some minor difficulty with towlines and chafing gear. Randall was still muttering about it as he took a cut of land tangents from his gyro pelorus on the port wing. The instrument had been blown out of line but still operated, though Randall struggled to hold the compass repeater level. Bell put down his coffee mug and started for the pilothouse door. Time to go back to sick bay. This had been a pleasant break.

"Fire! Fire!" Two sailors came running forward from the after end of the bridge house. "Fire in the flak magazine!" One of them grabbed the end of a heavy canvas firehose laid out on deck under full pressure, ready for use. The other rushed to the pilothouse and snatched a CO_2 extinguisher from the bulk-head.

MacDougall came scrambling across from the starboard wing of the bridge, brushing past Bell. As MacDougall came out on the port wing he saw flames pouring out the opened door to the magazine. There must have been a short circuit in the wiring; even so, he was amazed and dismayed to see such flames inside a steel compartment carefully kept clear of everything but ammunition. *Ammunition!* "Hey, you with the CO_2," shouted MacDougall. "Come back. Come back! You'll get blasted to bits! Get behind that hose, boys. Over here, three more of you. Hit that locker with solid stream. This is no time for fog. Knock that stuff out, whatever it is in there burning. Drown it out. The ammo—"

A big man pushed his way past MacDougall and ran aft towards the blazing magazine: Bell! "Come back, Frank! Come back, you fool!"

Bell held his elbows up to protect his face, crouched low and ran into the blazing magazine. He had not stopped to reason about this. He had just started back to the sick bay—healing was his business—then this fire and remembrance of the two sailors talking: Riley in there asleep. He must get him out. His mind was clear and of single purpose, uncluttered by reasoning and counter-reasoning about worthiness, risk or consequences. Inside the door it was easy enough to see smoldering clothing and blazing tins, but where was Riley? Not here? Not here at at all! Bell turned and took one fast stride for the door. He must get out of this place! Then the solid stream of hose water caught him in the left shoulder: one-hundred-ten pounds of salt water pressure from a three-inch diameter hose spun him around and knocked him into the middle of the blaze. For a moment there was no sensation but the cold water, then roaring flames cut into him deep. He was pinned here helpless and the flame was greater than the flood. Now the steel drums exploded, first one, then dozens of them. The water was off his back now, but Bell no longer had power to move back. The pain was nearly unbearable. Strange—that was his business: trying to ease pain for others—his turn now. Then, sharp as the cutting knife of fire, the realization came to him: this was his personal moment—here in flaming and blasting confusion. There was no time to figure things out. The pain . . . the pain *was* unbearable!

Within a minute more they got Bell out of the place. A second hose had been brought up, the flames died out and, with cooling, the crazy chain reaction of exploding 20-mm shells slackened and stopped. Willicut dropped the nozzle, dived in the door head first and got hold of Bell's ankles. Stanowski and Jones grasped Willicut's legs and dragged the two of them out. Bell was limp, apparently lifeless; blood flowed from a dozen deep wounds in his chest and legs. His trousers were burned to charred shreds; his face was terribly seared. MacDougall took one look and ran for the electric bull horn, snapped it on and, before the tubes were warm, began calling, "Dr. Gates, come to the bridge at once. Life and death emergency! Dr. Gates, come to the bridge at once!"

Bell lay perfectly still on the wet deck between snakelike lengths of firehose outside the flak magazine. Willicut was kneeling beside Bell, crying over and over, "It was all my fault, all my fault. I knocked him down with the hose. I was just trying to help and I killed him. The hose knocked him right back into the flames and then that twenty stuff went off. I killed him; it was all my fault."

Stanowski shook Willicut. "Cut it out, Wheels, cut it out!" Then he put an arm around Willicut's shoulder. "Take it easy, mate. It wasn't your fault; you did all you could. . . . It was my fault. I never should have left that alcohol there. I was afraid some knothead would run it through a loaf of bread and try to drink it, so I stashed it away there 'til morning. It wasn't your fault, John." Stanowski looked up to see MacDougall behind him. "Can't we do something? Respiration—something for the burns?"

"I think we'd better wait—those chest wounds. Dr. Gates should be here . . . There he is now."

Gates's hulking figure came up the ladder and along the deck fast, padding like a big bear in a hurry. "What's the trouble? Another fire they said. Somebody hurt? . . . Frank!" Gates was down on his knees in an instant, feeling Bell's pulse, unfastening the shirt. Little beads of perspiration stood out on Gates's broad, pale face, which otherwise remained void of any expression except the intense way he looked at Bell. It seemed to MacDougall that Gates was drained to the bottom of the barrel.

"Is there any . . . is there . . . life, Doc?"

Gates did not answer; he remained on one knee beside Bell's body, still holding to the lifeless pulse. Looking at him kneeling there, MacDougall could see that it was useless to ask.

There was a commotion on the signal bridge. Big Foots Boski was dragging Riley along the deck, down the ladder and aft on the bridge deck to the group outside the flak magazine.

"You dirty little rat! You done this. You killed Doc Bell, that's what you done!"

"I never. I tell you, Boski, I never; I never!"

"You're a liar by the clock. Look at them singed eyebrows of yours; look at them blisters on the palms of your hands. You never got them fighting fire; you got that running away. You weren't anywhere near while we was fighting fire. You was sacked out in there; you dragged in all them jackets. They was still out on deck an hour ago when I went past. You flaked out in that magazine, smoking; that's what you did. Fell asleep and set the place on fire."

"Honest, I . . . You see—Well—"

"No use lying. You're guilty as hell. Smell all that burned wool in there. It's strong as the powder smell, almost. I know what happened. You woke up in your little bonfire, slapped at a burning jacket a couple of times, then took a powder and hid in the flag bag, too yellow to even give the alarm. The best man on the ship went in there after you. How he knew you was there I'm sure I don't know. He must'a known: how'd he be dead now if it wasn't for you? He ran in there barehanded; he must'a known you was there!" Boski tightened his grip on Riley's collar and sent him crashing against the steel bulkhead of the bridge house, where he slumped to the deck, arms over his face, sobbing and trembling.

Ezra Gates allowed Bell's lifeless hand to drop. Still on his knees, the big man spoke for the first time—without hate or accusation in his tone, but with power and trembling as he said from the depths of his Irish soul: "Holy Mother of God!"

MacDougall looked back to the bridge, thinking, I must get back there; as long as there is a bridge and I am alive I must get back to the bridge. Then he said, "Riley, you're under arrest."

Riley looked at MacDougall in wordless fright. He had run away from a little trouble and gotten into worse; perhaps they'd hang him for this! At last he said in a weak, flat voice, "I didn't mean—"

"Of course you didn't; but Dr. Bell is dead, isn't he?" MacDougall turned to Boski. "Get the chief master-at-arms. Tell him I've placed Riley under arrest. He is to lock him up, but keep a man there to let him out at once if we have to abandon ship." MacDougall took a long look at Bell. Somehow his brain refused to settle down; something he wanted to say to Gates about Bell but all that came out of the whirl was: one good man dead, one useless man in the brig and another good man off the watch list to stand outside the brig and keep the useless one from drowning.

A group of pharmacist's mates arrived with a litter and carried Bell's remains below. Gates followed some distance behind, saying a prayer for Bell. His prayers were devout but automatic. Through the surge of deep emotion he recalled the first time the two of them had met years before when undergraduates at Jefferson Medical College. They were in the dissecting room and Bell was working on a femur. "I like bones," he had said.

459

"I'm going to be an orthopedist." And so he was, thought Gates, remembering the hundreds of war wounded able to walk because of Bell's skill with bones.

At last Maxwell showed up, shiny star of his police office pinned to faded chambray shirt. "Come along, Riley," he said.

Riley hung back for a moment, looked at Boski and said, "What'll they do to me? Shoot me? Hang me?"

"Worrying about your useless little carcass," snarled Boski. "They ought to set fire to that locker again and throw you back in! . . . I don't know what they'll do to you and I don't care; whatever it is it'll be too good. You ought to crawl on your hands and knees the rest of your life, but you won't. You're one of those guys who thinks the world owes him a living." Foots Boski spat on the deck in front of Riley, then jumped high, caught the lower railing of the signal bridge and climbed back to his gun station beside the flag bag. There were signs of dawn. If the Japs were coming back, this was the time.

CHAPTER 49

In the half-light of early morning, a small raid of kamikazes broke through combat air patrol and threw itself against those ships remaining off Hagushi and Naha. Watching red-flecked antiaircraft trajectory, burning planes and burning ships, Mac-Dougall waited anxiously on the *Belinda's* bridge. Every able-bodied man aboard, except those busy with damage control or out in the smaller landing craft attempting to tow ship, stood behind a gun. There was nothing he could do but wait and pray that the undamaged ships would handle the Japs. The PA system had been demolished, so that he could not exhort his crew; he might have used it if available but no advice from him to shoot well was needed. All hands realized that each sluggish rise of the *Belinda* in this moderate sea might be her last; each downward swoop might be the one which would take them all to the bottom. Knowing that another hit below the waterline, no matter how light, would undo all frantic efforts of the last twenty-four hours to save the ship, they would put everything they had into their shooting.

MacDougall looked around at the tanned faces under blue-gray helmets; these men of his in their faded dungarees somehow seemed a very part of the ship. He looked at the blue-gray decks, wet with morning dew, then up to pale silver of dying moon and first-magnitude stars fading out. Halfway to the eastern horizon was Okinawa, with her rocky little hills, where battle now raged, showing clear cut against the coming sun. He felt cold, shivering in spite of his zipped-up jacket. It seemed as if the world were dying; man could do only so much and faith

460

was pale like fading stars. Under his feet pulse of pumps and laboring air compressor; sea water waiting all about, pressing in, searching out every crack and popped rivet hole. The sea had a cold relentlessness which in the end could prove more deadly than all the flaming kamikazes they had absorbed. Those suicide Japs were dead but the sea still waited.

Then Randall let out a joyous shout, pointing with binoculars held in outstretched hand. MacDougall raised his own glasses and looked eastward. There under brightening skies and much nearer to the *Belinda* than to embattled Okinawa were four big LCM ramps tossing in the chop. The tank lighters were coming! Fifteen minutes later, megaphone in hand, he was shouting down to ruddy-faced John Marty, tall and serious in his salt-crusted khakis at the stern of the leading tank lighter. "We're broken down, Marty. Get your LCMs up under the bow; take a bridle and towline from Moran. Send the VPs back alongside."

"Aye, aye, sir. What course?"

"We'll give you instructions by voice radio. We're going to try and get her into that little cove up ahead—anchor there and patch her up. Give your boats the gun now; we're just barely floating."

"Aye, aye, sir." Marty looked along the *Belinda's* ruptured side, noted the diminished freeboard and hurried his tank lighters under the bow. They moved past the bridge and Marty's face wrinkled in a slow grin in response to some wisecrack called down to him from the foredeck. Then MacDougall saw the young boat officer searching the bridge with his usual serious expression. The kid's looking for something—the Old Man, I'll bet.

Marty's tank lighters, with large twin screws biting deep into the water and with their combined two thousand horsepower, moved the *Belinda* against the current at a five knot clip. These children she had carried vast distances nested upon her hatches —which she had launched so many times in assault waves against hostile shores—now towed the mother. While MacDougall conned, Randall plotted the ship along and Kruger watched the soundings flashing on the fathometer dial. Sixty fathoms shoaled to fifty, then to forty-three as they began rounding Kuro Shima to head south in the teeth of strong currents running past Kerama Retto's group of small and rocky islands. The *Belinda* hung across channel with the full three-knot current shoving against her shattered port side. Proud beachhead lady, apparently resisting the disparagement of being towed, she sheered toward the Jitsuru Rocks towering to starboard. Boatswain Torgeson stood by his anchors, ready to let go on order. As the rocks with their stunted pine trees frowned down within range of the *Belinda's* line-throwing

461

pistols, MacDougall began to sweat. The current was not only forcing into every gaping wound along the port side, but was also straightening up the port list. Quite suddenly it was easy to walk again on nearly level decks—frighteningly easy to MacDougall, who realized that if this carefully ballasted port list came out the ship would swing over to a cranky starboard list which could only end up with negative stability and a capsized ship. All night he had longed for the sanctuary of these islands, and now he was faced with any one of three unhappy chances: of running aground off this rocky, tide-ripped point which would tear open the *Belinda's* forepeak, thus sinking her; of sinking by loss of further buoyancy through current-pressed waters entering kamikaze-torn holes and overcoming thin, shored-up bulkheads; or by just rolling over on her better side and capsizing. He called the LCMs by voice radio: "Hang on to her, Marty. Hold her head up." Two miles further ahead was little Tokashiki Cove, offering the kind of protection which was a minimum requirement for this emergency. If he let go anchor now, delay in heaving up again might spell the difference between survival and sinking. At last, still sullen, but as if satisfied with her gesture of independence, the *Belinda* came grudgingly around and towing ahead was resumed.

Half an hour later the *Belinda's* anchor splashed ten fathoms down in the center of a toy-sized cove which provided bare swinging room to clear protecting rocks and reefs. Here, if only typhoons passed far away, she was reasonably safe from ordinary foul weather. Outsized and seeming out of place, the ship nestled under a steep and rocky hillside to which clung small, weather-gnarled pines, tiny native dwellings and midget-sized garden terraces. In addition to small Okinawan sampans, several wrecked Japanese suicide motor boats were beached near the village. Despite these reminders of bitter struggle, the *Belinda* seemed quite suddenly to be in a different world. The quaint pastoral atmosphere of the place seemed ages removed from modern warfare. There were, however, indications of time and place. A repair ship's boarding party swarmed up a debarkation net to help with soft patches inside the ruptured hull, which would make it possible to tow the *Belinda* across open sea between the combat area and some repair base having a dry dock, probably Samar. From the *Belinda's* stern, colors fluttered at half-mast in honor of the dead now being carried to the fantail.

MacDougall leaned over the bridge railing watching this activity while he worked with pencil and signal pad, puzzling out a message to the Senior Officer Present Afloat, Okinawa, reporting damages sustained and temporary remedial action being taken, together with a request for instructions as to whether to send the dead on shore for interment or to bury

462

them at sea. At this point his concentration was broken into by the voice of Russ Secor, energetic young boatswain's mate busy at number three winch handles on the deck below. Skillfully hoisting aboard a heavy slingload of shell plating from the repair shop, Secor was saying to Hatcher in a loud, uninhibited voice, "If my old man wants me back on the farm, he's going to have to get rid of the mules and buy a tractor!"

Then Boski, in charge of the signal watch on the deck above, shouted to his crew, "Signals: ship calling us. Stand by for a message." MacDougall finished his report to the SOPA, considered a moment, gave it Hawks's signature and sent it to the radio room for transmission. Crossing to the shattered port wing he watched a freshly painted supply ship now passing the little cove close aboard on her way to nearby anchorage. While MacDougall watched familiar preparations for anchoring taking place on her forecastle—chain and anchor walked out and made ready for dropping—Boski appeared at his elbow with a message. MacDougall read with astonishment:

FROM: COMMANDING OFFICER, U.S.S. *Peacock*
TO: COMMANDING OFFICER, U.S.S. *Belinda*
GREETINGS X DID BELINDA FORGET TO DUCK SOMETHING X IF YOU NEED RIVETS OR FRESH EGGS I HAVE PLENTY OF BOTH X

> QUIGLEY

Randall came from the chart room to have a look. MacDougall showed him the message, then focused his binoculars across the water. There was Quigley, leaning nonchalantly over the bridge railing, taking in the scenery and the damaged *Belinda*.

"They sure fixed him up with store choppers in a hurry," MacDougall remarked.

"Looks like they fixed him up with more than that," said Randall. "Look at that headgear: scrambled eggs!"

"What do you know! Full commander and a ship of his own!"

"I wonder who he has for exec," said Randall. "Better be a good man!"

MacDougall looked resentfully across the water at Quigley, who appeared to be quite unconcerned over the mooring of his command, while a shorter officer moved about the bridge in a competent manner, giving orders to helmsman and engine room.

"Quigley puts his finger on the easy way every time," he said at last. "I guess we don't live right."

Randall chuckled. "Oh, I don't know. Sometimes the hard way's a lot more fun."

"I've been having so much fun recently it's just killing me," said MacDougall. "Well, we'd better take him up on that egg deal. He's got all the eggs he needs on his cap!"

The pumps were definitely gaining. As Fraser confidently reported to MacDougall, "There's no longer any question about it." A growing bubble of air compressed into number three hold had shoved over two thousand tons of sea water back through the same ragged holes where it had rushed in during the preceding day. In spite of the dead aboard, the awesome damage to the ship and the persisting smell of death which permeated every compartment, most of the crew were lightheartedly enjoying the sensation of being alive on a pleasant morning.

The moment Fraser felt certain that the ship would not sink, he turned over routine supervision of damage control to his subordinates and went for a prowl of the ship. Specific damage to hull did not surprise him: sitting on his stool at damage control central station he had listened to reports and pictured things just about the way they were. The thing which struck him at once was the litter of empty shell cases, burned clothing and soggy paper, tangled hoses and soot-stained bulkheads. Five minutes later the newly repaired PA system gave out its first order, and shortly thereafter Fraser watched with dour satisfaction the sweepers fore and aft and groups of sailors scrubbing diligently before washdown hoses now advancing across battle-scarred decks. One such gang labored on the scorched and blasted bridge. "Back to the old routine," said Willicut, as he played his nozzle over a tangle of twisted steel which had once been Captain Hawks's high chair. "We're pumping water back into her again."

A sturdy collision mat girdled the shattered gasoline compartment in number five hold. Once the mat was in place, the thousand horsepower emergency pump at the stern made fast work of floodwater where Gonzales, Sanchez and Martinez had toiled unloading gasoline drums for the beach at Okinawa. When this compartment was dry enough, water began draining back into it from the flooded shaft alley which ran between the two tanks, enabling MacDougall and Walt Ingalls, the engineering officer, to get into the place and examine the shaft. Lighting circuits were waterlogged, so the two groped into the dank tunnel using flashlights. Ingalls led the way. A little over halfway along the hundred-foot shaft, which was solid steel and eighteen inches in diameter, Ingalls called out, "Here's the break. Look at that bearing; shoved more than a foot out of line!"

MacDougall looked at the fractured shaft, one end still resting in the cradle of the crooked bearing, the other end slanting down towards the double bottoms. "Isn't that just lovely! You won't mend that with a pot of glue."

Ingalls shook his head sadly as he ran his hand over the salt-encrusted surface of the once polished shaft. "We'll never fix it here; not a chance."

"No, there isn't a chance. I was hoping against hope that it would be the tail shaft at the business end of this thing. Then, after we'd patched the hull, we could flood the forward compartments, raising the propeller hub above water so that we could get the prop off, pull that tail shaft and put in the spare."

"Even that's quite a job."

"Yes, but it has been done. Well, that's all out now. We'll have to patch her up and request towage to the nearest available dry dock."

"What's the closest?"

"Samar—even that's a thousand miles over open water. We'll have to make those soft patches good!"

Lightened of some three thousand tons of sea water, the *Belinda* floated six feet higher in the water than when LCMs had towed her to anchorage at dawn. Stages rigged overside swarmed with Rinaldo's shipfitters, busy removing crumpled shell plating with cutting torches and welding temporary plating over all holes above waterline. Carpenter Long and his men started down into number five hold, where they would build wooden cribbing around the hole below waterline, then fill in with a "soft patch" of reinforced concrete.

Alvick grasped the coaming of the opened gasoline space, lowered himself until his feet found rungs, and went down the last section into the starboard tank. He waded across the storage tank, exploring with his flashlight. "Lower me a wire sling. We'll get this Jap engine out of here." Waiting for sling and cargo hook, Alvick poked around behind petallike scraps of exploded gas drums. Then he shouted to his men, "Belay that wire strap for now. Hook on a litter. I've found our little Mexicans!"

Dressed in cotton pajamas, Captain Hawks sat listlessly on the edge of his bunk. His feet rested on the edge of a drawer pulled out from the bunk a few inches, his elbows rested on his knees and his chin rested between cupped palms. Hawks raised his eyes slowly to look at MacDougall, who had just entered the cabin with a message in his hand, but the captain did not raise his head. MacDougall was thinking, that's the first time I've ever seen his spine curved; he always bent from the hips. The starch is gone from the man. Then he said, "Here's a message for you, Capt'n."

"I don't want any messages; messages are nothing but trouble." Hawks's diction was clear again, but the power and drive were gone from his voice and person; he spoke like a man exhausted from carrying too great a load uphill. "The ship is wrecked, MacDougall; she's on the reef."

"Oh, no, Capt'n. She's anchored safe: ten fathoms, coral bottom."

Hawks looked up slowly at a patch of reflected sunlight playing on the cabin overhead. "She's sunk." He said the words without heat or persuasiveness, but with finality. "I looked outside . . . and I remember the flames," he said very slowly. "No ship could live . . . We've lost her; we've lost the *Belinda*. I'm ruined; you're ruined too, MacDougall. We're all in this thing together: we lost our ship."

"Capt'n, you've been badly hurt; you've been very sick. I assure you, the *Belinda's* afloat and safely anchored. She's badly holed, but the pumps held out and we're patching her up."

Hawks shook his head slowly from side to side. "It's no use. You're just fooling yourself. I saw the flames." Then the first sign of irritation showed and his lower lip protruded in a suggestion of the old leer as he said, "You say I'm sick. How do you know I'm sick?"

"You told me that you were, Capt'n."

"That's right. I told you. Very well, then I'm sick. What are you going to do about it—make numbers on me? Take credit for everything? Oh, they'll blame me. The captain is always responsible. But they'll blame you too, don't think they won't. They have a very crafty way of getting everybody."

MacDougall shifted his weight uncomfortably, then stepped to the forward porthole and looked out at land, close and intimate: a bit of steep hillside with a small vegetable garden hanging incredibly above a cliff. An old woman toiled there, probably weeding onions. MacDougall turned back to Hawks, who had lifted his head and was looking at him directly. Those eyes, MacDougall thought. They used to burn right into you and now look at them—glazed like old porcelain and focused ten thousand miles through the bulkhead! He said, "Care for a cup of coffee, Capt'n?" Hawks nodded and MacDougall went to the pantry, where Jenkins, the cabin boy, sat patiently on a camp stool beside a simmering coffee pot. The tall Negro rose and began to get out the coffee gear, soft dark eyes questioning MacDougall as if to say, How's the captain, sir? MacDougall took the coffee without comment, returned to the cabin and handed the cup to Hawks, who stirred in cream and sugar mechanically and began to sip the coffee. Then MacDougall said, "Capt'n, I'm sure nobody could blame you for getting hit in three kamikaze raids. The *Belinda's* afloat and she's going to stay afloat. We did the job they sent us to do. They'll more than likely decorate you!"

Hawks did not seem to hear. MacDougall did not know that Hawks was back in Leyte, taking Chipchee for a sail. The sun shone brightly on sails perfectly dyed a rich maroon, while a twenty-one gun salute for the gallant *Albatross* boomed solemnly from the anchored fleet. Then Hawks shivered, shook his head back and forth in an effort to clear it and said in a startled, anxious voice, "What's that you said, MacDougall? A dispatch from ComTransron Eleven: orders to sortie?"

MacDougall hesitated for a moment, recalling in a flash the *Belinda* steaming in sparkling lagoon waters, standing out to sea between glaring sand beaches of blasted Eniwetok islands— the first lift of deep water swells, squadron joining up in formation ahead, a fast carrier speeding to windward while her brooding planes came home in rapid succession to her flight deck. Then he said, "No sir; no orders to sortie. . . . Orders for HT 177 to report to commanding officer, *Belinda,* and tow to Naval Repair Base, Samar."

Hawks rolled slowly back into his bunk and closed his eyes. At last he opened them again and said slowly, "I can't take this ship on a long, deep-water tow to dry dock, MacDougall. I'm so sick—all screwgied up inside. . . . Then they'll come aboard and ask questions, questions—find out about me."

"Don't worry about that, Capt'n. You'll be all right. You just get some rest. We'll get old *Belinda* there for you and make ready all reports."

Hawks nodded, but worry lifted him back to a sitting posture. Once more he swung long legs over the edge of his bunk, hooked heels in a partly opened lower drawer, sat slumping there, chin between hands, eyes staring through white-painted steel bulkhead.

Hearing some stir at the cabin door, MacDougall left Hawks's stateroom, passed out through the cabin curtains and found Biggs, the orderly, remonstrating with a communications messenger. "You can't go in there, Collins. The captain's—"

"All right, boys," MacDougall said. "I'll take the board." He paused beside the cabin table, noting the shattered clock still cushioned in Hawks's chair, then glanced through the sheaf of messages. With one exception, they were routine; MacDougall scrawled his initials to these and returned them to the messenger. Entering the cabin once more, MacDougall held out a yellow commanding officer's copy of a message to Hawks, who raised his head from cupped palms long enough to shake it slowly back and forth, then sank back into contemplation of the steel bulkhead. "It's good news, Capt'n," said MacDougall. "Message from Admiral Cromwell: 'TO COMMANDING

OFFICER AND ALL HANDS U.S.S. *BELINDA:* WELL DONE.' That's all it says, sir."

Hawks began to laugh, strange soundless laughter that shook him mirthlessly, ending in a queer cackle. Then, for the first time in forty-eight hours, his voice returned to full power. "Well done," he said. "WELL DONE!" he roared, laughing aloud and coughing painfully. "Why didn't he send me a poem? Do you know the verse, MacDougall?" MacDougall nodded but Hawks was not looking at him; he was looking straight through the bulkhead again as he chanted:

> *When in question or in doubt,*
> *Run in circles, scream and shout.*
> *Give them hell and fire a gun;*
> *Hoist the signal up:* Well Done.

Hawks slumped back into his bunk, mirthless chuckles fading into silence as the mattress took the full weight of his beaten body. After a time he said, "You can do anything in the Navy with that *Well Done*—except plug a hole in your bottom." He closed his eyes again, breathing slowly and deeply with a little shudder now and then, like a child waking from a bad dream. MacDougall tiptoed out and returned to the bridge.

Dr. Gates left the troop officers' mess hall, now serving as temporary sick bay, and hurried forward toward ladders leading up to the captain's cabin. As he passed the open door to the garbage room, hum of machinery and cracking sounds of bones and gristle stopped. A greasy hand reached out and grasped him by the slack of his white surgical jacket.

"Not now, Hubert," said Gates. "I've an emergency—"

"But my feet still hurt, Doc! My feet are an emergency. . . . Can't watch them mess cooks without running up and down ladders night and day. Wasn't going to mention it no more, but I tell you, Doc, my feet—"

"Hurry, Doctor, will you?" It was MacDougall, head and shoulders twisted over the pipe railing of the ladder from the deck above. "Hawks is in bad shape."

"I'm coming," said Gates, getting his big frame in motion once more.

"But my feet—" Hubert insisted.

"They'll have to wait."

Gates clattered up ladders after MacDougall, who paused outside the curtain leading into the cabin and whispered, "He's taken a turn for the worse, I'm sure. . . . Can't sleep; says a weight is pressing into his head. . . . Seems like he's going to pass out again, yet somehow keeps up that delirious talk."

Gates nodded. "There may be concussion complicating that heart condition. . . . X rays weren't very satisfactory."

"He's so weak—can't you give him more plasma?"

"Afraid to overload that heart, Mac. We gave him a pint of whole blood to replace what he lost from that head wound. He's had all the plasma he can take. There's a limit to everything. We've got a nasty combination here: nervous collapse, trauma and an overloaded heart. He needs a long rest. We've got to keep him quiet."

"I didn't realize: I was so busy trying to keep this pot afloat—"

"Sure . . . We'd better go in now." Parting the curtains, Gates strode through the cabin and entered Hawks's stateroom.

Hawks had somehow managed to dress himself in clean khaki trousers and shirt. He stood at the open porthole, looking out over the foredeck and at beginnings of sunset coloring the sky beyond Tokashiki Cove. Except for the obvious effort with which he clung for support to the brass rim of the opened port, he might have been waiting to receive readiness reports for getting the *Belinda* underway.

"Would you mind lying down awhile, Captain?" asked Gates quietly. "I'd like to examine that head wound of yours."

Hawks turned about slowly, now leaning his shoulders against the bulkhead for support. With difficulty he focused his opaque gaze upon Gates, who noted the set features, small beads of perspiration clinging to Hawks's brow, fresh blood staining the loose compress above his right temple.

"Where is Dr. Flynn?" Hawks asked slowly. "Flynn will prescribe for me."

"He was killed, Captain. I'd like to help you, sir. You need—"

"Flynn . . . Flynn killed?" Hawks said the words quietly, reflectively. Then his voice rose querulously, "But Flynn . . . But Flynn . . . Flynn dead!" A slow, shuddering sigh went out of Hawks.

"Captain," said Gates, "if you'll just let me check that head wound—"

"Don't rush me," said Hawks. "I'm going to have another look at this sunset. I like sunsets." Clinging to the brass porthole frame, Hawks got his face outside, looked long at the reddening sky, then off the port beam toward Naha and Hagushi. Freshness of evening breeze cleared his mind somewhat. "That anchorage over there . . . That's Okinawa, isn't it, MacDougall?"

"Yes, sir."

"Okinawa . . . Saipan . . . Kwajalein." Hawks shrugged. "Tarawa, Salerno, Guadalcanal—what's the difference? I've

469

seen them all—crowded with ships, crowded with landing craft heading for Germans or Japs. Look over there now— How long ago was Easter Sunday? Look at any of 'em! We've got a long string of empty beaches behind us. One more big push up Tokyo Bay and they can empty 'em all! . . . But I remember Guadalcanal that first morning." Hawks turned around facing Gates and MacDougall again, leaning for support against that bulkhead, pausing to catch his breath but carried along as if with some tremendous, moving force. "Guadalcanal," he repeated, savoring flavor of the word on his tongue. "It was a rough go to get in there those days; don't think it wasn't. We were outnumbered, almost outclassed, and the Tokyo Express came down the Slot on schedule every night. . . . Look out that porthole!" Hawks cried. "Look at Guadalcanal!" His eyes were glassy, wild, yet some great seeing power there shook MacDougall and Gates to their roots. "Look at those landing craft, half buried in sand! Which is Jap? Which is ours? Take an expert to tell the difference. Go into the jungle; hunt under morning glory vines. What do you see? Rust, rust and more rust! Tanks and cannibalized planes rust fast at Guadalcanal. Men rust. Dig down under the sand, under that jungle leaf mold and you'll find bones of men. Show me the Japs. Show me the boy from Nebraska. You can't tell one from another!" Breathing with difficult short gasps, Hawks clung with all his ebbing strength to the porthole frame, shaking away Gates and Mac-Dougall, who jumped to his side. "Morning glories grow fast on Guadalcanal. . . . New coconut trees grow fast on Kwajalein. . . . Sand's all smoothed over at Saipan. . . . Soon the tourists will come out to look see. . . . Somebody who's read up on the war will say, 'This happened here. . . . That happened over there.' And you know—" Hawks labored around from the porthole, balanced himself and pointed a shaking finger at MacDougall's face—"some numb brain will say, 'Oh? . . . When does the next plane leave for Eniwetok?' "

Gates moved beside Hawks, who was now gasping for breath. "You'd better lie down, Captain. You've got to rest." Hawks looked bad. If he could just get him to sleep now, perhaps that fighting heart could bring him back to this side of things. Somehow he seemed slipping away.

Hawks allowed Gates and MacDougall to assist him to his bunk. "Don't rush me," he said again, sticking out his lower jaw in a weak resemblance of his old defiant gesture. Then he sank back with his shoulder blades on the white spread, elbows dug in as if ready for a sudden dash to the bridge. At last the head went back on the pillow. Gates took Hawks's wrist in his hand, counting the pulse: fluttering and fast. Hawks was in a dangerous condition. If he could just sleep quietly . . . Dangerous to give sedatives now. Gates's mind traveled back over all the limp wrists he had held. There would be more; he was sure of that. Pay, pay, pay with life's blood—and it's never quite enough. We can't buy a deed to freedom; we have to pay for it as we go along. All that we've seen done—all that's gone before our time—is not enough, yet others will rise and stand fast when they must. . . . Sunset fire filled Okinawa's sky and a golden-red glow filtered through the porthole, flooding Hawks's cabin with glory light. They will rise, Gates thought, thrill suffusing his weary body. They will rise out of fire, cloud and mud and they will pay what has to be paid so that freedom will live beyond us and our small span and deeds. . . . The pulse under Gates's fingers was steadier now. Hawks's eyes were closed; his sharp nose and jaw brought back remembrance of his full strength, his driving energy which had given the *Belinda* her peculiar spark. Gates thought, he's made his contribution. We all lay down our contribution—sometimes pitiful enough. And yet, add it to all those who died unwitnessed and unsung: fellows who will never be rewarded by man; add Flynn and Bell—how bitter he had felt about their loss! Yes, somehow it all fits into the pattern. Somehow the leaking hole is plugged; somehow—after longer than we think we have strength and courage to hang on—we build the dam higher by a pebble, we lift a monument into the sky. Gates looked at MacDougall's shoulders hunched against the porthole: that man's stewing over repairs to the ship again! He looked at Hawks, quiet now on his white bedspread. The thrill ran up Gates's spine again. We all have a share in it: pushing, guiding, healing, standing fast. We don't have to be great to have a share in greatness!

MacDougall looked out from Hawks's stateroom porthole, watching Rinaldo hurrying aft, followed by his shipfitter gang with new shell plating and their welding gear. That Rinaldo: busy building a new ship! MacDougall looked out over the bow, far beyond the limits of Tokashiki Cove. Out on the red horizon was a sunset silhouette of Kruger's LCMs. They were stopped out there in deep water, gently sliding the last of those canvas-covered forms over the opened ramp: Doc Bell, Bud Foster, Ned Strange and the three little Mexicans. One at a time plunging deep into that warm salt water, down to join lost ships and shipmates on the quiet bottom. They'll have their peace, MacDougall thought. Nobody can take that away from them now. It seemed to him that he had fellowship with these shipmates —with all the ones who had gone on ahead. The *Belinda* would sail on; they'd patch her up and tow her to dry dock, new shaft and sound shell plating. Then she'd sail for invasion, the last tremendous landing: Kyushu.

Somehow they'd see it through to the end; there had to be an end somewhere. Over a ramp or home at last, a man had to have rest.

Now Hawks opened his eyes and struggled to a sitting position of his bunk. He waved off Gates's restraining hand. "The sunset! I've got to see the sunset!" MacDougall, looking anxiously at his captain, moved aside. Hawks staggered to his feet, grasping brass lugs at either side of the porthole. His breath came in ragged, difficult gasps, but he shook off the doctor and clung to the port, gazing into the sunset. Sky filled his vision. He could not see the ship any more.

"MacDougall."

"Yes, Capt'n."

"Watch out for old *Beachhead Belinda;* I'm going for a sail in the *Albatross.* I've found Chipchee. . . . It's time for a sail. . . ." Hawks's lips moved but no more words came. The *Belinda* was gone; he'd had to let her go. Red sails of the *Albatross* filled his vision; they'd never been so beautiful. That Jackson: stewing about red ink! If he'd only understood. . . . Hawks felt the tug of the sheet in his hand and the rudder's kick. Fine breeze, fair breeze—riding high now: no more sea slap under his bow. Full sheet and red sails filled, Chipchee on his shoulder and Louise waiting out there where sunset-sky and water met—out there as far as he could see and a little beyond, where there was no pain, no weakness, no fear and no foulups—where everything worked out all right at last.

The Old Man slipped down, crumpling to his knees. Gates jumped to his side, caught the pulse: very slow, weaker and weaker—and then it was gone altogether. Captain Hawks had found the sunset.

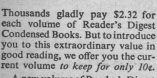

Only the most outstanding books from the hundreds published every month in hard-cover editions are chosen for the Bantam trademark.

That's why the book which carries the Bantam rooster is often one that has been a book club selection, a nationally listed bestseller, the basis for a great motion picture, and the choice of leading literary critics.

That's why Bantam's list of authors includes so many of the foremost writers of our time—novelists like Hemingway, Steinbeck, A. J. Cronin, Maugham, Costain, McCullers; mystery writers like Rex Stout, John Dickson Carr; Western writers like Luke Short, Peter Dawson; writers of science-fiction like Ray Bradbury, Fredric Brown.

Whether your choice is a mystery, a novel, a Western, or a work of non-fiction—if it carries the symbol of the Bantam rooster, you can be sure it is a book of exceptional merit, attractively printed, economically priced.